THE BERKSHIRE READER

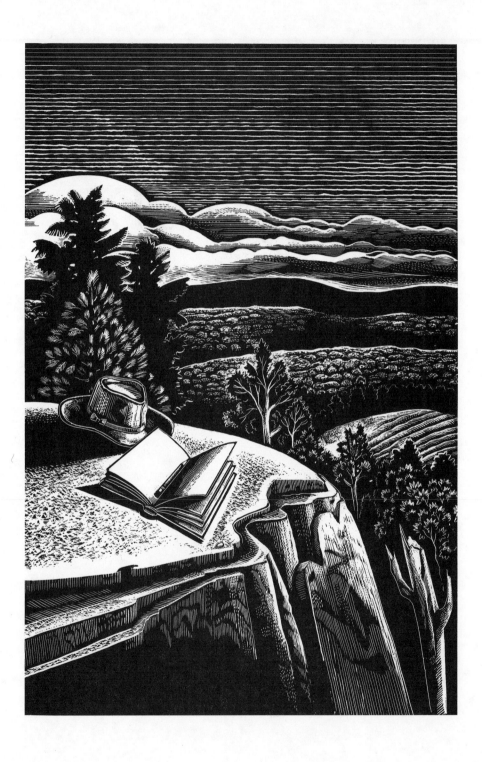

B<small>THE</small>ERKSHIRE READER

WRITINGS FROM NEW ENGLAND'S
SECLUDED PARADISE

Edited by RICHARD NUNLEY
Drawings by MICHAEL McCURDY

*The Valley of the Housatonic, locked in by walls of every shape
and size, from grassy knolls to bold basaltic cliffs — a 'Happy
Valley' indeed! A beautiful little river wanders singing from
side to side in this secluded Paradise; and from every mountain
cleft come running crystal springs to join it.*
Fanny Kemble, 1835

Berkshire House Publishers
Stockbridge, Massachusetts

Library of Congress Cataloging-in-Publication Data

The Berkshire reader: writings from New England's secluded paradise/edited
  by Richard Nunley; drawings by Michael McCurdy.
      p. cm.
  Includes bibliographical references.
  ISBN: 0-936399-33-3 : $29.95
    1. American literature—Massachusetts—Berkshire Hills.
  2. Berkshire Hills (Mass.)—Literary collections. I. Nunley, Richard, 1931-   .
  II. McCurdy, Michael.
  PS548.M4B47 1992
  810.8'097441—dc20
                                                                92-33106
                                                                     CIP

ISBN: 0-936399-33-3

Berkshire House books are available at substantial discounts for bulk purchases
by corporations and other organizations for promotions and premiums. Special
personalized editions can also be produced in large quantities. For more
information:

Berkshire House Publishers
PO Box 297
Stockbridge, Massachusetts 01262

Printed in the United States of America
10 9 8 7 6 5 4 3 2 1

In memory of Lawrence K. "Pete" Miller (1907-1991), editor and publisher of The Berkshire Eagle, whose lifelong fascination with and devotion to all things Berkshire have left all Berkshirites gratefully in his debt.

Contents

The Berkshires Observed

S ome years ago an attempt was made to count Berkshire authors —
residents or natives of the Berkshires who had published a book.
Somewhere past 270 the attempt was abandoned.

For one thing, it began to be uncomfortable to decide which contribu-
tors to the steady stream of scholarship flowing from Williams, North
Adams State College, and Simon's Rock to count as "Berkshire" writers.
For another, it began to be even more uncomfortable deciding what
counted as a book — a technical manual from the GE labs? A how-to
paperback on creative bow-tying? A picture book by a local historical
committee? And what about full-fledged Berkshirites who wrote well
and often but never published a book? These conundrums sapped enthusiasm for pressing on to an exhaustive count.

But those 270 undoubted Berkshire writers — that's a lot of writers
for a sparsely populated region to produce or attract in not much more
than 200 years. They attest to an unusual degree of bookishness in this
"secluded paradise" between its ranges of hills west of the Connecticut
and east of the Hudson.

It's hard to explain. Partly it must be due to the late development of
the region. Indian threats and uncertainty about where the jurisdiction of
Massachusetts ended and New York's began discouraged settlement of
the Berkshires until the fall of Quebec ended the French and Indian War.
Between 1760 and the first Federal census of 1790, the population of the
region surged from 500 or so to about 30,000.

This meant that settling the Berkshires was more like opening a
subdivision than creating a society from scratch. Extended families and
even sizable portions of towns moved up from eastern Massachusetts,
Rhode Island, and Connecticut bringing accumulated wealth, established
institutions, and developed intellectual traditions with them intact and
ready to go.

And the beauty of the region, early publicized by William Cullen
Bryant and Catharine Maria Sedgwick, attracted even more people of

bookish and artistic bent, first as tourists, later as residents.

If the Sedgwick family themselves account for a small regiment of Berkshire writers (this book could easily have become a Stockbridge sampler), then Williamstown with its college at the north end of the county accounts for a battalion. And Pittsfield consciously treasures its associations with Holmes and Melville.

Once a tradition of writing is established, local pride and appreciation of the enlargement it brings to life work to perpetuate it.

The Berkshire Reader grew out of a desire to survey this tradition both to afford local satisfaction in the Berkshire accomplishment and to introduce others to this interesting cultural phenomenon.

No one is more poignantly aware of what such an anthology leaves out than its compiler; the number of good Berkshire writers left unrepresented is painful to contemplate. The principles of selection were, first, that all selections be readable — or if unreadable, unreadable for interesting reasons; second, (with one or two exceptions) that every writer included have solid and significant Berkshire associations; and third, that each selection present a different angle of perception on the Berkshires — "the Berkshires observed."

It should be pointed out to geographical purists that "the Berkshires" as a region extend beyond the political boundaries of Berkshire County, Massachusetts — eastward toward Northampton and Springfield, southward into the "Connecticut Berkshires," westward into the eastern edge of Columbia County, New York, and northward into the bottom of Vermont.

As will be seen, effort has been made to enlarge the purview of the book beyond the narrowly literary; unfortunately, not too much that meets the principles of selection has been written on Berkshire's textile industry, its medical life, its machine, electrical, and plastics manufacturing, or its commerce.

But this is not a history, although it frequently wanted to become one, nor is it a cultural study. It is a reader, and if it gives pleasure, thanks are due to the many who so good-spiritedly contributed to its making, especially Ruth Degenhardt of the Berkshire Athenaeum in Pittsfield, Nancy Walker, Pat Tucker, Maryjane Fromm, and Wendy Hanson of the Jonathan Edwards Library at Berkshire Community College, Polly Pierce of the Stockbridge Library, Helen Southworth and Charles Bonenti of the *Berkshire Eagle*, Carolyn Banfield and Barbara Allen at the Berkshire County Historical Society, the Lenox Library, Williams College Library, Amherst College Library, University of Massachusetts Library, and the Special Collections of the United States Military Academy Library at West Point.

Special acknowledgments are due to Lion Miles of Stockbridge, Joanna Haight Adelberg of New Lebanon Center, New York, Wilson Kimnach of Woodbridge, Connecticut, and Peter and William Miles of Copake Falls, New York, and Mt. Washington, Massachusetts, for their suggestions and help.

Without the cheerful efficiency of Mary Osak and Joy Hayes in typing and proofreading a difficult text, and the unflappable expertise of Jane McWhorter, its designer, this book would still be a stack of folders in a milk crate.

And, finally, thanks are due to Sarah Novak, managing editor of Berkshire House. Her patience and amiable meticulousness are exceeded only by her tireless cooperativeness and quick discernment.

Wilderness to Settlement
1676 to 1800

WILLIAM HUBBARD

The earliest allusion in print to the Berkshire region, printed in Boston in 1677, appears to be the account by the Reverend William Hubbard, minister of Ipswich, of Major Talcott's attack on fugitives from King Philip's War, encountered at the crossing of the Housatonic at Great Barrington. Charles J. Taylor, in his 1882 History of Great Barrington, *quoting another source, says that Talcott, after a three days' march over the Berkshires from Westfield, came undetected upon the fugitives as they rested on the west side of the Housatonic. At dawn the next day, Talcott divided his forces to entrap the unsuspecting fugitives in an encircling movement, but the detachment being discovered by an Indian who had risen early to go fishing downstream, Talcott opened fire immediately on the slumbering encampment, with the disastrous results for the Indians which Hubbard enumerates, and Talcott's company losing "but one, and he a Mohegan."*

The Old Indian Burial Ground, Stockbridge, c. 1889, once thought to be the site of Talcott's raid. The Berkshire Athenaeum, Local History Department

Major Talcott's Raid, 1676

As for the Rest of the *Narragansetts* that joyned in Philip's Quarrel, it is already declared what End they were come unto. As for the Rest of the *Indians*, whether *Nipnet*, *Nashaway*, *Pacomptuk*, or *Hadly* or *Springfield* Indians; it is not so certain what has become of them: But after their Separation one from another about *July* last, it was observed by all the Tracts in those Woods, that they went still Westward, and about the Middle of *August* last, a great party of them were observed to pass by *Westfield*, a small Town to the West of *Springfield* and were judged to be about two hundred: News thereof being brought to Major *Talcot*, he with the Soldiers of *Connecticut Colony* under his Command, both English and Indians, pursued them as far as Ausotunnoog River (in the middle Way betwixt *Westfield* and the *Dutch River*, and *Fort-Albany*) where he overtook them, and fought with them; killing and taking Prisoners forty-five, whereof twenty-five were fighting Men, without the Loss of any one of his Company, besides a *Mohegin Indian*; many of the Rest were sorely wounded, as appeared by the dabling of the Bushes with Blood, as was observed by them that followed them a little further.

It is written since from *Albany*, that there were sundry Lost besides the forty-five forementioned, to the Number of threescore in all; and also that a hundred and twenty of them are since dead of Sickness: so as Vengeance seems to be persuing of them as well as the Rest.

From *The History of the Indian Wars in New England from the First Settlement to the Termination of the War with King Philip, in 1677*. By The Reverend William Hubbard, Minister of Ipswich. Boston, 1677.

KONKAPOT ET AL.

In 1724 Konkapot and other Housatonic Indians were induced to travel to Westfield to deed to a group of Connecticut Valley developers land which is now Sheffield, Great Barrington, and part of Stockbridge and Lee. A modern reader can only wonder what Konkapot and his forest associates made of the document's dense legalese, given in full herewith.

The Housatonack Deed

Know all Men by these presents that we, Conkepot Poneyote Partarwake Naurnauquin Waenenocow Nawnausquan Cauconaughfeet Nonamcaunet Naunhamiss Sunkhunk Popaqua Taunkhonkpus Tartakim Sauncokehe Cancannap Sunkiewe Nauheag Mauchewaufeet John VanGilder Pinaskenet all of Housatonack allias Westonook, in New England, in ye province of ye Massachusetts Bay: for & in consideration of a valuable sum well secured by bond viz Four Hundred and Sixty Pounds Three Barrels of Sider & thirty quarts of Rum: bearing date with these Presents, under ye hand & seal of Capt John Ashley of Westfield in ye County of Hampshire; we have given, granted, bargained, sold, aliened, conveyed & confirmed, and doe by these presents, fully, clearly and absolutely give, grant, bargain, sell, allinate, convey & confirm unto Col John Stoddard, Capt John Ashley, Capt Henry Dwight & Capt Luke Hitchcock, Esqrs, all in the County of Hampshire, Committee appointed by ye General Court to purchase a certain Tract of land lying upon Housatonack River, allias Westonook, in order for the settling two towns there, and unto such as ye Committee have or shall admit in order for ye settling of said Towns, to them, their Heirs & assigns a certain Tract or parcel of land, Meadow, swamp & upland lying on ye River aforesaid butted & bounded as followeth, viz: Southardly upon ye divisional line between the Province of Massachusetts Bay: and the colony of Connecticut in New England Westardly on ye patten or colony of New York, northardly upon ye Great mountain known by ye name of Manskuseehoank and Eastardly to run Four miles from ye aforesaid River and in a general way so to extend Furthermore it is to be understood that ye abovesaid Indians reserve to themselves within the aforesaid Tract of land, described by bounds and butments, Southardly on a Brook on ye west side Housatonack River, known by the name of Mannanpenokcan and Northardly to a small brook lying between ye aforesaid Brook and ye River called Wampanikseeport allias White River: viz All ye land between ye aforesaid Brooks from said Westonook River

Monument Mountain by Asher Durand. Courtesy of The Berkshire Eagle

extending unto ye patten of the Colleny of New York Together with a clear Meadow, between the aforesaid small Brook extending Northardly unto ye aforesaid White River; viz, the aforesaid Indians reserve to themselves all ye land between ye Brooks running due West line from ye mouth of sd Brooks unto ye patten of ye Colleny of New York aforesaid And we ye aforesaid Indians doe for ourselfs, our heirs Executors & Administrators, Covenant promise and grant to & with the aforesaid Committee & such as they have or shall admit of for Planters of sd Townships That before the ensealing hereof, we ye sd Indians are ye true, sole & lawful owners of ye aforegranted premises and are lawfully seized and possessed of the same in our own proper right, as a good perfect & absolute estate of inheritance in fee simple, and have in ourselfs good right, full power & lawful authority to grant, bargain, sell, convey & confirm sd bargained premises in manner aforesaid And ye sd Committee & such as they shall or may admit for Inhabitants of sd Townshipps to them their heirs and assigns shall & may from time to time and at all times hereafter by virtue of these Presents, lawfully & peacibly occupie, Possess and enjoy the said bargained Premises with all ye appurtenances, free & clear, and clearly & freely acquitted & discharged of, from all & all manner, former & other Gifts, Grants, Bargains, Sales, Jointures, Mortgages, Wills, Devises & Incumbrances whatsoever And furthermore We the sd Indians, for ourselfs and for sd Heirs, Executors & Administrators doe covenant & engage to secure & defend ye sd bargained Premises unto them the aforesaid Committee, and to such persons as the sd Committee have or shall admit in order to ye settling sd Towns, to them or their Heirs & Assigns forever against ye the lawful claims & demands of any Person or Persons whatsoever In witness whereof, we the aforesaid Indians have hereunto set our hands and seals this 25th day of April, in ye tenth year of his Majisty's rign and in ye year of or one thousand seven hundred & twenty four:

Signed, sealed & deld
in presence of us
Conreat Borghghart
Benjamin Smith
John Gun Jun
Samuel Bartlett

Conkepot,	his mark * seal
Poneyote,	his mark * seal
Pota wakeont,	his mark * seal
Naunausquan,	his mark * seal
Wanenocow,	his mark * seal
Naunauquin,	his mark * seal
Conconaughpeet,	his mark * seal
Nonaucauneet,	his mark * seal
Paunopescennot,	his mark * seal
Covconofeet,	his mark * seal
Naunhamiss,	his mark * seal
Sunkhonk,	his mark * seal
Popaqua,	his mark * seal
Taunkhonkpus,	his mark * seal
Tatakim,	his mark * seal
Saunkokehe,	his mark * seal
Cancanwap,	his mark * seal
Saunkewenaugheag,	his mark * seal
Manchewanfeet,	his mark * seal
John Vangilder,	his mark * seal
Ponaskenet,	his mark * seal

The aforesaid is a Copy of ye Deed given by the Indians for ye Housatonack Land Examined by me

Ebener Pomroy by order

Acknowledged before
John Ashly, J. P.

From *Indian Deeds of Hampden County*. Edited by Harry Andrew Wright. Springfield, Massachusetts, 1905.

BENJAMIN WADSWORTH

In August 1694, the Reverend Benjamin Wadsworth of Boston, later president of Harvard, traveled across the Berkshires to Albany, where as Commissioner for Massachusetts, he met with other colonial delegations to negotiate with the Five Nations, a confederation of Iroquois tribes. Going home, he chose a longer but easier route, riding by way of Claverack, Taghanic, down Tenmile River, to Gaylordsville, Woodbury, Waterbury, and Hartford.

Journey to Albany

Captain Sewal and Major Townsend, being commission'd to treat with the Mockways, set out from Boston about halfe an hour past 12 Moonday August 6, 1694. Several Gentlemen did accompany them to Watertown and then returned. At Watertown, we met with Livetenant Hammond and thirty troopers, who were appointed for a guard to Springfield. We came to our first stage, at Malberough, about halfe an hour past eight in the evening. We lodged at Abraham How's, and thence set forward the next morning about halfe an hour past seven of the clock.

There was nothing remarkable this day, but only Mr. Dwite of Hatford did accidentally fall into our company, and after the same manner, scil. accidentally, he and his horse both together fell into a brook; but both rose again without damage. This day we din'd in the woods. Pleasant descants were made upon the dining room: it was said that it was large, high, curiously hung with green; our dining place was also accomodated with the pleasancy of a murmuring rivulet. This day, some of our company saw a bear; but being near a thick swamp, he escaped our pursuit. Towards night, we heard (I think) 3 guns; but we knew not who shot them. Our whole company come this day to Quaboag, about sundown, not long before nor after; here we lodged this night. The next day, August 8th, we set out from Quaboag, about six of the clock, and came to Springfield at two or three of the clock in the afternoon. This night we went over to Westfeild, and the next morning, about halfe an hour past 8, we set outt from thence toward Albany, the nearest way through the woods, being accompanied with Collonel Pinchon, in commission with Cap. Sewal and Major Townsend, by the Council Of the Province of the Massachusets Bay, and Collonel Allen and Captain Stanley, Commissioners for Conneticutt Colony. For a guard, we had with us Cap. Wadsworth of Harford, and with him 60 Dragoons.

This day we traveled through the woods, about 24 or 25 miles, and might in an ordinary way have gone much farther, but that Collonel Allen was very much indispos'd by reason of a great pain in his back, which occasion'd his frequent dismounting and resting. The road which we travelled, this day, was very woody, rocky, mountanous, swampy; extream bad riding it was. I never yet saw so bad travelling as this was. We took up our quarters, this night, by the side of a river, about a quarter past 5.

We had a little hutt built for us, with pine-bows, under which we lodg'd very comfortably. We had some curious descants made upon our buildings, lodgings, and entertainment; one, lying some small distance from the fire, was said to ly out of doors. The next morning, it was queried whether the house should be pulled down or sold. On this morning, we set out from our green lodgings towards Albany, about sunrise or a little after.

Collonel Allen being very ill, we were hindered in our journeyings upon the account thereof, and so travelled this day but about 25 miles, and took up our lodgings, about sundown, in the woods, at a place called Ousetonuck, formerly inhabited by Indians. Through this place runs a very curious river, the same (which some say) runs through Stradford; and it has, on each side, several parcels of pleasant, fertile, intervale land.

In the morning, two of our souldiers could not find their horses, and were therefore left a while behind, at our night quarters, with about a dozen or more other souldiers with them; but, not finding their horses, they quickly came after us, and overtook us. This day, Cap. Wadsworth had his leg very much hurt, by his horse falling upon it. The greatest part of our road, this day, was a hidious, howling wilderness; some part of the road was not so extream bad.

This day we met a negro coming from Albany; but being very suspicious, we took him back with us, and that night they pinion'd him; but yet, before morning, he was gone, and we saw him no more. Though we saw him no more, yet we thought of him; for he stool a sword and gun, and escaped therewith.

The next morning, Aug. 11, we set forward about sunrise, and came, the foremost of us, to Kindarhook about 3 of the clock; the rest, which were hindered in their motion by reason of Collonel Allen's being not well, came to us about 2 or 3 hours after. Here we took up our quarters at the house of one John Tison. Here we keept the Sabbath; and they having no minister, we had the libertie of using that meeting house. In this place there is very rich land; a curious river runs through the town, on the banks of which there is some interval land. There are not many inhabitants; I think they say but twenty families, or thereabouts, at most. The houses are in three parcels in this town; and there are two forts, one

whereof I saw. Provisions were here very scarce; eggs, twelve pence a
score; lambs, twelve shillings a piece, &c. On Munday morning, Aug. 13,
we set out for Albany, and having rode about 20 miles through a pine
plane, we came to Greenbush, about twelve of the clock, or a little more.

From *Wadsworth's Journal* in Massachusetts Historical Society Collections, Volume 1, 4th
Series, 1851.

JONATHAN EDWARDS

In January 1750, Jonathan Edwards rode over the top of the Berkshires to visit the mission to the Indians at Stockbridge. He had been invited to take over the direction of the mission following the death of its founder, John Sergeant. Although offered prestigious posts elsewhere in the colonies and in Scotland, Edwards, America's greatest intellect in theology, metaphysics, and psychology, chose to come to Stockbridge, then a wilderness outpost a two-days' ride beyond the frontier, and here wrote one of the great polemical works of the eighteenth century, Freedom of the Will, *while ministering to some of the more primitive souls of the era, both settler and native, faithfully and tirelessly laboring for the special welfare of the latter.*

Given here in its entirety is a little-known sermon he delivered to the Indians in November 1753. Since he was unable to master the Mahican language, he adapted his preaching style to accommodate a translator. The sermon was published by Alexander B. Grosart in his Selections from the Unpublished Writings of Jonathan Edwards, of America *in an edition of 300 copies in Edinburgh in 1865. Edwards left the mission in 1757 to become president of Princeton. Within three months he was dead of complications following a smallpox vaccination.*

Sermon to Stockbridge Indians

2 Tim. iii. 16 — "All scripture is given by inspiration of God."
Doctrine: The scripture is the Word of God.

I. There must be some Word of God.

'Tis unreasonable to think that God would always keep silence and never say anything to mankind.

God has made mankind and given him Reason and Understanding.

Has made him the chief of all the creatures.

Given him reason that he might know God and serve Him.

Did not give the other creatures reason: He did make 'em to serve Him.

Other creatures are made for man.

Man was made for God: to serve God, or else he was made for nothing.

But how unreasonable is it to think that God would make us for Himself and never say anything to us.

God is the King that rules over all nations.

But how unreasonable is it to suppose that He should be a King and never say anything to His subjects .... be a King and never tell them what His will or what His commands are, that His subjects may obey Him.

Is as a Father: all His Family.

But will a father be always dumb and silent, &c.?

God has given mankind speech: so that they are able to speak and make known their minds to one another.

And therefore 'tis unreasonable to think that God never would speak to men and make known His mind to them.

We need to have God teach us as much as a child needs to be taught by his father.

And since God has given mankind understanding He doubtless will teach him and instruct him.

How can we know Him to worship God if we have no Word of God to tell us?

We should not know what way of worship would please Him .... whether to pray to Him or to sing or to keep the Sabbath, or be baptized, or come to sacrament, or what else we shall do.

'Tis certain God has made us for another world .... Men but a little while here.

And how shall we know how God will do with us in another world?

How shall we know how He will punish such as do wickedly in another world?

What He will do for good men in another world?

Whether He will forgive us after we have sinned?

How shall we know what He expects we should do that we may be forgiven?

In what He will save .... Whether He will forgive great sins.

What will men do when they come to die if there be no Word of God to tell 'em?

How should we ever know how the world was made?

How should we know how God made man at first?

We see men in this world are very wicked: the world is full of wickedness everywhere.

Certainly God did not make man so.

How shall we know how mankind came to be so wicked?

We see how the world is full of death: full of war and all manner of misery.

How shall we know how misery and death came, &c.?

And how shall we know what way of salvation there is?

Where shall we find one to be our Saviour that will stand for us ... if the Word of God don't tell us?

How shall we know what God will do with the world at last? how the world will come to an end?

    We see that God is kind to mankind: takes care of 'em.

    Therefore He can't leave 'em in darkness and take no care to teach 'em.

    We see what necessity mankind stand in, of a Word of God to teach 'em when we consider how it is in those countries where they have no Word of God.

    They are all in darkness and blindness about God and Divine things.

    They think there is a God.

    Yet don't know what He is.

    Many think there is a great many gods.

    Worship "graven images" and stones.

    Worship the devil.

    Don't know how to serve God.

    Know nothing how the world was made .... how man was made.

    Know nothing what God will do with men in another world.

    Don't know how men shall obtain forgiveness of their sin.

    Some think by offering their own children ....

    Thus we see there must certainly be some Word of God.

    But where is any Word of God if it ben't in the Bible?

    The Heathen han't no Word of God amongst them.

    The Bible therefore is the Word of God, must be.

    The Bible gives right notions concerning God.

    Tells how God made the world .... made men .... how men became wicked ....

    What God will do with men in another world.

    What way we may have the forgiveness of sin.

    What is the way of salvation?

    What God's mind, and will, is.

    All the Rules and Commandments in the Bible are holy.

    Here told what man's duty is in many things.

    All sin is forbidden.

    How God will be served.

    The great things God has done for His people through all ages.

    What the Saviour did and suffered: how He ascended into Heaven.

    How the world will come to an end.

    How God will judge the world.

    Another thing that shews that the Scriptures are the Word of God is this: —

    That when God told the wise and holy men to write the Bible He gave 'em power to work great MIRACLES, to convince men that it was His work.

    Moses was a man that wrote all the first part of the Bible.

And God, to shew that the Word he wrote was His word ....

And so the other Prophets that wrote other parts.

Jesus Christ gave us the Scriptures of the New Testament. He spoke the Word of God.

He, to shew that His Word was the Word of God, wrought great miracles.

He told His Disciples to write down what He said .... enabled them to do great miracles.

The Apostle Paul.

That there was such a man as Christ .... that great miracles were wrought even His enemies own: none deny it.

Another thing that shews the Scriptures to be the Word of God is that the Scripture FORETELLS a great many things.

The OLD TESTAMENT that was given to the Jews a great while before Christ was born foretold Christ's coming.

And a great many things concerning Him. All which are FULFILLED.

The Scriptures of the NEW TESTAMENT foretell a great many things .... all came to pass.

The Jews should become a *distinct* nation .... that the Pope shall arise .... many turn Papists .... just as it is.

The Scriptures we here read is the same Word that was given of old.

The same Word has been kept all along: it has not been changed.

Here it still is the same language in which it was written at first.

It must be the same that the Jews had, and that God's People had in Christ's and the Apostle's time.

It could not be altered since, because it was scattered about a great many nations all over the world .... which have had it ever since.

Therefore the world could not be cheated.

The Jews, to whom the Old Testament was given: they remain a distinct People still, and have had the Old Testament amongst 'em, written in their own language.

They are all over the world and can't alter it.

The Scripture has all along been among people that have been against one another in the OPINIONS.... could not agree to alter it .... if one altered the other would find it out.

Another thing that shews that the Scripture is the Word of God is this: —

That the Scripture has been the means of enlightening so many nations.

Many nations formerly in great darkness: but now ...

All the greatest nations of the world ...

No people in the world can come to have right notions of God and of another world any other way than by this Word.

Another thing that shews it, is ... Great opposition: the Devil and wicked men make against it.

Another thing that shews that it is the Word of God is this: it has PREVAILED against such great opposition.

When it first came abroad in the world all the wicked set themselves against it ... kings ... armies ... Christians put to cruel deaths ... yet it PREVAILED ... overcame all the greatest and strongest nations.

Then there is this thing: those who first preached were poor men.

So many nations never could have been made to believe it if men had made it.

Not only foolish men, little men, but great men and wise men.

Another thing: no other Word ever was used as the means of bringing men to know the true God but the Scriptures.

Where the Scriptures have come there has been light: all the rest of the world has remained in darkness. So 'tis now all over the world.

Another thing that shews it is this: no man could make such a Book as the Bible ....

It must be made by wicked men or good men .... Wicked men would not make it. Good men could not.

Another thing: no Book reaches the hearts of men so much. No word so AWAKENS the conscience. No word is so powerful to change the heart. Great many have been made 'new men:' very wicked men.

No word so powerful to comfort the hearts of men ... in death ... cruel deaths ...

Another: good men all love the Bible. Better they are the more they love it ... the more they are convinced that it is the Word of God. The more wicked men the more they are AGAINST it.

APPLICATION:

1. How thankful we should be to God ....

2. Hence we may learn that all the Scripture says to us is certainly true.

God knows ... God cannot lie ... God is very angry for sin.

About another world. There is another world. Good men die.

About Hell. The Scripture says there is a furnace of fire.

God will not hear. No rest.

Many are ready to think that it may be there is none.

About Heaven. About the Day of Judgment: rise again.

About the sorrowful, miserable condition man is in.

About the way of salvation.

Christ is the Son of God. No other Saviour. HE WILL SAVE ALL THAT COME TO HIM.

About the mystery of being 'born again.'

Some are ready to say in their hearts there is no such thing.

What we must be in order to go to Heaven —

Therefore let all men that are not 'born again' consider these things.

All these are not seeking their salvation.

3. Hence 'tis worth the while to take a great deal of pains to learn to read and understand the Scriptures.

I would have you all of you think of this.

When there is such a book that you may have, how can you be contented without being able to read it?

How does it make you feel when you think there is a Book that is God's own Word? That tells ...

And you think with yourself that you are not able to read it ... See and think about it. All that you know is only what others tell you ... see nothing with your own eyes.

Especially I would have you that are young people take notice of these things.

Parents should take care that their children learn ...

This will be the way to be kept from the Devil ... Devil can't bear the Bible. Kept from Hell. To be happy for ever.

But if you let the Word of God alone, and never use, and you can't expect the benefits of it ....

You must not only hear and read, &c., but you must have it sunk down into your heart. Believe. Be affected. Love the Word of God. Written in your heart.

Must not only read and hear, but DO the things. Otherwise no good; but will be the worse for it.

And you should endeavour to understand. To that end to learn the English tongue.

If you had the Bible in your own language, I should not say so much.

Endeavour to promote your children's learning English.

You that can read should often read ... meditate ... pray that God would enlighten you.

Consider how much it is worth the while to go often to your Bible to hear the great God Himself speak to you.

There you may hear Christ speak.

How much better must we think this is than the word of men. Better than the word of the wisest man of the world.

How much wiser is God than man.

Here all is true; nothing false.

Here all is wise; nothing foolish.

This is the GREAT LIGHT God has given to the world. To make use of this is the way to walk in the Light ... to have our souls filled with Light. If we neglect this we shall walk in darkness.

We should value this more than the light of the sun. We see the light of the sun does a great deal of good ... gives light ... pleasant to see ... 'tis comfortable ... it gives life.

So Scripture gives light ... gives life.

Should hear the Word: come to meeting. 'Tis the way to have God's mercy, to seek God in His Word. There we may expect to meet with God. God will respect His own Word for the good of men: what great good has been done.

God has often made it a means of great good. Conversion of many souls. Great joy of many. Many have been comforted in affliction ... in death.

This will be the way to be wise with the most excellent wisdom.

From *Selections from the Unpublished Writings of Jonathan Edwards, of America.* Transcribed by Alexander B. Grosart. Edinburgh, 1865.

Jonathan Edwards. Stockbridge Historical Society

ESTHER EDWARDS BURR

The daughter of Jonathan Edwards and Sarah Pierrepont Edwards, Esther Edwards at 20 left Stockbridge to marry the Reverend Aaron Burr of Newark, president of the College of New Jersey (later Princeton), a man sixteen years older than she. Four years later, a few months after the birth of her son, Aaron, Jr., later vice president of the United States, she returned to Stockbridge for a visit — unfortunately in the midst of an Indian scare. A little more than a year later, her husband suddenly died of malaria and overwork. The following March her father died, and in April Esther herself died at the age of 26.

In 1903, the Rev. Jeremiah E. Rankin of Washington, D.C., president of Howard University, published what purported to be "Esther Burr's Journal" as a gift book for women. (It was reprinted by a Washington department store.) Largely the product of his sentimental imagination and a rare item today, Rankin's fiction presents a saccharine Esther Burr glaringly at odds with reality.

Excerpts from Rankin's Bogus Journal

Stockbridge, June 8, 1752

This is my last day in Stockbridge, in this dear home, with my honored mother and sisters. The orchards are filled with apple-bloom as for a bridal. Dear beautiful Stockbridge; the sweetest place on earth, with her mountains tree-topped to the blue skies, her miniature meadows along the Housatonic, where the Indians have their picturesque encampments, the river, willow-embosomed, where the strong arms of my tawny friends have so often noiselessly guided the canoe, and we have glided as in a dream. Yes, also dear sanctuary of God, where the red man and the white man have dwelt together in peace, as in their own Father's House, and where my good father's instruction has so often fallen upon us all alike, as manna from Heaven. "Blessed are they that dwell in thy house; they shall still be praising thee."

Stockbridge

I have sometimes essayed a description to myself of Mr. Edwards. Let me do it again, before I leave my father's house for the house of my husband. His face is almost womanly in refinement and feature, and grace. There is a kind of sweet sedateness, an elevated, almost celestial serenity, to some, perhaps severity, of expression. And when he is speaking in the pulpit, it often seems that his voice has a supernatural, an angelic tenderness and authority. There is in his utterance no weakness or softness, though it is not a loud voice nor very masculine. There is such a holy loyalty to the truth in the speaker, as though he were one of God's swift messengers, unwinged indeed, save in the spirit, which often tries lofty flights, but coming straight from the ineffable glory, commissioned of infinite love to proclaim the truth and defend it. In person, he sometimes reminds me of Michael Angelo's arch-angel with drawn sword; of pictures of John the Evangelist, which our Scotland friends, the Erskines, have sent us, and which hang in our living room.

Stockbridge, June, 1752

The good man who has chosen me for his bride, has sent a young messenger from Newark, with two horses, to conduct my honored mother and myself to New Jersey. He says, there is plenty of Scripture for it. Did not Isaac thus send for Rebekah? I am to ride Nimrod, Mr. Burr's great admiration and pride. I am glad to go. I suppose I feel some as did Christiana, in "Pilgrim's Progress," when she had summons to follow her husband. Is it wrong to think of my new home as the type of heaven? I hope it is not wrong to feel so. I had to kiss the bark of the elm-tree, that stands in front of my window, and where I have so often watched the returning robins, as they built their nests and reared their young, and then taught them to fly away; and now I am to stretch my wings and go, after their example. But, mine are the wings of the dove!

When we mounted the hill, on our way toward West Stockbridge, I was fain to turn again and look back on the lovely little town in the valley, and the surrounding mountains in their grandeur. On either side stood the hills, lately clothed with new verdure; between them, the beautiful intervales, beneath which crept the river, the smooth-gliding Housatonic, and where were feeding the cattle. I shut my eyes if I might fix the picture and make it mine forever, and then rode on with my companions. And soon Nimrod, with his eager spirit, gave me enough to attend to. He seemed to know he was taking me to his master.

We took the turnpike to the Hudson. The road having been lately mended, our progress was slow. Indeed, there were some passages where the men were still at work picking out the stones and the stumps. But, even this gave us all the more leisure to look at the beautiful woods, and to hear the brooks full of glancing fish, bubbling by the roadside. The birds were very lively with their songs, and the bushy-tailed squirrels were full of their pranks. The early dews, too, were dropping on the leaves. And soon my steed having come to know his rider, moved on obediently, and as though more than satisfied with his burden. Our riding companion, who has just graduated at the College, was not very talkative, though quite enough so for me. My dear mother, who was with us — but, ah, only a mother could know the soliloquies going on in her heart. She hid all those mother-thoughts, even from me. I am afraid, it sometimes seemed to her, that she was accompanying her Isaac, to a place that God would tell her of — for the altar.

From *Esther Burr's Journal*. Edited by Jeremiah Eames Rankin. Washington, 1903.

Jonathan Edwards' house, built in 1737, where he wrote The Freedom of the Will. Stockbridge Historical Society

Excerpts from the Authentic Journal, 1756

29 Aug

Sabbath Morn (about 12 miles from Levingstons Manor) at a Dutch house in the Woods. Yesterday about 3 in the P.M. we arrived at Levingstons Manor, tarried just to drink Tea and then Mr Levingston was so good as to let me have a Waggon and servant to carry us to Stockbridge, and we thought it best to come to this place that we might have the easier days ride on Monday. But this morn before day our servant gives us the slip and goes home, so what we shall do God only knows — This is a very inconvenient place to spend a Sabbath. The whole house is but one room, and a large famaly and no relegion, but I desire to be thankfull tis a pleasant day so that one may walk out into the Woods and be retired — and O my dear I find God is here as well as in his house and among his people — Yes my Dear God is everywhere and does not forget his, be they where they will — as soon as Breakfast was over I took an English Bible (which is rare among the Dutch) and walked about a quarter of a mile with some longing desires that I might meet God, and I hope I found him. O how good is God to an unworthy Worm that has forsook him to meet me this Morn — I said surely God is in this place; and I hope I shall never forget it — truly my dear I hant found such freedom and delight in Gods servise for many weeks past — God does not want for means nor place — I have been long seeking God in this and the other duty and ordinance — but it has pleased him to hide his face and disappoint me in my hopes and expecttations when I was ready to think him near — but how little did I think of meeting him here — last Sabbath I lost and I greived at the loos and I was affraid I should lose this — O what shall I render to the Lord for his goodness to me? I can render nothing but myself, my poor wicked sinfull self.

Eve — 50 soldiers to sup at this House and lodge which surprzed me much, but they behaved better then I expected considering they came from Road-lsland — they are going for recrutes — how many difficulties one meets with in a journey, just so with our journy throu' this life.

Monday—30

Morn — before sun rise, set out in a Waggon for Stockbridge, was threttened with rain but cleared up and was pleasant, the road very bad but got along finely — when we had got within abot 10 miles of Stockbridge it set a raining very hard. We stoped as soon as we could find a convenient house which was abut 6 miles from my Fathers. I could not bare to stop for all night, and our waggonner was urgent to go along so we set out wet to the skin as we were and had not got far before it Raind as fast as ever I saw it in my life, and in a half an hour I had not a dry thread abot me, but kept along and just as we got to my Fathers it left raining (so some good came from bad *luck* as the vulgar say —) We came in and surprized em almost out of their witts. Lucy and Sueky were almost overcome. I need not tell you how glad they were to see us but the meloncholy news that I brought fild the house with gloom. I mean the news of Oswego's being taken which was not confermd here till I brought the dreadfull tidings [On August 14, 1756, the French Army under General Montcalm captured the British forts at Oswego on Lake Ontario.] — the first thing I did was to strip from Top to Toe — found my self very stiff and worried, so went to bed soon but could not sleep for fear of the Enemy.

Aug 31

Teusday — dark dull weather — feel very poorly hardly able to set up.

Wednsday—Septr-1

Mrs Dwight had a letter from the Colonel giving an account how Oswego was taken which was by Treachery — O how dark do things look! I fear I shall not be able to take any comfort in my friends nor they in me.

Thursday and Fryday—2 and 3

Almost overcome with fear. Last night and Thursday night we had a watch at this fort and most of the Indians come to lodge here — Some thought that they heard the enemy last night — O how distressing to live in fear every moment — This day had several friends come to see me.

Saturday 4

A very busy day with us for my Brother sets out for the Jersyes on Monday and on Teusday My Mother sets out for Northampton. My Sister Dwight is near her time, so I never said one Word against it altho' I am come 150 Miles to see my friends and am apt to think I shall not come again in many years if ever — I proposed when I came from home to tarry here till the second week in October but beleive I shall shorten my vissit since things are so ordered and I am so distracted with fears.

Sabbath-5

Out all day. Heard 4 excellent sermons tho so Ill for want of sleep that I am hardly my self — I hant had a nights sleep since I left Newyork — Since I have been here I may say I have had none.

Monday very hot-6

My brother set out for Newark and I had the pleasure of writing to Mr Burr, but Indeed I had nothing very pleasing to say, I am so poorly, and scared out of my Witts about the Enemy — a deal of company.

7 Teusday extream hot—

This Morn my mother set out for Northampton and hopes to return in about a month, but alas for me I shall not be able to wait her return, for I grow worse and worse, more affraid than ever — if I happen to drowse I am frighted to death with dreams. As for sleep tis gone, and I shall go two if things dont alter — My Mother gone! It adds double gloom to everything.
P.M. expected company but had none.

8 Wednsday still as hot as ever

O how dreadfully does this World look! Happy — thrice happy are those that have a sure title to a better — It looks to me that this Land is to be given into the hands of our enemies to be scurged and that severly — I am looking for persecution — but alas I fear, I fear, I am not able to stand the firery tryal! And O what an awful dreadfull thing to be left to deny Christ and loose our souls forever!

P.M. This place is in a very defenceless condicion — not a soldier in it, the fighting Indians all except a very few gone into the Army, many of the white people also, and this is a place that the enemy can easily get at, and if they do we cant defend our selves. 10. Indians might with all ease distroy us intirely. There has been a number seen at about 30 miles distance from this place.

I have had company and there has been a tirrable Thunder storm as ever I knew.

Thursday-9

I am full of news about Oswego and our Army and the Treachery of some officers at Oswego — but you will hear all sooner then by this Letter so I shant trouble you with it.

P.M. Vissitors a great many. I am sick for want of sleep.

Fryday Morn-10

I want to be made willing to die in any way God pleases, but I am not willing to be Buchered by a barbarous enemy nor cant make my self willing — I slept a little better last night then usual — but feel no easier this morn — *The Lord Reighns,* and why ant I sattisfied, he will order all for the best for the publick and for me, and he will be glorified let all the powers of Earth and Hell do their worst — I am to spend this day at my sister Parsonses.

Saturday-11

Last night 17 soldiers came to Town to our assistance. The number is two small by much to defend three Forts. Some of em are to lodge here. Hope I shant be so much affraid as before tho' they are but little better than none — P.M. heard from my Mother and Sister Dwight. All well as yet.

Teusday 14

P.M. Vissited again, kindly treated, heard from Northampton. My mother got down comfortably — the person that brought word from her says that my Sister Dwight was just taken in Travil — I feel very ancious for her, poor Woman, but I hope all is well over long before this — She was taken about 10 o'Clock Monday Morn — last Night I slept pretty comfortably, which is the first comfortable Night I have had since I have been here.

Sabbath—19

Last eve I had some free discourse with My Father on the great things that concern my best intrest — I opend my difeculties to him very freely and he as freely advised and directed. The conversation has removed some

distressing doubts that discouraged me much in my Christian warfare —
He gave me some excellent directions to be observed in secret that tend to
keep the soul near to God, as well as others to be observed in a more
publick way — What a mercy that I have such a Father! Such a Guide!

Sept 20 Monday A.M.

Vissit amongst the poor Indians, which excites in me a great concern
for the poor cretures best intrest.

P.M. Vissited an old aquaintance — Eve. Heard from the Waggoner
and he insists on going on Wednsday so I must set out afternoon on
Wednsday.

Teusday P.M.

Vissited again, and now all my vissiting is over. Eve Perswaded Mr
Woodbridge to let one of his Daughters go with him for company for me
and now feel easier.

Wednsday A.M. 22

Very busy in geting my things togather — just before noon heard Mr
Woodbridge is taken very ill with a Vomiting and Purging so cant think
of going at present — I was at a loss what to do but upon consideration
and advise concluded to go when the Waggon came, for perhaps I may
loose the oppertunity of Mr Fondas sloop which is the only one that I am
sertain is going down — My Father went to Mr Woodbridge and found
him a little better and hopes to be able to go before the sloop sails.

P.M. 5 o'Clock set out in the Waggon after an affectionate parting
with all my friends except Lucy. She rode as far as Sheffeild and will tarry
all Night with me.

23 Thursday Morn very Erly

Parted with Lucy and set forward with my honest Dutchman only. It
seemd very lonesome to go quite alone and could have no conversation not
much more then with the Horses, but found I could convers with my God
and did not think my self alone for he was present, and has brought me to Mr
Fondas more comfortably then I could expect — tho weary as you may think.

Sept 24 Fryday Morn 9. o'Clock
at Clavarack.

Mr Fonda says he cant go to Newyork till next Week on Teusday or
Wednsday — this very discourageing — What, lay here amongst a parsle
of dumb Dutch people a whole week? Tis trying I assure you my dear —
tho' the people are very sivel (but not like English) and I have reason to be

thankfull they are so — All is sertainly for the best, however dark and cross it may seem — I hope I am in some degree thankfull that I am in the hands of God. I would not have the ordering of my Voyage for the world — I think it will be my duty to seek some other conveyance then by Mr Fonda — several of the Albany sloops are about to sail and many of their Masters I am acquainted with and could trust — My Son is awake so must leve you.

Saturday—25

Yesterday about noon came Mr Woodbridge and Daughter very unexpectedly — you see providence is kind in sending me good company when I had no reason to expect any — Many have been Gods mercies.

P.M. All for the best that we are not gone yet, for tis very cold and Rainy as well as head-wind — We are such short sighted cretures we know not when a thing is for us nor when against us, but we must lern to trust *him* that does know all things and will order all for the best — 5 O'Clock, there is a sloop in sight and we are about to send to her to see whether she will drop ancor till the Morn and then take us in. Eve. Find the supposed sloop to be only a Boat with men sick of the Camp distemper — so must wait.

Sabbath—26

Must spend another Sabbath amongst the Dutch. O tis a tryal! But I will call to mind the Sabbath I spent at a Dutch house in the Woods as I went to Stockbridge — a Sabbath to be remembred — then God taught me and made me feel that he was every where, and that he could bless without the ordinary means of grace — O! just and righteous art thou O Lord in depriveing me of such precious means as I have been favoured with heretofore — for my shamefull abuse off them and unthankfullness for them — O that I might spend my Sabbaths better hereafter if God should grant me them — P.M. A deel of company — The Sabbath here is no more then a play day — I wonder what they think.

Monday—P.M. 27

Soon this morn a fine North Wind blew up and several Albany sloops appeared. We set out in a Boat and got on Board of one of them that has no passengers, so we have the Cabbin to our selves — and sail very finely — Eve. The wind gone and we are obliged to throw Ancor and lay till morn.

Teusday Morn—28

A fine wind but such a thick fog that we cant see three yerds from the sloop, so obliged to lay till about 10 o'Clock and then our tide will be almost spent — P.M. We came finely throu the Highlands, but then lost our Wind as is common in this place, the Mountains being so vastly high that no wind can find us that comes from the East, West, or North, so must wait for the tide in hopes that that will carry us out of the reach of these Mountains — Eve. Came prety fast with the tide and a small west breese within a mile of Dobbs's Ferry which is about 30 miles from Newyork and here forced to lay for Morn Tide, the Wind being gone.

Wednsday Morn—Sept 29

7 O'Clock set sail with the Tide but soon meet a strong south wind as much ahead as could blow but with tacking and going about 5 miles to gain one we made out to get half way between the ferry and York then lost our tide and wait the motion of the Waters and Wind.

Tis very crossing to lay here all day but tis all best — Wisely ordered — Mr Woodbridge went ashore and got some fruit and other things for our comfort and we made our selves as content as we could considering for our greatest comfort that God orders all — towards night set sail with a very violent head Wind, got along but very slowly but hoped to get in to york — 8 o'Clock the Wind blew so extream hard which made such a tirrable sea that we could not sail for we had not ballast — so lay all night abot 3 miles from Newyork. This was trying.

Thursday Morn—Sept 30

7 O'Clock landed safe at Newyork. What a Mercy! O how good is God to an Ill deserving creature! Called for Breakfast at an Inn, then got sombody to carry my little Son and went up to Mrs Merciers where I now am waiting for an oppertunity to go to Newark — here I have the pleasure to hear from Mr Burr and Sally that they are well — I am quite impatient to see them as you may guss, tho I shall find em all in confusion. Commencement is over, yet the synnod sets.

From *Esther Edward Burr: Journal, 1754-1757.* Edited by Carol F. Karlsen and Laurie Krumpacker. Yale University Press, 1984.

HENRIETTE-LUCY DILLON, MARQUISE DE LA TOUR DU PIN

When the French Revolution broke out in 1789, the nineteen-year old Ma-
dame de la Tour du Pin was lady-in-waiting to Queen Marie Antoinette. In
1794 she and her family dramatically escaped the Terror, fleeing on a ship
bound for Boston. Offered a farm near Albany by Philip Schuyler, they shipped
their belongings to Albany by water via New York City and the Hudson, but
decided to travel themselves overland, then thought a novel and daring way to
go. Here she describes their last night in the "wilderness." She means Massa-
chusetts when she says Connecticut.

The Last Night in the Wilderness

We all three [Mme. de La Tour du Pin, her husband, and M. de Chambeau] left Boston during the early days of June, taking the children with us. A fortnight later, we arrived in Albany, having travelled right across the State of Connecticut and greatly ad-mired its fertility and air of prosperity. But some very sad news made me so unhappy that I was unable to enjoy any of it: Before we left Boston, M. de La Tour du Pin had received news of my father's death. He did not tell me until we had started out, hoping that the journey itself and the movement would be a distraction and help to dull my grief. It was at Northampton, where we spent a night, that he decided to tell me, fearing I might read it in some gazette. Indeed, all the news from France was printed in the American papers as soon as it arrived, no matter at which port of the Union it was received.

My father's death distressed me very deeply, despite the fact that I had been expecting it for a long time. For many years I had seen him only on rare occasions, but nonetheless I had a most tender affection for him. I wrote to my stepmother, who was living in Martinique, and to my twelve-year-old stepsister, Fanny. Long afterwards, I had a reply from Mme. Dillon in which she told me that she was leaving for England with Fanny and Mlle. de La Touche, her daughter by her first marriage. It was a very cold letter and my stepmother showed not the slightest concern for the condition in which I was living in America.

Despite my grief, I did find distraction in the beauty of the forests we crossed on our way to Lebanon, the last stage where we were to spend the night before arriving in Albany. Unbroken forest, fifty miles wide, sepa-rated the State of Connecticut from that of, I think, New York, though doubtless by now it has disappeared. It offered a spectacle which I had never before seen: a forest in every stage of growth, from the tree which was a mere shoot, just showing above ground, to the tree which had fallen from age. The road through these magnificent forests was only wide enough for two carriages. It was no more than a cutting where the tree trunks had been felled at ground level, the mass of the tree falling to right and left to clear a path. But, what jolting we endured when those trunks had not been cut properly level with the ground! The remarkable fertility of this virgin land had encouraged the growth of an enormous number of parasitic plants, wild vines and lianas which wound themselves from one tree to the next. In the more open areas, there were thickets of flowering rhododendrons, some of them purple, others pale lilac, and roses of every kind. The flowers made a vivid splash of colour against the grassland, which was itself studded with mosses and flowering plants, while in the low-lying parts which were furrowed, and watered by small streams or creeks, as they are called, every kind of water plant was in full flower. This unspoiled nature enchanted me to such an extent that I spent the entire day in ecstasy.

Towards midday, we stopped for lunch at an inn set up not long before in the midst of this immense forest. In America, when a house is built in a forest and close to a road, the owner's first expenditure is for a sign, even if only one traveller is likely to pass in the whole of the year, and his first task the planting of a pole on which to hang it. Then under the sign, a letter box is nailed to the pole. The road may be barely visible, but thenceforward the place is marked on the map as a town.

The wooden house at which we stopped had reached the second stage of civilisation for it was a frame house, that is to say, a house with glazed windows. But it is the incomparable beauty of the family who lived in it that particularly remains in my memory and which I still never forget. There were three generations: first, the husband and wife, aged about forty to forty-five, both remarkable for their strength and beauty and gifted with that exquisite perfection of form which is to be found only in the paintings of the greatest masters; about them were grouped eight or ten children, boys and girls, and in them you could admire everything, from the young girl so like one of Raphael's beautiful virgins, to the smaller children with the faces of angels whom Rubens would not have disowned; also in this house lived a grandfather, most venerable in appearance, his hair whitened by the years, but quite unhampered by infirmity.

After we had finished lunch, which we ate together, he arose, took off his cap, and in a most respectful manner, announced: 'We shall drink to the health of our beloved President.' In those days there was not a single cabin, even among those most deeply buried in the forests, where this demonstration of love for the great Washington was not renewed at the end of every meal. Sometimes the health of 'The Marquis' was added. M.

de La Fayette had left a much-loved memory in the United States.

At Lebanon there was a sulphur bath establishment which was even then quite well known. The inn was very good, and above all, impeccably clean. But the luxury of white sheets was still unknown in that part of the United States. To ask for sheets that had not been used by others would have been considered a quite unreasonable caprice, and when the bed was fairly wide, you would even be asked, as if it were the most normal thing in the world, to allow someone to share it with you. This is what happened to M. de Chambeau that very evening at Lebanon. In the middle of the night, we suddenly heard a stream of French oaths, which could come only from him. In the morning we learned that towards midnight he had been awakened by a gentleman who was sliding, without so much as a 'by your leave' into the empty half of his double bed. Furious at this invasion, he promptly leaped out at the other side and spent the night in a chair listening to his companion's snores, for he had been in no way disturbed by M. de Chambeau's anger. This misadventure led to much teasing from everyone. When we arrived that evening at Albany, a small room was reserved for him alone, and that consoled him.

From *Memoirs of Madame de la Tour du Pin*. Translated by Felice Harcourt. Harville Press, 1969.

TIMOTHY DWIGHT

During his vacations while president of Yale (1795-1817), Timothy Dwight, a grandson of Jonathan Edwards, delighted to get into his carriage and travel the northeast corner of the new Republic, assessing its resources, collecting its statistics and historical information, and describing its beauties, curiosities, and advances. He was interested in everything, and conscious of being the first ever to study at first hand the conversion of a wilderness into civilization. In 1798 a tour to Vergennes, Vermont, took him up through the Berkshires, and the account excerpted here is based on his journal of that trip, with some information gathered and added later. (The "Bug in the Table" incident also interested a later observer, David Dudley Field.)

Travels in New England

SHEFFIELD

Sheffield lies on the southern border of Berkshire, and is the oldest settlement in that county. It occupies the principal part of the valley between the Green Mountains and Taconic on both sides of the river, which is everywhere bordered by a chain of rich and beautiful intervals. The rest of the valley is here principally a light, level ground, in some places fertile, but generally of an indifferent soil. The town is chiefly built on a single street, running about four miles and a half on the western border of the intervals. On the southern half the houses are thinly scattered. In the northern half they are more numerous and better. Upon the whole, it is rather a pretty settlement.

Among the interesting objects which are in full view, the river and its beautiful intervals and the mountains on the east and on the west hold a place of high distinction. Taconic, clad at this time in misty grandeur, partly embosomed and partly capped by clouds, particularly ornaments the landscape. Its height is about three thousand feet above the ocean. Its sides are not precipitous, nor its summits angular; but it is everywhere limited by lines which are flowing and graceful. This fact has always appeared to me sensibly to diminish its magnificence. Still it is a highly sublime object.

In the year 1781, I ascended the loftiest summit of this mountain, and found a most extensive and splendid prospect spread around me. On the north rose Saddle Mountain at the head of the Housatonic valley at the distance of forty miles. At the same distance the Catskill Mountains formed on the west the boundary of the vast valley of the Hudson. In the southwest rose Butter Hill, the most northern summit of the Highlands on the western side of that river, and the majestic front of an immense range receding gradually from the sight, limited the view beneath us toward that quarter of the horizon. The chain of the Green Mountains on the east stretched its long succession of summits from north to south a prodigious length, while over them, at the distance of forty miles, rose the single, solitary point of Mount Tom; and farther still, at the termination of fifty and sixty miles, ascended successively various eminences in the Lyme Range. Monadnock, at the distance of seventy miles on the northeast, is distinctly discernible in a day sufficiently clear, but to us, the weather being in a small degree hazy, was invisible. Immediately around us spread a collection of flourishing settlements, and finely varied the grandeur with their beauty.

Sheffield was incorporated in the year 1733, six years before any other town in this county, and twenty-two years before the commencement of the last Canadian war. The first settlers were, therefore, exposed to Indian depredations during a considerable period, without any possibility of obtaining timely assistance. They were emigrants from Westfield, and were allured hither by the fine intervals on the Housatonic. The character which they brought with them, their descendants still keep, and are just about as industrious, as moral, and as propense to improvements as their ancestors.

Sheffield has always been subject to the fever and ague, a calamity to which the slow motion of the Housatonic through its whole breadth may not improbably contribute. Several marshes also within its limits are supposed to have had a malignant influence on the health of the inhabitants. In the year 1795, they attempted to drain two of them, but did it imperfectly; as a consequence of which fact, an offensive fetor filled the atmosphere, the inhabitants were suddenly seized with a malignant bilious fever, and seventy persons died.

The number of inhabitants in 1790 was 1,899; in 1800, 2,050; and in 1810, 2,439.

GREAT BARRINGTON

Great Barrington lies immediately north of Sheffield. It is built on a single street upon the western bank of the Housatonic throughout the breadth of the township, and throughout half that distance on another street upon the eastern side of the river. The surface is pleasanter than that of Sheffield. The character of the inhabitants who had the same origin is a strong proof of the permanent influence which education of any sort has on the minds of men. It is probable that there has been more horse racing in these two towns than in all the state of Massachusetts besides. The soil of Great Barrington is excellent, yet we saw very few marks of thrift or prosperity. The houses are in many instances decayed; the Episcopal church, barely decent; and the Congregational, ruinous. A small number of houses are exceptions to this account, particularly on the eastern street, where the inhabitants are descendants from the Dutch of New York, and exhibit proofs of industry and wealth.

The following fact was recited to me many years since by a respectable man as having taken place in this town. I know no reason to question the truth of the recital, except what is furnished by the nature of the fact itself.

A Mr. Van Rensselaer, a young gentleman from Albany, came one evening into an inn kept by a Mr. Root, just at the eastern end of the bridge which crosses the Housatonic in this town. The innkeeper, who knew him, asked him where he had crossed the river. He answered, "On the bridge." Mr. Root replied that that was impossible, because it had been raised that very day, and that not a plank had been laid on it. Mr. Van Rensselaer said that this could not be true, because his horse had come over without any difficulty or reluctance, that the night was indeed so profoundly dark as to prevent him from seeing anything distinctly, but that it was incredible, if his horse could see sufficiently well to keep his footing anywhere, that he should not discern the danger, and impossible for him to pass over a bridge in that condition. Each went to bed dissatisfied, neither believing the story of the other. In the morning Mr. Van Rensselaer went, at the solicitation of his host, to view the bridge; and, finding it a naked frame, gazed for a moment with astonishment and fainted.

MONUMENT MOUNTAIN

From Barrington in our way to Stockbridge, we crossed Monument Mountain, a spur from the Green Mountain Range. The name is derived from a pile of stones about six or eight feet in diameter, circular at its base, and raised in the form of an obtuse cone over the grave of one of the aborigines. The manner in which it has been formed is the following. Every Indian who passes by the place throws a stone upon the tomb of his country-man. By this slow method of accumulation, the heap is risen in a long series of years to its present size.

After passing the ridge of the mountain, the country on the north opens beautifully to the eye of a traveler. The mountain itself presents on its eastern front a magnificent and awful precipice, formed by ragged, perpendicular cliffs of white quartz, and rising immediately west of the road between five and six hundred feet. Beyond it spreads the valley of the Housatonic, here running for several miles from east to west, and the fine hills by which it is bordered. In the valley and on the hills, the farms and houses ornament the landscape, while a variety of mountains by which the whole scene is encircled to the eye finish the view. Among these objects is the hill immediately north of the town. Its soil is rich and its vegetation vivid. Its summit is crowned with a grove, and immediately behind it Rattlesnake Mountain forms a background of the picture.

The Housatonic in its passage through Stockbridge takes from Lee a course to the west of not less, as I should judge, than eight miles; when, turning round a huge promontory formed by the western extremity of Monument Mountain, it pursues again its southern course to Great Barrington. Everywhere, and particularly in Stockbridge, it is bordered by the richest intervals, of elegant forms and covered with the most beautiful verdure. Upon the whole, few spots in New England are more romantically delightful than the township of Stockbridge.

ICE GLEN

One of these mountains, known here by the name of the East Mountain, a spur also from the same range, wears toward its southwestern limit evident proofs of having undergone a violent convulsion at some distant period. A huge mass of rocks tumbled from its summit and sides lies in confusion at the bottom. This event preceded the existence of the oldest trees in the valley and of any existing Indian tradition, for they exhibit no marks of the violence with which this heap of ruins descended. Amid the chaos, ice continues throughout the summer.

Still further south, a rock descended from this mountain within the last twenty years (1811), which was somewhat more than thirty feet in length, near twenty in breadth, and in different places from one to perhaps six in thickness. At the bottom of the precipice it lodged upon two others. On the top of one of these a round stone about fifteen inches in diameter, probably forced along with it in its fall, was caught between this and the descending rock where it now stands, and is the immediate support of the latter. The mind when surveying it can with difficulty conceive how it was possible for the stone to have been arrested in the course of a rapid descent on the top of a rock everywhere convex, and fixed by accident where it could hardly have been fixed by the hand. The large rock from its present position is called the Table. Under it eight or ten persons may sit without inconvenience.

THE REVEREND JOHN SERGEANT

Stockbridge was incorporated in 1739, six years after Sheffield, and twenty years before any other town in this county. For a considerable time it was almost merely an Indian settlement named Housatonic, containing perhaps three or four English families. Among these people a mission was begun in October 1734 by the Rev. John Sergeant, a clergyman of great respectability. This gentleman was born at Newark, New Jersey, in 1710, and was educated at Yale College, where he took the degree of A.B. in 1729. In 1731, he was appointed a tutor in that seminary, and continued in that office four years, in which time he was licensed to preach the Gospel. A few weeks after he quitted the tutorship, he entered upon his mission, and on the 31st of August, the following year, was ordained at Deerfield as an evangelist. He continued in the business of a missionary until his death, which happened July 22, 1749, in the thirty-ninth year of his age. Mr. Sergeant baptized 129 Indians during his ministry, of whom forty-two were communicants when he died. He translated the whole New Testament except the Revelation of St. John, and several parts of the Old Testament, into the language of the Mahicans.

During his ministry considerable efforts were made to civilize and Christianize the Indians of Stockbridge. A house was erected for the purpose of boarding, schooling, and instructing in religion, husbandry, and mechanical business a number of Indian children. Mr. Thomas Hollis, of London, had ordered twenty-four of these children to be educated at his own expense. To his efforts those of many other benevolent persons were united, and strong hopes were entertained that they would issue in the best consequences to this unhappy people. But the death of Mr. Sergeant and some other unfortunate incidents which took place about the same time, particularly the war which soon after broke out between France and England, frustrated these benevolent intentions.

THE REVEREND JONATHAN EDWARDS

The Rev. Mr. Edwards, afterwards president of Nassau Hall in New Jersey, having been dismissed from the ministry in Northampton, succeeded Mr. Sergeant in 1751, and continued in the mission until 1757. As he was unacquainted with the language of his parishioners, he preached to them by an interpreter. Their reverence for him was very great, and his family are still regarded by their descendants with peculiar respect. After a considerable interval Mr. Edwards was succeeded by the Rev. John Sergeant, youngest son of the gentleman mentioned above, who has nobly devoted his life to the service of these poor people. Since he began his ministry, the Oneidas have invited the Housatonic Indians to plant themselves in their neighborhood in the state of New York, and have given them the township of New Stockbridge. To that place Mr. Sergeant has removed with his flock, and has already done no small good in civilizing and Christianizing them. It has been supposed that in every state of society the Indian tribes have for a long period been diminishing in their numbers. At the last interview which I had with Mr. Sergeant, he informed me that his own people were increasing, not by accumulations from other tribes, but in the ordinary course of population.

This tribe has been known throughout New England by the name of Stockbridge Indians. In their own language they were called in the singular, Muhhekanneuw (Dr. Edwards writes it Mohekaneew), and Muhheakunnuk in the plural. This name, as interpreted by themselves, signifies *"the people of the great waters continually in motion."*

THE STOCKBRIDGE INDIANS

Their history, as derived from the traditions of their ancestors by one of the tribe, is summarily the following.

They came from a distant country, west by north, i.e., a country lying in that direction from their present residence, crossed over the great waters which separate that country from this, and after a series of pilgrimages arrived on the border of Hudson River. Here they settled and spread through the neighboring country. Their ancestors, they say, were much more civilized than their descendants, lived in towns and villages, and were very numerous; but, being dispersed by a famine, were obliged to seek for subsistence in distant regions. In the progress, they lost their arts and manners, or, in the language of the historian, "apostatized." Before they began sensibly to diminish, they could furnish on any emergency a thousand warriors, and of course consisted of about four or five thousand persons, probably, however, not more than four thousand.

The Stockbridge Indians have been uniform friends to the English colonists. They have acted for them as interpreters and spies, and have often fought in their armies. Yet I have never heard of an instance in which they were treacherous. Several of them have been respectable for their understanding, and more for their piety. Yet it must be owned that the body of them have in many respects sustained a very imperfect character. Upon the whole, they have behaved well in so many instances as to prompt in my mind an ardent wish that their present and future descendants may increase in numbers, virtue, and happiness.

LENOX

Lenox, the shire town of this county, is principally built on a single street upon a ridge declining rather pleasantly to the east and to the west, but disagreeably interrupted by several deep valleys crossing it at right angles. The soil and the buildings are good, and the town exhibits many proofs of prosperity. The public buildings consist of a church, a courthouse, a schoolhouse, and a jail.

PITTSFIELD

Pittsfield is a beautiful township lying in a noble expansion between the Taconic and Green Mountain Ranges. It is about twelve miles in breadth, and is sublimely bounded on the north by the lofty summits of Saddle Mountain. On the south, West Stockbridge, or as it ought to be called, Richmond Mountain, intrudes into it centrally, as a magnificent promontory into the ocean. Into Stockbridge this expansion extends on the eastern side through the townships of Lenox and Lee; and, on the western, through the beautiful valley of Richmond. The two head branches of the Housatonic unite in Pittsfield, and are both prettily bordered by rich intervals.

The soil of this township is excellent. A small, but handsome village is built in the center around the church. Elsewhere, it is distributed into farms.

Pittsfield was incorporated in the year 1761, about six years before Lenox. Its Indian name was Pontoosuc. Its English name was given it in honor of the Earl of Chatham. The settlement was begun before the last Canadian war, and four families continued in it through that war in fortified houses. After the peace of 1763, the beauty of the situation and the richness of the soil allured settlers here in great numbers.

There is a printing office in Pittsfield and another in Stockbridge. The road from Pittsfield to Lanesboro, which is very pleasant, lies along the western branch of the Housatonic and by the side of a lake, about a mile in length, commonly, but erroneously supposed to be the headwater of this river.

LANESBORO

The township of Lanesboro lies principally on two hills and an interjacent valley, commencing near the southern boundary of New Ashford, and extending five or six miles to the south, gradually increasing its breadth until it is lost in the greater valley of Pittsfield. The hill on the east is a spur of Saddle Mountain. That on the west is a part of the margin of the Taconic Range. Both the hills and the valley are beautiful. The valley is a vast meadow of the richest luxuriance and the most animated verdure, and is gaily ornamented by the fine lake mentioned above, and bounded to the eye, at the distance of eight or ten miles below the center of the town, by the northern front of West Stockbridge Mountain. The houses in Lanesboro are good farmers' habitations.

In this township is wrought a great quantity of white marble, a subject of which I shall say more hereafter.

Lanesboro from the south, with Saddleback (Mt. Greylock) in the distance, c. 1841.
The Berkshire Athenaeum, Local History Department

NEW ASHFORD

New Ashford is a rough, disagreeable township lying on the hills which connect Saddle Mountain with the Taconic Range. These hills are of uncouth forms and sudden acclivities. The valleys between them wear an aspect equally forbidding, and might with perhaps more propriety be denominated ravines. The soil also is lean; the houses are generally poor; and the inhabitants are plainly in indifferent circumstances. The settlement is recent and scattered. The only pleasant objects in our ride through it were the numerous rivulets which murmured down the valleys with a clean and sprightly current, and Saddle Mountain, the southwestern base of which is in this township. Among the rivulets, we passed the western branch of the Housatonic, about seven miles northward of the lake mentioned above. It is here a small brook, crossing the road from the hills on the west, and descending in a narrow valley by the roadside into Lanesboro. Before its entrance into the lake, it is swollen into a stream of a considerable size.

SADDLE MOUNTAIN

Saddle Mountain [later Greylock], which derives its name from its resemblance to a saddle, is the highest land in this state. Its whole length from northeast to southwest may be about six miles. Its southeastern front is extensively visible throughout Berkshire, and from high elevations in the states of New Hampshire, New York, Vermont, and Connecticut at very great distances. Its figure is remarkably fine, and its aspect majestic in the highest degree. On its northern side ascends the mountain of Williamstown, another part of the same spur of great elevation.

The southwestern summit has, by repeated mensurations differing very little in their results, been found to be about 3,700 feet above the subjacent valley, and therefore at least 4,000 above the level of the ocean. During a great part of the year, it is either embosomed or capped by clouds, and indicates to the surrounding inhabitants the changes of weather with not a little exactness.

WILLIAMSTOWN

The township of Williamstown lies principally in a triangular valley, bounded by Williamstown Mountain on the south, the range of the Green Mountains on the east, and that of Taconic on the west. These ranges approach near each other on the north, leaving a narrow opening into Pownal. Between the former of these mountains and the northeastern ends of Williamstown and Saddle Mountains, there is another opening on the southeast, through which Hoosic River enters Williamstown from Adams, as it does Pownal from Williamstown through the first of these openings. There is also a third passage out of this valley: viz., that in which our road lay, between the southwestern ends of these mountains and the range of Taconic.

This triangular area may, at a loose estimate, be six or seven miles on a side. Its surface is irregular in the extreme, being everywhere made up of varieties. The borders of the Hoosic and of Green River, which joins it from the south, are formed by beautiful successions of intervals. The scenery as a whole is pleasant, but more distinguished for sublimity than beauty.

Williamstown is almost wholly settled by farmers living on their respective plantations. The town is built near its center. The principal street runs along a declivity sloping from the Taconic Range toward the east. In its progress it passes over three small rising grounds, on the westernmost of which stands a handsome church, and on the others, the two colleges belonging to the institution denominated Williams College.

There are many good houses in Williamstown, and several handsome ones.

WILLIAMS COLLEGE

Williams College owes its existence to Colonel Ephraim Williams, a native of Newtown in Massachusetts. This gentleman spent a considerable part of his life in the county of Hampshire, then including all that part of the province of Massachusetts Bay which lies west of the county of

Worcester. During the war which commenced 1740, he commanded the line of forts built on the western side of Connecticut River, and resided principally at Hoosick, or Massachusetts Fort, which stood not far from the northeastern end of Saddle Mountain within the present township of Adams and on the eastern border of Hoosic River. At this time a small number of persons began a settlement within the limits of what is now Williamstown. The hardships suffered by these men were of course great, and appear to have excited in the mind of Colonel Williams an intention of extending his beneficence to them at some future period.

In 1755, he commanded a regiment destined to a post at the head of Lake George. As he was proceeding through Albany, he made his will in that city, on the 22nd of July. In this instrument, after giving certain legacies to his connections, he directed that the remainder of his land should be sold at the discretion of his executors, within five years after an established peace, and that the interest of the monies arising from the sale, and also the interest of his notes and bonds, should be applied to the support of a free school in a township west of Fort Massachusetts, provided the said township when incorporated should be named Williamstown.

The property designated in this bequest was loaned on interest and, after an accumulation of thirty years, was considered as a fund sufficient to warrant the institution of the free school contemplated in the will. The spot pointed out was, June 20, 1785, incorporated by the name of Williamstown. In 1785, nine gentlemen were appointed trustees for the management of the donation and the free school to which it was to give birth. In 1788, they voted to erect a building. The legislature granted them a lottery, which yielded four thousand dollars; and the inhabitants contributed two thousand more. In 1790, they built a brick edifice eighty-two feet in length and forty-two in breadth, of four stories, on the middle eminence in the principal street. It contained twenty-eight rooms and a chapel. The expense of erecting it was $11,700, and the remainder of the fund was about the same sum.

The school was opened in October 1791, under the superintendency of Mr. Ebenezer Fitch, now Rev. Dr. Fitch, president of Williams College. It consisted of two establishments: an academy and an English free school, and under the direction of this gentleman immediately became prosperous. A considerable number of students resorted to it from Massachusetts and the neighboring states, and even from Canada. In 1793, the legislature, being informed of its flourishing condition, erected it into a college, by the name of Williams College.

THE BUG IN THE TABLE

In September 1806, I passed through this town on a journey to Vermont. While I was here, President Fitch showed me an insect about an inch in length, of a brown color tinged with orange, with two antennae or feelers, not unlike a rosebug in form, but in every respect handsomer. This insect came out of a tea table made of the boards of an apple tree and belonging to Mr. Putnam, one of the inhabitants and a son of the Hon. Major General Putnam, late of Brooklyn in Connecticut.

I went with President Fitch to Mr. Putnam's to examine the spot whence the insect had emerged into light. We measured the cavity and found it about two inches in length, nearly horizontal, and inclining upward very little except at the mouth. Between the hole and the outside of the leaf of the table, there were forty grains of the wood. President Fitch supposed, with what I thought a moderate estimate, that the sawmill and the cabinet maker had cut off at least as many as thirteen more: making sixty in the whole. The tree had, therefore, been growing sixty years from the time when the egg was deposited in it out of which the insect was produced. How long a period had intervened between the day in which the apple tree was cut down and that in which the table was purchased by Mr. Putnam is unknown. It had been in his possession twenty years. Of course, eighty years had elapsed between the laying of the egg and the birth of the insect.

After its birth, it was placed under a tumbler and attempts were made by offering it for sustenance wood of the apple tree and bread to prolong its life. It ate a small quantity of the bread; but, either for want of more proper food, or from being lodged in too cold a temperature, or from some other cause, it died within a few days.

From *Travels in New-England and New-York* by Timothy Dwight. Edited by Barbara Miller Solomon. Harvard University Press, 1969.

ZENAS CRANE

The early days of the Republic saw a strong movement to encourage "domestic manufactures" to lessen dependence upon imported goods. In 1801 Zenas Crane, attracted by the purity of the region's water, brought this movement to the Berkshires when he proposed building a paper mill in Dalton. The industry established itself as a mainstay of the Berkshire economy, and the family and company Crane established continue today their exemplary leadership in responsible manufacturing and civic leadership. Here is the advertisment Crane placed in the Pittsfield Sun for February 17, 1801, soliciting rags as raw material for his new venture.

Americans !
Encourage your own Manufactories, and they will Improve.
LADIES, save your RAGS.

AS the Subscribers have it in contemplation to erect a PAPER-MILL in *Dalton*, the ensuing spring ; and the business being very beneficial to the community at large, they flatter themselves that they shall meet with due encouragement. And that every woman, who has the good of her country, and the interest of her own family at heart, will patronize them, by saving her rags, and sending them to their Manufactory, or to the nearest Storekeeper— for which the Subscribers will give a generous price.

HENRY WISWALL,
ZENAS CRANE,
JOHN WILLARD.

Worcester, Feb. 8, 1801.

From *The Pittsfield Sun,* 1801.

The Secluded Paradise
1810 to 1850

WILLIAM CULLEN BRYANT

William Cullen Bryant, born in Cummington in 1794, was America's reigning literary figure throughout much of the nineteenth century. His dignified yet ardent appreciation of nature (a love surely shaped by the Berkshire beauty he grew up in the midst of) inspired the generations which memorized his poems in school to view wilderness not as an enemy to be subdued but as a benign source of solace and moral uplift. Today's "environmental movement" may not implausibly be traced back to him.

In a similar way he softened his countrymen's Calvinist terror of death into a calmly rational Unitarian acceptance of death as part of the natural cycle of being.

Bryant attended Williams College for a couple of terms, then left to read law, practicing in Great Barrington until 1825 when, at the urging of the Sedgwicks, he went to New York City, where in time he became the foremost newspaper editor and publisher in the country, establishing the modern concept of fair and objective journalism.

Most of "Thanatopsis" was written before he was 21; it astonished his contemporaries and made him revered as a founder of our national literature. "Monument Mountain" invests the natural beauty of the Berkshires with the romance of legend. "The Murdered Traveller" poeticizes a body found between West Stockbridge and Stockbridge in the ravine just east of the turnpike tollgate. According to his son-in-law, Bryant composed "To a Waterfowl" in his head one spring evening as he walked from Cummington to Plainfield. "Green River" reflects his exasperation at the dryness and pettiness his Great Barrington practice involved him in. A few of his letters give an idea of the concerns that occupied the poet's days at that time.

Bryant's house in Great Barrington. The Berkshire Athenaeum, Local History Department

Poems

THANATOPSIS

To him who in the love of nature holds
  Communion with her visible forms, she speaks
  A various language; for his gayer hours
She has a voice of gladness, and a smile
And eloquence of beauty, and she glides
Into his darker musings, with a mild
And healing sympathy, that steals away
Their sharpness, ere he is aware. When thoughts
Of the last bitter hour come like a blight
Over thy spirit, and sad images
Of the stern agony, and shroud, and pall,
And breathless darkness, and the narrow house,
Make thee to shudder, and grow sick at heart; —
Go forth, under the open sky, and list
To Nature's teachings, while from all around —
Earth and her waters, and the depths of air, —
Comes a still voice —

                  Yet a few days, and thee
The all-beholding sun shall see no more
In all his course; nor yet in the cold ground,
Where thy pale form was laid, with many tears,
Nor in the embrace of ocean, shall exist
Thy image. Earth, that nourished thee, shall claim
Thy growth, to be resolved to earth again,
And, lost each human trace, surrendering up
Thine individual being, shalt thou go
To mix forever with the elements,
To be a brother to the insensible rock
And to the sluggish clod, which the rude swain
Turns with his share, and treads upon. The oak
Shall send his roots abroad, and pierce thy mould.
Yet not to thine eternal resting-place
Shalt thou retire alone — nor couldst thou wish
Couch more magnificent. Thou shalt lie down
With patriarchs of the infant world — with kings,
The powerful of the earth — the wise, the good,
Fair forms, and hoary seers of ages past,
All in one mighty sepulchre. — The hills

Rock-ribbed and ancient as the sun, — the vales
Stretching in pensive quietness between;
The venerable woods — rivers that move
In majesty, and the complaining brooks
That make the meadows green; and, poured round all,
Old ocean's gray and melancholy waste, —
Are but the solemn decorations all
Of the great tomb of man. The golden sun,
The planets, all the infinite host of heaven,
Are shining on the sad abodes of death,
Through the still lapse of ages. All that tread
The globe are but a handful to the tribes
That slumber in its bosom. — Take the wings
Of morning — and the Barcan desert pierce,
Or lose thyself in the continuous woods
Where rolls the Oregan, and hears no sound,
Save his own dashings — yet — the dead are there;
And millions in those solitudes, since first
The flight of years began, have laid them down
In their last sleep — the dead reign there alone.
So shalt thou rest — and what if thou withdraw
Unheeded by the living — and no friend
Take note of thy departure? All that breathe
Will share thy destiny. The gay will laugh
When thou art gone, the solemn brood of care
Plod on, and each one as before will chase
His favorite phantom; yet all these shall leave
Their mirth and their employments, and shall come,
And make their bed with thee. As the long train
Of ages glide away, the sons of men,
The youth in life's green spring, and he who goes
In the full strength of years, matron, and maid,
And the sweet babe, and the gray-headed man, —
Shall one by one be gathered to thy side,
By those, who in their turn shall follow them.

So live, that when thy summons comes to join
The innumerable caravan, that moves
To that mysterious realm, where each shall take
His chamber in the silent halls of death,
Thou go not, like the quarry-slave at night,
Scourged to his dungeon, but, sustained and soothed

By an unfaltering trust, approach thy grave,
Like one who wraps the drapery of his couch
About him, and lies down to pleasant dreams.

Calvin Coolidge with Bryant descendants at the dedication of the homestead.
Courtesy of The Berkshire Eagle

MONUMENT MOUNTAIN

Thou who wouldst see the lovely and the wild
Mingled in harmony on Nature's face,
Ascend our rocky mountains. Let thy foot,
Fail not with weariness, for on their tops
The beauty and the majesty of earth,
Spread wide beneath, shall make thee to forget
The steep and toilsome way. There, as thou stand'st,
The haunts of men below thee, and around
The mountain summits, thy expanding heart
Shall feel a kindred with that loftier world
To which thou art translated, and partake
The enlargement of thy vision. Thou shalt look
Upon the green and rolling forest tops,
And down into the secrets of the glens,

And streams, that with their bordering thickets strive
To hide their windings. Thou shalt gaze, at once,
Here on white villages, and tilth, and herds,
And swarming roads, and there on solitudes
That only hear the torrent, and the wind,
And eagle's shriek. There is a precipice
That seems a fragment of some mighty wall,
Built by the hand that fashioned the old world,
To separate its nations, and thrown down
When the flood drowned them. To the north a path
Conducts you up the narrow battlement.
Steep is the western side, shaggy and wild
With mossy trees, and pinnacles of flint,
And many a hanging crag. But, to the east,
Sheer to the vale go down the bare old cliffs,
Huge pillars, that in middle heaven upbear
Their weather-beaten capitals, here dark
With the thick moss of centuries, and there
Of chalky whiteness where the thunderbolt
Has splintered them. It is a fearful thing
To stand upon the beetling verge, and see
Where storm and lightning, from that huge wall,
Have tumbled down vast blocks, and at the base
Dashed them in fragments, and to lay thine ear
Over the dizzy depth, and hear the sound
Of winds, that struggle with the woods below,
Come up like ocean murmurs. But the scene
Is lovely round; a beautiful river there
Wanders amid the fresh and fertile meads,
The paradise he made unto himself,
Mining the soil for ages. On each side
The fields swell upward to the hills; beyond,
Above the hills, in the blue distance, rise
The mighty columns with which earth props heaven.

There is a tale about these gray old rocks,
A sad tradition of unhappy love,
And sorrows borne and ended, long ago,
When over these fair vales the savage sought
His game in the thick woods. There was a maid,
The fairest of the Indian maids, bright-eyed,
With wealth of raven tresses, a light form,

And a gay heart. About her cabin door
The wide old woods resounded with her song
And fairy laughter all the summer day.
She loved her cousin; such a love was deemed,
By the morality of those stern tribes,
Incestuous, and she struggled hard and long
Against her love, and reasoned with her heart,
As simple Indian maiden might. In vain.
Then her eye lost its lustre, and her step
Its lightness, and the gray old men that passed
Her dwelling, wondered that they heard no more
The accustomed song and laugh of her, whose looks
Were like the cheerful smile of Spring, they said,
Upon the Winter of their age. She went
To weep where no eye saw, and was not found
When all the merry girls were met to dance,
And all the hunters of the tribe were out;
Nor when they gathered from the rustling husk
The shining ear; nor when, by the river's side,
They pulled the grape and startled the wild shades
With sounds of mirth. The keen-eyed Indian dames
Would whisper to each other, as they saw
Her wasting form, and say, *the girl will die.*
　　One day into the bosom of a friend,
A playmate of her young and innocent years,
She poured her griefs. "Thou know'st, and thou alone,"
She said, "for I have told thee, all my love,
And guilt, and sorrow. I am sick of life.
All night I weep in darkness, and the morn
Glares on me, as upon a thing accursed,
That has no business on the earth. I hate
The pastimes and the pleasant toils that once
I loved; the cheerful voices of my friends
Have an unnatural horror in mine ear.
In dreams my mother, from the land of souls,
Calls me and chides me. All that look on me
Do seem to know my shame; I cannot bear
Their eyes; I cannot from my heart root out
The love that wrings it so, and I must die."

　　It was a summer morning, and they went
To this old precipice. About the cliffs

Lay garlands, ears of maize, and shaggy skins
Of wolf and bear, the offerings of the tribe
Here made to the Great Spirit, for they deemed,
Like worshippers of the elder time, that God
Doth walk on the high places and affect
The earth-o'erlooking mountains. She had on
The ornaments with which her father loved
To deck the beauty of his bright-eyed girl,
And bade her wear when stranger warriors came
To be his guests. Here the friends sat them down,
And sang, all day, old songs of love and death,
And decked the poor wan victim's hair with flowers,
And prayed that safe and swift might be her way
To the calm world of sunshine, where no grief
Makes the heart heavy and the eyelids red.
Beautiful lay the region of her tribe
Below her — waters resting in the embrace
Of the wide forest, and maize-planted glades
Opening amid the leafy wilderness.
She gazed upon it long, and at the sight
Of her own village peeping through the trees,
And her own dwelling, and the cabin roof
Of him she loved with an unlawful love,
And came to die for, a warm gush of tears
Ran from her eyes. But when the sun grew low
And the hill shadows long, she threw herself
From the steep rock and perished. There was scooped,
Upon the mountain's southern slope, a grave;
And there they laid her, in the very garb
With which the maiden decked herself for death
With the same withering wild flowers in her hair.
And o'er the mould that covered her, the tribe
Built up a simple monument, a cone
Of small loose stones. Thenceforward, all who passed,
Hunter, and dame, and virgin, laid a stone
In silence on the pile. It stands there yet.
And Indians from the distant West, who come
To visit where their fathers' bones are laid,
Yet tell the sorrowful tale, and to this day
The mountain where the hapless maiden died
Is called the Mountain of the Monument.

The Bryant homestead in Cummington.   Clemens Kalischer

THE MURDERED TRAVELLER

When spring, to woods and wastes around,
    Brought bloom and joy again,
The murdered traveller's bones were found,
    Far down a narrow glen.

The fragrant birch, above him, hung
    Her tassels in the sky;
And many a vernal blossom sprung,
    And nodded careless by.

The red-bird warbled, as he wrought
    His hanging nest o'erhead,
And fearless, near the fatal spot,
    Her young the partridge led.

But there was weeping far away,
    And gentle eyes, for him,
With watching many an anxious day,
    Were sorrowful and dim.

They little knew, who loved him so,
 The fearful death he met,
When shouting o'er the desert snow,
 Unarmed, and hard beset; —

Nor how, when round the frosty pole
 The northern dawn was red,
The mountain wolf and wild-cat stole
 To banquet on the dead; —

Nor how, when strangers found his bones,
 They dressed the hasty bier,
And marked his grave with nameless stones,
 Unmoistened by a tear.

But long they looked, and feared, and wept,
 Within his distant home;
And dreamed, and started as they slept,
 For joy that he was come.

So long they looked — but never spied
 His welcome step again,
Nor knew the fearful death he died
 Far down that narrow glen.

TO A WATERFOWL

Whither, 'midst falling dew,
While glow the heavens with the last steps of day
Far, through their rosy depths, dost thou pursue
 Thy solitary way?

Vainly the fowler's eye
Might mark thy distant flight to do thee wrong,
As, darkly painted on the crimson sky,
 Thy figure floats along.

Seek'st thou the plashy brink
Of weedy lake, or marge of river wide,
Or where the rocking billows rise and sink
 On the chafed ocean side?

There is a Power whose care
Teaches thy way along that pathless coast,
The desert and illimitable air —
    Lone wandering, but not lost.

All day thy wings have fanned,
At that far height, the cold thin atmosphere,
Yet stoop not, weary, to the welcome land,
    Though the dark night is near,

And soon that toil shall end;
Soon shalt thou find a summer home, and rest,
And scream among thy fellows; reeds shall bend,
    Soon, o'er thy sheltered nest.

Thou'rt gone, the abyss of heaven
Hath swallowed up thy form; yet, on my heart
Deeply hath sunk the lesson thou hast given,
    And shall not soon depart.

He who, from zone to zone,
Guides through the boundless sky thy certain flight,
In the long way that I must tread alone
    Will lead my steps aright.

GREEN RIVER

When breezes are soft and skies are fair,
I steal an hour from study and care,
And hie me away to the woodland scene,
Where wanders the stream with waters of green;
As if the bright fringe of herbs on its brink,
Had given their stain to the wave they drink;
And they, whose meadows it murmurs through,
Have named the stream from its own fair hue.

Yet pure its waters — its shallows are bright
With colored pebbles and sparkles of light,
And clear the depths where its eddies play,
And dimples deepen and whirl away,
And the plane-tree's speckled arms o'ershoot
The swifter current that mines its root,

Through whose shifting leaves, as you walk the hill,
The quivering glimmer of sun and rill,
With a sudden flash on the eye is thrown,
Like the ray that streams from the diamond stone.
Oh, loveliest there the spring days come,
With blossoms, and birds, and wild bees' hum;
The flowers of summer are fairest there,
And freshest the breath of the summer air
And sweetest the golden autumn day
In silence and sunshine glides away.

Yet fair as thou art, thou shun'st to glide,
Beautiful stream! by the village side;
But windest away from haunts of men,
To quiet valley and shaded glen;
And forest, and meadow, and slope of hill,
Around thee, are lonely, lovely, and still.
Lonely — save when, by thy rippling tides,
From thicket to thicket the angler glides;
Or the simpler comes with basket and book,
For herbs of power on thy banks to look;
Or haply, some idle dreamer, like me,
To wander, and muse, and gaze on thee.
Still — save the chirp of birds that feed
On the river cherry and seedy reed,
And thy own wild music gushing out
With mellow murmur and fairy shout,
From dawn to the blush of another day,
Like traveller singing along his way.

That fairy music I never hear,
Nor gaze on those waters so green and clear,
And mark them winding away from sight,
Darkened with shade or flashing with light,
While o'er them the vine to its thicket clings,
And the zephyr stoops to freshen his wings,
But I wish that fate had left me free
To wander these quiet haunts with thee,
Till the eating cares of earth should depart,
And the peace of the scene pass into my heart;
But I envy thy stream, as it glides along,
Through its beautiful banks in a trance of song.

Though forced to drudge for the dregs of men,
And scrawl strange words with the barbarous pen,
And mingle among the jostling crowd,
Where the sons of strife are subtle and loud —
I often come to this quiet place,
To breathe the airs that ruffle thy face,
And gaze upon thee in silent dream,
For in thy lonely and lovely stream,
An image of that calm life appears,
That won my heart in my greener years.

From *Poetical Works* by William Cullen Bryant. Thomas Y. Crowell, 1893.

Letters

To Peter Bryant   Great Barrington 1 Sept 1818

Yours of the 22d I received on the Friday evening following. On Saturday I was engaged so that it was out of my power to visit Cummington that week independent of other reasons. — As the Supreme Court is in session next week at Lenox you will see the propriety of my staying at home the present week — besides — though I should be happy to see my friends — I do not much relish Williamstown Commencements — nor indeed any thing that belongs to that place or that beggarly institution — You will therefore have the goodness to excuse me from attending — especially as I hope before long — at some time when there is no prospect of having any thing else to do, to have the pleasure of seeing my friends in Hampshire.

I have been in tolerable health this summer — I think I can perceive a gradual augmentation of my business. The gentlemen of our profession on the frontiers of Massachusetts are often employed to collect demands for creditors living in adjoining states which is not only a profitable but pleasant branch of our business. I have formed some acquaintances in the State of New York who already begin to be of use to me. —

Excuse the brevity of my letters.

[unsigned]

To Messrs. Robert B. Southwick & Co.

Great Barrington
Dec 27, 1823.

Gentlemen.

Sometime since I wrote you that I had seen Jno. C. Deming and that he promised to call on you and make some arrangement of the demand against him and Cyrenus Stevens. Since that time I have not heard from you.

At present I have some news to communicate concerning him and Stevens of no very agreeable nature.

A man in West Stockbridge, a creditor of Deming to a considerable amount, and who had given him money to discharge a certain debt, which he neglected to pay over & appropriated to his own use, was sued on that debt and called on Deming for security. Deming made to him an assignment of all his effects, and in the assignment stipulated that if the property assigned upon being sold should bring more than enough to pay this debt the surplus should be applied towards the payment of other claims which were mentioned in the assignment, and among which I cannot learn that yours was named. The property however, it is said, will not more than pay the debt it was first intended to secure. In the mean time Deming went off to the State of New York, and is now in Albany on the limits. — One of the creditors, whose name was mentioned in the assignment, has attached the property assigned — and the consequence, it is expected, will be a law suit.

While these things were transacting, Stevens was buying goods in the City of New York. He purchased, it is said, a considerable assortment, but he has not sent them to this state, nor is it expected that he will. Both they and he are somewhere in your state, and it is likely will not soon be seen here. Stevens it seems owed debts to a considerable amount, and both he and Deming have mutually been security for each other.

Such are the particulars as far as I have been able to learn them. It was impossible to secure any thing on your demand, the first news of Deming's failure being after the assignment of his property. —

I hope you may be able to get something of them in your State — though they will probably attempt to keep their property as much under cover as they can —

I am Gentlemen
Yrs. Respectfully
WM C BRYANT

To Messrs. Robert B. Southwick & Co.   Great Barrington
                                                           Feb 23 1824.

Gent.
    Yrs. of the 12th inst was duly received — You wish to know where Stevens is. A few days after I wrote you last he called on me, and said that he came to see about your demands against him. I told him what I had written to you, and in answer he said that he did not mean to leave the country — that he intended to remain in West Stockbridge — that he could not pay your debt at present — but would pay it if you would give him time — and finally that he intended before long to call on you and make some arrangement of the affair with you. I believe that one item of his information is true — namely that he does not mean to pay the debt at present. I do not know of any way to secure it. Stevens is now in West Stockbridge. What is become of his goods I cannot tell. Some hides purchased by him in New York were brought from Poughkeepsie by one Brown of Pittsfield who I am told claims them. —
Yours respectfully

                                                           Wm. C. Bryant

To Messrs. Robert B. Southwick & Co.   Great Barrington
                                                           Apl 10 1824.

Gentlemen.
    On last Monday all the hides in the vats of Cyrenus Stevens in West Stockbridge were attached and taken out on a writ in favour of Spencer & Crocker of West Stockbridge against Stevens. As soon as I learnt this fact which was yesterday I went to W. Stockbridge to learn more particularly what had been done. On my arrival I found that 500 hides had been attached, of which 400 were afterwards replevied as the property of Simeon Brown of Pittsfield who had taken them away with him to Pittsfield. The remaining 100 were slaughter hides. I have thought it my duty to give you this information that you might take such steps as you may think expedient. —
Yrs. respectfully

                                                  William C. Bryant

From *The Letters of William Cullen Bryant*, Volume I. Edited by W.C. Bryant III and T.G. Voss. Fordham University Press, 1975.

JOHN H.B. LATROBE

In 1821 a detachment of West Point cadets made a public relations march from Albany to Boston to cultivate good will for the recently reorganized military academy, at the time the only engineering school in the country. Their official "historian" was John Latrobe (1803-1891), the son of Benjamin Latrobe, the Greek Revival architect who completed the Capitol and White House. John Latrobe later became an important railroad lawyer and innovating engineer.

March Through the Berkshires

Tuesday, 24th. [Albany, July 24, 1821] At day light the tents were struck, and we commenced our march through the city to the ferry, in a cold and disagreeable rain, which accompanied us with little intermission during the day, but which enabled the battalion to proceed farther than would otherwise have been in their power. We crossed the river to Greenbush, a small village on the opposite bank, and marched rapidly to the place intended to breakfast, 4 miles distant from the ferry. After remaining here 2 hours, we continued towards Lebanon, through a hilly country highly cultivated, and bearing every mark of the wealth of its inhabitants. Schodack, Union Village, and Brainard's Bridge were the places we passed through this morning; and at half past 1 we halted to dine, 2 miles beyond the last mentioned village, making the distance we had reached from the place of our encampment 24 miles. It was near 4 when we resumed our march, and when within 2 miles of Lebanon, the rain which had continued all day, poured down in torrents, nor did it cease until after we had pitched our tents.

Wednesday, 25th. We remained at Lebanon, and bathed in the water for which the place is celebrated.

Lebanon, so deservedly celebrated for the beauty of its scenery, is situated near the head of a deep valley, in the highest possible state of cultivation. Even on the summits of the mountains around it, immense fields of grain are seen intermingled with the dark green foliage of the forest, and forming a scene more resembling an immense garden than a tract of country, including several counties, and terminated by the boundary line between New-York and Massachusetts.

Thursday, 26th. Having breakfasted at Lebanon, we started at 9 o'clock for Lenox, a distance of 12 miles, and soon reached the Shakers' village, (2 1-2 miles,) the neatness and regularity of which, together with the size and bright yellow colour of the buildings, form one of the most pleasing objects seen from the valley. Conspicuously placed on the side of a mountain, and every thing around them bearing marks of the greatest care and cultivation, it would seem that the beauty of the spot, and the certainty of support, would, exclusive of religious motives, be sufficient to induce many to enter a society and embrace a religion, where while living, they had no care for the morrow, and when dead were certain of a decent grave. Be this however as it may, during the hour's halt we made in the village, we had every kindness shewn us, refreshments were largely distributed among the corps, and we left them, highly gratified with the entertainment received from a body, who, (on account of their religious principles) we had as little to expect as from any.

Our road, on leaving the village, crossed Mount Hancock, one of the Hoosack range, on which is the boundary line between New-York and Massachusetts; and continued through a mountainous country, rivalling in some places the gloomy magnificence of Alpine scenery, and the contrast formed, when, on turning an angle in the road, Lenox, with its three steeples and houses of a brilliant white, appeared almost beneath our feet, was as striking as it was beautiful. From this spot we had a view as far as the eye could reach in the direction we were to proceed, and the endless succession of hills, among which the Becket Mountains were proudly conspicuous, gave us no favourable anticipation of the pleasure that would arise from the marching part of our expedition.

We entered Lenox at 3 o'clock, encamped — remained there that night.

Friday, 27th. We marched on, after having a dress parade at 9 in the morning. Two miles from the town, we crossed the Housatonick, here a narrow, rapid stream, turning several mills and a factory, which formed quite a village on the road side. From this spot the country begins to be less thickly settled; the land is evidently worse, and the inhabitants look poorer than those a few miles back — this appearance increases as we approach, and continues until we pass the mountains.

At 4 o'clock we halted to dine, in a large field by the road, 15 miles from Lenox, at the foot of the Becket Mountains, and remained there until near sun down, when we resumed the line of march for Chester Factory. It was the evening of a beautiful day; the heat, which was oppressive a few hours since, had moderated; the rest we had enjoyed, together with our dinner had refreshed us, and we started nearly all in good spirits.

We immediately entered the mountain defiles, where nothing was to be seen but precipices towering above you, scathed and blackened in many places to their very tops by fire, and nothing heard but the roar of the torrent, which is one of the sources of the Agawam, mingled with the hum of noises, as the battalion appeared and disappeared on the road which wound through this pass of the mountains. There was something in this evening's march none of us will ever forget; all the enthusiastic feelings of youth were excited; what we had read in the fictions of romance or the facts of history, seemed here to be realized or experienced; and as the column almost ran down the gloomy defile, we wanted but the roar of artillery and the noise of action, to transport us in imagination to the confines of Italy, and make our peaceful march, the passage of the Alps. After marching five miles in this manner, we reached Chester Factory, a miserable spot among the hills, where no field could be found fit for us to encamp on, and our tents were pitched along the road side.

This place, during the late war, was quite a respectable village, owing to a large glass manufactory established here, which, together with the dwellings of the workmen, we saw deserted, and presenting the very picture of poverty. Since the conclusion of the war, when the factory fell through, the place has fallen off considerably, and every thing appears as if it was going to ruin.

Saturday, 28th. At day light we struck our tents, and followed the course of the Agawam, which runs through a deep and narrow valley, having in many places scarcely width sufficient for the road, on its bank, we crossed and re-crossed the river several times, and at 6 o'clock arrived at Chester village, a pretty little spot at the entrance of the valley. Here we breakfasted, and after remaining an hour and a half, proceeded, still continuing with the Agawam, towards Westfield.

From Chester village the country becomes more open, the land better, and every thing bears the appearance of comfort and industry. The day was oppressively warm, the roads very dusty, owing to the long drought, and the march altogether fatiguing. Halting for a short time to rest under the shade on the bank of the river, the battalion were suffered to bathe, which enabled us to reach Westfield, (twenty miles from the factory,) with greater ease than otherwise would have been possible. We encamped on the green in the centre of the village, at 5 o'clock, and were indebted to the kindness of the ladies of Westfield for some additions to our late dinner, as agreeable as unexpected.

From *Journal of A March, Performed By the Corps of Cadets of the United States Military Academy, In the Year Eighteen Hundred and Twenty-One.* Ward M. Gazlay, Newburgh, New York, 1822.

ELKANAH WATSON

A tireless improver and promoter, Elkanah Watson came to Pittsfield after two or three careers, here and abroad, in which brilliant success alternated with spectacular failure. In the Berkshires he took up the cause of scientific agriculture, introducing Merino sheep and improved breeds of swine and cattle, and organizing in 1810 the Berkshire Agricultural Society, sponsor of the first county fair in America. His contributions to the improvement of wool production visibly modified the Berkshire landscape and stimulated the growth of the Berkshire textile industry.

The Berkshire Agricultural Society

In June, 1807, I purchased the elegant seat of Henry Van Schaick, Esquire, in Pittsfield, Massachusetts, thirty-six miles from Albany. The farm, containing two hundred and fifty acres, was much exhausted — yet from its high state of improvement, abounding with excellent fruit, and the convenience and elegance of the buildings, also a circular pond of twenty acres, and lying within one mile of a beautiful village — I was induced, at the age of fifty, to hazard my own, and my family's happiness, on the experiment of seeking *"rural felicity,"* — a life I had for twenty years sighed to enjoy; my only mistake was, I commenced too late. In consequence, I soon found my error — my habits were settled for city life: to retreat was impossible — to labour in person, *was impossible*. To fill up the void in an active mind, led me first to conceive the idea of an Agricultural Society on a plan different from all others.

With a view of writing this book, in conformity to the wishes of a respectable friend in North-Carolina, I have resorted to all my documents, to trace its commencement, and progress, which shall be faithfully narrated. In the fall of 1807, I procured the first pair of Merino sheep, which had appeared in Berkshire, if not in the state; even the name was new to every body. They were the first I had ever seen: although defective in the grade, I was led to expect, yet, as all who examined their wool, were delighted with its texture and fineness,* I was induced to notify an exhibition under the great elm tree in the public square, in Pittsfield, of these two sheep, on a certain day. Many farmers, and even women were excited by curiosity to attend this first novel, and humble exhibition. It

* The wool which came from these two sheep, was, with infinite pains, manufactured by the best artists then in the country, into a piece of blue cloth. It far excelled any other which had yet appeared — a detail of its manufacture, the expense per yard was published in all the papers and samples notified in our principal cities. — This was the origin of the present woollen factories, producing cloths which will vie with the best European.

was by this lucky accident, I reasoned thus — if two animals are capable of exciting so much attention, what will be the effect on a larger scale, with larger animals? The farmers present, responded to my remarks with approbation — We became acquainted, by this little incident; and from that moment, to the present, Agricultural Societies, Cattle Shows, and all in connection therewith, have predominated in my mind, greatly to the injury of my private affairs.

The winter following, I addressed (under the signature of Projector,) the farmers of Berkshire, with a view to the spread of the Merino sheep; which I considered as invaluable, especially in the hilly countries of New-England. In these first essays, the following *extracts* were an introduction to the subject of establishing an Agricultural Society.

"The most certain and direct road to effect this great object, appears to me, will be the organization of an Agricultural Society, which will ultimately embrace all the respectable farmers of the county, who will bring to this common fund, like bees to the hive, their stock of experience, for the good of the whole; whereas, for the want of such a central point of communication, how much useful information is necessarily swallowed up in the grave; which, of right, should be the common property of mankind," &c.

The following marginal note in a book containing several other printed essays to the same effect, was written some months after these publications.

"These essays, I appeal to the fountain of all truth, were written and published from the purest amor patriae; yet they have exposed me most unjustly in public and in private, to ridicule, to uncharitable inferences, to sarcasms, and to the imputation of every unworthy motive, yet I will persevere, and with the blessing of God, I will prevail, and if I live, I will humble these pigmy minds into confusion."

The public mind was gradually maturing to embrace the prize in full view, and feeling indignant at the scandalous treatment I had experienced, in being ridiculed at a public festival by professional men, my mind was intent, and settled, in neglecting nothing to revolutionize the public sentiment in the pursuit of their own good.

The breed of swine in Berkshire, was of the most unprofitable kind — long legs — tall — lank sides — large bones, requiring more to fat them than their value.

In 1808, I procured from Dutchess County, in the state of New-York, a pair of small boned, short-legged, grass-fed pigs, so called, and presented the male to the town of Pittsfield, upon condition that he should be alternately removed to different places. The conditions were disregarded, and he was left to wander from place to place, friendless, and even shot through the body — at length, barbarously mutilated on the highway.

The old breed, nevertheless, disappeared, and the community have gained largely by the exchange. In the same year, I purchased a young bull at Cherry Valley, of the celebrated English stock, with the view of ameliorating the breed of cattle. The winter of 1809, I introduced into my pond, in connection with a few friends, the first pickerel which had been seen in Berkshire, with the exception of a commencement at Stockbridge two years previous. Their prolific increase in all the ponds, and streams, now affords an essential item of delicious and increasing food for the inhabitants, which cost them nothing but the trouble of catching and eating them.

I stood alone, the butt of ridicule, till the 1st of August, 1810, when I wrote an appeal to the public, thus:

BERKSHIRE CATTLE-SHOW.

"The multiplication of useful animals is a common blessing to mankind."   WASHINGTON.

TO FARMERS.

"The subscribers take the liberty to address you on a momentous subject, which, in all probability, will materially affect the Agricultural interest of this county."

After several other remarks, it concludes:

"In a hope of being instrumental in commencing a plan so useful in its consequences, we propose to exhibit in the square in the village of Pittsfield on the 1st October next, from 9 to 8 o'clock, Bulls," &c. &c. "It is hoped this essay will not be confined to the present year, but will lead to permanent annual cattle shows, and that an incorporate Agricultural Society will emanate from these meetings, which will hereafter be possessed of funds sufficient to award premiums," &c. &c.

Signed, 1st August, 1810, Samuel H. Wheeler, and twenty-six farmers, among whom I include myself.

In consequence of this first step, on the 1st October, 1810, I find the following notice in the Pittsfield Sun.

"The first Berkshire Cattle Show was exhibited with considerable eclat on Monday last. This laudable measure cannot fail to be highly beneficial, considering its novelty in this part of the world, and that many had their doubts, and even a dread of being held up for the finger of scorn to point at. The display of fine animals, and the number exhibited, exceeded the most sanguine hopes of its promoters,* and a large collection of people participated in the display: the weather was delightful — the ice is now broke — all squeamish feelings buried — and a general satisfaction evinced. It will now be impossible to arrest its course; we have every thing to hope, and to expect, the year ensuing."

* The farmers held back their animals in the vicinity, for fear of being laughed at, which compelled me to lead the way with several prime animals.

A committee of fourteen respectable farmers, from different parts of the county, was appointed to take preparatory measures for a real exhibition in October, 1811. As I had thus far taken the lead in every thing, by common consent, I was placed at the head of a senseless procession of farmers, marching round the square, without motive, or object; having returned from whence we started, and to separate, with some eclat, I stopped in front, gave three cheers, in which they all united, we then parted, all pleased with the day, and with each other.

The following winter we were incorporated into an Agricultural Society, with ample powers to do good — but no funds. The persons named in the law, met to organize: I was chosen President, and devoted myself in preparation for a splendid exhibition, the following 24th of September.

From *History of The Berkshire Agricultural Society* by Elkanah Watson. E&E Hosford, Albany, 1819.

Elkanah Watson. Courtesy of The Berkshire Eagle

DAVID DUDLEY FIELD

*The Reverend David Dudley Field (1781-1867) was minister of Stockbridge
from 1819 to 1837, and after retirement in 1851 returned to live in Stockbridge
until his death. A pioneer in local history, he edited and wrote much of the*
History of the County of Berkshire *(1829) which still stands as the indispensable starting-point of any inquiry into the Berkshire past.*

*He is also notable as the father of four extraordinary sons — David, a rail-
road lawyer and legal reformer, Cyrus, the entrepreneur who laid the Atlantic
cable, Stephen, justice of the U.S. Supreme Court, and Henry, author and
liberal Presbyterian reformer.*

In this excerpt on Berkshire insects from the History, *Field records the
incident (also recounted by Timothy Dwight) that Melville worked up into his
story "The Apple Tree Table," and that Thoreau alludes to at the end of*
Walden.

Berkshire Insects

COMMON AND UNCOMMON INSECTS

The insects, though abundant, have not been sufficiently examined
to merit much notice. The *Firefly* or *Lightning Bug*, is common in
the summer months, shedding its light on the darkness of the
lower tracts in the evening. The *Glow Worm* is uncommon. The *Locust*
(cicada septendecem) appears in small numbers every year, but has never
been sufficiently numerous to be destructive to vegetables. The *Grasshop-
per*, especially two species, sometimes commit great devastation. In the
summer of 1818 they were abundant; and in 1826, far more numerous,
greatly injured fields of wheat, oats, grass, &c.; destroyed turnips entirely, and also fields of buckwheat in the north part of the County. They
were far more numerous in many places in Vermont.

THE TRANSFORMATION OF INSECTS

The organization of insects is probably as complete, certainly as wonderful, as that of the elephant. They are too often regarded as beneath the
consideration of men. Their wonderful transformation and economy is
well deserving of enlightened curiosity. To lead some to the consideration of these minute works of God, the following facts may be of some
consequence.

The *gad-fly*, or *goad fly*, so troublesome to cattle in July and August,
but not abundant in this part of the country, is produced from the *grubs*

which fall from the backs of cattle in the spring; the egg having been deposited by the fly in the skin of the cattle, the summer before.

The insect, so annoying to sheep in August and September, is produced from a grub in the nose of the sheep, the egg of which is deposited in the nostrils of the sheep the season before, and the deposition of whose eggs causes the sheep to attempt to hide their heads under logs and fences, and to run with such rapidity from place to place, to avoid the insects. These worms sometimes work their way into the head of the sheep, producing a fatal disease.

The *bot-fly* or *bot-bee*, is well known to originate from the *nits* deposited on the hairs of the horse, which are taken into the stomach of the animal, transformed into a grub, voided in winter and spring, and finally changed into the *bot-fly*.

The *ugly worm*, a caterpillar on the nettle, when put under a tumbler and fed with the leaves to its satisfaction, fastens itself by the its tail to the upper part of the tumbler; drops off its head, and changes into a rude sack; from which is a few days issues the common black *butterfly*, with scolloped wings, spangled with reddish-yellow spots.

The worm found upon *silk-weed*, by a similar process, becomes another beautiful butterfly.

The *canker worm*, or apple-tree caterpillar, rolls itself up in a leaf, and in a few days comes out a *brown miller* or *moth*, so common about our *lights* in the evenings of July.

The *cut-worm* changes also into a *brown* moth, which annoys people in the same way.

The *yellow cabbage* worm, often abundant on this plant in September and October, after having eaten sufficiently, drops its head; changes into a kind of *bot-worm* or *grub*; slowly works a passage into the earth; lies till spring, and then works upwards to the surface; changes also into a brown but very different *moth*, and deposits its eggs upon the cabbage for another generation.

The *horn-bug*, so annoying in our summer evenings, is produced from the *grub*, found in the rich earth of our chip-yards and rotten wood.

The large brown *butterfly*, whose wings are spangled with large golden spots, and are often four or five inches across, is produced from the larva found in the strong webbed covering attached to the limbs of the oak. This covering is often four inches in length and near an inch in diameter.

The *Libellula* or *dragon fly*, darting with such rapidity on its four horizontal wings of most delicate network, is produced from the larva, or kind of worm, which is found in the mud on the sides of ditches and the like.

The Reverend David Dudley Field. Stockbridge Historial Society

THE BUG IN THE TABLE

In 1806, a strong and beautiful *bug* eat out of a table made from an apple-tree, which grew on the farm of Maj. Gen. Putnam, in Brooklyn, Conn., and which was brought to Williamstown when his son, Mr. P. S. Putnam, removed to that town. It was cut down in 1786, sixty-five years after it was transplanted, and if the tree was then fifteen years old, it was 80 years old when cut down. As the *cortical* layers of the *leaf* of the table are about *sixty*, and extend within about *five* of the heart, as the inner ones are quite convex, about fifteen layers have been cut off from the outside.

In 1814, a third bug made his way out, the second having appeared two or three years before. The *last* bug came forth from nearest the heart, and 45 cortical layers distant, on the supposition of its age, from the outside. The tree had now been cut down 28 years. Of course, the egg must have been deposited in the wood *seventy-three* years before. This bug eat about three inches along the grain, till it emerged into the light. The eating of the insect was heard for weeks before its appearance. These *facts* were given by Mr. Putnam, in whose possession the table still remains, and were first published in the *Repertory* at Middlebury, Vt., in 1816. One of the bugs, preserved for some time by the Rev. Dr. Fitch, "was about an inch and one fourth long, and one third inch in diameter; colour, dark glistening brown, with tints of yellow." The facts here mentioned are remarkable, but not solitary; several similar cases are recorded. However difficult it may be to account for the preservation of the vivifying principle for so long a time, the facts will enable us to account for the periodical return of some insects, and for the actual appearance of some new ones in countries to which timber is transported. New insects actually occur, though rarely. But in relation to the preservation of the vivifying principle, the difficulty is caused more by our speculations, than by any thing *known* to the contrary. No man can account for the preservation of the vivifying principle for one week, a familiar fact, on any principle which will not apply equally well to the time of a month, a year, or a century. He can introduce only the peculiar constitution of the thing; which is in fact only the law of Divine operation in the case. A frequent recurrence to this principle, while it will manifest the ignorance of man, will remove his reasons for doubt and wonder, and lead him the oftener to the contemplation of the dependence of all things upon the operation of that amazing power and constant energy of the great Creator, who has brought these things into existence, and continues that existence according to his own wisdom and pleasure.

From *A History of the County of Berkshire, Massachusetts* by David Dudley Field. Pittsfield, 1829.

THOMAS MELVILL

Thomas Melvill (without the 'e') was the son of Major Melvill of Boston (who was one of the "Mohawks" at the Boston Tea Party) and the uncle of Herman Melville. After a career in banking in France, he came to Pittsfield during the War of 1812 as commissary officer of the large army camp established on what were then the northern outskirts of North Street. After the war he bought the Van Shaack farm and mansion "Broadhall" from Elkanah Watson. A supporter of Horace Mann, in 1837 he was appointed to chair a committee to report on Pittsfield's schools. Later that year economic difficulties caused him to sell out and move to Galena, Illinois. Until 1851 his son Robert operated Broadhall as a boarding house much frequented in summer by the literary. It is now the Pittsfield Country Club.

The Condition of Pittsfield's Schools

After a full investigation of the subject as well as from personal knowledge, the committee have come to the conclusion, that our Schools are not so good, and usefull *as they ought to be*, or as they *can be*; that they are behind the requirements of the age, both in topics of study, and in the modes of teaching; and consequently do not respond to the imperious wants of our growing population.

In the opinion of the committee, various causes have co-operated to produce this state of things; some of which it may be proper to notice. — First The deficientcy of *competent Teachers*; the natural consequence of *the low estimate* too generally made of their intrinsic *moral* and *mental* worth. —

Secondly   The general neglect of a systematic and thorough examination of *teachers*, and of *schools* ...

The Committee here present you with a gloomy picture of the actual state of our Schools — Is it not therefore our bounden duty, to commence the work of improvement without delay, and in good earnest? — or, shall we continue to present the strange anomaly of a town, always ready to aid institutions designed to educate *children from abroad*, whilst we supinely *suffer our own offspring* to lack the bread of knowledge? ...

by order of the Committee
Tho[s] Melvill

From *Report of the Committee on Schools*, April 17, 1837.

CATHARINE MARIA SEDGWICK

Catharine Maria Sedgwick (1789-1867) was an immensely loved woman; even today from the musty pages of her books emerges a sense of the kindly optimist she was, a constitutionally modest woman firmly convinced that even the worst person has a better nature which ladylike behavior will impel him to live up to. If today she is little read, in her day her novels sold in the tens of thousands and were widely translated. Along with Irving, Cooper, and her friend Bryant, she was regarded as one of the creators of a national literature.

Her lively depiction of American country life and country "characters," based on her close observation of Berkshire life, as in her first effort, A New-England Tale, *established the strain of "local color" in American fiction and put the Berkshires on the tourist map. In particular, the exciting "sacrifice scene" of* Hope Leslie, *in which the Indian maiden Magawisca miraculously scrambled up raw precipices to the top of Laurel Hill in the nick of time, brought a constant stream of pilgrims to the site of her noble deed. (Nor should the pointed relevance of Miss Sedgwick's favorable portrayal of native Americans to Jackson's policy of Indian removal be overlooked.)*

Having grown up in the family mansion in Stockbridge, in her mature years she was in residence part of every year at "The Hive," a school in Lenox run by her sister-in-law. Here she taught the art of conversation to the young ladies. Every foreign visitor to the United States wished to come to the Berkshires to meet the famous Miss Sedgwick.

Her uncompleted autobiography gives insight into the Berkshires' leading family.

A Hill Town Encounter

THE TRAVELERS APPROACH THE BERKSHIRES

From the Connecticut they passed by the romantic road that leads through the plains of West Springfield, Westfield, &c. There is no part of our country, abundant as it is in the charms of nature, more lavishly adorned with romantic scenery. The carriage slowly traced its way on the side of a mountain, from which the imprisoned road had with difficulty been won; a noisy stream dashed impetuously along at their left, and as they ascended the mountain, they still heard it before them, leaping from rock to rock, now almost losing itself in the deep pathway it had made, and then rushing with increased violence over its stony bed.

"This young stream," said Mr. Lloyd, "reminds one of the turbulence of headstrong childhood: I can hardly believe it to be the same we admired, so leisurely winding its peaceful way into the bosom of the Connecticut."

"Thou likest the sobriety of maturity," replied Rebecca; "but I confess that there is something delightful to my imagination in the elastic bound of this infant stream; it reminds me of the joy of untamed spirits, and undiminished strength."

A STORM THREATENS

The travellers' attention was withdrawn from the wild scene before them to the appearance of the heavens, by their coachman, who observed that "never in his days had he seen clouds make so fast; it was not," he said, "five minutes since the first speck rose above the hill before them, and now there was not enough blue sky for a man to swear by: — but," added he, looking with a lengthening visage to what he thought an interminable hill before them, "the lightning will be saved the trouble of coming down to us, for if my poor beasts ever get us to the top, we may reach up and take it."

SHELTER INVITES

Having reached the top of the next acclivity, they perceived by the roadside, a log hut; over the door was a slab, with a rude and mysterious painting (which had been meant for a foaming can and a plate of ginger-bread), explained underneath by "cake and beer for sale." This did not look very inviting, but it promised a better shelter from the rain, for the invalid, than the carriage could afford. Mr. Lloyd opened the door, and lifted his wife over a rivulet, which actually ran between the sill of the house and the floor-planks that had not originally been long enough for the dimensions of the apartment.

A BERKSHIRE HILL FAMILY

The mistress of the mansion, a fat middle-aged woman, who sat with a baby in her arms at a round table, at which there were four other children eating from a pewter dish placed in the middle, rose, and having ejected the eldest boy from a chair by a very unceremonious slap, offered it to Mrs. Lloyd, and resumed her seat, quietly finishing her meal. Her husband, a ruddy, good-natured, hardy-looking mountaineer, had had the misfortune, by some accident in his childhood, to lose the use of both his legs, which were now ingeniously folded into the same chair on which he sat. He turned to the coachman, who, having secured his horses, had just entered, and smiling at his consternation, said, "Why, friend, you look scare't, pretty pokerish weather, to be sure, but then we don't mind it up here;" then turning to the child next him, who, in gazing at the strangers, had dropped half the food she was conveying to her mouth, he said, —

"*Desdemony*, don't scatter the 'tatoes so." — "But last week," he continued, resuming his address to the coachman, "there was the most *tedious* spell of weather I have sen the week before last thanksgiving, when my wife and I went down into the lower part of Becket, to hear Deacon Hollister's funeral sarmont — Don't you remember, Tempy, that musical fellow that was there? — 'I don't see,' says he, 'the use of the minister preaching up so much about hell-fire,' says he, 'it is a very good doctrine,' says he, 'to preach down on Connecticut River, but,' says he, 'I should not think it would frighten any body in such a cold place as Becket.'"

A bright flash, that seemed to fire the heavens, succeeded by a tremendous clap of thunder, which made the hovel tremble, terrified all the group, except the fearless speaker.

"A pretty smart flash to be sure; but, as I was saying, it is nothing to that storm we had last week. — *Valorus*, pull that hat out of the window, so the gentleman can see. — There, sir," said he, "just look at that big maple tree, that was blown down, if it had come one yard nearer my house, it would have crushed it to atoms. Ah, this is a nice place as you will find any where," he continued (for he saw Mr. Lloyd was listening attentively to him, "to bring up boys; it makes them hardy and spirited, to live here with the wind roaring about them, and the thunder rattling right over their heads; why they don't mind it any more than my woman's spinning-wheel, which, to be sure, makes a dumb noise sometimes."

NAMES

Our travellers were not a little amused with the humour of this man, who had a natural philosophy that a stoic might have envied. "Friend," said Mr. Lloyd, "you have a singular fancy about names; what may be the name of that chubby little girl who is playing with my wife's fan?"

"Yes, sir, I am a little notional about names; that girl, sir, I call *Octavy*, and that lazy little dog that stands by her, is *Rodolphus*."

"And this baby," said Mr. Lloyd, kindly giving the astonished little fellow his watch chain to play with, "this must be Vespasian or Agricola."

"No, sir, no; I met with a disappointment about that boy's name — what you may call a slip between the cup and the lip — when he was born, the women asked me what I meant to call him? I told them I did not mean to be in any hurry; for you must know, sir, the way I get my names, I buy a book of one of them pedlers that are going over the mountain with tin-ware and brooms, and books and pamphlets, and one notion and another; that is, I don't buy out and out, but we make a swap; they take some of my wooden dishes, and let me have the *vally* in books; for you must know I am a great reader, and mean all my children shall have larning too, though it is pretty tough scratching for it. Well, sir, as I was saying about this boy, I found a name just to hit my fancy, for I can pretty generally suit myself; the name was Sophronius; but just about that time, as the deuce would have it, my wife's father died, and the gin'ral had been a very gin'rous man to us, and so to compliment the old gentleman, I concluded to call him Solomon Wheeler."

Portrait of Catharine Maria Sedgwick after Charles Ingham. Stockbridge Historical Society

THE TRAVELER'S GENEROSITY

Mr. Lloyd smiled, and throwing a dollar into the baby's lap, said, "There is something, my little fellow, to make up for your loss." The sight and the gift of a silver dollar produced a considerable sensation among the mountaineers. The children gathered round the baby to examine the splendid favour. The mother said, "The child was not old enough to make its manners to the gentleman, but he was as much beholden to him as if he could." The father only seemed insensible, and contented himself with remarking, with his usual happy nonchalance, that he "guessed it was easier getting money down country, than it was up on the hills."

"Very true, my friend," replied Mr. Lloyd, "and I should like to know how you support your family here. You do not appear to have any farm."

EARNING A LIVING IN BECKET

"No, Sir," replied the man, laughing, "it would puzzle me, with my legs, to take care of a farm; but then I always say, that as long as a man has his wits he has something to work with. This is a pretty cold sappy soil up here, but we make out to raise all our sauce, and enough besides to fat a couple of pigs on; then, Sir, as you see, my woman and I keep a stock of cake and beer, and tansy bitters — a nice trade for a cold stomach; there is considerable travel on the road, and people get considerable dry by the time they get up here, and we find it a good business; and then I turn wooden bowls and dishes, and go out peddling once or twice a year; and there is not an old woman, or a young one either, for the matter of that, but I can coax them to buy a dish or two; I take my pay in provisions or clothing; all the cash I get is by the beer and cake: and now Sir, though I say it, that may be should not say it, there is not a more independent man in the town of Becket than I am, though there is them that's more fore-handed; but I pay my minister's tax and my school-tax as reg'lar as any of them."

Mr. Lloyd admired the ingenuity and contentment of this man, his enjoyment of the privilege, the "glorious privilege," of every New-England man, of "being independent." But his pleasure was somewhat abated by an appearance of a want of neatness and order, which would have contributed so much to the comfort of the family, and which, being a Quaker, he deemed essential to it.

From *A New-England Tale* by Catharine Maria Sedgwick. E. Bliss and E. White, New York, 1822.

The Sacrifice

THE NATIVE AMERICAN BERKSHIRES

T he lower valley of the Housatonick, at the period to which our
history refers, was inhabited by a peaceful, and, as far as that
epithet could ever be applied to our savages, an agricultural tribe,
whose territory, situate midway between the Hudson and the Connecticut, was bounded and defended on each side by mountains, then deemed
impracticable to a foe. These inland people had heard from the hunters of
distant tribes, who occasionally visited them, of the aggressions and
hostility of the English strangers, but regarding it as no concern of theirs,
they listened, much as we listen to news of the Burmese war — Captain
Symmes' theory — or lectures on phrenology. One of their hunters, it is
true, had penetrated to Springfield, and another had passed over the hills
to the Dutch fort at Albany, and returned with the report that the strangers' skin was the colour of cowardice — that they served their women,
and spoke an unintelligible language. There was little in this account to
interest those who were so ignorant as to be scarcely susceptible of
curiosity, and they hardly thought of the dangerous strangers at all, or
only thought of them as a people from whom they had nothing to hope or
fear, when the appearance of the ruined Pequod chief, with his English
captives, roused them from their apathy.

THE VILLAGE

The village was on a level, sandy plain, extending for about half a
mile, and raised by a natural and almost perpendicular bank fifty feet
above the level of the meadows. At one extremity of the plain, was the hill
we have described; the other was terminated by a broad green, appropriated to sports and councils.

The huts of the savages were irregularly scattered over the plain —
some on cleared ground, and others just peeping out of copses of pine
trees — some on the very verge of the plain, overlooking the meadows —
and others under the shelter of a high hill that formed the northern
boundary of the valley, and seemed stationed there to defend the inhabitants from their natural enemies — cold, and wind.

The huts were the simplest structures of human art; but, as in no
natural condition of society a perfect equality obtains, some were more
spacious and commodious than others. All were made with flexible poles
firmly set in the ground, and drawn and attached together at the top.
Those of the more indolent, or least skilful, were filled in with branches of
trees and hung over with coarse mats; while those of the better order

were neatly covered with bark, prepared with art, and considerable labour for the purpose. Little garden patches adjoined a few of the dwellings, and were planted with beans, pumpkins, and squashes; the seeds of these vegetables, according to an Indian tradition, (in which we may perceive the usual admixture of fable and truth,) having been sent to them, in the bill of a bird, from the south-west, by the Great Spirit.

The Pequod chief and his retinue passed, just at twilight, over the plain, by one of the many foot-paths that indented it. Many of the women were still at work with their stone-pointed hoes, in their gardens. Some of the men and children were at their sports on the green. Here a straggler was coming from the river with a string of fine trout; another fortunate sportsman appeared from the hill-side with wild turkeys and partridges; while two emerged from the forest with still more noble game, a fat antlered buck.

This village, as we have described it, and perhaps from the affection its natural beauty inspired, remained the residence of the savages long after they had vanished from the surrounding country. Within the memory of the present generation the remnant of the tribe migrated to the west; and even now some of their families make a summer pilgrimage to this, their Jerusalem, and are regarded with a melancholy interest by the present occupants of the soil.

MAGAWISCA AND EVERELL SEPARATED

Mononotto directed his steps to the wigwam of the Housatonick chief, which stood on one side of the green. The chief advanced from his hut to receive him, and by the most animated gestures expressed to Mononotto his pleasure in the success of his incursion, from which it seemed that Mononotto had communicated with him on his way to the Connecticut.

A brief and secret consultation succeeded, which appeared to consist of propositions from the Pequod, and assent on the part of the Housatonick chief, and was immediately followed by a motion to separate the travellers. Mononotto and Everell were to remain with the chief, and the rest of the party to be conducted to the hut of his sister.

Magawisca's prophetic spirit too truly interpreted this arrangement; and thinking or hoping there might be some saving power in her presence, since her father tacitly acknowledged it by the pains he took to remove her, she refused to leave him. He insisted vehemently; but finding her unyielding, he commanded the Mohawks to force her away.

Resistance was vain, but resistance she would still have made, but for the interposition of Everell. "Go with them, Magawisca," he said, "and leave me to my fate. — We shall meet again."

"Never!" she shrieked; "your fate is death."

"And after death we shall meet again," replied Everell, with a calmness that evinced his mind was already in a great degree resigned to the event that now appeared inevitable. "Do not fear for me, Magawisca. Better thoughts have put down my fears. When it is over, think of me."

"And what am I to do with this scorching fire till then?" she asked, pressing both her hands on her head. "Oh, my father, has your heart become stone?"

Her father turned from her appeal, and motioned to Everell to enter the hut. Everell obeyed; and when the mat dropped over the entrance and separated him from the generous creature, whose heart had kept true time with his through all his griefs, who he knew would have redeemed his life with her own, he yielded to a burst of natural and not unmanly tears.

If this could be deemed a weakness, it was his last. Alone with his God, he realized the sufficiency of His presence and favour. He appealed to that mercy which is never refused, nor given in stinted measure to the humble suppliant. Every expression of pious confidence and resignation, which he had heard with the heedless ear of childhood, now flashed like an illumination upon his mind.

MAGAWISCA UNDER GUARD

But we must leave him to his solitude and silence, only interrupted by the distant hootings of the owl, and the heavy tread of the Pequod chief, who spent the night in slowly pacing before the door of the hut.

Magawisca and her companions were conducted to a wigwam standing on that part of the plain on which they had first entered. It was completely enclosed on three sides by dwarf oaks. In front there was a little plantation of the edible luxuries of the savages. On entering the hut, they perceived it had but one occupant, a sick emaciated old woman, who was stretched on her mat covered with skins.

Her hut contained all that was essential to savage hospitality. A few brands were burning on a hearth-stone in the middle of the apartment. The smoke that found egress, passed out by a hole in the centre of the roof over which a mat was skilfully adjusted, and turned to the windward-side by a cord that hung within. The old woman, in her long pilgrimage, had accumulated stores of Indian riches: piles of sleeping-mats laid in one corner; nicely dressed skins garnished the walls; baskets, of all shapes and sizes, gaily decorated with rude images of birds and flowers, contained dried fruits, medicinal herbs, Indian corn, nuts, and game. A covered pail, made of folds of birch-bark, was filled with a kind of beer —

a decoction of various roots and aromatic shrubs. Neatly turned wooden spoons and bowls, and culinary utensils of clay supplied all the demands of the inartificial housewifery of savage life.

Magawisca seated herself at the feet of the old woman, and had neither spoken nor moved since she entered the hut. She watched anxiously and impatiently the movements of the Indian, whose appointed duty it appeared to be, to guard her. He placed a wooden bench against the mat which served for a door, and stuffing his pipe with tobacco from the pouch slung over his shoulder, and then filling a gourd with the liquor in the pail and placing it beside him, he quietly sat himself down to his night-watch.

The old woman became restless, and her loud and repeated groans, at last, withdrew Magawisca from her own miserable thoughts. She inquired if she could do aught to allay her pain; the sufferer pointed to a jar that stood on the embers in which a medicinal preparation was simmering. She motioned to Magawisca to give her a spoonful of the liquor; she did so, and as she took it, "it is made," she said, "of all the plants on which the spirit of sleep has breathed," and so it seemed to be; for she had scarcely swallowed it, when she fell asleep.

The night wore slowly and painfully away, as if, as in the fairy tale, the moments were counted by drops of heart's-blood. But the most wearisome nights will end; the morning approached; the familiar notes of the birds of earliest dawn were heard, and the twilight peeped through the crevices of the hut, when a new sound fell on Magawisca's startled ear. It was the slow measured tread of many feet. The poor girl now broke silence, and vehemently entreated the Mohawk to let her pass the door, or at least to raise the mat.

MAGAWISCA'S RESOURCEFULNESS

He shook his head with a look of unconcern, as if it were the petulant demand of a child, when the old woman, awakened by the noise, cried out that she was dying — that she must have light and air, and the Mohawk started up, impulsively, to raise the mat. It was held between two poles that formed the door-posts, and while he was disengaging it, Magawisca, as if inspired, and quick as thought, poured the liquor from the jar on the fire into the hollow of her hand, and dashed it into the gourd which the Mohawk had just replenished. The narcotic was boiling hot, but she did not cringe; she did not even feel it; and she could scarcely repress a cry of joy when the savage turned round and swallowed, at one draught, the contents of the cup.

Magawisca looked eagerly through the aperture, but though the sound of the footsteps had approached nearer, she saw no one. She saw nothing but a gentle declivity that sloped to the plain, a few yards from the hut, and was covered with a grove of trees; beyond and peering above them, was the hill, and the sacrifice-rock: the morning star, its rays not yet dimmed in the light of day, shed a soft trembling beam on its summit. This beautiful star, alone in the heavens, when all other lights were quenched, spoke to the superstitious, or, rather, the imaginative spirit of Magawisca. 'Star of promise,' she thought, 'thou dost still linger with us when day is vanished, and now thou art there, alone, to proclaim the coming sun, thou dost send in upon my soul a ray of hope; and though it be but as the spider's slender pathway, it shall sustain my courage.' She had scarcely formed this resolution, when she needed all its efficacy, for the train, whose footsteps she had heard, appeared in full view.

THE PROCESSION TO THE ROCK

First came her father, with the Housatonick chief; next, alone, and walking with a firm undaunted step, was Everell; his arms folded over his breast, and his head a little inclined upward, so that Magawisca fancied she saw his full eye turned heavenward; after him walked all the men of the tribe, ranged according to their age, and the rank assigned to each by his own exploits.

They were neither painted nor ornamented according to the common usage at festivals and sacrifices, but every thing had the air of hasty preparation. Magawisca gazed in speechless despair. The procession entered the wood, and for a few moments, disappeared from her sight — again they were visible, mounting the acclivity of the hill, by a winding narrow foot-path, shaded on either side by laurels. They now walked singly and slowly, but to Magawisca, their progress seemed rapid as a falling avalanche. She felt that, if she were to remain pent in that prison-house, her heart would burst, and she sprang towards the door-way in the hope of clearing her passage, but the Mohawk caught her arm in his iron grasp, and putting her back, calmly retained his station. She threw herself on her knees to him — she entreated — she wept — but in vain: he looked on her with unmoved apathy. Already she saw the foremost of the party had reached the rock, and were forming a semicircle around it — again she appealed to her determined keeper, and again he denied her petition, but with a faltering tongue, and a drooping eye.

Magawisca, in the urgency of a necessity that could brook no delay, had forgotten, or regarded as useless, the sleeping potion she had infused into the Mohawk's draught; she now saw the powerful agent was at work for her, and with that quickness of apprehension that made the operations of her mind as rapid as the impulses of instinct, she perceived that every emotion she excited but hindered the effect of the potion, suddenly seeming to relinquish all purpose and hope of escape, she threw herself on a mat, and hid her face, burning with agonizing impatience, in her mantle. There we must leave her, and join that fearful company who were gathered together to witness what they believed to be the execution of exact and necessary justice.

EVERELL FACES HIS FATE

Seated around their sacrifice-rock — their holy of holies — they listened to the sad story of the Pequod chief, with dejected countenances and downcast eyes, save when an involuntary glance turned on Everell, who stood awaiting his fate, cruelly aggravated by every moment's delay, with a quiet dignity and calm resignation, that would have become a hero, or a saint. Surrounded by this dark cloud of savages, his fair countenance kindled by holy inspiration, he looked scarcely like a creature of earth.

There might have been among the spectators, some who felt the silent appeal of the helpless courageous boy; some whose hearts moved them to interpose to save the selected victim; but they were restrained by their interpretation of natural justice, as controlling to them as our artificial codes of laws to us.

Others of a more cruel, or more irritable disposition, when the Pequod described his wrongs, and depicted his sufferings, brandished their tomahawks, and would have hurled them at the boy, but the chief said — "Nay, brothers — the work is mine — he dies by my hand — for my firstborn — life for life — he dies by a single stroke, for thus was my boy cut off. The blood of sachems is in his veins. He has the skin, but not the soul of that mixed race, whose gratitude is like that vanishing mist," and he pointed to the vapour that was melting from the mountain tops into the transparent ether; "and their promises are like this," and he snapped a dead branch from the pine beside which he stood, and broke it in fragments. "Boy, as he is, he fought for his mother, as the eagle fights for its young. I watched him in the mountain-path, when the blood gushed from his torn feet; not a word from his smooth lip, betrayed his pain."

Mononotto embellished his victim with praises, as the ancients wreathed theirs with flowers. He brandished his hatchet over Everell's head, and cried, exultingly, "See, he flinches not. Thus stood my boy, when they flashed their sabres before his eyes, and bade him betray his father. Brothers — My people have told me I bore a woman's heart towards the enemy. Ye shall see. I will pour out this English boy's blood to the last drop, and give his flesh and bones to the dogs and wolves."

He then motioned to Everell to prostrate himself on the rock, his face downward. In this position the boy would not see the descending stroke.

Even at this moment of dire vengeance, the instincts of a merciful nature asserted their rights.

Everell sunk calmly on his knees, not to supplicate life, but to commend his soul to God. He clasped his hands together. He did not — he could not speak: his soul was

"Rapt in still communion that transcends
The imperfect offices of prayer."

"FORBEAR!"

At this moment a sun-beam penetrated the trees that enclosed the area, and fell athwart his brow and hair, kindling it with an almost supernatural brightness. To the savages, this was a token that the victim was accepted, and they sent forth a shout that rent the air. Everell bent forward, and pressed his forehead to the rock. The chief raised the deadly weapon, when Magawisca, springing from the precipitous side of the rock, screamed — "Forbear!" and interposed her arm. It was too late. The blow was levelled — force and direction given — the stroke aimed at Everell's neck, severed his defender's arm, and left him unharmed. The lopped quivering member dropped over the precipice. Mononotto staggered and fell senseless, and all the savages, uttering horrible yells, rushed toward the fatal spot.

"Stand back!" cried Magawisca. "I have bought his life with my own. Fly, Everell — nay, speak not, but fly — thither — to the east!" she cried, more vehemently.

Everell's faculties were paralyzed by a rapid succession of violent emotions. He was conscious only of a feeling of mingled gratitude and admiration for his preserver. He stood motionless, gazing on her. "I die in vain then," she cried, in an accent of such despair, that he was roused. He threw his arms around her, and pressed her to his heart, as he would a sister that had redeemed his life with her own, and then tearing himself from her, he disappeared. No one offered to follow him. The voice of nature rose from every heart, and responding to the justice of Magawisca's claim, bade him "God speed!" To all it seemed that his deliverance had been achieved by miraculous aid. All — the dullest and coldest, paid involuntary homage to the heroic girl, as if she were a superior being, guided and upheld by supernatural power.

From *Hope Leslie* by Catharine Maria Sedgwick. White, Gallaher, and White, New York, 1827.

The Laurel Hill Association observes its 100th Anniversary in 1953 near the "Sacrifice Rock."
Bishop Anson Phelps Stokes is seated at right. Mrs. Margaret French Cresson, daughter of
Daniel Chester French, looks over her shoulder at the band.
Stockbridge Historical Society

Autobiographical Selections

FATHER

No bickering or dissension was ever permitted. Love was the habit, the life of the household rather than the law, or rather it was the law of our nature. Neither the power of despots nor the universal legislation of our republic can touch this element, for as God is love, so love is God, is life, is light. We were born with it — it was our inheritance. But the duty and the virtue of guarding all its manifestations, of never failing in its demonstrations, of preserving its interchanges and smaller duties, was most vigilantly watched, most peremptorily insisted on. A querulous tone, a complaint, a slight word of dissension, was met by that awful frown of my father's. Jove's thunder was to a pagan believer but as a summer day's drifting cloud to it. It was not so dreadful because it portended punishment — it was punishment; it was a token of a suspension of the approbation and love that were our life.

Have I given you an idea of the circumstances and education that made a family of seven children all honorable men and women — all, I think I may say without exaggeration, having noble aspirations and strong affections, with the fixed principle that these were holy and inviolable?

I have always considered country life with outlets to the great world as an essential advantage in education. Besides all the teaching and inspiration of Nature, and the development of the faculties from the necessity of using them for daily exigencies, one is brought into close social relations with all conditions of people. There are no barriers between you and your neighbors. There are grades and classes in our democratic community seen and acknowledged. These must be everywhere, as Scott truly says, "except among the Hottentots," but with us one sees one's neighbor's private life unveiled. The highest and the lowest meet in their joys and sorrows, at weddings and funerals, in sicknesses and distresses of all sorts. Not merely as alms-bearers, but the richest and highest go to the poorest to "watch" with them in sickness, and perform the most menial offices for them; and though your occupations, your mode of life may be very different from the artisan's, your neighbor, you meet him on an apparent equality, and talk with him as members of one family. In my youth there was something more of the old valuation than now. My mother's family was of the old established gentry of Western Massachusetts, connected by blood and friendship with the families of the "River-gods," as the Hawleys, Worthingtons, and Dwights of Connecticut River were then designated. My father had attained an elevated position in political life, and his income was ample and liberally expended. He was born too soon to relish the freedoms of democracy, and I have seen his brow lower when a free-and-easy mechanic came to the *front* door, and upon one occasion I remember his turning off the "east steps" (I am *sure* not kicking, but the demonstration was unequivocal) a grown-up lad who kept his hat on after being told to take it off (would the President of the United States dare do as much now!); but, with all this tenacious adherence to the habits of the elder time, no man in life was kindlier than my father. One of my contemporaries, now a venerable missionary, told me last summer an anecdote, perhaps worth preserving, as characterizing the times and individuals. He was a gentle boy, the son of a shoemaker, and then clerk to the clerk of the court. The boy had driven his master to Lenox, and all the way this gentleman, conscious that his dignity must be preserved by vigilance, had maintained silence. When they came to their destination, he ordered the boy to take his trunk into the house. As he set it down in the entry, my father, then judge of the Supreme Judicial Court, was coming down stairs, bringing his trunk himself. He set it down, accosted the boy most kindly, and gave him his cordial hand. The lad's feelings, chilled by his master's haughtiness, at once melted, and took an impression of my father's kindness that was never effaced.

MOTHER

My father decided for public life, and I believe my mother never again expressed one word of remonstrance or dissatisfaction. She, no doubt, was gratified with his honorable public career, inasmuch as it proved his worth, but I think she had no sympathy with what is called honor and distinction; she was essentially modest and humble, and she *looked beyond.*

She was oppressed with cares and responsibilities; her health failed; she made no claims, she uttered no complaints; she knew she was most tenderly beloved, and held in the very highest respect by my father, but her physical strength was not equal to the demands upon her, and her reason gave way. She had two or three turns of insanity, which lasted each, I believe, some months; I know not how long, for I was too young to remember any thing but being told that my "mamma was sick, and sent away to a good doctor." This physician, I have since learned, was a Dr. Waldo, of Richmond, who took my mother to his house, and was supposed to treat her judiciously and most kindly. But oh! I can not bear to think — it has been one of the saddest sorrows of my life to think how much aggravated misery my dear, gentle, patient mother must have suffered from the ignorance of the right mode of treating mental diseases which then existed.*

My mother may have had a constitutional tendency to insanity, but I believe the delicate construction of a sensitive and reserved temperament, a constitution originally fragile, and roughly handled by the medical treatment of the times, and the terrible weight of domestic cares, will sufficiently account for her mental illness without supposing a cerebral tendency which her descendants may have inherited. But this fear may be wholesome to them, if it lead them to a careful physical training, to guarding against nervous susceptibilities and weakness, and to avoiding the stimulants and excitements so unfavorable to nervous constitutions. I firmly believe that people may be educated out of a hereditary tendency to insanity more surely than one can eradicate a liability to consumption, or any other scrofulous poison.

* Mumbet was the only person who could tranquillize my mother when her mind was disordered — the only one of her friends whom she liked to have about her — and why? She treated her with the same respect she did when she was sane. As far as was possible, she obeyed her commands and humored her caprices; in short, her superior instincts hit upon the mode of treatment that science has since adopted.

GRIPPY

How trivial, too, are the recollections of childhood! The next notch on my memory is of being sent over to Mrs. Caroline Dwight, to borrow a boy's dress of Frank Dwight's, which was to be the model of your "father Charles's" first male attire. Then come thronging recollections of my childhood, its joys and sorrows — "Papa's going away," and "Papa's coming home;" the dreadful clouds that came over our sunny home when mamma was sick — my love of Mumbet, that noble woman, the main pillar of our household — distinctly the faces of the favorite servants, *Grippy*, Sampson Derby, Sampson the cook, a runaway slave, "Lady Prime," and various others who, to my mind's eye, are still young, vigorous, and alert! Not Agrippa, for him I saw through the various stages of manhood to decrepit old age. Grippy is one of the few who will be immortal in our village annals. He enlisted in the army of the Revolution, and, being a very well-trained and adroit servant, he was taken into the personal service of the noble Pole, Kosciusko. Unlike most heroes, he always remained a hero to his valet Grippy, who many a time has charmed our childhood with stories of his soldier-master. One I remember, of which the catastrophe moved my childish indignation. Kosciusko was absent from camp, and Agrippa, to amuse his fellow-servants, dressed in his master's most showy uniform, and blacked with shining black-ball his legs and feet to resemble boots.

Just as he was in full exhibition, his master returned, and, resolved to have his own fun out of the joke, he bade "Grip" follow him, and took him to the tents of several officers, introducing him as an African prince. Poor Grippy, who had as mortal an aversion practically as our preachers of temperance have theoretically to every species of spirituous liquor, was received at each new introduction by a soldier's hospitality, and compelled, by a nod from his master, to taste each abhorrent cup, brandy, or wine, or "Hollands," or whatever (to Grippy poisonous) potion it might chance to be, till, when his master was sated with the joke, he gave him a kick, and sent him staggering away. I think Grippy was fully compensated by the joke for the ignominy of its termination. He had a fund of humor and mother-wit, and was a sort of Sancho Panza in the village, always trimming other men's follies with a keen perception, and the biting wit of wisdom. Grippy was a capital subaltern, but a very poor officer. As a servant he was faultless, but in his own domain at home a tyrant. Mumbet (mamma Bet), on the contrary, though absolutely perfect in service, was never servile. Her judgment and will were never subordinated by mere authority; but when she went to her own little home, like old Eli, she was the victim of her affections, and was weakly indulgent to her riotous and ruinous descendants.

MUMBET

Mumbet had a clear and nice perception of justice, and a stern love of it, an uncompromising honesty in word and deed, and conduct of high intelligence, that made her the unconscious moral teacher of the children she tenderly nursed.

I do not believe that any amount of temptation could have induced Mumbet to swerve from truth. She knew nothing of the compromises of timidity or the overwrought conscientiousness of bigotry. Truth was her nature — the offspring of courage and loyalty. In my childhood I clung to her with instinctive love and faith, and the more I know and observe of human nature, the higher does she rise above others, whatever may have been their instruction or accomplishment. In her the image of her Maker was cast in material so hard and pure that circumstances could not alter its outline or cloud its lustre. This may seem rhodomontade to you, my child. "Why," you may exclaim, "my aunt could say nothing more of Washington, and this woman was once a slave, born a slave, and always a servant!" Yes, so she was, and yet I well remember that during her last sickness, when I daily visited her in her little hut — her then independent home — I said then, and my sober after judgment ratified it, that I felt awed as if I had entered the presence of Washington. Even protracted suffering and mortal sickness, with old age, could not break down her spirit. When Dr. F. said to her, with the proud assurance of his spiritual office, "Are you not afraid to meet your God ?" "No, sir," she replied, "I am not afeard. I have tried to do my duty, and I am *not* afeard!" This was truth, and she spoke it with calm dignity. Creeds crumble before such a faith.

Speaking to me of the mortal nature of her disease, she said, "It is the last stroke, and it is the best stroke."

Her expressions of feeling were simple and comprehensive. When she suddenly lost a beloved grandchild, the only descendant of whom she had much hope — she was a young mother, and died without an instant's warning — I remember Mumbet walking up and down the room with her hands knit together and great tears rolling down her cheeks, repeating, as if to send back into her soul its swelling sorrow, "Don't say a word; it's God's will!" And when I was sobbing over my dead mother, she said, "We must be quiet. Don't you think I am grieved? Our hair has grown white together." Even at this distance of time I remember the effect on me of her still, solemn sadness. Her virtues are recorded, with a truth that few epitaphs can boast, on the stone we placed over her grave.

From *Life and Letters of Catharine Maria Sedgwick*. Edited by Mary E. Dewey. Harper & Bros., New York, 1872.

HARRIET MARTINEAU

Harriet Martineau (1802-1876) was a great British intellect, Unitarian and Liberal, with voluble opinions on everything notable. In 1834 she traveled to the Berkshires to visit Catharine Maria Sedgwick, one American woman she deemed worthy of her attention. Here are her observations.

Notable Berkshirites

MISS SEDGWICK

The Sedgwicks were beginning to be interested in the great controversy [slavery]; but they were not only constitutionally timid, — with that American timidity which we English can scarcely conceive of, — but they worshipped the parchment idol, — the Act of Union; and they did not yet perceive, as some of them have done since, that a human decree which contravenes the laws of Nature must give way when the two are brought into conflict. I remember Miss Sedgwick starting back in the path, one day when she and I were walking beside the sweet Housatonic, and snatching her arm from mine when I said, in answer to her inquiry, what I thought the issue of the controversy must be. "The dissolution of the Union!" she cried. "The Union is sacred, and must be preserved at all cost." My answer was that the will of God was sacred too, I supposed; and if the will of God which, as she believed, condemned slavery should come into collision with the federal constitution which sanctioned it, the only question was which should give way, — the Divine will or a human compact. It did not appear to me then, any more than now, that the dissolution of the Union need be of a hostile character. That the elimination of the two pro-slavery clauses from the constitution must take place sooner or later was always clear to me; but I do not see why the scheme should not be immediately and peaceably reconstituted, if the Americans will but foresee the necessity in time. The horror expressed by the Sedgwicks at what seemed so inevitable a consequence of the original compromise surprised me a good deal: and I dare say it seems strange to themselves by this time: for Miss Sedgwick and others of her family have on occasion spoken out bravely on behalf of the liberties of the republic, when they were most compromised.

I had a great admiration of much in Miss Sedgwick's character, though we were too opposite in our natures, in many of our views, and in some of our principles, to be very congenial companions. Her domestic attachments and offices were charming to witness; and no one could be further from all conceit and vanity on account of her high reputation in her own country. Her authorship did not constitute her life; and she led a complete life, according to her measure, apart from it: and this is a spectacle which I always enjoy, and especially in the case of a woman. The insuperable difficulty between us, — that which closed our correspondence, though not our good will, was her habit of flattery; — a national weakness, to which I could have wished that she had been superior. But her nature was a timid and sensitive one; and she was thus predisposed to the national failing; — that is, to one side of it; for she could never fall into the cognate error, — of railing and abuse when the flattery no longer answers. She praised or was silent. The mischief was that she praised people to their faces, to a degree which I have never considered it necessary to permit. I told her that I dreaded receiving her letters because, instead of what I wished to hear, I found praise of myself. She informed me that, on trial, she found it a *gêne* to suppress what she wanted to say, and thus it was natural for us to cease from corresponding. I thought she wanted courage, and shrank from using her great influence on behalf of her own convictions; and she thought me rash and rough. She thought "safety" a legitimate object of pursuit in a gossipping state of society; and I did not care for it, — foreigner as I was, and witnessing as I did, as critical a struggle as has ever agitated society. I said what I thought and what I knew of the Websters and the Everetts, and other northern men who are now universally recognised as the disgrace rather than the honour of the region they represented. Their conduct, even then, authorised my judgment of them: but she, a northern woman, shared the northern caution, if not the sectional vanity, which admired and upheld, as long as possible, the men of genius and accomplishment who sustained the intellectual reputation of New England.

Through all our differences of view and temperament, I respected and admired Miss Sedgwick, and I was sorry to be absent from England in 1839 when she was in London, and when I should have enjoyed being of any possible use to her and her connexions, who showed me much hospitality and kindness in their own country. What I think of Miss Sedgwick's writings I told in a review of her works in the Westminster Review of October, 1837. Her novels, and her travels, published some years later, had better be passed over with the least possible notice; but I think her smaller tales wonderfully beautiful; — those which, as "Home" and "Live and Let Live," present pictures of the household life of New England which she knows so well, and loves so heartily.

From *Autobiography* by Harriet Martineau. J.R. Osgood, 1877.

MUM BETT AND SHAYS'S REBELS

Her services to the Sedgwick family are gratefully remembered by them. She is believed to have saved her master's life by following her own judgment in his treatment when she was nursing him in a dangerous fever. When her master was in Boston, and the rural districts were liable to nightly visitations from marauders after Shay's [sic] war, the village of Stockbridge, in the absence of the gentlemen, depended on Mum Bett for its safety, so general was the confidence in her wisdom and courage. The practice of the marauders was to enter and plunder gentlemen's houses in the night, on pretence of searching for ammunition and prisoners. Mum Bett declared that she could have no cowards in the village; as many as were afraid had better go up the hills in the evening to farm-houses which were safe from intrusion. All brought their valuables of small bulk to Mum Bett for security. Everybody's watches, gold chains, rings, and other trinkets were deposited in an iron chest in the garret where Mum Bett slept.

The marauders arrived one night when Mrs. Sedgwick was very ill, and Mum Bett was unwilling to admit them. She quietly told her mistress that her pistols were loaded, and that a few shots from the windows would probably scare the wretches away, as they could not be sure but that there were gentlemen in the house. Her mistress, however, positively ordered her to let the people in without delay. Mum Bett obeyed the order with much unwillingness. She appeared at the door with a large kitchen shovel in one hand and a light in the other, and assured the strangers that they would find nothing of what they asked for, neither Judge Sedgwick, nor ammunition and prisoners. They chose to search the house, however, as she had expected. Her great fear was that they would drink themselves intoxicated in the cellar, and become unmanageable; and she had prepared for this by putting rows of porter bottles in front of the wine and spirits, having drawn the corks to let the porter get flat, and put them in again. The intruders offered to take the light from her hand, but she held it back. Here was the way to the cellar, and there was the way to the chambers; she would light the gentlemen wherever they chose to go, but she would not let the house be set on fire. "The gentlemen" went down to the cellar first. One of the party broke the neck of a bottle of porter, for which she rebuked him, saying that if they wished to drink, she would fetch the corkscrew and draw the cork, but that if anyone broke the neck of another bottle, she would lay him low with her shovel. The flat porter was not to the taste of the visitors.

At the foot of the cellar stairs stood a barrel of pickled pork, out of which the intruders began helping themselves. In a tone of utter scorn

Mum Bett exclaimed, "Ammunition and prisoners indeed! You come for ammunition and prisoners and take up with pickled pork!" They were fairly ashamed and threw the pork back into the barrel. They went through all the chambers, poking under the beds lest Judge Sedgwick should be there. At last, to Mum Bett's sorrow, they decided to search the garrets. In hers the iron chest came into view. She hoped in vain they would pass it over. Mum Bett put down the light, kneeled on the chest, and brandished her weapon, saying, "This is my chest, and let any man touch it at his peril." The men considered the matter not worth contesting, and went down stairs, they without having met with a single article of value enough to carry away.

From *Retrospect of Western Travel* by Harriet Martineau. Saunders and Otley, London, 1838.

FANNY APPLETON

Fanny Appleton was the granddaughter of Thomas Gold, an original corporator and first president of the Agricultural Bank in Pittsfield, and Maria Theresa Gold, a first cousin once removed of Catharine Maria Sedgwick. A woman of spirited vivacity, she visited her Berkshire grandparents frequently. Their mansion on East Street stood where Pittsfield High School now is. Her letters to friends record her lively impressions of Berkshire personalities and places.

After her marriage (following several refusals) to Henry Wadsworth Longfellow in 1843 at age 25, they continued to be familiar visitors, even buying land for a house on a bend of the Housatonic in Stockbridge. She tragically died at 44 of burns suffered when her summer dress caught fire from a candle, and the house was never built.

"Crazy Sue" was a local character made famous by Miss Sedgwick in her novel A New-England Tale.

Berkshire Letters

"CRAZY SUE"

Pittsfield, July 13, 1835

After dinner "Crazy Sue" made us a visit to my delight, for I was crazy to see her. She was not so frantically demented as I expected, but rambled on, a thousand thoughts pushing away others half formed, with now and then an amazingly shrewd "hit" at matters and things. Religion is her main topic, which she seems to view more rationally than many sounder heads. Tom tried to sketch her, but you might as well take hold of a streak of lightning. She was in tolerably fanciful garb with roses stuck through a hole in her antique bonnet, one whole shoe, and another strapped round her foot all manner of ways, which she called her "cloven foot." She sung us an old ballad, of a youth crazed for love, pretty much her own story as I supposed, though she gives a much more rational and less romantic cause for her madness, namely that it runs in the family. She must have been beautiful once, for weatherbeaten as she is, she is very fine looking, and her straight nose and black bright eyes bear evidence of better days. I was infinitely amused with her odd comparisons and quick retorts. Mary gave her a dollar to buy a pair of shoes and she strode off for them at a most majestic pace.

MISS SEDGWICK AND MRS. BUTLER

Lenox, Mass., September 5, 1838

We are sojourning for a week at this quiet little village, having left our kith and kin at Pittsfield to enjoy the society of our friends the Sedgwicks and are now sharing with Mrs. Butler parlor and board — (our beds and dinners could both come under that head) — at a staring brick hotel with Grecian columns in front, looking forth, however, on a noble sweep of hill beyond hill, steeped just now in an Italian mist and clothed in as fresh a green as June. I am enjoying myself excessively, for it is a rare good fortune to be in the constant influence of such rich minds and noble hearts as our friends here are gifted withal. Miss Sedgwick — or my own Aunt Kitty, as she is always called — you know I am enthusiastically fond of. She always seems to me a female St. John, breathing forth, on all who come near her, an atmosphere of goodness and love that is irresistibly winning and heart-warming. All the children great and small run to her ever open arms as to a sanctuary, and there is no human creature she will not bless with some corner of her great heart. Her noble qualities of mind are forgotten beside these divine capacities of heart, and she herself seems to forget them, her extreme simplicity of manner being one of her most striking gifts. More and more does she wind round your heart-strings, adapting herself to the feelings of every age and mood beyond any person I ever saw.

Curtis Hotel in 1886, 48 years after Fanny Appleton stayed there.
Courtesy of The Berkshire Eagle

You asked me to write about her; it is difficult for one to write or think about anything else when in her neighborhood. Thus go the days: About nine, Mary and I emerge from our straw couch into the breakfast room, where we find Mrs. Butler *en robe de chambre* ready to sit down with us. Then, having performed her maternal duties, she arrays herself in her riding costume — white pants (*tout à fait à la mode des messieurs*) and habit, with a black velvet jacket and cap, very picturesque, and when mounted on her own fine steed a picture that puts Miss Sedgwick in raptures. She bends to every motion with such grace and perfect control of a sufficiently fiery quadruped. Either Mary or Kate accompany her, and I usually go walk — yesterday such a one with Aunt Kitty, through sunchequered woods to a rocky precipice, a wide valley at our feet and pine woods at our back! Then we dine on whatever the charity of our landlord assigns us. Then drives or walks infinite in number and beauty hereabouts lure us out, and the evening usually is passed at Mrs. Sedgwick's, Mrs. Butler always in white muslin, bare arms and neck if it be cold as November, charming us with singing old ballads with a thrilling pathos, and such nervous excitement herself that she often turns cold as marble for a few moments after dancing the *cachucha* with castanets, and great spirit of discoursing on deep topics, with an earnestness and far-reaching intelligence which kindles her face to wonderful shiftings beyond any countenance I ever saw. Her soul seems always boiling at fever heat, and she reminds me in her various accomplishments and brilliant expressions of some gypsy Fenella. There is surely some southern, un-Saxon blood in her veins. Such a German story she told the other night, that sent us all shuddering home in the moonlight to our beds.... Little Dr. Holmes we met t'other day in Pittsfield, and he was raving about the country here, owning a fine farm near there, on the river too, so he was planning rowing adown it to make me a visit!

SHAKER DANCING AT MOUNT LEBANON

Pittsfield, September 15, 1839

Entered with a flock of other "females" the female door and left the gents to seek their kind also, got a good seat in the middle of the side appropriated for "world's people" and awaited the performances as at a theatre. Very gradually Shakeress after Shakeress opened noiselessly their side door, glided on tiptoe noiselessly, across the beautiful floor, to their respective pegs, hung thereon their white shawls, fichus, and straw bonnets (which resembled *en masses* huge hornets' nests), then sat down, as jointed dolls do, upon the wall benches, handkerchief straight across lap and hands folded over, turning not an eyelash to the right or left, like so many draped sphinxes or corpses set on end. The little girls copying so well the same rigid repose — so unlike the fidgetiness of youth — is a horrible sight, as if they were under a spell.

The men came in later, but visitors flocked in so fast that half their benches were civilly resigned to them by a patriarch elder. After utter repose the men and women staring at each other from their respective benches, rather dangerously if eyes are ammunition to such sanctified shadows of humanity, they all rose, or rather stiffened up their joints like a machine, and putting back the benches began to sing, one of the elders addressing them in unconnected, drawling scraps of morality at one end of the aisle they formed, and then stepping tip-toe to our gay ranks, held forth on the desirableness of proprietous behavior, non-mounting of benches, as it would soil them, etc., pitying us for our poor, lost condition, declaring *them* the favored of Heaven, the "salt of the earth" (rather savorless I should think) and prophesying that one day we should lament we were not Shakers! Confessed there was some virtue in the world, though grossly obscured, but no *faith* — a dim belief in former miracles but utter infidelity about those of the present day, which were vouchsafed much more marvelously. An unhinged, stuttering discourse, as if the petrifaction extended over the man's body was reaching his brain.

They then ploughed up and down (for it can't be called dancing), with their backs to us, and sang again very gay airs, terribly shrill under the large sounding board but sometimes sweeping through the gamut with great effect. I could only catch a few words: "Press on, press on to thy happy kingdom," etc. They then filed off into a double circle, one circle going one way, another two or three abreast, "laboring" round this large hall, knees bent, with a sort of galvanized hop, hands paddling like fins and voices chanting these wild airs, with a still smaller circle of elders and children in the center, stationary, giving the pitch of the songs, like so many old witches or enchanters, working over the caldron while the younger ones skipped through the force of their incantations. But no witch's sabbath, no bacchanal procession could be more unearthly, revolting, oppressive, and bewildering. The machinery of their stereotyped steps, plunging on in this way so long without rest, the constrained attitude forward, the spasmodic jumps and twists of the neck, and the ghastly visages of the women in their corpse-like caps, the waving of so many shrill voices, and the rigid expression of their faces combined to form a spectacle as piteous as disgusting, fit only for the dancing hall of the lower regions or the creation of a nightmare.

There was one woman whose horrible contortions will haunt me forever. She wrenched her head nearly over her shoulder on one side and the other, and then jerked it nearly to her knee, with a regularity of manner for such an immense time that I thought I should have rushed out for relief, as my eye saw always this dreadful figure. I supposed at first it was St. Vitus dance, or a fit, but she stopped at the end and varied it by spinning like a dervish, twisting her arms round her head like snakes. Shrouded in such a dress, and carried to such a pitch, it was the most frightful human gesticulation ever perpetrated. Doubtless they regard her as a saint, for I saw a faint imitation of it in others. After interminable dancing, varied by changing of feet with great energy, we were relieved of this constant repassing of the same faces, mostly very disagreeable: one head like an idiot or a thief, one full of cunning and self conceit, with thin, prononcé features, and a lank fringe of hair behind I shall never forget, and one youth, evidently wrought upon intensely by a devotional excitation leaping higher than the rest, with painful earnestness of expression, among the women all frightful but one tall girl with a fine profile, who seemed to curl her lip in some scorn at this insane mummery and waved her hands very languidly. There was a fat novice in worldly gear except the cap who presented an amusing contrast to her lank sisters. At one time they all knelt silently, like spectres rising from their graves, as awful a spectacle as the nuns in Robert le Diable, then sat waving their hands as if scattering cobwebs from their faces or spirits.

The stupified elder at the end thanked us for our good behavior and right gladly we emerged into fresh air after the close heat and wearisome exhibition we had been forced to endure for so many hours. The concourse of visitors is extraordinary, for surely no mortal could wish to see this twice. I remember as a child being painfully impressed by it but that was nothing to the shock the maturer judgment receives from such pitiful delusions; however, if this exercise excites in any one of them devotional feeling, doubtless God cares little by what means it is brought to light.

From *Mrs. Longfellow: Selected Letters and Journals of Fanny Appleton Longfellow*. Edited by Edward Wagenknecht. Longman Green & Co., 1956.

HENRY WADSWORTH LONGFELLOW

Longfellow's marriage in 1843 to Fanny Appleton, daughter of Boston textile tycoon Nathan Appleton, brought him to her grandparents' mansion on East Street in Pittsfield, which was the inspiration of "The Old Clock on the Stairs," written in 1845.

Longfellow's thin novel, Kavanaugh *(1849), is supposed by some to be set in Pittsfield and by others, in Lenox, but the vagueness of the writing reveals next to nothing of Longfellow's impressions of either town. This excerpt does, however, hint that Longfellow could take a wry view of the literary controversies of his day.*

The Old Clock on the Stairs

Somewhat back from the village street
Stands the old-fashioned country-seat.
Across its antique portico
Tall poplar-trees their shadows throw;
And from its station in the hall
An ancient timepiece says to all, —
    "Forever — never!
    Never — forever!"

Half-way up the stairs it stands,
And points and beckons with its hands
From its case of massive oak,
Like a monk, who, under his cloak,
Crosses himself, and sighs, alas!
With sorrowful voice to all who pass, —
    "Forever — never!
    Never — forever!"

By day its voice is low and light;
But in the silent dead of night,
Distinct as a passing footstep's fall,
It echoes along the vacant hall,
Along the ceiling, along the floor,
And seems to say, at each chamber-door, —
    "Forever — never!
    Never — forever!"

Through days of sorrow and of mirth,
Through days of death and days of birth,
Through every swift vicissitude
Of changeful time, unchanged it has stood,
And as if, like God, it all things saw,
It calmly repeats those words of awe, —
    "Forever — never!
     Never — forever!"

In that mansion used to be
Free-hearted Hospitality;
His great fires up the chimney roared;
The stranger feasted at his board;
But, like the skeleton at the feast,
That warning timepiece never ceased, —
    "Forever — never!
     Never — forever!"

There groups of merry children played,
There youths and maidens dreaming strayed;
O precious hours! O golden prime,
And affluence of love and time!
Even as a miser counts his gold,
Those hours the ancient timepiece told, —
    "Forever — never!
     Never — forever!"

From that chamber, clothed in white,
The bride came forth on her wedding night;
There, is that silent room below,
The dead lay in his shroud of snow;
And in the hush that followed the prayer,
Was heard the old clock on the stair,—
    "Forever — never!
     Never — forever!"

All are scattered now and fled,
Some are married, some are dead;
And when I ask, with throbs of pain,
"Ah! when shall they all meet again?'
As in the days long since gone by,
The ancient timepiece makes reply, —

"Forever — never!
Never — forever!"

Never here, forever there,
Where all parting, pain, and care,
And death, and time shall disappear, —
Forever there, but never here!
The horologe of Eternity
Sayeth this incessantly, —
"Forever — never!
Never — forever!"

1845

From *The Belfry of Bruges and Other Poems,* by Henry Wadsworth Longfellow. J. Owen, 1846.

The Influence of Scenery on the Mind

One evening, as he was sitting down to begin at least the hundredth time the great Romance, — subject of so many resolves and so much remorse, so often determined upon, but never begun, — a loud knock at the street-door, which stood wide open, announced a visitor. Unluckily, the study-door was likewise open; and consequently, being in full view, he found it impossible to refuse himself; nor in fact, would he have done so, had all the doors been shut and bolted, — the art of refusing one's self being at that time but imperfectly understood in Fairmeadow. Accordingly, the visitor was shown in.

He announced himself as Mr. Hathaway. Passing through the village, he could not deny himself the pleasure of calling on Mr. Churchill, whom he knew by his writings in the periodicals, though not personally. He wished, moreover, to secure the co-operation of one already so favorably known to the literary world, in a new Magazine he was about to establish, in order to raise the character of American literature, which, in his opinion, the existing reviews and magazines had entirely failed to accomplish. A daily increasing want of something better was felt by the public; and the time had come for the establishment of such a periodical as he proposed. After explaining in rather florid and exuberant manner his plans and prospects, he entered more at large into the subject of American literature, which it was his design to foster and patronize.

"I think, Mr. Churchill," said he, "that we want a national literature commensurate with our mountains and rivers, — commensurate with Niagara, and the Alleghanies, and the Great Lakes!"

"Oh!"

"We want a national epic that shall correspond to the size of the country; that shall be to all other epics what Banvard's Panorama of the Mississippi is to all other paintings, — the largest in the world!"

"Ah!"

"We want a national drama in which scope enough shall be given to our gigantic ideas, and to the unparalleled activity and progress of our people!"

"Of course."

"In a word, we want a national literature altogether shaggy and unshorn, that shall shake the earth, like a herd of buffaloes thundering over the prairies!"

"Precisely," interrupted Mr. Churchill; "but excuse me! — are you not confounding things that have no analogy? Great has a very different meaning when applied to a river, and when applied to a literature. Large and shallow may perhaps be applied to both. Literature is rather an image of the spiritual world, than of the physical, is it not? — of the internal, rather than the external. Mountains, lakes, and rivers are, after all, only its scenery and decorations, not its substance and essence. A man will not necessarily be a great poet because he lives near a great mountain. Nor, being a poet, will he necessarily write better poems than another, because he lives nearer Niagara."

"But, Mr. Churchill, you do not certainly mean to deny the influence of scenery on the mind?"

"No, only to deny that it can create genius. At best, it can only develop it. Switzerland has produced no extraordinary poet; nor, as far as I know, have the Andes, or the Himalaya mountains, or the Mountains of the Moon in Africa."

"But, at all events," urged Mr. Hathaway, "let us have our literature national. If it is not national, it is nothing."

From *Kavanaugh* by Henry Wadsworth Longfellow. Ticknor, Reed & Fields, Boston, 1849.

HARRIET BEECHER STOWE

Harriet Beecher Stowe grew up in Litchfield, Connecticut. In her novel Oldtown Folks *(1869) she preserves memories of the "life-ways" of the generation before, as she heard them from her elders while growing up, and so furnishes us today with the flavor of Berkshire life in the late 18th and early 19th century.*

Her daughter Georgianna May married Henry Allen, rector of St. Paul's Church in Stockbridge. When visiting, Mrs. Stowe stayed with them in Laurel Cottage, which was then the rectory, and is now the site of the town tennis courts.

How We Kept Thanksgiving at Oldtown

Are there any of my readers who do not know what Thanksgiving day is to a child? Then let them go back with me, and recall the image of it as we kept it in Oldtown.

When the apples were all gathered and the cider was all made, and the yellow pumpkins were rolled in from many a hill in billows of gold, and the corn was husked, and the labors of the season were done, and the warm, late days of Indian Summer came in, dreamy and calm and still, with just frost enough to crisp the ground of a morning, but with warm trances of benignant, sunny hours at noon, there came over the community a sort of genial repose of spirit, — a sense of something accomplished, and of a new golden mark made in advance on the calendar of life, — and the deacon began to say to the minister, of a Sunday, "I suppose it's about time for the Thanksgiving proclamation."

Rural dress-makers about this time were extremely busy in making up festival garments, for everybody's new dress, if she was to have one at all, must appear on Thanksgiving day.

Aunt Keziah and Aunt Lois and my mother talked over their bonnets, and turned them round and round on their hands, and discoursed sagely of ribbons and linings, and of all the kindred bonnets that there were in the parish, and how they would probably appear after Thanksgiving. My grandmother, whose mind had long ceased to wander on such worldly vanities, was at this time officiously reminded by her daughters that her bonnet wasn't respectable, or it was announced to her that she must have a new gown. Such were the distant horizon gleams of the Thanksgiving festival.

We also felt its approach in all departments of the household, — the conversation at this time beginning to turn on high and solemn culinary mysteries and receipts of wondrous power and virtue. New modes of elaborating squash pies and quince tarts were now ofttimes carefully discussed at the evening fireside by Aunt Lois and Aunt Keziah, and notes seriously compared with the experiences of certain other Aunties of high repute in such matters. I noticed that on these occasions their voices often fell into mysterious whispers, and that receipts of especial power and sanctity were communicated in tones so low as entirely to escape the vulgar ear. I still remember the solemn shake of the head with which my Aunt Lois conveyed to Miss Mehitable Rossiter the critical properties of *mace*, in relation to its powers of producing in corn fritters a suggestive resemblance to oysters. As ours was an oyster-getting district, and as that charming bivalve was perfectly easy to come at, the interest of such an imitation can be accounted for only by the fondness of the human mind for works of art.

For as much as a week beforehand, "we children" were employed in chopping mince for pies to a most wearisome fineness, and in pounding cinnamon, allspice, and cloves in a great lignum-vitae mortar; and the sound of this pounding and chopping re-echoed through all the rafters of the old house with a hearty and vigorous cheer, most refreshing to our spirits.

In those days there were none of the thousand ameliorations of the labors of housekeeping which have since arisen, — no ground and pre-pared spices and sweet herbs; everything came into our hands in the rough, and in bulk, and the reducing of it into a state for use was deemed one of the appropriate labors of childhood. Even the very salt that we used in cooking was rock-salt, which we were required to wash and dry and pound and sift, before it became fit for use.

At other times of the year we sometimes murmured at these labors, but those that were supposed to usher in the great Thanksgiving festival were always entered into with enthusiasm. There were signs of richness all around us, — stoning of raisins, cutting of citron, slicing of candied orange-peel. Yet all these were only dawnings and intimations of what was coming during the week of real preparation, after the Governor's proclamation had been read.

The glories of that proclamation! We knew beforehand the Sunday it was to be read, and walked to church with alacrity, filled with gorgeous and vague expectations.

The cheering anticipation sustained us through what seemed to us the long waste of the sermon and prayers; and when at last the auspicious moment approached, — when the last quaver of the last hymn had died out, — the whole house rippled with a general movement of compla-cency, and a satisfied smile of pleased expectation might be seen gleam-ing on the faces of all the young people, like a ray of sunshine through a garden of flowers.

Thanksgiving now was dawning! We children poked one another, and fairly giggled with unreproved delight as we listened to the crackle of the slowly unfolding document. That great sheet of paper impressed us as something supernatural, by reason of its mighty size, and by the broad seal of the State affixed thereto; and when the minister read therefrom, "By his Excellency, the Governor of the Commonwealth of Massachusetts, a Proclamation," our mirth was with difficulty repressed by admonitory glances from our sympathetic elders. Then, after a solemn enumeration of the benefits which the Commonwealth had that year received at the hands of Divine Providence, came at last the naming of the eventful day, and, at the end of all the imposing heraldic words, "God save the Commonwealth of Massachusetts." And then as the congregation broke up and dispersed, all went their several ways with schemes of mirth and feasting in their heads.

And now came on the week in earnest. In the very watches of the night preceding Monday morning, a preternatural stir below stairs, and the thunder of the pounding-barrel, announced that the washing was to be got out of the way before daylight, so as to give "ample scope and room enough" for the more pleasing duties of the season.

The making of *pies* at this period assumed vast proportions that verged upon the sublime. Pies were made by forties and fifties and hundreds, and made of everything on the earth and under the earth.

The pie is an English institution, which, planted on American soil, forthwith ran rampant and burst forth into an untold variety of genera and species. Not merely the old traditional mince pie, but a thousand strictly American seedlings from that main stock, evinced the power of American housewives to adapt old institutions to new uses. Pumpkin pies, cranberry pies, huckleberry pies, cherry pies, green-currant pies, peach, pear, and plum pies, custard pies, apple pies, Marlborough-pudding pies, — pies with top crusts, and pies without, — pies adorned with all sorts of fanciful flutings and architectural strips laid across and around, and otherwise varied, attested the boundless fertility of the feminine mind, when once let loose in a given direction.

Fancy the heat and vigor of the great pan-formation, when Aunt Lois and Aunt Keziah, and my mother and grandmother, all in ecstasies of creative inspiration, ran, bustled, and hurried, — mixing, rolling, tasting, consulting, — alternately setting us children to work when anything could be made of us, and then chasing us all out of the kitchen when our misinformed childhood ventured to take too many liberties with sacred mysteries. Then out we would all fly at the kitchen door, like sparks from a blacksmith's window.

In the corner of the great kitchen, during all these days, the jolly old oven roared and crackled in great volcanic billows of flame, snapping and gurgling as if the old fellow entered with joyful sympathy into the frolic of the hour; and then, his great heart being once warmed up, he brooded over successive generations of pies and cakes, which went in raw and came out cooked, till butteries and dressers and shelves and pantries were literally crowded with a jostling abundance.

A great cold northern chamber, where the sun never shone, and where in winter the snow sifted in at the window-cracks, and ice and frost reigned with undisputed sway, was fitted up to be the storehouse of these surplus treasured. There, frozen solid, and thus well preserved in their icy fetters, they formed a great repository for all the winter months; and the pies baked at Thanksgiving often came out fresh and good with the violets of April.

Moreover, my grandmother's kitchen at this time began to be haunted by those occasional hangers-on and retainers, of uncertain fortunes, whom a full experience of her bountiful habits led to expect something at her hand at this time of the year. All the poor, loafing tribes, Indian and half-Indian, who at other times wandered, selling baskets and other light wares, were sure to were back to Oldtown a little before Thanksgiving time, and report themselves in my grandmother's kitchen.

The great hogshead of cider in the cellar, which my grandfather called the Indian Hogshead, was on tap at all hours of the day; and many a mugful did I draw and dispense to the tribes that basked in the sunshine at our door.

"Now," says my Aunt Lois, "I s'pose we've got to have Betty Poganut and Sally Wonsamug, and old Obscue and his wife, and the whole tribe down, roosting around our doors. till we give 'em something. That's just mother's way; she always keeps a whole generation at her heels."

"How many times must I tell you, Lois, to read your Bible?" was my grandmother's rejoinder; and loud over the sound of pounding and chopping in the kitchen could be heard the voice of her quotations: "If there be among you a poor man in any of the gates of the land which the Lord thy God giveth thee, thou shalt not harden thy heart, nor shut thy hand, from thy poor brother. Thou shalt surely give him; and thy heart shall not be grieved when thou givest to him, Because that for this thing the Lord thy God shall bless thee in all thy works; for the poor shall never cease from out of the land."

These words seemed to resound like a sort of heraldic proclamation to call around us all that softly shiftless class, who, for some reason or other, are never to be found with anything in hand at the moment that it is wanted.

"There, to be sure," said Aunt Lois, one day when our preparations were in full blast, — "there comes Sam Lawson down the hill, limpsy as ever; now he'll have his doleful story to tell, and mother'll give him one of the turkeys."

And so, of course, it fell out.

Sam came in with his usual air of plaintive assurance, and seated himself a contemplative spectator in the chimney-corner, regardless of the looks and signs of unwelcome on the part of Aunt Lois.

"Lordy massy, how prosperous everything does seem here!" he said, in musing tones, over his inevitable mug of cider; "so different from what 't is t' our house. There's Hepsy, she's all in a stew, an' I've just been an' got her thirty-seven cents' wuth o' nutmegs, yet she says she's sure she don't see how she's to keep Thanksgiving, an' she's down on me about it, just as ef't was my fault. Yeh see, last winter our old gobbler got froze. You know, Mis' Badger, that 'ere cold night we hed last winter. Wal, I was off with Jake Marshall that night; ye see, Jake, he hed to take old General Dearborn's corpse into Boston, to the family vault, and Jake, he kind o' hated to go alone; 't was a dreful cold time, and he ses to me, 'Sam, you jes' go 'long with me'; so I was sort o' sorry for him, and I kind o' thought I'd go 'long. Wal, come 'long to Josh Bissel's tahvern, there at the Halfway House, you know, 't was so swinging cold we stopped to take a little suthin' warmin', an' we sort o' sot an' sot over the fire, till, fust we knew, we kind o' got asleep; an' when we woke up we found we'd left the old General hitched up t' th' post pretty much all night. Wal, didn't hurt him none, poor man; 't was allers a favorite spot o' his'n. But, takin' one thing with another, I didn't get home till about noon next day, an', I tell you, Hepsy she was right down on me. She said the baby was sick, and there hadn't been no wood split, nor the barn fastened up, nor nothin'. Lordy massy, I didn't mean no harm; I thought there was wood enough, and I thought likely Hepsy'd git out an' fasten up the barn. But Hepsy, she was in one o' her contrary streaks, an' she wouldn't do a thing; an', when I went out to look, why, sure 'nuff, there was our old tom-turkey froze as stiff as a stake, — his claws jist a stickin' right straight up like this." Here Sam struck an expressive attitude, and looked so much like a frozen turkey as to give a pathetic reality to the picture.

"Well now, Sam, why need you be off on things that's none of your business?' said my grandmother. "I've talked to you plainly about that a great many times, Sam," she continued, in tones of severe admonition. "Hepsy is a hard-working woman, but she can't be expected to see to everything, and you oughter 'ave been at home that night to fasten up your own barn and look after your own creeturs."

Sam took the rebuke all the more meekly as he perceived the stiff black legs of a turkey poking out from under my grandmother's apron while she was delivering it. To be exhorted and told of his shortcomings, and then furnished with a turkey at Thanksgiving, was a yearly part of his family programme. In time he departed, not only with the turkey, but with us boys in procession after him, bearing a mince and a pumpkin pie for Hepsy's children.

"Poor things!" my grandmother remarked; "they ought to have something good to eat Thanksgiving day; 't ain't their fault that they've got a shiftless father."

Sam, in his turn, moralized to us children, as we walked beside him: "A body'd think that Hepsy'd learn to trust in Providence," he said, "but she don't. She allers has a Thanksgiving giving dinner pervided; but that 'ere woman ain't grateful for it, by no manner o' means. Now she'll be jest as cross as she can be, 'cause this 'ere ain't *our* turkey, and these 'ere ain't our pies. Folks doos lose so much, that hes sech dispositions."

A multitude of similar dispensations during the course of the week materially reduced the great pile of chickens and turkeys which black Caesar's efforts in slaughtering, picking, and dressing kept daily supplied.

Besides these offerings to the poor, the handsomest turkey of the flock was sent, dressed in first-rate style, with Deacon Badger's dutiful compliments, to the minister; and we children, who were happy to accompany black Caesar on this errand, generally received a seed-cake and a word of acknowledgment from the minister's lady.

Well, at last, when all the chopping and pounding and baking and brewing, preparatory to the festival, were gone through with, the eventful day dawned. All the tribes of the Badger family were to come back home to the old house, with all the relations of every degree, to eat the Thanksgiving dinner. And it was understood that in the evening the minister and his lady would look in upon us, together with some of the select aristocracy of Oldtown.

Great as the preparations were for the dinner, everything was so contrived that not a soul in the house should be kept from the morning service of Thanksgiving in the church, and from listening to the Thanksgiving sermon, in which the minister was expected to express his views freely concerning the politics of the country, and the state of things in society generally, in a somewhat more secular vein of thought than was deemed exactly appropriate to the Lord's day. But it is to be confessed, that, when the good man got carried away by the enthusiasm of his subject to extend these exercises beyond a certain length, anxious glances, exchanged between good wives, sometimes indicated a weakness of the flesh, having a tender reference to the turkeys and chickens and chicken pies, which might possibly be overdoing in the ovens at home. But your old brick oven was a true Puritan institution, and backed up the devotional habits of good housewives, by the capital care which he took of whatever was committed to his capacious bosom. A truly well-bred oven would have been ashamed of himself all his days, and blushed redder than his own fires, if a God-fearing house-matron, away at the temple of the Lord, should come home and find her pie-crust either burned or underdone by his over or under zeal; so the old fellow generally managed to bring things out exactly right.

When sermons and prayers were all over, we children rushed home to see the great feast of the year spread.

What chitterings and chatterings there were all over the house, as all the aunties and uncles and cousins came pouring in, taking off their things, looking at one another's bonnets and dresses, and mingling their comments on the morning sermon with various opinions on the new millinery outfits, and with bits of home news, and kindly neighborhood gossip.

Uncle Bill, whom the Cambridge college authorities released, as they did all the other youngsters of the land, for Thanksgiving day, made a breezy stir among them all, especially with the young cousins of the feminine gender.

The best room on this occasion was thrown wide open, and its habitual coldness had been warmed by the burning down of a great stack of hickory logs, which had been heaped up unsparingly since morning. It takes some hours to get a room warm, where a family never sits, and which therefore has not in its walls one particle of the genial vitality which comes from the in-dwelling of human beings. But on Thanksgiving day, at least, every year, this marvel was effected in our best room.

Although all servile labor and vain recreation on this day were by law forbidden, according to the terms of the proclamation, it was not held to be a violation of the precept, that all the nice old aunties should bring their knitting-work and sit gently trotting their needles around the fire; nor that Uncle Bill should start a full-fledged romp among the girls and children, while the dinner was being set on the long table in the neighboring kitchen. Certain of the good elderly female relatives, of serious and discreet demeanor, assisted at this operation.

But who shall do justice to the dinner, and describe the turkey, and chickens, and chicken pies, with all that endless variety of vegetables which the American soil and climate have contributed to the table, and which, without regard to the French doctrine of courses, were all piled together in jovial abundance upon the smoking board? There was much carving and laughing and talking and eating, and all showed that cheerful ability to despatch the provisions which was the ruling spirit of the hour. After the meat came the plum-puddings, and then the endless array of pies, till human nature was actually bewildered and overpowered by the tempting variety; and even we children turned from the profusion offered to us, and wondered what was the matter that we could eat no more.

———————

From *Oldtown Folks* by Harriet Beecher Stowe. Fields, Osgood, Boston, 1869.

FRANCIS PARKMAN

America's greatest writer of history, Francis Parkman (1823-1893), de-cided early on that he wanted to write "the history of the American forest," and decided, too, that he wanted to observe in person as many of the sites of his story as possible. He crossed the Berkshires in 1842 on his way to Lake George, an early passenger on the railroad newly extended to Albany, and returned in August, 1844, after graduation from Harvard, to visit the country, soaking up topography and collecting old-timers' recollections of what they had heard about the French and Indian War. His Berkshire impressions did not necessarily strengthen his faith in democracy. Henry Dwight Sedgwick of Stockbridge wrote his biography.

The site of Fort Massachusetts is now part of the North Adams Price Chopper parking lot.

Through the Berkshires by Train in 1842

July 15th, 42, Albany.

L eft Boston this morning at half past six, for this place, where I am now happily arrived, it being the longest day's journey I ever made. For all that, I would rather have come thirty miles by stage than the whole distance by railroad, for of all methods of progressing, that by steam is incomparably the most disgusting. We were whisked by Worcester and all the other intermediate towns, and reached Springfield by noon, where White ran off to see his sister, and I staid and took "refreshment" in a little room at the end of the car-house, where about thirty people were standing around a table in the shape of a horse-shoe, eating and drinking in lugubrious silence. The train got in motion again, and passed the Connecticut. Its shores made a perspective of high, woody hills, closed in the distance by the haughty outline of Mount Tom. The view from the railroad-bridge was noble, or rather would have been so, had not the Company taken care to erect a parapet on both sides, which served the double purpose of intercepting the view, and driving all the sparks into the eyes of the passengers. A few miles farther, and we came upon the little river Agawam [Westfield]; and an hour after, high mountains began to rise before us. We dashed by them; dodged under their cliffs; whirled round their bases; only seeing so much as to make us wish to see more, and more than half-blinded meanwhile by showers of red hot sparks which poured in at the open windows like a hail storm. I have scarcely ever seen a wilder and more picturesque country. We caught tantalizing glimpses of glittering streams and waterfalls, rocks and mountains, woods and lakes, and before we could rub our scorched eyes to look again, the scene was left miles behind. A place called Chester Factory, where we stopped five minutes, is beautifully situated among encircling mountains which rise like an amphitheatre around it, to the height of many hundred feet, wooded to the summit. It almost resembled New Hampshire scenery. I learned the names of some of the mountains — Pontoosac — Bear — Becket — The Summit [Washington] — the last being the highest. The road here is ascending for a considerable distance through the townships of North Becket, Hinsdale, &c. The whole is a succession of beautiful scenes. The Irishmen who worked on the road made a most praiseworthy selection of places for their shanties, which many of them are wise enough to occupy still. Three or four of these outlandish cabins, ranged along the banks of a stream flowing through a woody glen extending back among the hills, made with their turf walls and slant roofs a most picturesque addition to the scene. We crossed the boundary line to Chatham, the first New York village. The country was as level as that about Boston. We passed through Kinderhook and Schodack — or however else it is spelled — and at half past six saw the Hudson, moping dismally between its banks under a cloudy sky, with a steamboat solemnly digging its way through the leaden waters. In five minutes the spires and dirt of Albany rose in sight on the opposite shore. We crossed in a steamboat and entered the old city, which, indeed, impressed us once with its antiquity by the most ancient and fish-like smell which saluted our shrinking nostrils, the instant we set foot on the wharf. We have put up at the Eagle Hotel — a good house. Nevertheless, we are both eager to leave cities behind us.

Locomotive "Hampshire" of the Western Railroad of Massachusetts; the afternoon fast passenger train from Albany to Pittsfield on its way to Boston, 1841.
Courtesy of The Berkshire Eagle

Berkshire Journal of 1844

C *abotville.* The Negro family, who sell "refreshments beer & cake." The old man, the boy with the pears and water-melons, and the woman with the money-box.

The landlord of Chester Factory, sitting cross-legged on his chair, took no notice of me as I came in; but on my asking if the landlord was in, he said, "Yes, here I be."

Parties — dances — ministers.

The stage and driver from Ches[ter] Fac[tory]. A fellow with hollow eyes, and peculiar sullenness and discontent on his features. He had travelled all over the State, sometimes driving, and sometimes singing at cows — but usually following his inclinations. Nothing pleased him. He hated the country, the road, and everything else. He had engaged on it for a year, but intended to get away at the first opportunity. He hated hard labor, and set such a value on his services that he refused to be coachman to a southern gent, who offered him $15 when he demanded $25. He intended never to marry, but liked "training with the girls." We past the house of a man who was rich for the country, having about $20,000. "I suppose he likes this place," said the driver, looking up with contemptuous discontent, and giving his horses a switch under the bellies. He says he could be rich in a month, if he chose to try, but he "always wanted to take comfort, and have nothing to think on when even'g came. Working in the day-time was enough for him."

There are occasional dances in the villages. The Methodist ministers are changed every two years. Beside their salary, they receive contributions and presents. The people are in the habit of coming to tea, sending or bringing the materials to the minister's house.

The driver turned to me with a surly envy, and said he guessed I "warn't used to hard labor." The lazy rascal envies all who can live without labor. As we were driving on, I remarked on the beauty of the road. "*Humph!* Wouldn't you like to live here?" I enquired who were the occupants of a certain house. "Paddies" — with exquisite surly indifference. "Where does that road lead?" — "Don't know," in the same tone.

Lee is full of factory girls. The very devil beset me there. I never suffered so much from certain longings which I resolved not to gratify, and which got me into such a nervous state that I scarcely slept all night.

Stockbridge. Maple and beech have followed the fir of the original growth. The railroad has lessened the value of land by the influx of western produce. These towns never sent produce to Boston and do not now — the expense of the R.R. transportation is too great.

Stockbridge. An old man at the church told me that the original meeting-house where Sergeant preached stood on the green in front. About half a mile off is the site of the church of 1784 where, in the mound on which it was built, were found a number of Indian bodies. An old man, present when the grave was opened, said that they were heaped confusedly together, without instruments of any kind with them. Perhaps they were flung there by the whites after Wolcott's [Talcott's] fight in [King] Philip's War. The Stockbridge Indians had a burying ground, the care of which they consigned, on leaving the place, to old Mr. Partridge, who keeps it carefully for them. It is in the village, and seems to contain a large number of bodies.

The old Negro at the church. He remembered all about the Indians and exchanged recollections with the old man aforesaid. He had been a soldier in W's [Washington's] army. He had four children in the churchyard, he said with a solemn countenance, but "These are my children," he added, stretching his cane over a host of little boys. "Ah, how much we are consarned to fetch them up well and virtuous," etc. He was very philosophical, and every remark carried the old patriarch into lengthy orations on virtue and temperance. He looked on himself as father to all Stockbridge.

Agrippa Hull — the "African Prince."

The "full-blooded Yankee girl," of whom I asked the way to Monument Mt. "She'd been up there going arter the cows." Bold, lively, and talkative. "Would she go and show me the way?" "Well, that *would* be rather curious!"

The group by the road-side — the beautiful girl with her hand in that of the man on horseback, and her friend sitting close by on the bank.

House of Jones. His kindness and obliging disposition. He had two large bowls of ash knots — a beautiful material — made by the Indians. The largest is used only for making wedding-cake. Also a mortar, of a piece of the trunk of a maple, made by the Indians for his grandfather. The pestle was of stone. The conch which was used to call the Indians to church now calls his household to dinner. His brother, Mr. Stephen Jones, is a great geologist, and very talkative. I got of him a chisel and two arrowheads.

Dr. Partridge. The old man was in his laboratory, bedroom, etc. among his old tables, book-cases, etc., with shelves of medicines, and scales suspended hard by. He is about 94, and remembered Williams well, who he describes as a large stout man, who used often to visit his father, and taken him on his knee. And once went out the door and blew a trumpet to amuse him. He says he remembers the face as if he saw it yesterday, especially the swelling of the ruddy cheeks.

The Dr. tells some familiar anecdotes of Williams, and says that Kunkapot and some other Indians accompanied him to the war. He remembered nothing of the affair of William Henry.

Great Barrington. On entering the bar-room, an old man with a sun-burnt wrinkled face and no teeth, a little straw hat set on one side of his gray head — and who was sitting on a chair leaning his elbows on his knees and straddling his legs apart — thus addressed me: "Hullo! hullo!! What's agoin' on, now? Ye ain't off to the wars aready, be ye? Ther' ain't no war now as I knows on, though there's agoin' to be one afore long, as damned bloody as ever was fit this side o' hell!" He proceeded to inform me that he was an old soldier, and always fought on the side of Liberty. He swore like a trooper at every sentence. He cursed the temperance reform which has run mad all over Berkshire.

Someone speaking of a girl's uncle — "Uncle, is it; uncle ain't the thing. You must look farder up" — and then laughed between his toothless gums. "The' ain't none o' them thing now-a-days, now the temperance folks says you mustn't," remarked a man. "You mustn't," said the old farmer, "G-d d—m you mustn't."

He then began to speak of some of his neighbors, one of whom he mentioned as "that G-d damnedest sneakingest, nastiest puppy that ever went this side of Hell!" Another he likened to a "sheep's cod dried"; another was "not fit to carry guts to a bear." His features were remarkably bold and well formed, but thoroughly Yankee, as also were his positions. "That d—d rascal's brother," said he, pointing to a man near him, "played me the meanest trick you ever seed," etc. The man was rather amused.

Stopped to get a dinner at a house in Mt. Washington. One was provided, such as it was. The old woman was very kind. Speaking of the difficulty of finding the way to the falls, she said in the peculiar whining tone, "Well, I should think the folks at the house might accommodate a stranger with somebody to show the way." "Well," replied the daughter, "I guess they a'nt got nobody that's big enough."

Bash Bish Falls, c. 1889. The Berkshire Athenaeum, Local History Department

Bash-a-bish lower Fall. A noble spectacle. Rocks covered with pine, maple, yellow birch, and hemlock sweep round in a semi-circular form, the water plunging through a crevice in the middle.

The cliffs stretch away above, thick-set with vegetation — you see but a small patch of sky from the deep gorge. The basin at the foot of the fall is filled with foam, and the stream escapes downward in a deep gulf, full of rocks and shadowed by the trees of the opposite mountain declivity.

Mt. Washington. As I rested by the road, a little boy came up with a kettle full of vinegar in his hand. He said he lived near the head of the falls. But was going to move soon, and go off he did not know where, but "Mr. Jenkins said it was a great ways." I showed him how to fire my gun, which very much pleased [him]. After clambering up the steep path for a mile or more, we reached the top; and the path led on into a very wild and narrow valley, with a house at the foot of it. The brook ran down through the middle, till it flung itself over the cliffs at the foot, some hundred feet down, into the deep gorge we had just come up. The mountains of this little valley were very steep, and drew nearer to each other as we proceeded up the brook. There was a delapidated barn, some old potato fields, etc., but the woods of birch and maple came close down on each side, and all was wild enough. At length a high dam and a mill appeared up stream, and a new log-house on the other side among the pine trees. We came opposite to it, where, though drift-rotten logs enough were laying about, there was no means to pass the stream. A woman [Mrs. Comstock] came down to the other side and tried to lay a plank across, but without success, so I waded through with the little boy. The woman immediately began to apologize for her bare feet, saying that she had mistaken me for her cousin, and was so glad to see an acquaintance in that place that [she] had "ran right down to see." She showed me her house, which was remarkably neat, with a little sheltered porch before it, and a rude garden fenced with the outside slabs of boards from the mill. There were plenty of ducks and geese about. She did not wish to give me lodging as she was alone, her husband being gone; but she sent "Abel" to the spring for water, killed a duck, and gave me an excellent supper. "I warn't never rich," she said, "but I a'nt always lived in a log hut." The place she stigmatized as a "Hell on earth," which she was going to leave as soon as possible. She described her terror when, sitting alone, she hears the footstep of a man about the house. Once, she says, she thought nothing of it; but now, in that lonely place, it frightens her. A wild cat from the mountains has invested the house, and stolen her ducks and hens. She has seen it; and one night, hearing the hens cackling, she went out, though in great terror, and made a fire to keep it off.

I went to Mr. Murray's — the other house — to spend the night. His wife was Dutch. He is a broken tradesman. His house is neatly plastered; and he, the picture of ill-health and leanness, sat smoking his pipe, and talking slowly between the whiffs. The room where I slept contained various relics of departed prosperity. A handsomely curtained bed — images and french toys on the mantel. A table with books, vases, pamphlets, and a *basket of cards* upon it. His girls' dresses were hung up around, with a few maps, etc. The furniture, though a little old, evidently belonged to his better days; and these various articles contrasted queerly with the hearth of rough stones, and the rude whitewashed fireplace, filled by way of ornament with pine and hemlock boughs.

Murray is a broken man every way — duns are frequently upon him, Mrs. Comstock says, but he says that he is pleased with that place, because it is *"retired."* He has had enough of company, and wants to be by himself, and his wife echoes his words. "Well," says Mrs. C. in a true woman's strain, "I should think Mrs. Murray might wait till she *feels* what she says, and not pretend to be so Christain like and humble, when we all know she don't like the mounting no more than I do."

I breakfasted with Mrs. C. in the morning, who on my departure refused to take any remuneration, which I was obliged to throw into the form of a gift to her little boy; and took my leave of this very kind and hospitable woman.

The falls from the top of the rock are an extraordinarily fine scene — almost as fine below and seem to me one of the finest scenes in New England.

The Patroon's (or the "Patteroon's") tenure is in peril. The tenants refuse to pay rent. I went to Stephentown to see the gathering for resistance. All along the road occurred boards with "Down with the rent" — and flags in the village and the gathering place, which was on a hill at a mean tavern surrounded by a group of houses. The assembly was of the very lowest kind. The barroom full to suffocation, and vilely perfumed. One old man sat and talked for a long time. He had been with Indians, and kept remarking on their good qualities; which remarks were received with great applause. The chief actors were to appear in the disguise of Indians. There was another old fellow who had been with the Indians and kept constantly talking of their friendship for him, perfuming all near with the stench of his filthy, rotten teeth. Another fellow had been at Plattsburg, and distinguished himself by the vileness of his appearance and conversation. Another old fool, with a battered straw hat, and a dirty shirt for his only upper garment, kept retailing his grievances, lashing himself into enthusiasm and exclaiming "Down with the rent!" The "Indians" at length appeared, and went through some meaningless manoevres. A hole in a block of cast iron was charged with powder, and a plug being driven hard into it, it was repeatedly fired. After a while, it was attempted to come to business. A few of the more decent squatted themselves on the bank of grass before the platform erected for the directors, but were listless and inattentive while the directors, who managed the whole affair, nominated deputies from the different districts to arrange the matter. Those loudest in their noise were not of the number on the bank. The voice of the old man with the straw hat could be heard declaiming, and sharply exclaiming, "Down with the rent!" while the rest were eating or watching the clumsy and absurd movements of the "Indians."

The other towns of the Patroon's domain have also revolted; and his feudal tenure, so strangely out of place in America, has probably lived its time.

I have never seen a viler concourse in America.

The "Hopper." A great mountain rises before me, covered with trees — birch, beech and fir; and near the top and down its sides light vapors are resting among the tree tops — now sinking below them, now rising up and obscuring them; sometimes a line of firs will be relieved against the white cloud, turning nearly black by the contrast. A ridge beyond is black with firs, with a few light green birches dotted among them and a rough, bare avalanche slide. They are stiff and erect all along the top of the ridge.

The clouds rise upward from the forest like smoke from firs below. The shadows of the clouds pass over it — now it is dark and now light — now the brightness is on the wet smooth stones of the slide. The clouds move rapidly overhead, and the weather grows clearer. The stream makes a loud noise below. The hillside where I sit is scattered with the remains of large pines — lying with their branches tangled and twisted together — and numberless dead ones stand erect, burnt about the roots by fire. The living pines above raise their arms out towards the light — opposite the declivity they stand on.

The little brown wren hopping among the fallen pine trees.

Ft. Massachusetts. It stood on wide green meadows, surrounded on every side by hills. The Hoosic on the other, some 6 or 8 hundred yds. distant, with a high forest-covered hill — a ridge of Saddle Mt., I think, beyond. Wooded hills on the other side, sloping down to the meadow, less distant. In front and behind, as I stand, distant, undulating hills. The crows caw loudly among the woods. Under an apple tree is a broken head-stone with a fragment of inscription, where the bones of the officer who was shot — bones now in the W [Williams] college — were found. The bullet was in the spine.

It is a beautiful situation, this fine day.

French hatchets have been found here, beside Indian weapons of stone.

Horse radish planted by the soldiers grows here quite abundantly. I got a hatchet and gouge from Capt. B[adger].

From *Journals of Francis Parkman.* Massachusetts Historical Society.

The Attack on Fort Massachusetts

The chaplain said mass, and the party marched in a brisk rain up the Williamstown valley, till after advancing about ten miles they encamped again. Fort Massachusetts was only three or four miles distant. Rigaud held a talk with the Abenaki chiefs who had acted as guides, and it was agreed that the party should stop in the woods near the fort, make scaling-ladders, battering-rams to burst the gates, and other things needful for a grand assault, to take place before daylight; but their plan came to nought through the impetuosity of the young Indians and Canadians, who were so excited at the first glimpse of the watch-tower of the fort that they dashed forward, as Rigaud says, "like lions." Hence one might fairly expect to see the fort assaulted at once; but by the maxims of forest war this would have been reprehensible rashness, and nothing of the kind was attempted. The assailants spread to right and left, squatted behind stumps, and opened a distant and harmless fire, accompanied with unearthly yells and howlings.

Fort Massachusetts was a wooden enclosure formed, like the fort at Number Four, of beams laid one upon another, and interlocked at the angles. This wooden wall seems to have rested, not immediately upon the ground, but upon a foundation of stone, designated by Mr. Norton, the chaplain, as the "underpinning," — a name usually given in New England to foundations of the kind. At the northwest corner was a block-house, crowned with the watch-tower, the sight of which had prematurely kindled the martial fire of the Canadians and Indians. This wooden structure, at the apex of the blockhouse, served as a lookout, and also supplied means of throwing water to extinguish fire-arrows shot upon the roof. There were other buildings in the enclosure, especially a large log-house on the south side, which seems to have overlooked the outer wall, and was no doubt loop-holed for musketry. On the east side there was a well, furnished probably with one of those long well-sweeps universal in primitive New England. The garrison, when complete, consisted of fifty-one men under Captain Ephraim Williams, who has left his name to Williamstown and Williams College, of the latter of which he was the founder. He was born at Newton, near Boston; was a man vigorous in body and mind; better acquainted with the world than most of his countrymen, having followed the seas in his youth, and visited England, Spain, and Holland; frank and agreeable in manners, well fitted for such a command, and respected and loved by his men. When the proposed invasion of Canada was preparing, he and some of his men went to take part in it, and had not yet returned. The fort was left in charge of a sergeant, John Hawks, of Deerfield, with men too few for the extent of the works, and a supply of ammunition nearly exhausted. Canada being then put on the defensive, the frontier forts were thought safe for a time. On the Saturday before Rigaud's arrival, Hawks had sent Thomas Williams, the surgeon, brother of the absent captain, to Deerfield, with a detachment of fourteen men, to get a supply of powder and lead. This detachment reduced the entire force, including Hawks himself and Norton, the chaplain, to twenty-two men, half of whom were disabled with dysentery, from which few of the rest were wholly free. There were also in the fort three women and five children.

The site of Fort Massachusetts is now a meadow by the banks of the Hoosac. Then it was a rough clearing, encumbered with the stumps and refuse of the primeval forest, whose living hosts stood grimly around it, and spread, untouched by the axe, up the sides of the neighboring Saddleback Mountain. The position of the fort was bad, being commanded by high ground, from which, as the chaplain tells us, "the enemy could shoot over the north side into the middle of the parade," — for which serious defect, John Stoddard, of Northampton, legist, capitalist, colonel of militia, and "Superintendent of Defence," was probably answerable. These frontier forts were, however, often placed on low ground with a view to an abundant supply of water, fire being the most dreaded enemy in Indian warfare.

Sergeant Hawks, the provisional commander, was, according to tradition, a tall man with sunburnt features, erect, spare, very sinewy and strong, and of a bold and resolute temper. He had need to be so, for counting every man in the fort, lay and clerical, sick and well, he was beset by more than thirty times his own number; or, counting only his effective men, by more than sixty times, — and this at the lowest report of the attacking force. As there was nothing but a log fence between him and his enemy, it was clear that they could hew or burn a way through it, or climb over it with no surprising effort of valor. Rigaud, as we have seen, had planned a general assault under cover of night, but had been thwarted by the precipitancy of the young Indians and Canadians. These now showed no inclination to depart from the cautious maxims of forest warfare. They made a terrific noise, but when they came within gunshot of the fort, it was by darting from stump to stump with a quick zigzag movement that made them more difficult to hit than birds on the wing. The best moment for a shot was when they reached a stump, and stopped for an instant to duck and hide behind it. By seizing this fleeting opportunity, Hawks himself put a bullet into the breast of an Abenaki chief from St. Francis, — "which ended his days," says the chaplain. In view of the nimbleness of the assailants, a charge of buckshot was found more to the purpose than a bullet. Besides the slain Abenaki, Rigaud reports sixteen

Indians and Frenchmen wounded, — which, under the circumstances, was good execution for ten farmers and a minister; for Chaplain Norton loaded and fired with the rest. Rigaud himself was one of the wounded, having been hit in the arm and sent to the rear, as he stood giving orders on the rocky hill about forty rods from the fort. Probably it was a chance shot, since, though rifles were invented long before, they were not yet in general use, and the yeoman garrison were armed with nothing but their own smooth-bore hunting-pieces, not to be trusted at long range. The supply of ammunition had sunk so low that Hawks was forced to give the discouraging order not to fire except when necessary to keep the enemy in check, or when the chance of hitting him should be unusually good. Such of the sick men as were strong enough aided the defence by casting bullets and buckshot.

The outrageous noise lasted till towards nine in the evening, when the assailants greeted the fort with a general war-whoop, and repeated it three or four times; then a line of sentinels was placed around it to prevent messengers from carrying the alarm to Albany or Deerfield. The evening was dark and cloudy. The lights of a camp could be seen by the river towards the southeast, and those of another near the swamp towards the west. There was a sound of axes, as if the enemy were making scaling-ladders for a night assault; but it was found that they were cutting fagots to burn the wall. Hawks ordered every tub and bucket to be filled with water, in preparation for the crisis. Two men, John Aldrich and Jonathan Bridgman, had been wounded, thus farther reducing the strength of the defenders. The chaplain says: "Of those that were in health, some were ordered to keep the watch, and some lay down and endeavored to get some rest, lying down in our clothes with our arms by us.... We got little or no rest; the enemy frequently raised us by their hideous outcries, as though they were about to attack us. The latter part of the night I kept the watch."

Rigaud spent the night in preparing for a decisive attack, "being resolved to open trenches two hours before sunrise, and push them to the foot of the palisade, so as to place fagots against it, set them on fire, and deliver the fort a prey to the fury of the flames." It began to rain, and he determined to wait till morning. That the commander of seven hundred French and Indians should resort to such elaborate devices to subdue a sergeant, seven militiamen, and a minister, — for this was now the effective strength of the besieged, — was no small compliment to the spirit of the defence.

The firing was renewed in the morning, but there was no attempt to open trenches by daylight. Two men were sent up into the watch-tower, and about eleven o'clock one of them, Thomas Knowlton, was shot through the head. The number of effectives was thus reduced to eight, including the chaplain. Up to this time the French and English witnesses are in tolerable accord; but now there is conflict of evidence. Rigaud says that when he was about to carry his plan of attack into execution, he saw a white flag hung out, and sent the elder De Muy, with Montigny and D'Auteuil, to hear what the English commandant — whose humble rank he nowhere mentions — had to say. On the other hand, Norton, the chaplain, says that about noon the French "desired to parley," and that "we agreed to it." He says farther that the sergeant, with himself and one or two others, met Rigaud outside the gate, and that the French commander promised "good quarter" to the besieged if they would surrender, with the alternative of an assault if they would not. This account is sustained by Hawks, who says that at twelve o'clock an Indian came forward with a flag of truce, and that he, Hawks, with two or three others, went to meet Rigaud, who then offered honorable terms of capitulation. The sergeant promised an answer within two hours; and going back to the fort with his companions, examined their means of defence. He found that they had left but three or four pounds of gunpowder, and about as much lead. Hawks called a council of his effective men. Norton prayed for divine aid and guidance, and then they fell to considering the situation. "Had we all been in health, or had there been only those eight of us that were in health, I believe every man would willingly have stood it out to the last. For my part, I should," writes the manful chaplain. But besides the sick and wounded, there were three women and five children, who, if the fort were taken by assault, would no doubt be butchered by the Indians, but who might be saved by a capitulation. Hawks therefore resolved to make the best terms he could. He had defended his post against prodigious odds for twenty-eight hours. Rigaud promised that all in the fort should be treated with humanity as prisoners of war, and exchanged at the first opportunity. He also promised that none of them should be given to the Indians, though he had lately assured his savage allies that they should have their share of the prisoners.

At three o'clock the principal French officers were admitted into the fort, and the French flag was raised over it. The Indians and Canadians were excluded, on which some of the Indians pulled out several of the stones that formed the foundation of the wall, crawled through, opened the gate, and let in the whole crew. They raised a yell when they saw the blood of Thomas Knowlton trickling from the watch-tower where he had been shot, then rushed up to where the corpse lay, brought it down, scalped it, and cut off the head and arms. The fort was then plundered, set on fire, and burned to the ground.

The prisoners were led to the French camp; and here the chaplain was presently accosted by one Doty, Rigaud's interpreter, who begged him to persuade some of the prisoners to go with the Indians. Norton replied that it had been agreed that they should all remain with the French; and that to give up any of them to the Indians would be a breach of the capitulation. Doty then appealed to the men themselves, who all insisted on being left with the French, according to the terms stipulated. Some of them, however, were given to the Indians, who, after Rigaud's promise to them, could have been pacified in no other way. His fault was in making a stipulation that he could not keep. Hawks and Norton, with all the women and children, remained in the French camp.

From *A Half Century of Conflict* by Francis Parkman. Little, Brown, 1897.

HENRY DAVID THOREAU

In July 1844, not long after he had disgraced himself by accidentally caus-ing a fire that burned several hundred acres of woodlots, Thoreau set off on a "summit" walking tour. Mt. Monadnock, his first summit, can be seen from the top of Greylock, his second; looking the other way on Greylock, one can see Hunter Mountain in the Catskills, his third, on the brink of which stood the Catskill Mountain House, one of the most dramatic scenic sites in North America. Next year he described the night he spent with Luke Rice of Florida on his way from Monadnock to Greylock and the night he spent on Greylock in A Week on the Concord and Merrimack Rivers, *the book he went to Walden to write as a memorial to his brother John.*

His companion from Pittsfield to the Catskills and back again was Ellery Channing, who noted in his copy of A Week *that they walked back through Mount Washington to Chester, where they picked up a train to Concord.*

Mount Greylock from the south, c. 1887.
The Berkshire Athenaeum, Local History Department

With Luke Rice of Florida

Early one summer morning I had left the shores of the Connecticut, and for the livelong day travelled up the bank of a river, which came in from the west; now looking down on the stream, foaming and rippling through the forest a mile off, from the hills over which the road led, and now sitting on its rocky brink and dipping my feet in its rapids, or bathing adventurously in mid-channel. The hills grew more and more frequent, and gradually swelled into mountains as I advanced, hemming in the course of the river, so that at last I could not see where it came from, and was at liberty to imagine the most wonderful meanderings and descents. At noon I slept on the grass in the shade of a maple, where the river had found a broader channel than usual, and was spread out shallow, with frequent sand-bars exposed. In the names of the towns I recognized some which I had long ago read on teamsters' wagons, that had come from far up country; quiet, uplandish towns, of mountainous fame. I walked along, musing and enchanted, by rows of sugar-maples, through the small and uninquisitive villages, and sometimes was pleased with the sight of a boat drawn up on a sand-bar, where there appeared no inhabitants to use it. It seemed, however, as essential to the river as a fish, and to lend a certain dignity to it. It was like the trout of mountain streams to the fishes of the sea, or like the young of the land-crab born far in the interior, who have never yet heard the sound of the ocean's surf. The hills approached nearer and nearer to the stream, until at last they closed behind me, and I found myself just before nightfall in a romantic and retired valley, about half a mile in length, and barely wide enough for the stream at its bottom. I thought that there could be no finer site for a cottage among mountains. You could anywhere run across the stream on the rocks, and its constant murmuring would quiet the passions of mankind forever. Suddenly the road, which seemed aiming for the mountainside, turned short to the left, and another valley opened, concealing the former, and of the same character with it. It was the most remarkable and pleasing scenery I had ever seen. I found here a few mild and hospitable inhabitants, who, as the day was not quite spent, and I was anxious to improve the light, directed me four or five miles farther on my way to the dwelling of a man whose name was Rice, who occupied the last and highest of the valleys that lay in my path, and who, they said, was a rather rude and uncivil man. But "what is a foreign country to those who have science? Who is a stranger to those who have the habit of speaking kindly?"

At length, as the sun was setting behind the mountains in a still darker and more solitary vale, I reached the dwelling of this man. Except for the narrowness of the plain, and that the stones were solid granite, it was the counterpart of that retreat to which Belphoebe bore the wounded Timias, —

> "In a pleasant glade,
> With mountains round about environed
> And mighty woods, which did the valley shade,
> And like a stately theatre it made
> Spreading itself into a spacious plain;
> And in the midst a little river played
> Amongst the pumy stones which seemed to plain,
> With gentle murmur, that his course they did restrain."

I observed, as I drew near, that he was not so rude as I had antici- pated, for he kept many cattle, and dogs to watch them, and I saw where he had made maple-sugar on the sides of the mountains, and above all distinguished the voices of children mingling with the murmur of the torrent before the door. As I passed his stable I met one whom I supposed to be a hired man, attending to his cattle, and I inquired if they enter- tained travellers at that house. "Sometimes we do," he answered gruffly, and immediately went to the farthest stall from me, and I perceived that it was Rice himself whom I had addressed. But pardoning this incivility to the wildness of the scenery, I bent my steps to the house. There was no sign-post before it, nor any of the usual invitations to the traveller, though I saw by the road that many went and came there, but the owner's name only was fastened to the outside; a sort of implied and sullen invitation, as I thought. I passed from room to room without meeting any one, till I came to what seemed the guests' apartment, which was neat, and even had an air of refinement about it, and I was glad to find a map against the wall which would direct me on my journey on the morrow. At length I heard a step in a distant apartment, which was the first I had entered, and went to see if the landlord had come in; but it proved to be only a child, one of those whose voices I had heard, probably his son, and between him and me stood in the doorway a large watch-dog, which growled at me, and looked as if he would presently spring, but the boy did not speak to him; and when I asked for a glass of water, he briefly said, "It runs in the corner." So I took a mug from the counter and went out of doors, and searched round the corner of the house, but could find neither well nor spring, nor any water but the stream which ran all along the front. I came back, therefore, and, setting down the mug, asked the child if the stream was good to drink; whereupon he seized the mug, and, going to the corner of the room, where a cool spring which issued from the mountain behind trickled through a pipe into the apartment, filled it, and drank, and gave it to me empty again, and, calling to the dog, rushed out of doors. Erelong some of the hired men made their appearance, and drank at the spring, and lazily washed themselves and combed their hair in silence, and some sat down as if weary, and fell asleep in their seats. But all the while I saw no women, though I sometimes heard a bustle in that part of the house from which the spring came.

At length Rice himself came in, for it was now dark, with an ox-whip in his hand, breathing hard, and he too soon settled down into his seat not far from me, as if, now that his day's work was done, he had no farther to travel, but only to digest his supper at his leisure. When I asked him if he could give me a bed, he said there was one ready, in such a tone as implied that I ought to have known it, and the less said about that the better. So far so good. And yet he continued to look at me as if he would fain have me say something further like a traveller. I remarked, that it was a wild and rugged country he inhabited, and worth coming many miles to see. "Not so very rough neither," said he, and appealed to his men to bear witness to the breadth and smoothness of his fields, which consisted in all of one small interval, and to the size of his crops; "and if we have some hills," added he, "there's no better pasturage anywhere." I then asked if this place was the one I had heard of, calling it by a name I had seen on the map, or if it was a certain other; and he answered, gruffly, that it was neither the one nor the other; that he had settled it and cultivated it, and made it what it was, and I could know nothing about it. Observing some guns and other implements of hunting hanging on brackets around the room, and his hounds now sleeping on the floor, I took occasion to change the discourse, and inquired if there was much game in that country, and he answered this question more graciously, having some glimmering of my drift; but when I inquired if there were any bears, he answered impatiently that he was no more in danger of losing his sheep than his neighbors; he had tamed and civilized that region. After a pause thinking of my journey on the morrow, and the few hours of daylight in that hollow and mountainous country, which would require me to be on my way betimes, I remarked that the day must be shorter by an hour there than on the neighboring plains; at which he gruffly asked what I knew about it, and affirmed that he had as much daylight as his neighbors; he ventured to say, the days were longer there than where I lived, as I should find if I stayed, that in some way, I could not be expected to understand how, the sun came over the mountains half an hour earlier, and stayed half an hour later there than on the neighboring plains. And more of like sort he said. He was, indeed, as rude as a fabled satyr. But I suffered him to pass for what he was, — for why should I quarrel with nature? — and was even pleased at the discovery of such a singular natural phenomenon. I dealt with him as if to me all manners were indifferent, and he had a sweet, wild way with him. I would not question nature, and I would rather have him as he was than as I would have him. For I had come up here not for sympathy, or kindness, or society, but for novelty and adventure, and to see what nature had produced here. I therefore did not repel his rudeness, but quite innocently welcomed it all, and knew how to appreciate it, as if I were reading in an old drama a part well sustained. He was indeed a coarse and sensual man, and, as I have said, uncivil, but he had his just quarrel with nature and mankind, I have no doubt, only he had no artificial covering to his ill humors. He was earthy enough, but yet there was good soil in him, and even a long-suffering Saxon probity at bottom. If you could represent the case to him, he would not let the race die out in him, like a red Indian.

At length I told him that he was a fortunate man, and I trusted that he was grateful for so much light; and, rising, said I would take a lamp, and that I would pay him then for my lodging, for I expected to recommence my journey even as early as the sun rose in his country; but he answered in haste, and this time civilly, that I should not fail to find some of his household stirring, however early, for they were no sluggards, and I could take my breakfast with them before I started, if I chose; and as he lighted the lamp I detected a gleam of true hospitality and ancient civility, a beam of pure and even gentle humanity, from his bleared and moist eyes. It was a look more intimate with me, and more explanatory, than any words of his could have been if he had tried to his dying day. It was more significant than any Rice of those parts could even comprehend, and long anticipated this man's culture, — a glance of his pure genius, which did not much enlighten him, but did impress and rule him for the moment, and faintly constrain his voice and manner. He cheerfully led the way to my apartment, stepping over the limbs of his men, who were asleep on the floor in an intervening chamber, and showed me a clean and comfortable bed. For many pleasant hours after the household was asleep I sat at the open window, for it was a sultry night, and heard the little river

> "Amongst the pumy stones, which seemed to plain,
> With gentle murmur, that his course they did restrain."

But I arose as usual by starlight the next morning, before my host, or his men, or even his dogs, were awake; and, having left a ninepence on the counter, was already half-way over the mountain with the sun before they had broken their fast.

Alone on Greylock's Summit

I had come over the hills on foot and alone in serene summer days, plucking the raspberries by the wayside, and occasionally buying a loaf of bread at a farmer's house, with a knapsack on my back which held a few traveler's books and a change of clothing, and a staff in my hand. I had that morning looked down from the Hoosack Mountain, where the road crosses it, on the village of North Adams in the valley three miles away under my feet, showing how uneven the earth may sometimes be, and making it seem an accident that it should ever be level and convenient for the feet of man. Putting a little rice and sugar and a tin cup into my knapsack at this village, I began in the afternoon to ascend the mountain, whose summit is three thousand six hundred feet above the level of the sea, and was seven or eight miles distant by the path. My route lay up a long and spacious valley called the Bellows, because the winds rush up or down it with violence in storms, sloping up to the very clouds between the principal range and a lower mountain. There were a few farms scattered along at different elevations, each commanding a fine prospect of the mountains to the north, and a stream ran down the middle of the valley, on which, near the head, there was a mill. It seemed a road for the pilgrim to enter upon who would climb to the gates of heaven. Now I crossed a hayfield, and now over the brook on a slight bridge, still gradually ascending all the while with a sort of awe, and filled with indefinite expectations as to what kind of inhabitants and what kind of nature I should come to at last. It now seemed some advantage that the earth was uneven, for one could not imagine a more noble position for a farmhouse than this vale afforded, farther from or nearer to its head, from a glenlike seclusion overlooking the country at a great elevation between these two mountain walls.

It reminded me of the homesteads of the Huguenots, on Staten Island, off the coast of New Jersey. The hills in the interior of this island, though comparatively low, are penetrated in various directions by similar sloping valleys on a humble scale, gradually narrowing and rising to the centre, and at the head of these the Huguenots, who were the first settlers, placed their houses quite within the land, in rural and sheltered places, in leafy recesses where the breeze played with the poplar and the gum-tree, from which, with equal security in calm and storm, they looked out through a widening vista, over miles of forest and stretching salt marsh, to the Huguenot's Tree, an old elm on the shore, at whose root they had landed, and across the spacious outer bay of New York to Sandy Hook and the Highlands of Neversink, and thence over leagues of the Atlantic, perchance to some faint vessel in the horizon, almost a day's sail on her voyage to that Europe whence they had come. When walking in the interior there, in the midst of rural scenery, where there was as little to remind me of the ocean as amid the New Hampshire hills, I have suddenly, through a gap, a cleft or 'clove road,' as the Dutch settlers called it, caught sight of a ship under full sail, over a field of corn, twenty or thirty miles at sea. The effect was similar, since I had no means of measuring distances, to seeing a painted ship passed backwards and forwards through a magic lantern.

But to return to the mountain. It seemed as if he must be the most singular and heavenly-minded man whose dwelling stood highest up the valley. The thunder had rumbled at my heels all the way, but the shower passed off in another direction, though if it had not, I half believed that I should get above it. I at length reached the last house but one, where the path to the summit diverged to the right, while the summit itself rose directly in front. But I determined to follow up the valley to its head, and then find my own route up the steep as the shorter and more adventurous way. I had thoughts of returning to this house, which was well kept and so nobly placed, the next day, and perhaps remaining a week there, if I could have entertainment. Its mistress was a frank and hospitable young woman, who stood before me in a dishabille, busily and unconcernedly combing her long black hair while she talked, giving her head the necessary toss with each sweep of the comb, with lively, sparkling eyes, and full of interest in that lower world from which I had come, talking all the while as familiarly as if she had known me for years, and reminding me of a cousin of mine. She at first had taken me for a student from Williamstown, for they went by in parties, she said, either riding or walking, almost every pleasant day, and were a pretty wild set of fellows; but they never went by the way I was going. As I passed the last house, a man called out to know what I had to sell, for, seeing my knapsack, he thought that I might be a peddler who was taking this unusual route over the ridge of the valley into South Adams. He told me that it was still four or five miles to the summit by the path which I had left, though not more than two in a straight line from where I was, but that nobody ever went this way; there was no path, and I should find it as steep as the roof of a house. But I knew that I was more used to woods and mountains than he, and went along through his cow-yard, while he, looking at the sun, shouted after me that I should not get to the top that night. I soon reached the head of the valley, but as I could not see the summit from this point, I ascended a low mountain on the opposite side, and took its bearing with my compass. I at once entered the woods, and began to climb the steep side of the mountain in a diagonal direction, taking the bearing of a tree every dozen rods. The ascent was by no means difficult or unpleasant, and occupied much less time than it would have taken to follow the path. Even country people, I have observed, magnify the difficulty of traveling in the forest, and especially among mountains. They seem to lack their usual common sense in this. I have climbed several higher mountains without guide or path, and have found, as might be expected, that it takes only more time and patience commonly than to travel the smoothest highway. It is very rare that you meet with obstacles in this world which the humblest man has not faculties to surmount. It is true we may come to a perpendicular precipice, but we need not jump off, nor run our heads against it. A man may jump down his own cellar stairs, or dash his brains out against his chimney, if he is mad. So far as my experience goes, travelers generally exaggerate the difficulties of the way. Like most evil, the difficulty is imaginary; for what's the hurry? If a person lost would conclude that after all he is not lost, he is not beside himself, but standing in his own old shoes on the very spot where he is, and that for the time being he will live there; but the places that have known him, *they* are lost — how much anxiety and danger would vanish. I am not alone if I stand by myself. Who knows where in space this globe is rolling? Yet we will not give ourselves up for lost, let it go where it will.

I made my way steadily upward in a straight line, through a dense undergrowth of mountain laurel, until the trees began to have a scraggy and infernal look, as if contending with frost goblins, and at length I reached the summit, just as the sun was setting. Several acres here had been cleared, and were covered with rocks and stumps, and there was a rude observatory in the middle which overlooked the woods. I had one fair view of the country before the sun went down, but I was too thirsty to waste any light in viewing the prospect, and set out directly to find water. First, going down a well-beaten path for half a mile through the low, scrubby wood, till I came to where the water stood in the tracks of the horses which had carried travelers up, I lay down flat, and drank these dry, one after another, a pure, cold, spring-like water, but yet I could not fill my dipper, though I contrived little siphons of grass stems, and ingenious aqueducts on a small scale; it was too slow a process. Then, remembering that I had passed a moist place near the top, on my way up, I returned to find it again, and here, with sharp stones and my hands, in the twilight, I made a well about two feet deep, which was soon filled with pure cold water, and the birds too came and drank at it. So I filled my dipper, and, making my way back to the observatory, collected some dry sticks, and made a fire on some flat stones which had been placed on the floor for that purpose, and so I soon cooked my supper of rice, having already whittled a wooden spoon to eat it with.

I sat up during the evening, reading by the light of the fire the scraps of newspapers in which some party had wrapped their luncheon — the prices current in New York and Boston, the advertisements, and the singular editorials which some had seen fit to publish, not foreseeing under what critical circumstances they would be read. I read these things at a vast advantage there, and it seemed to me that the advertisements, or what is called the business part of a paper, were greatly the best, the most useful, natural, and respectable. Almost all the opinions and sentiments expressed were so little considered, so shallow and flimsy, that I thought the very texture of the paper must be weaker in that part and tear the more easily. The advertisements and the prices current were more closely allied to nature, and were respectable in some measure as tide and meteorological tables are; but the reading-matter, which I remembered was most prized down below, unless it was some humble record of science, or an extract from some old classic, struck me as strangely whimsical, and crude, and one-idea'd, like a school-boy's theme, such as youths write and after burn. The opinions were of that kind that are doomed to wear a different aspect tomorrow, like last year's fashions; as if mankind were very green indeed, and would be ashamed of themselves in a few years, when they had outgrown this verdant period. There was, moreover, a singular disposition to wit and humor, but rarely the slightest real success; and the apparent success was a terrible satire on the attempt; the Evil Genius of man laughed the loudest at his best jokes. The advertisements, as I have said, such as were serious, and not of the modern quack kind, suggested pleasing and poetic thoughts; for commerce is really as interesting as nature. The very names of the commodities were poetic, and as suggestive as if they had been inserted in a pleasing poem — Lumber, Cotton, Sugar, Hides, Guano, Logwood. Some sober, private, and original thought would have been grateful to read there, and as much in harmony with the circumstances as if it had been written on a mountain-top; for it is of a fashion which never changes, and as respectable as hides and logwood, or any natural product. What an inestimable companion such a scrap of paper would have been, containing some fruit of a mature life! What a relic! What a recipe! It seemed a divine invention, by which not mere shining coin, but shining and current thoughts, could be brought up and left there.

As it was cold, I collected quite a pile of wood and lay down on a board against the side of the building, not having any blanket to cover me, with my head to the fire, that I might look after it, which is not the Indian rule. But as it grew colder towards midnight, I at length encased myself completely in boards, managing even to put a board on top of me, with a large stone on it, to keep it down, and so slept comfortably. I was reminded, it is true, of the Irish children, who inquired what their neighbors did who had no door to put over them in winter nights as they had; but I am convinced that there was nothing very strange in the inquiry. Those who have never tried it can have no idea how far a door, which keeps the single blanket down, may go toward making one comfortable. We are constituted a good deal like chickens, which, taken from the hen, and put in a basket of cotton in the chimney-corner, will often peep till they die, nevertheless; but if you put in a book, or anything heavy, which will press down the cotton, and feel like the hen, they go to sleep directly. My only companions were the mice, which came to pick up the crumbs that had been left in those scraps of paper; still, as everywhere, pensioners on man, and not unwisely improving this elevated tract for their habitation. They nibbled what was for them; I nibbled what was for me. Once or twice in the night, when I looked up, I saw a white cloud drifting through the windows and filling the whole upper story.

This observatory was a building of considerable size, erected by the students of Williamstown College, whose buildings might be seen by daylight gleaming far down in the valley. It would be no small advantage if every college were thus located at the base of a mountain, as good at least as one well-endowed professorship. It were as well to be educated in the shadow of a mountain as in more classical shades. Some will remember, no doubt, not only that they went to the college, but that they went to the mountain. Every visit to its summit would, as it were, generalize the particular information gained below, and subject it to more catholic tests.

I was up early and perched upon the top of this tower to see the daybreak, for some time reading the names that had been engraved there, before I could distinguish more distant objects. An 'untamable fly' buzzed at my elbow with the same nonchalance as on a molasses hogshead at the end of Long Wharf. Even there I must attend to his stale humdrum. But now I come to the pith of this long digression. As the light increased, I discovered around me an ocean of mist, which by chance reached up exactly to the base of the tower, and shut out every vestige of the earth, while I was left floating on this fragment of the wreck of a world, on my carved plank, in cloudland; a situation which required no aid from the imagination to render it impressive. As the light in the east steadily increased, it revealed to me more clearly the new world into which I had risen in the night, the new *terra firma* perchance of my future life. There was not a crevice left through which the trivial places we name Massachusetts or Vermont or New York could be seen, while I still inhaled the clear atmosphere of a July morning — if it were July there. All around beneath me was spread for a hundred miles on every side, as far as the eye could reach, an undulating country of clouds, answering in the varied swell of its surface to the terrestrial world it veiled. It was such a country as we might set in dreams, with all the delights of paradise. There were immense snowy pastures, apparently smooth shaven and firm, and shady vales between the vaporous mountains; and far in the horizon I could see where some luxurious misty timber jutted into the prairie, and trace the windings of a watercourse, some unimagined Amazon or Orinoko, by the misty trees on its brink. As there was wanting the symbol, so there was not the substance of impurity, no spot nor stain. It was a favor for which to be forever silent to be shown this vision. The earth beneath had become such a flitting thing of lights and shadows as the clouds had been before. It was not merely veiled to me, but it had passed away like the phantom of a shadow, *skias onar*, and this new platform was gained. As I had climbed above storm and cloud, so by successive days' journeys I might reach the region of eternal day, beyond the tapering shadow of the earth; ay,

> "Heaven itself shall slide,
> And roll away like melting stars that glide
> Along their oily threads."

But when its own sun began to rise on this pure world, I found myself a dweller in the dazzling halls of Aurora, into which poets have had but a partial glance over the eastern hills, drifting amid the saffron-colored clouds, and playing with the rosy fingers of the Dawn, in the very path of the Sun's chariot, and sprinkled with its dewy dust, enjoying the benignant smile, and near at hand the far-darting glances of the god. The inhabitants of earth behold commonly but the dark and shadowy under side of heaven's pavement; it is only when seen at a favorable angle in the horizon, morning or evening, that some faint streaks of the rich lining of the clouds are revealed. But my muse would fail to convey an impression of the gorgeous tapestry by which I was surrounded, such as men see faintly reflected afar off in the chambers of the east. Here, as on earth, I saw the gracious god

> "Flatter the mountain-tops with sovereign eye,
> Gilding pale streams with heavenly alchemy."

But never here did 'Heaven's sun' stain himself.

But, alas, owing, as I think, to some unworthiness in myself, my private sun did stain himself, and

> "Anon permit the basest clouds to ride
> With ugly wrack on his celestial face" —

for before the god had reached the zenith the heavenly pavement rose and embraced my wavering virtue, or rather I sank down again into that 'forlorn world,' from which the celestial sun had hid his visage,

> "How may a worm that crawls along the dust,
> Clamber the azure mountains, thrown so high,
> And fetch from thence thy fair idea just,
> That in those sunny courts doth hidden lie,
> Clothed with such light as blinds the angel's eye?
> How may weak mortal ever hope to file
> His unsmooth tongue, and his deprostrate style?
> Oh, raise thou from his corse thy now entombed exile!"

In the preceding evening I had seen the summits of new and yet higher mountains, the Catskills, by which I might hope to climb to heaven again, and had set my compass for a fair lake in the southwest, which lay in my way, for which I now steered, descending the mountain by my own route, on the side opposite to that by which I had ascended, and soon found myself in the region of cloud and drizzling rain, and the inhabitants affirmed that it had been a cloudy and drizzling day wholly.

From *A Week on the Concord and Merrimack Rivers* by Henry David Thoreau. James Munroe, Boston and Cambridge, 1849.

SUSAN B. WARNER

Susan Bogert Warner (1819-1885), who spent much of her girlhood in the ancestral home in Canaan, New York, wrote sentimental and moralistic novels that were extremely popular. She was the first American author whose books sold in the millions of copies. Queechy (1852), much of which is recognizably set in Canaan and Lebanon Springs, inspired the town of Canaan to rename Whiting's Pond Queechy Lake.

Queechy Scenes

AN AUTUMN RIDE

It was a pleasant day in autumn. Fleda thought it particularly pleasant for riding, for the sun was veiled with thin hazy clouds. The air was mild and still, and the woods, like brave men, putting the best face upon falling fortunes. Some trees were already dropping their leaves; the greater part standing in all the varied splendour which the late frosts had given them. The road, an excellent one, sloped gently up and down across wide arable country, in a state of high cultivation and now shewing all the rich variety of autumn. The reddish buckwheat patches, and fine wood tints of the fields where other grain had been; the bright green of young rye or winter wheat, then soberer coloured pasture or meadow lands, and ever and anon a tuft of gay woods crowning a rising ground, or a knot of the everlasting pines looking sedately and steadfastly upon the fleeting glories of the world around them, these were mingled and interchanged and succeeded each other in ever-varying fresh combinations. With its high picturesque beauty the whole scene had a look of thrift and plenty and promise which made it eminently cheerful. So Mr. Ringgan and his little granddaughter both felt it to be. For some distance the grounds on either hand the road were part of the old gentleman's farm; and many a remark was exchanged between him and Fleda as to the excellence or hopefulness of this or that crop or piece of soil; Fleda entering into all his enthusiasm, and reasoning of clover leys and cockle and the proper harvesting of Indian corn and other like matters, with no lack of interest or intelligence.

"O grandpa," she exclaimed suddenly, "won't you stop a minute and let me get out. I want to get some of that beautiful bittersweet."

"What do you want that for?" said he. "You can't get out very well."

"O yes I can — please, grandpa! I want some of it very much — just one minute!"

He stopped, and Fleda got out and went to the roadside, where a bittersweet vine had climbed into a young pine tree and hung it as it were with red coral. But her one minute was at least four before she had succeeded in breaking off as much as she could carry of the splendid creeper; for not until then could Fleda persuade herself to leave it. She came back and worked her way up into the wagon with one hand full as it could hold of her brilliant trophies.

"Now what good'll that do you?" inquired Mr. Ringgan good-humouredly, as he lent Fleda what help he could to her seat.

"Why grandpa, I want it to put with cedar and pine in a jar at home — it will keep for ever so long, and look beautiful. Isn't that handsome? — only it was a pity to break it."

Fleda settled herself again to enjoy the trees, the fields, the roads, and all the small handiwork of nature, for which her eyes had a curious intelligence. But this was not fated to be a ride of unbroken pleasure.

"Why what are those bars down for?" she said as they came up with a field of winter grain. "Somebody's been in here with a wagon. O grandpa! Mr. Didenhover has let the Shakers have my butternuts! — the butternuts that you told him they mustn't have."

The old gentleman drew up his horse. "So he has!" said he.

Their eyes were upon the far end of the deep lot, where at the edge of one of the pieces of woodland spoken of, a picturesque group of men and boys in frocks and broad-brimmed white hats were busied in filling their wagon under a clump of the now thin and yellow leaved butternut trees.

"The scoundrel!" said Mr. Ringgan under his breath.

"Would it be any use, grandpa, for me to jump down and run and tell them you don't want them to take the butternuts? — I shall have so few."

"No, dear, no," said here grandfather, "they have got 'em about all by this time; the mischief's done. Didenhover meant to let 'em have 'em unknown to me, and pocket the pay himself. Get up!"

Fleda drew a long breath, and gave a hard look at the distant wagon where *her* butternuts were going in by handfuls. She said no more.

QUEECHY MILL

A few hundred yards from Mr. Ringgan's gate the road began to wind up a very long heavy hill. Just at the hill's foot it crossed by a rude bridge the bed of a noisy brook that came roaring down from the higher grounds, turning sundry mill and factory wheels in its way. About half way up the hill one of these was placed, belonging to a mill for sawing boards. The little building stood alone, no other in sight, with a dark background of wood rising behind it on the other side of the brook; the stream itself running smoothly for a small space above the mill, and leaping down madly below, as if it disdained its bed and would clear at a bound every impediment in its way to the sea. When the mill was not going the quantity of water that found its way down the hill was indeed very small, enough only to keep up a pleasant chattering with the stones; but as soon as the stream was allowed to gather all its force and run free its loquacity was such that it would prevent a traveller from suspecting his approach to the mill, until, very near, the monotonous hum of its saw could be heard. This was a place Fleda dearly loved. The wild sound of the waters and the lonely keeping of the scene, with the delicious smell of the new-sawn boards, and the fascination of seeing the great logs of wood walk up to the relentless, tireless up-and-down-going steel; as the generations of men in turn present themselves to the course of those sharp events which are the teeth of Time's saw; until all of a sudden the master spirit, the man-regulator of this machinery, would perform some conjuration on lever and wheel, — and at once, as at the touch of an enchanter, the log would be still and the saw stay its work; — the business of life came to a stand, and the romance of the little brook sprang up again.

DEEPWATER

After reaching the brow of the hill the road continued on a very gentle ascent towards a little settlement half a quarter of a mile off; passing now and then a few scattered cottages or an occasional mill or turner's shop. Several mills and factories, with a store and a very few dwelling-houses were all the settlement; not enough to entitle it to the name of a village. Beyond these and the mill-ponds, of which in the course of the road there were three or four, and with a brief intervening space of cultivated fields, a single farm-house stood alone; just upon the borders of a large and very fair sheet of water from which all the others had their supply. — So large and fair that nobody cavilled at its taking the style of a lake and giving its own pretty name of Deepwater both to the settlement and the farm that half embraced it.

PROVISIONING THE PARSONAGE

The parsonage-house was about a quarter of a mile, a little more, from the saw-mill, in a line at right angles with the main road. The road ran north, keeping near the level of the mid-hill where it branched off a little below the saw-mill; and as the ground continued rising towards the east and was well clothed with woods, the way at this hour was still pleasantly shady. To the left the same slope of ground carried down to the foot of the hill gave them an uninterrupted view over a wide plain or bottom, edged in the distance with a circle of gently swelling hills. Close against the hills, in the far corner of the plain, lay the little village of Queechy Run, hid from sight by a slight intervening rise of ground; not a chimney shewed itself in the whole spread of country. A sunny landscape just now; but rich in picturesque associations of hay-cocks and winrows, spotting it near and far; and close by below them was a field of mowers at work; they could distinctly hear the measured rush of the scythes through the grass, and then the soft clink of the rifles would seem to play some old delicious tune of childish days. It was a warm day, but "the sweet south that breathes upon a bank of violets," could hardly be more sweet than the air which coming to them over the whole breadth of the valley had been charged by the new-made hay.

Two or three wagons were standing outside the parsonage, but nobody to be seen. Fleda went up the steps and crossed the broad piazza, brown and unpainted, but picturesque still, and guided by the sound of tongues turned to the right where she found a large low room the very centre of the stir. But the stir had not by any means reached the height yet. Not more than a dozen people were gathered. Here were aunt Syra and Mrs. Douglass, appointed a committee to receive and dispose the offerings as they were brought in.

"Why there is not much to be seen yet, said Fleda. "I did not know I was so early."

"Time enough," said Mrs. Douglass. "They'll come the thicker when they do come. Good-morning, Dr. Quackenboss! — I hope you're a going to give us something else besides a bow? and I won't take none of your physic, neither."

"I humbly submit," said the doctor graciously, "that nothing ought to be expected of gentlemen that — a — are so unhappy as to be alone; for they really — a — have nothing to give, — but themselves."

There was a shout of merriment.

"And suppos'n that's a gift that nobody wants?" said Mrs. Douglass's sharp eye and voice at once.

There was certainly a promising beginning made for the future minister's comfort. One shelf was already completely stocked with pies, and another shewed a quantity of cake, and biscuits enough to last a good-sized family for several meals.

"That is always the way," said Mrs. Douglass; — "it's the strangest thing that folks has no sense! Now one-half o' them pies'll be dried up afore they can eat the rest; — tain't much loss, for Mis' Prin sent 'em down, and if they are worth anything it's the first time anything ever come out of her house that was. Now look at them biscuit!" —

"How many are coming to eat them?" said Fleda.

"How?"

"How large a family has the minister?"

"He ha'n't a bit of a family! He ain't married.'

"Not!"

At the grave way in which Mrs. Douglass faced around upon her and answered, and at the idea of a single mouth devoted to all that closetful, Fleda's gravity gave place to most uncontrollable merriment.

"No," said Mrs. Douglass, with a curious twist of her mouth but commanding herself, — "he ain't to be sure — not yet. He ha'n't any family but himself and some sort of a housekeeper, I suppose; they'll divide the house between 'em."

"And the biscuits, I hope," said Fleda. "But what will he do with all the other things, Mrs. Douglass?"

"Sell 'em if he don't want 'em," said Mrs. Douglass quizzically. "Shut up, Fleda, I forget who sent them biscuit — somebody that calculated to make a shew for a little, I reckon. — My sakes! I believe it was Mis' Springer herself! — she didn't hear me though," said Mrs. Douglass peeping out of the half-open door. "It's a good thing the world ain't all alike; — there's Mis' Plumfield — stop now, and I'll tell you all she sent; — that big jar of lard, there's as good as eighteen or twenty pound, — and that basket of eggs, I don't know how many there is, — and that cheese, a real fine one I'll be bound, she wouldn't pick out the worst in her dairy, — and Seth fetched down a hundred weight of corn meal and another of rye flour; now that's what I call doing things something like; if everybody else would keep up their end as well as they keep up their'n the world wouldn't be quite so one-sided as it is. I never see the time yet when I couldn't tell where to find Mis' Plumfield."

People were constantly arriving now, in wagons and on foot; and stores of all kinds were most literally pouring in. Bags and even barrels of meal, flour, pork, and potatoes; strings of dried apples, salt, hams and beef; hops, pickles, vinegar, maple sugar and molasses; rolls of fresh butter, cheese, and eggs; cake, bread, and pies, without end. Mr. Penny, the storekeeper, sent a box of tea. Mr. Winegar, the carpenter, a new ox-sled. Earl Douglass brought a handsome axe-helve of his own fashioning; his wife a quantity of rolls of wool. Zan Finn carted a load of wood into the wood-shed, and Squire Thornton another. Home-made candles, custards, preserves, and smoked liver, came in a batch from two or three miles off up on the mountain. Half a dozen chairs from the factory man. Half a dozen brooms from the other store-keeper at the Deepwater settlement. A carpet for the best room from the ladies of the township, who had clubbed forces to furnish it; and a home-made concern it was, from the shears to the loom.

The room was full now, for every one after depositing his gift turned aside to see what others had brought and were bringing; and men and women, the young and old, had their several circles of gossip in various parts of the crowd. Apart from them all Fleda sat in her window, probably voted "elegant" by others than the doctor, for they vouchsafed her no more than a transitory attention and sheered off to find something more congenial. She sat watching the people; smiling very often as some odd figure, or look or some peculiar turn of expression or tone of voice, caught her ear or her eye.

Both ear and eye were fastened by a young countryman with a particularly fresh face whom she saw approaching the house. He came up on foot, carrying a single fowl slung at his back by a stick thrown across his shoulder, and without stirring hat or stick he came into the room and made his way through the crowd of people, looking to the one hand and the other evidently in a maze of doubt to whom he should deliver himself and his chicken, till brought up by Mrs. Douglass's sharp voice.

"Well, Philetus! what are you looking for?"

"Do, Mis' Douglass!" — it is impossible to express the abortive attempt at a bow which accompanied this salutation, — "I want to know if the minister'll be in town to day?"

"What do you want of him?"

"I don't want nothin' of him. I want to know if he'll be in town to-day?"

"Yes — I expect he'll be along directly — why, what then?"

"Cause I've got teu chickens for him here, and mother said they hadn't ought to be kept no longer, and if he wa'n't to hum I were to fetch 'em back, straight."

"Well he'll be here, so let's have 'em," said Mrs. Douglass biting her lips.

"What's become o' t'other one?" said Earl, as the young man's stick was brought round to the table; — "I guess you've lost it, ha'n't you?"

"My gracious!" was all Philetus's powers were equal to. "Du tell! — I *am* beat! —"

"Where's t'other one?" said Mrs. Douglass between paroxysms.

"Why I ha'n't done nothin' to it," said Philetus dismally, — "there was teu on 'em afore I started, and I took and tied 'em together and hitched 'em onto the stick, and that one must ha' loosened itself off some way. — I believe the darned thing did it o' purpose."

"I guess your mother knowed that one wouldn't keep till it got here," said Mrs. Douglass.

From *Queechy* by Susan B. Warner. J.P. Lippincott, 1895.

MARK HOPKINS

Time has altered President James Garfield's definition of the ideal college as "a student on one end of a bench and Mark Hopkins at the other" into "a log in the woods" instead of "a bench" (see the selection by Washington Gladden). Whatever the image, Mark Hopkins (1802-1887) remains the exemplar of a teacher of character and understanding.

Born in Stockbridge, Hopkins became a doctor after graduating from Berkshire Medical College in Pittsfield but practiced only a year before being called back to Williams as professor in moral philosophy and rhetoric.

Related to John Sergeant, missionary to the Stockbridge Indians, and to Ephraim Williams, founder of the college, Hopkins served as president of Williams from 1836 to 1872. Although he never went to a theological school, he was ordained by the Berkshire Association of Congregational Ministers in 1836.

Here are the beginning and end of his lengthy sermon at the Pittsfield Jubilee in 1844. Temperance was a cause dear to his heart, and the Jubilee was a dry affair.

Sermon

And this is the Berkshire Jubilee! We have come — the sons and daughters of Berkshire — from our villages, and hill sides, and mountain tops; from the distant city, from the far west, from every place where the spirit of enterprise and of adventure bears men — we have come. The farmer has left his field, the mechanic his work-shop, the merchant his counting-room, the lawyer his brief, and the minister his people, and we have come to revive old and cherished associations, and to renew former friendships — to lengthen the cords and strengthen the stakes of every kind and time-hallowed affection.

And coming thus from these wide dispersions, under circumstances which must carry our minds back to the first dawnings of life, and cause us to review all the path of our pilgrimage; coming too as natives and citizens of a State on the eastern border of which is Plymouth rock, what so suitable as that our first public act should be to assemble ourselves for the worship of the God of our fathers, and our God, and to do honor to those institutions of religion through the influence of which, chiefly, we are what we are, and without which the moral elements in which this occasion has originated could not have existed. Coming thus to celebrate a local thanksgiving — local in one sense, but extended in another, since this day our family affection is thrown around a whole county, — how fit is it, while we look back on all the way in which God has led us, while our kind feelings towards our fellow men are awakened and strengthened, that we should suffer all the goodness of God to lead us to him — that we should adopt, as I am sure every one of us has reason to do, the language of the Psalmist, and say, "Return unto thy rest, O my soul; for the Lord hath dealt bountifully with thee."

This passage of Scripture, which I have selected as my text on this occasion, will be found in the 116th Psalm and the 7th verse:

"RETURN UNTO THY REST, O MY SOUL; FOR THE LORD HATH DEALT BOUNTIFULLY WITH THEE."

Pittsfield from Jubilee Hill, around the time of the Jubilee. Courtesy of The Berkshire Eagle

It was in the hope that this occasion might do something towards bringing forward a consummation [the cause of temperance] so desirable, that I was willing to take part in it; that, in connexion with this sacred service, I was willing to be the organ of my fellow-citizens to welcome home those who had gone out from us. And this I now do. Natives, and former citizens of Berkshire, I welcome you — not to bacchanalian revels, not to costly entertainments, not to the celebration of any party or national triumph, but to the old homestead, to these scenes of your early days, to these mountains and vallies, and streams, and skies, to the hallowed resting places of the dear departed; I welcome you to the warm grasp of kindred and friends, to rational festivity — to the Berkshire Jubilee.

So far as I know, this gathering is unprecedented. More than any thing else in modern times, it reminds us of those gatherings of ancient Israel, when the tribes went up to Mount Zion; and if we look to the future, it cannot fail to remind us of that greater gathering, of that better home, of those higher joys which there shall be when "they shall come from the East, and the West, and the North, and the South, and shall sit down with Abraham and Isaac and Jacob in the kingdom of God." With that great assembly may we all be gathered. Amen!

From *The Berkshire Jubilee* celebrated at Pittsfield, August 1844.

FRANCES ANNE KEMBLE

Fanny Kemble (1809-1893), the celebrated English actress, was attracted to the Berkshires by her friendship with the Sedgwicks, first with Catharine Maria, and then with Elizabeth, Catharine's sister-in-law. For forty years she charmed and terrified the Berkshires with her beauty, intelligence, generosity, and unconventional, energetic, and sometimes imperious appetite for life. She was a tireless writer of letters, which from time to time were published.

Letters

THE SHAKERS

1835

In one part of this romantic hill-region exists the strangest worship that ever the craving need of religious excitement suggested to the imagination of human beings.

I do not know whether you have ever heard of a religious sect called the Shakers; I never did till I came into their neighborhood: and all that was told me before seeing them fell short of the extraordinary effect of the reality. Seven hundred men and women, whose profession of religion has for one of its principal objects the extinguishing of the human race and the end of the world, by devoting themselves and persuading others to celibacy and the strictest chastity. They live all together in one community, and own a village and a considerable tract of land in the beautiful hill country of Berkshire. They are perfectly moral and exemplary in their lives and conduct, wonderfully industrious, miraculously clean and neat, and incredibly shrewd, thrifty and money-making.

Their dress is hideous, and their worship, to which they admit spectators, consists of a fearful species of dancing, in which the whole number of them engage, going round and round their vast hall or temple of prayer, shaking their hands like the paws of a dog sitting up to beg, and singing a deplorable psalm-tune in brisk jig time. The men without their coats, in their shirt-sleeves, with their lank hair hanging on their shoulders, and a sort of loose knee-breeches — knickerbockers — have a grotesque air of stage Swiss peasantry. The women without a single hair escaping beneath their hideous caps, mounted upon very high-heeled shoes, and every one of them with a white handkerchief folded napkin-fashion and hanging over her arm. In summer they all dress in white, and what with their pale, immovable countenances, their ghost-like figures, and ghastly, mad spiritual dance, they looked like the nuns in "Robert the Devil," condemned, for their sins in the flesh, to post-mortem decency and asceticism, to look ugly, and to dance like ill-taught bears.

The whole exhibition was at once so frightful and so ludicrous, that I very nearly went off into hysterics, when I first saw them.

Postcard of "The Perch," Fanny Kemble's Lenox home. Courtesy of The Berkshire Eagle

"THIS SECLUDED PARADISE"

A "Happy Valley" indeed! — the Valley of the Housatonic, locked in by walls of every shape and size, from grassy knolls to bold basaltic cliffs. A beautiful little river wanders singing from side to side in this secluded Paradise, and from every mountain cleft come running crystal springs to join it; it looks only fit for people to be baptized in (though I believe the water is used for cooking and washing purposes).

LOVE OF PLACES

1838

My love for certain places is inexplicable to myself. They have, for some reasons which I have not detected, so powerfully affected my imagination, that it will thenceforth never let them go. I retain the strongest impression of some places where I have stayed the shortest time; thus there is a certain spot in the hill country of Massachusetts, called Lebanon, where I once spent two days.

I was going to tell you how like Paradise that place was to my memory, and with what curious yearning I have longed to visit it again. I

believe we shall go to the hill country of Berkshire, to visit our friends the
Sedgwicks. I wonder whether your love for heat would have made agreeable to you a six-mile ride I took to-day, at about eleven o'clock, the
thermometer standing at 94 degrees in the shade.

ON LENOX HILL

Monday, September 3d, 1838

I am sitting "on top," as the Americans say, of the hill of Lenox,
looking out at that prospect upon which your eyes have often rested, and
making common cause in the eating and living way with Mary and
Fanny Appleton, who have taken up their abode here for a week. Never
was village hostelry so graced before surely! There is a pretty daughter of
Mr. Dewey's staying in the house besides, with a pretty cousin; and it
strikes me that the old Red Inn is having a sort of blossoming season, with
all these sweet, handsome young faces shining about it in every direction.

You know the sort of life that is lived here: the absence of all form,
ceremony, or inconvenient conventionality whatever. We laugh, and we
talk, sing, play, dance, and discuss; we ride, drive, walk, run, scramble,
and saunter, and amuse ourselves extremely with little materials (as the
generality of people would suppose) wherewith to do so.

The Sedgwicks are under a cloud of sorrow just now. They are none
of them, however, people who suffer themselves to be absorbed by their
own personal interest, whether sad or gay; and as in their most prosperous and happy hours they would have sympathy to spare to the sufferings of others, so the sickness and sorrow of these members of their
family circle, and the consequent depression they all labor under (for
where was a family more united?), does not prevent our enjoying every
day delightful seasons of intercourse with them.

AFTER A RIDE

Lenox, August 9th, 1839

I am ashamed to say that I am exceedingly sleepy. I have been riding
sixteen miles over these charming hills. The day is bright and breezy, and
full of shifting lights and shadows, playing over a landscape that com-
bines every variety of beauty, — valleys, in the hollows of which lie small
lakes glittering like sapphires; uplands, clothed with grain-fields and
orchards, and studded with farm-houses, each the centre of its own free
domain; hills clothed from base to brow with every variety of forest tree;
and woods, some wild, tangled, and all but impenetrable, others clear of
underbrush, shady, moss-carpeted and sun-checkered; noble masses of

granite rock, great slabs of marble (of which there are fine quarries in the neighborhood), clear mountain brooks and a full, free-flowing, sparkling river; — all this, under a cloud-varied sky, such as generally canopies mountain districts, the sunset glories of which are often magnificent. I have good friends, and my precious children, an easy, cheerful, cultivated society, my capital horse, and, in short, most good things that I call mine — on this side of the water — with one heavy exception....

My drowsiness grows upon me, so that my eyelids are gradually drawing together as I look out at the sweet prospect, and the blue shimmer of the little lake and sunny waving of the trees are fading all away into a dream before me.

READING FOR LENOX LIBRARY

A similar blessed exemption from the curse of pauperism existed in the New England village of Lenox, where I owned a small property, and passed part of many years. Being asked by my friends there to give a public reading, it became a question to what purpose the proceeds of the entertainment could best be applied. I suggest "the poor of the village," but, "We have no poor," was the reply, and the sum produced by the reading was added to a fund which established an excellent public library; for though Lenox had no paupers, it had numerous intelligent readers among its population.

MISS KEMBLE'S BEER

Some years after, when I found the men employed in mowing a meadow of mine at Lenox with no refreshment but "water from the well," I sent in much distress a considerable distance for a barrel of beer, which seemed to me an indispensable adjunct to such labor under the fervid heat of that summer sky; and was most seriously expostulated with by my admirable friend, Mr. Charles Sedgwick, as introducing among the laborers of Lenox a mischievous need and deleterious habit, till then utterly unknown there, and setting a pernicious example to both employers and employed throughout the whole neighborhood. In short, my poor barrel of beer was an offense to the manners and morals of the community I lived in; and my meadow was mowed upon cold "water from the well"; of which indeed the water was so delicious, that I often longed for it as King David did for that which, after all, he would not drink, because his mighty men had risked their lives in procuring it for him.

———————

From *Records of Later Life* by Frances Anne Kemble. Henry Holt & Co., 1882.

Jubilee Ode

Darkness upon the mountain and vale,
The woods, the lakes, the fields, are buried deep,
In the still silent solemn star-watched sleep,
    No sound, no motion, and o'er hill and dale
A calm and lovely death seems to embrace
Earth's fairest realms, and Heaven's unfathomed space.

But hark! the woody depths of green
            Begin to stir,
Light breaths of life creep fresh between
            Oak, beech, and fir:
Faint rustling sounds of trembling leaves
            Whisper around,
The world at waking, slowly heaves,
            A sigh profound;
And showers of tears, night-gathered in her eyes,
Fall from fair nature's face, as she doth rise.

The Housatonic River by A. F. Bellows (1872–1874). Courtesy of The Berkshire Eagle

Hail to this day! that brings ye home
    Ye distant wanderers from the mountain land,
Hail to this hour! that bids ye come
    Again upon your native hills to stand.

Hail, hail! from rocky peak,
 And wood embowered dale,
A thousand loving voices speak,
 Hail! home-turn'd pilgrims hail!
Oh, welcome! from the meadow and the hill
  Glad greetings rise,
From flowing river, and from bounding rill,
Bright level lake, and dark green wood depths still,
And the sharp thunder-splinter'd crag, that strikes
  Its rocky spikes
  Into the skies.

Grey-Lock, cloud girdled, from his purple throne,
  A voice of welcome sends,
And from green sunny fields, a warbling tone
  The Housatonic blends.

Welcome ye absent long, and distant far!
 Who from the roof-tree of your childhood turn'd,
Have waged mid strangers, life's relentless war,
 While at your hearts, the ancient home-love burn'd.

Ye, that have plough'd the barren briny foam,
 Reaping hard fortunes from the stormy sea,
The golden grain fields rippling round your home,
 Roll their rich billows from all tempests free.

On each bald granite brow, and forest crest,
 Each stony hill path, and each lake's smooth shore,
Blessings of noble exil'd patriots rest,
 Liberty's altars are they evermore.

And on this air, there lingers yet the tone,
 Of those last sacred words to freedom given,
The mightiest utterance of that sainted one,
 Whose spirit from these mountains soar'd to Heaven.

Ye that have prosper'd bearing hence with ye,
 The virtues that command prosperity;
To the green threshold of your youth, ah! come!
 And hang your trophies round your early home.

Hail, hail!
Bright hill and dale,
    With joy resound!
Join in the joyful strain!
Ye have not wept in vain,
The parted meet again,
    The lost shall yet be found!

And may God guard thee, oh, thou lovely land!
  Danger, nor evil, nigh thy borders come.
Green towers of freedom may thy hills still stand.
  Still, be each valley, peace and virture's home:
The stranger's grateful blessing rest on thee,
And firm as Heaven, be thy prosperity!

———————

From *The Berkshire Jubilee* by Frances Anne Kemble (Mrs. F.K. Butler). 1844.

More Letters

AMERICAN WOMEN

July 28, 1875

The men and women of the United States are upon the whole the least animal race of human beings that I have ever seen. The men have no backs to their heads, and the women no backs to their bodies, and their animal nature appears to me weaker than that of either English, French, Italian, or German people.* The Americans love their children, I should say, much more morally and intellectually than physically, which is the reverse of all coarse and powerfully animal natures. The American women do not care to have children, and have, I think, generally (compared with woman of other nations) little baby and little nursery love; for all which their general infirm health and terrible climate

* The brain development in this country is earlier, and its action more rapid than elsewhere, and the *mental* processes of the Americans quicker and more vivid than those of any other people. Their intellect is subtler than that of the English, and there is a tendency to insanity with them which does not exist with us. They want our heavy, sound, material ballast to qualify their higher and finer brain. The Americans, as a rule, are wanting in animal spirits, properly so called, because they are generally the result of vigorous animal health, and abound in the young, in whom the animal vital element preponderates. The Americans know nothing of the nursery life of English children, that existence so carefully devoted to physical habits of the wholesomest simplicity and regularity, so carefully deprived of all intellectual influence or nervous excitement. There is no American childhood, and the athletic sports of Englishmen are comparatively little cultivated by American. Business life begins much earlier in the United States, and the carelessness of youth is shorter lived there than in any other country.

and miserable lack of domestic assistance for the proper care of their children (rendering the periods of their infancy one of absolute slavery to the mothers) would be reasons enough.

I believe the climate has been assigned as the reason of the comparatively unsensual character of the Red Indian savages; and I have always thought that part of the dislike of the Americans for the negroes as a race, was due to the fact that the negro is among the most animal of human beings. But I think many causes tend to make American women hard, or, at any rate, less tender, caressing, soft, and affectionate in their outward demonstrations than other women.

Of course the immense influx of foreign people, Irish and German, keeps modifying the American character in all respects the whole time; but then, again, the American climate and institutions modify the constitution of the emigrants and their children, in the course of a couple of generations, very perceptibly.

THE LONGFELLOWS

Longfellow was my friend for a great many years, and one of the most amiable men I have ever known. His home being near Boston, I saw him oftenest, and always when I was there, but for two summers he took a charming old-fashioned country house on the outskirts of the beautiful village of Pittsfield, six miles from my own summer residence in Lenox, and during those seasons I saw him and his wife very frequently, and was often in that house, on the staircase landing of which stood the famous clock whose hourly song, "Never — for ever; ever — never," has long been familiar to all English speaking people.

Fanny Longfellow, the charming Mary of the poet's "Hyperion," had a certain resemblance to myself, which on one occasion caused some amusement in our house, my father coming suddenly into the room and addressing her as "Fanny," which rather surprised her, as, though it was her name, they were not sufficiently intimate to warrant his so calling her. She was seated, however, otherwise he could not have committed the mistake, as besides being very much handsomer than I, she had the noble stature and bearing of "a daughter of the gods, divinely tall."

MR. CURTIS

Lenox, July 26, 1879

I am staying now in the same old inn which has always had the monopoly of lightening the traveling public ever since I first came here. Many years ago it was bought by the son of the village baker, who, when a lad of about eighteen, used to come out with me on my fishing excursions on the lake to manage my boat, let down and haul up anchor, and otherwise make himself useful as my attendant. I remember a droll and characteristic conversation which once took place between us while we were sitting on the bank eating our luncheon one day. After gazing round him for some time at the charming landscape far and near, my companion said to me, "Now, Mrs. Kemble, I want to know" (the invariable Yankee form of interrogation) "what would be the difference between all that we see here now if we were in England instead of America?" I thought awhile what feature of difference would be at once the most comprehensive and the most striking to him that I could name, and, looking round at the fair hillsides, the meadows, orchards, woods, and farmsteads, all cultivated and inhabited by their owners, I said, "Well, William, in England, all that we see here now would probably be the property of one man." "Oh, my! that's bad!" was his sole reply, as with a solemn shake of the head he bit a huge mouthful out of his bread and cheese. "Well, now I want to know," are the words oftenest in the mouths of these people. This fellow was as ignorant as it is possible for a Massachusetts man to be; but think of the intelligence evinced by both his question and answer.

He was absolutely ignorant and desperately idle, but good-tempered and good-looking, with a sort of coarse likeness to my brother Henry, which was a recommendation to me. As he grew up, he took to working about a livery stable which his brother established in the village, and having the liking for horses that most idle fellows seem to have, he became one of the finest drivers I ever saw; so that on all her mountain expeditions with her school-girls, my friend E. S_____ invariably had him to drive the huge four-horse omnibus, which, what with its freight of screaming, gabbling girl-geese, and the terrible dangerous roads he often had to go over, was a very considerable proof of skill, as well as of steadiness and courage.

He was recalling to my memory the other day a day's drive he had taken this lively freight, when I was one of the party, when he brought the whole caravan safely down a steep and execrably bad mountain-road that skirted a precipice the greater part of the way, and towards the end of which day the daylight was beginning to fail him, and said that when he arrived safe at the bottom of it, at the village where we stopped for the night, his hands shook so that he could hardly use them — not with effort of driving his team, but with the nervous tension of the anxiety he had felt during the whole descent.

Well, this Jehu contrived to captivate the good will of a very pretty Lenox young woman, refined and delicate, and of so much more education and better breeding that himself, that she was a teacher in Mrs.

S____'s school; and my friend E____ considered her marrying him quite a *mésalliance*. He had had perception enough, however, of her superiority to fall in love with it; and I think her name being Evelina must have had something to do with his admiration for her. However, he presently purchased the Lenox Hotel, and has gone on thriving and prospering ever since; and one fine day was sent up by his fellow-citizens as their representative to the Legislative State Assembly at Boston, where he took his place by the side of one of the best educated, best bred, most refined, and every way distinguished men that I have ever known anywhere. Now E____ will be sure, if you do not, to echo my Yankee lad's exclamation, only probably not in his vernacular, "Oh, my! that's bad;" but it isn't so bad, for reasons which I have now neither time, space, nor inclination to give you.

Mr. Curtis has gone on thriving and prospering and becoming a well-to-do "hotel" keeper — a position supposed in this country to require administrative faculties and a certain intelligence of no common order, the familiar saying being, in speaking of a man's abilities, "Oh, well, so-and-so's smart enough; couldn't keep a hotel, though;" but my friend William walks about with his hands in his pockets, while his pretty ladylike wife lives retired in her own apartments, the house being managed by three grown-up sons and two daughters; their father only occasionally condescending to give a sample of his former skill by driving a four-horse omnibus full of gay summer visitors, who throng his house from Boston and New York, to some of the especially beautiful points of view, hills or lakes, of this picturesque region.

The beauty of the place and the temperate healthy summer atmosphere bring more and more visitors every season; and as the house is really thriving, though there are occasional complaints of want of progress in the establishment, and even sometimes threats of the opening of a rival Lenox house, I dare say there will before long be set up by the young people some horrible, *modern*, big, new, fine, city-looking building, which will keep pace with the times in all the latest "improvements" (six stories high, with *alleviators*, as the Irish servants wisely and wittily call elevators), which will give more general satisfaction, and supersede the old-fashioned, red-brick, ugly, dear old house, which I loved for its memories of many years, by something really much uglier, but which will be an object of pride and pleasure to the Curtis's family and the whole neighborhood.

The Perch, my former property and home in Lenox, is called a mile from the village. It never seemed to me more than three-quarters of that distance, if so much. I walked down there and found it looking very pretty, the trees grown, and the whole place much improved. It is the only place in all this neighborhood where there are any oak trees, and there are about half a dozen fine ones scattered round the house, and I was assured the other day that it was always supposed that my English love for the English tree had made me select that particular place; whereas it was bought for me, without my eyes having seen it, or knowing whether oaks or willows grew on it, but merely because it was a ready-furnished house for sale, which I wanted at once. I find myself, however, in consequence of that purchase, invested with a dignity which none of my more distinguished kinsfolk achieved. Not only is the little "Perch" designated as the Kemble place, but the road that leads from the village to it is set down in the maps of Lenox and its neighborhood as Kemble Street or Road, which struck me as strange and comical and melancholy enough.

FAREWELL TO LENOX

My plans were all overturned, and I was compelled to give up my rooms at Lenox at a few days' notice, by a mistake in the arrangement when they were taken. The hotel-keeper understood me to have retained them only for two months, and immediately gave the prospective reversion of them to other people, for whom I was obliged to vacate them. This has occasioned me a good deal of inconvenience and annoyance, especially in the inevitable uncertainty and confusion of all my plans. Moreover, I am afraid you will be without any letter from me a longer time than usual, because packing up and departing suddenly in this way, and traveling from place to place are, of course, impediments to correspondence.

I left Lenox last Thursday in terrible heat. I looked my last with very tender affection at the lovely country we drive through for six miles, from the village to the station, where I take the railroad. Of course it is *possible* that I may live to return to see it again, but very highly improbable, and so I looked my farewell at it. I have enjoyed its improved beauty and increased cultivation and agricultural prosperity extremely this summer. It will become more and more attractive and charming with time, for the natural features of the landscape cannot be spoiled, and will admit of infinite improvement from tasteful cutting and planting of trees, and general cultivation.

From *Further Records 1848-1883: A Series of Letters by Frances Anne Kemble*. Henry Holt & Co., 1891.

THOMAS ROBBINS

Thomas Robbins, D.D., (1777-1856) was an energetic antiquarian who assembled an invaluable collection of materials relating to the early history of New England, the nucleus of the holdings of the Connecticut Historical Society. He grew up in Norfolk, Connecticut, where his father was minister and prepared boys for college. For his senior year, Robbins transferred from Yale to the new Williams College, of which his father was a trustee. Later he taught school in Sheffield and studied theology under the famous Reverend Stephen West in Stockbridge, where his aunt lived.

Early on, Robbins served as missionary to Connecticut emigrants in Vermont and Ohio. His diaries, 1796 to 1854, cover his incessant travels through the Berkshires. His brothers lived in Lenox, and his election to the board of trustees of Williams brought him to Williamstown at least annually. His Diaries, *edited by Increase Tarbox and published by his nephew Joseph Battell in 1888, are a mine of fascinating daily information.*

Williams College from the west, c. 1841. The Berkshire Athenaeum, Local History Department

Diary Excerpts

THE '96 CAMPAIGN

13 October 1796 [at Williamstown]

Electioneering runs higher than ever in the county of Berkshire. If such a spirit becomes prevalent in our republic, adieu freedom of elections.

STUDYING HOMILETICS

25 June 1798 [at Stockbridge]

In the morning Dr. West told me that I must write a sermon.

26 June 1798

Began to write a sermon on John iii.5. Read newspaper etc. Had green peas.

27 June 1798

Wrote most of the day. O, for assistance!

BUYS A HORSE

1 September 1801

Left Becket. Rode to Tyringham. Bought a horse of Mr. Avery [pastor at Tyringham]. Paid thirty dollars and gave a note for thirty-five, payable next January. The horse is six years old. May I find him useful and serviceable.

2 September 1801

My brother was offered seventy dollar for my horse.

WINTER TRAVEL

7 December 1807

Set out on a journey to Berkshire. Rode on the Farmington River turnpike. A good road. Very windy and cold. Tarried at a tavern in Sandisfield.

14 February 1815

The morning extreme cold. Rode to Lenox. Made very welcome at my brother's. He is very well situated here. There is a great awakening here. People were greatly animated with the news of peace all the way that I came. I rode fifty miles in a little less than ten hours. The Lenox turnpike is a very good winter road.

A BAD SEASON

4 September 1816

At sundown left Williamstown with my brother, and by the light of the full moon rode to Lenox. Got to his house at one o'clock. The drought is very extreme and severe.

5 September 1816

Left Lenox a little before ten o'clock and rode home; a little more than sixty miles. Further than I have ever travelled in a day before. Got home about half after twelve at night. Warm and very dusty. I presume no person living has known so poor a crop of corn in New England, at this season, as now.

PROSPERING PITTSFIELD

1 July 1836, Worthington

Left my kind host, Col. Wood, and rode over huge hills to Pittsfield. This town is large and flourishing.

20 August 1840

Rode [from Williamstown] with brother Francis and wife to Lenox, except that he went from Pittsfield to New Lebanon. The heat very oppressive. Saw the great Western Railroad at Pittsfield, now making.

21 August 1840

Called on Miss Sedgwick. The mercury said to beat 98 degrees.

22 August 1840

Rode with my two sisters-in-law over a mountain to Richmond, and visited nephew Clark and his wife. I hope after repeated dismissions, he will here spend his days. There was a very fine shower at Richmond, but none at Lenox.

THE BERKSHIRE JUBILEE

22 August 1844

Cool. I have left my surtout somewhere; I believe in a Connecticut River steamboat. Rode in a stage to Pittsfield. A very great gathering here at the county jubilee. The first thing of the kind in the country.

DISAPPOINTING ELECTION RESULTS

8 November 1844

New York and Pennsylvania appear to have gone for the miserable Polk, and the wicked are triumphing. God's ways with our country are unsearchable.

A MOURNFUL JOURNEY

26 March 1847

In the evening had a letter from my nephew at Lenox, Ammi Robbins, announcing the death of my dear brother James, at two o'clock last night. Holy, holy is the Lord. Just one half of our family now sleep. I shall, most likely, next follow.

The Reverend Dr. Stephen West (1735–1819), Minister of Stockbridge.
Stockbridge Historical Society

29 March 1847

Took the cars for my mournful journey. It snowed a little, which much increased as we ascended the high lands after leaving Springfield. At Washington we had a long hindrance. Went on to Pittsfield, thence to Lenox in a public sleigh.

30 March 1847

A mournful day. The snow is nearly a foot deep. People move in sleighs. In the afternoon we buried my good brother.

31 March 1847

It snowed pretty fast in the morning. Was carried to Pittsfield and took the cars. Came to Springfield, and the Hartford cars had been gone an hour. Had to wait till evening.

UP-TO-DATE TRAVEL

16 August 1847

Took the cars and rode to Springfield, Pittsfield, North Adams; a new railroad from Pittsfield. Dined and took the stage, five miles, to Williamstown. Much fatigued. Visited the new library building; a very fine one. It has a noble new portrait of Mr. Lawrence, the donor of the building.

A DISTRESSING OCCURRENCE

7 May 1853

There has been a most terrible disaster on the railroad in Norwalk. A train from New York ran into an open drawbridge. The train carried many of the leading physicians of New England, returning from a medical convention in New York.

9 May 1853

The fatal event, which we have feared, has been confirmed. Mrs. Robbins of Lenox, widow of my brother James, with her daughter, drowned at the great catastrophe. I believe such a distressing occurrence has not taken place in this country.

From *Diaries of Thomas Robbins*. Edited by Increase Tarbox, 1888.

CHARLES DICKENS

When in 1842 Charles Dickens traveled to the Berkshires expressly to visit the Shakers, they were in the midst of a spiritualistic phase known as "Mother's Work," marked by ecstatic visions and messages from the spirit world. Because the manifestations of spiritual enthusiasm are seldom regarded sympathetically by those who do not share it, meetings had been closed to "the world's people," and no exception was made for the 30-year-old Dickens, who everywhere else in America had been welcomed as an exciting celebrity. He seems to have remained impervious to the appeal which other visitors to Mount Lebanon responded to in Shaker neatness, wholesomeness, cleanliness, good work, and inner peace.

A Visit to Mount Lebanon

I had a great desire to see "the Shaker Village," which is peopled by a religious sect from whom it takes its name. To this end, we went up the North River again as far as the town of Hudson, and there hired an extra to carry us to Lebanon, thirty miles distant.

THE HUTS OF IRISH RAILROAD LABORERS

The country through which the road meandered was rich and beautiful; the weather very fine; and for many miles the Kaatskill Mountains, where Rip Van Winkle and the ghastly Dutchmen played at ninepins one memorable gusty afternoon, towered in the blue distance like stately clouds. At one point, as we ascended a steep hill, athwart whose base a railroad, yet constructing, took its course, we came upon an Irish colony. With means at hand of building decent cabins, it was wonderful to see how clumsy, rough, and wretched its hovels were. The best were poor protection from the weather; the worst let in the wind and rain through wide breaches in the roofs of sodden grass, and in the walls of mud; some had neither door nor window; some had nearly fallen down, and were imperfectly propped up by stakes and poles; all were ruinous and filthy. Hideously ugly old women and very buxom young ones, pigs, dogs, men, children, babies, pots, kettles, dunghills, vile refuse, rank straw, and standing water all wallowing together in an inseparable heap, composed the furniture of every dark and dirty hut.

AT LEBANON SPRINGS

Between nine and ten o'clock at night we arrived at Lebanon; which is renowned for its warm baths, and for a great hotel, well adapted, I have no doubt, to the gregarious taste of those seekers after health or pleasure who repair here, but inexpressibly comfortless to me. We were shown into an immense apartment, lighted by two dim candles, called the drawing-room: from which there was a descent, by a flight of steps, to another vast desert called the dining-room: our bedchambers were among certain long rows of little whitewashed cells, which opened from either side of a dreary passage; and were so like rooms in a prison that I half expected to be locked up when I went to bed, and listened involuntarily for the turning of the key on the outside. There need be baths somewhere in the neighborhood, for the other washing arrangements were on as limited a scale as I ever saw, even in America: indeed, these bedrooms were so very bare of even such common luxuries as chairs, that I should say they were not provided with enough of anything, but that I bethink myself of our having been most bountifully bitten all night.

The house is very pleasantly situated, however, and we had a good breakfast. That done, we went to visit our place of destination, which was some two miles off, and the way to which was soon indicated by a finger-post, whereon was painted, "To the Shaker Village."

As we rode along, we passed a party of Shakers, who were at work upon the road; who wore the broadest of all broad-brimmed hats; and were in all visible respects such very wooden men, that I felt about as much sympathy for them, and as much interest in them, as if they had been so many figureheads of ships. Presently we came to the beginning of the village, and, alighting at the door of a house where the Shaker manufactures are sold, and which is the headquarters of the elders, requested permission to see the Shaker worship.

AN IMPRESSION OF GRIMNESS

Pending the conveyance of this request to some person in authority, we walked into a grim room, where several grim hats were hanging on grim pegs, and the time was grimly told by a grim clock, which uttered every tick with a kind of struggle, as if it broke the grim silence reluctantly, and under protest. Ranged against the wall were six or eight stiff, high-backed chairs, and they partook so strongly of the general grimness, that one would much rather have sat on the floor than incurred the smallest obligation to any of them.

Presently, there stalked into this apartment a grim old Shaker, with eyes as hard, and dull, and cold as the great round metal buttons on his coat and waistcoat; a sort of calm goblin. Being informed of our desire, he produced a newspaper wherein the body of elders, whereof he was a member, had advertised, but a few days before, that in consequence of certain unseemly interruptions which their worship had received from

"Fernside," the old Shaker Village in Tyringham, c. 1890.
The Berkshire Athenaeum, Local History Department

strangers, their chapel was closed to the public for the space of one year.

As nothing was to be urged in opposition to this reasonable arrangement, we requested leave to make some trifling purchases of Shaker goods; which was grimly conceded. We accordingly repaired to a store in the same house, and on the opposite side of the passage, where the stock was presided over by something alive in a russet case, which the elder said was a woman; and which I suppose *was* a woman, though I should not have suspected it.

On the opposite side of the road was their place of worship: a cool, clean edifice of wood, with large windows and green blinds: like a spacious summerhouse. As there was no getting into this place, and nothing was to be done but walk up and down, and look at it and the other buildings in the village (which were chiefly of wood, painted a dark red like English barns, and composed of many stories like English factories), I have nothing to communicate to the reader beyond the scanty results I gleaned the while our purchases were making.

SHAKERISM DESCRIBED

These people are called Shakers from their peculiar form of adoration, which consists of a dance, performed by the men and women of all ages, who arrange themselves for that purpose in opposite parties: the men first divesting themselves of their hats and coats, which they gravely hang against the wall before they begin; and tying a ribbon round their shirt-sleeves, as though they were going to be bled. They accompany themselves with a droning humming noise, and dance until they are quite exhausted, alternately advancing and retiring in a preposterous sort of trot. The effect is said to be unspeakably absurd: and if I may judge from a print of this ceremony which I have in my possession; and which, I am informed by those who have visited the chapel, is perfectly accurate; it must be infinitely grotesque.

They are governed by a woman, and her rule is understood to be absolute, though she has the assistance of a council of elders. She lives, it is said, in strict seclusion, in certain rooms above the chapel, and is never shown to profane eyes. If she at all resemble the lady who presided over the store, it is a great charity to keep her as close as possible, and I cannot too strongly express my perfect concurrence in this benevolent proceeding.

All the possessions and revenues of the settlement are thrown into a common stock, which is managed by the elders. As they have made converts among people who were well to do in the world, and are frugal and thrifty, it is understood that this fund prospers: the more especially as they have made large purchases of land. Nor is this at Lebanon the only Shaker settlement: there are, I think, at least three others.

They are good farmers, and all their produce is eagerly purchased and highly esteemed. "Shaker seeds," "Shaker herbs," and "Shaker distilled waters" are commonly announced for sale in the shops of towns and cities. They are good breeders of cattle, and are kind and merciful to the brute creation. Consequently, Shaker beasts seldom fail to find a ready market.

They eat and drink together, after the Spartan model, at a great public table. There is no union of the sexes; and every Shaker, male and female, is devoted to a life of celibacy. Rumor has been busy upon this theme, but here again I must refer to the lady of the store, and say, that if many of the sister Shakers resemble her, I treat all such slander as bearing on its face the strongest marks of wild improbability. But that they take as proselytes persons so young that they cannot know their own minds, and cannot possess much strength of resolution in this or any other respect, I can assert from my own observation of the extreme juvenility of certain youthful Shakers whom I saw at work among the party on the road.

They are said to be good drivers of bargains, but to be honest and just in their transactions, and even in horse-dealing to resist those thievish tendencies which would seem, for some undiscovered reason, to be almost inseparable from that branch of traffic. In all matters they hold their own course quietly, live in their gloomy, silent commonwealth, and show little desire to interfere with other people.

DICKENS'S OPINION

This is well enough, but nevertheless I cannot, I confess, incline towards the Shakers; view them with much favor, or extend towards them any very lenient construction. I so abhor, and from my soul detest, that bad spirit, no matter by what class or sect it may be entertained, which would strip life of its healthful graces, rob youth of its innocent pleasures, pluck from maturity and age their pleasant ornaments, and make existence but a narrow path towards the grave: that odious spirit which, if it could have had full scope and sway upon the earth, must have blasted and made barren the imaginations of the greatest men, and left them, in their power of raising up enduring images before their fellow-creatures yet unborn, no better than the beasts: that, in these very broad-brimmed hats and very sombre coats — in stiff-necked, solemn-visaged piety, in short, no matter what its garb, whether it have cropped hair as in a Shaker village, or long nails as in a Hindu temple — I recognize the worst among the enemies of Heaven and earth, who turn the water at the marriage feasts of this poor world, not into wine, but gall. And if there must be people vowed to crush the harmless fancies and the love of innocent delights and gayeties, which are a part of human nature: as much a part of it as any other love or hope that is our common portion: let them, for me, stand openly revealed among the ribald and licentious; the very idiots know that *they* are not on the Immortal road, and will despise them, and avoid them readily.

Leaving the Shaker village with a hearty dislike of the old Shakers, and a hearty pity for the young ones: tempered by the strong probability of their running away as they grow older and wiser, which they not uncommonly do: we returned to Lebanon, and so to Hudson.

From *American Notes* by Charles Dickens. Estes & Lauriat, 1892.

RALPH WALDO EMERSON

Emerson enjoyed visiting the Berkshires and alluded to the region in his writing as an example of beautiful, unspoiled nature, but he was disinclined to move here himself in the mid-century back-to-the-land movement championed by Samuel Gray Ward and Caroline Sturgis Tappan, owners of the farms on the Lenox-Stockbridge line which now comprise Tanglewood. (Mrs. Tappan had better luck in persuading her friend Sophia Hawthorne to take up residence here.) Emerson did, however, send his daughter to Mrs. Sedgwick's school in Lenox, "The Hive." She loved it. Other students there were Harriet Hosmer, the sculptor, and Jennie Jerome, Winston Churchill's mother.

Journal Excerpts

POTS AND KETTLES

Caroline Sturgis inquired why I would not go to Berkshire? But the great inconvenience is sufficient answer. If I could freely and manly go to the mountains, or to the prairie, or to the sea, I would not hesitate for inconvenience: but to cart all my pots & kettles, kegs & clothespins & all that belongs thereunto, over the mountains seems not worth while. I should not be nearer to sun or star. (1844)

SECLUSION AND SOLITUDE

The young people do not like the town, they do not like the seashore, they will go inland, find a dear cottage deep in the mountains, secret as their hearts. They set forth on their travels in search of a home: they reach Berkshire, they reach Vermont, they look at the farms, good farms, high mountain sides, but where is the seclusion? The farm 'tis near this, 'tis near that. They have got far from Boston, but 'tis near Albany, or near Brattleboro, or near Montreal. They explore this farm, but the house is small, old, thin; discontented people lived there, & are gone: there's too much sky, too much outdoor, too public: This is not solitude. (1855)

From *Journals and Miscellaneous Notebooks of Ralph Waldo Emerson.* Belknap Press of Harvard University Press, 1971.

Literature and Luxury
1850 to 1914

OLIVER WENDELL HOLMES

Oliver Wendell Holmes's great-grandfather, Col. Jacob Wendell, a Boston merchant, in 1737 invested in the 24,040-acre Pontoosuc Tract, which eventually became Pittsfield. Dr. Holmes, professor of anatomy at Harvard Medical School, was distinguished as a pioneer of scientific medicine. Early famous as the poet who wrote "Old Ironsides," he was celebrated as the foremost essayist of his day. In 1849, Holmes built himself a summer villa at Canoe Meadows, the 280-acre farm which was the remnant of the Wendell family landholdings in the Berkshires. Here he spent "seven happy summers," eventually selling the place because keeping it up became too expensive. The whole family loved the place by the river; it was he who said in The Autocrat of the Breakfast Table, *"The best tonic is the Housatonic."*

Witty, gregarious, and renowned as a conversationalist, he entered Berkshire social life with gusto, but not without a professional humorist's amused appreciation of rural pretension. In this extract from his novel, Elsie Venner *(1861), "Rockland" is Pittsfield. In later life, in letters to Berkshire friends he looked back tenderly to his years at Canoe Meadows.*

Scenes from Berkshire Localities

PIGWACKET CENTER

Whether the Student advertised for a school, or whether he fell in with the advertisement of a school-committee, is not certain. At any rate, it was not long before he found himself the head of a large district, or, as it was called by the inhabitants, "deestric" school, in the flourishing inland village of Pequawkett, or, as it is commonly spelt, Pigwacket Centre. The natives of this place would be surprised, if they should hear that any of the readers of a work published in Boston were unacquainted with so remarkable a locality. As, however, some copies of it may be read at a distance from this distinguished metropolis, it may be well to give a few particulars respecting the place, taken from the Universal Gazetteer.

"PIGWACKET, sometimes spelt Pequawkett. A post-village and township in ____ Co., State of ____, situated in a fine agricultural region, 2 thriving villages, Pigwacket Centre and Smithville, 3 churches, several school houses, and many handsome private residences. Mink River runs through the town, navigable for small boats after heavy rains. Muddy Pond at N. E. section, well stocked with horn pouts, eels, and shiners. Products, beef, pork, butter, cheese. Manufactures, shoe-pegs, clothes-pins, and tin-ware. Pop. 1373."

The reader may think there is nothing very remarkable implied in this description. If, however, he had read the town-history, by the Rev. Jabez Grubb, he would have learned that it was distinguished by many *very* remarkable advantages. Thus:

"The situation of Pigwacket is eminently beautiful, looking down the lovely valley of Mink River, a tributary of the Musquash. The air is salubrious, and many of the inhabitants have attained great age, several having passed the allotted period of 'three-score years and ten' before succumbing to any of the various 'ills that flesh is heir to.' Widow Comfort Leevins died in 1836, AEt. LXXXVII. years. Venus, an African, died in 1841, supposed to be C. years old. The people are distinguished for intelligence, as has been frequently remarked by eminent lyceum-lecturers, who have invariably spoken in the highest terms of a Pigwacket audience. There is a public library, containing nearly a hundred volumes, free to all subscribers. The preached word is well attended, there is a flourishing temperance society, and the schools are excellent. It is a residence admirably adapted to refined families who relish the beauties of Nature and the charms of society. The Honorable John Smith, formerly a member of the State Senate, was a native of this town."

That is the way they all talk. After all, it is probably pretty much like other inland New England towns in point of "salubrity," — that is, gives people their choice of dysentery or fever every autumn, with a season-ticket for consumption, good all the year round. And so of the other pretences. "Pigwacket audience," forsooth! Was there ever an audience anywhere, though there wasn't a pair of eyes in it brighter than pickled oysters, that didn't think it was "distinguished for intelligence"? — "The preachèd word"! That means the Rev. Jabez Grubb's sermons. "Temperance society"! "Excellent schools"! Ah, that is just what we were talking about.

The truth was, that District No. 1, Pigwacket Centre, had had a good deal of trouble of late with its schoolmasters. The committee had done their best, but there were a number of well-grown and pretty rough young fellows who had got the upperhand of the masters, and meant to keep it. Two dynasties had fallen before the uprising of this fierce democracy. This was a thing that used to be not very uncommon; but in so "intelligent" a community as that of Pigwacket Centre, in an era of public libraries and lyceum-lectures, it was portentous and alarming.

ROCKLAND

It was a comfort to get to a place with something like society, with residences which had pretensions to elegance, with people of some breeding, with a newspaper, and "stores" to advertise in it, and with two or three churches to keep each other alive by wholesome agitation. Rockland was such a place.

Some of the natural features of the town have been described already. The Mountain, of course, was what gave it its character, and redeemed it from wearing the commonplace expression which belongs to ordinary country-villages. Beautiful, wild, invested with the mystery which belongs to untrodden spaces, and with enough of terror to give it dignity, it had yet closer relations with the town over which it brooded than the passing stranger knew of. Thus, it made a local climate by cutting off the northern winds and holding the sun's heat like a garden-wall. Peach-trees, which, on the northern side of the mountain, hardly ever came to fruit, ripened abundant crops in Rockland.

But Rockland had other features which helped to give it a special character. First of all, there was one grand street which was its chief glory. Elm Street it was called, naturally enough, for its elms made a long, pointed-arched gallery of it through most of its extent. No natural Gothic arch compares, for a moment, with that formed by two American elms, where their lofty jets of foliage shoot across each other's ascending curves, to intermingle their showery flakes of green. When one looks through a long double row of these, as in that lovely avenue which the poets of Yale remember so well, —

"Oh, could the vista of my life but now as bright appear
As when I first through Temple Street looked down thine espalier!"

he beholds a temple not built with hands, fairer than any minster, with all its clustered stems and flowering capitals, that ever grew in stone.

Nobody knows New England who is not on terms of intimacy with one of its elms. The elm comes nearer to having a soul than any other vegetable creature among us. It loves man as man loves it. It is modest and patient. It has a small flake of a seed which blows in everywhere and makes arrangements for coming up by and by. So, in spring, one finds a crop of baby-elms among his carrots and parsnips, very weak and small compared to those succulent vegetables. The baby-elms die, most of them, slain, unrecognized or unheeded, by hand or hoe, as meekly as Herod's innocents. One of them gets overlooked, perhaps, until it has established a kind of right to stay. Three generations of carrot and parsnip consumers have passed away, yourself among them, and now let your great-grandson look for the baby-elm. Twenty-two feet of clean girth, three hundred and sixty feet in the line that bounds its leafy circle, it covers the boy with such a canopy as neither glossy-leafed oak nor insect-haunted linden ever lifted into the summer skies.

Elm Street was the pride of Rockland, but not only on account of its

Gothic-arched vista. In this street were most of the great houses, or "mansion-houses," as it was usual to call them. Along this street, also, the more nicely kept and neatly painted dwellings were chiefly congregated. It was the correct thing for a Rockland dignitary to have a house in Elm Street.

Daguerreotype identified as "Grandfather Peck," mid-19th century, Pittsfield. Berkshire County Historical Society Collection

THE MANSION-HOUSE

A New England "mansion-house" is naturally square, with dormer windows projecting from the roof, which has a balustrade with turned posts round it. It shows a good breadth of front-yard before its door, as its owner shows a respectable expanse of clean shirt-front. It has a lateral margin beyond its stables and offices, as its master wears his white wristbands showing beyond his coat-cuffs. It may not have what can properly be called grounds, but it must have elbow-room at any rate. Without it, it is like a man who is always tight-buttoned for want of any linen to show. The mansion-house which has had to button itself up tight in fences, for want of green or gravel margin, will be advertising for boarders presently.

THE GENTEEL HOUSE

Next to the mansion-houses, came the two-story trim, white-painted, "genteel" houses, which, being more gossipy and less nicely bred, crowded close up to the street, instead of standing back from it with arms akimbo, like the mansion-houses. Their little front-yards were very commonly full of lilac and syringa and other bushes, which were allowed to smother the lower story almost to the exclusion of light and air, so that, what with small windows and small windowpanes, and the darkness made by these choking growths of shrubbery, the front parlors of some of these houses were the most tomb-like, melancholy places that could be found anywhere among the abodes of the living. Their garnishing was apt to assist this impression. Large-patterned carpets, which always look discontented in little rooms, hair-cloth furniture, black and shiny as beetles' wing cases, and centre-tables, with a sullen oil-lamp of the kind called astral by our imaginative ancestors, in the centre, — these things were inevitable. In set piles round the lamp was ranged the current literature of the day, in the form of Temperance Documents, unbound numbers of one of the Unknown Public's Magazines with worn-out steel engravings and high-colored fashion-plates, the Poems of a distinguished British author whom it is unnecessary to mention, a volume of sermons, or a novel or two, or both, according to the tastes of the family, and the Good Book, which is always Itself in the cheapest and commonest company. The father of the family with his hand in the breast of his coat, the mother of the same in a wide-bordered cap, sometimes a print of the Last Supper, by no means Morghen's, or the Father of his Country, or the old General, or the Defender of the Constitution, or an unknown clergyman with an open book before him, — these were the usual ornaments of the walls, the first two a matter of rigor, the others according to politics and other tendencies.

This intermediate class of houses, wherever one finds them in New England towns, are very apt to be cheerless and unsatisfactory. They have neither the luxury of the mansion-house nor the comfort of the farmhouse. They are rarely kept at an agreeable temperature. The mansion-house has large fireplaces and generous chimneys, and is open to the sunshine. The farm-house makes no pretensions, but it has a good warm kitchen, at any rate, and one can be comfortable there with the rest of the family, without fear and without reproach. These lesser country-houses of genteel aspirations are much given to patent subterfuges of one kind and another to get heat without combustion. The chilly parlor and the slippery hair-cloth seat take the life out of the warmest welcome. If one would make these places wholesome, happy, and cheerful, the first precept would be, — The dearest fuel, plenty of it, and let half the heat go up the chimney. If you can't afford this, don't try to live in a "genteel" fashion, but stick to the ways of the honest farm-house.

THE FARM HOUSE

There were a good many comfortable farm-houses scattered about Rockland. The best of them were something of the following pattern, which is too often superseded of late by a more pretentious, but infinitely less pleasing kind of rustic architecture. A little back from the road, seated directly on the green sod, rose a plain wooden building, two stories in front, with a long roof sloping backwards to within a few feet of the ground. The walls were unpainted, but turned by the slow action of sun and air and rain to a quiet dove or slate color. An old broken millstone at the door, — a well-sweep pointing like a finger to the heavens, which the shining round of water beneath looked up at like a dark unsleeping eye, — a single large elm a little at one side, — a barn twice as big as the house, — a cattle-yard, with

"The white horns tossing above the wall," —

some fields, in pasture or in crops, with low stone walls round them, — a row of beehives, — a garden-patch, with roots, and currant-bushes, and many-hued hollyhocks, and swollen-stemmed, globe-headed, seedling onions, and marigolds and flower-de-luces, and lady's-delights, and peonies, crowding in together, with southernwood in the borders, and woodbine and hops and morning-glories climbing as they got a chance, — these were the features by which the Rockland-born children remembered the farm-house, when they had grown to be men. Such are the recollections that come over poor sailor-boys crawling out on reeling yards to reef topsails as their vessels stagger round the stormy Cape; and such are the flitting images that make the eyes of old country-born merchants look dim and dreamy, as they sit in their city palaces, warm with the after-dinner flush of the red wave out of which Memory arises, as Aphrodite arose from the green waves of the ocean.

THE MEETING HOUSES

Two meeting-houses stood on two eminences, facing each other, and looking like a couple of fighting-cocks with their necks straight up in the air, — as if they would flap their roofs, the next things, and crow out of their upstretched steeples, and peck at each other's glass eyes with their sharp-pointed weathercocks.

The first was a good pattern of the real old-fashioned New England meeting-house. It was a large barn with windows, fronted by a square tower crowned with a kind of wooden bell inverted and raised on legs, out of which rose a slender spire with the sharp-billed weathercock at its summit. Inside, tall, square pews with flapping seats, and a gallery running round three sides of the building. On the fourth side the pulpit, with a huge, dusty sounding-board hanging over it. Here preached the Reverend Pierrepont Honeywood, D.D., successor, after a number of generations, to the office and parsonage of the Reverend Didymus Bean, before mentioned, but not suspected of any of his alleged heresies.

THE REVEREND PIERREPONT HONEYWOOD, D.D.

He held to the old faith of the Puritans, and occasionally delivered a discourse which was considered by the hard-headed theologians of his parish to have settled the whole matter fully and finally, so that now there was a good logical basis laid down for the Millennium, which might begin at once upon the platform of his demonstrations. Yet the Reverend Dr. Honeywood was fonder of preaching plain, practical sermons about the duties of life, and showing his Christianity in abundant good works among his people. It was noticed by some few of his flock, not without comment, that the great majority of his texts came from the Gospels, and this more and more as he became interested in various benevolent enterprises which brought him into relations with ministers and kind-hearted laymen of other denominations. He was in fact a man of a very warm, open, and exceedingly *human* disposition, and, although bred by a clerical father, whose motto was "*Sit anima mea cum Puritanis,*" he exercised his human faculties in the harness of his ancient faith with such freedom that the straps of it got so loose they did not interfere greatly with the circulation of the warm blood through his system. Once in a while he seemed to think it necessary to come out with a grand doctrinal sermon, and then he would lapse away for a while into preaching on men's duties to each other and to society, and hit hard, perhaps, at some of the actual vices of the time and place, and insist with such tenderness and eloquence on the great depth and breadth of true Christian love and charity, that his oldest deacon shook his head, and wished he had shown as much interest when he was preaching, three Sabbaths back, on Predestination, or in his discourse against the Sabellians. But he was sound in the faith; no doubt of that. Did he not preside at the council held in the town of Tamarack, on the other side of the mountain, which expelled its clergy-man for maintaining heretical doctrines? As presiding officer, he did not vote, of course, but there was no doubt that he was all right; he had some of the Edwards blood in him, and that couldn't very well let him go wrong.

The meeting-house on the other and opposite summit was of a more modern style, considered by many a great improvement on the old New England model, so that it is not uncommon for a country parish to pull down its old meeting-house, which has been preached in for a hundred years or so, and put up one of these more elegant edifices. The new building was in what may be called the florid shingle-Gothic manner. Its pinnacles and crockets and other ornaments were, like the body of the building, all of pine wood, — an admirable material, as it is very soft and easily worked, and can be painted of any color desired. Inside, the walls were stuccoed in imitation of stone, — first a dark brown square, then two light brown squares, then another dark brown square, and so on, to represent the accidental differences of shade always noticeable in the real stones of which walls are built. To be sure, the architect could not help getting his party-colored squares in almost as regular rhythmical order as those of a chess-board; but nobody can avoid doing things in a systematic and serial way; indeed, people who wish to plant trees in natural clumps know very well that they cannot keep from making regular lines and symmetrical figures, unless by some trick or other, as that one of throw-ing a peck of potatoes up into the air and sticking in a tree wherever a potato happens to fall. The pews of this meeting-house were the usual oblong ones, where people sit close together, with a ledge before them to support their hymn-books, liable only to occasional contact with the back of the next pew's heads or bonnets, and a place running under the seat of that pew where hats could be deposited, — always at the risk of the owner, in case of injury by boots or crickets.

THE REVEREND CHAUNCY FAIRWEATHER

In this meeting-house preached the Reverend Chauncy Fairweather, a divine of the "Liberal" school, as it is commonly called, bred at that famous college which used to be thought, twenty or thirty years ago, to have the monopoly of training young men in the milder forms of heresy. His ministrations were attended with decency, but not followed with enthusiasm. "The beauty of virtue" got to be an old story at last. "The moral dignity of human nature" ceased to excite a thrill of satisfaction, after some hundred repetitions. It grew to be a dull business, this preaching against stealing and intemperance, while he knew very well that the thieves were prowling round orchards and empty houses, instead of being there to hear the sermon, and that the drunkards, being rarely church-goers, get little good by the statistics and eloquent appeals of the preacher. Every now and then, however, the Reverend Mr. Fairweather let off a polemic discourse against his neighbor opposite, which waked his people up a little; but it was languid congregation, at best, — very apt to stay away from meeting in the afternoon, and not at all given to extra evening services. The minister, unlike his rival of the other side of the way, was a down-hearted and timid kind of man. He went on preaching as he had been taught to preach, but he had misgivings at times. There was a little Roman Catholic church at the foot of the hill where his own was placed, which he always had to pass on Sundays. He could never look on the thronging multitudes that crowded its pews and aisles or knelt bare-headed on its steps, without a longing to get in among them and do gown on his knees and enjoy that luxury of devotional contact which makes a worshipping throng as different from the same numbers praying apart as a bed of coals is from a trail of scattered cinders.

"Oh, if I could but huddle in with those poor laborers and working-women!" he would say to himself. "If I could but breathe that atmosphere, stifling though it be, yet made holy by ancient litanies, and cloudy with the smoke of hallowed incense, for one hour, instead of droning over these moral precepts to my half-sleeping congregation!" The intellectual isolation of his sect preyed upon him; for, of all terrible things to natures like his, the most terrible is to belong to a minority. No person that looked at his thin and sallow cheek, his sunken and sad eye, his tremulous lip, his contracted forehead, or who hears his querulous, though not unmusical voice, could fail to see that his life was an uneasy one, that he was engaged in some inward conflict. His dark, melancholic aspect contrasted with his seemingly cheerful creed, and was all the more striking, as the worthy Dr. Honeywood, professing a belief which made him a passenger on board a shipwrecked planet, was yet a most good-humored and companionable gentleman, whose laugh on week-days did one as much good to listen to as the best sermon he ever delivered on a Sunday.

A mile or two from the centre of Rockland was a pretty little Episcopal church, with a roof like a wedge of cheese, a square tower, a stained window, and a trained rector, who read the service with such ventral depth of utterance and rrreduplication of the rrresonant letter, that his own mother would not have known him for her son, if the good woman had not ironed his surplice and put it on with her own hands.

PUBLIC HOUSES

There were two public-houses in the place: one dignified with the name of the Mountain House, somewhat frequented by city people in the summer months, large-fronted, three-storied, balconied, boasting a distinct ladies'-drawing-room, and spreading a *table d'hôte* of some pretensions; the other, "Pollard's Tahvern," in the common speech, — a two-story building, with a bar-room, once famous, where there was a great smell of hay and boots and pipes and all other bucolic-flavored elements, — where games of checkers were played on the back of the bellows with red and white kernels of corn, or with beans and coffee, — where a man slept in a box-settle at night, to wake up early passengers, — where teamsters came in, with wooden-handled whips and coarse frocks, reinforcing the bucolic flavor of the atmosphere, and middle-aged male gossips, sometimes including the squire of the neighboring law-office, gathered to exchange a question or two about the news, and then fall into that solemn state of suspended animation which the temperance bar-rooms of modern days produce in human beings, as the Grotta del Cane does in dogs in the well-known experiments related by travellers. This bar-room used to be famous for drinking and story-telling, and sometimes fighting, in old times. That was when there were rows of decanters on the shelf behind the bar, and a hissing vessel of hot water ready, to make punch, and three or four *loggerheads* (long irons clubbed at the end) were always lying in the fire in the cold season, waiting to be plunged into sputtering and foaming mugs of flip, — a goodly compound, speaking according to the flesh, made with beer and sugar, and a certain suspicion of strong waters, over which a little nutmeg being grated, and in it the hot iron being then allowed to sizzle, there results a peculiar singed aroma, which the wise regard as a warning to remove themselves at once out of the reach of temptation.

But the bar of Pollard's Tahvern no longer presented its old attractions, and the loggerheads had long disappeared from the fire. In place of the decanters, were boxes containing "lozengers," as they were commonly called, sticks of candy in jars, cigars in tumblers, a few lemons, grown hard-skinned and marvellously shrunken by long exposure, but still feebly suggestive of possible lemonade, — the whole ornamented by festoons of yellow and blue cut fly-paper. On the front shelf of the bar stood a large German-silver pitcher of water, and scattered about were ill-conditioned lamps, with wicks that always wanted picking, which burned red and smoked a good deal, and were apt to go out without any obvious cause, leaving strong reminiscences of the whale-fishery in the circumambient air.

From *Elsie Venner* by Oliver Wendell Holmes. Houghton, Mifflin, 1883.

Memories of Pittsfield

In 1883 Holmes wrote to John O. Sargent: "I am glad, my dear John, to know that you are taking your comfort in the midst of your own acres in my dear old Berkshire, where I once thought I should have a permanent summer home. I have never regretted my seven summers passed in Pittsfield, and never had the courage, though often asked, to visit the place since I left it. I have one particularly pleasant remembrance about my place, — that I in a certain sense created it. The trees about are all, or almost all, of my planting, — many of them not more than a foot high from English nurseries, others transplanted by myself and my tenant. Look at them as you pass my old place, and see how much better I have deserved the gratitude of posterity than the imbecile who only accomplished a single extra blade of grass."

And later still, to Mrs. Kellogg: —

"A happy New Year, my dear Mrs. Kellogg, and as many such as you can count until you reach a hundred, and then begin again, if you like the planet well enough.

"But how good you are to send me all those excellent and to me most interesting photographs! I delight in recalling the old scenes in this way; changed as they are, I yet seem to be carried back to the broad street — East Street, down which I — we — used to drive on our way to the 'Four Corners' and 'Canoe Meadow,' as my mother told me they used to call our old farm. I wonder that Pittsfield is not a city by this time. It seems almost too bad to take away its charming rural characteristics, — but such a beautiful, healthful, central situation could not resist its destiny, and you must have a mayor, I suppose, by and by, and a common council, and a lot of aldermen. But you cannot lose the sight of Greylock, nor turn the course of the Housatonic. I can hardly believe that it is almost thirty years since I bade good-by to the old place, expecting to return the next season. We passed through the gate — under the maple which used to stand there, and is probably in its old place, took a look at the house, and the great pine that stood, and I hope stands, in its solitary beauty and grandeur, — rode on — passed the two bridges, reached the station — the old one, — I think you have a better since — and good-by, dear old town — well, that is the way."

From *Life & Letters of Oliver Wendell Holmes*, Volume I, by J.T. Morse. Houghton Mifflin, 1896.

NATHANIEL HAWTHORNE

Nathaniel Hawthorne was probably the best observer the Berkshires have ever had. His 18-month residence in the "Red Cottage" in Lenox (actually over the line in Stockbridge) in 1850-51 — during which time he wrote A Wonder Book *wherein he gave Tanglewood its name — is the more famous of his Berkshire sojourns. But equally of interest is his summer vacation in North Adams in 1838, of which he kept a full account in his journal.*

He was of the party on the famous Monument Mountain picnic on Monday, August 5, 1850, where he met Melville and began the friendship that lasted while both were in the area. In 1851, while his wife was away, Hawthorne kept a running daily report detailing for her enjoyment how he and Julian, their little boy, spent their days in her absence.

"Ethan Brand" shows the fictional use he made of his 1838 recollections of Greylock.

Journal Extracts, 1838

NORTHAMPTON TO PITTSFIELD

July 24, 1838

Left Northampton next morning between 1 & 2 o'clock. Three other passengers, whose faces were not visible for some hours; so we went on through unknown space, saying nothing, — glancing forth sometimes, to see the gleam of the lanterns on wayside objects. How very desolate looks a forest, when seen in this way, — as if, should you venture one step within its wild, tangled, many-stemmed, and dark-shadowed verge, you would inevitably be lost forever. Sometimes we passed a house, or rumbled through a village — stopping, perhaps, to arouse some drowsy postmaster, who appeared at the door in shirt and pantaloons, yawning, received the mail, returned it again, and was yawning when last seen. A few words exchanged among the passengers, as they roused themselves from their half-slumbers, or dreamy slumber like abstraction. Meantime, dawn came on, our faces became partially visible, the morning air grew colder, and finally cloudy day came on. We found ourselves driving through quite a romantic country, with hills, or mountains, on all sides, a stream on one side — bordered by a high precipitous bank, up which would have grown pines, only that, losing their foothold, many of them had slipt downward. The road was not the safest in the world, for often the carriage approached within two or three feet of a precipice — but the driver, a merry fellow, lolled on his box, with his feet protruding horizontally, and rattled on at the rate of ten miles an hour. Breakfast between four and five, newly caught trout, salmon, ham, boiled eggs, and other niceties — truly excellent. A bunch of pickerel, intended for a tavern-keeper farther on, was carried by the stage-driver. The drivers carry a "time-watch," enclosed in a small wooden case with a lock, so that it may be known in what time they perform their stages — they are allowed so many hours and minutes to do their work, and their desire to go as fast as possible, combined with that of keeping their horses in good order, produces about a right medium. One of the passengers was a young man who had been in Pennsylvania, keeping a school — a genteel enough young man, but not a gentleman. He took neither supper nor breakfast, excusing himself from one as being weary with riding all day, and from the other, because it was so early. He attacked me for a sub-scription for "building up a destitute church" — of which he had taken an agency, and had collected two or three hundred dollars, but wanted as many thousands. Betimes in the morning, on the descent of a mountain, we arrived at a house where dwelt the married sister of the young man, whom he was going to visit. He alighted, saw his trunk taken off, and then, having perceived his sister at the door, and turning to bid us farewell, there was a broad smile, even laugh, of pleasure, which did him more credit with me than anything else; for hitherto there had been a disagreeable, scornful twist upon his face, — perhaps, however, merely superficial. I saw, as the stage drove off, his comely sister, coming with a lighted-up face to greet him, and one passenger on the front seat beheld them meet. "Is it an affectionate greeting?" inquired I. "Yes" said he, "I should like to share it." — whereby I concluded that there was a kiss ex-changed. The highest point of our journey was at Windsor, where we could see leagues around over the mountain — a terrible bare, bleak spot, fit for nothing but sheep, and without shelter of woods. We rattled downward into a warmer region, beholding, as we went, the sun shining on portions of the landscape miles ahead of us, while we were yet in chillness and gloom. It is probable, that, during part of the stage, the mists around us looked like sky clouds to those in the lower regions. Think of riding in a stagecoach through the clouds! Seasonably in the forenoon, we arrived at Pittsfield.

PITTSFIELD

Pittsfield is a large village, quite shut in by mountain-walls, generally extending like a rampart on all sides of it, but with insulated great hills rising here and there in the outline. The area of the town is level; its houses are handsome, mostly wooden and white, but some are of brick, painted a deep red — the bricks being of not a healthy natural color. There are handsome churches, gothic and others, and a court-house, and academy — the court-house having a marble front. There is a small mall

The center of Pittsfield, c. 1841. The Berkshire Athenaeum, Local History Department

in the centre of the town, and in the centre of the mall rises an elm, of the loftiest and straightest stem that ever I beheld — without a branch or leaf upon it, till it has soared seventy or perhaps a hundred feet into the air. The top branches, unfortunately, have been shattered somehow or other, so that it does not cast a broad shade — probably broken by their own ponderous foliage. The central square of Pittsfield presents all the bustle of a thriving village — the farmers of the vicinity in light wagons, sulkies, or on horseback; stages at the door of the Berkshire Hotel, under the stoop of which sit or lounge the guests, stage-people, and idlers, observing or assisting the arrivals and departures — huge trunks and bandboxes un-laded and laded. The courtesy shown to ladies in assisting them to alight, in a shower, under umbrellas. The dull looks of passengers, who have ridden all night, scarcely brightened by the excitement of arriving at a new place. The stage agent demanding the names of those who are going on: — some to Lebanon Springs, some to Albany. The toddy-stick is still busy at these Berkshire public houses. At dinner, soup preliminary, in city style — guests, the court-people, Briggs, member of congress, attend-ing a trial here; horse-dealers, country squires, store-keepers in the village &c &c. My room, a narrow crib, overlooking a back court-yard, where a young man and a lad were drawing water for the maid-servants. Their jokes — especially those of the lad, at whose wit the elder fellow, being a blockhead himself, was in great admiration — declaring to another — that he knew as much as them both. Yet he was not witty to kill, either. Once in a while the servant would come to the door, and hear and respond to their jokes with a kind of restraint, yet both permitting them and enjoying them. After, or about sunset, there was a heavy shower — the thunder rumbling round and round the mountain wall, and the clouds stretching from rampart to rampart. When it abated, the clouds in all parts of the visible heavens were tinged with glory from the west; some that hung low being purple and gold, while the higher ones were gray. The slender curve of the new moon was also visible, brightening among the fading brightness of the sunny part of the sky. There are marble-quarries in and near Pittsfield; which accounts for the fact, that there are none but marble gravestones in the burialgrounds — some of the monuments well carved; but the marble does not stand the wear and tear of time and weather so well as the imported; and the sculpture soon loses its sharp outline. The door of one tomb — a wooden door, opening in the side of a green mound, surmounted by a marble obelisk — having been shaken from its hinges by the late explosion of the powder-house, and incompletely repaired, I peeped in at the crevices, and saw the coffins. It was the tomb of Rev. Thomas Allen, first minister of Pittsfield, deceased in 1810. It contained three coffins, all with white mould on the top. One, a small child's, rested on the top of another. The other, was on the opposite side of the tomb, and the lid was considerably displaced; but the tomb being dark, I could see neither corpse nor skeleton. Marble also occurs here in North Adams; and thus some very ordinary houses have marble door-steps, and even the stone walls are built of fragments of marble.

THE TRIP TO NORTH ADAMS

Wednesday, 26th.

Left Pittsfield about eight o'clock in the Bennington stage, intending to go to Williamstown. Inside passengers, a new married couple, taking a jaunt — The lady, with a clear, pale complexion, rather pensive cast of countenance, slender, and a genteel figure; the bridegroom, a shopkeeper in New York; probably; a young man with a stout black beard, black eyebrows which formed one line across his forehead, — They were very loving; and while the stage stopt, I watched them quite entranced in each other, both leaning sideways against the back of the coach, and perusing their mutual comeliness, and apparently making complimentary observations on one another's comeliness. The bride appeared the most absorbed and devoted, referring her whole being to him. The gentleman seemed in a most Paradisaical mood, smiling ineffably upon his bride, and when she spoke, responding to her with a sort of benign expression, of matrimonial sweetness, and as it were compassion for the weaker vessel, mingled with great love and pleasant humor that was dreadful queer. The driver peeped into the coach once, and said that he had his arm round her waist. He took little freedoms with her — tapping her, if I mistake not, with his cane — love pats; and she seemed to see nothing amiss. It would be pleasant to meet them again next summer, and note the change. They kept eating gingerbread all along the road; and dined heartily, notwithstanding.

Our driver was a slender, lath, round-backed, rough-bearded, thin-visaged, middle-aged Yankee, who became very communicative during our ride. He was not bred a stage-driver, but had undertaken the business temporarily, as a favor to his brother-in-law. He was a native of these Berkshire mountains, but had formerly emigrated to Ohio, and had returned for a time to try the benefit of her native air on his wife's declining health — she having complaints of a consumptive nature. He pointed out the house where he was married to her, and told the name of the country-squire who tied the knot. His wife has little or no chance of recovery; and he said he would never marry again: — this resolution being expressed in answer to a remark of mine relative to a second marriage. He has no children by his wife. I pointed to a hill at some distance before us, and asked what it was. "That, Sir," said he, "is a very high hill. It is known by the name of Graylock." He seemed to feel that this was a more poetical epithet than Saddleback, which is a more usual name for it. Graylock, or Saddleback, is quite a respectable mountain; and I suppose the former name has been given it, because it often has a gray cloud, or lock of gray mist, upon his head; it does not ascend into a peak, but heaves up a round ball, and has supporting ridges on each side. Its summit is not bare, like Mt Washington, but covered with forest. The driver said, that several years since the students of Williams' college erected a building for an observatory on the top of this mountain, and employed him to haul the materials for constructing it; and he was the only man that had ever driven an ox-team up Graylock. It was necessary to drive the team round and round, in ascending. President Griffin rode up on horseback.

Along our road, we passed villages, and often factories, the machinery whizzing, and girls looking out of the windows at the stage, with heads averted from their tasks, but still busy. These factories have two, three, or more, boarding houses near them, two stories high, and of double length — often with bean vines &c. running up round the doors; and altogether a domestic look. There are several factories in different parts of North-Adams, along the banks of a stream, a wild highland rivulet, which, however, does vast work of a civilized nature. It is strange to see such a rough and untamed stream as it looks to be, so tamed down to the purposes of man, and making cottons, woollens &c — sawing boards, marbles, and giving employment to so many men and girls; and there is a sort of picturesqueness in finding these factories, supremely artificial establishments, in the midst of such wild scenery. For now the stream will be flowing through a rude forest, with the trees erect and dark, as when the Indians fished there; and it brawls, and tumbles, and eddies, over its rock-strewn current. Perhaps there is a precipice hundreds of feet high, beside it, down which, by heavy rains or the melting of snows, great pinetrees have slid or tumbled headlong, and lie at the bottom or half-way down; while their brethren seem to be gazing at their fall from the summit, and anticipating a like fate. And taking a turn in the road, behold these factories and their range of boarding-houses, with the girls looking out of the window as aforesaid. And perhaps the wild scenery is all around the very site of the factory, and mingles its impression strangely with those opposite ones. These observations were made during a walk yesterday. I bathed in a part of the stream that was out of sight, and where its brawling waters were deep enough to cover me, when I lay at length. Parts of the road, along which I walked, lay on the edge of a precipice, falling down straight towards the stream; and in one place, the passage of heavy loads had sunk the road, so that soon, probably, there will be an avalanche, perhaps carrying a stage-coach or heavy wagon down into the bed of the stream. I met occasional wayfarers, sometimes two women in a wagon, decent, brown visaged country matrons, sometimes an apparent doctor, of whom there are seven or thereabouts, in North Adams; for though the vicinity is very healthy, yet they have to ride considerable distances among the mountain-towns; and their practice is very laborious. A nod is always exchanged between strangers meeting on the road.

The morning was cloudy; and all the near landscape lay unsunned; but there was sunshine on distant tracts in the vallies, and in specks upon the mountain tops. Between the ridges of hills, there are long, wide, hollow vallies extending for miles and miles; with houses scattered along them. A bulky company of mountains, swelling round head over round head, rises insulated by such broad vallies from the surrounding ridges. I ought to have mentioned that I arrived at North-Adams in the forenoon of the 26th; and liking the aspect of matters indifferently well, determined to make my headquarters here, for a short time.

NORTH ADAMS IMPRESSIONS

July 29th.

Remarkable characters: — a disagreeable figure, waning from middle-age, clad in a pair of tow homespun pantaloons and very dirty shirt, barefoot, and with one of his feet maimed by an axe: also, an arm amputated two or three inches below the elbow. His beard of a week's growth, grim and grisly, with a general effect of black; — altogether a filthy and disgusting object. Yet he has signs of having been a handsome man in his idea, though now such a beastly figure that, probably, no living thing but his great dog would touch him without an effort. Coming to the stoop, where several persons were sitting, — "Good morning, gentlemen," said the wretch. Nobody answered for a time, till at last one said, "I don't know who you speak to; — not me, I'm sure;" meaning that he did not claim to be a gentleman. "Why, I thought you all speak at once," replied the figure laughing. So he sat himself down on the lower step of the stoop, and began to talk; and the conversation being turned upon his bare feet, by one of the company, he related the story of his losing his toes by the glancing aside of an axe, and with what grim fortitude he bore it. Then he made a transition to the loss of his arm — and setting his teeth and drawing in his breath, said that the pain was dreadful; but this, too, he seems to have borne like an Indian; and a person testified to his fortitude by saying that he did not suppose that there was any feeling in him, from observing how he bore it. The man spoke of the pain of cutting the muscles, and the particular agony at one moment, while the bone was being sawed asunder; and there was a strange expression of remembered agony, as he shrugged his half-limb, and described the matter. After-wards, in a reply to a question of mine whether he still seemed to feel the hand that had been amputated, he answered that he did, always — and baring the stump, he moved the severed muscles, saying, "There is the thumb, there the forefinger &c. Then he talked to me about phrenology, of which he seems a firm believer and skilful practitioner, telling how he had hit upon the true characters of many people. There was a great deal of sense and acuteness in his talk, and something of elevation in his expression; perhaps a studied elevation — and a sort of courtesy in his manner; but his sense had something out of the way in it; something wild, and ruined, and desperate, in his talk, though I can hardly say what it was. There was something of the gentleman and man of intellect in his deep degradation; and a pleasure in intellectual pursuits, and an acuteness and trained judgment, which bespoke a mind once strong and culti-vated. "My study is man," said he. And looking at me "I do not know your name," said he, "but there is something of the hawk-eye about you too." This man was formerly a lawyer in good practice, but taking to drinking, was reduced to this lowest state. Yet not the lowest; for, after the amputation of his arm, being advised by divers persons to throw himself upon the public for support, he told them that, even if he should lose his other arm, he would still be able to support himself and a waiter. Certainly he is a strong minded and iron-constitutioned man; but, look-ing at the stump of his arm, he said "that the pain of the mind was a thousand times greater than the pain of the body — "That hand could make the pen go fast," said he. Among people in general, he does not seem to have any greater consideration in his ruin, for the sake of his former standing in society. He supports himself by making soap; and on

North Adams from the west, c. 1841. The Berkshire Athenaeum, Local History Department

account of the offals used in that business, there is probably rather an evil smell in his domicile. Talking about a dead horse, near his house, he said that he could not bear the scent of it. "I should not think you could smell carrion in that house," said a stage-agent. Whereupon the soap-maker dropped his head, with a little snort, as it were, of wounded feeling; but immediately said that he took all in good part. There was an old squire of the village, a lawyer probably, whose demeanor was different — with a distance, yet a kindliness; for he remembered the times when they met on equal terms. "You and I," said the squire, alluding to their respective troubles and sicknesses, "would have died long ago, if we had not had the courage to live." The poor devil kept talking to me long after everybody else had left the stoop, giving vent to much practical philosophy and just observation on the ways of men, mingled with rather more assumption of literature and cultivation than belonged to the present condition of his mind. Meantime his great dog — a cleanly looking, and not ill-bred dog, being the only decent attribute appertaining to his master — a well natured dog, too, and receiving civilly any demonstration of courtesy from other people, though preserving a certain distance of deportment — this great dog grew weary of his master's lengthy talk, and expressed his impatience to be gone, by thrusting himself between his legs, rolling over on his back, seizing his ragged trowsers, or playfully taking his maimed bare foot into his mouth — using, in short, the kindly and humorous freedom of a friend, with a wretch to whom all are free enough, but none other kind. His master rebuked him, but with kindness too, and not so that the dog felt himself bound to desist, though he seemed willing to allow his master all the time that could possibly be spared. And, at last, having said many times that he must go and shave and dress himself — and as his beard had been at least a week growing, it might have seemed almost a week's work to get rid of it — he rose from the stoop, and went his way, a forlorn and miserable thing in the light of the cheerful summer Sabbath morning. Yet he seems to keep his spirits up, and still preserves himself a man among men, asking nothing from them — nor is it clearly perceptible what right they have to scorn him.

VILLAGE DOGS

There are a great many dogs kept in the village, and many of the travellers also have dogs. Some are almost always playing about, and if a cow or a pig be passing, two or three of them scamper forth to attack her. Some of the younger sort chase pigeons, wheeling as they wheel. If a contest arises between two dogs, a number of others come with huge barking to join the fray; though I believe that they do not really take any active part in the contest, but swell the uproar, by way of encouraging the combatants. When a traveller is starting from the door, his dog often gets in front of the horse, placing his forefeet down, looking the horse in the face, and barking loudly, then, as the horse comes on, running a little farther, and repeating the process; and this he does in spite of his master's remonstrances, till the horse being fairly started, the dog follows on quietly. One dog, a diminutive little beast, has been taught to stand on his hind legs and rub his face with his paw, which he does with an aspect of much endurance and deprecation. Another springs at people whom his master points out to him, barking and pretending to bite. These tricks make much mirth in the bar-room. All dogs, of whatever different sizes and dissimilar varieties, acknowledge the common bond of species among themselves; and the largest one does not disdain to suffer his tail to be smelt of, nor to reciprocate that courtesy, to the smallest. They appear to take much interest in one another, but there is always a degree of caution between two strange dogs, in approaching one another.

HUDSON'S CAVE

July 31st.

A visit to what is called "Hudson's Cave," or "Hudson's Falls" — the tradition being, that a man by the name of Henry Hudson, many years ago, chasing a deer, the deer fell over this place, which then first became known to white men. It is not properly a cave, but a fissure in a huge ledge of marble, through which a stream has been for ages forcing its way, and has left marks of its gradually wearing power on the tall crags, having made curious hollows from the summit down to the level which it has reached at the present day. The depth of the fissure, in some places, is at least fifty or sixty feet, perhaps more, and at several points, it nearly closes over, and often the sight of the sky is hidden by the interposition of masses of the marble crags. The fissure is very irregular, so as not to be describable in words, and scarcely to be painted — jutting buttresses, moss grown — impending crags, with tall trees growing on their verge, nodding over the head of the observer at the bottom of the chasm, and rooted as it were in air. The part where the water works its way down is very narrow; but the chasm widens, after the descent, so as to form a spacious chamber between the crags, open to the sky, and its floor strewn with fallen fragments of marble, trees that have been precipitated long ago, and are heaped with fragments of drift wood, left there by the freshets, when the scanty stream becomes a considerable waterfall. One crag, with a narrow ridge, which might be climbed without much difficulty, protrudes from the middle of the rock, and divides the fall. The passage through the cave, made by the stream, is very crooked, and is interrupted, not only by fallen fragments, but by deep pools of water, which probably have been forded by few. As the deepest pool occurs in the most uneven part of the chasm, where the hollows in the side of the crag are deepest, so that each hollow is almost a cave by itself, I determined to wade through it. There was an accumulation of soft stuff on the bottom, so that the water did not look more than knee-deep; but, finding that my feet sunk in it, I took off my pantaloons, and waded through, up to my middle. Thus I reached the most interesting part of the cave, where the whirlings of the stream had left the marks of its eddies in the solid marble, all up and down the two sides of the chasm. The water is now sluiced and dammed for the construction of two marble saw-mills; else it would have been impossible to effect the passage; and I presume that, for years after the cave was discovered, the waters roared and tore their way in a torrent through this part of the chasm. While I was there, I heard voices, and a small stone tumbled down the chasm; and looking up towards the narrow strip of bright, and the sunny verdure that peeped over the top — looking up thither from the deep gloomy depth, I saw two or three men; and not liking to be to them the most curious part of the spectacle, I waded back, and put on my clothes. The marble crags are overspread with a concretion which makes them look as gray as granite, only where the continual flow of water keeps them of a snowy whiteness. If they were so white all over, it would be a splendid spectacle. There is a marble quarry close in the rear, above the cave; and in process of time, the whole of the crags will be quarried into tombstones, door-steps, fronts of edifices, fire-places &c. That will be a pity. On such portions of the walls as are within reach, visitors have sculptured their initials, or names at full length; — and the white letters showing plainly in the gray surface, it has a more obvious effect than such inscriptions generally do. There was formerly, I believe, a complete arch of marble, forming a natural bridge over the top of the cave; but this is no longer so. At the bottom of the broad chamber of the cave, standing in its shadow, the effect of the morning sunshine on the dark or bright foliage of the pines and other trees, that cluster on the summits of the crags, was particularly beautiful; and it was strange how such great trees had rooted themselves in solid marble, for so it seemed. After passing through this romantic and most picturesque spot, the stream goes onward to turn factories. Here its voice resounds within the hollow crags; then it goes onward, talking to itself, with babbling din of its own wild thoughts and fantasies — the voice of solitude and the wilderness — loud and continual, but which yet does not seem to disturb the thoughtful wanderer, so that he forgets there is a noise. It talks along its stone-strewn path; it talks beneath tall precipices, and high banks — a voice that has been the same innumerable ages; and yet, if you listen, you will perceive a continual change and variety in its babble, and sometimes it seems to swell louder upon the ear than at others — in the same spot, I mean. By and bye, man makes a dam for it; and it pours over it, still making its voice heard, while it labors.

At one shop for manufacturing the marble, I saw the disk of a sun-dial, as large as the top of a hogshead, — intended for Williams' College. Also a small obelisk and numerous grave-stones. The marble is coarse-grained, but of a very brilliant whiteness. It is rather a pity that the cave is not formed of some worthless stone.

EVENING CLOUDS

In the deep vallies of this neighborhood, where the shadows at sunset are thrown from mountain to mountain, the clouds have a beautiful effect, flitting high over the valley, bright with heavenly gold; — it seems as if the soul might soar up from the gloom, and alight upon them, and soar away. Walking along one of the vallies, the other evening, while a pretty fresh breeze blew along it, the clouds that were skimming the length of the valley, over my head, seemed to conform themselves to the valley's shape.

At a distance, mountain ridges look close together, and almost form-ing one mountain, though in reality, a village lies in the depth between them.

A steam engine in a factory to be supposed to possess a malignant spirit; it catches one man's arm, and pulls it off; seizes another by the coat-tails, and almost grapples him bodily; — catches a girl by the hair, and scalps her; — and finally draws a man, and crushes him to death.

The one-armed soap-maker, lawyer Haynes, wears an iron hook, which serves him instead of a hand for the purpose of holding on. They nickname him Black Hawk.

The village viewed from the top of a hill to the westward, at sunset, has a peculiarly happy and peaceful look; it lies on a level, surrounded by hills, and seems as if it lay in the hollow of a large hand. The Union Village may be seen, a manufacturing place, extending from the main village up a gorge of the hills. It is amusing to see all the distributed property, the aristocracy and commonalty, the various and conflicting interests of the town, the loves and hates, compressed into a space which the eye takes in as completely as the arrangement of a tea-table. The rush of the streams comes up the hill, somewhat like the sound of a city.

The hills about the village appear very high and steep sometimes, when the shadows of the clouds are thrown blackly upon them, while there is sunshine elsewhere; so that, seen in front; the effect of their gradual slope is lost. These hills, surrounding the town on all sides, give it a snug and insulated air; and viewed from certain points, it would be difficult to tell how to get out, without climbing the mountain ridges; but the roads wind away and accomplish the passage without ascending very high. Sometimes the notes of a horn or bugle may be heard, sounding afar among these passes of the mountains, announcing the coming of the stage-coach from Bennington, or Troy, or Greenfield, or Pittsfield.

SHEEP

There are multitudes of sheep among the hills; and they appear very tame and gentle; though sometimes, like the wicked, they "flee when no man pursueth." But climbing a rude, rough, rocky, stumpy, ferny height yesterday, one or two of them stood and stared at me with great earnestness; I passed on quietly, but soon heard an immense baa-ing up the hill; and all the sheep came galloping and scrambling after me, baa-ing with all their might with innumerable voices, running in a compact body, expressing the utmost eagerness, as if they sought the greatest imaginable favor from me; and so they accompanied me down the hillside — a most ridiculous cortège. Doubtless they had taken it into their heads that I brought them salt.

The peculiarly beautiful aspect of the village, towards sunset, and when there are masses of cloud about the sky — the remnants of a thunderstorm. These clouds throw a shade upon large portions of the rampart of hills, and the hills towards the west are shaded of course; the clouds, also, make the shades deeper in the village; and thus the sunshine on the houses and trees, and along the street, is a bright, rich gold. The green is deeper, in consequence of the recent rain.

Doctors walk about the village with their saddlebags on their arms. One always with a pipe in his mouth.

A little dog named Snapper — the same who stands on his hind-legs. He appears to be a roguish little dog; and the other day, he stole one of the girl's shoes and ran into the street with it. Being pursued, he would lift the shoe in his mouth (it almost dragging on the ground) and run a little ways; then lie down with his paws on it, and wait to be pursued again.

FURTHER IMPRESSIONS

Aug 11th.

This morning, it being cloudy and boding of rain, the clouds had settled upon the mountains, both summits and ridges, all round the town, so that there seemed to be no way of gaining access to the rest of the world, unless by climbing above the clouds. By and bye, they partially dispersed, giving glimpses of the mountain ramparts through their ob-scurity; separate clouds lay heavily upon the mountain's breast. In warm mornings, after rain, the mist breaks forth from the forests on the ascent of the mountains, like smoke, the smoke of a volcano, — then it soars up, and becomes a cloud in heaven. But these clouds were real rain clouds. Sometimes, it is said, while laboring up the mountain-side, they suddenly burst, and pour down their moisture in a cataract, sweeping all before it.

Every new aspect of the mountains, or view from a prise position, creates a surprise in the mind.

Scenes and characters — A young country fellow, twenty or there-abouts, decently dressed, pained with the toothache. A country doctor — passing on horseback, with his black leather saddle-bags behind him, a thin frosty-haired man. Being asked to operate, he looks at the tooth, lances the gum; and the fellow being content to be operated upon on the spot, he seats himself in a chair on the stoop, with great heroism. The doctor produces a rusty pair of iron forceps; a man holds the patient's head; the doctor perceives, that it being a difficult tooth, wedged between the two largest in the head, he shall pull very moderate; and the forceps are introduced. A turn of the doctor's hand; the patient begins to utter a cry; but the tooth comes out first, all bloody, with four prongs. The patient gets up, half amazed, spits out a mouthfull of blood, pays the doctor ninepence, pockets the tooth; and the spectators are in glee and admiration.

Fat woman, stage-passenger to-day — a wonder how she could pos-sibly get through the door, which seemed not so wide as she. When she put her foot on the steps, the stage gave a great lurch. She joking all the while — a great, coarse, redfaced dame. Other passengers, three or four slender Williamstown students, a young girl, and a man with one leg and two crutches.

One of the most sensible men in this village is a plain, tall, elderly person, who is overseeing the mending of a road — humorous, intelligent, with much thought about matters and things; and while at work, a sort of dignity in handling the hoe or crow-bar, which shows him the chief. In the evening he sits under the stoop, silent much and observant from under the brim of his hat; but occasion calling, he holds an argument about the benefit or otherwise of manufactories &c. A simplicity characterizes him more than most Yankees.

A man in a pea-green frock coat, with velvet collar. Another in a flowered chintz frock coat. There is a great diversity of hues in garments. A doctor, a stout, tall, round-paunched, red-faced, brutal looking old fellow, who gets drunk daily. He sat down on the step of our stoop, looking surly, and speaking to nobody; then got up and walked homeward, with a surly swagger, and a slight unevenness of track, attended by a fine Newfoundland dog.

A barouche and driver returning from beyond Greenfield or Troy — empty, having left his passengers at the former place. He stops here for the night, and while washing, enters into talk with an old man, about the different roads over the mountain.

People washing themselves at the common basin in the bar-room, and using the common hair-brush — perhaps with a consciousness of praiseworthy neatness.

A man with a cradle on his shoulder, having been cradling oats.

Attended a funeral (child's) yesterday afternoon. An assemblage of people in a plain, homely apartment. Most of the men were dressed in their ordinary clothes, and one or two in their shirt-sleeves. The coffin was placed in the midst of us, covered with a velvet-pall. A baptist clergyman prayed (the audience remaining seated, while he stood up at the head of the coffin) read a passage of Scripture, and commented upon it. While he read, and prayed, and expounded, there was a heavy thunder-storm rumbling among the surrounding hills; and the lightning flashed fiercely through the gloomy room; and the preacher alluded to God's voice of thunder.

It is the custom in this part of the country — and perhaps extensively in the interior of New-England — to bury the dead first in a Charnel-House, or common tomb, where they remain till decay has so far progressed as to secure them from the resurrectionists. They are then reburied, with certain ceremonies, in their own peculiar graves.

COMMENCEMENT AT WILLIAMS

Wednesday Aug 15th 1838.

To commencement at Williams College — five miles distant. At the tavern, students, with ribbons, pink or blue, fluttering from their button-holes — these being the badges of rival societies. A considerable gathering of people, chiefly arriving in wagons or buggies — some barouches — very few chaises. The most characteristic part of the scene, was where the pedlers, gingerbread-sellers &c were collected, a few hundred yards from the meeting-house. There was a pedler there from New-York state, who sold his wares by auction; and I could have stood and listened to him all day long. Sometimes he would put up a heterogeny of articles in a lot — as a paper of pins, a lead pencil, and a shaving-box — and knock them all down, perhaps, for ninepence. Bunches of lead pencils, steel pens; pound cakes of shaving soap, gilt finger rings, bracelets, clasps, and other jewelry, cards of pearl buttons, or steel — "there is some steel about them, gentlemen; for my brother stole 'em, and I bore him out in it," bundles of wooden combs, boxes of loco-focos, suspenders, &c, &c &c — in short everything — dipping his hand down into his boxes, with the promise of a wonderful lot, and producing, perhaps, a bottle of opodeldoc, and joining it with a lead pencil — and when he had sold several things of the same kind, pretending huge surprise at finding "just one more" — if the lads lingered, saying, "I could not afford to steal them for the price; for the remorse of conscience would be worth more" — all the time, keeping an eye upon those who bought, calling for the pay, making change with silver or bills, and deciding on the goodness of banks, — and saying to the boys who climbed upon his cart — "Fall down, roll down, tumble down — only get down" — and everything in the queer humorous recitative, in which he sold his articles. Sometimes he pretended that a person had bid, either by word or wink, and raised a laugh thus. Never losing his self-possession, nor getting out of humor; — When a man asked whether a bill was good "No!! Do you suppose I'd give you good money." When he delivered an article, You're the lucky man. Setting off his wares with the most extravagant eulogies. The people bought very freely, and seemed also to enjoy the fun. One little boy bought a shaving box — perhaps meaning to speculate upon it. This character could not possibly be over-drawn; and he was really excellent, with his allusions to what was passing, intermingled, doubtless with a good deal that was studied. He was a man between thirty and forty, with a face expressive of other ability, as well as humor.

From *The American Notebooks* of Nathaniel Hawthorne. Edited by Randall Stewart. Yale University Press, 1932.

Journal Extracts, 1850-1851

RESIDENCE AT TANGLEWOOD

August 4th. (Sunday) 1850

Dined at hotel with J.T. Fields and wife: afternoon, rode with them to Pittsfield, and called on Dr. Holmes.

August 5th (Monday)

Rode with Fields & wife to Stockbridge, being thereto invited by Mr. Field of S. — in order to ascend Monument Mountain. Found at Mr. F's Dr. Holmes, Mr. Duyckink of New-York, also Messrs Cornelius Mathews & Herman Melville. Ascended the mountain — that is to say, Mrs. Fields & Miss Jenny Field — Messrs Field & Fields — Dr. Holmes, Messrs. Duyckinck, Mathews, Melville, Mr. Henry Sedgewick, & I. — and were caught in a shower. Dined at Mr. F's. Afternoon, under guidance of J.T. Headley, the party scrambled through the Ice Glen. Left Stockbridge and arrived at home, about 8. P.M.

August 7th. (Wednesday)

Messrs. Duyckinck, Mathews, Melville, Melville, Jr, called in the forenoon. Gave them a couple of bottles of Mr Mansfield's champagne, and walked down to the lake with them. At twilight, Mr. Edwin P. Whipple and wife called, from Lenox.

August 8th.

E. P. Whipple & wife took tea.

August 12th.

Seven chickens hatched. Afternoon, J.T. Headley and brother called. — Eight chickens.

August 19th.

Monument Mountain in the early sunshine; its base enveloped in mist, parts of which are floating in the sky; so that the great hill looks really as if it were founded on a cloud. Just emerging from the mist is seen a yellow field of rye, and above that, forest.

August 21st. (Wednesday)

Eight more chickens hatched. — Ascended a mountain with wife — a beautiful, mellow, autumnal sunshine.

August 24th.

In the afternoons, now-a-days, this valley in which I dwell seems like a vast basin, filled with golden sunshine as with wine.

Stockbridge Bowl, with Monument Mountain in the distance. Clemens Kalischer

August 31st.
J.R. Lowell called in the evening. Septr 1st. He and Mrs. Lowell called in the forenoon, on their way to Stockbridge or Lebanon, to meet Miss Bremer. Septr 2d. "When I grow up;" quoth Julian, in illustration of the might to which he means to attain to, "when I grow up, I shall be *two* men!" Septr 3d. Foliage of maples begins to change.

Septr 3d. (Tuesday)
Herman Melville came, in the forenoon.

Septr 4th.
Rode with Mr Tappan and Melville (in T's wagon,) to Pittsfield; left T. there, to take the cars for Albany; and spent the day with Melville at his cousin's, near Pittsfield. Reached home, with Melville, at about 8. P.M.

Septr 7th (Saturday)
Herman Melville went away, after breakfast.

Septr 19th.
Lying by the lake, yesterday afternoon, with my eyes shut, while the

breeze and sunshine were playing together on the water, the quick glimmer of the wavelets was perceptible through my closed eyelids.

October 13th.

A north-west windy day, cool, with a general prevalence of dull grey clouds over the sky, but with brief, quick glimpses of sunshine. The foliage having its autumn hues, Monument Mountain looks like a headless sphinx, wrapt in a rich Persian shawl. Yesterday, through a prevalent mist, with the sun shining on it, it had the aspect of burnished copper. The sun-gleams on the hills are peculiarly magnificent, just in these days.

October 16th.

A morning mist filling up the whole length and breadth of the valley, betwixt here and Monument Mountain; the summit of the mountain emerging. The mist reaches to within perhaps a hundred yards of our house, so dense as to conceal everything, except that, near its hither boundary, a few ruddy or yellow tree-tops emerge, glorified by the early sunshine; as is likewise the whole mist cloud. There is a glen between our house and the lake, through which winds a little brook, with pools, and tiny waterfalls over the great roots of trees. The glen is deep and narrow, and filled with trees; so that, in the summer, it is all a dense shadow of obscurity. Now, the foliage of the trees being almost entirely a golden yellow, instead of being full of shadow, the glen is absolutely full of sunshine, and its depths are more brilliant than the open plain or the mountain-tops. The trees are sunshine, and many of their golden leaves being freshly fallen, the glen is strewn with sunshine, amid which winds and gurgles the bright, dark little brook.

October 28th.

On a walk, yesterday forenoon, my wife and children gathered Housatonias. Before night, it snowed — mingled with rain. The trees are now generally bare.

Decr 1st.

I saw a dandelion in bloom, near the lake, in a pasture, by the brookside.

A WALK ACROSS STOCKBRIDGE BOWL

Febry 12th, 1851.

A walk across the lake, with Una. A heavy rain, some days ago, has melted a good deal of the snow on the intervening descent between our house and the lake; but many drifts, depths, and levels, yet remain; and there is a frozen crust, sufficient to bear a man's weight, and very slippery. Adown the slopes, there are tiny rivulets, which exist only for this winter. Bare, brown spaces of grass, here and there, but still so infrequent as only to diversify the scene a little. In the woods, rocks emerging; and where there is a slope immediately towards the lake, the snow is pretty much gone; and we see partridge-berries frozen; and outer shells of walnuts, and chesnut-burrs, heaped or scattered among the roots of the trees. The walnut-husks mark the place where boys, after nutting, sat down to clear the walnuts of their outer-shell. The various species of pine look exceedingly brown, just now; less beautiful than those trees which shed their leaves. An oak-tree, with almost all its brown foliage still rustling on it. We clamber down the bank, and step upon the frozen lake. It was snow covered for a considerable time; but the rain overspread it with a surface of water, or imperfectly melted snow, which is now hard frozen again; and the thermometer having been frequently below zero, I suppose there may be four or five feet thickness of ice. Frequently, there are great cracks across it, caused, I suppose, by the air beneath, and giving an idea of greater firmness than if there were no cracks; round holes, which have been hewn into the marble pavement by fishermen, and are now frozen over again, looking darker than the rest of the surface; spaces where the snow was more imperfectly dissolved than elsewhere; little crackling spots, where a thin surface of ice, over the real mass, crumples beneath one's foot; the track of a line of footsteps, most of them vaguely formed, but some quite perfectly, where a person passed across the lake while its surface was in a state of slush, but which are now as hard as adamant; and remind one of the traces discovered by geologists in rocks, that hardened thousands of ages ago. It seems as if the person passed when the lake was in an intermediate state between ice and water. In one spot some pine-boughs which somebody had cut, and heaped there, for an unknown purpose. In the centre of the lake, we see the surrounding hills in a new attitude; this being a basin in the midst of them. Where they are covered with wood, the aspect is grey or black; then there are bare slopes of unbroken snow; the outlines and indentations being much more hardly and firmly defined than in summer. We went across the lake southward, directly towards Monument Mountain, which reposes like a headless sphinx; its prominences, projections, and roughnesses are very evident, and it does not present a smooth and placid front, as when the grass is green and the trees in leaf; at one end, too, we are sensible of precipitous descents; black and shaggy with the forest that is likely always to grow there; and, in one streak, a headlong sweep downward of snow. We just set our feet on the farther shore, and then immediately set out on our return, facing the north-west wind, which blew very sharp against our faces.

After landing, we returned homeward, tracing up the little brook, so far as it lay in our course. It was considerably swollen, and rushed fleetly on its course between overhanging banks of snow and ice, from which depended adamantine icicles. The little waterfalls, with which we had impeded it in the summer and autumn, could do little more than form a large ripple, so much greater was the volume of water. In some places the crust of frozen snow made a bridge quite over the brook; so that you only knew it was there by its brawling sound beneath.

The sunsets of winter are incomparably splendid; and, when the ground is covered with snow, no brilliancy of tint, expressible by words, can come within an infinite distance of the effect. Our southern view, at that time, with the clouds and atmospherical hues, is quite indescribable and unimaginable; and the various distances of the hills, which lie between us and the remote Dome of Taconic, are brought out with an accuracy unattainable in summer. The transparency of the air, at this season, has the effect of a telescope, in bringing objects apparently near, while it leaves the scene all its breadth. The sunset sky, amidst its splendor, has a softness and delicacy, that impart themselves to a white-marble world.

May 23d.

I think the face of Nature can never look more beautiful than now, with this so fresh and youthful green: the trees not being fully leaved out, yet enough so to give airy shade to the woods. The sunshine fills them with green light. Monument Mountain and its brethren are green; and the lightness of the tint takes away something from their massiveness and ponderosity, and they respond with livelier effect to the shine and shade or the sky. Each tree now within sight stands out in its own individuality of hue. This is a very windy day (from the south-west, I believe) and the lights shift with magical alternation. In a walk to the lake, just now, with the children, we found abundance of flowers — wild geranium, violets of all families, red columbines, and many others, known and unknown; besides innumerable blossoms of the wild strawberry, which have been in bloom for a fortnight past. The housatonias seem quite to overspread some pastures, when viewed from a distance. Not merely the flowers, but the various shrubs which one sees, seated for instance on the decayed trunk of a tree, are well worth looking at; such a variety, and such enjoyment as they have of their new growth. Amid these new creations, we see others that have already run their course, and done with warmth and sunshine; — the hoary periwigs, I mean, of dandelions gone to seed.

The Julian Diaries

August 7, 1851.

I t has continued quite showery, through the afternoon. Just now, there was a very picturesque scene, if I could but paint it in words. Across our valley, from east to west, there was a heavy canopy of clouds, almost resting on the hills on either side. It did not extend southward so far as Monument Mountain, which lay in sunshine, and with a sunny cloud mid-way on its bosom; and from the midst of our storm, beneath our black roof of clouds, we looked out upon this bright scene, where the people were enjoying beautiful weather. The clouds hung so low over us, that it was like being in a tent, the entrance of which was drawn up, permitting us to see the sunny landscape. This lasted for several minutes; but at last the shower stretched southward, and quite snatched away Monument Mountain, and made it invisible; although now it is mistily re-appearing.

Julian has got rid of the afternoon in a miscellaneous way; making a whip, and a bow and arrow, and playing jack straws with himself for an antagonist. It was less than an hour, I think, after dinner, when he began to tease for something to eat; although he dined abundantly on rice and string-beans. I allowed him a slice of bread in the middle of the afternoon; and an hour afterwards, he began to bellow at the full stretch of his lungs for more, and beat me terribly, because I refused it. He is really as strong as a little giant. He asked me just now — "What are sensible questions?" — I suppose with a view to asking me some.

After the most rampageous resistance, the old gentleman was put to bed at seven o'clock. I ought to mention that Mrs Peters is quite attentive to him, in her grim way. To-day, for instance, we found two ribbons on his old straw hat, which must have been of her sewing on. She encourages no familiarity on his part, nor is he in the least drawn towards her, nor, on the other hand, does he exactly seem to stand in awe; but he recognizes that there is to be no communication beyond the inevitable — and, with that understanding, she awards him all substantial kindness. To bed not long after nine.

August 8th. Friday.

It was not much later than six when we got up. A pleasant morning, with a warm sun, and clouds lumbering about, especially to the north-ward and eastward; the relics of yesterday's showeriness, and perhaps foreboding similar weather today. When we went for the milk, Mrs. Butler told me that she could not let us have any more butter, at present; so that we must have recourse to Highwood. Before breakfast, the little man heard a cat mewing; and on investigation, we found that the noise proceeded from the cistern. I removed a plank, and, sure enough, there seemed to be a cat swimming for her life in it. Mrs. Peters heard her, last night; and probably she had been there ten or twelve hours, paddling in that dismal hole. After many efforts to get her out, I at last let down a bucket, into which she made shift to scramble, and so I drew her out. The poor thing was almost exhausted, and could scarcely crawl; and no wonder, after such a night as she must have spent. We gave her some milk, of which she lapped a little. It was one of the kittens.

Early in the forenoon, came Deborah with Ellen, to see Julian and Bunny. Julian was quite silent. Between eleven and twelve, came Herman Melville, and the two Duyckincks, in a barouche and pair. Melville had spoken, when he was here, of bringing these two expected guests of his to call on me; and I intended, should it be any wise practicable, to ask them to stay to dinner; but we had nothing whatever in the house to-day. It passed well enough, however; for they proposed a ride and a pic-nic, to which I readily consented. In the first place, however, I produced our only remaining bottle of Mr Mansfield's champagne; after which we set out, taking Julian, of course. It was an admirable day; neither too cold nor too hot — with some little shadow of clouds, but no appearance of impending rain. We took the road over the mountain toward Hudson, and by and by came to a pleasant grove, where we alighted and arranged matters for our pic-nic.

After all, I suspect they had considered the possibility, if not probability, of my giving them a dinner; for the repast was neither splendid nor particularly abundant — only some sandwiches and gingerbread. There was nothing whatever for Julian, except the gingerbread; for the bread, which encased the sandwiches, was buttered, and moreover had mustard on it. So I had to make the little man acquainted, for the first time in his life, with gingerbread; and he seemed to be greatly pleased until he had eaten a considerable quantity — when he began to discover that it was not quite the thing to make a meal of. However, his hunger was satisfied and no harm done; besides that there were a few nuts and raisins at the bottom of the basket, whereof he ate and was contented. He enjoyed the ride and the whole thing exceedingly, and behaved like a man experienced in pic-nics.

After talk about literature and other things, we set forth again, and resolved to go and visit the Shaker establishment at Hancock, which was but two or three miles off. I don't know what Julian expected to see — some strange sort of quadruped or other, I suppose — at any rate, the term Shakers was evidently a subject of great puzzlement with him; and probably he was a little disappointed when I pointed out an old man in a gown and a gray, broad-brimmed hat, as a Shaker. This old man was one of the fathers and rulers of the village; and under his guidance, we visited the principal dwelling-house in the village. It was a large brick edifice, with admirably convenient arrangements, and floors and walls of polished wood, and plaster as smooth as marble, and everything so neat that it was a pain and constraint to look at it; especially as it did not imply any real delicacy or moral purity in the occupants of the house. There were spit-boxes (bearing no appearance of ever being used, it is true) at equal distances up and down the long and broad entries. The sleeping apartments of the two sexes had an entry between them, on one side of which hung the hats of the men, on the other the bonnets of the women. In each chamber were two particularly narrow beds, hardly wide enough for one sleeper, but in each of which, the old elder told us, two people slept. There were no bathing or washing conveniences in the chambers; but in the entry there was a sink and wash-bowl, where all their attempts at purification were to be performed. The fact shows that all their miserable pretence of cleanliness and neatness is the thinnest superficiality; and that the Shakers are and must needs be a filthy set. And then their utter and systematic lack of privacy; the close function of man with man, and supervision of one man over another — it is hateful and disgusting to think of; and the sooner the sect is extinct the better — a consummation which, I am happy to hear, is thought to be not a great many years distant.

In the great house, we saw an old woman — a round, fat, cheerful little old sister — and two girls, from nine to twelve years old; these looked at us and at Julian with great curiosity, though slily and with side glances. At the doors of other dwellings, we saw women sewing or otherwise at work; and there seemed to be a kind of comfort among them, but of no higher kind than is enjoyed by their beasts of burden. Also, the women looked pale, and none of the men had a jolly aspect. They are certainly the most singular and bedevilled set of people that ever existed in a civilized land; and one of these days, when their sect and system shall have passed away, a History of the Shakers will be a very curious book. All through this outlandish village went our little man hopping and dancing in excellent spirits.

I think it was about five o'clock when we left the village. Lenox was probably seven or eight miles distant; but we mistook the road, and went up hill and down, through unknown regions, over at least twice as much ground as there was any need. It was by far the most picturesque ride that I ever had in Berkshire. On one height, just before sunset, we had a view for miles and miles around, with the Kaatskills blue and far on the horizon. Then the road ran along the verge of a deep gulf — deep, deep, deep, and filled with foliage of trees that could not reach half way up to us; and on the other side of the chasm up rose a mountainous precipice.

This continued for a good distance; and on the other side of the road there were occasional openings through the forest, that showed the low country at the base of the mountain. If I could find the way, I should like to go back to this scene on foot; for I had no idea that there was such a region within a few miles of us.

By and by, we saw Monument Mountain, and Rattlesnake hill, and all the familiar features of our own landscape, except the lake, which (by some witchcraft that I cannot possibly explain to myself) had utterly vanished. It appeared as if we ought to see the lake, and our little red-house, and Highwood; but none of these objects were discoverable, although the scene was certainly that of which they make a part. It was now after sunset; and we found that as we went we were approaching the village of Lenox from the west, and must pass through it before reaching home. I got out at the post office, and received, among other things, a letter from Phoebe. By the time we were out of the village, it was beyond twilight; indeed, but for the full moon, it would have been quite dark. The little man behaved himself still like an old traveller; but sometimes he looked round at me from the front seat (where he sat between Herman Melville and Evert Duyckinck), and smiled at me with a peculiar expression, and put back his hand to touch me. It was a method of establishing a sympathy in what doubtless appeared to him the wildest and unprecedentedest series of adventures that had ever befallen mortal travellers. Anon, we drew up at the little gate of the old red house.

Now, with many doubts as to the result, but constrained by the necessity of the case, I had asked the party to take tea and rest the horses, before returning to Pittsfield. I did not know but Mrs Peters would absolutely refuse to co-operate, at such an hour, and with such poor means as were at hand. However, she bestirred herself at once, like a colored angel as she is; and for my own part, I went over to Highwood, a humble suppliant for some loaf sugar and for whatever else Mrs Tappan should be pleased to bestow. She too showed herself angelically disposed, and gave me not only the sugar, but a pot of raspberry jam, and some little bread-cakes — an inestimable gift, inasmuch as our own bread was sour.

Immediately on our arrival, Julian had flung himself on the couch, without so much as taking off his hat, and fallen asleep. When I got back from Highwood, I found that Mrs Peters had already given him his supper, and that he was munching his final piece of bread. So I undressed him, and asked him, meanwhile, whether he had had a good time. But the naughty little man said, 'no'; whereas, until within the last half hour, never had he been happier in his life; but the bitter weariness had effaced the memory of all that enjoyment. I never saw such self-gratulation and contentment as that wherewith he stretched himself out in bed, and doubtless was asleep before I reached the foot of the stairs.

In a little while more, Mrs Peters had supper ready — no very splendid supper, but not nearly so meagre as it might have been. Tea, bread and butter, dropt eggs, little bread-cakes, raspberry jam; and I truly thanked Heaven, and Mrs Peters, that it was no worse! After tea, we had some pleasant conversation; and at ten o'clock the guests departed. I looked over one or two newspapers, and went to bed before eleven. It was a most beautiful night, with full, rich, cloudless moonlight, so that I would rather have ridden the six miles to Pittsfield, than have gone to bed.

The Red Cottage at Tanglewood. Courtesy of The Berkshire Eagle

THE G.P.R. JAMESES CALL

August 9th. Saturday.

Julian awoke in bright condition, this morning; and we arose at about seven. I felt the better for the expedition of yesterday; and asking Julian whether he had a good time, he answered with great enthusiasm in the affirmative, and that he wanted to go again, and that he loved Mr Melville as well as me, and as mamma, and as Una.

It being so fair and fine weather, last night, it followed as a matter of course that it should be showery, this morning; and so it was. The rain was pouring when we got up; and though it held up when I went for the milk, the atmosphere was very vaporish and juicy. From all the hill sides mists were steaming up, and Monument Mountain seemed to be enveloped as if in the smoke of a great battle. I kept Julian within doors till about eleven, when, the sun glimmering out, we went to the barn, and afterwards to the garden. The rest of the time, he had played at jack-straws, and ridden on his horse, and through all and above all, has deafened and confounded me with his interminable babble. I read him, in the course of the morning, a portion of his mother's letter that was addressed to himself; and he chuckled immeasurably.

We could not venture away from the house and its environment, on account of the weather; and so we got rid of the day as well as we could, within those precincts. I think I have hardly ever known Julian talk so incessantly as he has today; if I did not attend to him, he talked to himself. He has been in excellent spirits all the time.

Between four and five o'clock, came on one of the heaviest showers of the day; and in the midst of it there was a succession of thundering knocks at the front door. Julian and I ran as quickly as possible to see whom it might be; and on opening the door, there was a young man on the door-step, and a carriage at the gate, and Mr James thrusting his head out of the carriage window, and beseeching shelter from the storm! So here was an invasion. Mr. & Mrs. James, their oldest son, their daughter, their little son Charles, their maid-servant, and their coachman; — not that the coachman came in; and as for the maid, she staid in the hall. Dear me, where was Phoebe in this time of need! All taken aback as I was, I made the best of it. Julian helped me somewhat, but not much. Little Charlie is a few months younger than he, and between them, they at least furnished subject for remark. Mrs. James, luckily, seemed to be very much afraid of thunder and lightning; and as these were loud and sharp, she might be considered *hors de combat*. The son, who seemed to be about twenty, and the daughter, of seventeen or eighteen, took the part of saying nothing; which I suppose is the English fashion, as regards such striplings. So Mr. James was the only one to whom it was necessary to talk; and we got along tolerably well. He said that this was his birthday, and that he was keeping it by a pleasure-excursion, and that therefore the rain was a matter of course. We talked of periodicals, English and American, and of the Puritans, about whom we agreed pretty well in our opinions; and Mr. James told how he had been recently thrown out of his wagon, and how the horse ran away with Mrs James; — and we talked about green lizards and red ones. And Mr. James told Julian how, when he was a child, he had twelve owls at the same time, and, at another time, a raven, who used to steal silver spoons and money; he also mentioned a squirrel, and various other pets — and Julian laughed most obstreperously.

As to little Charlie, he was much interested with Bunny, and likewise with the rocking-horse, which luckily happened to be in the sitting-room.

He examined the horse most critically and asked a thousand questions about him, with a particularly distinct utterance, and not the slightest bashfulness; finally, he got upon the horse's back, but did not show himself quite so good a rider as Julian. Our old boy hardly said a word; indeed it could hardly be expected, on the first brunt of such an irruption as we were undergoing. Finally, the shower past over, and the invaders passed away; and I do hope, that, on the next occasion of the kind, my wife may be there to see.

Immediately on their departure, Mrs Peters brought in Julian's supper; being in a hurry to arrange matters and go home. It is now twenty minutes past six.

I spent a rather forlorn evening, and to bed at nine.

August 10th. Sunday.

Uprose we at not much after six. It was a particularly cool and northwest windy morning; and sullen and angry clouds were scattered about, especially to the northward. When we went for the milk, Luther Butler expressed his opinion that Indian corn would not do very well, this season. In fact, it hardly seems like a summer at all.

I got the breakfast, and the morning passed away without any incident, till about ten, when we set out for the lake. There the little man took an old branch of a tree, and set very earnestly to fishing. Such perseverance certainly does deserve a better reward than it is likely to meet with; although he seems to enjoy it, and always comes away without any apparent disappointment. Afterwards, we threw stones into the lake; and I lay on the bank, under the trees, and watched his little busyness — his never-wearying activity — as cheerful as the sun, and shedding a reflected cheer upon my sombreness. From the lake, we strolled upward, fighting mulleins and thistles, and I sat down on the edge of the tall pine wood. He finds so much to amuse him in every possible spot we light upon, that he always contends stoutly against a removal. After spending a little time here, we passed through the wood, to the field beyond, when he insisted that I should sit down on a great rock, and let him dig in the sand; and so I did. Here the old boy made little holes, and heaped up the sand, and imagined his constructions to be fairy houses; and I believe he would willingly have spent the rest of the day there, had I been as content as he. We came homeward by the cold spring, out of which we drank — and when we reached the house, it was after one.

From *American Notebooks*, 1850-1851.

Ethan Brand: A Chapter from an Abortive Romance

Bartram the lime-burner, a rough, heavy-looking man, begrimed with charcoal, sat watching his kiln at nightfall, while his little son played at building houses with the scattered fragments of marble, when, on the hillside below them, they heard a roar of laughter, not mirthful, but slow, and even solemn, like a wind shaking the boughs of the forest.

"Father, what is that?" asked the little boy, leaving his play, and pressing betwixt his father's knees.

"Oh, some drunken man, I suppose," answered the lime-burner, "some merry fellow from the barroom in the village, who dared not laugh loud enough within doors lest he should blow the roof of the house off. So here he is, shaking his jolly sides at the foot of Graylock."

"But, Father," said the child, more sensitive than the obtuse, middle-aged clown, "he does not laugh like a man that is glad. So the noise frightens me!"

"Don't be a fool, child!" cried his father, gruffly. "You will never make a man, I do believe; there is too much of your mother in you. I have known the rustling of a leaf startle you. Hark! Here comes the merry fellow now. You shall see that there is no harm in him."

Bartram and his little son, while they were talking thus, sat watching the same limekiln that had been the scene of Ethan Brand's solitary and meditative life, before he began his search for the Unpardonable Sin. Many years, as we have seen, had now elapsed, since that portentous night when the Idea was first developed. The kiln, however, on the mountainside, stood unimpaired, and was in nothing changed since he had thrown his dark thoughts into the intense glow of its furnace, and melted them, as it were, into the one thought that took possession of his life. It was a rude, round, tower-like structure about twenty feet high, heavily built of rough stones, and with a hillock of earth heaped about the larger part of its circumference; so that the blocks and fragments of marble might be drawn by cartloads, and thrown in at the top. There was an opening at the bottom of the tower, like an oven mouth, but large enough to admit a man in a stooping posture, and provided with a massive iron door. With the smoke and jets of flame issuing from the chinks and crevices of this door, which seemed to give admittance into the hillside, it resembled nothing so much as the private entrance to the infernal regions, which the shepherds of the Delectable Mountains were accustomed to show to pilgrims.

There are many such limekilns in that tract of country, for the purpose of burning the white marble which composes a large part of the substance of the hills. Some of them, built years ago, and long deserted, with weeds growing in the vacant round of the interior, which is open to the sky, and grass and wild flowers rooting themselves into the chinks of the stones, look already like relics of antiquity, and may yet be overspread with the lichens of centuries to come. Others, where the lime-burner still feeds his daily and nightlong fire, afford points of interest to the wanderer among the hills, who seats himself on a log of wood or a fragment of marble, to hold a chat with the solitary man. It is a lonesome, and, when the character is inclined to thought, may be an intensely thoughtful occupation; as it proved in the case of Ethan Brand, who had mused to such strange purpose, in days gone by, while the fire in this very kiln was burning.

The man who now watched the fire was of a different order, and troubled himself with no thoughts save the very few that were requisite to his business. At frequent intervals, he flung back the clashing weight of the iron door, and, turning his face from the insufferable glare, thrust in huge logs of oak, or stirred the immense brands with a long pole. Within the furnace were seen the curling and riotous flames, and the burning marble, almost molten with the intensity of heat; while without, the reflection of the fire quivered on the dark intricacy of the surrounding forest, and showed in the foreground a bright and ruddy little picture of the hut, the spring beside its door, the athletic and coal-begrimed figure of the lime-burner, and the half-frightened child, shrinking into the protection of his father's shadow. And when, again, the iron door was closed, then reappeared the tender light of the half-full moon, which vainly strove to trace out the indistinct shapes of the neighboring mountains; and, in the upper sky, there was a flitting congregation of clouds, still faintly tinged with the rosy sunset, though thus far down into the valley the sunshine had vanished long and long ago.

The little boy now crept still closer to his father, as footsteps were heard ascending the hillside, and a human form thrust aside the bushes that clustered beneath the trees.

"Halloo! who is it?" cried the lime-burner, vexed at his son's timidity, yet half infected by it. "Come forward, and show yourself, like a man, or I'll fling this chunk of marble at your head!"

"You offer me a rough welcome," said a gloomy voice, as the unknown man drew nigh. "Yet I neither claim nor desire a kinder one, even at my own fireside."

To obtain a distincter view, Bartram threw open the iron door of the kiln, whence immediately issued a gush of fierce light, that smote full upon the stranger's face and figure. To a careless eye, there appeared nothing very remarkable in his aspect, which was that of a man in a coarse, brown, country-made suit of clothes, tall and thin, with the staff and heavy shoes of a wayfarer. As he advanced, he fixed his eyes — which were very bright — intently upon the brightness of the furnace, as if he beheld, or expected to behold, some object worthy of note within.

"Good evening, stranger," said the lime-burner. "Whence come you, so late in the day?"

"I come from my search," answered the wayfarer, "for, at last, it is finished."

"Drunk! or crazy!" muttered Bartram to himself. "I shall have trouble with the fellow. The sooner I drive him away, the better."

The little boy, all in a tremble, whispered to his father, and begged him to shut the door of the kiln, so that there might not be so much light; for that there was something in the man's face which he was afraid to look at, yet could not look away from. And, indeed, even the lime-burner's dull and torpid sense began to be impressed by an indescribable something in that thin, rugged, thoughtful visage, with the grizzled hair hanging wildly about it, and those deeply sunken eyes, which gleamed like fires within the entrance of a mysterious cavern. But, as he closed the door, the stranger turned towards him, and spoke in a quiet, familiar way that made Bartram feel as if he were a sane and sensible man, after all.

"Your task draws to an end, I see," said he. "This marble has already been burning three days. A few hours more will convert the stone to lime."

"Why, who are you?" exclaimed the lime-burner. "You seem as well acquainted with my business as I am myself."

"And well I may be," said the stranger, "for I followed the same craft many a long year, and here, too, on this very spot. But you are a new-comer in these parts. Did you never hear of Ethan Brand?"

"The man that went in search of the Unpardonable Sin?" asked Bartram, with a laugh.

"The same," answered the stranger. "He has found what he sought, and therefore he comes back again."

"What! then you are Ethan Brand himself?" cried the lime-burner, in amazement. "I am a newcomer here, as you say, and they call it eighteen years since you left the foot of Graylock. But, I can tell you, the good folks still talk about Ethan Brand, in the village yonder, and what a strange errand took him away from his limekiln. Well, and so you have found the Unpardonable Sin?"

"Even so!" said the stranger, calmly.

"If the question is a fair one," proceeded Bartram, "where might it be?"

Ethan Brand laid his finger on his own heart.

"Here!" replied he.

And then, without mirth in his countenance, but as if moved by an involuntary recognition of the infinite absurdity of seeking throughout the world for what was the closest of all things to himself, and looking into every heart, save his own, for what was hidden in no other breast, he broke into a laugh of scorn. It was the same slow, heavy laugh that had almost appalled the lime-burner when it heralded the wayfarer's approach.

The solitary mountainside was made dismal by it. Laughter, when out of place, mistimed, or bursting forth from a disordered state of feeling may be the most terrible modulation of the human voice. The laughter of one asleep, even if it be a little child — the madman's laugh — the wild, screaming laugh of a born idiot — are sounds that we sometimes tremble to hear, and would always willingly forget. Poets have imagined no utterance of fiends or hobgoblins so fearfully appropriate as a laugh. And even the obtuse lime-burner felt his nerves shaken, as this strange man looked inward at his own heart, and burst into laughter that rolled away into the night, and was indistinctly reverberated among the hills.

"Joe," said he to his little son, "scamper down to the tavern in the village, and tell the jolly fellows there that Ethan Brand has come back, and that he has found the Unpardonable Sin!"

The boy darted away on his errand, to which Ethan Brand made no objection, nor seemed hardly to notice it. He sat on a log of wood, looking steadfastly at the iron door of the kiln. When the child was out of sight, and his swift and light footsteps ceased to be heard treading first on the fallen leaves and then on the rocky mountain path, the lime-burner began to regret his departure. He felt that the little fellow's presence had been a barrier between his guest and himself, and that he must now deal, heart to heart, with a man who, on his own confession, had committed the one only crime for which Heaven could afford no mercy. That crime, in its indistinct blackness, seemed to overshadow him. The lime-burner's own sins rose up within him, and made his memory riotous with a throng of evil shapes that asserted their kindred with the Master Sin, whatever it might be, which it was within the scope of man's corrupted nature to conceive and cherish. They were all of one family; they went to and fro between his breast and Ethan Brand's, and carried dark greetings from one to the other.

Then Bartram remembered the stories which had grown traditionary in reference to this strange man, who had come upon him like a shadow of the night, and was making himself at home in his old place, after so long absence that the dead people, dead and buried for years, would have had more right to be at home, in any familiar spot, than he. Ethan Brand, it was said, had conversed with Satan himself in the lurid blaze of this very kiln. The legend had been matter of mirth heretofore, but looked grisly now. According to this tale, before Ethan Brand departed on his search, he had been accustomed to evoke a fiend from the hot furnace of the limekiln, night after night, in order to confer with him about the Unpardonable Sin; the man and the fiend each laboring to frame the image of some mode of guilt which could neither be atoned for nor forgiven. And, with the first gleam of light upon the mountaintop, the fiend crept in at the iron door, there to abide the intensest element of fire until again summoned forth to share in the dreadful task of extending man's possible guilt beyond the scope of Heaven's else infinite mercy.

While the lime-burner was struggling with the horror of these thoughts, Ethan Brand rose from the log, and flung open the door of the kiln. The action was in such accordance with the idea in Bartram's mind, that he almost expected to see the Evil One issue forth, red hot, from the raging furnace.

"Hold! hold!" cried he, with a tremulous attempt to laugh; for he was ashamed of his fears, although they overmastered him. "Don't, for mercy's sake, bring out your Devil now!"

"Man!" sternly replied Ethan Brand, "what need have I of the Devil? I have left him behind me, on my track. It is with such halfway sinners as you that he busies himself. Fear not because I open the door. I do but act by old custom, and am going to trim your fire, like a lime-burner, as I was once."

He stirred the vast coals, thrust in more wood, and bent forward to gaze into the hollow prison house of the fire, regardless of the fierce glow that reddened upon his face. The lime-burner sat watching him, and half suspected this strange guest of a purpose, if not to evoke a fiend, at least to plunge bodily into the flames, and thus vanish from the sight of man. Ethan Brand, however, drew quietly back, and closed the door of the kiln.

"I have looked," said he, "into many a human heart that was seven times hotter with sinful passions than yonder furnace is with fire. But I found not there what I sought. No, not the Unpardonable Sin!"

"What is the Unpardonable Sin?" asked the lime-burner; and then he shrank farther from his companion, trembling lest his question should be answered.

"It is a sin that grew within my own breast," replied Ethan Brand, standing erect, with a pride that distinguishes all enthusiasts of his stamp. "A sin that grew nowhere else! The sin of an intellect that triumphed over the sense of brotherhood with man and reverence for God, and sacrificed everything to its own mighty claims! The only sin that deserves a recompense of immortal agony! Freely, were it to do again, would I incur the guilt. Unshrinkingly I accept the retribution!"

"The man's head is turned," muttered the lime-burner to himself. "He may be a sinner like the rest of us — nothing more likely — but, I'll be sworn, he is a madman, too "

Nevertheless, he felt uncomfortable at his situation, alone with Ethan Brand on the wild mountainside, and was right glad to hear the rough murmur of tongues, and the footsteps of what seemed a pretty numerous party, stumbling over the stones and rustling through the underbrush. Soon appeared the whole lazy regiment that was wont to infest the village tavern, comprehending three or four individuals who had drunk flip beside the barroom fire through all the winters, and smoked their pipes beneath the stoop through all the summers, since Ethan Brand's departure. Laughing boisterously, and mingling all their voices together in unceremonious talk, they now burst into the moonshine and narrow streaks of firelight that illuminated the open space before the limekiln. Bartram set the door ajar again, flooding the spot with light, that the whole company might get a fair view of Ethan Brand, and he of them.

There, among other old acquaintances, was a once ubiquitous man, now almost extinct, but whom we were formerly sure to encounter at the hotel of every thriving village throughout the country. It was the stage agent. The present specimen of the genus was a wilted and smoke-dried man, wrinkled and red-nosed, in a smartly cut, brown, bobtailed coat with brass buttons, who, for a length of time unknown, had kept his desk and corner in the barroom, and was still puffing what seemed to be the same cigar that he had lighted twenty years before. He had great fame as a dry joker, though, perhaps, less on account of any intrinsic humor than from a certain flavor of brandy toddy and tobacco smoke, which impreg-nated all his ideas and expressions, as well as his person. Another well remembered, though strangely altered, face was that of Lawyer Giles, as people still called him in courtesy; an elderly ragamuffin, in his soiled shirt sleeves and tow-cloth trousers. This poor fellow had been an attor-ney, in what he called his better days, a sharp practitioner, and in great vogue among the village litigants; but flip, and sling, and toddy, and cocktails, imbibed at all hours, morning, noon, and night, had caused him to slide from intellectual to various kinds and degrees of bodily labor, till at last, to adopt his own phrase, he slid into a soap vat. In other words, Giles was now a soap-boiler, in a small way. He had come to be but the fragment of a human being, a part of one foot having been chopped off by an ax, and an entire hand torn away by the devilish grip of a steam engine. Yet, though the corporeal hand was gone, a spiritual member remained; for, stretching forth the stump, Giles steadfastly averred that he felt an invisible thumb and fingers with as vivid a sensation as before the real ones were amputated. A maimed and miserable wretch he was;

but one, nevertheless, whom the world could not trample on, and had no right to scorn, either in this or any previous stage of his misfortunes, since he had still kept up the courage and spirit of a man, asked nothing in charity, and with his one hand — and that the left one — fought a stern battle against want and hostile circumstances.

Among the throng, too, came another personage, who, with certain points of similarity to Lawyer Giles, had many more of difference. It was the village doctor; a man of some fifty years, whom, at an earlier period of his life, we introduced as paying a professional visit to Ethan Brand during the latter's supposed insanity. He was now a purple-visaged, rude, and brutal, yet half-gentlemanly figure, with something wild, ruined, and desperate in his talk, and in all the details of his gesture and manners. Brandy possessed this man like an evil spirit, and made him as surly and savage as a wild beast, and as miserable as a lost soul; but there was supposed to be in him such wonderful skill, such native gifts of healing, beyond any which medical science could impart, that society caught hold of him, and would not let him sink out of its reach. So, swaying to and fro upon his horse, and grumbling thick accents at the bedside, he visited all the sick chambers for miles about among the mountain towns, and sometimes raised a dying man, as it were, by miracle, or quite as often, no doubt, sent his patient to a grave that was dug many a year too soon. The doctor had an everlasting pipe in his mouth, and, as somebody said, in allusion to his habit of swearing, it was always alight with hell-fire.

These three worthies pressed forward, and greeted Ethan Brand each after his own fashion, earnestly inviting him to partake of the contents of a certain black bottle, in which, as they averred, he would find something far better worth seeking for than the Unpardonable Sin. No mind, which has wrought itself by intense and solitary meditation into a high state of enthusiasm, can endure the kind of contact with low and vulgar modes of thought and feeling to which Ethan Brand was now subjected. It made him doubt — and, strange to say, it was a painful doubt — whether he had indeed found the Unpardonable Sin, and found it within himself. The whole question on which he had exhausted life, and more than life, looked like a delusion.

"Leave me," he said bitterly, "ye brute beasts, that have made yourselves so, shriveling up your souls with fiery liquors! I have done with you. Years and years ago, I groped into your hearts and found nothing there for my purpose. Get ye gone!"

"Why, you uncivil scoundrel," cried the fierce doctor, "is that the way you respond to the kindness of your best friends? Then let me tell you the truth. You have no more found the Unpardonable Sin than yonder boy

Joe has. You are but a crazy fellow — I told you so twenty years ago — neither better nor worse than a crazy fellow, and the fit companion of old Humphrey, here!"

He pointed to an old man, shabbily dressed, with long white hair, thin visage, and unsteady eyes. For some years past, this aged person had been wandering about among the hills, inquiring of all travelers whom he met for his daughter. The girl, it seemed, had gone off with a company of circus performers, and occasionally tidings of her came to the village, and fine stories were told of her glittering appearance as she rode on horseback in the ring, or performed marvelous feats on the tightrope.

The white-haired father now approached Ethan Brand, and gazed unsteadily into his face.

"They tell me you have been all over the earth," said he, wringing his hands with earnestness. "You must have seen my daughter, for she makes a grand figure in the world, and everybody goes to see her. Did she send any word to her old father, or say when she was coming back?"

Ethan Brand's eye quailed beneath the old man's. That daughter, from whom he so earnestly desired a word of greeting, was the Esther of our tale, the very girl whom, with such cold and remorseless purpose, Ethan Brand had made the subject of a psychological experiment, and wasted, absorbed, and perhaps annihilated her soul, in the process.

"Yes," murmured he, turning away from the hoary wanderer, "it is no delusion. There is an Unpardonable Sin!"

While these things were passing, a merry scene was going forward in the area of cheerful light, beside the spring and before the door of the hut. A number of the youth of the village, young men and girls, had hurried up the hillside, impelled by curiosity to see Ethan Brand, the hero of so many a legend familiar to their childhood. Finding nothing, however, very remarkable in his aspect — nothing but a sunburnt wayfarer, in plain garb and dusty shoes, who sat looking into the fire as if he fancied pictures among the coals — these young people speedily grew tired of observing him. As it happened, there was other amusement at hand. An old German Jew traveling with a diorama on his back was passing down the mountain road towards the village just as the party turned aside from it, and, in hopes of eking out the profits of the day, the showman had kept them company to the limekiln.

"Come, old Dutchman," cried one of the young men, "let us see your pictures, if you can swear they are worth looking at!"

"Oh, yes, Captain," answered the Jew — whether as a matter of courtesy or craft, he styled everybody Captain — "I shall show you, indeed, some very superb pictures!"

So, placing his box in a proper position, he invited the young men and girls to look through the glass orifices of the machine, and proceeded to exhibit a series of the most outrageous scratchings and daubings, as specimens of the fine arts, that ever an itinerant showman had the face to impose upon his circle of spectators. The pictures were worn out, moreover, tattered, full of cracks and wrinkles, dingy with tobacco smoke, and otherwise in a most pitiable condition. Some purported to be cities, public edifices, and ruined castles in Europe; others represented Napoleon's battles and Nelson's sea fights; and in the midst of these would be seen a gigantic, brown, hairy hand — which might have been mistaken for the Hand of Destiny, though, in truth, it was only the showman's — pointing its forefinger to various scenes of the conflict, while its owner gave historical illustrations. When, with much merriment at its abominable deficiency of merit, the exhibition was concluded, the German bade little Joe put his head into the box. Viewed through the magnifying glasses, the boy's round, rosy visage assumed the strangest imaginable aspect of an immense Titanic child, the mouth grinning broadly, and the eyes and every other feature overflowing with fun at the joke. Suddenly, however, that merry face turned pale, and its expression changed to horror, for this easily impressed and excitable child had become sensible that the eye of Ethan Brand was fixed upon him through the glass.

"You make the little man to be afraid, Captain," said the German Jew, turning up the dark and strong outline of his visage from his stooping posture. "But look again, and, by chance, I shall cause you to see somewhat that is very fine, upon my word!"

Ethan Brand gazed into the box for an instant, and then, starting back, looked fixedly at the German. What had he seen? Nothing, apparently; for a curious youth, who had peeped in almost at the same moment, beheld only a vacant space of canvas.

"I remember you now," muttered Ethan Brand to the showman.

"Ah, Captain," whispered the Jew of Nuremberg, with a dark smile, "I find it to be a heavy matter in my show box, this Unpardonable Sin! By my faith, Captain, it has wearied my shoulders, this long day, to carry it over the mountain."

"Peace," answered Ethan Brand, sternly, "or get thee into the furnace yonder!"

The Jew's exhibition had scarcely concluded, when a great, elderly dog — who seemed to be his own master, as no person in the company laid claim to him — saw fit to render himself the object of public notice. Hitherto, he had shown himself a very quiet, well-disposed old dog, going round from one to another, and, by way of being sociable, offering his rough head to be patted by any kindly hand that would take so much trouble. But now, all of a sudden, this grave and venerable quadruped, of his own mere motion, and without the slightest suggestion from anybody else, began to run round after his tail, which, to heighten the absurdity of the proceeding, was a great deal shorter than it should have been. Never was seen such headlong eagerness in pursuit of an object that could not possibly be attained, never was heard such a tremendous outbreak of growling, snarling, barking, and snapping — as if one end of the ridiculous brute's body were at deadly and most unforgivable enmity with the other. Faster and faster, round about went the cur; and faster and still faster fled the unapproachable brevity of his tail; and louder and fiercer grew his yells of rage and animosity; until, utterly exhausted, and as far from the goal as ever, the foolish old dog ceased his performance as suddenly as he had begun it. The next moment, he was as mild, quiet, sensible, and respectable in his deportment as when he first scraped acquaintance with the company.

As may be supposed, the exhibition was greeted with universal laughter, clapping of hands, and shouts of encore, to which the canine performer responded by wagging all that there was to wag of his tail, but appeared totally unable to repeat his very successful effort to amuse the spectators.

Meanwhile, Ethan Brand had resumed his seat upon the log, and moved, it might be, by a perception of some remote analogy between his own case and that of this self-pursuing cur, he broke into the awful laugh which, more than any other token, expressed the condition of his inward being. From that moment, the merriment of the party was at an end; they stood aghast, dreading lest the inauspicious sound should be reverberated around the horizon, and that mountain would thunder it to mountain, and so the horror be prolonged upon their ears. Then, whispering one to another that it was late — that the moon was almost down — that the August night was growing chill — they hurried homewards, leaving the lime-burner and little Joe to deal as they might with their unwelcome guest. Save for these three human beings, the open space on the hillside was a solitude, set in a vast gloom of forest. Beyond that darksome verge, the firelight glimmered on the stately trunks and almost black foliage of pines, intermixed with the lighter verdure of sapling oaks, maples, and poplars, while here and there lay the gigantic corpses of dead trees, decaying on the leaf-strewn soil. And it seemed to little Joe — a timorous and imaginative child — that the silent forest was holding its breath until some fearful thing should happen.

Ethan Brand thrust more wood into the fire, and closed the door of the kiln; then, looking over his shoulder at the lime-burner and his son, he bade rather than advised them to retire to rest.

"For myself, I cannot sleep," said he. "I have matters that it concerns me to meditate upon. I will watch the fire, as I used to do in the old time."

"And call the Devil out of the furnace to keep you company, I suppose," muttered Bartram, who had been making intimate acquaintance with the black bottle above mentioned. "But watch, if you like, and call as many devils as you like! For my part, I shall be all the better for a snooze. Come, Joe!"

As the boy followed his father into the hut, he looked back at the wayfarer, and the tears came into his eyes, for his tender spirit had an intuition of the bleak and terrible loneliness in which this man had enveloped himself.

When they had gone, Ethan Brand sat listening to the crackling of the kindled wood, and looking at the little spirits of fire that issued through the chinks of the door. These trifles, however, once so familiar, had but the slightest hold of his attention, while deep within his mind he was reviewing the gradual but marvelous change that had been wrought upon him by the search to which he had devoted himself. He remembered how the night dew had fallen upon him — how the dark forest had whispered to him — how the stars had gleamed upon him — a simple and loving man, watching his fire in the years gone by, and ever musing as it burned. He remembered with what tenderness, with what love and sympathy for mankind, and what pity for human guilt and woe, he had first begun to contemplate those ideas which afterwards became the inspiration of his life; with what reverence he had then looked into the heart of man, viewing it as a temple originally divine, and, however desecrated, still to be held sacred by a brother; with what awful fear he had deprecated the success of his pursuit, and prayed that the Unpardonable Sin might never be revealed to him. Then ensued that vast intellectual development, which, in its progress, disturbed the counterpoise between his mind and heart. The Idea that possessed his life had operated as a means of education; it had gone on cultivating his powers to the highest point of which they were susceptible; it had raised him from the level of an unlettered laborer to stand on a starlit eminence, whither the philosophers of the earth, laden with the lore of universities, might vainly strive to clamber after him. So much for the intellect! But where was the heart? That, indeed, had withered — had contracted — had hardened — had perished! It had ceased to partake of the universal throb. He had lost his hold of the magnetic chain of humanity. He was no longer a brother man, opening the chambers or the dungeons of our common nature by the key of holy sympathy, which give him a right to share in all its secrets; he was now a cold observer, looking on mankind as the subject of his experiment, and, at length, converting man and woman to be his puppets, and pulling the wires that moved them to such degrees of crime as were demanded for his study.

Thus Ethan Brand became a fiend. He began to be so from the moment that his moral nature had ceased to keep the pace of improvement with his intellect. And now, as his highest effort and inevitable development — as the bright and gorgeous flower, and rich, delicious fruit of his life's labor — he had produced the Unpardonable Sin!

"What more have I to seek? what more to achieve?" said Ethan Brand to himself. "My task is done, and well done!"

Starting from the log with a certain alacrity in his gait and ascending the hillock of earth that was raised against the stone circumference of the limekiln, he thus reached the top of the structure. It was a space of perhaps ten feet across, from edge to edge, presenting a view of the upper surface of the immense mass of broken marble with which the kiln was heaped. All these innumerable blocks and fragments of marble were red hot and vividly on fire, sending up great spouts of blue flame, which quivered aloft and danced madly, as within a magic circle, and sank and rose again, with continual and multitudinous activity. As the lonely man bent forward over this terrible body of fire, the blasting heat smote up against his person with a breath that, it might be supposed, would have scorched and shriveled him up in a moment.

Ethan Brand stood erect, and raised his arms on high. The blue flames played upon his face, and imparted the wild and ghastly light which alone could have suited its expression; it was that of a fiend on the verge of plunging into his gulf of intensest torment.

"O Mother Earth," cried he, "who art no more my mother, and into whose bosom this frame shall never be resolved! O mankind, whose brotherhood I have cast off, and trampled thy great heart beneath my feet! O stars of heaven, that shone on me of old, as if to light me onward and upward! Farewell all, and forever. Come, deadly element of Fire, henceforth my familiar friend! Embrace me, as I do thee!"

That night the sound of a fearful peal of laughter rolled heavily through the sleep of the lime-burner and his little son; dim shapes of horror and anguish haunted their dreams, and seemed still present in the rude hovel when they opened their eyes to the daylight.

"Up, boy, up!" cried the lime-burner, staring about him. "Thank Heaven, the night is gone, at last; and rather than pass such another, I would watch my limekiln, wide awake, for a twelvemonth. This Ethan Brand, with his humbug of an Unpardonable Sin, has done me no such mighty favor, in taking my place!"

He issued from the hut, followed by little Joe, who kept fast hold of his father's hand. The early sunshine was already pouring its gold upon the mountaintops, and though the valleys were still in shadow, they smiled cheerfully in the promise of the bright day that was hastening onward. The village, completely shut in by hills, which swelled away gently about it, looked as if it had rested peacefully in the hollow of the great hand of Providence. Every dwelling was distinctly visible; the little spires of the two churches pointed upwards, and caught a fore-glimmering of brightness from the sun-gilt skies upon their gilded weathercocks. The tavern was astir, and the figure of the old, smoke-dried stage agent, cigar in mouth, was seen beneath the stoop. Old Graylock was glorified with a golden cloud upon his head. Scattered likewise over the breasts of the surrounding mountains, there were heaps of hoary mist, in fantastic shapes, some of them far down into the valley, others high up towards the summits, and still others, of the same family of mist or cloud, hovering in the gold radiance of the upper atmosphere. Stepping from one to another of the clouds that rested on the hills, and thence to the loftier brotherhood that sailed in air, it seemed almost as if a mortal man might thus ascend into the heavenly regions. Earth was so mingled with sky that it was a daydream to look at it.

To supply that charm of the familiar and homely, which Nature so readily adopts into a scene like this, the stagecoach was rattling down the mountain road, and the driver sounded his horn, while Echo caught up the notes, and intertwined them into a rich and varied and elaborate harmony, of which the original performer could lay claim to little share. The great hills played a concert among themselves, each contributing a strain of airy sweetness.

Little Joe's face brightened at once.

"Dear Father," cried he, skipping cheerily to and fro, "that strange man is gone, and the sky and the mountains all seem glad of it!"

"Yes," growled the lime-burner, with an oath, "but he has let the fire go down, and no thanks to him if five hundred bushels of lime are not spoiled. If I catch the fellow hereabouts again, I shall feel like tossing him into the furnace!"

With his long pole in his hand, he ascended to the top of the kiln. After a moment's pause, he called to his son.

"Come up here, Joe!" said he.

So little Joe ran up the hillock, and stood by his father's side. The marble was all burnt into perfect, snow-white lime. But on its surface, in the midst of the circle — snow white, too, and thoroughly converted into lime — lay a human skeleton, in the attitude of a person who, after long toil, lies down to long repose. Within the ribs — strange to say — was the shape of a human heart.

"Was the fellow's heart made of marble?" cried Bartram, in some perplexity at this phenomenon. "At any rate, it is burnt into what looks like special good lime; and, taking all the bones together, my kiln is half a bushel the richer for him."

So saying, the rude lime-burner lifted his pole, and, letting it fall upon the skeleton, the relics of Ethan Brand were crumbled into fragments.

Written in 1847. First published in the "Boston Weekly Museum," January 1850.

HERMAN MELVILLE

It is often overlooked that Melville, who turned 18 in the midst of the 1837 crash, took to writing because he could not find remunerative employment in the long-drawn-out depression that ensued. And easily forgotten, too, is the fact that all of his fiction, with the exception of Billy Budd, *appeared within 11 years, between 1846 and 1857. He kept up an exhaustingly intense creative pace.*

The Melvilles moved to Pittsfield from New York City in 1850 to live cheaply and to have the space and quiet writing at such a rate needed. Through visits to his uncle Thomas Melvill, Melville had been acquainted with Pittsfield from boyhood, and had even taught for a term in the Sykes District School (now disappeared) at the foot of Washington Mountain. His Berkshire friendship with Hawthorne coincided with his seeing new possibilities for Moby Dick, *which he had brought from New York almost finished (or so he thought); re-writing it occupied his first year at Arrowhead. He dedicated it to Hawthorne. The first chapter of* Israel Potter *(1855) evidences Melville's perceptive explo-ration of the Berkshire countryside, just as "Cock-a-Doodle-Doo!" — in which story he gave October Mountain its name — evidences his unconventional grasp of religious faith as an affirmation of the goodness of life (cf. Bonhoffer's later observation that "one who has been baptized already has death behind him.")*

The "College Colonel" was Colonel (later General) William Francis Bartlett, who left Harvard as a junior to take a commission in the 20th Massa-chusetts Infantry. He lost a leg at Yorktown and endured imprisonment in Libby Prison. Melville saw him parade the 49th Infantry, a Berkshire regiment which he had commanded in Louisiana, through Pittsfield on Saturday, August 22, 1863.

Lake Pontoosuc, with Greylock rising in the distance, lies at the north end of Pittsfield. In the dedication of "Weeds and Wildings" to his wife — in his copy Melville crossed out "Winnefred" and pencilled in "Lizzie" — he recalls, back in New York City, their days at Arrowhead.

Selected Letters

TEACHING SCHOOL

Pittsfield Dec 31st 1837

My Dear Uncle [Peter Gansevoort]

At my departure from Albany last fall with Robert you expressed a desire that I should write you when my school should have gone into operation.

I should have taken up my pen at an earlier day had not the variety &

importance of the duties incident to my vocation been so numerous and pressing, that they absorbed a large portion of my time.

But now, having become somewhat acquainted with the routine of business, — having established a systim in my mode of instruction, — and being familiar with the charactars & dispositions of my schollars: in short, having brought my school under a proper organization — a few intervals of time are afforded me, which I improve by occasional writting & reading.

My scholars are about thirty in number, of all ages, sizes, ranks, charaterrs, & education; some of them who have attained the ages of eighteen can not do a sum in addition, while others have travelled through the Arithmatic: but with so great swiftness that they can not recognize objects in the road on a second journey: & are about as ignorant of them as though they had never passed that way before.

My school is situated in a remote & secluded part of the town about five miles from the village, and the house at which I am now boarding is a mile and a half from any other tenement whatever — being located on the summit of as savage and lonely a mountain as ever I ascended. The scenery however is most splendid & unusual, — embracing an extent of country in the form of an Amphitheatre sweeping around for many miles & encircling a portion of your state in its compass.

The man with whom I am now domicilated is a perfect embodiment of the traits of Yankee character, — being shrewd bold & independant, carrying himself with a genuine republican swagger, as hospitable as "mine host" himself, perfectly free in the expression of his sentiments, and would as soon call you a fool or a scoundrel, if he thought so — as, button up his waistcoat. — He has reared a family of nine boys and three girls, 5 of whom are my pupils — and they all burrow together in the woods — like so many foxes.

The books you presented me (and for which I am very gratefull) I have found of eminent usefulness, particularly John O Taylors "Dristict School" — an admirable production by the by, which if generally read is calculated to exert a powerful influence and one of the most salutary & beneficial charactar.—

I have given his work a diligent and attentive perusal: and am studying it, to the same advantage, — which a scholar traveling in a country — peruses its hystory, — being surrounded by the scenes it describes.

I think he has treated his theme in a masterly manner, and displays that thourough knowledge of his subject — which is only to be obtained by Experience.

Had he been perfectly familiar with the circumstances of this school, — the difficultys under which it labours, and in short with every thing pertaining to it, — he could not have sketched it in a more graphic manner, than he has, in his description of the style in which schools of this species are genneraly conducted.

Intimatly am I acquainted with the prevalence of those evils which he alledges to exist in Common-Schools.

Orators may declaim concerning the universally-diffused blessings of education in our Country, and Essayests may exhaust their magazine of adjectives in extolling our systim of Common School instruction, — but when reduced to practise, the high and sanguine hopes excited by its imposing appearance in *theory* — are a little dashed. —

My Taylor has freely pointed out its defects, and has not been deterred from reproving them by any feelings of delicacy. — If he had, he would have proved a traitor to the great cause, in which he is engaged. — But I have almost usurped the province of the Edinburgh Review — so as I am approaching the confines of my sheet I will subscribe myself

> Your affectionate nephew
> Herman Melville

My love to Aunt Mary, & a kiss to Henry — Remember me to Uncle Herman

"DOLLARS DAMN ME"

Pittsfield June 1851

My Dear Hawthorne, — I should have been rumbling down to you in my pine-board chariot a long time ago, were it not that for some weeks past I have been more busy than you can well imagine, — out of doors, — building and patching and tinkering away in all directions. Besides, I had my crops to get in, — corn and potatoes (I hope to show you some famous ones by and by), — and many other things to attend to, all accumulating upon this one particular season. I work myself; and at night my bodily sensations are akin to those I have so often felt before, when a hired man, doing my day's work from sun to sun. But I mean to continue visiting you until you tell me that my visits are both supererogatory and superfluous. With no son of man do I stand upon any etiquette or ceremony, except the Christian ones of charity and honesty. I am told, my fellow-man, that there is an aristocracy of the brain. Some men have boldly advocated and asserted it. Schiller seems to have done so, though I don't know much about him. At any rate, it is true that there have been those who, while earnest in behalf of the political equality, still accept the intellectual estates. And I can well perceive, I think, how a man of superior mind can, by its intense cultivation, bring himself, as it were, into a certain spontaneous aristocracy of feeling, — exceedingly nice and fastidious, — similar to that which, in an English Howard, conveys a torpedo-fish thrill at the slightest contact with a social plebeian. So, when you see or hear of my ruthless democracy on all sides, you may possibly feel a touch of a shrink, or something of that sort. It is but nature to be shy of a mortal who boldly declares that a thief in jail is as honorable a personage as Gen. George Washington. This is ludicrous. But Truth is the silliest thing under the sun. Try to get a living by the Truth — and go to the Soup Societies. Heavens! Let any clergyman try to preach the Truth from its very strong-hold, the pulpit bannister. It can hardly be doubted that all Reformers are bottomed upon the truth, more or less; and to the world at large are not reformers almost universally laughing-stocks? Why so? Truth is ridiculous to men. Thus easily in my room here do I, conceited and garrulous, reverse the test of my Lord Shaftesbury.

It seems an inconsistency to assert unconditional democracy in all things, and yet confess a dislike to all mankind — in the mass. But not so. — But it's an endless sermon, — no more of it. I began by saying that the reason I have not been to Lenox is this, — in the evening I feel completely done up, as the phrase is, and incapable of the long jolting to get to your house and back. In a week or so, I go to New York, to bury myself in a third-story room, and work and slave on my "Whale" while it is driving through the press. *That* is the only way I can finish it now, — I am so pulled hither and thither by circumstances. The calm, the coolness, the silent grass-growing mood in which a man *ought* always to compose, — that, I fear, can seldom be mine. Dollars damn me; and the malicious Devil is forever grinning in upon me, holding the door ajar. My dear Sir, a presentiment is on me, — I shall at last be worn out and perish, like an old nutmeg-grater, grated to pieces by the constant attrition of the wood, that is, the nutmeg. What I feel most moved to write, that is banned, — it will not pay. Yet, altogether, write the *other* way I cannot. So the product is a final hash, and all my books are botches. I'm rather sore, perhaps, in this letter; but see my hand! — four blisters on this palm, made by hoes and hammers within the last few days. It is a rainy morning; so I am indoors, and all work suspended. I feel cheerfully disposed, and therefore I write a little bluely. Would the Gin were here! If ever, my dear Hawthorne, in the eternal times that are to come, you and I shall sit down in Paradise, in some little shady corner by ourselves; and if we shall by any means be able to smuggle a basket of champagne there (I won't believe in a Temperance Heaven), and if we shall then cross our celestial legs in the celestial grass that is forever tropical, and strike our glasses and our heads together, till both musically ring in concert, — then, O my dear fellow-mortal, how shall we pleasantly discourse of all the things manifold which now so distress us, — when all the earth shall be but a reminis-

cence, yea, its final dissolution an antiquity. Then shall songs be composed as when wars are over; humorous, comic songs, — "Oh, when I
lived in that queer little hole called the world," or, "Oh, when I toiled and
sweated below," or, "Oh, when I knocked and was knocked in the fight"
— yes, let us look forward to such things. Let us swear that, though now
we sweat, yet it is because of the dry heat which is indispensable to the
nourishment of the vine which is to bear the grapes that are to give us the
champagne hereafter.

But I was talking about the "Whale." As the fishermen say, "he's in
his flurry" when I left him some three weeks ago. I'm going to take him
by his jaw, however, before long, and finish him up in some fashion or
other. What's the use of elaborating what, in its very essence, is so short-
lived as a modern book? Though I wrote the Gospels in this century, I
should die in the gutter. — I talk all about myself, and this is selfishness
and egotism. Granted. But how help it? I am writing to you; I know little
about you, but something about myself. So I write about myself, — at
least, to you. Don't trouble yourself, though, about writing; and don't
trouble yourself about visiting; and when you do visit, don't trouble
yourself about talking. I will do all the writing and visiting and talking
myself. — By the way, in the last "Dollar Magazine" I read "The
Unpardonable Sin." He was a sad fellow, that Ethan Brand. I have no
doubt you are by this time responsible for many a shake and tremor of the
tribe of "general readers." It is a frightful poetical creed that the cultivation of the brain eats out the heart. But it's my *prose* opinion that is most
cases, in those men who have fine brains and work them well, the heart
extends down to hams. And though you smoke them with the fire of
tribulation, yet like veritable hams, the head only gives the richer and the
better flavor. I stand for the heart. To the dogs with the head! I had rather
be a fool with a heart, than Jupiter Olympus with his head. The reason the
mass of men fear God, and *at bottom dislike* Him, is because they rather
distrust His heart, and fancy Him all brain like a watch. (You perceive I
employ a capital initial in the pronoun referring to the Deity; don't you
think there is a slight dash of flunkeyism in that usage?) Another thing. I
was in New York for four-and-twenty hours the other day, and saw a
portrait of N.H. And I have seen and heard many flattering (in a publisher's
point of view) allusions to the "Seven Gables." And I have seen "Tales,"
and "A New Volume" announced, by N.H. So upon the whole, I say to
myself, this N.H. is in the ascendant. My dear Sir, they begin to patronize.
All Fame is patronage. Let me be infamous: there is no patronage in that.

What "reputation" H.M. has is horrible. Think of it! To go down to
posterity is bad enough, any way; but to go down as a "man who lived
among the cannibals"! When I speak of posterity, in reference to myself, I

Portrait of Melville at age 29, painted c. 1847-48 by Asa W. Twitchell of Albany.
The Berkshire Athenaeum, Local History Department; photo by Clemens Kalischer

only mean the babies who will probably be born in the moment immediately ensuing upon my giving up the ghost. I shall go down to some of them, in all likelihood. "Typee" will be given to them, perhaps, with their gingerbread. I have come to regard this matter of Fame as the most transparent of all vanities. I read Solomon more and more, and every time see deeper and deeper and unspeakable meanings in him. I did not think of Fame, a year ago, as I do now. My development has been all within a few past. I am like one of those seeds taken out of the Egyptian Pyramids, which, after being three thousand years a seed and nothing but a seed, being planted in English soil, it developed itself, grew to greenness, and then fell to mould. So I. Until I was twenty-five, I had no development at all. From my twenty-fifth year I date my life. Three weeks have scarcely passed, at any time between then and now, that I have not unfolded within myself. But I feel that I am now come to the inmost leaf of the bulb, and that shortly the flower must fall to the mould. It seems to me now that Solomon was the truest man who ever spoke, and yet that he a little *managed* the truth with a view to popular conservatism; or else there have been many corruptions and interpolations of the text. — In reading some of Goethe's sayings, so worshipped by votaries, I came across this, *"Live in the all."* That is to say, your separate identity is but a wretched one, — good; but get out of yourself, spread and expand yourself, and bring to yourself the tinglings of life that are felt in the flowers and the woods, that are felt in the planets Saturn and Venus, and the Fixed Stars. What nonsense! Here is a fellow with a raging toothache. "My dear boy," Goethe says to him, "you are sorely afflicted with that tooth; but you must *live in the all*, and then you will be happy!" As with all great genius, there is an immense deal of flummery in Goethe, and in proportion to my own contact with him, a monstrous deal of it in me.

H. Melville.

P.S. "Amen!" saith Hawthorne.

N.B. This "all" feeling, though, there is some truth in. You must often have felt it, lying on the grass on a warm summer's day. Your legs seem to send out shoots into the earth. Your hair feels like leaves upon your head. This is the *all* feeling. But what plays the mischief with the truth is that men will insist upon the universal application of a temporary feeling or opinion.

P.S. You must not fail to admire my discretion in paying the postage on this letter.

"NOT A LETTER"

Pittsfield 22 July 1851, Tuesday afternoon.

My dear Hawthorne:

This is not a letter, or even a note — but only a passing word said to you over your garden gate. I thank you for your easy-flowing long letter (received yesterday) which flowed through me, and refreshed all my meadows, as the Housatonic — opposite me — does in reality. I am now busy with various things — not incessantly though; but enough to require my frequent tinkerings; and this is the height of the haying season, and my nag is dragging me home his winter's dinners all the time. And so, one way and another, I am not yet a disengaged man; but shall be, very soon. Meantime, the earliest good chance I get, I shall roll down to you, my good fellow, seeing we — that is, you and I — must hit upon some little bit of vagabondism, before Autumn comes. Graylock — we must go and vagabondize there. But ere we start, we must dig a deep hole, and bury all Blue Devils, there to abide till the Last Day.

    Goodbye,

    his x mark.

From *Letters of Herman Melville*. Edited by Merrill Davis and William Gilman. Yale University Press, 1960.

North From Otis

The traveller who at the present day is content to travel in the good old Asiatic style, neither rushed along by a locomotive, nor dragged by a stage-coach; who is willing to enjoy hospitalities at far-scattered farm-houses, instead of paying his bill at an inn; who is not to be frightened by any amount of loneliness, or to be deterred by the roughest roads or the highest hills; such a traveller in the eastern part of Berkshire, Massachusetts, will find ample food for poetic reflection in the singular scenery of a country, which, owing to the ruggedness of the soil and its lying out of the track of all public conveyances, remains almost as unknown to the general tourist as the interior of Bohemia.

Travelling northward from the township of Otis, the road leads for twenty or thirty miles toward Windsor, lengthwise upon that long broken spur of heights which the Green Mountains of Vermont send into Massachusetts. For nearly the whole of the distance you have the continual sensation of being upon some terrace in the moon. The feeling of the plain or the valley is never yours; scarcely the feeling of the earth. Unless by a sudden precipitation of the road you find yourself plunging into some gorge, you pass on, and on, and on, upon the crests or slopes of pastoral mountains, while far below, mapped out in its beauty, the valley of the Housatonic lies endlessly along at your feet. Often, as your horse gaining some lofty level tract, flat as a table, trots gaily over the almost deserted and sodded road, and your admiring eye sweeps the broad landscape beneath, you seem to be Boötes driving in heaven. Save a potato field here and there, at long intervals, the whole country is either in wood or pasture. Horses, cattle, and sheep are the principal inhabitants of these mountains. But all through the year lazy columns of smoke, rising from the depths of the forest, proclaim the presence of that half-outlaw, the charcoal-burner; while in early spring added curls of vapour show that the maple sugar-boiler is also at work. But as for farming as a regular vocation, there is not much of it here. At any rate, no man by that means accumulates a fortune from this thin and rocky soil, all whose arable parts have long since been nearly exhausted.

Yet during the first settlement of the country, the region was not unproductive. Here it was that the original settlers came, acting upon the principle well known to have regulated their choice of site, namely, the high land in preference to the low, as less subject to the unwholesome miasmas generated by breaking into the rich valleys and alluvial bottoms of primeval regions. By degrees, however, they quitted the safety of this sterile elevation, to brave the dangers of richer though lower fields. So that, at the present day, some of those mountain townships present an aspect of singular abandonment. Though they have never known aught but peace and health, they, in one lesser aspect at least, look like countries depopulated by plague and war. Every mile or two a house is passed untenanted. The strength of the frame-work of these ancient buildings enables them long to resist the encroachments of decay. Spotted gray and green with the weather-stain, their timbers seem to have lapsed back into their woodland original, forming part now of the general picturesqueness of the natural scene. They are of extraordinary size compared with modern farm-houses. One peculiar feature is the immense chimney, of a light gray stone, perforating the middle of the roof like a tower.

On all sides are seen the tokens of ancient industry. As stone abounds throughout these mountains, that material was, for fences, as ready to the hand as wood, besides being much more durable. Consequently the landscape is intersected in all directions with walls of uncommon neatness and strength.

The number and length of these walls is not more surprising than the size of some of the blocks comprising them. The very Titans seemed to have been at work. That so small an army as the first settlers must needs have been, should have taken such wonderful pains to enclose so ungrateful a soil; that they should have accomplished such herculean undertakings with so slight prospect of reward; this is a consideration which gives us a significant hint of the temper of the men of the revolutionary era.

Nor could a fitter country be found for the birthplace of the devoted patriot, Israel Potter.

To this day the best stone-wall builders, as the best wood-choppers, come from those solitary mountain towns; a tall, athletic, and hardy race, unerring with the axe as the Indian with the tomahawk; at stone-rolling, patient as Sisyphus, powerful as Samson.

In fine clear June days the bloom of these mountains is beyond expression delightful. Last visiting these heights ere she vanishes, spring, like the sunset, flings her sweetest charms upon them. Each tuft of upland grass is musked like a bouquet with perfume. The balmy breeze swings to and fro like a censer. On one side the eye follows for the space of an eagle's flight, the serpentine mountain chains, southward from the great purple dome of Taconic — the St. Peter's of these hills — northward to the twin summits of Saddleback, which is the two-steepled natural cathedral of Berkshire; while low down to the west the Housatonic winds on in her watery labyrinth, through charming meadows basking in the reflected rays from the hillsides. At this season the beauty of everything around you populates the loneliness of your way. You would not have the country more settled if you could. Content to drink in such loveliness at all your senses, the heart desires no company but Nature.

With what rapture you behold, hovering over some vast hollow of the hills, or slowly drifting at an immense height over the far sunken Housatonic valley, some lordly eagle, who in unshared exaltation looks down equally upon plain and mountain. Or you behold a hawk sallying from some crag, like a Rhenish baron of old from his pinnacled castle, and darting down toward the river for his prey. Or perhaps, lazily gliding about in the zenith, this ruffian fowl is suddenly beset by a crow, who with stubborn audacity pecks at him, and, spite of all his bravery, finally persecutes him back to his stronghold. The otherwise dauntless bandit, soaring at his topmost height, must needs succumb to this sable image of death. Nor are there wanting many smaller and less famous fowl, who without contributing to the grandeur, yet greatly add to the beauty of the scene. The yellow-bird flits like a winged jonquil here and there; like knots of violets the blue-birds sport in clusters upon the grass; while hurrying from the pasture to the grove, the red robin seems an incendiary putting torch to the trees. Meanwhile the air is vocal with their hymns, and your own soul joys in the general joy. Like a stranger in an orchestra, you cannot help singing yourself when all around you raise such hosannas.

But in autumn, those gay northerners, the birds, return to their southern plantations. The mountains are left bleak and sere. Solitude settles down upon them in drizzling mists. The traveller is beset, at perilous turns, by dense masses of fog. He emerges for a moment into more penetrable air; and passing some gray, abandoned house, sees the lofty vapours plainly eddy by its desolate door; just as from the plain you may see it eddy by the pinnacles of distant and lonely heights. Or, dismounting from his frightened horse, he leads him down some scowling glen, where the road steeply dips among grim rocks, only to rise as abruptly again; and as he warily picks his way, uneasy at the menacing scene, he sees some ghost-like object looming through the mist at the roadside; and wending toward it, beholds a rude white stone, uncouthly inscribed, marking the spot where, some fifty or sixty years ago, some farmer was upset in his wood-sled, and perished beneath the load.

In winter this region is blocked up with snow. Inaccessible and impassable, those wild, unfrequented roads, which in August are overgrown with high grass, in December are drifted to the arm-pit with the white fleece from the sky. As if an ocean rolled between man and man, inter-communication is often suspended for weeks and weeks.

Such, at this day, is the country which gave birth to our hero; prophetically styled Israel by the good Puritans, his parents, since, for more than forty years, poor Potter wandered in the wild wilderness of the world's extremest hardships and ills.

How little he thought, when, as a boy, hunting after his father's stray cattle among these New England hills, he himself like a beast should be hunted through half of Old England, as a runaway rebel. Or, how could he ever have dreamed, when involved in the autumnal vapours of these mountains, that worse bewilderments awaited him three thousand miles across the sea, wandering forlorn in the coal-fogs of London. But so it was destined to be. This little boy of the hills, born in sight of the sparkling Housatonic, was to linger out the best part of his life a prisoner or a pauper upon the grimy banks of the Thames.

From *Israel Potter* by Herman Melville. G.P. Putnam & Co., 1855.

Cock-A-Doodle-Doo!
Or The Crowing of the Noble Cock Beneventano

In all parts of the world many high-spirited revolts from rascally despotisms had of late been knocked on the head; many dreadful casualties, by locomotive and steamer, had likewise knocked hundreds of high-spirited travellers on the head (I lost a dear friend in one of them); my own private affairs were also full of despotisms, casualties, and knockings on the head, when early one morning in Spring, being too full of hypos to sleep, I sallied out to walk on my hill-side pasture.

It was a cool and misty, damp, disagreeable air. The country looked underdone, its raw juices squirting out all round. I buttoned out this squitchy air as well as I could with my lean, double-breasted dress-coat — my overcoat being so long-skirted I only used it in my wagon — and spitefully thrusting my crab-stick into the oozy sod, bent my blue form to the steep ascent of the hill. This toiling posture brought my head pretty well earthward, as if I were in the act of butting it against the world. I well earthward, as if I were in the act of butting it against the world. I marked the fact, but only grinned at it with a ghastly grin.

All round me were tokens of a divided empire. The old grass and the new grass were striving together. In the low wet swales the verdure peeped out in vivid green; beyond, on the mountains, lay light patches of snow, strangely relieved against their russet sides; all the humped hills looked like brindled kine in the shivers. The woods were strewn with dry dead boughs, snapped off by the riotous winds of March, while the young trees skirting the woods were just beginning to show the first yellowish tinge of the nascent spray.

I sat down for a moment on a great rotting log nigh the top of the hill, my back to a heavy grove, my face presented toward a wide, sweeping circuit of mountains enclosing a rolling, diversified country. Along the base of one long range of heights ran a lagging, fever-and-agueish river, over which was a duplicate stream of dripping mist, exactly corresponding in every meander with its parent water below. Low down, here and there, shreds of vapour listlessly wandered in the air, like abandoned or helmless nations or ships — or very soaky towels hung on criss-cross clothes-lines to dry. Afar, over a distant village lying in a bay of the plain formed by the mountains, there rested a great flat canopy of haze, like a pall. It was the condensed smoke of the chimneys, with the condensed, exhaled breath of the villagers, prevented from dispersion by the imprisoning hills. It was too heavy and lifeless to mount of itself; so there it lay, between the village and the sky, doubtless hiding many a man with the mumps, and many a queasy child.

My eye ranged over the capacious rolling country, and over the mountains, and over the village, and over a farmhouse here and there, and over woods, groves, streams, rocks, fells — and I thought to myself, what a slight mark, after all, does man make on this huge great earth. Yet the earth makes a mark on him. What a horrid accident was that on the Ohio, where my good friend and thirty other good fellows were sloped into eternity at the bidding of a thick-headed engineer, who knew not a valve from a flue. And that crash on the railroad just over yon mountains there, where two infatuate trains ran pell-mell into each other, and climbed and clawed each other's backs; and one locomotive was found fairly shelled, like a chick, inside of a passenger car in the antagonist train; and near a score of noble hearts, a bride and her groom, and an innocent little infant, were all disembarked into the grim hulk of Charon, who ferried them over, all baggageless, to some clinkered iron-foundry country or other. Yet what's the use of complaining? What justice of the peace will right this matter? Yea, what's the use of bothering the very heavens about it? Don't the heavens themselves ordain these things — else they could not happen?

Melville's writing table in the northeast chamber at Arrowhead. Clemens Kalischer

A miserable world! Who would take the trouble to make a fortune in it, when he knows not how long he can keep it; for the thousand villains and asses who have the management of railroads and steamboats, and innumerable other vital things in the world. If they would make me Dictator in North America a while, I'd string them up, and hang, draw, and quarter; fry, roast, and boil; stew, grill, and devil them, like so many turkey-legs — the rascally numskulls of stokers; I'd set them to stokering in Tartarus — I would!

Great improvements of the age! What! to call the facilitation of death and murder an improvement! Who wants to travel so fast? My grandfather did not, and he was no fool. Hark! here comes that old dragon again — that gigantic gad-fly of a Moloch — snort! puff! scream! — here he comes straight-bent through these vernal woods, like the Asiatic cholera cantering on a camel. Stand aside! here he comes, the chartered murderer! the death monopoliser! judge, jury, and hangman all together, whose victims die always without benefit of clergy. For two hundred and fifty miles that iron fiend goes yelling through the land, crying 'More! more! more!' Would that fifty conspiring mountains would fall atop of him! And, while they were about it, would they also fall atop of that smaller dunning fiend, my creditor, who frightens the life out of me more than any locomotive — a lantern-jawed rascal, who seems to run on a railroad track, too, and duns me even on Sunday, all the way to church and back, and comes and sits in the same pew with me, and pretending to be polite and hand me the prayer-book opened at the proper place, pokes his pesky bill under my nose in the very midst of my devotions, and so shoves himself between me and salvation; for how can one keep his temper on such occasions?

I can't pay this horrid man; and yet they say money was never so plentiful — a drug in the market; but blame me if I can get any of the drug, though there never was a sick man more in need of that particular sort of medicine. It's a lie; money ain't plenty — feel of my pocket. Ha! here's a powder I was going to send to the sick baby in yonder hovel, where the Irish ditcher lives. That baby has the scarlet fever. They say the measles are rife in the country, too, and the varioloid, and the chicken-pox, and it's bad for teething children. And after all, I suppose many of the poor little ones, after going through all this trouble, snap off short; and so they had the measles, mumps, croup, scarlet fever, chicken-pox, cholera-morbus, summer-complaint, and all else, in vain! Ah! there's that twinge of the rheumatics in my right shoulder. I got it one night on the North River, when, in a crowded boat, I gave up my berth to a sick lady, and stayed on deck till morning in drizzling weather. There's the thanks one gets for charity! Twinge! Shoot away, ye rheumatics! Ye couldn't lay on worse if I were some villain who had murdered the lady instead of befriending her. Dyspepsia, too — I am troubled with that.

Hallo! here come the calves, the two-year-olds, just turned out of the barn into the pasture, after six months of cold victuals. What a miserable-looking set, to be sure! A breaking up of a hard winter, that's certain: sharp bones sticking out like elbows; all quilted with a strange stuff dried on their flanks like layers of pancakes. Hair worn quite off too, here and there; and where it ain't pancaked, or worn off, looks like the rubbed sides of mangy old hair-trunks. In fact, they are not six two-year-olds, but six abominable old hair-trunks wandering about here in this pasture.

Hark! By Jove, what's that? See! the very hair-trunks prick their ears at it, and stand and gaze away down into the rolling country yonder.

Hark again! How clear! how musical! how prolonged! What a triumphant thanksgiving of a cock-crow! *'Glory be to God in the highest!'* It says those very words as plain as ever cock did in this world. Why, why, I begin to feel a little in sorts again. It ain't so very misty, after all. The sun yonder is beginning to show himself: I feel warmer.

Hark! There again! Did ever such a blessed cock-crow so ring out over the earth before! Clear, shrill, full of pluck, full of fire, full of fun, full of glee. It plainly says —*'Never say die!'* My friends, it is extraordinary, is it not?

Unwittingly, I found that I had been addressing the two-year-olds — the calves — in my enthusiasm; which shows how one's true nature will betray itself at times in the most unconscious way. For what a very two-year-old, and calf, I had been to fall into the sulks, on a hill-top too, when a cock down in the lowlands there, without discourse of reason, and quite penniless in the world, and with death hanging over him at any moment from his hungry master, sends up a cry like a very laureate celebrating the glorious victory of New Orleans.

Hark! there it goes again! My friends, that must be a Shanghai; no domestic-born cock could crow in such prodigious exulting strains. Plainly, my friends, a Shanghai of the Emperor of China's breed.

But my friends the hair-trunks, fairly alarmed at last by such clamor-ously-victorious tones, were now scampering off, with their tails flirting in the air, and capering with their legs in clumsy enough sort of style, sufficiently evincing that they had not freely flourished them for the six months last past.

Hark! there again! Whose cock is that? Who in this region can afford to buy such an extraordinary Shanghai? Bless me — it makes my blood bound — I feel wild. What? jumping on this rotten old log here, to flap my elbows and crow too? And just now in the doleful dumps. And all this from the simple crow of a cock. Marvellous cock! But soft — this fellow now crows most lustily; but it's only morning; let's see how he'll crow about noon, and toward nightfall. Come to think of it, cocks crow mostly in the beginning of the day. Their pluck ain't lasting, after all. Yes, yes; even cocks have to succumb to the universal spell of tribulation: jubilant in the beginning, but down in the mouth at the end.

> ... 'Of fine mornings,
> We fine lusty cocks begin our crows in gladness;
> But when eve does come we don't crow quite so much,
> For then cometh despondency and madness.'

The poet had this very Shanghai in his mind when he wrote that. But stop. There he rings out again, ten times richer, fuller, longer, more obstreperously exulting than before! Why, this is equal to hearing the great bell of St. Paul's rung at a coronation! In fact, that bell ought to be taken down, and this Shanghai put in its place. Such a crow would jollify all London, from Mile-End (which is no end) to Primrose Hill (where there ain't any primroses), and scatter the fog.

Well, I have an appetite for my breakfast this morning, if I have not had it for a week before. I meant to have only tea and toast; but I'll have coffee and eggs — no, brown stout and a beefsteak. I want something hearty. Ah, here comes the down-train: white cars, flashing through the trees like a vein of silver. How cheerfully the steam-pipe chirps! Gay are the passengers. There waves a handkerchief — going down to the city to eat oysters, and see their friends, and drop in at the circus. Look at the mist yonder; what soft curls and undulations round the hills, and the sun weaving his rays among them. See the azure smoke of the village, like the azure tester over a bridal-bed. How bright the country looks there where the river overflowed the meadows. The old grass has to knock under to the new. Well, I feel the better for this walk. Home now, and walk into that steak, and crack that bottle of brown stout, and by the time that's drunk — a quart of stout — by that time, I shall feel about as stout as Samson. Come to think of it, that dun may call, though. I'll just visit the woods and cut a club. I'll club him, by Jove, if he duns me this day.

Hark! there goes Shanghai again. Shanghai says, 'Bravo!' Shanghai says, 'Club him!'

Oh, brave cock!

I felt in rare spirits the whole morning. The dun called about eleven. I had the boy Jake send the dun up. I was reading *Tristram Shandy*, and could not go down under the circumstances. The lean rascal (a lean farmer, too — think of that!) entered, and found me seated in an arm-chair, with my feet on the table, and the second bottle of brown stout handy, and the book under eye.

'Sit down,' said I; 'I'll finish this chapter, and then attend to you. Fine morning. Ha! ha! — this is a fine joke about my Uncle Toby and the Widow Wadman! Ha! ha! ha! let me read this to you.'

'I have no time; I've got my noon *chores* to do.'

'To the deuce with your *chores*!' said I. 'Don't drop your old tobacco about here, or I'll turn you out.'

'Sir!'

'Let me read you this about the Widow Wadman. Said the Widow Wadman — '

'There's my bill, sir.'

'Very good. Just twist it up, will you; it's about my smoking-time; and hand a coal, will you, from the hearth yonder!'

'My bill, sir!' said the rascal, turning pale with rage and amazement at my unwonted air (formerly I had always dodged him with a pale face), but too prudent as yet to betray the extremity of his astonishment. 'My bill, sir!' — and he stiffly poked it at me.

'My friend,' said I, 'what a charming morning! How sweet the country looks! Pray, did you hear that extraordinary cock-crow this morning? Take a glass of my stout!'

'Yours? First pay your debts before you offer folks your stout!'

'You think, then, that, properly speaking, I have no stout,' said I, deliberately rising. 'I'll undeceive you. I'll show you stout of a superior brand to Barclay and Perkins.'

Without more ado, I seized that insolent dun by the slack of his coat — (and, being a lean, shad-bellied wretch, there was plenty of slack to it) — I seized him that way, tied him with a sailor-knot, and thrusting his bill between his teeth, introduced him to the open country lying round about my place of abode.

'Jake,' said I, 'you'll find a sack of blue-nosed potatoes lying under the shed. Drag it here, and pelt this pauper away; he's been begging pence of me, and I know he can work, but he's lazy. Pelt him away, Jake!'

Bless my stars, what a crow! Shanghai sent up such a perfect paean and laudamus — such a trumpet-blast of triumph, that my soul fairly snorted in me. Duns! — I could have fought an army of them! Plainly, Shanghai was of the opinion that duns only came into the world to be kicked, hanged, bruised, battered, choked, walloped, hammered, drowned, clubbed!

Returning indoors, when the exultation of my victory over the dun had a little subsided, I fell to musing over the mysterious Shanghai. I had no idea I would hear him so nigh my house. I wondered from what rich gentleman's yard he crowed. Nor had he cut short his crows so easily as I had supposed he would. This Shanghai crowed till midday, at least. Would he keep a-crowing all day? I resolved to learn. Again I ascended the hill. The whole country was now bathed in a rejoicing sunlight. The warm verdure was bursting all round me. Teams were afield. Birds, newly arrived from the south, were blithely singing in the air. Even the crows cawed with a certain unction, and seemed a shade or two less black than usual.

Hark! there goes the cock! How shall I describe the crow of the Shanghai at noontide? His sunrise crow was a whisper to it. It was the loudest, longest, and most strangely musical crow that ever amazed mortal man. I had heard plenty of cock-crows before, and many fine ones; but this one! so smooth and flute-like in its very clamour; so self-possessed in its very rapture of exultation; so vast, mounting, swelling, soaring, as if spurted out from a golden throat, thrown far back. Nor did it sound like the foolish, vain-glorious crow of some young sophomorean cock, who knew not the world, and was beginning life in audacious gay spirits, because in wretched ignorance of what might be to come. It was the crow of a cock who crowed not without advice; the crow of a cock who knew a thing or two; the crow of a cock who had fought the world and got the better of it, and was now resolved to crow, though the earth should heave and the heavens should fall. It was a wise crow; an invincible crow; a philosophic crow; a crow of all crows.

I returned home once more full of reinvigorated spirits, with a dauntless sort of feeling. I thought over my debts and other troubles, and over the unlucky risings of the poor oppressed *peoples* abroad, and over the railroad and steamboat accidents, and over even the loss of my dear friend, with a calm, good-natured rapture of defiance, which astounded myself. I felt as though I could meet Death, and invite him to dinner, and toast the Catacombs with him, in pure overflow of self-reliance and a sense of universal security.

Toward evening I went up to the hill once more to find whether, indeed, the glorious cock would prove game even from the rising of the sun unto the going down thereof. Talk of Vespers or Curfew! — the evening crow of the cock went out of his mighty throat all over the land and inhabited it, like Xerxes from the East with his double-winged host. It was miraculous. Bless me, what a crow! The cock went game to roost that night, depend upon it, victorious over the entire day, and bequeathing the echoes of his thousand crows to night.

After an unwontedly sound, refreshing sleep I rose early, feeling like a carriage-spring — light, elliptical, airy, buoyant as sturgeon-nose — and, like a football, bounded up the hill. Hark! Shanghai was up before me. The early bird that caught the worm — crowing like a bugle worked by an engine — lusty, loud, all jubilation. From the scattered farm-houses a multitude of other cocks were crowing, and replying to each other's crows. But they were as flageolets to a trombone. Shanghai would suddenly break in, and overwhelm all their crows with his one domineering blast. He seemed to have nothing to do with any other concern. He replied to no other crow, but crowed solely by himself, on his own account, in solitary scorn and independence.

Oh, brave cock! — oh, noble Shanghai! — oh, bird rightly offered up by the invincible Socrates, in testimony of his final victory over life.

As I live, thought I, this blessed day will I go and seek out the Shanghai, and buy him, if I have to clap another mortgage on my land.

I listened attentively now, striving to mark from what direction the crow came. But it so charged and replenished, and made bountiful and overflowing all the air, that it was impossible to say from what precise point the exultation came. All that I could decide upon was this: the crow came from out of the east, and not from out of the west. I then considered with myself how far a cock-crow might be heard. In this still country, shut in, too, by mountains, sounds were audible at great distances. Besides, the undulations of the land, the abuttings of the mountains into the rolling hill and valley below, produced strange echoes, and reverberations, and multiplications, and accumulations of resonance, very remarkable to hear, and very puzzling to think of. Where lurked this valiant Shanghai — this bird of cheerful Socrates — the game-fowl Greek who died unappalled? Where lurked he? Oh, noble cock, where are you? Crow once more, my Bantam! my princely, my imperial Shanghai! my bird of the Emperor of China! Brother of the Sun! Cousin of great Jove! where are you? — one crow more, and tell me your number!

Hark! like a full orchestra of the cocks of all nations, forth burst the crow. But where from? There it is; but where? There was no telling, further than it came from out the east.

After breakfast I took my stick and sallied down the road. There were many gentlemen's seats dotting the neighbouring country, and I made no doubt that some of these opulent gentlemen had invested a hundred-dollar bill in some royal Shanghai recently imported in the ship Trade Wind, or the ship White Squall, or the ship Sovereign of the Seas; for it must needs have been a brave ship with a brave name which bore the fortunes of so brave a cock. I resolved to walk the entire country, and find this noble foreigner out; but thought it would not be amiss to inquire on the way at the humblest homesteads, whether, peradventure, they had heard of a lately-imported Shanghai belonging to any of the gentlemen settlers from the city; for it was plain that no poor farmer, no poor man of any sort, could own such an oriental trophy, such a Great Bell of St. Paul's swung in a cock's throat.

I met an old man, ploughing, in a field nigh the roadside fence.

'My friend, have you heard an extraordinary cock-crow of late?'

'Well, well,' he drawled, 'I don't know — the Widow Crowfoot has a cock — and Squire Squaretoes has a cock — and I have a cock, and they all crow. But I don't know of any on 'em with 'strordinary crows.'

'Good morning to you,' said I, shortly; 'it's plain that you have not heard the crow of the Emperor of China's chanticleer.'

Presently I met another old man mending a tumble-down old rail-fence. The rails were rotten, and at every move of the old man's hand they crumbled into yellow ochre. He had much better let the fence alone, or else get him new rails. And here I must say, that one cause of the sad fact why idiocy more prevails among farmers than any other class of people, is owing to their undertaking the mending of rotten rail-fences in warm, relaxing spring weather. The enterprise is a hopeless one. It is a laborious one; it is a bootless one. It is an enterprise to make the heart break. Vast pains squandered upon a vanity. For how can one make rotten rail-fences stand up on their rotten pins? By what magic put pith into sticks which have lain freezing and baking through sixty consecutive winters and summers? This it is, this wretched endeavour to mend rotten rail-fences with their own rotten rails, which drives many farmers into the asylum.

On the face of the old man in question incipient idiocy was plainly marked. For, about sixty rods before him extended one of the most unhappy and desponding broken-hearted Virginia rail-fences I ever saw in my life. While in a field behind, were a set of young steers, possessed as by devils, continually butting at this forlorn old fence, and breaking through it here and there, causing the old man to drop his work and chase them back within bounds. He would chase them with a piece of rail huge as Goliath's beam, but as light as cork. At the first flourish, it crumbled into powder.

'My friend,' said I, addressing this woeful mortal, 'have you heard an extraordinary cock-crow of late?'

I might as well have asked him if he had heard the death-tick. He stared at me with a long, bewildered, doleful, and unutterable stare, and without reply resumed his unhappy labours.

What a fool, thought I, to have asked such an uncheerful and uncheerable creature about a cheerful cock!

I walked on. I had now descended the high land where my house stood, and being in a low tract could not hear the crow of the Shanghai, which doubtless overshot me there. Besides, the Shanghai might be at lunch of corn and oats, or taking a nap, and so interrupted his jubilations for a while.

At length I encountered riding along the road, a portly gentleman — nay, a *pursy* one — of great wealth, who had recently purchased him some noble acres, and built him a noble mansion, with a goodly fowl-house attached, the fame whereof spread through all that country. Thought I, Here now is the owner of the Shanghai.

'Sir,' said I,' excuse me, but I am a countryman of yours, and would ask, if so be you own any Shanghais?'

'Oh, yes; I have ten Shanghais.'

'Ten!' exclaimed I in wonder; 'and do they all crow?'

'Most lustily; every soul of them; I wouldn't own a cock that wouldn't crow.'

'Will you turn back, and show me those Shanghais?'

'With pleasure: I am proud of them. They cost me, in the lump, six hundred dollars.'

As I walked by the side of his horse, I was thinking to myself whether possibly I had not mistaken the harmoniously combined crowings of ten Shanghais in a squad, for the supernatural crow of a single Shanghai by himself.

'Sir,' said I, 'is there one of your Shanghais which far exceeds all the others in the lustiness, musicalness, and inspiring effects of his crow?'

'They crow pretty much alike, I believe,' he courteously replied; 'I really don't know that I could tell their crow apart.'

I began to think that after all my noble chanticleer might not be in the possession of this wealthy gentleman. However, we went into his fowl-yard, and I saw his Shanghais. Let me say that hitherto I had never clapped eye on this species of imported fowl. I had heard what enormous prices were paid for them, and also that they were of an enormous size, and had somehow fancied they must be of a beauty and brilliancy pro-portioned both to size and price. What was my surprise, then, to see ten carrot-coloured monsters, without the smallest pretension to effulgence of plumage. Immediately I determined that my royal cock was neither among these, nor could possibly be a Shanghai at all; if these gigantic gallows-bird fowl were fair specimens of the true Shanghai.

I walked all day, dining and resting at a farm-house, inspecting various fowl-yards, interrogating various owners of fowls, hearkening to various crows, but discovered not the mysterious chanticleer. Indeed, I had wandered so far and deviously, that I could not hear his crow. I began to suspect that this cock was a mere visitor in the country, who had taken his departure by the eleven o'clock train to the south, and was now crowing and jubilating somewhere on the verdant banks of Long Island Sound.

But next morning, again I heard the inspiring blast, again felt my blood bound in me, again felt superior to all the ills of life, again felt like turning my dun out of doors. But displeased with the reception given him at his last visit, the dun stayed away, doubtless being in a huff. Silly fellow that he was, to take a harmless joke in earnest.

Several days passed, during which I made sundry excursions in the regions round about, but in vain sought the cock. Still, I heard him from the hill, and sometimes from the house, and sometimes in the stillness of the night. If at times I would relapse into my doleful dumps, straightway at the sound of the exultant and defiant crow, my soul, too, would turn chanticleer, and clap her wings, and throw back her throat, and breathe forth a cheerful challenge to all the world of woes.

At last, after some weeks I was necessitated to clap another mortgage on my estate in order to pay certain debts, and among others the one I owed the dun, who of late had commenced a civil-process against me. The way the process was served was a most insulting one. In a private room I had been enjoying myself in the village tavern over a bottle of Philadelphia porter, and some Herkimer cheese, and a roll, and having apprised the landlord, who was a friend of mine, that I would settle with him when I received my next remittances, stepped to the peg where I had hung my hat in the bar-room, to get a choice cigar I had left in the hall, when lo! I found the civil-process enveloping the cigar. When I unrolled the cigar, I unrolled the civil-process, and the constable standing by rolled out, with a thick tongue, 'Take notice!' and added, in a whisper, 'Put that in your pipe and smoke it!'

I turned short round upon the gentlemen then and there present in that bar-room. Said I, 'Gentlemen, is this an honourable — nay, is this a lawful way of serving a civil-process? Behold!'

One and all they were of opinion that it was a highly inelegant act in the constable to take advantage of a gentleman's lunching on cheese and porter, to be so uncivil as to slip a civil-process into his hat. It was ungenerous; it was cruel; for the sudden shock of the thing coming instanter upon the lunch would impair the proper digestion of the cheese, which is proverbially not so easy of digestion as blanc-mange.

Arrived home, I read the process, and felt a twinge of melancholy. Hard world! hard world! Here I am, as good a fellow as ever lived — hospitable — open-hearted — generous to a fault: and the Fates forbid that I should possess the fortune to bless the country with my bounteous-ness. Nay, while many a stingy curmudgeon rolls in idle gold, I, heart of nobleness as I am, I have civil-processes served on me! I bowed my head, and felt forlorn — unjustly used — abused — unappreciated — in short, miserable.

Hark! like a clarion! yea, like a jolly bolt of thunder with bells to it — came the all-glorious and defiant crow! Ye gods, how it set me up again! Right on my pins! Yea, verily on stilts!

Oh, noble cock!

Plain as cock could speak, it said: 'Let the world and all aboard of it go to pot. Do you be jolly, and never say die. What's the world compared to you? What is it anyhow but a lump of loam? Do you be jolly!'

Oh, noble cock!

'But my dear and glorious cock,' mused I, upon second thought,' one can't so easily send this world to pot; one can't so easily be jolly with civil-processes in his hat or hand.'

Hark! the crow again. Plain as cock could speak, it said: 'Hang the process, and hang the fellow that sent it! If you have not land or cash, go and thrash the fellow, and tell him you never mean to pay him. Be jolly!'

Now this was the way — through the imperative intimations of the cock — that I came to clap the added mortgage on my estate; paid all my debts by fusing them into this one added bond and mortgage. Thus made at ease again, I renewed my search for the noble cock. But in vain, though I heard him every day. I began to think there was some sort of deception in this mysterious thing: some wonderful ventriloquist prowled around my barns, or in my cellar, or on my roof, and was minded to be gaily mischievous. But no — what ventriloquist could so crow with such an heroic and celestial crow?

At last, one morning there came to me a certain singular man, who had sawed and split my wood in March — some five-and-thirty cords of it — and now he came for his pay. He was a singular man, I say. He was tall and spare, with a long, saddish face, yet somehow a latently joyous eye, which offered the strangest contrast. His air seemed staid, but undepressed. He wore a long, gray, shabby coat, and a big battered hat. This man had sawed my wood at so much a cord. He would stand and saw all day long in a driving snowstorm, and never wink at it. He never spoke unless spoken to. He only sawed. Saw, saw, saw — snow, snow, snow. The saw and the snow went together like two natural things. The first day this man came, he brought his dinner with him, and volunteered to eat it sitting on his buck in the snowstorm. From my window, where I was reading Burton's *Anatomy of Melancholy*, I saw him in the act. I burst out of doors bare-headed. 'Good heavens!' cried I; 'what are you doing? Come in. *This* your dinner!'

He had a hunk of stale bread and another hunk of salt beef, wrapped in a wet newspaper, and washed his morsels down by melting a handful of fresh snow in his mouth. I took this rash man indoors, planted him by the fire, gave him a dish of hot pork and beans, and a mug of cider.

'Now,' said I, 'don't you bring any of your damp dinners here. You work by the job, to be sure, but I'll dine you for all that.'

He expressed his acknowledgments in a calm, proud, but not un-grateful way, and dispatched his meal with satisfaction to himself, and me also. It afforded me pleasure to perceive that he quaffed down his mug of cider like a man. I honoured him. When I addressed him in the way of business at his buck, I did so in a guardedly respectful and deferential manner. Interested in his singular aspect, struck by his won-drous intensity of application at his saw — a most wearisome and dis-gustful occupation to most people — I often sought to gather from him who he was, what sort of a life he led, where he was born, and so on. But he was mum. He came to saw my wood, and eat my dinners — if I chose to offer them — but not to gabble. At first I somewhat resented his sullen silence under the circumstances. But better considering it, I honoured him

the more. I increased the respectfulness and deferentialness of my address toward him. I concluded within myself that this man had experienced hard times; that he had had many sore rubs in the world; that he
was of a solemn disposition; that he was of the mind of Solomon; that he
lived calmly, decorously, temperately; and though a very poor man, was,
nevertheless, a highly respectable one. At times I imagined that he might
even be an elder or deacon of some small country church. I thought it
would not be a bad plan to run this excellent man for President of the
United States. He would prove a great reformer of abuses.

His name was Merrymusk. I had often thought how jolly a name for
so unjolly a wight. I inquired of people whether they knew Merrymusk.
But it was some time before I learned much about him. He was by birth a
Marylander, it appeared, who had long lived in the country round about;
a wandering man; until within some ten years ago, a thriftless man,
though perfectly innocent of crime; a man who would work hard a month
with surprising soberness, and then spend all his wages in one riotous
night. In youth he had been a sailor, and run away from his ship at
Batavia, where he caught the fever, and came nigh dying. But he rallied,
reshipped, landed home, found all his friends dead, and struck for the
Northern interior, where he had since tarried. Nine years back he had
married a wife, and now had four children. His wife was become a
perfect invalid; one child had the white-swelling, and the rest were rickety. He and his family lived in a shanty on a lonely barren patch nigh the
railroad-track, where it passed close to the base of a mountain. He had
bought a fine cow to have plenty of wholesome milk for his children; but
the cow died during an accouchement, and he could not afford to buy
another. Still, his family never suffered for lack of food. He worked hard
and brought it to them.

Now, as I said before, having long previously sawed my wood, this
Merrymusk came for his pay.

'My friend,' said I, 'do you know of any gentleman hereabouts who
owns an extraordinary cock?'

The twinkle glittered quite plain in the wood-sawyer's eye.

'I know of no *gentleman*,' he replied, 'who has what might well be
called an extraordinary cock.'

Oh, thought I, this Merrymusk is not the man to enlighten me. I am
afraid I shall never discover this extraordinary cock.

Not having the full change to pay Merrymusk, I gave him his due, as
nigh as I could make it, and told him that in a day or two I would take a
walk and visit his place, and hand him the remainder. Accordingly one
fine morning I sallied forth upon the errand. I had much ado finding the
best road to the shanty. No one seemed to know where it was exactly. It

lay in a very lonely part of the country, a densely-wooded mountain on one side (which I call October Mountain, on account of its bannered aspect in that month), and a thicketed swamp on the other, the railroad cutting the swamp. Straight as a die the railroad cut it; many times a day tantalising the wretched shanty with the sight of all the beauty, rank, fashion, health, trunks, silver and gold, dry-goods and groceries, brides and grooms, happy wives and husbands, flying by the lonely door — no time to stop — flash! here they are — and there they go! — out of sight at both ends — as if that part of the world were only made to fly over, and not to settle upon. And this was about all the shanty saw of what people call 'life.'

Though puzzled somewhat, yet I knew the general direction where the shanty lay, and on I trudged. As I advanced, I was surprised to hear the mysterious cock crow with more and more distinctness. Is it possible, thought I, that any gentleman owning a Shanghai can dwell in such a lonesome, dreary region? Louder and louder, nigher and nigher, sounded the glorious and defiant clarion. Though somehow I may be out of the track to my wood-sawyer's, I said to myself, yet, thank Heaven, I seem to be on the way toward that extraordinary cock. I was delighted with this auspicious accident. On I journeyed; while at intervals the crow sounded most invitingly, and jocundly, and superbly; and the last crow was ever nigher than the former one. At last, emerging from a thicket of elders, straight before me I saw the most resplendent creature that ever blessed the sight of man.

A cock, more like a golden eagle than a cock. A cock, more like a field-marshal than a cock. A cock, more like Lord Nelson with all his glittering arms on, standing on the *Vanguard*'s quarter-deck going into battle, than a cock. A cock, more like the Emperor Charlemagne in his robes at Aix-la-Chapelle, than a cock.

Such a cock!

He was of a haughty size, stood haughtily on his haughty legs. His colours were red, gold, and white. The red was on his crest alone, which was a mighty and symmetric crest, like unto Hector's helmet, as delineated on antique shields. His plumage was snowy, traced with gold. He walked in front of the shanty, like a peer of the realm; his crest lifted, his chest heaved out, his embroidered trappings flashing in the light. His pace was wonderful. He looked like some noble foreigner. He looked like some Oriental king in some magnificent Italian opera.

Merrymusk advanced from the door.

'Pray, is not that the Signor Beneventano?'

'Sir!'

'That's the cock,' said I, a little embarrassed. The truth was, my enthusiasm had betrayed me into a rather silly inadvertence. I had made a somewhat learned sort of allusion in the presence of an unlearned man. Consequently, upon discovering it by his honest stare, I felt foolish; but carried it off by declaring that *this was the cock.*

Now, during the preceding autumn I had been to the city, and had chanced to be present at a performance of the Italian Opera. In that opera figured in some royal character a certain Signor Beneventano — a man of a tall, imposing person, clad in rich raiment, like to plumage, and with a most remarkable, majestic, scornful stride. The Signor Beneventano seemed on the point of tumbling over backward with exceeding haughtiness. And, for all the world, the proud pace of the cock seemed the very stage-pace of the Signor Beneventano.

Hark! Suddenly the cock paused, lifted his head still higher, ruffled his plumes, seemed inspired, and sent forth a lusty crow. October Mountain echoed it; other mountains sent it back; still others rebounded it; it overran the country round. Now I plainly perceived how it was I had chanced to hear the gladdening sound on my distant hill.

'Good heavens! do you own the cock? Is that cock yours?'

'Is it my cock!' said Merrymusk, looking slyly gleeful out of the corner of his long, solemn face.

'Where did you get it?'

'It chipped the shell here. I raised it.'

'You?'

Hark! Another crow. It might have raised the ghosts of all the pines and hemlocks ever cut down in that country. Marvellous cock! Having crowed, he strode on again, surrounded by a bevy of admiring hens.

'What will you take for Signor Beneventano?'

'Sir?'

'That magic cock! — what will you take for him?

'I won't sell him.'

'I will give you fifty dollars.'

'Pooh!'

'One hundred!'

'Pish!'

'Five hundred!'

'Bah!'

'And you a poor man?'

'No; don't I own that cock, and haven't I refused five hundred dollars for him?'

'True,' said I, in profound thought; 'that's a fact. You won't sell him, then?'

'No.'

'Will you give him?'

'No.'

'Will you *keep* him, then!' I shouted, in a rage.

'Yes.'

I stood a while admiring the cock, and wondering at the man. At last I felt a redoubled admiration of the one, and a redoubled deference for the other.

'Won't you step in?' said Merrymusk.

'But won't the cock be prevailed upon to join us?' said I.

'Yes. Trumpet! hither, boy! hither!'

The cock turned round, and strode up to Merrymusk.

'Come!'

The cock followed us into the shanty.

'Crow!'

The roof jarred.

Oh, noble cock!

I turned in silence upon my entertainer. There he sat on an old battered chest, in his old tattered gray coat, with patches at his knees and elbows, and a deplorably bunged hat. I glanced round the room. Bare rafters overhead, but solid junks of jerked beef hanging from them. Earth floor, but a heap of potatoes in one corner, and a sack of Indian meal in another. A blanket was strung across the apartment at the farther end, from which came a woman's ailing voice and the voices of ailing children. But somehow in the ailing of these voices there seemed no complaint.

'Mrs. Merrymusk and children?'

'Yes.'

I looked at the cock. There he stood majestically in the middle of the room. He looked like a Spanish grandee caught in a shower, and standing under some peasant's shed. There was a strange supernatural look of contrast about him. He irradiated the shanty; he glorified its meanness. He glorified the battered chest, and tattered gray coat, and the bunged hat. He glorified the very voices which came in ailing tones from behind the screen.

'Oh, father,' cried a little sickly voice, 'let Trumpet sound again.'

'Crow,' cried Merrymusk.

The cock threw himself into a posture.

The roof jarred.

'Does not this disturb Mrs. Merrymusk and the sick children?'

'Crow again, Trumpet.'

The roof jarred.

'It does not disturb them, then?'

'Didn't you hear 'em *ask* for it?'

'How is it, that your sick family like this crowing?' said I. 'The cock is a glorious cock, with a glorious voice, but not exactly the sort of thing for a sick-chamber, one would suppose. Do they really like it?'

'Don't *you* like it? Don't it do *you* good? Ain't it inspiring? Don't it impart pluck? give stuff against despair?'

'All true,' said I, removing my hat with profound humility before the brave spirit disguised in the base coat.

'But then,' said I, still with some misgivings, 'so loud, so wonderfully clamorous a crow, methinks might be amiss to invalids, and retard their convalescence.'

'Crow your best now, Trumpet!'

I leaped from my chair. The cock frightened me, like some overpowering angel in the Apocalypse. He seemed crowing over the fall of wicked Babylon, or crowing over the triumph of righteous Joshua in the vale of Askalon. When I regained my composure somewhat, an inquisitive thought occurred to me. I resolved to gratify it.

'Merrymusk, will you present me to your wife and children?'

'Yes. Wife, the gentleman wants to step in.'

'He is very welcome,' replied a weak voice.

Going behind the curtain, there lay a wasted, but strangely cheerful human face; and that was pretty much all; the body, hid by the counterpane and an old coat, seemed too shrunken to reveal itself through such impediments. At the bedside sat a pale girl, ministering. In another bed lay three children, side by side: three more pale faces.

'Oh, father, we don't mislike the gentleman, but let us see Trumpet too.'

At a word, the cock strode behind the screen, and perched himself on the children's bed. All their wasted eyes gazed at him with a wild and spiritual delight. They seemed to sun themselves in the radiant plumage of the cock.

'Better than a 'pothecary, eh?' said Merrymusk. 'This is Dr. Cock himself.'

We retired from the sick ones, and I reseated myself again, lost in thought over this strange household.

'You seem a glorious independent fellow!' said I.

'And I don't think you a fool, and never did. Sir, you are a trump.'

'Is there any hope of your wife's recovery?' said I, modestly seeking to turn the conversation.

'Not the least.'

'The children?'

'Very little.'

'It must be a doleful life, then, for all concerned. This lonely solitude

— this shanty — hard work — hard times.'

'Haven't I Trumpet? He's the cheerer. He crows through all; crows at the darkest: Glory to God in the highest! Continually he crows it.'

'Just the import I first ascribed to his crow, Merrymusk, when first I heard it from my hill. I thought some rich nabob owned some costly Shanghai; little weening any such poor man as you owned this lusty cock of a domestic breed.'

'*Poor* man like *me*? Why call *me* poor? Don't the cock I own glorify this otherwise inglorious, lean, lantern-jawed land? Didn't *my* cock encourage *you*? And *I* give you all this glorification away gratis. I am a great philanthropist. I am a rich man — a very rich man, and a very happy one. Crow, Trumpet.'

The roof jarred.

I returned home in a deep mood. I was not wholly at rest concerning the soundness of Merrymusk's views of things, though full of admiration for him. I was thinking on the matter before my door, when I heard the cock crow again. Enough. Merrymusk is right.

Oh, noble cock! oh, noble man!

I did not see Merrymusk for some weeks after this; but hearing the glorious and rejoicing crow, I supposed that all went as usual with him. My own frame of mind remained a rejoicing one. The cock still inspired me. I saw another mortgage piled on my plantation; but only bought another dozen of stout, and a dozen-dozen of Philadelphia porter. Some of my relatives died; I wore no mourning, but for three days drank stout in preference to porter, stout being of the darker colour. I heard the cock crow the instant I received the unwelcome tidings.

'Your health in this stout, oh, noble cock!'

I thought I would call on Merrymusk again, not having seen or heard of him for some time now. Approaching the place, there were no signs of motion about the shanty. I felt a strange misgiving. But the cock crew from within doors, and the boding vanished. I knocked at the door. A feeble voice bade me enter. The curtain was no longer drawn; the whole house was a hospital now. Merrymusk lay on a heap of old clothes; wife and children were all in their beds. The cock was perched on an old hogshead hoop, swung from the ridge-pole in the middle of the shanty.

'You are sick, Merrymusk,' said I, mournfully.

'No, I am well,' he feebly answered. 'Crow, Trumpet.'

I shrunk. The strong soul in the feeble body appalled me.

But the cock crew.

The roof jarred.

'How is Mrs. Merrymusk?'

'Well.'

'And the children?'

'Well. All well.'

The last two words he shouted forth in a kind of wild ecstasy of triumph over ill. It was too much. His head fell back. A white napkin seemed dropped upon his face. Merrymusk was dead.

An awful fear seized me.

But the cock crew.

The cock shook his plumage as if each feather were a banner. The cock hung from the shanty roof as erewhile the trophied flags from the dome of St. Paul's. The cock terrified me with exceeding wonder.

I drew nigh the bedsides of the woman and children. They marked my look of strange affright; they knew what had happened.

'My good man is just dead,' breathed the woman lowly. 'Tell me true?'

'Dead,' said I.

The cock crew.

She fell back, without a sigh, and through long-loving sympathy was dead.

The cock crew.

The cock shook sparkles from his golden plumage. The cock seemed in a rapture of benevolent delight. Leaping from the hoop, he strode up majestically to the pile of old clothes, where the wood-sawyer lay, and planted himself, like an armorial supporter, at his side. Then raised one long, musical, triumphant, and final sort of crow, with throat heaved far back, as if he meant the blast to waft the wood-sawyer's soul sheer up to the seventh heaven. Then he strode, king-like, to the woman's bed. Another upturned and exultant crow, mated to the former.

The pallor of the children was changed to radiance. Their faces shone celestially through grime and dirt. They seemed children of emperors and kings, disguised. The cock sprang upon their bed, shook himself, and crowed, and crowed again, and still and still again. He seemed bent upon crowing the souls of the children out of their wasted bodies. He seemed bent upon rejoining instanter this whole family in the upper air. The children seemed to second his endeavours. Far, deep, intense longings for release transfigured them into spirits before my eyes. I saw angels where they lay.

They were dead.

The cock shook his plumage over them. The cock crew. It was now like a Bravo! like a Hurrah! like a Three-times-three! hip! hip! He strode out of the shanty. I followed. He flew upon the apex of the dwelling, spread wide his wings, sounded one supernatural note, and dropped at my feet.

The cock was dead.

If now you visit that hilly region, you will see, nigh the railroad track, just beneath October Mountain, on the other side of the swamp — there you will see a gravestone, not with skull and cross-bones, but with a lusty cock in act of crowing, chiselled on it, with the words beneath: —

'O death, where is thy sting?
O grave, where is thy victory?'

The wood-sawyer and his family, with the Signor Beneventano, lie in that spot; and I buried them, and planted the stone, which was a stone made to order; and never since then have I felt the doleful dumps, but under all circumstances crow late and early with a continual crow.

Cock-a-doodle-doo! — oo! — oo! — oo! — oo!

First published in *Harper's Magazine*, 1853.

Poems

THE COLLEGE COLONEL

He rides at their head;
    A crutch by his saddle just slants in view,
One slung arm is in splints, you see,
    Yet he guides his strong steed — how coldly too.

He brings his regiment home —
    Not as they filed two years before,
But a remnant half-tattered, and battered, and worn,
Like castaway sailors, who — stunned
        By the surf's loud roar,
    Their mates dragged back and seen no more —
Again and again breast the surge,
    And at last crawl, spent, to shore.

A still rigidity and pale —
    An Indian aloofness lones his brow;
He has lived a thousand years
Compressed in battle's pains and prayers,
    Marches and watches slow.
There are welcoming shouts, and flags;
    Old men off hat to the Boy,

Wreaths from gay balconies fall at his feet,
    But to *him* — there comes alloy.

It is not that a leg is lost,
    It is not that an arm is maimed,
It is not that the fever has racked —
    Self he has long disclaimed.

But all through the Seven Days' Fight,
    And deep in the Wilderness grim,
And in the field-hospital tent,
    And Petersburg crater, and dim
Lean brooding in Libby, there came —
    Ah heaven! — what *truth* to him.

1863

Colonel (later General) William
Francis Bartlett.
Courtesy of The Berkshire Eagle

PONTOOSUCE

Crowning a bluff where gleams the lake below,
Some pillared pines in well-spaced order stand,
And like an open temple show,
And here in best of seasons bland,
Autumnal noontide, I look out
From dusk arcades on sunshine all about.

Beyond the lake, in upland cheer,
Field, pastoral fields and barns appear,
They skirt the hills where lovely roads
Revealed in links through tiers of woods
Wind up to indistinct abodes
And faery-peopled neighbourhoods;
While further, fainter mountains keep
Hazed in romance impenetrably deep.
Look, corn in stacks, on many a farm
And orchards ripe in languorous charm
As dreamy nature, feeling sure
Of all her genial labour done,
And the last mellow fruitage won,
Would idle out her term mature;
Reposing like a thing reclined
In kinship with man's meditative mind.

For me, within the brown arcade,
Rich life, methought; sweet here in shade,
And pleasant abroad in air! — But, nay,
A counter thought intrusive played,
A thought as old as thought itself,
And who shall lay it on the shelf! —
I felt the beauty bless the day,
I knew the opulence of Autumn's dower;
But evanescence will not stay!
A year ago was such an hour
As this, which but foreruns the blast
Shall sweep these live leaves to the dead leaves past.

All dies!

I stood in reverie long,
Then to forget death's ancient wrong
I turned me in the deep arcade,
And there by chance in lateral glade
I saw low tawny mounds in lines,
Relics of trunks of stately pines,
Ranked erst in colonnades where, lo,
Erect succeeding pillars show!

All dies! and not alone
The aspiring trees and men and grass;
The poet's forms of beauty pass,
And noblest deeds they are undone,
Even truth itself decays, and lo,
From truth's sad ashes pain and falsehood grow.

All dies!

The workman dies, and, after him, the work;
Like to those pines whose graves I trace,
Statue and statuary fall upon their face:
In every amaranth the worm doth lurk,
Even stars, Chaldaeans say, fade from the starry space,
Andes and Appalachee tell
Of havoc ere our Adam fell,
And present Nature as a moss doth show
Of the ruins of the Nature of the aeons of long ago.

But look — and hark!

Adown the glade,
Where light and shadow sport at will,
Who cometh vocal, and arrayed
As in the first pale tints of morn —
So pure, rose-clear, and fresh and chill!
Some ground-pine sprigs her brow adorn,
The earthly rootlets tangled clinging.
Over tufts of moss which dead things made,
Under vital twigs which danced or swayed,
Along she floats, and slightly singing:

'Dies, all dies!
The grass it dies, but in vernal rain
Up it springs, and it lives again;
Over and over, again and again,
It lives, it dies, and it lives again,
Who sighs that all dies?
Summer and winter, and pleasure and pain,
And everything everywhere in God's reign,
They end, and anon they begin again:
Wane and wax, wax and wane:
Over and over and over amain,
End, ever end, and begin again —
End, ever end, and forever and ever begin again!'

She ceased, and nearer slid, and hung
In dewy guise; then softlier sung:
'Since light and shade are equal set,
And all revolves, nor more ye know;
Ah, why should tears the pale cheek fret
For aught that waneth here below.
Let go, let go!'

With that, her warm lips thrilled me through,
She kissed me, while her chaplet cold
Its rootlets brushed against my brow,
With all their humid clinging mould.
She vanished, leaving fragrant breath
And warmth and chill of wedded life and death.

Probably written in 1859

From *The Works of Herman Melville*. Constable, London, 1922.

A Dedication

CLOVER DEDICATION
TO
WINNEFRED

With you and me, Winnie, Red Clover has always been one of the dearest of the flowers of the field: an avowal — by the way — as you well ween, which implies no undelight as to this ruddy young brother's demure little half-sister, White Clover. Our feeling for both sorts originates in no fanciful associations egotistic in kind. It is not, for example, because in any exceptional way we have verified in experience the aptness of that pleasant figure of speech, *Living in clover* — not for this do we so take to the Ruddy One, for all that we once dwelt annually surrounded by flushed acres of it. Neither have we, jointly or severally, so frequently lighted upon that rare four-leaved variety accounted of happy augury to the finder; though, to be sure, on my part, I yearly remind you of the coincidence in my chancing on such a specimen by the wayside on the early forenoon of the fourth day of a certain bridal month, now four years more than four times ten years ago.

But, tell, do we not take to this flower — for flower it is, though with the florist hardly ranking with the floral clans — not alone that in itself it is a thing of freshness and beauty, but also that being no delicate foster-child of the nurseryman, but a hardy little creature of out-of-doors accessible and familiar to every one, no one can monopolise its charm. Yes, we are communists here.

Sweet in the mouth of that brindled heifer, whose breath you so loved to inhale, and doubtless pleasant to her nostril and eye; sweet as well to the like senses in ourselves; prized by that most radical of men, the farmer, to whom wild amaranths in a pasture, though emblems of immortality, are but weeds and anathema; finding favor even with so peevish a busybody as the bee; is it not the felicitous fortune of our favourite to incur no creature's displeasure, but to enjoy, and without striving for it, the spontaneous goodwill of all? Why it is that this little peasant of the flowers revels in so enviable an immunity and privilege, not in equal degree shared by any of us mortals however gifted and good; that indeed is something the reason whereof may not slumber very deep. But — *In pace*; always leave a sleeper to his repose.

How often at our adopted homestead on the hillside — now ours no more — the farm-house, long ago shorn by the urbane barbarian succeeding us in the proprietorship — shorn of its gambrel roof and dormer windows, and when I last saw it indolently settling in serene contentment of natural decay; how often, Winnie, did I come in from my ramble early cheery roses of the meek, newly purloined from the fields to consecrate them on that bit of a maple-wood mantel — your altar, somebody called it — in the familiar room facing your belovèd South! And in October most did I please myself in gathering them from the moist matted aftermath in an enriched little hollow near by, soon to be snowed upon and for consecutive months sheeted from view. And once — you remember it — having culled them in a sunny little flurry of snow, winter's frolic skirmisher in advance, the genial warmth of your chamber melted the fleecy flakes into dewdrops rolling off from the ruddiness, 'Tears of the happy,' you said.

Well, and to whom but to thee, Madonna of the Trefoil, should I now dedicate these 'Weeds and Wildings,' thriftless children of quite another and yet later spontaneous aftergrowth, and bearing indications, too apparent it may be, of that terminating season on which the offerer verges. But take them. And for aught suggestion of the 'melting mood' that any may possibly betray, call to mind the dissolved snowflakes on the ruddy oblation of old, and remember your 'Tears of the Happy.'

———————

From "Weeds and Wildings," probably written in 1891. Published posthumously in 1924.

EVERT A. DUYCKINCK

Evert A. Duyckinck (1816-1878), editor and owner of the "Literary World," the best literary weekly in the country at the time, was a good friend of Melville's. He visited the Melvilles shortly after they had moved to Pittsfield, and in a letter to his wife gives an account of the famous picnic expedition up Monument Mountain, a climb now informally reenacted each summer on the Sunday nearest August 5 by any and all interested. "Miss Panton" was Mrs. Duyckinck's sister and "Mr. Wolfe" her uncle. Joel T. Headley, a prolific biographer and popular historian, lived for a time in Stockbridge. "Darley and Henry" are F.O.C. Darley, the artist, and Mrs. Duyckinck's brother. "Magarnsca" is Duyckinck's garbling of "Magawisca," Miss Sedgwick's native American heroine.

In another letter the following week, he describes to his wife an expedition up Greylock under Melville's guidance.

Picnic Letters

THE PICNIC ON MONUMENT MOUNTAIN

The Melville House, Pittsfield
Tuesday August 6. 1850

My dear wife,

Monday came and the visit to Stockbridge with it. You drop down by the cars fifteen miles or so and find yourself on a lower level in a Chinese painted green saucer, with water, trees and verandahs, edged by blue mountains. We found at the station house Oliver Wendell Holmes whom Mr Field had reached with his lion lasso. He was on the spot himself at Stockbridge and drove us to his cottage, convenient and rambling and pitched down in the verdure — There we saw Mrs. F. and the daughter a nice young lady. The family goes to Europe in the Pacific to be at Rome in the fall. I said they must look out for Mr Wolfe & Miss Panton — "Miss Panton?" said the daughter. I know a Miss Panton — They call her Cassy and Julia Bryant talks about her. The pleasant Julia had been there a week & gone away among the hills. Presently James T. Fields the Boston publisher drove up with his newly married wife and Nathaniel Hawthorne. A young whiskered Harry Sedgwick came on on horseback and we fell in line in three conveyances for Monument Mountain. You will find the legend and the poem in Bryant's poems. It is a rough projection of the cliffs, scarred and blasted. We took to our feet on its sides and strode upward Hawthorne and myself in advance, talking of the Scarlet Letter. As we scrambled over the rocks at the summit which

Summer boarders at the Old Coffee House, South Street, Pittsfield, c. 1870.
The Berkshire Athenaeum, Local History Department

surveys a wide range of country on either side, a black thunder cloud from the south dragged its ragged edges toward us — the thunder rolling in the distance. They talked of shelter and shelter there proved to be though it looked unpromising but these difficulties, like others, vanish on trial and a few feet of rock with a damp underground of mosses and decay actually sheltered publisher Fields curled whiskers, his patent leathers and his brides delicate blue silk. Dr Holmes cut three branches for an umbrella and uncorked the champagne which was drunk from a silver mug. The rain did not do its worst and we scattered over the cliffs, Herman Melville to seat himself, the boldest of all, astride a projecting low stick of rock while Dr Holmes peeped about the cliffs and protested it affected him like ipecac. Hawthorne looked wildly about for the great carbuncle. Mathews read Bryant's poem. The exercise was glorious. We shed rain like ducks and for wet feet — I boated about in Mr Fields parlors on the return in *his* stockings and slippers — Then came the dinner — a three hour's business from turkey to ice cream, well moistened by the way. Dr Holmes said some of his best things and drew the whole company out by laying down various propositions of the superiority of the Englishmen. Melville attacked him vigorously. Hawthorne looked on and Fields his publisher smiled with internal satisfaction underneath his curled whiskers at the good tokens of a brilliant poem from Holmes in a few days at the Yale College celebration. Joel Tyler Headley dropped in with his brother in law — I forget his name but he was shot at the Astor Riots.

It was a merciless thing to get us off from such a dinner in the afternoon to the Icy Glen, a break in one of the hills of tumbled huge, damp, mossy rocks in whose recesses ice is said to be found all the year round. Headley led the way and a scramble it was such as you would not have effected — nasty and sublime though the ladies get up torch light parties here — we came out on the peaceful fields of the Housatonic and skirting a meadow crossed the river to our host's again. Talk and tea and a tall Mrs Sedgewick and a cross examination which I did not stand very well on Hope Leslie and Magarnsca — and at 10 o'clock the railway home, a short walk under the stars and we turned in at the Melville house — a vigorous Creole lady & her husband having departed in the forenoon.

Mr. Field's hospitalities & kindness were of the rarest & altogether it was a rare meeting was it not —

The best part of the scenery they say is yet to be seen — Salisbury Lakes I think they call them and the ascent of the Dome &c. We were urged to visit these at once but this I thought was a day to be left by itself and I shall need your help in discovering the rest. I wish you could see the view from my window now & breathe this fine air. It is warm but you do not *swelter* — If you were here with the children I could be content to remain till October — You must see Pittsfield — The fat woman of Davis' stoop does not compare — I am in earnest — with Saddleback and the small birds sing sweeter than the Sunday newsboys or the demented milk man. Headley is to visit us to day. He has been looking for Darley & Henry. As he will remain here some six weeks they can not do better than to overhaul him at Stockbridge. Tomorrow we shall drive over six or eight miles to Lebanon & look up Mrs. Long & Dambman & get something out of the Shakers for you and the children. Another day for a visit to Hawthorne & Monday, at the latest, a call upon dear Margaret.

Hers truly
Evert A Duyckinck

A NIGHT ON GREYLOCK

Pittsfield, August 13

The ascent of Saddleback the highest mountain in Massachusetts came off grandly with a party of eleven Allan Melville & wife, Herman Melville & his sister Augusta, Mrs Morewood, her sisters Mrs Pollock and Miss Henderson & an adjacent clergyman Mr Entler — with the best Pic-nic-ian appliances.

By railway to North Adams — but go on to Williamstown ... for there is a cripple land lord and a stage contractor at the first place who will swindle you.

The ascent — We did this with four horses in a four seated wagon from the northerly side of the Mt. Ascending you get to a passage, with Saddleback or Saddleball or Greylock as they call him for its southerly side which they cant easily deface. It is the "Bellows Pipe" or "Notch" pass to South Adams. Then you have the ascent proper taking to horseback or foot — *three* miles of the toughest bog and stumbling which could well be got up by the forces of mountain torrents, the rotting of mists, snows and ever falling vegetation. The last mile of that is tough.

I was a blown horse when I reached the summit, gasping with open mouth and dripping at every pore. A half tumbler of Port was the thing then.

The Observatory. This is a structure some seventy feet high without which you would see nothing of the view. It was put up some twenty years since by the neighboring Williams' College for observations on the winds &c.

To dinner — spread on boards in the damp saturated sleeping story of the Observatory. How that Heidsieck is emptied into the silver gilt mug and the throats of the company! How those multitudinous layers of ham disappear and well they may — for when you go up into the heavens 3500 ft you must strengthen the stomach.

The Fire. It is dark. Melville's axe is ringing against the fallen trees lying about and with a fireplace among the roots of a huge decaying stump a pyramid is created fanned by the wind. The ladies are lying around in buffalo robes borrowed from the sleighing parties of last winter and thus, with Mrs Morewood's ringing laugh till midnight.

Sleep. "Sleep no more, Morewood has murdered sleep." We are all stretched in a row on quilts and buffalo robes. While Mrs M surveys and describes the company satirically enough, not forgetting my position alongside of the English lady. You drink strong liquor and make strong jokes up in the clouds. Then she feeds us with brandy cherries — while Miss Augusta sits bolt upright in a corner all the night to report in the morning the number of rats which have passed over the coverlets! You must not be too nice in the clouds. Allan Melville had the effrontery to go to sleep and snore defiance to the sleepless. A champagne bottle had contained a sperm candle but it was extinguished out of respect to the moon.

Sunrise. At four we were aloft — a dull cloudy sky. Later in the morning the sun did break through the mists and showed us below mountains and clouds which rolled away from each other with the sublimity with which mountains are invested in the O. Testament. It was worth while to see that.

Breakfast. The cloth is spread out of doors and shows stains of the fast devoured supper — Herman Melville and the clergyman are tossing a pair of fine fowls (hurriedly snatched from the landlord's larder at North Adams) amidst the smoke & heated stones of a fire which wont make coals. They taste well however and the water (which cost us $2 for the pail to the guides) is relieved of its taste of mountain ferns by the rinsings of the cherry jar. There would be a poor prospect for a dinner.

The Descent. I go ahead, Mrs Morewood and George straggling along to gather the mosses and wild flowers and pick the strawberries (which she only can find) and yellow raspberries by the way — the rest of the party waiting for the horses to ascend to them. I enjoyed that walk of solitary mountain, descending to the Hopper.

The Arrest. A piece of sharp practice at North Adams. We had directed the vehicle contractor to take us directly to the Railway station. It suited his plans better to carry us, at the dinner hour, to the hotel only a few yards off, but we had baggage to shift. He would not carry the ladies farther & proceeded to unload. It was concluded to let him follow us who marched off with the luggage, to the Railway for his pay. The next thing we hear is at the car office. A couple of gentlemen of no business apparently in particular drop down and tell me that it was best to settle, the *Sheriff* was coming, and says he, there he is & lo and behold the driver bearing down with a couple of attendants. The sheriff presently produces a writ, doubtless impersonal & tells Mr Melville he is arrested and must go with him. Go where — Why to the hotel and settle — You have no business to take me to the hotel — I have had no demand. Where is your bill — So much & my fees. Your arrest is worth nothing — make your demand. A bill was made out & paid. But you have no idea of the downright English they got from us or of the lots of vagabonds who hung on at the proceedings — Allan M put into them pretty much as Henry would have done.

What do you think? After our hot and wearied return from all this Mrs Morewood proposed a fishing party for the afternoon!

From *Glimpses of Herman Melville's Life in Pittsfield 1850-51; Some Unpublished Letters of Evert A. Duyckinck* by Luther Stearns Mansfield (Williams College); reprinted from American Literature, Vol. 9 No. 1, March 1937.

JAMES T. FIELDS

James T. Fields (1817-1881) of Boston was Hawthorne's publisher. Here he recollects the famous Monument Mountain picnic when Melville and Hawthorne first met. Although shy on the surface, with those he knew well Fields was a true and jovial friend — surely a significant element of his emi-nence as a publisher in American literary history.

The Devil's Pulpit, Monument Mountain. Stockbridge Historical Society

The Picnic

One beautiful summer day, twenty years ago, I found Hawthorne in his little red cottage at Lenox, surrounded by his happy young family. He had the look, as somebody said, of a banished lord, and his grand figure among the hills of Berkshire seemed finer than ever. His boy and girl were swinging on the gate as we drove up to his door, and with their sunny curls formed an attractive feature in the landscape. As the afternoon was cool and delightful, we proposed a drive over to Pittsfield to see Holmes, who was then living on his ancestral farm. Hawthorne was in a cheerful condition, and seemed to enjoy the beauty of the day to the utmost. Next morning we were all invited by Mr. Dudley Field, then living at Stockbridge, to ascend Monument Mountain. Holmes, Hawthorne, Duyckinck, Herman Melville, Headley, Sedgwick, Matthews, and several ladies, were of the party. We scrambled to the top with great spirit, and when we arrived, Melville, I remember, bestrode a peaked rock, which ran out like a bowsprit, and pulled and hauled imaginary ropes for our delectation. Then we all assembled in a shady spot, and one of the party read to us Bryant's beautiful poem commemorating Monument Mountain. Then we lunched among the rocks, and somebody proposed Bryant's health, and "long life to the dear old poet." This was the most popular toast of the day, and it took, I remember, a considerable quantity of Heidsieck to do it justice. In the afternoon, pioneered by Headley, we made our way, with merry shouts and laughter, through the Ice-Glen. Hawthorne was among the most enterprising of the merry-makers; and being in the dark much of the time, he ventured to call out lustily and pretend that certain destruction was inevitable to all of us. After this extemporaneous jollity, we dined together at Mr. Dudley Field's in Stockbridge, and Hawthorne rayed out in a sparkling and unwonted manner. I remember the conversation at table chiefly ran on the physical differences between the present American and English men, Hawthorne stoutly taking part in favor of the American. This 5th of August was a happy day throughout, and I never saw Hawthorne in better spirits.

From *Yesterdays With Authors* by James T. Fields. Osgood & Co., 1873.

J.E.A. SMITH

J.E.A. Smith (1822-1896), Pittsfield socialite and editor of the Berkshire County Eagle *for a time, was an excellent local historian who was a good friend and memorialist of Melville, with whom he went on some of the long tramps Melville loved to Berkshire destinations of interest.*

In these excerpts from his History of Pittsfield, *Smith discusses the county's loss of population, a perennial problem; and the explosion of the magazine, which occurred a few days before Hawthorne's arrival. Under the name of "Godfrey Greylock" Smith wrote several books of Berkshire lore, including an account of the Richmond Boulder Train, which figured internationally in the theorizing about glaciation and an Ice Age.*

Pages from Pittsfield's History

EMIGRATION TO THE WEST

But of those losses most felt and least compensated, in Pittsfield, between 1820 and 1840, was the constant drain, especially upon the farming-portion of its population, by emigration to the west. Much as had been accomplished by the Agricultural Society, it had not been able to perform the miracle of making the soil of New England rival that of the Genessee valley and Ohio — then the wheat-growing west. Speculating companies, taking advantage of the severe winters and cold summers, about the year 1816, stimulated the western fever by painting the new country as at once the paradise and the El Dorado of the farmer, and, by offering lands upon the most favorable terms. And, as if this were not enough, religious enthusiasm was brought to aid in the depletion of the population of the town. In 1835, while a great revival was in progress at the Baptist church, a preacher from the west portrayed the wants of that region to the assembled crowds, so vividly that one hundred and six of the most valuable members of the church — and it is to be presumed equally valuable citizens — at once emigrated, and were followed soon after by a second migration in such numbers that only three men were left in the organization.

THE MAGAZINE EXPLODES

One of the most vividly remembered of the minor events in the history of Pittsfield was the explosion of the public powder-magazine in July, 1838. This building was located, with singular disregard to public safety, in the north-east corner of the old burial-ground near the center of

The Boston and Albany Roundhouse in Pittsfield, c. 1865, with Jubilee Hill in the background.
The Berkshire Athenaeum, Local History Department

the village; and, at the time of the explosion contained about seven hundred pounds of gunpowder; of which four hundred pounds, intended for use in testing the arms manufactured at Lemuel Pomeroy's armory, was owned by the United States government, and the remainder by various merchants.

For several months previous to the explosion the inhabitants of the village had been annoyed by the nocturnal misdemeanors of disorderly young men. Gates were unhinged, signs removed, fences defaced, and other like petty crimes were endured with little resistance by those who suffered from them. Finally, the artillery-pieces belonging to the state were frequently taken out of their house and discharged at dead of night, while the firing of muskets and smaller arms was incessant night after night. Emboldened by the neglect of efficient measures to bring them to justice, the authors of these disturbances, sometime previous to the fourth of July, stole both the cannon and secreted them until, on the night of the seventh of July, one of them was planted in the earth in front of the house of Lemuel Pomeroy, and after being loaded to the muzzle was discharged, ruining the piece and inflicting considerable injury upon the house of Mr. Pomeroy and that opposite to it.

Proceeding to more dangerous practices, the disturbers of the peace several times entered the magazine, by means of false keys, and obtained considerable quantities of gunpowder.

Now, at last, active measures were taken to bring them to justice; and, at the request of Mr. Pomeroy, the Adjutant-General ordered the artillery pieces to Boston. Provoked by this threatened interruption of their discreditable exploits, they threw out menaces to which little attention was paid, that the magazine should be exploded. Even their previous reck-lessness had not prepared the magistrates or the people to believe that they would perpetrate an act fraught with such danger to life and prop-erty, and likely to bring swift and extreme punishment upon themselves. No watch was therefore set over the exposed property, or any other measures of precaution taken. On the night of the 12th of July, however, the threats were put in execution, and at half-past eleven o'clock, the magazine was exploded, the great mass of gunpowder contained in it having been fired by a slow-match.

By remarkable good fortune no loss of life ensued; but the destruction of property was very great. The house owned by Nelson Strong, situated on Fenn street, very near the magazine, was a perfect wreck. Windows, doors, and whatever else could be loosened by the explosion were thrown upon the beds where the family were sleeping. Every piece of crockery in the house was broken. On the opposite side of Fenn street, the house of Mr. Henry Callender was much injured in a similar way, and a brick was thrown entirely through it. The brick school-house on the corner of Pearl and Fenn streets, and a neighboring house lost their windows. The dwell-ing-house of James Warriner on East street, James H. Dunham on North street, the Medical Institution, the town-hall, the Congregational and Baptist churches suffered severely. Some twenty other buildings suffered considerably, but chiefly from the breakage of glass.

Intense excitement prevailed on the following morning, and at a large meeting of the citizens, after speeches such as the occasion would natu-rally call out, a committee, of which Edward A. Newton was chairman, was appointed to bring the authors of the outrage to justice. The select-men also offered a reward of two hundred dollars for their conviction. The committee reported on the 19th of July, that they were "engaged in a course of investigations and suits which promised to bring the guilty parties to justice." But, nevertheless, and although several young men connected with highly respectable families were generally believed to be implicated, no one was ever convicted.

From *History of Pittsfield* by J.E.A. Smith. Lee and Shepard, 1869.

The Richmond Boulder Trains

THE FIELD-MEETING

The phenomenon which has drawn to Richmond so many eminent geologists is the occasional arrangement of the exposed boulders in well-defined trains; which is exceptional, if not unique, so far as observations have been made and published.

These remarkable trains were discovered, about the year 1840, by Dr. Stephen Reed, who, as President of our Scientific Association, led our field-meeting on Perry's Peak. When the feast was over, that day, and we had fraternized with our genial and hospitable Richmond hosts, we listened to local story, told by venerable speakers from Lenox and Stockbridge, concerning Parson Perry, the second minister, and his parishioner, Col. Rossiter, who, as second in command of the Berkshire militia at the Battle of Bennington, did good service; recalling his men from plundering to fighting, and thereby saving the day which was well nigh lost after it had been once won.

When we had thus done due honor to some of the old-time local worthies, our venerable president — who might well have served the most fastidious painter as a model for "an old geologist" — told the story of his discovery, illustrating his method very simply. "If," said he "you should see a cart loaded with apples of a peculiar variety, which, dropping from a leaky tail-board, were strewn all the way back to a certain orchard which alone bore that kind of fruit, you would have no difficulty in determining where that apple train came from."

By a similar process it is easy to trace the principal, and most perfect, of the Richmond Boulder Trains to its source; since it is an exceedingly well defined and nearly continuous succession of large angular masses of a peculiar chloritic schist, wholly unlike the general bed-rocks of the vicinity, and also differing totally from most of the neighboring boulders.

Following up this train, Dr. Reed found it terminate, three miles northwest of the Richmond meeting house, on the summit of Fry's Hill, the highest, and almost the central point of the Canaan Mountains in Columbia county, N.Y.; one of the short ranges which run along the Taconics. The top of this hill is composed of a chloritic schist, precisely like that of the boulders, and unlike any other bed-rock in all that region. Of course no doubt remained of the source of that train, and its discoverer, retracing his steps, continued his investigations until he had followed it in the opposite direction across the towns of Richmond, Lenox and Lee, some ten or twelve miles in all. He believed that it reached still further, and perhaps even to Connecticut. I think he afterwards obtained some evidence that this supposition was correct, but of how conclusive a nature I cannot say. Subsequently he found another train of the chloritic schist, originating, like the first, on the Canaan Mountains, and five of limestone derived from the Taconic range; but none so complete as the first.

In 1842, Dr. Reed published an account of his discovery in the "Lenox Farmer," predicting for the boulders a host of distinguished visitors and a wide fame; a prophecy which has been amply verified; for during his life he piloted among them Dr. Birney of Boston, Professors Chester Dewey, Hitchcock, Hosford, Hall and the Brothers Rogers, Sir Charles Lyell, Count Pourtales, and Professor De Saurre.

The result has been a dozen or more learned essays, of which the most interesting are those of Sir Charles Lyell and Rev. John B. Perry.

LYELL'S THEORY

Lyell in his "Antiquity of Man," gives a spirited account of his visit and a graphic description of the rocks, making some very fascinating reading. His theory is that "at the time of the drift period, the highest points of the Canaan, Richmond and Lenox ranges formed chains of islands in an ocean; and that the gaps in the Richmond and Lenox ranges were straits through which floated ice-bergs bearing the chloritic blocks from the exposed parts of the Canaan range, and dropping them in their present positions." So strongly did this notion impress itself upon Sir Charles, that he illustrated his work with a view of the islands, and the rock-laden ice-floes — not ice-bergs — floating between them. He has also given views of some of the larger boulders, and a diagram of the seven trains.

PERRY'S THEORY

Mr. Perry divides the boulders which rest upon the surface of the drift into two classes, according as they are rounded or angular: those which make up the trains being rounded, while the angular are distributed without definite arrangement. He considers that the trains owe their formation to the movement of the general ice-mass which rested upon the region during the glacial period; the boulders, which are found in trains; and which he believes to be rounded, having been torn from prominent peaks, and forced along under the ice-sheet, while the scattered ones were transported to their present position much later, when the ice-mass had become so much reduced in thickness that the peaks in question projected above the surface, so that masses of rock could be lodged upon the ice as well as dragged along under it.

Since Dr. Reed's death, which occurred in 1876, Mr. E.R. Benton of Boston has made an exhaustive survey of the locality of the boulders and a thorough study of their phenomena, and has published the result in a pamphlet of forty-two pages, forming Number Three of the Fifth Volume of the Bulletin of the Harvard College Museum of Comparative Zoölogy.

BENTON'S CONCLUSION

Having given a concise resumé of the statements and opinions of his predecessors, Mr. Benton proceeds to a geological and topographical description of the Boulder Region, which is illustrated by maps showing the contours of the hills, their bed-rocks and the course of the trains.

The crest of Fry's Hill in the town of Canaan, has an elevation of six hundred and twenty feet above the track of the Boston and Albany railroad in Richmond, which is one thousand and fifty feet above the level of the sea. This crest, extending one hundred and fifty feet down from its summit, is composed of a fine-grained foliaceous mica chloritic schist, very tough and of a green color. It is identical with the boulders of the main train, is of narrow extent here, and has been found, in place, in only one other locality on the range. To its limited extent Mr. Benton attributes the distinctness of the train, whose width varies from two hundred and fifty to five hundred feet; the difference being caused apparently by the varying contours of the hills in its path.

From the summit of Fry's Hill the train descends in a south 54 degrees east direction; then bends gradually to the southward till, at the base of the range, it has a south 27 degrees east direction. Thence it extends just south of the North Family of the Shakers, and up the face and along the crest of a westerly spur of the Richmond range, called Merriman's Mount, to the crest of the western branch of the range. In so doing it gradually changes its direction, to the south 68 degrees east; and so crosses the Haskell valley and begins the descent of the Richmond range. In making this descent, it bends considerably to the south, crossing the main road in Richmond two miles north of the railroad station, till it attains a south 25 degrees east direction, where it crosses the railroad. From the railroad the train continues on across the Richmond valley, but curves to the eastward as it mounts the western slope of the Lenox range, crosses its two parallel ridges and descends into the Lenox and Stockbridge valley, where its direction is south 50 degrees east. A half a mile south-east of Mr. Luther Butler's house, near the Lenox and Stockbridge line, the train seems to lose its continuous character; the chloritic schist boulders in the same line, to the south-east, being few, small, and widely separated.

Far the largest boulders of the train, averaging fifteen feet in length — are found on the eastern slope of the Canaan range; two of them measuring ninety and one hundred and twenty-five feet in circumference respectively, and being about thirty feet in height. One the western slope of this range there are no chloritic schist boulders. Near the Lebanon Shakers they average twelve feet in length; one having a circumference of seventy-five feet. Lyell mentions two with circumferences of seventy, and one hundred and twenty feet respectively, and a height of twenty feet above the soil, lying two miles north of Richmond station. Thence there is a constant diminution in size until, in the Lenox and Stockbridge valley, the average length does not exceed two feet.

By the Richmond range, Mr. Benton means that portion of the Taconic Mountains which lies in Richmond and the adjoining town of Canaan on the west; and is separated by a narrow valley from the Canaan or Columbia range. Fry's Hill is two and a half miles south of Douglas Knob, the picturesque elevation which almost over-hangs Columbia Hall, and forms the northern terminus of the range.

The Lenox range is a spur thrown off by the Taconics at Egremont, which, broken by the Williams River at West Stockbridge, extends northeastward to Pittsfield, where it terminates in South Mountain and Melville Hill. Its domes and peaks form some of the most striking and beautiful features in the views, looking north from the Lenox, and south from the Pittsfield valley; while its southern extension, reaching to Stockbridge, is filled with the most delicious scenery.

But to return to the Boulder trains: in accounting for the transportation of the boulders to the positions in which they are now found, Mr. Benton discards Lyell's theory of floating ice, since it implies that, during the period in which they were deposited, the level of the ocean stood above the crest of the Canaan range, or sixteen hundred and fifty feet higher than it now does. Other writers have shown that the same line of reasoning which leads to Lyell's conclusions would require a depression of parts of the glaciated region to a depth of five thousand feet below their present level; a depression which all the evidence indicates did not exist.

Mr. Benton's own solution of the problem is based upon the fact, now generally admitted by geologists, that in the Post-Pliocene age, this region, in common with a large part of the northern hemisphere, was covered with an ice-sheet several thousand feet thick, which had a slow motion in this district from the north-west to the south-east. But he shows that the boulders could not have rested, and been borne along, upon the upper surface of this ice-sheet; since that pre-supposes cliffs upon the Canaan range which towered above that surface, whereas an ice-sheet which could move across valleys six hundred feet deep, without being materially deflected from its course, must have covered the highest land to the depth of many hundred feet. Nor could the boulders have been dragged along under the ice-mass, without leaving marks of abrasion of which none are to be seen.

It is probable, he thinks, that the boulders were torn from their original bed by the ice sheet, and became imbedded in its mass instead of being dragged along under it. The sharpness of the knob called Fry's Hill favors this supposition, since boulders torn from its upper part would be at least one hundred feet above the lower surface of the ice along the neighboring parts of the crest; and the mass, closing again as soon as it had passed the sharp knob, would hold many of them firmly in its grasp, without allowing them to reach the rocks below, until the ice-sheet had ceased its grinding march and was in process of dissolution. Nevertheless, under the incessant influence of gravity, the imbedded fragments would be constantly working their way downward, and many of them, finally reaching the under surface, would be ground up by the crunching, superincumbent, moving mass; and the farther from the source, the greater would be the amount of material lost to the trains, and added to the underlying gravel beds.

OTHER INTERESTING ERRATICS

The boulder and drift deposits in the valley at the base of the Taconics, north of Richmond, offer a fresh and interesting field of investigation. At some points there are indications of arrangement in trains; but, whether or not if followed up those indications should lead to discoveries of that character, they could not fail of valuable and curious results. Some of the local deposits of boulders are strikingly suggestive. I have already spoken of the Balanced Rock group. In the romantic town of New Marlboro', next east of Great Barrington, is another rocking stone, quite as firmly based, and with a more pronounced and easy oscillation. Between Onota street and Lake Onota, in Pittsfield, some most singular boulders are strewn. One variety is composed of what appears upon the surface to be a net work, but in reality is a honey comb, of quartz cells filled with a hard schist. Sometimes cells, which were probably filled with a softer rock, are empty, leaving a skeleton of quartz walls. Another variety of soft rock enclosed rounded pebbles sometimes six or eight inches long. I think some summer or autumn days could be pleasantly passed in tracing these queer erratics to their source, and trying to imagine how they were made; and when; and why.

From *Taghconic* by "Godfrey Greylock" (J.E.A. Smith). Eagle Printing & Binding, 1908.

HENRY WARD BEECHER

It is an interesting coincidence that the three greatest leaders of American Protestantism — Jonathan Edwards, Henry Ward Beecher, and Reinhold Niebuhr — each of whom turned Protestant thought into decisively new directions, lived (in their different times, of course) within a few miles of one another in the Berkshires.

Beecher fashioned the sort of non-denominational "civic religion" based upon ideals of forgiveness, brotherhood, and uplift that made him an immensely influential figure in an age weary of sectarian hair-splitting, increasingly skeptical of literal fundamentalism as science advanced, and apprehensive about slavery, urban slums, immigration, and the abuses of capitalism.

In 1853, his congregation in Brooklyn made it possible for him to buy John Hotchkin's farm in Lenox for $4000. There he spent several summers and wrote his Star Papers, *in which he amusingly informed his readers of the delights of Berkshire living. Subsequently his house was torn down and the farm incorporated into Cranwell.*

Mid-October Days

Lenox, October, 1854.

A t this season of the year it requires but a few weeks, and often but a few days, to work great changes upon the face of Nature. Lenox in the middle of September stood in untarnished green. Grass and flowers were plump and succulent with copious juices. Here and there a coquetting maple leaf displayed gay colors among its yet sober fellow leaves. A shade of yellow, a bright streak of red, might be seen in single trees, as if Nature, like an artist, was trying its colors, to make sure of the right shades before laying them upon the gorgeous canvas. Yet all these made no impression upon the vast front of the mountains around us, that still lay patiently, like mighty dromedaries, camped down against the horizon — a caravan that shall never rise up to the voice of a driver, nor move, until He who formed them shall scatter them!

It is now mid-October. All things are changed. Of all the railroads near New York none can compare for beauty of scenery with the Housatonic from Newtown up to Pittsfield, but especially from New Milford to Lenox.

That scenery which a few weeks ago stood in summer green now seemed enchanted. The Housatonic was the same. The skies were the same. The mountain forms were unchanged. But they had blossomed into resplendent colors from top to base. It was strange to see such huge mountains, that are images of firmness and majesty, now tricked out with fairy pomp, as if all the spirits of the air had reveled there, and hung their glowing scarfs on every leaf and bough. We were almost sorry to reach our destination and leave the cars. But the first step on our own ground brought content.

Once more I am upon this serene hill-top! The air is very clear, very still, and very solemn, or, rather, tenderly sad, in its serene brightness. It is not that moist spring air, full of the smell of wood, of the soil, and of the odor of vegetation, which warm winds bring to us from the south. It is not that summer atmosphere, full of alternations of haze and fervent clearness, as if Nature were brewing every day some influence for its myriad children; sometimes in showers, and sometimes with coercive heat upon root and leaf; and, like a universal taskmaster, was driving up the hours to accomplish the labors of the year. No! In these autumn days there is a sense of leisure and of meditation. The sun seems to look down upon the labors of its fiery hands with complacency. Be satisfied, O seasonable Sun! Thou hast shaped an ample year, and art garnering up harvests which well may swell thy rejoicing heart with gracious gladness.

One who breaks off in the summer, and returns in autumn to the hills, needs almost to come to a new acquaintance with the most familiar things. It is another world; or it is the old world a-masquerading; and you halt, like one scrutinizing a disguised friend, between the obvious dissemblance and the subtile likeness.

Southward of our front door there stood two elms, leaning their branches toward each other, forming a glorious arch of green. Now, in faint yellow they grow attenuated and seem as if departing; they are losing their leaves and fading out of sight, as trees do in twilight. Yonder, over against that young growth of birch and evergreen, stood, all summer long, a perfect maple tree, rounded out on every side, thick with luxuriant foliage, and dark with greenness, save when the morning sun, streaming through it, sent transparency to its very heart. Now it is a tower of gorgeous red. So sober and solemn did it seem all summer that I should think as soon to see a prophet dancing at a peasants' holiday, as *it* transfigured to such intense gayety! Its fellows, too, the birches and the walnuts, burn from head to foot with fires that glow but never consume.

But these holiday hills! Have the evening clouds, suffused with sunset, dropped down and become fixed into solid forms? Have the rainbows that followed autumn storms faded upon the mountains and left their mantles there? Yet, with all their brilliancy, how modest do they seem; how patient when bare, or burdened with winter; how cheerful when flushed with summer-green; and how modest when they lift up their wreathed and crowned heads in the resplendent days of autumn!

Henry Ward Beecher. Engraving by H.B. Hall's Sons, New York, 1888

I stand alone upon the peaceful summit of this hill, and turn in every direction. The east is all a-glow; the blue north flushes all her hills with radiance; the west stands in burnished armor; the southern hills buckle the zone of the horizon together with emeralds and rubies, such as were never set in the fabled girdle of the gods! Of gazing there can not be enough. The hunger of the eye grows by feeding.

Only the brotherhood of evergreens — the pine, the cedar, the spruce, and the hemlock — refuse to join this universal revel. They wear their sober green straight through autumn and winter, as if they were set to keep open the path of summer through the whole year, and girdle all seasons together with a clasp of endless green. But in vain do they give solemn examples to the merry leaves which frolic with every breeze that runs sweet riot in the glowing shades. Gay leaves will not be counseled, but will die bright and laughing. But both together — the transfigured leaves of deciduous trees and the calm unchangeableness of evergreens — how more beautiful are they than either alone! The solemn pine brings color to the cheek of the beeches, and the scarlet and golden maples rest gracefully upon the dark foliage of the million-fingered pine.

All summer long these leaves have wrought their tasks. They have plied their laboratory, and there that old chemist, the Sun, hath prepared all the juices of the trees. Now hath come their play-spell. Nature gives them a jubilee. It is a concert of colors for the eye. What a mighty chorus of colors do the trees roll down the valleys, up the hill-sides, and over the mountains!

Before October we sought and found colors in single tones, in flowers, in iris-winking dew-drops, in westward trooping clouds. But when the Year, having wrought and finished her solid structures, unbends and consecrates the glad October month to fancy, then all hues that were before scattered in lurking flowers, in clouds, upon plumed birds, and burnished insects, are let loose like a flood and poured abroad in the wild magnificence of Divine bounty. The earth lifts up its head crowned as no monarch was ever crowned, and the seasons go forth toward winter, chanting to God a hymn of praise that may fitly carry with it the hearts of all men, and bring, forth in kindred joy the sympathetic spirits of the dead.

These are the days that one fain would be loose from the earth and wander forth as a spirit, or lie bedded in some buoyant cloud, to float above the vast expanse, in the silence of the upper air. How we would fain be voyagers, pursuing the seasons through all their latitudes, and no longer stand to wait their coming and going about our fixed habitations.

When we were here in August, the odorous barns were full of new mown hay, and the hay was full of buried crickets and locusts, that chirped away as merrily from the smothered mow as if it were no prison. The barns now are still. The field-crickets are gone, the locust is gone, and the hay has lost its clover-smell. In August we loved to throw wide open the doors, upon the threshing floor, and let the wind through. But now only the sunny door looking south stands open. No lithe swallow twitters in and out, or in his swift flight marks dark circles in the sky, gone as soon as made.

There are two barns. The floor of the one is covered with shocks of corn, whose golden ears, split through the husk, are showing their burnished rows of grain. The other floor is heaped with unwinnowed buckwheat. O! what cakes shall yet rise out of that dusky pile! But now the buckwheat lies in heaps of chaff that swell the bulk, but diminish the value. If we could sell grain in the chaff as we can books, farming would be very profitable.

I love to sit just within the sunny edge of the south door, whose prospect is large and beautiful, with an unread book for company. For a book is set to sharpen, not to feed the appetite. It whets the drowsy thought, and puts observation into the eye. The best books do not think for us, but stir us to think. They are lenses through which we look — not mere sacks stuffed with knowledge.

A wagon rolls past, rattling over the stones. From under the unthreshed straw mice squeak and quarrel; lonesome spiders are repairing their webs in the windows that catch nothing but dust and chaff. Yet these bum-bailiffs have grown plump on something. I wonder what a spider is thinking about for hours together, down in the dark throat of his web, where he lies as still as if he were dead.

Our old Shanghai steps up with a pert how-do-ye-do-sir, cocking his eye one-sidedly at you, and uttering certain nondescript guttural sounds. He walks off crooning to himself and his dames. It is all still again. There are no flies now to buzz in the air. There is not wind enough to quiver a hanging straw, or to pipe a leaf-dance along the fence. You fall into some sweet fancy that inhabits silence, when all at once, with a tremendous vociferation, out flies a hen from over your head, with an outrageous noise, clattering away as if you had been throwing stones at her, or abusing her beyond endurance. The old Shanghai takes up the case, and the whole mob of hens join the outcry. The whole neighborhood is raised, and distant roosters from far off farms echo the shrill complaints. An egg is all very well in its way, but we never could see any justification for such vociferous cackling. Every hen in the crowd is as much excited as if she had performed the deed herself. And the cock informs the whole region round about that there never was so smart a crowd of hens as he leads.

Nothing seems so aimless and simple as a hen. She usually goes about in a vague and straggling manner, articulating to herself cacophonous remarks upon various topics. The greatest event in a hen's life is compound, being made up of an egg and a cackle. Then only she shows enthusiasm when she descends from the nest of duty and proclaims her achievement. If you chase her, she runs cackling; if you pelt her with stones, she streams through the air cackling all abroad till the impulse has run out, when she subsides quietly into a silly, gadding hen. Now and then an eccentric hen may be found stepping quite beyond the limits of hen-propriety. One such has persisted in laying her daily egg in the house. She would steal noiselessly in at the open door, walk up stairs, and leave a plump egg upon the children's bed. The next day she would honor the sofa. On one occasion she selected my writing table, and scratching my papers about, left her card, that I might not blame the children or servants for scattering my manuscripts. Her persistent determination was amusing. One Sabbath morning we drove her out of the second-story window, then again from the front hall. In a few moments she was heard behind the house, and on looking out the window, she was just disappearing into the bed-room window on the ground floor! Word was given, but before any one could reach the place, she had bolted out of the window with victorious cackle, and her white, warm egg lay upon the lounge. I proposed to open the pantry-window, set the egg-dish within her reach, and let her put them up herself; but those in authority would not permit such a deviation from propriety. Such a breed of hens could never be popular with the boys. It would spoil that glorious sport of hunting hen's nests.

How utterly different are birds from their gross congeners. Already the snow-sparrows have come down from the north, and are hopping in our hedges, sure precursors of winter. Robins are gathering in flocks in the orchards, and preparing for their southern flight. May his gun for ever miss fire that would thin the ranks of singing-birds!

Lifted far above all harm of fowler or impediment of mountain, wild fowl are steadily flying southward. The simple sight of them fills the imagination with pictures. They have all summer long called to each other from the reedy fens and wild oat-fields of the far north. Summer is already extinguished there. Winter is following their track, and marching steadily toward us. The spent flowers, the seared leaves, the thinning tree tops, the morning rime of frost, have borne witness of the change on earth; and these caravans of the upper air confirm the tidings. Summer *is* gone; winter *is* coming!

The wind has risen to-day. It is not one of those gusty, playful winds, that frolic with the trees. It is a wind high up in the air, that moves steadily with a solemn sound, as if it were the spirit of summer journeying past us; and, impatient of delay, it doth not stoop to the earth, but touches the tops of the trees, with a murmuring sound, sighing a sad farewell, and passing on.

Such days fill one with pleasant sadness. How sweet a pleasure is there in sadness! It is not sorrow; it is not despondency; it is not gloom! It is one of the moods of joy. At any rate I am very happy, and yet it is sober, and very sad happiness. It is the shadow of joy upon the soul! I can reason about these changes. I can cover over the dying leaves with imaginations as bright as their own hues; and, by christian faith, transfigure the whole scene with a blessed vision of joyous dying and glorious resurrection. But what then? Such thoughts glow like evening clouds, and not far beneath them are the evening twilights, into whose dusk they will soon melt away. And all communions, and all admirations, and all associations, celestial or terrene, come alike into a pensive sadness, that is even sweeter than our joy. It is the minor key of the thoughts. A right sadness will sometimes cure a sorrow.

The asters, which are the floral rear-guards of the year, are saying to me, that no more flowers shall come after them. The very brightness of their faces makes me sad to think that the next blossoms shall be frost-blooms. I know that seeds and roots do not die; that the winter is but a vacation, in which the year rests from its works; that all things shall come again. What then? It is sad nevertheless to see summer dying out. There is some influence in this hush of the heavens, in the helplessness of vegetation, that by leaves and root striving against the cold nights, can only gather strength to die in glorious colors, which makes one glad and sad together. Your smiles end in tears, and tears exhale to smiles again.

Among all the grateful gifts of summer, none, I think, has been deeper and more various than the sight of the enjoyment of the children. I do pity children in a city. There is no place for them. The streets are full of bad boys that they must not play with, and the house is rich in furniture that they must not touch. They are always in somebody's way, or making a noise out of proper time — for the twenty-fifth hour of the day is the only time when people are willing that children should be noisy. There is no grass in the fieldless, parkless city for their feet, no trees for climbing, no orchards or nut-laden trees for their enterprise.

But here has been a troop of children, of three families, nine that may be called children, (without offense to any sweet fifteen,) that have had the summer before them to disport themselves as they chose. There are no ugly boys to be watched, no dangerous places to fall from, no bulls or wicked hippogriffs to chase them. They are up and fledged by breakfast, and then they are off in uncircumscribed liberty till dinner. They may go to the barn, or to either of three orchards, or to either of two woods, or to either of two springs, or to grandma's, who is the very genius of comfort and gingerbread to children! They can build all manner of structures in wet sand, or paddle in the water, and even get their feet wet, their clothes dirty, or their pantaloons torn, without being aught reckoned against them. They scuffle along the road to make a dust in the world, they chase the hens, hunt sly nests, build fires on the rocks in the pastures, and fire off Chinese crackers, until they are surfeited with noise; they can run, wade, halloo, stub their toes, lie down, climb, tumble down, with or without hurting themselves, just as much as they please. They may climb in and out of wagons, sail chips in the water-trough at the barn, fire apples from the sharpened end of a limber stick, pick up baskets full of brilliant apples in competition with the hired men, proud of being "almost men." Their hands, thank fortune, are never clean, their faces are tanned, their hair is tangled within five minutes after combing, and a button is always off somewhere.

The dog is a creation especially made for children. Our Noble has been at least equal to one hand and one foot extra for frolic and mischief, to each of the urchins. But grandest of all joy, highest in the scale of rapture, the last thing talked of before sleep, and the first thing remembered in the morning, is the going out *a-nutting*. O! the hunting of little baskets, the irrepressible glee, as bags and big baskets, into which little ones are to disembogue, come forth! Then the departure, the father or uncle climbing the tree — "O! how high" — the shaking of limbs, the rattle of hundreds of chestnuts, which squirrels shall never see again, the eager picking up, the merry ohs! and ouches! as nuts come plump down on their bare heads, the growing heap, the approaching dinner by the brook, on leaves yellow as gold, and in sunlight yellower still, the mysterious baskets to be opened, the cold chicken, the bread slices — ah me! one would love to be twenty boys, or a boy twenty times over, just to experience the simple, genuine, full, unalloyed pleasure of children going with father and mother to the woods "a-nutting!"

From *Star Papers, or, Experiencing Art and Nature* by Henry Ward Beecher. J.C. Derby, New York, 1855.

WASHINGTON GLADDEN

Washington Gladden (1836-1918) was an eminent Protestant clergyman and editor, particularly influential·as an interpreter of the "social gospel," which sought to ameliorate the severe social problems of later 19th century capitalism by translating New Testament ethical principles into practical action and legislation. He wrote his alma mater's song, The Mountains, the Mountains!, *which echoes across Williamstown every commencement. He also wrote* O Master Let Me Walk with Thee *and several other favorite hymns. He was minister of the First Congregational Church in North Adams from 1866-1871.*

Williams in 1856

STUDENTS AND STUDIES

It was a beautiful September evening, half an hour before sunset, when I mounted the Williamstown stage at North Adams; recent rains had freshened the meadows, the forests on the mountain-sides still wore their summer dress, the fleecy clouds touched with crimson, that rested upon the Taghkanics in the west, or crowned the Saddle profile on the south, set off the bluest of skies. I had never seen anything so beautiful as that Williamstown valley appeared to me that evening; and I cannot say that I have seen anything since that has robbed it of its charm.

The entrance examinations the next day were not formidable, and before night I was matriculated as a sophomore, and established in the southwest corner of West College on the lower floor. Thus opens a chapter of this history which must have far more significance to the writer of it than it can have to any of its readers.

Williams College in 1856 was an institution of modest pretensions. Its faculty consisted of but nine members, all of them full professors, and the four classes averaged less than sixty each. There may have been half-a-dozen "special" students who were taking a partial course; but almost all were candidates for the degree of bachelor of arts. The curriculum was perfectly rigid; all the work was required; the only electives were in the junior year, when we were permitted to choose between French and German. The classes were not divided, the instructional force did not admit of that; the whole class met, three times a day, in the recitation-room; naturally a student became pretty well acquainted with all his classmates. There was some advantage in the fact that all the instruction was given by full professors; tutorial assistance had been called in, in former years, but there was none of it in my day.

The teaching was mainly by means of text-books and oral recitations;

lectures were few; in the last two years there were a few courses, but notebooks were not much used in my time. The range of teaching was not wide. In the first two years Greek, Latin, and mathematics took up nearly all the time; in the sophomore year there was a course in Weber's "Universal History." No English was required for entrance, and the only English work of the first two years was one or two themes each term, with an occasional declamation before the class. There was also a speaking exercise, every Wednesday afternoon at the chapel, which the entire college was required to attend, and there were two speakers from each class; seniors and juniors presented original orations, sophomores and freshmen declaimed. The president and the professor of rhetoric presided, and criticised each speaker at the close of his performance.

Waiting for the Williamstown stage to leave North Adams, 1865.
Courtesy of The Berkshire Eagle

In the junior year there were lessened rations of Latin and Greek, and some elementary instruction in science was given, so that every graduate might have some notion of the groundwork of botany and chemistry and physics and astronomy and mineralogy and geology; a single term was sufficient for political economy, and the tale of the themes was slightly increased. The senior year was devoted largely to mental and moral science, logic, the elements of rhetoric, and criticism, and the evidences of Christianity, with Paley's "Natural Theology" and Butler's "Analogy." I have reproduced the curriculum wholly from memory, but I think that I have not omitted anything essential.

Better than the methods of instruction was the personal contact with the instructors. Every student in college was personally known by every member of the faculty, and the personal interest of the teachers in the students was as paternal as the students would permit. This is not, indeed, saying a great deal, for in that time there was much of that traditional antagonism which makes it a point of honor for a student to refuse all friendly relations with teachers, as members of a hostile class, and which stigmatizes as "bootlicks" all those who seek such relations. Nevertheless, the association between teachers and students was, of necessity, so close that the personal touch could not be wholly evaded, and most Williams men of that time are ready now to confess that the best gains of their college course came to them in this way.

PRESIDENT HOPKINS

The conspicuous figure of the college was its president, Mark Hopkins, one of the four or five great teachers that America has produced. In 1856 he was in his prime, fifty-four years of age, tall, with a slight stoop, but stalwart, with a swinging gait. Over the great dome which crowned the broad forehead, and which was now nearly denuded of its covering, long brown locks were coaxed; and the strong chin and the Roman nose, with the eyes that glanced from under beetling brows, made up a countenance of great dignity and benignity. There was but one opinion about Dr. Hopkins in college; among the students his intellectual prowess was not disputed, and the wisdom and integrity of his character were never questioned. Every man has his foibles, and those who stood nearest to President Hopkins must have known what were his; but the student body, generally quick enough to spy out inconsistencies and weaknesses, was always singularly unanimous and enthusiastic in its loyalty to the great president.

He preached, frequently, in the village church, whose galleries the students occupied; and these extemporaneous discourses, delivered with

Mark Hopkins. Stockbridge Historical Society

great deliberation and dignity, while they always held our attention, were not apt to awaken our enthusiasm; but the baccalaureate sermon was always an event. That was fully written; its philosophical framework was strong, its logic was convincing, and it was delivered with a power and fervor which made a lasting impression.

It was in the senior year that the students came in touch with Dr. Hopkins; a large share of the work of that year was in his hands; the seniors met him every day and sometimes twice; in philosophy and ethics, in logic and theology, he was their only teacher. The tradition of his masterful instruction was always descending; the freshmen heard of it from all above them; it was the expectation of every student that, however unsatisfactory other parts of the course might turn out to be, there would be something worth while in the senior year. The expectation was not disappointed. There was nothing sensational in Dr. Hopkins's teaching; his method was quiet and familiar; his bearing was modest and dignified; but he was a past-master in the art of questioning; he knew how by adroit suggestion to kindle the interest of his pupils in the subject under discussion, and by humor and anecdote he made dry topics vital and deep waters clear. What his best students got from him was not so much conclusions or results of investigation, as a habit of mind, a method of philosophical approach, a breadth and balance of thought, which might serve them in future study. What Garfield said (and I heard him say it, at a Williams banquet at Delmonico's in New York) expressed the feeling of many another graduate of the Berkshire college: "A pine bench, with Mark Hopkins at one end of it and me at the other, is a good enough college for me!"

A unique exercise was the conversation on the Catechism every Saturday morning in senior year. Following the Westminster Assembly's Shorter Catechism, Dr. Hopkins led his seniors carefully over the whole field of theology. The questions and answers, while not furnishing in all cases an adequate statement of doctrine, served as a convenient guide in the investigation of the deep things of God; and there was no other exercise in which the peculiar quality of this teacher appeared more strikingly. These Saturday morning discussions would have been a good equivalent for a Seminary course in systematic theology.

PROFESSOR BASCOM

Of all the instructors, however, the one to whom I am most indebted was John Bascom, then professor of rhetoric, later, for many years, President of the University of Wisconsin, and now resting, after his long day's work, in his old home among the stately trees planted by his own hand in Williamstown. I was not a little irritated by my first interview with Professor Bascom; I had carried to him a theme for criticism; I thought it a meritorious performance, but his blue pencil seriously disfigured it. I went away much exasperated, but on looking it over, I had to confess that the points were well taken. Of that just and penetrating judgment I gradually learned to avail myself; before the end of the course, respect had deepened into affection, and all my life long my debt to that brave and veracious soul has been growing. The score of volumes of which Dr. Bascom is the author have had but a limited circulation; but there are few books of the last half-century, dealing with applications of philosophy to life, which are better worth knowing.

COLLEGE LIFE

College life in that time was very simple. The college buildings were plainness itself, wholly devoid of architectural pretensions; the furniture of most of the rooms was far from luxurious; the expense of living was light. My board, in a club, the first term, cost me two dollars and thirty cents a week; it never exceeded two dollars and seventy-five cents a week. The entire expense of my college course, for the three years, including clothing, was less than nine hundred dollars. Several of the students who boarded themselves, in their own rooms, brought the cost far within that figure.

Several Greek-letter fraternities were flourishing, and there was an anti-secret confederation which made war upon them, but was quite as clannish as they were. None of these societies had houses of their own; they were content with humble quarters, which they rented in private houses, or in lofts over village stores.

A large place in the life of the college was taken by the two rival literary societies, — the Philologian and the Philotechnian, — to the one or the other of which every student belonged. These societies had well-furnished rooms in one of the dormitories, with libraries of three or four thousand volumes each. Their weekly meetings were events of no little interest to the college community; the programme generally included one or two original orations, a debate, sometimes a poem, an essay or two, and the report of the censor upon the performance of the previous meeting. The two societies were united in the Adelphic Union, which gave three or four debates or exhibitions annually, in the chapel or the village church.

The summer vacation was short, not more than five or six weeks, and there was a long winter vacation, beginning at Thanksgiving and continuing into January, that students who were supporting themselves might teach in the winter terms of country schools. All my winters were thus employed.

CONTEMPORARIES

Of the men in my time some names are well known. First among them was Garfield, of the class of '56, who was a senior when my class were freshmen, and whom, therefore, I did not personally know. The fame of him, however, was large when I entered college. He had distinguished himself as debater and orator; there were many reminiscences of his brilliant performances in the Logian forum and on the chapel stage. When my class graduated, he returned and took his second degree, delivering a "master's oration" on our Commencement stage. He had taken to himself a wife, who accompanied him to the scene of his former triumphs, and proudly witnessed his induction into the new honors. He was then President of Hiram College, in Ohio, and must then have been a candidate for the state senate at Columbus, to which, in October of that year, he was chosen. He was a fine, strong young fellow, with a ruddy face, a massive head, a cordial manner, and an air of mastership. The hour that I spent with him on this occasion gave me a large sense of his power. Few who knew him in those days were surprised at his swift ascent to the places of command.

Two of our best-known magazine editors, Mr. Henry M. Alden, of "Harper's Monthly," and Mr. Horace E. Scudder, of the "Atlantic," were contemporaries of mine at Williams. Alden's forte was metaphysics; he was supposed to be occupied mainly with interest purely transcendental, absorbed in investigating the "Thing-ness of the Here"; and if the Messrs. Harper had come to Williamstown inquiring for a young man who would be a skillful purveyor of short stories and poems and sketches for a popular magazine, the last man to whom they would have been sent was Henry Mills Alden. Nor is it probable that our veteran managing editor ever dreamed, at that day, of the kind of occupation in which he was destined to spend his years and to render to the world a service so high and fine. Just how Alden ever got down from cloudland to Franklin Square I have never been able to find out, but it is well for the world that he came, and perhaps the world has been the gainer by his early residence in cloudland. We get our best training for work in this world by living above it.

As for Scudder, whether he ever dreamed of editing the "Atlantic Monthly," I know not; he might, for his pen had a dainty nib, even then; we counted him one of our most graceful writers; what he wrote had an air of distinction and refinement to which undergraduate prose does not often attain. The "Atlantic," in those days, was in its pristine glory. Its life began in Scudder's senior year, and every number, with possible contributions from Emerson or Longfellow or Hawthorne or Lowell or Whittier, and with "The Autocrat of the Breakfast-Table" running its bright career, was an event in our little college community. How we canvassed those first numbers, guessing the authorship of the contributions, all of which were anonymous, and glorying in the new light that had arisen upon American letters!

Scudder was a shy and modest fellow; I doubt if he ever conceived of climbing into Lowell's seat.

EXTRACURRICULAR ACTIVITIES

We were, indeed, so unfortunate as to have few interests which were not intellectual. Athletics were not yet; we sometimes kicked a football rather aimlessly about the campus, never having seen a football game; we played, among ourselves, an occasional game of what we called baseball — class against class; and in our senior year we had one match game with Amherst; but the interest in athletic sports was a negligible quantity. Some of our more adventurous spirits found vent for their surplus force in natural history expeditions to Newfoundland and South America, and an occasional picnic at Lanesboro Pond, or a tramp to the top of Greylock, gave zest to life. But for the most part, the subjects which claimed our attention were those which had some reference to the work of the college.

College music at the middle of the nineteenth century was not of a high order. At Yale and Harvard there had been some singing; in the fresh-water colleges the repertoire of the singers was scanty. At Williams, in my sophomore year, two or three old Latin songs were occasionally sung, — "Gaudeamus Igitur," to a good German choral; "Integer Vitae," to Flemming's strong setting; and "Lauriger Horatius," to the air since better known as "Maryland, my Maryland." For the rest there was a meagre collection of nonsense songs, like the lines, set to Rousseau's "Greenville," "Go tell Aunt Nancy her old gray goose is dead," and several drinking songs, like "Landlords, fill your flowing bowls," and "Roll, roll, rolling home!" Longfellow's "Psalm of Life" was also chanted to a rollicking melody with the refrain of "Cocachelunk-chelunk-chelaly," which was a little like dressing up the Apollo Belvidere in a sweater and tennis shoes.

During my junior year one or two men came to us from Yale, bringing some of the nonsense songs which were current there, and groups began to gather in the summer evenings on the benches in front of East College for the singing of these new songs. It must have been early in my senior year that a musical organization was formed which called itself "The Mendelssohn Society," of which I was made the conductor. This society made some ambitious attempts at glees and male choruses, giving, in the course of the year, a few concerts in the surrounding towns. By these various measures so much interest in college singing was awakened that I ventured to publish, at the close of our senior year, a collection of the "Songs of Williams." Most of the songs were written for the collection, and many of them were, of course, lyrically defective; it is not an easy thing to write a singable song. But I find in the latest Williams song-book fourteen numbers from my old compilation. How many of them are sung in these days I do not know. One of these I had the good fortune to write. I had been wishing that I might write a song which could be sung at some of our exhibitions; and one winter morning, walking down Bee Hill, the lilt of the chorus of "The Mountains" came to me. I had a little music-paper in my room in the village, and on my arrival I wrote down the notes. Then I cast about for words to fit them, and the refrain, "The Mountains, the Mountains!" suggested itself. I wrote the melody of the stanza next, and fitted the verses to it. We were soon to have a public debate, in the Chapel, for which the Mendelssohn Society was to furnish the music; we learned this song and sang it on that occasion. The next morning I heard the melody whistled by students in the halls and by town boys in the streets; it was evident that it had caught on.

COMMENCEMENTS

Commencement, in those days, was a high festival. It drew to the village all the people of the countryside, and there were booths for gingerbread and root beer, and sellers of whips and toy balloons, and the usual assortment of fakirs. Few of the hundreds of country people who flocked to the show paid much attention to the graduating exercises; the occasion simply supplied them with an out-of-door holiday.

The Commencement occurred during the first week in August, and the day was sacred to the graduating class. Out of a total of fifty or sixty, from thirty to thirty-five men presented original orations. The speaking began in the village church about nine o'clock in the morning, and continued until noon; after an intermission of two hours for dinner, the floodgates of oratory were reopened, and it was after four o'clock before the valedictorian made his final bow to the applauding crowd. With such powers of endurance were the audiences of those days endowed!

It was a heavy heart that I carried out of that valley when the Commencement festivities were ended, in the summer of 1859. I had tarried for a day after my classmates were gone; and I was alone on the train that bore me away to the westward that August afternoon. I sat at the window and looked backward till Greylock and Prospect were shut from sight, and I knew that the curtain had gone down on the happiest time that I had ever known.

From *Recollections* by Washington Gladden. Houghton Mifflin, 1909.

HENRY WHEELER SHAW ("Josh Billings")

*Abraham Lincoln supposedly thought Henry Wheeler Shaw, born in
Lanesborough in 1818, the "funniest man in America." After some years as a
rolling stone out West, he returned to farm in Lanesborough, but after a few
years went west again. Eventually he became an auctioneer and real estate
agent in Poughkeepsie. His early attempts at humor, published in the* Berkshire Eagle *and Poughkeepsie papers, attracted no attention until he mis-
spelled them, and then his cracker-barrel philosophical wise-cracks took off and
his fame made him much in demand on the lecture circuit.*

In his misspellings one may detect the Berkshire accent, now happily extinct.

The Bliss ov Living up in New Ashford

The village ov New Ashford iz lokated in the state ov Massachusetts, and iz about 150 miles west ov Plymouth rok.

It iz one ov them towns that dont make enny fuss, but for pure
water, pure morals, and good rye, and injun bread, it stands on tiptoze.

It was settled soon after the landing ov the pilgrims, bi sum ov that
party, and like all the Nu England towns, waz, at one time, selebrated for
its stern religious creed, and its excellent rum and tanzy.

It may seem a leetle strange, tew these latter day saints, tew hear me
mix up rum and religion together, but i had an Unkle, who preached
God's word in the next town south ov New Ashford, 80 years ago, who
died in due time, and went to heaven.

This genial old saint alwus took, on week daze, three magnificent
horns ov rum and tanzy, and Sundaze he took four.

I hav no doubt it lengthened out hiz time, and braced up hiz faith.

But i wouldn't advise enny ov the yung klergy ov to-day tew meddle
with rum and tanzy, az a fertilizer.

The tanzy iz all rite — it grows az green and az bitter az ever; for man
kant adulturate it, but rum haz bin bedeviled into rank pizon.

One sich horn az mi old unkle used tew absorb between hiz sermons
on Sunday (5 inches, good and strong) would disfranchise a whole drove
ov preachers now.

In them daze, the preacher was a stalwart man, and could mo his
swarth in the hay field, with the best ov them, and could ride a hard
trotting cob or a hoss, 6 miles an hour, all day, akrost the mountains, and
set doun at night, to biled pork and kabbage, and kold injun puddin, and
after thanking the Lord for his menny mersys, eat hiz way klean to the
middle ov the table.

Leaving New Ashford for Lanesboro. Courtesy of The Berkshire Eagle

But times, and men, hav altered, and so haz rum and tanzy.

I dont want them good old times tew cum back agin, we aint pure enuff now tew stand them, neither are we tuff enuff.

Our virtews may be az pure in the eyes ov heaven, but they kant stand the biled pork, and rum, ov one hundred years ago.

We are told that mankind are growing weaker and wizer; weaker i admit, but wisdum that is gained at the expense ov simplicity may be a doubtful gain.

I never hav met an old man yet, who didn't mourn the degeneracy ov the times.

Wisdum don't konsist in knowing more that iz new, but in knowing less that iz false.

But, dear Mr. ___, i will now git back tew whare i am, and tell yu sumthin about New Ashford.

If yu luv a mountain, cum up here and see me.

Right in front ov the little tavern, whare i am staying, rizes up a chunk ov land, that will make yu feel weak tew look at it.

I hav bin on its top, and far above waz the brite blu ski, without a kloud swimming in it, while belo me the rain shot slanting on the valley, and the litening played its mad pranks.

How is this for hi?

But what a still place this New Ashford iz.

At sunrize the roosters crow all around, one apiece; at sunset the cows cum hollering home tew be milked; and at twilite out steal the krickets, with a song, the burden ov which seems sad and weary.

This iz all the racket thare iz in New Ashford. It is so still here that you can hear a feather drop from a blujay's tail.

Out ov this mountain, squeezed bi the weight ov it, leaks a little brook ov water, and up and down this brook each day i loiter.

In mi hand i hav a short pole, on the end ov the pole a short line, on the line a sharp hook, looped on the hook a grub, or a worm.

Every now and and then thare cums dancing out ov this little brook a live trout no longer than yure finger, but az sweet az a stick ov kandy, and in he goes at the op ov mi baskit.

This iz what i am here for; trout for breakfast, trout for dinner and trout for supper.

I am az happy and az lazy az a yerling heifer.

I hav not a kare on mi mind, not an ake in mi boddy.

I haven't read a nuzepaper for a week, and wouldn't read one for a dollar.

I shall stay here till mi munny givs out, and shall cum bak tew the senseless crash ov the city, with a tear in mi eye, and holes in both ov mi boots.

This world iz phull ov fun, but most pholks look too hi for it.

On one side ov this mountain they say thare iz rattlesnaix, on that side of the mountain, iz whare i dont go.

I am just az fraid ov a snaix as a woman iz, i had rather meet the devil, ennytime, on a bust, than a three foot snaik. A striped snaik in the morning spiles the rest ov that day for me.

I am coming home, dear Friends in two months, and then i will set down, in yure little sanktum, and whisper to you.

It iz so still here, that a whisper sounds loud; a still noize iz another name i beleave, for happiness. The bible sez: *"peace, be still."*

The fust thing i do in the morning, when i git up, iz tew go out and look at the mountain, and see if it iz thare, if this mountain should go away, how lonesum i should be.

Yesterday i picked one quart ov field strawberrys, kaught 27 trout, and gathered a whole parcell ov wintergreen leaves, a big daze work.

When i got home last night tired, no man kould hav bought them ov me for 700 dollars, but i suppoze, after all, that it waz the *tired* that waz wuth the munny.

Thare is a grate deal ov raw bliss, in gitting tired.

Dear Mr.___, good-bye, it iz now 9 oclk, P.M., and every thing, in New Ashford, iz fast asleep, inkluding the krickets, I will just step out and see if the mountain iz thare, and then I will go to bed too.

Oh! the bliss ov living up in New Ashford, cluss bi the side ov a grate giant mountain tew guard yu, whare every thing iz az still as a boys tin whissell at midnite, a musketo couldn't liv long enuff tew take one bite, whare board iz only 4 dollars a week, and everyboddy, kats and all, at 9 clok, P.M., are fast asleep, and snoreing.

From *Josh Billings: His Works, Complete.* G.W. Carlton & Co., 1876.

Henry Wheeler Shaw ("Josh Billings"). Courtesy of The Berkshire Eagle

DORA GOODALE

The Goodale sisters of Mount Washington were the infant phenomena of the 1879 publishing season (see Gerard Chapman's article about them in the following section). Here is a sample of their verse.

Our Chickens

A gentle pullet on the stoop, —
　　A rooster where the cream is rising, —
　　A hen who doubtless likes our soup,
And eats it without criticizing!

A mild-eyed chicken calmly stands
　　And on the kitchen table lingers, —
And why? of course he understands
　　The bread is fresh from mamma's fingers.

An angry "shoo!" — he thinks it vain,
　　But then of course there is no knowing, —
He smashes through a windowpane
　　And fears it's time that he was going.

A pullet, *not* upon the stoop,
　　But with cream gravy on a platter;
A hen who's grown so fat on soup
　　That what she makes is no small matter.

Ah, chickens! 'tis no use to beg,
　　Tho' you were bold, we, we are bolder, —
And mamma, will you take a leg?
　　Or would you rather have a shoulder?

You make a most delicious pie!
　　Your time is past and ours beginning, —
Not long upon my plate you'll lie, —
　　This is the penalty of sinning!

From *Apple Blossoms: Verses of Two Children* by Elaine Goodale and Dora Read Goodale. G.P. Putnam's, New York, 1879.

W.E.B. DU BOIS

As the "grandfather" of the modern civil rights movement which has left no aspect of American life unaltered, Great Barrington native William Edward Burghardt Du Bois (1868-1966) affected life in this country more pervasively and profoundly than any other Berkshirite has ever done, with the possible exception of William Stanley, whose invention of the transformer made feasible the long-distance transmission of electricity. (Stanley demonstrated his invention by electrifying Great Barrington's Main Street two years after Du Bois had graduated from Great Barrington High School.)

Du Bois broke ground as the historian of slavery and the sociologist of race relations, laying the theoretical foundations of the civil rights movement, and, as the founder and organizer of the NAACP, giving it its activist force. As an editor and writer, he shaped new attitudes, both black and white, towards race relations.

A strongly poetic sensitivity, unusual in polemical or scholarly writing, distinguishes his prose and thought. In his long life he wrote three autobiographies, Darkwater *(1921),* Dusk of Dawn *(1940), and the* Autobiography *of 1960, by which time, reviled by his own country and despairing of its ever surmounting racism, he had embraced socialism and become a citizen of Ghana.*

His observations about his Great Barrington boyhood are followed by a letter home to the Reverend Scudder, pastor of the Congregational Church; the four Protestant churches in Great Barrington helped with the cost of his education at Fisk University in Tennesee.

By A Golden River

I was born by a golden river and in the shadow of two great hills, five years after the Emancipation Proclamation. The house was quaint, with clapboards running up and down, neatly trimmed, and there were five rooms, a tiny porch, a rosy front yard, and unbelievably delicious strawberries in the rear. A South Carolinian, lately come to the Berkshire Hills, owned all this — tall, thin and black, with golden earrings, and given to religious trances. We were his transient tenants for the time.

My own people were part of a great clan. Fully two hundred years before, Tom Burghardt had come through the western pass from the Hudson with his Dutch captor, "Coenraet Burghardt," sullen in his slavery and achieving his freedom by volunteering for the Revolution at a time of sudden alarm. His wife was a little, black, Bantu woman, who never became reconciled to this strange land; she clasped her knees and rocked and crooned:

"Do bana coba — gene me, gene me!
Ben d'nuli, ben d'le —"

Tom died about 1787, but of him came many sons, and one, Jack, who helped in the War of 1812. Of Jack and his wife, Violet, was born a mighty family, splendidly named: Harlow and Ira, Cloe, Lucinda, Maria, and Othello! I dimly remember my grandfather, Othello, — or "Uncle Tallow," — a brown man, strong-voiced and redolent with tobacco, who sat stiffly in a great high chair because his hip was broken. He was probably a bit lazy and given to wassail. At any rate, grandmother had a shrewish tongue and often berated him. This grandmother was Sarah — "Aunt Sally" — a stern, tall, Dutch-African woman, beak-nosed, but beautiful-eyed and golden-skinned. Ten or more children were theirs, of whom the youngest was Mary, my mother.

Long years before him Louis XIV drove two Huguenots, Jacques and Louis Du Bois, into wild Ulster County, New York. One of them in the third or fourth generation had a descendant, Dr. James Du Bois, a gay, rich bachelor, who made his money in the Bahamas, where he and the Gilberts had plantations. There he took a beautiful little mulatto slave as his mistress, and two sons were born: Alexander in 1803 and John, later. They were fine, straight, clear-eyed boys, white enough to "pass." He brought them to America and put Alexander in the celebrated Cheshire School, in Connecticut. Here he often visited him, but one last time, fell dead. He left no will, and his relations made short shrift of these sons. They gathered in the property, apprenticed grandfather to a shoemaker; then dropped him.

Grandfather took his bitter dose like a thoroughbred. Wild as was his inner revolt against this treatment, he uttered no word against the thieves and made no plea. He tried his fortunes here and in Haiti, where, during his short, restless sojourn, my own father was born. Eventually, grandfather became chief steward on the passenger boat between New York and New Haven; later he was a small merchant in Springfield; and finally he retired and ended his days at New Bedford. Always he held his head high, took no insults, made few friends. He was not a "Negro"; he was a man! Yet the current was too strong even for him. Then even more than now a colored man had colored friends or none at all, lived in a colored world or lived alone. A few fine, strong, black men gained the heart of this silent, bitter man in New York and New Haven. If he had scant sympathy with their social clannishness, he was with them in fighting discrimination. So, when the white Episcopalians of Trinity Parish, New Haven, showed plainly that they no longer wanted black folk as fellow Christians, he led the revolt which resulted in St. Luke's Parish, and was for years its senior warden. He lies dead in the Grove Street Cemetery, beside Jehudi Ashmun.

Beneath his sternness was a very human man. Slyly he wrote poetry, — stilted, pleading things from a soul astray. He loved women in his masterful way, marrying three beautiful wives in succession and clinging to each with a certain desperate, even if unsympathetic, affection. As a father he was, naturally, a failure, — hard, domineering, unyielding. His four children reacted characteristically: one was until past middle life a thin spinster, the mental image of her father; one died; one passed over into the white world and her children's children are now white, with no knowledge of their Negro blood; the fourth, my father, bent before grandfather, but did not break — better if he had. He yielded and flared back, asked forgiveness and forgot why, became the harshly-held favorite, who ran away and rioted and roamed and loved and married my brown mother.

So with some circumstance having finally gotten myself born, with a flood of Negro blood, a strain of French, a bit of Dutch, but, thank God! no "Anglo-Saxon," I came to the days of my childhood.

They were very happy. Early we moved back to Grandfather Burghardt's home, — I barely remember its stone fireplace, big kitchen, and delightful woodshed. Then this house passed to other branches of the clan and we moved to rented quarters in town, — to one delectable place "upstairs," with a wide yard full of shrubbery, and a brook; to another house abutting a railroad, with infinite interests and astonishing playmates; and finally back to the quiet street on which I was born, — down a long lane and in a homely, cozy cottage, with a living-room, a tiny sitting-room, a pantry, and two attic bedrooms. Here mother and I lived until she died, in 1884, for father early began his restless wanderings. I last remember urgent letters for us to come to New Milford, where he had started a barber shop. Later he became a preacher. But mother no longer trusted his dreams, and he soon faded out of our lives into silence.

From the age of five until I was sixteen I went to school on the same grounds, — down a lane, into a widened yard, with a big choke-cherry tree and two buildings, wood and brick. Here I got acquainted with my world, and soon had my criterions of judgment.

Wealth had no particular lure. On the other hand, the shadow of wealth was about us. That river of my birth was golden because of the woolen and paper waste that soiled it. The gold was theirs, not ours; but the gleam and glint was for all. To me it was all in order and I took it philosophically. I cordially despised the poor Irish and South Germans, who slaved in the mills, and annexed the rich and well-to-do as my natural companions. Of such is the kingdom of snobs!

Most of our townfolk were, naturally, the well-to-do, shading downward, but seldom reaching poverty. As playmate of the children I saw the homes of nearly every one, except a few immigrant New Yorkers, of whom none of us approved. The homes I saw impressed me, but did not overwhelm me. Many were bigger than mine, with newer and shinier things, but they did not seem to differ in kind. I think I probably surprised my hosts more than they me, for I was easily at home and perfectly happy and they looked to me just like ordinary people, while my brown face and frizzled hair must have seemed strange to them.

Yet I was very much one of them. I was a center and sometimes the leader of the town gang of boys. We were noisy, but never very bad, — and, indeed, my mother's quiet influence came in here, as I realize now. She did not try to make me perfect. To her I was already perfect. She simply warned me of a few things, especially saloons. In my town the saloon was the open door to hell. The best families had their drunkards and the worst had little else.

Very gradually, — I cannot now distinguish the steps, though here and there I remember a jump or a jolt — but very gradually I found myself assuming quite placidly that I was different from other children. At first I think I connected the difference with a manifest ability to get my lessons rather better than most and to recite with a certain happy, almost taunting, glibness, which brought frowns here and there. Then, slowly, I realized that some folks, a few, even several, actually considered my brown skin a misfortune; once or twice I became painfully aware that some human beings even thought it a crime. I was not for a moment daunted, — although, of course, there were some days of secret tears — rather I was spurred to tireless effort. If they beat me at anything, I was grimly determined to make them sweat for it! Once I remember challenging a great, hard farmer-boy to battle, when I knew he could whip me; and he did. But ever after, he was polite.

As time flew I felt not so much disowned and rejected as rather drawn up into higher spaces and made part of a mightier mission. At times I almost pitied my pale companions, who were not of the Lord's anointed and who saw in their dreams no splendid quests of golden fleeces.

From *Darkwater* by W.E.B. Du Bois. Harcourt Brace, 1921.

Growing Up in Great Barrington

reat Barrington was a town of middle-class people, mostly native white Americans of English and Dutch descent. There were differences of property and income and yet all the men worked and seemed at least to be earning their living. Naturally the income was not proportioned to the effort; some men worked three hours a day and earned several thousand dollars a year; carpenters worked 12 hours a day for a dollar, and servants toiled day and night for two dollars a week. But we did not dream of a day when a man doing nothing could be a millionaire at 35, while his fellow broke back and heart and starved.

The women were housekeepers, with a few exceptions, like teachers, the postmistress, and a clerk now and then in stores like Fassett's shop for women's apparel. The ownership of property, of homes and stores, of a few mills of various sorts, was fundamental, and the basis of social prestige. Most families owned their homes. There was some inherited wealth but not in very large amounts. There were no idle rich and no outstanding "society."

There were two hotels; the Berkshire catered to summer visitors, chiefly from New York; the Miller House depended on local trade. There was for a time a steam bakery which turned out delicious food until the National Biscuit Company swallowed it up and it disappeared. There was a bank, the Mahaiwe National.

Of course there was also the usual contradiction: while property and income were the main bases of social status, at the same time the facts concerning them were a carefully guarded secret. No one knew exactly how rich the Russells were or just what was the financial status of the Coffins and Churches. There were, of course, rumors and general estimates which were in all probability not far from the truth, but few knew with any exactitude the economic status of the important persons of the town.

There was no great exhibition of wealth. The homes of the Russells, the Churches and Dr. Collins were comparatively large with perhaps eight or ten rooms and built of wood or, more rarely, of stone. There was an abundance of cheap blue granite in the neighboring mountains. Most of the houses were of wood, four to six rooms, and all of them were furnished according to a common pattern: horse-hair sofas and chairs in the "parlors," with old-fashioned wooden furniture and corner "whatnots." They were usually heated by coal stove; one in each room, anthracite coal and wood from the vicinity were used. Bathrooms and indoor toilets were rare; each home had its outdoor privy, often nicely arranged.

In general living, the contrast between the well-to-do and the poor was not great. Living was cheap and there was little real poverty. Some food like local fruit was almost common property; vegetables like potatoes, navy beans and cabbage were grown in small home gardens; corned beef and chickens fetched low prices and eggs could often be raised at home; "greens" and rhubarb grew in back yards and in the Fall canning and preserving cost only the sugar. There were no flashy carriages and the social life was quite private. When the *Berkshire Courier*, our local weekly newspaper, made social announcements it was usually marriages, births, and deaths, visiting relatives from out of town, and trips to New York or the West by local residents.

I grew up in the midst of definite ideas as to wealth and poverty, work and charity. Wealth was the result of work and saving and the rich rightly inherited the earth. The poor, on the whole, were themselves to be blamed. They were unfortunate and if so their fortunes could easily be mended with care. But chiefly, they were "shiftless," and "shiftlessness" was unforgivable.

The chief criterion of local social standing was property and ancestry; but the ancestors were never magnates like the patroons of the manors along the Hudson to the west; nor were they persons of great prestige and learning with aristocratic connections like the residents of Boston and eastern Massachusetts. They were usually ordinary folk of solid respectability, farm owners, or artisans merging into industry. Standing did not depend on what the ancestor did, or who he was, but rather that he existed, lived decently and thus linked the individual to the community. Physically and socially our community belonged to the Dutch valley of the Hudson rather than to Puritan New England, and travel went south to New York more often and more easily than east to Boston.

After I entered high school, I began to feel the pressure of the "veil of color"; in little matters at first and then in larger. There were always certain compensations. For instance, George Beebe was a handsome classmate in high school, two or three years older than I, and extravagantly dressed. My own clothes were never ragged, but seldom new and certainly not in current style. Yet George and I were excellent friends because with all his clothes he was rather dumb in class and knew it, while I was bright and just this side of shabby, so that we balanced each other. The Sabins, Clarence and Ralph, lived near me on the opposite street. Clarence was serious and studious, and Ralph a little devil. We were friends and playmates. Art Benham, whose father was a railroad engineer, was a pixie, red-haired, ugly and gifted. He and I were joint editors of the only paper that was ever published during my day. It was the high school *Howler*, gotten out by hand, and lasting only for two or three issues.

Of the other town folk outside my schoolmates, I remember espe-

W.E.B. Du Bois in 1957. Courtesy of The Berkshire Eagle

cially Johnny Morgan. He was a small man, I think of Welsh descent, and ran a bookstore in the front part of the little shop where the village post office occupied the rear. I went to the post office daily, not because I was expecting mail or often got any, but because of the intriguing exhibition of periodicals and books in Johnny Morgan's store. He became interested in me and very sympathetic. He did not repel me by asking too many questions or trying to find out my plans and ideas. But he made little suggestions and did not object to my looking at the illustrations in *Puck* and *Judge*. I looked them over each week.

I remember one momentous transaction. From early days I had been intrigued by books as books. In our living room I took possession of an old "secretary" which had come down in the family and gathered together in it a number of stray volumes which I found about the house. One I distinctly remember, *Opie on Lying*. There were a few others. I did not read them, but they formed my library. Then one Fall — it was in 1882 and I was in my second year in high school — I saw in Johnny Morgan's window a gorgeous edition of Macaulay's *History of England*, in five volumes, and I wanted it fiercely. Its price was, of course, far beyond my ability to pay, but Johnny Morgan suggested that I buy it on installments. This was not a usual method at that time in Great Barrington. It was our rule to "pay as you go." But I seized on Morgan's suggestion and for several months paid installments of, I think, 25 cents a week. At Christmas time I took my precious purchase home and it still stands in my library.

The first glimpse in the outer and wider world was through Johnny Morgan's store. There I remember very early seeing pictures of U.S. Grant and Tweed, who was beginning his extraordinary career in New York; and later of Hayes and the smooth and rather cruel face of Tilden. Johnny Morgan made other suggestions to me. He arranged while I was in high school that I become the local Great Barrington correspondent of the *Springfield Republican*, which was the most influential and widely circulated paper in western Massachusetts. I sent it from time to time some items of interest, but not many, as I was soon graduated from high school.

Outside my school, my chief communication with the people of the town was through the church. In Great Barrington there were three leading Protestant churches, and later a fourth. The most important church was the Congregational. It had the largest attendance of all the churches, including merchants and farmers, and professional men of the town. My own family on both sides had been Episcopalians, but because we lived near the Congregational church, and because my mother had many acquaintances there, and because the minister, Scudder, was especially friendly, my mother early joined this church. I think we were the only colored communicants.

In the festivities of the whole year, when strawberries became ripe, when harvest brought in fruit and vegetables, and at Christmas time, there were celebrations in Sunday School, and I was always there. I felt absolutely no discrimination, and I do not think there was any, or any thought of it. When the great church was burned down, I was a sensitive mourner and oversaw at every period its pretentious rebuilding. I remember the altar, whose Greek inscription I was proudly able to read:

"*He alethia eleutherosi humas.*" (The truth shall make you free.) I heard the dedicatory sermon: "For thus said the High and Mighty One, who inhabiteth eternity, Whose Name is Holy. I dwell in the high and lofty place. With him also that is of a contrite and humble spirit to revive the spirit of the humble, to revive the heart of the contrite ones."

The new Sunday School building was my chief pride and joy. It had climbed out of the basement and had broad and beautiful rooms with sunlit windows looking out on lawn and flowers. The carpet, the chairs, the tables, were all new, and the teachers were inspired to new efforts with their growing classes. I was quite in my element and led in discussions, with embarrassing questions, and long disquisitions. I learned much of the Hebrew scriptures. I think I must have been both popular and a little dreaded, but I was very happy.

From early years, I attended the town meeting every Spring and in the upper room in that little red brick Town Hall, fronted by a Roman "victory" commemorating the Civil War, I listened to the citizens discuss things about which I knew and had opinions: streets and bridges and schools, and particularly the high school, an institution comparatively new. We had in the town several picturesque hermits, usually retrograde Americans of old families. There was Crosby, the gunsmith, who lived in a lovely dale with brook, waterfall and water wheel. He was a frightful apparition but we boys often ventured to visit him. Particularly there was Baretown Beebe, who came from forest fastnesses which I never penetrated. He was a particularly dirty, ragged, fat old man, who used to come down regularly from his rocks and woods and denounce high school education and expense.

I was 13 or 14 years of age and a student in the small high school with two teachers and perhaps 25 pupils. The high school was not too popular in this rural part of New England and received from the town a much too small appropriation. But the thing that exasperated me was that every Spring at Town Meeting, which I religiously attended, this huge, ragged old man came down from the hills and for an hour or more reviled the high school and demanded its discontinuance.

I remember distinctly how furious I used to get at the stolid town folk, who sat and listened to him. He was nothing and nobody. Yet the town heard him gravely because he was a citizen and property-holder on a small scale and when he was through, they calmly voted the usual funds for the high school. Gradually as I grew up, I began to see that this was the essence of democracy: listening to the other man's opinion and then voting your own, honestly and intelligently.

I presume I was saved evidences of a good deal of actual discrimination by my own keen sensitiveness. My companions did not have a chance to refuse me invitations; they must seek me out and urge me to come as indeed they often did. When my presence was not wanted they had only to refrain from asking. But in the ordinary social affairs of the village — the Sunday School with its picnics and festivals; the temporary skating rink in the Town Hall; the coasting in crowds on all the hills — in all of these, I took part with no thought of discrimination on the part of my fellows, for that I would have been the first to notice.

Later, I was protected in part by the fact that there was little social activity in the high school; there were no fraternities; there were no school dances; there were no honor societies. Whatever of racial feeling gradually crept into my life, its effect upon me in these earlier days was rather one of exaltation and high disdain. They were the losers who did not ardently court me, and not I, which seemed to be proven by the fact that I had no difficulty in outdoing them in nearly all competition, especially intellectual. In athletics I was not outstanding. I was only moderately good at baseball and football; but at running, exploring, story-telling and planning of intricate games, I was often if not always the leader.

After I entered the high school, economic problems and questions of the future began to loom. They were partly settled by my own activities. My mother's limited sources of income were helped through boarding the barber, my uncle, supplemented infrequently by her own day's work, and by some kindly unobtrusive charity. But I was keen and eager to eke out this income by various jobs; splitting kindling, mowing lawns, doing chores. I early came to understand that to be "on the town," the recipient of public charity, was the depth not only of misfortune but of a certain guilt. I presume some of my folk sank to that, but not to my knowledge. We earned our way.

My first regular wage began as I entered the high school: I went early of mornings and filled with coal one or two of the new so-called "base burning" stoves in the millinery shop of Madame L'Hommedieu. From then on, all through my high school course, I worked after school and on Saturdays.

For some time too I sent weekly letters to a colored weekly *New York Age* and sold copies, and before the A&P stores dealt in groceries and simply were selling tea, I was one of their local agents. Thus in all sorts of little ways I managed to earn some money and never asked or thought of gifts.

From *Autobiography* by W.E.B. Du Bois. International Publishers, 1968.

From Great Barrington to the Wider World

In Great Barrington there were perhaps twenty-five, certainly not more than fifty, colored folk in a population of five thousand. My family was among the oldest inhabitants of the valley. The family had spread slowly through the county intermarrying among cousins and other black folk with some but limited infiltration of white blood. Other dark families had come in and there was some intermingling with local Indians. In one or two cases there were groups of apparently later black immigrants, near Sheffield for instance. There survives there even to this day an isolated group of black folk whose origin is obscure. We knew little of them but felt above them because of our education and economic status.

The economic status was not high. The early members of the family supported themselves on little farms of a few acres; then drifted to town as laborers and servants, but did not go into the mills. Most of them rented homes, but some owned little homes and pieces of land; a few had very pleasant and well-furnished homes, but none had anything like wealth.

For several generations my people had attended schools for longer or shorter periods so most of them could read and write. I was brought up from earliest years with the idea of regular attendance at school. This was partly because the schools of Great Barrington were near at hand, simple but good, well-taught, and truant laws were enforced. I started on one school ground, which I remember vividly, at the age of five or six years, and continued there in school until I was graduated from high school at sixteen. I was seldom absent or tardy, and the school ran regularly ten months in the year with a few vacations. The curriculum was simple: reading, writing, spelling and arithmetic; grammar, geography and history. We learned the alphabet; we were drilled rigorously on the multiplication tables and we drew accurate maps. We could spell correctly and read clearly.

Meantime the town and its surroundings were a boy's paradise: there were mountains to climb and rivers to wade and swim; lakes to freeze and hills for coasting. There were orchards and caves and wide green fields; and all of it was apparently property of the children of the town. My earlier contacts with playmates and other human beings were normal and pleasant. Sometimes there was a dearth of available playmates but that was peculiar to the conventions of the town where families were small and children must go to bed early and not loaf on the streets or congregate in miscellaneous crowds. Later, in the high school, there came some rather puzzling distinctions which I can see now were social and racial; but the racial angle was more clearly defined against the Irish than against me. It was a matter of income and ancestry more than color.

When, however, during my high school course the matter of my future career began to loom, there were difficulties. The colored population of the town had been increased a little by "contrabands," who on the whole were well received by the colored group; although the older group held some of its social distinctions and the newcomers astonished us by forming a little Negro Methodist Zion Church, which we sometimes attended. The work open to colored folk was limited. There was day labor; there was farming; there was house-service, particularly work in summer hotels; but for a young, educated and ambitious colored man, what were the possibilities? And the practical answer to this inquiry was: Why encourage a young colored man toward such higher training? I imagine this matter was discussed considerably among my friends, white and black, and in a way it was settled partially before I realized it.

My high school principal was Frank Hosmer, afterward president of Oahu College, Hawaii. He suggested, quite as a matter of fact, that I ought to take the college preparatory course which involved algebra, geometry, Latin and Greek. If Hosmer had been another sort of man, with definite ideas as to a Negro's "place," and had recommended agricultural "science" or domestic economy, I would doubtless have followed his advice, had such "courses" been available. I did not then realize that Hosmer was quietly opening college doors to me, for in those days they were barred with ancient tongues. This meant a considerable expenditure for books which were not free in those days — more than my folk could afford; but the wife of one of the mill-owners, or rather I ought to describe her as the mother of one of my playmates, after some hesitation offered to furnish all the necessary school books. I became therefore a high school student preparing for college and thus occupying an unusual position in the town even among whites, although there had been one or two other colored boys in the past who had gotten at least part of a high school education. In this way I was thrown with the upper rather than the lower social classes and protected in many ways. I came in touch with rich folk, summer boarders, who made yearly incursions from New York. Their beautiful clothes impressed me tremendously but otherwise I found them quite ordinary. The children did not have much sense or training; they were not very strong and rather too well dressed to have a good time playing.

In general thought and conduct I became quite thoroughly New England. It was not good form in Great Barrington to express one's thought volubly, or to give way to excessive emotion. We were even sparing in our daily greetings. I am quite sure that in a less restrained and conventional atmosphere I should have easily learned to express my emotions with far greater and more unrestrained intensity; but as it was I had the social heritage not only of a New England clan but Dutch taciturnity. This was later reinforced and strengthened by inner withdrawals in the face of real and imagined discriminations. The result was that I was early thrown in upon myself. I found it difficult and even unnecessary to approach other people and by that same token my own inner life perhaps grew the richer; but the habit of repression often returned to plague me in after years, for so early a habit could not easily be unlearned. The Negroes in the South, when I came to know them, could never understand why I did not naturally greet everyone I passed on the street or slap my friends on the back.

I was graduated from high school in 1884 and was of course the only colored student. Once during my course another young dark man had attended the school for a short time but I was very much ashamed of him because he did not excel the whites as I was quite used to doing. All thirteen of us had orations and mine was on "Wendell Phillips." The great anti-slavery agitator had just died in February and I presume that some of my teachers must have suggested the subject, although it is quite possible that I chose it myself. But I was fascinated by his life and his work and took a long step toward a wider conception of what I was going to do. I spoke in June and then came face to face with the problem of my future life.

My mother lived proudly to see me graduate but died in the fall and I went to live with an aunt. I was strongly advised that I was too young to enter college. Williams had been suggested, because most of our few high school graduates who went to college had attended there; but my heart was set on Harvard. It was the greatest and oldest college and I therefore quite naturally thought it was the one I must attend. Of course I did not realize the difficulties: some difficulties in entrance examinations because our high school was not quite up to the Harvard standard; but a major difficulty of money. There must have been in my family and among my friends a good deal of anxious discussion as to my future but finally it was temporarily postponed when I was offered a job and promised that the next fall I should begin my college work.

The job brought me in unexpected touch with the world. There had been a great-uncle of mine, Tom Burghardt, whose tombstone I had seen often in the town graveyard. My family used to say in undertones that the money of Tom Burghardt helped to build the Pacific Railroad and that this came about in this wise: nearly all his life Tom Burghardt had been a servant in the Kellogg family, only the family usually forgot to pay him; but finally they did give him a handsome burial. Then Mark Hopkins, a son or relative of the great Mark, appeared on the scene and married a daughter of the Kelloggs. He became one of the Huntington-Stanford-Crocker Pacific Associates who built, manipulated and cornered the Pacific railroads and with the help of the Kellogg nest-egg, Hopkins made nineteen million dollars in the West by methods not to be inquired into. His widow came back to Great Barrington in the eighties and planned a mansion out of the beautiful blue granite which formed our hills. A host of workmen, masons, stone-cutters and carpenters were assembled, and in the summer of 1884 I was made time-keeper for the contractors who carried on this job. I received the fabulous wage of a dollar a day. It was a most interesting experience and had new and intriguing bits of reality and romance. As time-keeper and the obviously young and inexperienced agent of superiors, I was the one who handed the discharged workers their last wage envelopes. I talked with contractors and saw the problems of employers. I pored over the plans and specifications and even came in contact with the elegant English architect Searles who finally came to direct the work.

The widow had a steward, a fine, young educated colored fellow who had come to be her right-hand man; but the architect supplanted him. He had the glamour of an English gentleman. The steward was gradually pushed aside and down into his place. The architect eventually married the widow and her wealth and the steward killed himself. So the Hopkins millions passed strangely into foreign hands and gave me my first problem of inheritance. But in the meantime the fabrication and growth of this marvelous palace, beautiful beyond anything that Great Barrington had seen, went slowly and majestically on, and always I could sit and watch it grow.

Finally in the fall of 1885, the difficulty of my future education was solved. The whole subtlety of the plan was clear neither to me nor my relatives at the time. Merely I was offered through the Reverend C.C. Painter, once an excellent Federal Indian Agent, a scholarship to attend Fisk University in Nashville, Tennessee; the funds were to be furnished by four Connecticut churches which Mr. Painter had formerly pastored. Disappointed though I was at not being able to go to Harvard, I merely regarded this as a temporary change of plan; I would of course go to Harvard in the end. But here and immediately was adventure. I was going into the South; the South of slavery, rebellion and black folk; and above all I was going to meet colored people of my own age and education, of my own ambitions. Once or twice already I had had swift glimpses of the colored world: at Rocky Point on Narragansett Bay, I had attended an annual picnic beside the sea, and had seen in open-mouthed astonishment the whole gorgeous color gamut of the American Negro world; the swaggering men, the beautiful girls, the laughter and gaiety, the unhampered self-expression. I was astonished and inspired. I became aware, once a chance to go to a group of such young people was opened up for me, of the spiritual isolation in which I was living. I heard too in these days for the first time the Negro folk songs. A Hampton Quartet had sung them in the Congregational Church. I was thrilled and moved to tears and seemed to recognize something inherently and deeply my own. I was glad to go to Fisk.

On the other hand my people had undoubtedly a more discriminating and unromantic view of the situation. They said frankly that it was a shame to send me South. I was Northern born and bred and instead of preparing me for work and giving me an opportunity right there in my own town and state, they were bundling me off to the South. This was undoubtedly true. The educated young white folk of Great Barrington became clerks in stores, bookkeepers and teachers, while a few went into professions. Great Barrington was not able to conceive of me in such local position. It was not so much that they were opposed to it, but it did not occur to them as a possibility.

On the other hand there was the call of the black South; teachers were needed. The crusade of the New England schoolmarm was in full swing. The freed slaves, if properly led, had a great future. Temporarily deprived of their full voting privileges, this was but a passing set-back. Black folk were bound in time to dominate the South. They needed trained leadership. I was sent to help furnish it.

From *Dusk of Dawn* by W.E.B. Du Bois. Harcourt Brace, 1940.

Letter Home

Fisk, Feb. 3, 1886.

Dear Pastor:

You have no doubt expected to hear of my welfare before this, but nevertheless you must know I am very grateful to you and the Sunday-School for what you have done. In the first place I am glad to tell you that I have united with the Church here and hope that the prayers of my Sunday-school may help guide me in the path of Christian duty. During the revival we had nearly forty conversions. The day of prayer for Colleges was observed here with two prayer meetings. The Rev. M. Aitkins, the Scotch revivalist spoke to us a short time ago, and tomorrow Mr. Moody will be present at our chapel exercises.

Our University is very pleasantly situated, overlooking the city, and the family life is very pleasant indeed. Some mornings as I look about upon the two or three hundred of my companions assembled for morning prayers I can hardly realize they are all my people; that this great assembly of youth and intelligence are the representatives of a race which twenty years ago was in bondage. Although this sunny land is very pleasant, notwithstanding its squalor misery and ignorance spread broad-cast; and although it is a bracing thought to know that I stand among those who do not despise me for my color, yet I have not forgotten to love my New England hills, and I often wish I could join some of your pleasant meetings in person as I do in spirit. I remain

Respectfully yours,

William E Du Bois

From *The Correspondence of W.E.B. Du Bois*, Volume I. Edited by Herbert Aptheker. University of Massachusetts Press, 1973.

EDITH WHARTON

Edith Wharton spent some of the most contented seasons of her life writing, gardening, and motoring in the Berkshires. In 1899, on a site overlooking Laurel Lake, she began building The Mount, designed to reflect her strong ideas about proportion, harmony, restraint, and utility in architecture, interior decoration, and gardens. She relished driving through the Berkshire hill towns which were only then, at the birth of the automobile age, beginning to emerge from their old-fashioned quaintness and overcome their soul-dislocating isolation. In "Xingu" we may enjoy her acid view of Berkshire ladies, and in the excerpt from Summer *her perception of the realities under the surface of bustling mill towns like Pittsfield.*

Life at The Mount

BUILDING THE MOUNT

We sold our Newport house, and built one near Lenox, in the hills of western Massachusetts, and at last I escaped from watering-place trivialities to the real country. If I could have made the change sooner I daresay I should never have given a thought to the literary delight of Paris or London; for life in the country is the only state which has always completely satisfied me, and I had never been allowed to gratify it, even for a few weeks at a time. Now I was to know the joys of six or seven months a year among fields and woods of my own, and the childish ecstasy of that first spring outing at Mamaroneck swept away all restlessness in the deep joy of communion with the earth. On a slope overlooking the dark waters and densely wooded shores of Laurel Lake we built a spacious and dignified house, to which we gave the name of my great-grandfather's place, the Mount. There was a big kitchen-garden with a grape pergola, a little farm, and a flower-garden outspread below the wide terrace overlooking the lake. There for over ten years I lived and gardened and wrote contentedly, and should doubtless have ended my days there had not a grave change in my husband's health made the burden of the property too heavy. But meanwhile the Mount was to give me country cares and joys, long happy rides and drives through the wooded lanes of that loveliest region, the companionship of a few dear friends, and the freedom from trivial obligations which was necessary if I was to go on with my writing. The Mount was my first real home, and though it is nearly twenty years since I last saw it (for I was too happy there ever to want to revisit it as a stranger) its blessed influence still lives in me.

Entrance façade of The Mount.
Courtesy of Edith Wharton
Restoration, Inc. Photograph
by Victoria Beller Smith

MOTORING IN THE BERKSHIRES

About this time we set up a motor, or perhaps I should say a series of them, for in those days it was difficult to find one which did not rapidly develop some organic defect; and selling, buying and exchanging went on continuously, though without appreciably better results. One summer, when we were all engaged on the first volumes of Mme Karénine's absorbing life of George Sand, we had a large showy car which always started off brilliantly and then broke down at the first hill, and this we christened "Alfred de Musset", while the small but indefatigable motor which subsequently replaced "Alfred" was naturally named "George." But those were the days when motor-guides still contained carefully drawn gradient-maps like fever-charts, and even "George" sometimes balked at the state of the country roads about Lenox; I remember in particular one summer night when Henry James, Walter Berry, my husband and I sat by the roadside till near dawn while our chauffeur tried to persuade "George" to carry us back to the Mount. The other day, in going over some old letters written to Bay Lodge by Walter Berry, I came on one dated from the Mount. "Great fun here," the writer exulted; "we motor every day, and yesterday *we did sixty-five miles*" (in triumphant italics). In those epic days roads and motors were an equally unknown quantity, and one set out on a ten-mile run with more apprehension than would now attend a journey across Africa. But the range of country-lovers like myself had hitherto been so limited, and our imagination so tantalized by the mystery beyond the next blue hills, that there was inexhaustible delight in penetrating to the remoter parts of Massachusetts and New Hampshire, discovering derelict villages with Georgian churches and balustraded house-fronts, exploring slumbrous mountain valleys, and coming back, weary but laden with a new harvest of beauty, after sticking fast in ruts, having to push the car up hill, to rout out the village black-smith for repairs, and suffer the jeers of horse-drawn travellers trotting gaily past us. My two New England tales, "Ethan Frome" and "Summer", were the result of explorations among villages still bedrowsed in a decaying rural existence, and sad slow-speaking people living in conditions hardly changed since their forbears held those villages against the Indians.

FIRST MEETING WITH HENRY JAMES

Since I have already spoken of Henry James's visits to the Mount, it is perhaps best to put his name first on the list of the friends who composed my closest group during the years I spent there, and those that followed. In fact, however, my first meeting with Henry James happened many years earlier, probably in the late 'eighties; though it is at the Mount that he first comes into the foreground of the picture.

For a long time there seemed small hope of his ever figuring there, for when we first met I was till struck dumb in the presence of greatness, and I had never doubted that Henry James was great, though how great I could not guess till I came to know the man as well as I did his books. The encounter took place at the house of Edward Boit, the brilliant water-colour painter whose talent Sargent so much admired. Boit and his wife, both Bostonians, and old friends of my husband's had lived for many years in Paris, and it was there that one day they asked us to dine with Henry James. I could hardly believe that such a privilege could befall me, and I could think of only one way of deserving it — to put on my newest Doucet dress, and try to look my prettiest! I was probably not more than twenty-five, those were the principles in which I had been brought up, and it would never have occurred to me that I had anything but my

youth, and my pretty frock, to commend me to the man whose shoe-
strings I thought myself unworthy to unloose. I can see the dress still —
and it *was* pretty; a tea-rose pink, embroidered with iridescent beads. But,
alas, it neither gave me the courage to speak, nor attracted the attention of
the great man. The evening was a failure, and I went home humbled and
discouraged.

*A publicity shot of Edith Wharton at her desk at The Mount about 1905. (She actually
did her writing in bed.)* Courtesy of Edith Wharton Restoration, Inc.

JAMES AT THE MOUNT

I believe James enjoyed those days at the Mount as much as he did (or
could) anything connected with the American scene; and the proof of it is
the length of his visits and their frequency. But on one occasion his stay
with us coincided with a protracted heat-wave; a wave of such unusual
intensity that even the nights, usually cool and airy at the Mount, were as
stifling as the days. My own dislike of heat filled me with sympathy for
James, whose sufferings were acute and uncontrollable. Like many men
of genius he had a singular inability for dealing with the most ordinary
daily incidents, such as giving an order to a servant, deciding what to

wear, taking a railway ticket, or getting from one place to another.

During a heat-wave this curious inadaptability to conditions or situations became positively tragic. His bodily surface, already broad, seemed to expand to meet it, and his imagination to become a part of his body, so that the one dripped words of distress as the other did moisture. Always uneasy about his health, he became visibly anxious in hot weather, and this anxiety added so much to his sufferings that his state was pitiful. Electric fans, iced drinks and cold baths seemed to give no relief; and finally we discovered that the only panacea was incessant motoring.

Luckily by that time we had a car which would really go, and go we did, daily, incessantly, over miles and miles of lustrous landscape lying motionless under the still glaze of heat. While we were moving he was refreshed and happy, his spirits rose, the twinkle returned to lips and eyes; and we never halted except for tea on a high hillside, or for a "cooling drink" at a village apothecary's — on one of which occasions he instructed one of us to bring him "something less innocent than Apollinaris", and was enchanted when this was interpreted as meaning an "orange phosphate", a most sophisticated beverage for that day.

From *A Backward Glance* by Edith Wharton. Appleton-Century, 1934.

Excerpts From Summer

TO NETTLETON ON THE FOURTH OF JULY

W hen they reached Hepburn the full heat of the airless morning descended on them. At the railway station the platform was packed with a sweltering throng, and they took refuge in the waiting-room, where there was another throng, already dejected by the heat and the long waiting for retarded trains. Pale mothers were struggling with fretful babies, or trying to keep their older offspring from the fascination of the track; girls and their "fellows" were giggling and shoving, and passing about candy in sticky bags, and older men, collarless and perspiring, were shifting heavy children from one arm to the other, and keeping a haggard eye on the scattered members of their families.

At last the train rumbled in, and engulfed the waiting multitude. Harney swept Charity up on to the first car and they captured a bench for two, and sat in happy isolation while the train swayed and roared along through rich fields and languid tree-clumps. The haze of the morning had become a sort of clear tremor over everything, like the colourless vibration about a flame; and the opulent landscape seemed to droop under it. But to Charity the heat was a stimulant: it enveloped the whole world in the same glow that burned at her heart. Now and then a lurch of the train flung her against Harney, and through her thin muslin she felt the touch of his sleeve. She steadied herself, their eyes met, and the flaming breath of the day seemed to enclose them.

The train roared into the Nettleton station, the descending mob caught them on its tide, and they were swept out into a vague dusty square thronged with seedy "hacks" and long curtained omnibuses drawn by horses with tasselled fly-nets over their withers, who stood swinging their depressed heads drearily from side to side.

A mob of 'bus and hack drivers were shouting "To the Eagle House," "To the Washington House," "This way to the Lake," "Just starting for Greytop;" and through their yells came the popping of fire-crackers, the explosion of torpedoes, the banging of toy-guns, and the crash of a firemen's band trying to play the Merry Widow while they were being packed into a waggonette streaming with bunting.

The ramshackle wooden hotels about the square were all hung with flags and paper lanterns, and as Harney and Charity turned into the main street, with its brick and granite business blocks crowding out the old low-storied shops, and its towering poles strung with innumerable wires that seemed to tremble and buzz in the heat, they saw the double line of flags and lanterns tapering away gaily to the park at the other end of the perspective. The noise and colour of this holiday vision seemed to transform Nettleton into a metropolis. Charity could not believe that Springfield or even Boston had anything grander to show, and she wondered if, at this very moment, Annabel Balch, on the arm of as brilliant a young man, were threading her way through scenes as resplendent.

"Where shall we go first?" Harney asked; but as she turned her happy eyes on him he guessed the answer and said: "We'll take a look round, shall we?"

The street swarmed with their fellow-travellers, with other excursionists arriving from other directions, with Nettleton's own population, and with the mill-hands trooping in from the factories on the Creston. The shops were closed, but one would scarcely have noticed it, so numerous were the glass doors swinging open on saloons, on restaurants, on drugstores gushing from every soda-water tap, on fruit and confectionery shops stacked with strawberry-cake, cocoanut drops, trays of glistening molasses candy, boxes of caramels and chewing-gum, baskets of sodden strawberries, and dangling branches of bananas. Outside of some of the doors were trestles with banked-up oranges and apples, spotted pears and dusty raspberries; and the air reeked with the smell of fruit and stale coffee, beer and sarsaparilla and fried potatoes.

Even the shops that were closed offered, through wide expanses of

Fourth of July parade in Pittsfield, 1909. Courtesy of The Berkshire Eagle

plate-glass, hints of hidden riches. In some, waves of silk and ribbon broke over shores of imitation moss from which ravishing hats rose like tropical orchids. In others, the pink throats of gramophones opened their giant convolutions in a soundless chorus; or bicycles shining in neat ranks seemed to await the signal of an invisible starter; or tiers of fancy-goods in leatherette and paste and celluloid dangled their insidious graces; and, in one vast bay that seemed to project them into exciting contact with the public, wax ladies in daring dresses chatted elegantly, or, with gestures intimate yet blameless, pointed to their pink corsets and transparent hosiery.

Presently Harney found that his watch had stopped, and turned in at a small jeweller's shop which chanced to be still open. While the watch was being examined Charity leaned over the glass counter where, on a background of dark blue velvet, pins, rings and brooches glittered like the moon and stars. She had never seen jewellery so near by, and she longed to lift the glass lid and plunge her hand among the shining treasures. But already Harney's watch was repaired, and he laid his hand on her arm and drew her from her dream.

"Which do you like best?" he asked leaning over the counter at her side.

"I don't know...." She pointed to a gold lily-of-the-valley with white flowers.

"Don't you think the blue pin's better?" he suggested, and immediately she saw that the lily of the valley was mere trumpery compared to the small round stone, blue as a mountain lake, with little sparks of light all round it. She coloured at her want of discrimination.

"It's so lovely I guess I was afraid to look at it," she said.

He laughed, and they went out of the shop; but a few steps away he exclaimed: "Oh, by Jove, I forgot something," and turned back and left her in the crowd. She stood staring down a row of pink gramophone throats till he rejoined her and slipped his arm through hers.

"You mustn't be afraid of looking at the blue pin any longer, because it belongs to you," he said; and she felt a little box being pressed into her hand. Her heart gave a leap of joy, but it reached her lips only in a shy stammer. She remembered other girls whom she had heard planning to extract presents from their fellows, and was seized with a sudden dread lest Harney should have imagined that she had leaned over the pretty things in the glass case in the hope of having one given to her....

A little farther down the street they turned in at a glass doorway opening on a shining hall with a mahogany staircase, and brass cages in its corners. "We must have something to eat," Harney said; and the next moment Charity found herself in a dressing-room all looking-glass and lustrous surfaces, where a party of showy-looking girls were dabbing on powder and straightening immense plumed hats. When they had gone she took courage to bathe her hot face in one of the marble basins, and to straighten her own hat-brim, which the parasols of the crowd had indented. The dresses in the shops had so impressed her that she scarcely dared look at her reflection; but when she did so, the glow of her face under her cherry-coloured hat, and the curve of her young shoulders through the transparent muslin, restored her courage; and when she had taken the blue brooch from its box and pinned it on her bosom she walked toward the restaurant with her head high, as if she had always strolled through tessellated halls beside young men in flannels.

FIREWORKS OVER THE LAKE

Presently the thought of the cool trolley-run to the Lake grew irresistible, and they struggled out of the theatre. As they stood on the pavement, Harney pale with the heat, and even Charity a little confused by it, a young man drove by in an electric run-about with a calico band bearing the words: "Ten dollars to take you round the Lake." Before Charity knew what was happening, Harney had waved a hand, and they were climbing in. "Say, for twenny-five I'll run you out first to see the ball-game and back," the driver proposed with an insinuating grin; but Charity said quickly: "Oh, I'd rather go rowing on the Lake." The street was so thronged that progress was slow; but the glory of sitting in the little carriage while it wriggled its way between laden omnibuses and trolleys made the moments seem too short. "Next turn is Lake Avenue," the young man called out over his shoulder; and as they paused in the wake of a big omnibus groaning with Knights of Pythias in cocked hats and swords, Charity looked up and saw on the corner a brick house with a conspicuous black and gold sign across its front. "Dr. Merkle; Private Consultations at all hours. Lady Attendants," she read; and suddenly she remembered Ally Hawes's words: "The house was at the corner of Wing Street and Lake Avenue ... there's a big black sign across the front...." Through all the heat and the rapture a shiver of cold ran over her.

The Lake at last — a sheet of shining metal brooded over by drooping trees. Charity and Harney had secured a boat and, getting away from the wharves and the refreshment-booths, they drifted idly along, hugging the shadow of the shore. Where the sun struck the water its shafts flamed back blindingly at the heat-veiled sky; and the least shade was black by contrast. The Lake was so smooth that the reflection of the trees on its edge seemed enamelled on a solid surface; but gradually, as the sun declined, the water grew transparent, and Charity, leaning over, plunged her fascinated gaze into depths so clear that she saw the inverted tree-tops interwoven with the green growths of the bottom.

They rounded a point at the farther end of the Lake, and entering an inlet pushed their bow against a protruding tree-trunk. A green veil of willows overhung them. Beyond the trees, wheat-fields sparkled in the sun; and all along the horizon the clear hills throbbed with light. Charity leaned back in the stern, and Harney unshipped the oars and lay in the bottom of the boat without speaking.

She was still thinking of the ten dollars he had handed to the driver of the run-about. It had given them twenty minutes of pleasure, and it seemed unimaginable that anyone should be able to buy amusement at that rate. With ten dollars he might have bought her an engagement ring; she knew that Mrs. Tom Fry's, which came from Springfield, and had a diamond in it, had cost only eight seventy-five. But she did not know why the thought had occurred to her. Harney would never buy her an engagement ring: they were friends and comrades, but no more. He had been perfectly fair to her: he had never said a word to mislead her. She wondered what the girl was like whose hand was waiting for his ring....

Boats were beginning to thicken on the Lake and the clang of incessantly arriving trolleys announced the return of the crowds from the ball-field. The shadows lengthened across the pearl-grey water and two white clouds near the sun were turning golden. On the opposite shore men were hammering hastily at a wooden scaffolding in a field. Charity asked what it was for.

"Why, the fireworks. I suppose there'll be a big show." Harney looked at her and a smile crept into his moody eyes. "Have you never seen any good fireworks?"

"Miss Hatchard always sends up lovely rockets on the Fourth," she answered doubtfully.

"Oh —" his contempt was unbounded. "I mean a big performance like this: illuminated boats, and all the rest."

She flushed at the picture. "Do they send them up from the Lake, too?"

"Rather. Didn't you notice that big raft we passed? It's wonderful to see the rockets completing their orbits down under one's feet." She said nothing, and he put the oars into the rollicks. "If we stay we'd better go and pick up something to eat."

"But how can we get back afterward?" she ventured, feeling it would break her heart if she missed it.

He consulted a time-table, found a ten o'clock train and reassured her. "The moon rises so late that it will be dark by eight, and we'll have over an hour of it."

Twilight fell, and lights began to show along the shore. The trolleys roaring out from Nettleton became great luminous serpents coiling in and out among the trees. The wooden eating-houses at the Lake's edge danced with lanterns, and the dusk echoed with laughter and shouts and the clumsy splashing of oars.

Harney and Charity had found a table in the corner of a balcony built over the Lake, and were patiently awaiting an unattainable chowder. Close under them the water lapped the piles, agitated by the evolutions of a little white steamboat trellised with coloured globes which was to run passengers up and down the Lake. It was already black with them as it sheered off on its first trip.

Suddenly Charity heard a woman's laugh behind her. The sound was familiar, and she turned to look. A band of showily dressed girls and dapper young men wearing badges of secret societies, with new straw hats tilted far back on their square-clipped hair, had invaded the balcony and were loudly clambering for a table. The girl in the lead was the one who had laughed. She wore a large hat with a long white feather, and from under its brim her painted eyes looked at Charity with amused recognition.

"Say! if this ain't like Old Home Week," she remarked to the girl at her elbow; and giggles and glances passed between them. Charity knew at once that the girl with the white feather was Julian Hares. She had lost her freshness, and the paint under her eyes made her face seem thinner; but her lips had the same lovely curve, and the same cold mocking smile, as if there were some secret absurdity in the person she was looking at, and she had instantly detected it.

Charity flushed to the forehead and looked away. She felt herself humiliated by Julia's sneer, and vexed that the mockery of such a creature should affect her. She trembled lest Harney should notice that the noisy troop had recognized her; but they found no table free, and passed on tumultuously.

Presently there was a soft rush through the air and a shower of silver fell from the blue evening sky. In another direction, pale Roman candles shot up singly through the trees, and a fire-haired rocket swept the horizon like a portent. Between these intermittent flashes the velvet curtains of the darkness were descending, and in the intervals of eclipse the voices of the crowds seemed to sink to smothered murmurs.

Charity and Harney, dispossessed by newcomers, were at length obliged to give up their table and struggle through the throng about the boat-landings. For a while there seemed no escape from the tide of late arrivals; but finally Harney secured the last two places on the stand from which the more privileged were to see the fireworks. The seats were at the end of a row, one above the other. Charity had taken off her hat to have an uninterrupted view; and whenever she leaned back to follow the curve of some dishevelled rocket she could feel Harney's knees against her head.

After awhile the scattered fireworks ceased. A longer interval of darkness followed, and then the whole night broke into flower. From every point of the horizon, gold and silver arches sprang up and crossed each other, sky-orchards broke into blossom, shed their flaming petals and hung their branches with golden fruit; and all the while the air was filled with a soft supernatural hum, as though great birds were building their nests in those invisible tree-tops.

Now and then there came a lull, and a wave of moonlight swept the Lake. In a flash it revealed hundreds of boats, steel-dark against lustrous ripples; then it withdrew as if with a furling of vast translucent wings. Charity's heart throbbed with delight. It was as if all the latent beauty of things had been unveiled to her. She could not imagine that the world held anything more wonderful; but near her she heard someone say, "You wait till you see the set piece," and instantly her hopes took a fresh flight. At last, just as it was beginning to seem as though the whole arch of the sky were one great lid pressed against her dazzled eyeballs, and striking out of them continuous jets of jewelled light, the velvet darkness settled down again, and a murmur of expectation ran through the crowd.

"Now — now!" the same voice said excitedly; and Charity, grasping the hat on her knee, crushed it tight in the effort to restrain her rapture.

For a moment the night seemed to grow more impenetrably black; then a great picture stood out against it like a constellation. It was surmounted by a golden scroll bearing the inscription, "Washington crossing the Delaware," and across a flood of motionless golden ripples the National Hero passed, erect, solemn and gigantic, standing with folded arms in the stern of a slowly moving golden boat.

A long "Oh-h-h" burst from the spectators: the stand creaked and shook with their blissful trepidations. "Oh-h-h," Charity gasped: she had forgotten where she was, had at last forgotten even Harney's nearness. She seemed to have been caught up into the stars....

The picture vanished and darkness came down. In the obscurity she felt her head clasped by two hands: her face was drawn backward, and Harney's lips were pressed on hers. With sudden vehemence he wound his arms about her, holding her head against his breast while she gave him back his kisses. An unknown Harney had revealed himself, a Harney who dominated her and yet over whom she felt herself possessed of a new mysterious power.

But the crowd was beginning to move, and he had to release her. "Come," he said in a confused voice. He scrambled over the side of the stand, and holding up his arm caught her as she sprang to the ground. He passed his arm about her waist, steadying her against the descending rush of people; and she clung to him, speechless, exultant, as if all the crowding and confusion about them were a mere vain stirring of the air.

A SADDER VISIT TO NETTLETON

Charity descended from the train at Nettleton, and walked out of the station into the dusty square. The brief interval of cold weather was over, and the day was as soft, and almost as hot, as when she and Harney had emerged on the same scene on the Fourth of July. In the square the same broken-down hacks and carry-alls stood drawn up in a despondent line, and the lank horses with fly-nets over their withers swayed their heads drearily to and fro. She recognized the staring signs over the eating-houses and billiard saloons, and the long lines of wires on lofty poles tapering down the main street to the park at its other end. Taking the way the wires pointed, she went on hastily, with bent head, till she reached a wide transverse street with a brick building at the corner. She crossed this street and glanced furtively up at the front of the brick building; then she returned, and entered a door opening on a flight of steep brass-rimmed stairs. On the second landing she rang a bell, and a mulatto girl with a bushy head and a frilled apron let her into a hall where a stuffed fox on his hind legs proffered a brass card-tray to visitors. At the back of the hall was a glazed door marked: "Office." After waiting a few minutes in a handsomely furnished room, with plush sofas surmounted by large gold-framed photographs of showy young women, Charity was shown into the office....

When she came out of the glazed door Dr. Merkle followed, and led her into another room, smaller, and still more crowded with plush and gold frames. Dr. Merkle was a plump woman with small bright eyes, an immense mass of black hair coming down low on her forehead, and unnaturally white and even teeth. She wore a rich black dress, with gold chains and charms hanging from her bosom. Her hands were large and smooth, and quick in all their movements; and she smelt of musk and carbolic acid.

She smiled on Charity with all her faultless teeth. "Sit down, my dear. Wouldn't you like a little drop of something to pick you up? ... No.... Well, just lay back a minute then.... There's nothing to be done just yet; but in about a month, if you'll step round again ... I could take you right into my own house for two or three days, and there wouldn't be a mite of trouble. Mercy me! The next time you'll know better'n to fret like this...."

Charity gazed at her with widening eyes. This woman with the false hair, the false teeth, the false murderous smile — what was she offering her but immunity from some unthinkable crime? Charity, till then, had been conscious only of a vague self-disgust and a frightening physical distress; now, of a sudden, there came to her the grave surprise of motherhood. She had come to this dreadful place because she knew of no other way of making sure that she was not mistaken about her state; and the woman had taken her for a miserable creature like Julia.... The thought was so horrible that she sprang up, white and shaking, one of her great rushes of anger sweeping over her.

Dr. Merkle, still smiling, also rose. "Why do you run off in such a hurry? You can stretch out right here on my sofa...." She paused, and her smile grew more motherly. "Afterwards — if there's been any talk at home, and you want to get away for a while ... I have a lady friend in Boston who's looking for a companion ... you're the very one to suit her, my dear...."

Charity had reached the door. "I don't want to stay. I don't want to come back here," she stammered, her hand on the knob; but with a swift movement Dr. Merkle edged her from the threshold.

"Oh, very well. Five dollars, please."

Charity looked helplessly at the doctor's tight lips and rigid face. Her last savings had gone in repaying Ally for the cost of Miss Balch's ruined blouse, and she had had to borrow four dollars from her friend to pay for her railway ticket and cover the doctor's fee. It had never occurred to her that medical advice could cost more than two dollars.

"I didn't know ... I haven't got that much ..." she faltered, bursting into tears.

Dr. Merkle gave a short laugh which did not show her teeth, and inquired with concision if Charity supposed she ran the establishment for her own amusement ? She leaned her firm shoulders against the door as she spoke, like a grim gaoler making terms with her captive.

"You say you'll come round and settle later? I've heard that pretty often too. Give me your address, and if you can't pay me I'll send the bill to your folks.... What? I can't understand what you say.... That don't suit you either? My, you're pretty particular for a girl that ain't got enough to settle her own bills...." She paused, and fixed her eyes on the brooch with a blue stone that Charity had pinned to her blouse.

"Ain't you ashamed to talk that way to a lady that's got to earn her living, when you go about with jewellery like that on you? ... It ain't in my line, and I do it only as a favour ... but if you're a mind to leave that brooch as a pledge, I don't say no.... Yes, of course, you can get it back when you bring me my money...."

From *Summer* by Edith Wharton. Harper & Row Perennial Library. Reprinted by arrangement with D. Appleton & Co.

Moonrise Over Tyringham

Now the high holocaust of hours is done,
  And all the west empurpled with their death,
  How swift oblivion drinks the fallen sun,
How little while the dusk remembereth!

Though some there were, proud hours that marched in mail,
And took the morning on auspicious crest,
Crying to fortune "Back for I prevail!" —
Yet now they lie disfeatured with the rest;

And some that stole so soft on destiny
Methought they had surprised her to a smile;
But these fled frozen when she turned to see,
And moaned and muttered through my heart awhile.

But now the day is emptied of them all,
And night absorbs their life-blood at a draught;
And so my life lies, as the gods let fall
An empty cup from which their lips have quaffed.

Yet see — night is not ... by translucent ways,
Up the grey void of autumn afternoon
Steals a mild crescent, charioted in haze,
And all the air is merciful as June.

The lake is a forgotten streak of day
That trembles through the hemlocks' darkling bars,
And still, my heart, still some divine delay
Upon the threshold holds the earliest stars.

O pale equivocal hour, whose suppliant feet
Haunt the mute reaches of the sleeping wind,
Art thou a watcher stealing to entreat
Prayer and sepulture for thy fallen kind?

Poor plaintive waif of a predestined race,
Their ruin gapes for thee. Why linger here?
Go hence in silence. Veil thine orphaned face,
Lest I should look on it and call it dear.

For if I love thee thou wilt sooner die;
Some sudden ruin will plunge upon thy head,
Midnight will fall from the revengeful sky
And hurl thee down among thy shuddering dead.

Avert thine eyes. Lapse softly from my sight,
Call not my name, nor heed if thine I crave,
So shalt thou sink through mitigated night
And bathe thee in the all-effacing wave.

But upward still thy perilous footsteps fare
Along a high-hung heaven drenched in light,
Dilating on a tide of crystal air
That floods the dark hills to their utmost height.

Strange hour, is this thy waning face that leans
Out of mid-heaven and makes my soul its glass?

What victory is imaged there? What means
Thy tarrying smile? Oh, veil thy lips and pass.

Nay ... pause and let me name thee! For I see,
O with what flooding ecstasy of light,
Strange hour that wilt not loose thy hold on me,
Thou'rt not day's latest, but the first of night!

And after thee the gold-foot stars come thick,
From hand to hand they toss they flying fire,
Till all the zenith with their dance is quick
About the wheeling music of the Lyre.

Dread hour that lead'st the immemorial round,
With lifted torch revealing one by one
The thronging splendours that the day held bound,
And how each blue abyss enshrines its sun —

Be thou the image of a thought that fares
Forth from itself, and flings its ray ahead,
Leaping the barriers of ephemeral cares,
To where our lives are but the ages' tread,

And let this year be, not the last of youth,
But first — like thee! — of some new train of hours,
If more remote from hope, yet nearer truth,
And kin to the unpetitionable powers.

From Artemis to Arcturus by Edith Wharton. Charles Scribner, 1909.

Xingu

I

Mrs. Ballinger is one of the ladies who pursue Culture in bands, as though it were dangerous to meet alone. To this end she had founded the Lunch Club, an association composed of herself and several other indomitable huntresses of erudition. The Lunch Club, after three or four winters of lunching and debate, had acquired such local distinction that the entertainment of distinguished strangers became one of its accepted functions; in recognition of which it duly extended to the celebrated Osric Dane, on the day of her arrival in Hillbridge, an invitation to be present at the next meeting.

The club was to meet at Mrs. Ballinger's. The other members, behind her back, were of one voice in deploring her unwillingness to cede her rights in favor of Mrs. Plinth, whose house made a more impressive setting for the entertainment of celebrities; while, as Mrs. Leveret observed, there was always the picture gallery to fall back on.

Mrs. Plinth made no secret of sharing this view. She had always regarded it as one of her obligations to entertain the Lunch Club's distinguished guests. Mrs. Plinth was almost as proud of her obligations as she was of her picture gallery; she was in fact fond of implying that the one possession implied the other, and that only a woman of her wealth could afford to live up to a standard as high as that which she had set herself. An all-round sense of duty, roughly adaptable to various ends, was, in her opinion, all that Providence exacted of the more humbly stationed; but the power which had predestined Mrs. Plinth to keep a footman clearly intended her to maintain an equally specialized staff of responsibilities. It was the more to be regretted that Mrs. Ballinger, whose obligations to society were bounded by the narrow scope of two parlormaids, should have been so tenacious of the right to entertain Osric Dane.

The question of that lady's reception had for month past profoundly moved the members of the Lunch Club. It was not that they felt themselves unequal to the task, but that their sense of the opportunity plunged them into the agreeable uncertainty of the lady who weighs the alternatives of a well-stocked wardrobe. If such subsidiary members as Mrs. Leveret were fluttered by the thought of exchanging ideas with the author of *The Wings of Death*, no forebodings disturbed the conscious adequacy of Mrs. Plinth, Mrs. Ballinger and Miss Van Vluyck. *The Wings of Death* had, in fact, at Miss Van Vluyck's suggestion, been chosen as the subject of discussion at the last club meeting, and each member had thus been enabled to express her own opinion or to appropriate whatever sounded well in the comments of the others.

Mrs. Roby alone had abstained from profiting by the opportunity but it was now openly recognized that, as a member of the Lunch Club, Mrs. Roby was a failure. "It all comes," as Miss Van Vluyck put it, "of accepting a woman on a man's estimation." Mrs. Roby, returning to Hillbridge from a prolonged sojourn in exotic lands — the other ladies no longer took the trouble to remember where — had been heralded by the distinguished biologist, Professor Foreland, as the most agreeable woman he had ever met; and the members of the Lunch Club, impressed by an encomium that carried the weight of a diploma, and rashly assuming that the Professor's social sympathies would follow the line of his professional bent, had seized the chance of annexing a biological member. Their disillusionment was complete. At Miss Van Vluyck's first offhand mention of the pterodactyl Mrs. Roby had confusedly murmured: "I know so little about meters —" and after that painful betrayal of incompetence she had prudently withdrawn from further participation in the mental gymnastics of the club.

"I suppose she flattered him," Miss Van Vluyck summed up — "or else it's the way she does her hair."

The dimensions of Miss Van Vluyck's dining room having restricted the membership of the club to six, the nonconductiveness of one member was a serious obstacle to the exchange of ideas, and some wonder had already been expressed that Mrs. Roby should care to live, as it were, on the intellectual bounty of the others. This feeling was increased by the discovery that she had not yet read *The Wings of Death*. She owned to having heard the name of Osric Dane; but that — incredible as it appeared — was the extent of her acquaintance with the celebrated novelist. The ladies could not conceal their surprise; but Mrs. Ballinger, whose pride in the club made her wish to put even Mrs. Roby in the best possible light, gently insinuated that, though she had not had time to acquaint herself with *The Wings of Death*, she must at least be familiar with its equally remarkable predecessor, *The Supreme Instant*.

Mrs. Roby wrinkled her sunny brows in a conscientious effort of memory, as a result of which she recalled that, oh, yes, she *had* seen the book at her brother's, when she was staying with him in Brazil, and had even carried it off to read one day on a boating party; but they had all got to shying things at each other in the boat, and the book had gone overboard, so she had never had the chance —

The picture evoked by this anecdote did not increase Mrs. Roby's credit with the club, and there was a painful pause, which was broken by Mrs. Plinth's remarking: "I can understand that, with all your other pursuits, you should not find much time for reading; but I should have thought you might at least have got up *The Wings of Death* before Osric Dane's arrival."

Mrs. Roby took this rebuke good-humoredly. She had meant, she owned, to glance through the book; but she had been so absorbed in a novel of Trollope's that —

"No one reads Trollope now," Mrs. Ballinger interrupted.

Mrs. Roby looked pained. "I'm only just beginning," she confessed.

"And does he interest you?" Mrs. Plinth inquired.

"He amuses me."

"Amusement," said Mrs. Plinth, "is hardly what I look for in my choice of books."

"Oh, certainly, *The Wings of Death* is not amusing," ventured Mrs.

Leveret, whose manner of putting forth an opinion was like that of an obliging salesman with a variety of other styles to submit if his first selection does not suit.

"Was it *meant* to be?" inquired Mrs. Plinth, who was fond of asking questions that she permitted no one but herself to answer. "Assuredly not."

"Assuredly not — that is what I was going to say," assented Mrs. Leveret, hastily rolling up her opinion and reaching for another. "It was meant to — to elevate."

Miss Van Vluyck adjusted her spectacles as though they were the black cap of condemnation. "I hardly see," she interposed, "how a book steeped in the bitterest pessimism can be said to elevate, however much it may instruct."

"I meant, of course, to instruct," said Mrs. Leveret, flurried by the unexpected distinction between two terms which she had supposed to be synonymous. Mrs. Leveret's enjoyment of the Lunch Club was frequently marred by such surprises; and not knowing her own value to the other ladies as a mirror for their mental complacency she was sometimes troubled by a doubt of her worthiness to join in their debates. It was only the fact of having a dull sister who thought her clever that saved her from a sense of hopeless inferiority.

"Do they get married in the end?" Mrs. Roby interposed.

"They — who?" the Lunch Club collectively exclaimed.

"Why, the girl and man. It's a novel, isn't it? I always think that's the one thing that matters. If they're parted it spoils my dinner."

Mrs. Plinth and Mrs. Ballinger exchanged scandalized glances, and the latter said: "I should hardly advise you to read *The Wings of Death* in that spirit. For my part, when there are so many books one *has* to read, I wonder how any one can find time for those that are merely amusing."

"The beautiful part of it," Laura Glyde murmured, "is surely just this — that no one can tell how *The Wings of Death* ends. Osric Dane, overcome by the awful significance of her own meaning, has mercifully veiled it — perhaps even from herself — as Apelles, in representing the sacrifice of Iphigenia, veiled the face of Agamemnon."

"What's that? Is it poetry?" whispered Mrs. Leveret to Mrs. Plinth, who, disdaining a definite reply, said coldly: "You should look it up. I always make it a point to look things up." Her tone added — "Though I might easily have it done for me by the footman."

"I was about to say," Miss Van Vluyck resumed, "that it must always be a question whether a book can instruct unless it elevates."

"Oh —" murmured Mrs. Leveret, now feeling herself hopelessly astray.

"I don't know," said Mrs. Ballinger, scenting in Miss Van Vluyck's tone a tendency to depreciate the coveted distinction of entertaining Osric Dane; "I don't know that such a question can seriously be raised as to a book which has attracted more attention among thoughtful people than any novel since *Robert Elsmere*."

"Oh, but don't you see," exclaimed Laura Glyde, "that it's just the dark hopelessness of it all — the wonderful tone scheme of black on black — that makes it such an artistic achievement? It reminded me when I read it of Prince Rupert's *manière noire* ... the book is etched, not painted, yet one feels the color values so intensely ..."

"Who is *he*?" Mrs. Leveret whispered to her neighbor. "Someone she's met abroad?"

"The wonderful part of the book" Mrs. Ballinger conceded, "is that it may be looked at from so many points of view. I hear that as a study of determinism Professor Lupton ranks it with *The Data of Ethics*."

"I'm told that Osric Dane spent ten years in preparatory studies before beginning to write it," said Mrs. Plinth. "She looks up everything — verifies everything. It has always been my principle, as you know. Nothing would induce me, now, to put aside a book before I'd finished it, just because I can buy as many more as I want."

"And what do *you* think of *The Wings of Death*?" Mrs. Roby abruptly asked her.

It was the kind of question that might be termed out of order, and the ladies glanced at each other as though disclaiming any share in such a breach of discipline. They all knew there was nothing Mrs. Plinth so much disliked as being asked her opinion of a book. Books were written to read; if one read them what more could be expected? To be questioned in detail regarding the contents of a volume seemed to her as great an outrage as being searched for smuggled laces at the Custom House. The club had always respected this idiosyncrasy of Mrs. Plinth's. Such opinions as she had were imposing and substantial: her mind, like her house, was furnished with monumental "pieces" that were not meant to be disarranged; and it was one of the unwritten rules of the Lunch Club that, within her own province, each member's habits of thought should be respected. The meeting therefore closed with an increased sense, on the part of the other ladies, of Mrs. Roby's hopeless unfitness to be one of them.

II

Mrs. Leveret, on the eventful day, arrived early at Mrs. Ballinger's, her volume of *Appropriate Allusions* in her pocket.

It always flustered Mrs. Leveret to be late at the Lunch Club: she liked to collect her thoughts and gather a hint, as the others assembled, of the turn the conversation was likely to take. Today, however, she felt herself completely at a loss; and even the familiar contact of *Appropriate Allusions*, which stuck into her as she sat down, failed to give her any reassurance. It was an admirable little volume compiled to meet all the social emergencies; so that, whether on the occasion of Anniversaries, joyful or melancholy (as the classification ran), of Banquets, social or municipal, or of Baptisms, Church of England or sectarian, its student need never be at a loss for a pertinent reference. Mrs. Leveret, though she had for years devoutly conned its pages, valued it, however, rather for its moral support than for its practical services; for though in the privacy of her own room she commanded an army of quotations, these invariably deserted her at the critical moment, and the only phrase she retained — *Canst thou draw out leviathan with a hook?* — was one she had never yet found occasion to apply.

Today she felt that even the complete mastery of the volume would hardly have insured her self-possession; for she thought it probable that, even if she *did*, in some miraculous way, remember an Allusion, it would be only to find that Osric Dane used a different volume (Mrs. Leveret was convinced that literary people always carried them), and would consequently not recognize her quotations.

Mrs. Leveret's sense of being adrift was intensified by the appearance of Mrs. Ballinger's drawing room. To a careless eye its aspect was unchanged; but those acquainted with Mrs. Ballinger's way of arranging her books would instantly have detected the marks of recent perturbation. Mrs. Ballinger's province, as a member of the Lunch Club, was the Book of the Day. On that, whatever it was, from a novel to a treatise on experimental psychology, she was confidently, authoritatively "up." What became of last year's books, or last week's even; what she did with the "subjects" she had previously professed with equal authority; no one had ever yet discovered. Her mind was an hotel where facts came and went like transient lodgers, without leaving their address behind, and frequently without paying for their board. It was Mrs. Ballinger's boast that she was "abreast with the Thought of the Day," and her pride that this advanced position should be expressed by the books on her table. These volumes, frequently renewed, and almost always damp from the press, bore names generally unfamiliar to Mrs. Leveret, and giving her, as she furtively scanned them, a disheartening glimpse of new fields of knowledge to be breathlessly traversed in Mrs. Ballinger's wake. But today a number of maturer-looking volumes were adroitly mingled with the *primeurs* of the press — Karl Marx jostled Professor Bergson, and the *Confessions of St. Augustine* lay beside the last work on "Mendelism"; so that even to Mrs. Leveret's fluttered perceptions it was clear that Mrs. Ballinger didn't in the least know what Osric Dane was likely to talk about, and had taken measures to be prepared for anything. Mrs. Leveret felt like a passenger on an ocean steamer who is told that there is no immediate danger, but that she had better put on her lifebelt.

It was a relief to be roused from these foreboding by Miss Van Vluyck's arrival.

"Well, my dear," the newcomer briskly asked her hostess, "what subjects are we to discuss today?"

Mrs. Ballinger was furtively replacing a volume of Wordsworth by a copy of Verlaine. "I hardly know," she said, somewhat nervously. "Perhaps we had better leave that to circumstances."

"Circumstances?" said Miss Van Vluyck drily. "That means, I suppose, that Laura Glyde will take the floor as usual, and we shall be deluged with literature."

Philanthropy and statistics were Miss Van Vluyck's province, and she resented any tendency to divert their guest's attention from these topics.

Mrs. Plinth at this moment appeared.

"Literature?" she protested in a tone of remonstrance. "But this is perfectly unexpected. I understood we were to talk of Osric Dane's novel."

Mrs. Ballinger winced at the discrimination, but let it pass. "We can hardly make that our chief subject — at least not *too* intentionally," she suggested. "Of course we can let our talk *drift* in that direction; but we ought to have some other topic as an introduction, and that is what I wanted to consult you about. The fact is, we know so little of Osric Dane's tastes and interests that it is difficult to make any special preparation."

"It may be difficult," said Mrs. Plinth with decision, "but it is necessary. I know what that happy-go-lucky principle leads to. As I told one of my nieces the other day, there are certain emergencies for which a lady should always be prepared. It's in shocking taste to wear colors when one pays a visit of condolence, or a last year's dress when there are reports that one's husband is on the wrong side of the market; and so it is with conversation. All I ask is that I should know beforehand what is to be talked about; then I feel sure of being able to say the proper thing."

"I quite agree with you." Mrs. Ballinger assented; "but —"

And at that instant, heralded by the fluttered parlormaid, Osric Dane appeared upon the threshold.

Mrs. Leveret told her sister afterward that she had known at a glance what was coming. She saw that Osric Dane was not going to meet them halfway. That distinguished personage had indeed entered with an air of compulsion not calculated to promote the easy exercise of hospitality. She looked as though she were about to be photographed for a new edition of her books.

The desire to propitiate a divinity is generally in inverse ratio to its responsiveness, and the sense of discouragement produced by Osric Dane's entrance visibly increased the Lunch Club's eagerness to please her. Any lingering idea that she might consider herself under an obligation to her entertainers was at once dispelled by her manner: as Mrs. Leveret said afterward to her sister, she had a way of looking at you that made you feel as if there was something wrong with your hat. This evidence of greatness produced such an immediate impression on the ladies that a shudder of awe ran through them when Mrs. Roby, as their hostess led the great personage into the dining room, turned back to whisper to the others: "What a brute she is!"

The hour about the table did not tend to revise this verdict. It was passed by Osric Dane in the silent deglutition of Mrs. Ballinger's menu, and by the members of the club in the emission of tentative platitudes which their guest seemed to swallow as perfunctorily as the successive courses of the luncheon.

Mrs. Ballinger's reluctance to fix a topic had thrown the club into a mental disarray which increased with the return to the drawing room, where the actual business of discussion was to open. Each lady waited for the other to speak; and there was a general shock of disappointment when their hostess opened the conversation by the painfully commonplace inquiry: "Is this your first visit to Hillbridge?"

Even Mrs. Leveret was conscious that this was a bad beginning, and a vague impulse of deprecation made Miss Glyde interject: "It is a very small place indeed."

Mrs. Plinth bristled. "We have a great many representative people," she said in the tone of one who speaks for her order.

Osric Dane turned to her. "What do they represent?" she asked.

Mrs. Plinth's constitutional dislike to being questioned was intensified by her sense of unpreparedness; and her reproachful glance passed the question on to Mrs. Ballinger.

"Why," said that lady, glancing in turn at the other members, "as a community I hope it is not too much to say that we stand for culture."

"For art —" Miss Glyde interjected.

"For art and literature," Mrs. Ballinger amended.

"And for sociology, I trust," snapped Miss Van Vluyck.

"We have a standard," said Mrs. Plinth, feeling herself suddenly secure on the vast expanse of a generalization; and Mrs. Leveret, thinking there must be room for more than one on so broad a statement, took courage to murmur: "Oh, certainly, we have a standard."

"The object of our little club," Mrs. Ballinger continued, "is to concentrate the highest tendencies of Hillbridge — to centralize and focus its intellectual effort."

This was felt to be so happy that the ladies drew an almost audible breath of relief.

"We aspire," the President went on, "to be in touch with whatever is highest in art, literature and ethics."

Osric Dane again turned to her. "What ethics?" she asked.

A tremor of apprehension encircled the room. None of the ladies required any preparation to pronounce on a question of morals; but when they were called ethics it was different. The club, when fresh from the *Encyclopedia Britannica*, the *Reader's Handbook* or *Smith's Classical Dictionary*, could deal confidently with any subject; but when taken unawares it had been known to define agnosticism as a heresy of the Early Church and Professor Froude as a distinguished histologist; and such minor members as Mrs. Leveret sill secretly regarded ethics as something vaguely pagan.

Even to Mrs. Ballinger, Osric Dane's question was unsettling, and there was a general sense of gratitude when Laura Glyde leaned forward to say, with her most sympathetic accent: "You must excuse us, Mrs. Dane, for not being able, just at present, to talk of anything but *The Wings of Death*."

"Yes," said Miss Van Vluyck, with a sudden resolve to carry the war into the enemy's camp. "We are so anxious to know the exact purpose you had in mind in writing your wonderful book."

"You will find," Mrs. Plinth interposed, "that we are not superficial readers."

"We are eager to hear from you," Miss Van Vluyck continued, "if the pessimistic tendency of the book is an expression of your own convictions or —"

"Or merely," Miss Glyde thrust in, "a somber background brushed in to throw your figures into more vivid relief. *Are* you not primarily plastic?"

"I have always maintained," Mrs. Ballinger interposed, "that you represent the purely objective method —"

Osric Dane helped herself critically to coffee. "How do you define objective?" she then inquired.

There was a flurried pause before Laura Glyde intensely murmured: "In reading *you* we don't define, we feel."

Osric Dane smiled. "The cerebellum," she remarked, "is not infrequently the seat of the literary emotions." And she took a second lump of sugar.

The sting that this remark was vaguely felt to conceal was almost neutralized by the satisfaction of being addressed in such technical language.

"Ah, the cerebellum," said Miss Van Vluyck complacently. "The club took a course in psychology last winter."

"Which psychology?" asked Osric Dane.

There was an agonizing pause, during which each member of the club secretly deplored the distressing inefficiency of the others. Only Mrs. Roby went on placidly sipping her chartreuse. At last Mrs. Ballinger said, with an attempt at a high tone: "Well, really, you know, it was last year that we took psychology, and this winter we have been so absorbed in —"

Mrs. Roby put down her liqueur glass and drew near the group with a smile.

"In Xingu?" she gently prompted.

A thrill ran through the other members. They· exchanged confused glances, and then, with one accord, turned a gaze of mingled relief and interrogation on their rescuer. The expression of each denoted a different phase of the same emotion. Mrs. Plinth was the first to compose her features to an air of reassurance: after a moment's hasty adjustment her look almost implied that it was she who had given the word to Mrs. Ballinger.

"Xingu, of course!" exclaimed the latter with her accustomed promptness, while Miss Van Vluyck and Laura Glyde seemed to be plumbing the depths of memory, and Mrs. Leveret, feeling apprehensively for *Appropriate Allusions*, was somehow reassured by the uncomfortable pressure of its bulk against her person.

Osric Dane's change of countenance was no less striking than that of her entertainers. She too put down her coffee cup, but with a look of distinct annoyance; she too wore, for a brief moment, what Mrs. Roby afterward described as the look of feeling for something in the back of her head; and before she could dissemble these momentary signs of weakness, Mrs. Roby, turning to her with a deferential smile, had said: "And we've been so hoping that today you would tell us just what you think of it."

Osric Dane received the homage of the smile as a matter of course; but the accompanying question obviously embarrassed her, and it became clear to her observers that she was not quick at shifting her facial scenery. It was as though her countenance had so long been set in an expression of unchallenged superiority that the muscles had stiffened, and refused to obey her orders.

"Xingu —" she said, as if seeking in her turn to gain time.

Mrs. Roby continued to press her. "Knowing how engrossing the subject is, you will understand how it happens that the club has let everything else go to the wall for the moment. Since we took up Xingu I might almost say — were it not for your books — that nothing else seems to us worth remembering."

Osric Dane's stern features were darkened rather than lit up by an uneasy smile. "I am glad to hear that you make one exception," she gave out between narrowed lips.

"Oh, of course," Mrs. Roby said prettily; "but as you have shown us that — so very naturally! — you don't care to talk of your own things, we really can't let you off from telling us exactly what you think about Xingu; especially," she added, with a still more persuasive smile, "as some people say that one of your last books was saturated with it."

It was an *it*, then — the assurance sped like fire through the parched minds of the other members. In their eagerness to gain the least little clue to Xingu they almost forgot the joy of assisting at the discomfiture of Mrs. Dane.

The latter reddened nervously under her antagonist's challenge. "May I ask," she faltered out, "to which of my books you refer?"

Mrs. Roby did not falter. "That's just what I want you to tell us; because, though I was present, I didn't actually take part."

"Present at what?" Mrs. Dane took her up, and for an instant the trembling members of the Lunch Club thought that the champion Providence had raised up for them had lost a point. But Mrs. Roby explained herself gaily: "At the discussion, of course. And so we're dreadfully anxious to know just how it was that you went into the Xingu."

There was a portentous pause, a silence so big with incalculable dangers that the members with one accord checked the words on their lips, like soldiers dropping their arms to watch a single combat between their leaders. Then Mrs. Dane gave expression to their inmost dread by saying sharply: "Ah — you say *the* Xingu, do you?"

Mrs. Roby smiled undauntedly. "It is a shade pedantic, isn't it? Personally, I always drop the article: but I don't know how the other members feel about it."

The other members looked as though they would willingly have dispensed with this appeal to their opinion, and Mrs. Roby, after a bright glance about the group, went on: "They probably think, as I do, that nothing really matters except the thing itself — except Xingu."

No immediate reply seemed to occur to Mrs. Dane, and Mrs. Ballinger gathered courage to say: "Surely everyone must feel that about Xingu."

Mrs. Plinth came to her support with a heavy murmur of assent, and Laura Glyde sighed out emotionally: "I have known cases where it has changed a whole life."

"It has done me worlds of good," Mrs. Leveret interjected, seeming to herself to remember that she had either taken it or read it the winter before.

"Of course," Mrs. Roby admitted, "the difficulty is that one must give up so much time to it. It's very long."

"I can't imagine," said Miss Van Vluyck, "grudging the time given to such a subject."

"And deep in places," Mrs. Roby pursued; (so then it was a book!) "And it isn't easy to skip."

"I never skip," said Mrs. Plinth dogmatically.

"Ah, it's dangerous to, in Xingu. Even at the start there are places where one can't. One must just wade through."

"I should hardly call it *wading*," said Mrs. Ballinger sarcastically.

Mrs. Roby sent her a look of interest. "Ah — you always found it went swimmingly?"

Mrs. Ballinger hesitated. "Of course there are difficult passages," she conceded.

"Yes, some are not at all clear — even," Mrs. Roby added, "if one is familiar with the original."

"As I suppose you are?" Osric Dane interposed suddenly fixing her with a look of challenge.

Mrs. Roby met it by a deprecating gesture. "Oh, it's really not difficult up to a certain point; though some of the branches are very little known, and it's almost impossible to get at the source."

"Have you ever tried?" Mrs. Plinth inquired, still distrustful of Mrs. Roby's thoroughness.

Mrs. Roby was silent for a moment; then she replied with lowered lids: "No — but a friend of mine did; a very brilliant man; and he told me it was best for women — not to...."

A shudder ran around the room. Mrs. Leveret coughed so that the parlormaid, who was handing the cigarettes, should not hear; Miss Van Vluyck's face took on a nauseated expression, and Mrs. Plinth looked as if she were passing someone she did not care to bow to. But the most remarkable result of Mrs. Roby's words was the effect they produced on the Lunch Club's distinguished guest. Osric Dane's impassive features suddenly softened to an expression of the warmest human sympathy, and edging her chair toward Mrs. Roby she asked: "Did he really? And — did you find he was right?"

Mrs. Ballinger, in whom annoyance at Mrs. Roby's unwonted assumption of prominence was beginning to displace gratitude for the aid she had rendered, could not consent to her being allowed, by such dubious means, to monopolize the attention of their guest. If Osric Dane had not enough self-respect to resent Mrs. Roby's flippancy, at least the Lunch Club would do so in the person of its President.

Mrs. Ballinger laid her hand on Mrs. Roby's arm. "We must not forget," she said with a frigid amiability, "that absorbing as Xingu is to *us*, it may be less interesting to —"

"Oh, no, on the contrary, I assure you," Osric Dane intervened.

"— to others," Mrs. Ballinger finished firmly; "and we must not allow our little meeting to end without persuading Mrs. Dane to say a few words to us on a subject which, today, is much more present in all our thoughts. I refer, of course, to *The Wings of Death*."

The other members, animated by various degrees of the same sentiment, and encouraged by the humanized mien of their redoubtable guest, repeated after Mrs. Ballinger: "Oh, yes, you really *must* talk to us a little about your book."

Osric Dane's expression became as bored, though not as haughty, as when her work had been previously mentioned. But before she could respond to Mrs. Ballinger's request, Mrs. Roby had risen from her seat, and was pulling down her veil over her frivolous nose.

"I'm so sorry," she said, advancing toward her hostess with outstretched hand, "but before Mrs. Dane begins I think I'd better run away. Unluckily, as you know, I haven't read her books, so I should be at a terrible disadvantage among you all, and besides, I've an engagement to play bridge."

If Mrs. Roby had simply pleaded her ignorance of Osric Dane's works as a reason for withdrawing, the Lunch Club, in view of her recent prowess, might have approved such evidence of discretion; but to couple this excuse with the brazen announcement that she was foregoing the privilege for the purpose of joining a bridge party was only one more instance of her deplorable lack of discrimination.

The ladies were disposed, however, to feel that her departure — now that she had performed the sole service she was ever likely to render them — would probably make for greater order and dignity in the impending discussion, besides relieving them of the sense of self-distrust which her presence always mysteriously produced. Mrs. Ballinger therefore restricted herself to a formal murmur of regret, and the other members were just grouping themselves comfortably about Osric Dane when the latter, to their dismay, started up from the sofa on which she had been seated.

"Oh wait — do wait, and I'll go with you!" she called out to Mrs. Roby; and, seizing the hands of the disconcerted members, she administered a series of farewell pressures with the mechanical haste of a railway conductor punching tickets.

"I'm so sorry — I'd quite forgotten —" she flung back at them from the threshold; and as she joined Mrs. Roby, who had turned in surprise at her appeal, the other ladies had the mortification of hearing her say, in a voice which she did not take the pains to lower: "If you'll let me walk a little way with you, I should so like to ask you a few more questions about Xingu...."

III

The incident had been so rapid that the door closed on the departing pair before the other members had time to understand what was happening. Then a sense of the indignity put upon them by Osric Dane's unceremonious desertion began to contend with the confused feeling that they had been cheated out of their due without exactly knowing how or why.

There was a silence, during which Mrs. Ballinger, with a perfunctory hand, rearranged the skillfully grouped literature at which her distinguished guest had not so much as glanced; then Miss Van Vluyck tartly pronounced: "Well, I can't say that I consider Osric Dane's departure a great loss."

This confession crystallized the resentment of the other members, and Mrs. Leveret exclaimed: "I do believe she came on purpose to be nasty!"

It was Mrs. Plinth's private opinion that Osric Dane's attitude toward the Lunch Club might have been very different had it welcomed her in the majestic setting of the Plinth drawing room; but not liking to reflect on the inadequacy of Mrs. Ballinger's establishment she sought a roundabout satisfaction in deprecating her lack of foresight.

"I said from the first that we ought to have had a subject ready. It's what always happens when you're unprepared. Now if we'd only got up Xingu —"

The slowness of Mrs. Plinth's mental processes was always allowed for by the club; but this instance of it was too much for Mrs. Ballinger's equanimity.

"Xingu!" she scoffed. "Why, it was the fact of our knowing so much more about it than she did — unprepared though we were — that made Osric Dane so furious. I should have thought that was plain enough to everybody!"

This retort impressed even Mrs. Plinth, and Laura Glyde, moved by an impulse of generosity, said: "Yes, we really ought to be grateful to Mrs. Roby for introducing the topic. It may have made Osric Dane furious, but at least it made her civil."

"I am glad we were able to show her," added Miss Van Vluyck, "that a broad and up-to-date culture is not confined to the great intellectual centers."

This increased the satisfaction of the other members, and they began to forget their wrath against Osric Dane in the pleasure of having contributed to her discomfiture.

Miss Van Vluyck thoughtfully rubbed her spectacles. "What surprised me most," she continued, "was that Fanny Roby should be so up on Xingu."

This remark threw a slight chill on the company, but Mrs. Ballinger said with an air of indulgent irony: "Mrs. Roby always has the knack of making a little go a long way; still, we certainly owe her a debt for happening to remember that she'd heard of Xingu." And this was felt by the other members to be a graceful way of canceling once and for all the club's obligation to Mrs. Roby.

Even Mrs. Leveret took courage to speed a timid shaft of irony. "I fancy Osric Dane hardly expected to take a lesson in Xingu at Hillbridge!"

Mrs. Ballinger smiled. "When she asked me what we represented — do you remember? — I wish I'd simply said we represent Xingu!"

All the ladies laughed appreciatively at this sally, except Mrs. Plinth, who said, after a moment's deliberation: "I'm not sure it would have been wise to do so."

Mrs. Ballinger, who was already beginning to feel as if she had launched at Osric Dane the retort which had just occurred to her, turned ironically on Mrs. Plinth. "May I ask why?" she inquired.

Mrs. Plinth looked grave. "Surely," she said, "I understood from Mrs. Roby herself that the subject was one it was as well not to go into too deeply?"

Miss Van Vluyck rejoined with precision: "I think that applied only to an investigation of the origin of the — of the —"; and suddenly she found that her usually accurate memory had failed her. "It's a part of the subject I never studied myself," she concluded.

"Nor I, " said Mrs. Ballinger.

Laura Glyde bent toward them with widened eyes. "And yet it seems — doesn't it — the part that is fullest of an esoteric fascination?"

"I don't know on what you base that," said Miss Van Vluyck argumentatively.

"Well, didn't you notice how intensely interested Osric Dane became as soon as she heard what the brilliant foreigner — he was a foreigner, wasn't he — had told Mrs. Roby about the origin — the origin of the rite — or whatever you call it?"

Mrs. Plinth looked disapproving, and Mrs. Ballinger visibly wavered. Then she said: "It may not be desirable to touch on the — on that part of the subject in general conversation; but, from the importance it evidently has to a woman of Osric Dane's distinction, I feel as if we ought not to be afraid to discuss it among ourselves — without gloves — though with closed doors, if necessary."

"I'm quite of your opinion," Miss Van Vluyck came briskly to her support; "on condition, that is, that all grossness of language is avoided."

"Oh, I'm sure we shall understand without that," Mrs. Leveret tittered; and Laura Glyde added significantly: "I fancy we can read between the lines," while Mrs. Ballinger rose to assure herself that the doors were really closed.

Mrs. Plinth had not yet given her adhesion. "I hardly see," she began, "what benefit is to be derived from investigating such peculiar customs —"

But Mrs. Ballinger's patience had reached the extreme limit of tension. "This at least," she returned; "that we shall not be placed again in the humiliating position of finding ourselves less up on our own subjects than Fanny Roby!"

Even to Mrs. Plinth this argument was conclusive. She peered furtively abut the room and lowered her commanding tones to ask: "Have you got a copy?"

"A — a copy?" stammered Mrs. Ballinger. She was aware that the other members were looking at her expectantly, and that this answer was inadequate, so she supported it by asking another question. "A copy of what?"

Her companions bent their expectant gaze on Mrs. Plinth, who, in turn, appeared less sure of herself than usual. "Why, of — of — the book," she explained.

"What book?" snapped Miss Van Vluyck, almost as sharply as Osric Dane.

Mrs. Ballinger looked at Laura Glyde, whose eyes were interrogatively fixed on Mrs. Leveret. The face of being deferred to was so new to the latter that it filled her with an insane temerity. "Why, Xingu, of course!" she exclaimed.

A profound silence followed this challenge to the resources of Mrs. Ballinger's library, and the latter, after glancing nervously toward the Books of the Day, returned with dignity: "It's not a thing one cares to leave about."

"I should think *not!*" exclaimed Mrs. Plinth.

"It *is* a book, then?" said Miss Van Vluyck.

This again threw the company into disarray, and Mrs. Ballinger, with an impatient sigh, rejoined: "Why — there *is* a book — naturally...."

"Then why did Miss Glyde call it a religion?"

Laura Glyde started up. "A religion? I never —"

"Yes, you did," Miss Van Vluyck insisted; "you spoke of rites; and Mrs. Plinth said it was a custom."

Miss Glyde was evidently making a desperate effort to recall her statement; but accuracy of detail was not her strongest point. At length she began in a deep murmur: "Surely they used to do something of the kind at the Eleusinian mysteries —"

"Oh —" said Miss Van Vluyck, on the verge of disapproval; and Mrs. Plinth protested: "I understood there was to be no indelicacy!"

Mrs. Ballinger could not control her irritation. "Really, it is too bad

that we should not be able to talk the matter over quietly among ourselves. Personally, I think that if one goes into Xingu at all —"

"Oh, so do I!" cried Miss Glyde.

"And I don't see how one can avoid doing so, if one wishes to keep up
with the Thought of the Day —"

Mrs. Leveret uttered an exclamation of relief. "There — that's it!" she
interposed.

"What's it?" the President took her up.

"Why — it's a — a Thought: I mean a philosophy."

This seemed to bring a certain relief to Mrs. Ballinger and Laura
Glyde, but Miss Van Vluyck said: "Excuse me if I tell you that you're all
mistaken. Xingu happens to be a language."

"A language!" the Lunch Club cried.

"Certainly. Don't you remember Fanny Roby's saying that there were
several branches, and that some were hard to trace? What could that
apply to but dialects?"

Mrs. Ballinger could no longer restrain a contemptuous laugh. "Really,
if the Lunch Club has reached such a pass that it has to go to Fanny Roby
for instruction on a subject like Xingu, it had almost better cease to exist!"

"It's really her fault for not being clearer," Laura Glyde put in.

"Oh, clearness and Fanny Roby!" Mrs. Ballinger shrugged. "I dare
say we shall find she was mistaken on almost every point."

"Why not look it up?" said Mrs. Plinth.

As a rule this recurrent suggestion of Mrs. Plinth's was ignored in the
heat of discussion, and only resorted to afterward in the privacy of each
member's home. But on the present occasion the desire to ascribe their
own confusion of thought to the vague and contradictory nature of Mrs.
Roby's statements caused the members of the Lunch Club to utter a
collective demand for a book of reference.

At this point the production of her treasured volume gave Mrs.
Leveret, for a moment, the unusual experience of occupying the center
front; but she was not able to hold it long, for *Appropriate Allusions*
contained no mention of Xingu.

"Oh, that's not the kind of thing we want!" exclaimed Miss Van
Vluyck. She cast a disparaging glance over Mrs. Ballinger's assortment of
literature, and added impatiently: "Haven't you any useful books?"

"Of course I have," replied Mrs. Ballinger indignantly; "I keep them
in my husband's dressing room."

From this region, after some difficulty and delay, the parlormaid
produced the W-Z volume of an *Encyclopedia* and, in deference to the fact
that the demand for it had come from Miss Van Vluyck, laid the ponderous tome before her.

There was a moment of painful suspense while Miss Van Vluyck rubbed her spectacles, adjusted them, and turned to Z; and a murmur of surprise when she said: "It isn't here."

"I suppose," said Mrs. Plinth, "it's not fit to be put in a book of reference."

"Oh, nonsense!" exclaimed Mrs. Ballinger. "Try X."

Miss Van Vluyck turned back through the volume, peering shortsightedly up and down the pages, till she came to a stop and remained motionless, like a dog on a point.

"Well, have you found it?" Mrs. Ballinger inquired after a considerable delay.

"Yes I've found it," said Miss Van Vluyck in a queer voice.

Mrs. Plinth hastily interposed: "I beg you won't read it aloud if there's anything offensive."

Miss Van Vluyck, without answering, continued her silent scrutiny.

"Well, what *is* it?" exclaimed Laura Glyde excitedly.

"*Do* tell us!" urged Mrs. Leveret, feeling that she would have something awful to tell her sister.

Miss Van Vluyck pushed the volume aside and turned slowly toward the expectant group.

"It's a river."

"A *river*?"

"Yes: in Brazil. Isn't that where she's been living?"

"Who? Fanny Roby? Oh, but you must be mistaken. You've been reading the wrong thing," Mrs. Ballinger exclaimed, leaning over her to seize the volume.

"It's the only Xingu in the *Encyclopedia*; and she *has* been living in Brazil," Miss Van Vluyck persisted.

"Yes: her brother has a consulship there," Mrs. Leveret interposed.

"But it's too ridiculous! I — we — why we *all* remember studying Xingu last year — or the year before last," Mrs. Ballinger stammered.

"I thought I did when *you* said so," Laura Glyde avowed.

"*I* said so?" cried Mrs. Ballinger.

"Yes. You said it had crowded everything else out of your mind."

"Well *you* said it had changed your whole life!"

"For that matter Miss Van Vluyck said she had never grudged the time she'd given it."

Mrs. Plinth interposed: "I made it clear that I knew nothing whatever of the original."

Mrs. Ballinger broke off the dispute with a groan. "Oh, what does it all matter if she's been making fools of us? I believe Miss Van Vluyck's right — she was talking of the river all the while!"

"How could she? It's too preposterous," Miss Glyde exclaimed.

"Listen." Miss Van Vluyck had repossessed herself of the Encyclopedia, and restored her spectacles to a nose reddened by excitement. " 'The Xingu, one of the principal rivers of Brazil, rises on the plateau of Mato Grosso, and flows in a northerly direction for a length of no less than one-thousand one-hundred and eighteen miles, entering the Amazon near the mouth of the latter river. The upper course of the Xingu is auriferous and fed by numerous branches. Its source was first discovered in 1884 by the German explorer von den Steinen, after a difficult and dangerous expedition through a region inhabited by tribes still in the Stone Age of culture.' "

The ladies received this communication in a state of stupefied silence from which Mrs. Leveret was the first to rally. "She certainly *did* speak of its having branches."

The word seemed to snap the last thread of their incredulity. "And of its great length," gasped Mrs. Ballinger.

"She said it was awfully deep, and you couldn't skip — you just had to wade through," Miss Glyde added.

The idea worked its way more slowly through Mrs. Plinth's compact resistances. "How could there be anything improper about a river?" she inquired.

"Improper?"

"Why, what she said about the source — that it was corrupt?"

"Not corrupt, but hard to get at," Laura Glyde corrected. "Someone who'd been there had told her so. I dare say it was the explorer himself — doesn't it say the expedition was dangerous?"

" 'Difficult and dangerous,' " read Miss Van Vluyck.

Mrs. Ballinger pressed her hands to her throbbing temples. "There's nothing she said that wouldn't apply to a river — to this river!" She swung about excitedly to the other members. "Why, do you remember her telling us that she hadn't read *The Supreme Instant* because she'd taken it on a boating party while she was staying with her brother, and someone had 'shied' it overboard — 'shied' of course was her own expression."

The ladies breathlessly signified that the expression had not escaped them.

"Well — and then didn't she tell Osric Dane that one of her books was simply saturated with Xingu? Of course it was, if one of Mrs. Roby's rowdy friends had thrown it into the river!"

This surprising reconstruction of the scene in which they had just participated left the members of the Lunch Club inarticulate. At length, Mrs. Plinth, after visibly laboring with the problem, said in a heavy tone: "Osric Dane was taken in too."

Mrs. Leveret took courage at this. "Perhaps that's what Mrs. Roby did it for. She said Osric Dane was a brute, and she may have wanted to give her a lesson."

Miss Van Vluyck frowned. "It was hardly worthwhile to do it at our expense."

"At least," said Miss Glyde with a touch of bitterness, "she succeeded in interesting her, which was more than we did."

"What chance had we?" rejoined Mrs. Ballinger. "Mrs. Roby monopolized her from the first. And *that*, I've no doubt, was her purpose — to give Osric Dane a false impression of her own standing in the club. She would hesitate at nothing to attract attention: we all know how she took in poor Professor Foreland."

"She actually makes him give bridge teas every Thursday," Mrs. Leveret piped up.

Laura Glyde struck her hands together. "Why, this is Thursday, and it's *there* she's gone, of course; and taken Osric with her!"

"And they're shrieking over us at this moment," said Mrs. Ballinger between her teeth.

This possibility seemed too preposterous to be admitted. "She would hardly dare," said Miss Van Vluyck, "confess the imposture to Osric Dane."

"I'm not so sure: I thought I saw her make a sign as she left. If she hadn't made a sign, why should Osric Dane have rushed out after her?"

"Well, you know, we'd all been telling her how wonderful Xingu was, and she said she wanted to find out more about it," Mrs. Leveret said, with a tardy impulse of justice to the absent.

This reminder, far from mitigating the wrath of the other members, gave it a stronger impetus.

"Yes — and that's exactly what they're both laughing over now," said Laura Glyde ironically.

Mrs. Plinth stood up and gathered her expensive furs about her monumental form. "I have no wish to criticize," she said; "but unless the Lunch Club can protect its members against the recurrence of such — such unbecoming scenes, I for one —"

"Oh, so do I!" agreed Miss Glyde, rising also.

Miss Van Vluyck closed the Encyclopedia and proceeded to button herself into her jacket. "My time is really too valuable —" she began.

"I fancy we are all of one mind," said Mrs. Ballinger, looking searchingly at Mrs. Leveret, who looked at the others.

"I always deprecate anything like a scandal —" Mrs. Plinth continued.

"She has been the cause of one today!" exclaimed Miss Glyde.

Mrs. Leveret moaned: "I don't see how she *could*!" and Miss Van Vluyck said, picking up her notebook: "Some women stop at nothing."

"— But if," Mrs. Plinth took up her argument impressively, "anything of the kind had happened in my house" (it never would have, her tone implied), "I should have felt that I owed it to myself either to ask for Mrs. Roby's resignation — or to offer mine."

"Oh, Mrs. Plinth —" gasped the Lunch Club.

"Fortunately for me," Mrs. Plinth continued with an awful magnanimity, "the matter was taken out of my hands by our President's decision that the right to entertain distinguished guests was a privilege vested in her office; and I think the other members will agree that, as she was alone in this opinion, she ought to be alone in deciding on the best way of effacing its — its really deplorable consequences."

A deep silence followed this outbreak of Mrs. Plinth's long-stored resentment.

"I don't see why I should be expected to ask her to resign —" Mrs. Ballinger at length began; but Laura Glyde turned back to remind her; "You know she made you say that you'd got on swimmingly in Xingu."

An ill-timed giggle escaped from Mrs. Leveret, and Mrs. Ballinger energetically continued "— But you needn't think for a moment that I'm afraid to!"

The door of the drawing room closed on the retreating backs of the Lunch Club, and the President of that distinguished association, seating herself at her writing table, and pushing away a copy of *The Wings of Death* to make room for her elbow, drew forth a sheet of the club's notepaper, on which she began to write: "My dear Mrs. Roby —"

From *Xingu and Other Stories* by Edith Wharton. Scribners, 1916.

HENRY JAMES

Henry James and Edith Wharton were alike in their inclinations toward exclusive discrimination. He was her guest at The Mount for 10 days in the fall of 1904, for five days in June, 1905, and again for eight days in July, 1911.

In The American Scene *(1907), James described his impressions of the Berkshires in 1904-5, although, given his aversion to specificity, a reader may easily miss what he is talking about.*

The Berkshire Scene

"THE SMUTCH OF IMPUTATION"

These appeared to be, over the land, always possible adventures; obviously I should have others of the same kind; I could let them, in all confidence, accumulate and wait. But, if that was one kind of extreme, what meanwhile was the other kind, the kind portentously alluded to by those of the sagacious who had occasionally put it before me that the village street, the arched umbrageous vista, half so candid and half so cool, is too frequently, in respect to "morals," but a whited sepulchre? They had so put it before me, these advisers, but they had as well, absolutely and all tormentingly, so left it: partly as if the facts were too abysmal for a permitted distinctness, and partly, no doubt, as from the general American habit of indirectness, of positive primness, of allusion to those matters that are sometimes collectively spoken of as "the great facts of life." It had been intimated to me that the great facts of life are in high fermentation on the other side of the ground glass that never for a moment flushes, to the casual eye, with the hint of a lurid light: so much, at least, one had no alternative, under pressure, but to infer. The inference, however, still left the question a prey to vagueness — it being obvious that vice requires forms not less than virtue, or perhaps even more, and that forms, up and down the prospect, were exactly what one waited in vain for. The theory that no community *can* live wholly without by-play, and the confirmatory word, for the particular case, of more initiated reporters, these things were all very well; but before a scene peeled as bare of palpable pretext as the American sky is often peeled of clouds (in the interest of the slightly acid juice of its light), where and how was the application to be made? It came at last, the application — that, I mean, of the portentous hint; and under it, after a fashion, the elements fell together. Why the picture *shouldn't* bristle with the truth — that was all conceivable; that the truth could only strike inward, horribly inward, not playing up to the surface — this too needed no insistence; what was sharpest for reflection being, meanwhile, a couple of minor appearances, which one gathered as one went. That our little arts of pathetic, of humorous, portrayal may, for all their claim to an edifying "realism," have on occasion small veracity and courage — that again was a remark pertinent to the matter. But the strangest link in the chain, and quite the horridest, was this other, of high value to the restless analyst — that, as the "interesting" puts in its note but where it can and where it will, so the village street and the lonely farm and the hillside cabin became positively richer objects under the smutch of imputation; twitched with a grim effect the thinness of their mantle, shook out of its folds such crudity and levity as they might, and borrowed, for dignity, a shade of the darkness of Cenci-drama, of monstrous legend, of old Greek tragedy, and thus helped themselves out for the story-seeker more patient almost of anything than of flatness.

MOTORING IN HILL COUNTRY

There was not flatness, accordingly, though there might be dire dreariness, in some of those impressions gathered, for a climax, in the Berkshire country of Massachusetts, which forced it upon the fancy that here at last, in far, deep mountain valleys, where the winter is fierce and the summer irresponsible, was that heart of New England which makes so pretty a phrase for print and so stern a fact, as yet, for feeling. During the great loops thrown out by the lasso of observation from the wonder-working motor-car that defied the shrinkage of autumn days, this remained constantly the best formula of the impression and even of the emotion; it sat in the vehicle with us, but spreading its wings to the magnificence of movement, and gathering under them indeed most of the meanings of the picture. The heart of New England, at this rate, was an ample, a generous, heart, the largest demands on which, as to extent and variety, seemed not to overstrain its capacity. But it was where the mountain-walls rose straight and made the valleys happiest or saddest — one couldn't tell which, as to the felicity of the image, and it didn't much matter — that penetration was, for the poetry of it, deepest; just as generalization, for an opposite sort of beauty, was grandest on those several occasions when we perched for a moment on the summit of a "pass," a real little pass, slowly climbed to and keeping its other side, with an art all but Alpine, for a complete revelation, and hung there over the full vertiginous effect of the long and steep descent, the clinging road, the precipitous fall, the spreading, shimmering land bounded by blue horizons. We liked the very vocabulary, reduced to whatever minimum, of these romanticisms of aspect; again and again the land would do beautifully, if that were all that was wanted, and it deserved, the dear

Central Auto Station Company, 57-59 West Street, Pittsfield, c. 1908.
Berkshire County Historical Society Collection

thing, thoroughly, any verbal caress, any tenderness of term, any share in
a claim to the grand manner, to which we could responsively treat it. The
grand manner was in the winding ascent, the rocky defile, the sudden
rest for wonder, and all the splendid reverse of the medal, the world
belted afresh as with purple sewn with pearls — melting, in other words,
into violet hills with vague white towns on their breasts.

MOUNT LEBANON SHAKER VILLAGE

That was, at the worst, for October afternoons, the motor helping, our
frequent fare; the habit of confidence in which was, perhaps, on no
occasion so rewarded as on that of a particular plunge, from one of the
highest places, through an ebbing golden light, into the great Lebanon
"bowl," the vast, scooped hollow in one of the hither depths of which
(given the quarter of our approach) we found the Shaker settlement once
more or less, I believe, known to fame, ever so grimly planted. The
grimness, even, was all right, when once we had admiringly dropped
down and down and down; it would have done for that of a Buddhist

monastery in the Himalayas — though more savagely clean and more economically impersonal, we seemed to make out, than the communities of older faiths are apt to show themselves. I remember the mere chill of contiguity, like the breath of the sepulchre, as we skirted, on the wide, hard floor of the valley, the rows of gaunt windows polished for no whitest, stillest, meanest face, even, to look out; so that they resembled the parallelograms of black paint criss-crossed with white lines that represent transparency in Nuremberg dolls'-houses. It wore, the whole settlement, as seen from without, the strangest air of active, operative death; as if the state of extinction were somehow, obscurely, administered and applied — the final hush of passions, desires, dangers, converted into a sort of huge stiff brush for sweeping away rubbish, or still more, perhaps, into a monstrous comb for raking in profit. The whole thing had the oddest appearance of mortification made to "pay." This was really, however, sounding the heart of New England beyond its depth, for I am not sure that the New York boundary had not been, just there, overpassed; there flowered out of that impression, at any rate, another adventure, the very bravest possible for a shortened day, of which the motive, whether formulated or not, had doubtless virtually been to feel, with a far-stretched arm, for the heart of New York. *Had* New York, the miscellaneous monster, a heart at all? — this inquiry, amid so much encouraged and rewarded curiosity, might have been well on the way to become sincere, and we kept groping, between a prompt start and an extremely retarded return, for any stray sign of an answer.

DIFFERENCE BETWEEN BERKSHIRE AND NEW YORK

The answer, perhaps, in the event, still eluded us, but the pursuit itself, away across State lines, through zones of other manners, through images of other ideals, through densities of other values, into a separate sovereign civilization in short — this, with "a view of the autumnal Hudson" for an added incentive, became, in all the conditions, one of the finer flowers of experience. To be on the lookout for differences was, not unnaturally, to begin to meet them just over the border and see them increase and multiply; was, indeed, with a mild consistency, to feel it steal over us that we were, as we advanced, in a looser, shabbier, perhaps even rowdier world, where the roads were of an easier virtue and the "farms" of a scantier pride, where the absence of the ubiquitous sign-post of New England, joy of lonely corners, left the great spaces with an accent the less; where, in fine, the wayside bravery of the commonwealth of Massachusetts settled itself, for memory, all serenely, to suffer by no comparison whatever. And yet it wasn't, either, that this other was not also a big, bold country, with ridge upon ridge and horizon by horizon to deal with, insistently, pantingly, puffingly, pausingly, before the great river showed signs of taking up the tale with its higher hand; it wasn't, above all, that the most striking signs by which the nearness of the river was first announced, three or four fine old houses overlooking the long road, reputedly Dutch manors, seats of patriarchs and patroons, and unmistakably rich "values" in the vast, vague scene, had not a nobler archaic note than even the best of the New England colonial; it wasn't that, finally, the Hudson, when we reached the town that repeats in so minor a key the name of the stream, was not autumnal indeed, with majestic impenetrable mists that veiled the waters almost from sight, showing only the dim Catskills, off in space, as perfunctory graces, cheaply thrown in, and leaving us to roam the length of a large straight street which was, yes, decidedly, for comparison, for curiosity, not as the streets of Massachusetts.

REPAIRS AND DINNER IN HUDSON

The best here, to speak of, was that the motor underwent repair and that its occupants foraged for dinner — finding it indeed excellently at a quiet cook-shop, about the middle of the long-drawn way, after we had encountered coldness at the door of the main hotel by reason of our French poodle. This personage had made our group, admirably composed to our own sense as it was, only the more illustrious; but minds indifferent to an opportunity of intercourse, if but the intercourse of mere vision, with fine French poodles, may be taken always as suffering where they have sinned. The hospitality of the cook-shop was meanwhile touchingly, winningly unconditioned, yet full of character, of local, of national truth, as we liked to think: documentary, in a high degree — we talked it over — for American life. Wasn't it interesting that with American life so personally, so freely affirmed, the superstition of cookery should yet be so little denied? It was the queer old complexion of the long straight street, however, that most came home to me: Hudson, in the afternoon quiet, seemed to stretch back, with fumbling friendly hand, to the earliest outlook of my consciousness. Many matters had come and gone, innumerable impressions had supervened; yet here, in the stir of the senses, a whole range of small forgotten things revived, things intensely Hudsonian, more than Hudsonian; small echoes and tones and sleeping lights, small sights and sounds and smells that made one, for an hour, *as* small — carried one up the rest of the river, the very river of life indeed, as a thrilled, roundabouted pilgrim, by primitive steamboat, to a mellow, mediaeval Albany.

From *The American Scene* by Henry James. Chapman and Hall, 1907.

ELLERY SEDGWICK

After growing up in the Sedgwick house in Stockbridge, Ellery Sedgwick (1872-1960) went into magazine editing. In 1908 he bought the Atlantic Monthly *and over the next 30 years built it into the country's most distinguished periodical.*

Happy Valley

Within a year [of my birth] my father moved his family to Stockbridge, Massachusetts, but curiously enough in that migration he did not break with tradition but caught up with it. Even in that remote era Sedgwicks had lived in Stockbridge for a century or so, and it was in the house of my father's grandfather that we finally installed ourselves. Stockbridge is a village of little importance, but it is ours if love can make it so. It is seven decades at least since Tom Appleton, the wit who had the inspiration of tying a shorn lamb to a Beacon Street fence so that God would temper the wind there, chatting of the natural history of Stockbridge, used to maintain that "even the crickets there say nothing but Sedg'ick, Sedg'ick, Sedg'ick." The sixth generation is now growing up in the dear old house. This mansion house of happy memories replaced a wigwam; for it was built in 1785 on land purchased directly from the Indians. The last of the tribe, an ancient squaw known as Elizabeth, has given her name to an adjoining field, still, in family nomenclature, the Elizabeth Lot. Elizabeth had another name for it. In her day it was *Manwootania,* meaning "middle of the town." The town itself is six miles square. Elizabeth and the Sedgwicks too once lived in the heart of it.

Through all the country round the scant history that could be recalled had drifted into legend. The Yankee tongue is not good at a double twist and Indian names screw it into contortions. *Awestonook* became Housatonic. Grateful as we may be for that, it is interesting to remember that in Indian times the name *Awestonook,* meaning "over the mountain," was given not only to the river but to the entire valley. The little brook that goes sparkling through it bore a name more easily assimilated and remains Konkapot Brook, but when it came to the mountain which frames the valley to the north, guardian of Stockbridge simplicities against the sophistications of Lenox, the native *Takeecanuck* made too large a mouthful, and there was no transliteration. Rattlesnake Mountain it became. Now *Takeecanuck* means "the heart," and apparently stood as a kind of memorial to some friendly interchange between red men and white, but Rattlesnake has a sinister meaning. Behind such a transformation there seems to lie some story of treachery, some bloody drama forgotten these hundred years. It was also simply the impossibilities of linguistics which translated *Masswassehaich* (the euphonious name for "nest") into Monument Mountain.

The Reverend Theodore Sedgwick, Henry Dwight Sedgwick, and Ellery Sedgwick at the reception after the wedding of Christina Sedgwick Marquand and Richard E. Welch, September 4, 1948. Stockbridge Historical Society

Wherever I am, it is always from the windows of the old house on Main Street that I look out on the world and take a Stockbridge-eye-view of it. Ours is not a great house nor a beautiful, but it is delightful and built to endure. The ground plan follows the best of all designs for family living — an ample square, with four generous rooms, one at each corner, and a broad hall running through the center, opening on the view of Monument Mountain, which is the hallmark of the village. My great-grandfather had a family suited to his day, four sons and four daughters, but it was customary for the sons to offer their wives the protection of the paternal rooftree and guests in unbroken succession were collectively quite as permanent residents as the family. In the absence of inns, any traveler with a letter to introduce him could find a night's lodging there, and humble wayfarers were invariably provided with a shakedown. Hospitality was endless and boundless. By what magic the four walls could have contained such a company mystifies the present generation.

How could the less contain the greater? In my father's day a substantial wing was added for the accommodation of a much more moderate household, and I doubt whether my children would think it physically possible to find room for a company less by a third than my grandparents considered normal. Nowadays a guest or two alter the pattern of family life. It was different then. Guests simply enlarged the domestic circle.

From the beginning the Sedgwicks loved their house. It was part of them, almost the dearest part. My old Latin professor at Harvard taught me once for all that *domus* was a house but not a home. And I well know the distinction. But our Stockbridge house was certainly different from the other houses on the village street. Perhaps I can find what the difference was by quoting from a letter of a Sedgwick three generations back.

"I came down," wrote my Great-aunt Catherine in 1844, "to pass a few days at the old homestead — my only home — the only place on earth where forms, common and mute to others, have to me soul and speech; where voices linger in the walls of the rooms, and make their secret and by-gone cheerfulness and tenderness ring in my ears in the dead of night; where the stems of the old trees are still warm with the hands that once pressed them; where, in short, the dead are *not* dead."

Life with its joys and heartbreaks, death "with its train of infinite hopes," there they abide together.

Like all beloved communities, Stockbridge wears two aspects. There is the Stockbridge of guidebooks and motorcars, of rockers on hotel piazzas, and of swarms of the music-struck conjured by Koussevitzky and siphoned into his showplace at Tanglewood. Pure Philistinism mingled with the titillated, the genuine, and the passionate. So far as the real Stockbridge is concerned, these are but trespassers and vagrants. The real Stockbridge is the subjective Stockbridge. It is made of a thousand memories, older than the arching elms of Main Street and more luxuriant than they, memories of the neighborliness of two hundred years, of odd characters twisted into odder shapes, of Yankee speech and Yankee silences, of sunsets over Housatonic meadows, of births and deaths intimately shared by every villager. When a Stockbridgian goes abroad he takes Stockbridge with him. To this day my yardstick of height is Monument Mountain. Marveling at the Andes I have wondered how many Monument Mountains it would take to top the crest of Illimani. Besides, it is convenient to have fixed standards like Stockbridge Bowl or Hatch's Pond when you are called on to appraise the loveliness of Lucerne or Lake Louise!

LARRY LYNCH OF LARRYWANG

Neither Stockbridge is what it was. The census credits eighteen hundred souls or so against the twelve hundred of my time, but so many of them now are Irish or Italian souls. They are souls worth saving too, but then they have the Church to shepherd them through the Gates. My interest is in the souls of the Yankees of my youth which certainly needed salvation and as surely found it. All of us, Yankees, Irish, Italians, and the rest, are of immigrant stock of course, but we Yankees like to remember that we came over for different reasons and by earlier ships. It is interesting to trace the first trickle towards Stockbridge of the Irish blood. The spearhead of the invasion was one Larry Lynch, indentured servant of Brigadier General Joseph Dwight, a Berkshire warrior of the first magnitude in the French wars. Larry settled at the foot of West Stockbridge Mountain, outstripped his Yankee neighbors by raising fourteen children, and about the turn of the eighteenth century built a homestead for them: and Larrywang it is until this day. *Wang* is Indian for a cluster of houses, but the transliteration from Indian into American affords the learned men of Stockbridge some latitude in spelling. This I mention because the "Seelectmen" of this day seem to prefer the alternative of Larrywaug.

I owe a personal debt to Larry for in the strength of his youth, a century before I was born, he did me a signal service. An Indian raid was on. Tomahawks were in the air and my great-great-grandmother, Abigail Dwight, wife of the Brigadier and sister of that Ephraim Williams who founded Williams College, was hard put to it to bring her children to safety. Her little daughter Pamela (of whom I am an ultimate fruit), just three years old, was hurriedly entrusted to the care of a black manservant, but the chase grew hot and the Negro, incommoded by his burden, chucked it into a raspberry patch and looked out for number one. Then who should come that way, find the child and save it, but Larry of Larrywang.

COLONEL DWIGHT

The Stockbridge of my youth was almost as far removed in time from Larry Lynch as it is from his great-great-grandsons of today. We worried our heads over many things but who would have thought then that we were started toward the highroad of socialism? Since Cranford there has not been a more individualistic community. Even as a boy I felt myself no cog in the machine but an individual item in creation. The village street was and is a mile long. At one end of it just before the road drops down to The Indian Burial Ground, where a monolith dedicated To the Friends of Our Fathers testifies to a decided change in the hearts of Red Men since

Larry's day, lived Colonel Dwight. To us children there was a certain aura about his florid face and substantial figure, for had he not been a personal crony of President Arthur? Arthur, you remember, had disappointed "the boys" by becoming a good President, and I suspect that as a young man, Colonel Dwight had shared substantially in that disappointment. Anyway he gave the impression of a lost, more jovial age, the substance of which had largely disappeared. Certainly he sought solace, for on his sideboard there were always a bottle or two, and we boys used to watch him take up each in turn and hold it sadly to the light to make certain one final drink was not left at the bottom of it. Then with a melancholy shake of the head he would set the bottle down, exclaiming:

Not one damn drop o' rum
Glory hallelujahrum!

Colonel Dwight had a witty tongue. I remember meeting him on the morning of the annual flower parade of boats which in our midsummer festival drifted down the Housatonic at very low water. The sky had a lowering look. "Colonel Dwight," I said, "I do hope it doesn't rain."

"Well," he drawled, "won't a little rain help to lay the dust in the river?"

UNCLE BUTLER

A full mile beyond Colonel Dwight's, high above long reaches of the wandering river, stood Linwood. There in frosty isolation lived my Uncle Butler, ogre of my childhood. Charles E. Butler was a great man, there was no denying that. Had he not gone, a poor boy, to New York, and become the architect of the greatest law firm of the American ages, Butler, Evarts, and Southmayd? Uncle Butler was a notably handsome man, with bold classical features and a heart tender as a granite block. So impressive was his personality that on his entrance, conversation would flag and soon come to a full stop. In a child's ears at least, his humor roused no mirth. Often my family went for their Sunday roasts to the cold stone house, decorated with marble statuary, with marbleized wallpaper to set it off and chairs that looked immutable in their several stations. Uncle Butler would meet us at the forbidding walnut-paneled entrance. He loved my mother, nobody could help that, but he would turn to me as the youngest of the party with the air of a playful mastodon.

"Well, Stick-in-the-mud, brought your dinner with you? If you've left it behind, go down to the coal hole." The inevitable greeting froze the cockles of my heart.

MR. SOUTHMAYD

Half a mile below the gates of Linwood on the way back to the village lived Mr. Butler's junior partner, Mr. Charles F. Southmayd. He was the only man I ever saw who dressed after the pattern of Mr. Pickwick in black broadcloth with the characteristic square flap of the trouser buttoned up in front, and a huge collar which was only the slightest modification of a stock. On Sundays he would walk to church in his gray beaver hat and never without a silver-headed cane, exclusively I imagine a Sunday ornament. His costume never altered. For nigh forty years it had been Mr. Southmayd's custom to save time and trouble by writing a brief semiannual note to his tailor ordering "two more of the same." Pinched and alert, caustic and formidable, Mr. Southmayd looked for all the world as if "Phiz" had just drawn him for a new novel by Charles Dickens. Certainly Dickens in all his rambles never picked up a more congenial subject for his artist's pencil or his own pen.

Charles Southmayd's education was remarkable. As a child he was sent to a small private school and there displayed so unusual a precocity that at the age of twelve years and six months his schoolmaster confided to his astonished father that since he had taught the boy all he knew and since the boy had perfectly assimilated the whole of that learning, he could do nothing more for him. It was the beatific quandary parents dream of before they wake to the realities. How was the boy to go on from there? Providence, responsible for the conundrum, stood ready with an answer. A lawyer of distinction, one Elisha P. Hurlbut, heard of the young prodigy through a friend of his and asked to have a look at the phenomenon. Now this Mr. Hurlbut, very wise in the ways of the law, had as an amateur practised a "science" much in vogue at the time. Phrenology he thought might give the answer, and phrenology did. Mr. Hurlbut passed his hands over the small boy's bumpy head and announced that inside of it was the very stuff lawyers are made of. And so it was that, long before his thirteenth birthday, Charles was presented with Blackstone and a Kent's *Commentaries* and went to work as office boy for the firm of Hurlbut and Johnson, 73 Cedar Street, New York City.

Charles was not a boy to let the grass grow under his feet. During the next four years he read, marked, learned, and inwardly digested the principles of the law. He learned them from top to bottom, outside and in, and by the time he was seventeen the whole office knew him as the "Chancellor." Legends began to grow about his phrenologic head. It was said that when clients turned up they would find the two senior members of the firm in the front office discussing public questions and that one of them was sure to say, "Do you want to talk politics? If so, here we are. But if you happen to come on law business, you will find the Chancellor inside." Boys like this are very different from your sons or mine but they get on. Charles worked in the office. He lived in the office. He slept in the office. After the shutters were closed for the night, he would eat his bread and cheese and wash his supper down with water from the tap. Then out would come the *Commentaries* and he was lost in them till midnight. As the clock struck twelve, he would slip into his cot conveniently made up under the counter and squander six hours in idle sleep.

Charles was not a poor boy to begin with, and having no rent to pay nor fees for instruction he began early to grow rich. Unencumbered he shot ahead. He became the office partner in the firm of Butler, Evarts, and Choate (he was Choate's senior), living his own shrewd, ingrowing life, seldom going into court, and making himself utterly indispensable to Mr. Choate, whose forensic brilliance rested squarely on Mr. Southmayd's briefs.

Mr. Southmayd was a man of intense conviction. That was the interesting part of him. Property was a sacred thing, immutable, ordained of God. When the Elevated Railroad was built, destroying property rights without one penny of damages to the abutters, as its engines rattled every pane of glass the length of Sixth Avenue, he made the resolution never to pay tribute to that iniquity. Daily he traveled four miles by the slow streetcar, up and down from Forty-seventh Street to his office, losing one hour every day. After years of litigation, righteousness triumphed and the Elevated was compelled to pay for the evil it had wrought. But Mr. Southmayd's sense of injustice was not to be assuaged. "No," said he, "it's a fraud anyway and I will never ride in it." And he never did.

"Thou shalt not speculate" was Mr. Southmayd's first and great commandment, and he embraced speculation to mean a probable return of more than three per cent unless a prime mortgage was concerned. He was saving. Almost he was penurious. He held out to himself the decent hope of living on his income's income. But he was not mean and, as I can affirm from personal knowledge, he could be generous — provided he could be generous in secret. Mr. Gradgrind was not more a man of principle than he.

Such was Charles F. Southmayd. Dickens would have made of him an avaricious Scrooge. Not so his Maker. Beneath the reinforced concrete of his principles, utterly hidden from the world, glowed a strain of romance. Who would have suspected it! Who could have imagined it! One solitary flame of devotion kindled in his youth (assuming that he had a youth) burned to the very end.

Before Uncle Butler married my Aunt Susan, his first wife had borne him a large family. The eldest daughter, noble in mind, manners, and appearance, moved like a goddess across Mr. Southmayd's field of vision. He adored her, this weazened, narrow, intelligent man, as much as the rights of property; as much as the majestic law itself, he worshiped her. It was not in the stars she should accept him. She was kind, but she was obdurate. He understood. He had no hope, but his affection was unchanged. And so without a glimmer of expectancy, but knowing that at least he should see her pass on her way to church, he bought a large and beautiful place, bounded by the Oxbow of the Housatonic, put up a large and ugly house just below the hill whereon she lived, and there for decades spent his summers. He retired at sixty, but it was ten years later that he volunteered to write the most brilliant brief of his life, the brief by whose aid Mr. Choate won his great income tax case and quashed an Act of Congress. I never knew Mr. Southmayd to go into another man's house, I never but once knew another to go into his, but when I was old enough to understand his story I felt the magnificence of his lonely devotion. Under his quaint American disguise he was a Cyrano. And how he would have sniffed at the comparison!

Poor Mr. Southmayd! Toward the end of his gnarled and twisted life he had a terrible adventure. One night he was undressing and had tossed those Pickwickian trousers of his across a chair, when a violent knock came at the door and a rough voice cried: "Your house is afire!" Mr. Southmayd ran to the window. Light was streaming from the parlor below. He threw open the door and there stood a gigantic Negro, a mask over his eyes and in his hand a naked axe. The burglar had lighted the lamps below. His ruse succeeded. He stripped the pitiful old gentleman of his watch and cash. The loot was small but the terror remained and the next season the house was empty.

Before I leave Mr. Southmayd I want to pay his memory a personal tribute which I have carried in my heart for sixty years. Perhaps there is no one left who holds him in affectionate remembrance, but it is his due, and I set the story down.

For some reason deep in the human heart, my father, the looting of whose comfortable fortune had left him in chronic difficulties, found it impossible to talk of his troubles to grown-up people and found relief in making a confidant of his youngest son, scarcely fourteen years old. Bills, mortgages, and notes of ninety days crept into my dreams. Of course I did not understand them, but I felt the aura of horror that surrounds such things and my sympathies could always be relied on.

There came a summer day when my father said to me: "Ell, if I am to save the Old House, I must borrow seven thousand dollars and I have decided to ask Mr. Southmayd for it." Now I did not regard Mr. Southmayd as an ogre; our greetings on Sunday mornings were too manly for that, but more than once I had heard our farmer, Jimmy MacMonigle, speak of him as "near," and I had a notion of what that meant. I knew too that Mr. Southmayd was formidable and felt certain he was a man not easily to be dispossessed; so although I fell in with my father's plan, there was fear in my heart where hope ought to be. At any rate, it was arranged that on the following day we two were to drive over behind old Conrad in the pony phaeton, and that I was to hold the horse while my father transacted business in the grim parlor.

That drive might have happened yesterday. Somehow or other Conrad walked the entire way. Papa's spirits were at an all-time low, so I held the reins while he bit his nails. The crunch of the gravel before the door is still in my ears, and I see my father with the desperate look of the debtor doomed, visible across his face. In a moment he had gone within and I was left to loop the reins about the whip and sit back shivering in the warm sun. Visions of the Old House slipping inexorably into the river were before my eyes. We were homeless; I had little doubt of it. Then suddenly the door was flung open and out came my father, his ruddy face glowing with happiness. There was no need for words, but as we trotted home, my father kept exclaiming: "What a kind man! What a good man!"

Mr. Southmayd, it seemed, had made everything easy. He had agreed to give his check for seven thousand dollars and take in exchange our meadows lying beyond the river. The Old House was safe.

The full extent of Mr. Southmayd's generosity my father never knew. Those meadows, which must have been a mere encumbrance to him, were left by his will as a bequest to my brother, Alexander, who in those days ruled as master in the Old House.

From *The Happy Profession* by Ellery Sedgwick. Little Brown, 1946.

The cortege of Henry Dwight Sedgwick passing the Mission House, Stockbridge.
Clemens Kalischer

ADELE SLOANE

When Florence Adele Sloane of Elm Court, Lenox, married James Burden, Jr., of Troy, N.Y., on June 6, 1895, private trains were laid on to bring guests from New York, Vanderbilt relatives one day, others the day before. The Journal of Lincoln, Nebraska, in reporting the affair, informed its readers that the bride had "two uncles worth $80 million apiece, and half a dozen worth $20 million each." Two summers before, Adele had described in her diary Jay's visit to Elm Court.

Today Elm Court is a boarded-up ruin.

A Perfect Week

Elm Court, Lenox. Sunday, July 9.

I don't think I have ever spent a more perfect week than this last one; every minute of it has been absolute pleasure to me, and I can't think that it is almost over. I am sure it will have been the most perfect week of my summer. We have had beautiful weather, almost cold, with two hard thunderstorms, and we have been out morning, noon, and night. I must write what I have done every day.

Monday: Beatrice [Bend] and Alonzo [Potter] arrived early; I drove over to Pittsfield for them. That afternoon Alonzo and I went riding. Every day I think I like Alonzo better; he is so nice. Jay Burden and George [Vanderbilt] arrived in the evening. Always after dinner we would sit on the piazza talking and then, when it was later, half past ten or so, we went for a walk. Quite often we played "willing" games and mesmerism — made tables fly around the rooms, lifted ourselves up, and other extraordinary things. Jay has a wonderful power of willing a person to do a thing. He has a great deal of magnetism at all times and is fascinating in the true sense of the word, but when he really wills you to do a thing, it has the most peculiar effect on me, and over and over again, blindfolded, we did exactly what he wanted us to do.

Tuesday: We did a lot of things, riding, driving, and walking, etc., but Wednesday: Oh, what a perfect day Wednesday was! I shall never forget it. Beatrice, Jay, Alonzo, and I started on horseback at ten in the morning and rode over to Lebanon. Papa had sent a buckboard on ahead with our luncheon, so when we arrived at one of the first houses of this settlement, we dismounted, bought some maple sugar in the house and a pitcher of milk, then carried our luncheon up in the apple orchard and sat down under an apple tree and had a perfect picnic. I am sure that I have never enjoyed anything more. We were way off from anyone we knew, and we all felt wild. We stayed there about three hours, played games, climbed trees, and did various other things, and then rode home in the late afternoon. None of us have gotten over caring about that day yet.

Thursday afternoon was almost the loveliest of any. Jay and I went out at half past two and rode over to Stevens Glen. There we got the funny old farmer to put our horses in the barn, and after a good deal of talking, I persuaded him that we could find our way alone to the Glen, as he always persists in showing one down and explaining everything. I have never seen the Glen so beautiful; I have never seen any spot more beautiful than it was that afternoon when we got way down and climbed over the little bridge at the bottom of the ravine and sat down on a moss-covered rock in the middle of the stream. The rocks rise straight up some two or three hundred feet, leaving the watermark on their sides where the stream has gradually worn its way down. Huge rocks have fallen into the stream and are now covered with soft, bright-green moss where the water leaps over in little waterfalls or nestles round in sleeping pools. The afternoon was cloudless, and up through the opening of the rocks and through the trees we could see the blue sky, and the sunshine poured down leaving everywhere its lines of light and shade. We both said we never could forget how we felt when we first sat down on that rock and realized suddenly what the beauty of everything around us was. And then we talked, a lovely long talk of two hours. He has such interesting thoughts on different subjects, I enjoyed talking to him more almost than to any man I know. He gives himself up to you entirely, and the way he looks at you, straight in the eyes, makes you know that he is simply talking to *you* and not thinking of twenty other things. We were both wild on our ride home, it was all through the woods, and we felt like shrieking and screaming for the happiness of it all. I have not felt so absolutely well and brimming over with life since I was in Biltmore. Jay says he cannot imagine me sad or depressed; he had never seen such spirit in anyone. I suppose I will have a reaction next week. He is attractive in every way, and especially in his half indifference. He is extremely good-looking, very tall, very bright, and very interesting.

Yesterday I rode twenty-two miles with Jay, one of the most beautiful rides up here. Up West Brook, where the valley is only wide enough for the road and the wild brook that goes racing down the mountain; across the top of Washington Mountain, which is like a high plateau with only low trees and shrubs and not the sign of a living abode for miles. It was on top of there that we saw the storm blowing up, the black clouds pushing each other forward, and heard the low rumbling of the thunder. We were at least twelve miles from home, and there was no place to put up for shelter. Then we realized what fun it would be to be caught in a thunderstorm way up there on that lovely grass-grown road, and every time we heard the peal of thunder it was more exciting. Finally in the narrow wood road, it was almost dark; then the flashes of lightning came, and then the torrents of rain. Jay made me put on his coat, although I protested as long as I could, and he rode in his thin shirt sleeves, and in five minutes was soaked through. From that time we rode home at a good fast canter, never pulling in the horses up hill or down.

We rode ten miles, Jay said, faster than he had ever been before; it is probably that which kept him from taking cold. I have never laughed more than on that ride, and every time I think of it I laugh again. The whole thing was such a ludicrously funny picture. Both of us galloping along in the drenching rain, laughing as if it was the greatest fun we had ever had in our lives; I with my hat tied on in front, for it fell off so often, and little streams of water and mud pouring down from it, wearing Jay's coat with the sleeves a great deal too long for me, and buttoned tight up to the throat. While Jay's white duck trousers and light-blue shirt looked appropriate for a hot day with the thermometer ninety! When we got on the main Pittsfield road, everyone turned around and stared at us, which only made us laugh all the more. I wish I could have that ride over again; I wish, I wish I could have the whole week over again.

From *Maverick in Mauve* by Florence Adele Sloane, with commentary by Louis Auchincloss. Doubleday, 1983.

Elm Court 100 years later. Clemens Kalischer

FREDERICK VANDERBILT FIELD

In his life after High Lawn, Frederick V. Field became radically concerned to promote social and economic equality in this country, moving from the Democratic Party to the Socialist Party under Norman Thomas to the Communist Party. He spent nine months in federal prison for refusing to reveal in questioning before the Senate Internal Security Committee under Senator McCarran the names of his CPUSA associates, and in 1953, to escape continuing FBI harrassment, moved to Mexico City, where he became an expert on pre-Columbian stamps.

The Elegance of High Lawn

We occupied High Lawn in Lenox, Massachusetts, in 1909, when I was five years old. I was too young to have overheard any thing about the planning of the house and grounds and farm buildings, and in spite of having at least once having seen them under construction, I don't remember any of it as new. High Lawn came into my consciousness full-blown. The house, the gardens, the long driveway through woods, the tennis court, the farm on the other side of a small valley — these had, to me, always been there. Much later I came to understand that the whole caboodle had been a gift to my mother from her father. He had made similar gifts, one in Mt. Kisco and the other in Syosset, Long Island, to his other two daughters. Such gifts were not taxable in those days and were a way of passing on the family fortune to the next generation.

High Lawn was and remains a beautiful place. The architecture is Georgian, as are several other mansions in Lenox. Red brick with shuttered windows, the house was an oblong three stories high with a full cellar and large porches on the ground and second levels. A low curving wall led on one side to a billiard room and on the other to the laundry. Later, the addition of a large wing doubled the size of the work end of the house. For the family and guests, there were thirteen bedrooms and eight bathrooms. On the ground floor were a huge living room, a library, a dining room, a children's dining room, a pantry, a boudoir, an office for my father and another for my parents' secretary and still another bathroom. All that and extensive servants' quarters existed for two parents and four children and their guests.

A hundred yards away was a so-called "playhouse," with enough rooms, including kitchen and bath, to accommodate an average-size family comfortably. It served various purposes, but I best remember the occasional picnics. The picnic procedure never varied. In the middle of the afternoon preceding the outing, an observer would have seen the butler carrying a large tray of silverware, plates and linen from the big house. Sometime later, he would be followed by the "fourth man" carrying cooking utensils, eggs, cream, salt and pepper. We participants would then gather at the appointed hour around the electric stove, and the picnic would get underway. An outstanding feature was that everyone was in good humor. I wonder if that was not because we were, for a change, relatively on our own, away from the servants for a whole meal. Another characteristic that graced these occasions was lavish praise for the outstandingly delicious scrambled eggs my mother had managed to serve. My mother, whose accomplishments did not include cooking, could, however, stir eggs to scramble them. They tasted better than eggs at the big house, because it was such fun to rough it at the playhouse. After the fiesta was over, our observer, if still observing, would have noticed a maid on the way to the playhouse to clean up and the earlier procession returning.

While we children were small, fifteen domestics lived and worked in the house. Two chauffeurs lived in the garage, which had two small bedrooms, a bath and room for many cars and a workshop, but they ate in the big house. As a result, the total for meals was a minimum of twenty-three, and if we had guests, as we often did, the count went even higher.

Two of the butlers stand out in my memory, one for the silly reason that he had a pimple on the end of his tongue. As he stood behind my mother's chair during meals, he would incessantly roll the protuberance around his mouth, thus diverting me for minutes at a time from my food and the guest next to me. The other butler, Charles Harris, had a splendid personality and the even disposition that the job required. He was considerably more attractive than most of the gentleman guests. He and my mother, both strong characters, got along famously and worked together many years. Early in their relationship, they had settled on a *modus vivendi* which thereafter served them well.

Right after Mama's breakfast, the two met in the great marble hall that bisected the house lengthwise. Their agenda was the day's events for the household, which Charles would then pass on to the appropriate underling. There would be so many for lunch and dinner. Guests would be arriving at either the Stockbridge or Hillsdale station and a car should meet them. Master Freddy would be playing tennis at the Blakes at three and should be picked up again at five-thirty. My mother herself wanted to go to England Brothers in Pittsfield for shopping and, on the return, should be left off at her mother's, and she would walk home from there. After dropping her off, the chauffeur should pick up a basket of fruit at

Miss Katie Schermerhorn in her pony cart. Lenox, 1900.
Berkshire County Historical Society Collection

the Elm Court greenhouses. Another car could meanwhile take Mr. Field and three guests to the Stockbridge golf club and wait to bring them home. Mr. and Mrs. So-and-so would be coming from New York for the weekend, and Elizabeth should be told to prepare the large guest room. My mother had left a small package with Rose, her maid, which should be delivered to the wife of one of the cowmen who had just had a baby. Miss Peto, the secretary, had telephoned that she was not well and would therefore not have to be picked up in Lenox.

The meeting was regularly interrupted by Mama's sudden preoccupation with one of her favorite pastimes, sneezing. As everyone addicted to this habit knows, the instant the desire approaches the periphery of one's consciousness it must be nurtured, lest it drift away. In order to coax it to a successful explosion, one should look up at the sun or another strong light. The middle of the hallway where my mother and Charles conferred was about fifteen yards from the nearest window. In the middle of a sentence my mother would gather her skirts and rush, not run, to the nearest sunbeam and in a few moments return to resume the day's directives with a contented smile on her face. Having inherited this taste for one of the finer things of life, I write as an expert. I have enjoyed it all my life, often to the consternation of others. "So sorry, Fred, that you have a cold." "Fred, you must immediately get out of the draft." Now that I'm in my seventies, my pleasure has been slightly impaired. Not that I don't sneeze as well as I ever did; decades of practice have made me well nigh perfect and noisier than ever. The impairment comes from jealousy; one of my daughters, Federica, sneezes better and more often than I do.

Our nurses were important in our young lives because we saw more of them than of our parents. They housebroke us and taught us the basics of living with other people. Through them I learned to speak French before English. Alas, while I still can understand and read a little, I have forgotten the spoken language entirely. I visited one of them much later, when she was living comfortably on her savings and a pension in a small village on Lake Geneva. It gave me much pleasure to see that she was no longer a servant.

Other servants were also very real people during my childhood, more often than not of greater importance than guests or relatives. One, for instance, was Albert Spiller, a man well under five feet in height. He had been a jockey before joining our family as coachman, and with the passing of the horses and carriages, he became the family chauffeur. When the demand on the cars increased, he became the number one chauffeur, driving the family exclusively while his assistant drove the servants and ran errands. Albert first drove me in carriages and sleighs, later in town cars and country cars, and later still he taught me to drive myself. He made excuses for me with the local cops on the few occasions I got tickets, and when I had my own car, he never let it leave the family premises without a full tank.

John Burke, the "fourth man," was the downstairs of the downstairs, for he took orders from everyone. A lifelong bachelor, of Irish descent and a faithful Catholic, either devoted to or emotionally imprisoned by — we never knew which — a mother to whom he turned over his wages, he was an outstanding personality in the household. His duties — coal for the furnace, wood for the fireplaces, garbage and such — kept him in the cellar regions much of the time. At one period we were short a male servant for the upstairs duties, and John was given an unwanted promotion and put in livery to wait on table. It was a disaster for him and for my mother. He was ill-suited to play the role of flunky and John returned to the cellar. He wrote poetry; at one time or another I listened to a good deal of it. I have no idea whether it was any good or not, but it was his way of expressing himself. It couldn't have been too bad, for one of his poems won a contest run by the old *New York World*, the prize for which was one of those large box-like portrait cameras that you operate with a black hood over your head. With it John became a proficient photographer, and was allowed to set up a small darkroom for himself somewhere in the nether regions of 645 [Fifth Avenue, their home in New York City]. One Christmas he presented the family with a volume of eight-by-tens of the interior of that mansion, the best I believe that were ever taken. He was still around working the downstairs of the downstairs when some of my nieces and nephews were growing up. He won their respect and affection as he had, many years before, won mine.

I also respected other servants of my early days, but there is no need to name them. The important thing is that these men and women were individual personalities to me, people of pride and dignity. They were in all ways as meritorious as my parents' fancy relatives and friends who lived in the upstairs. These servants formed as much a part of my human environment as did those they served. They played a positive role in my life, and their class status, their "position" in our household, played a significant part in developing my understanding of the world. I am grateful to these early friends.

Of course, we had an unequal relationship. According to the ridiculous measurements of our society, I was their superior, they my servants. If I wanted a horse, my parents bought me one, and a coachman groomed and fed it and brought it from the barn to the front door whenever the young master felt like riding. We had a baseball team made up of the farm hands, some of the men from the house, and other employees. Osgood and I played with them. We had nice uniforms with "High Lawn" spread across the front. The pitcher threw a strike and I yelled, "Great, Jack, strike him out!" I got a base hit and the second houseman exclaimed, "Good hit, Master Freddy!" I didn't think that inequality made any sense. I didn't like it.

High Lawn was a large "gentleman's farm" in that it did not pay for itself and was not meant to. When taxes began to hit the upper classes, the losses helped. The farm's chief asset was a fine herd of Jersey cows that produced the richest milk in the world. After my mother's death, my sister Marjorie acquired the rest of our interests in the farm, and she and her husband turned it into a successful commercial venture.

In my early years, aside from the cattle at High Lawn, there were chickens, pigs, sheep and even bees. The farmland produced hay, corn, alfalfa and whatever else was required to feed the livestock. The house was supplied by the farm and a large vegetable garden. All this had to be manned by a staff under the direction of a superintendent. The setup was about as feudal as you could get back to in the first quarter of the twentieth century. It did not, however, function as well as a truly feudal unit where the help were serfs and the whole enterprise nearly self-

The Pittsfield-Lenox Road near Brushwood Farm. Courtesy of The Berkshire Eagle

sufficient. At High Lawn, wages had to be paid, employees moved in and out of the place, and father and sons had their clothes made in London from material woven in Australia. Nevertheless, High Lawn made a pretty good stab at keeping itself in an earlier century. In the twentieth, it was an anachronism.

It need hardly be said that, for a young boy, life at High Lawn was easy. There were no responsibilities whatsoever, unless you consider showing up on time for meals or keeping your fingernails clean responsibilities. Except when school made its unreasonable demands, I woke up in the morning whenever I pleased and pushed the bell button which connected with the pantry three times as a signal that I would shortly be down for breakfast. Then I paused to decide whether to wear white flannels or crash knickerbockers, and another heavy day began. Tennis or golf might be on the morning schedule and tennis or golf on the afternoon schedule. According to the standards of those days, I got to be fair at tennis. I collected several cups in junior tournaments at the country club, a couple of which were for mixed doubles in which I teamed with Margaret Blake, who later went far beyond me to become nationally ranked.

I never got to be a good player. Had there been tennis camps in those days, I might have rounded out my game, perfected an unreliable backhand, done something with the second serve and learned more about volley-ing. But as it was, there was no one to teach me. I learned something by playing a great deal, and for a while I was a little better than most of the other boys. That was all, and after eighteen, I hardly played again.

My father gave me a .22 rifle at an early age, taught me to squeeze instead of jerk the trigger and to point the weapon toward the ground when not firing. I got up one morning at dawn and went into the woods that lined the long driveway to the house. There was a chipmunk on the branch of a tree. I hit it with the second shot. Its guts came out, but it stayed on the branch. It took two more bullets to knock it to the ground, and by that time I didn't want to look at it. After that, I shot at tin cans and bottles. From the .22 I graduated, at about eleven or twelve, to a light but effective rifle for big game hunting called a Mannlicher. I never got good with it or particularly enjoyed using it.

But a rod and reel were a different matter. My mother, strangely enough for both the times and her upbringing, was an avid fisher. Before Osgood and I were old enough to join such adventures, she and my father had several times fished for tarpon off the Florida coast. The early family albums were full of pictures of my mother hauling in one of those mon-strous animals or standing next to one that had been caught and hauled up on the beach to be weighed. When we came of fishing age, the site for that sport had been shifted to the Little Cascapedia River on the Gaspé Peninsula in eastern Quebec. There, in September, just before school opened, we would spend two weeks casting for freshwater salmon and trout and living the simple life. Simple is a relative term. There was no plumbing in the camps; we experienced the joys of outhouses. But each of us had two guides because the river current was swift and there were rapids up which the loaded canoes had to be poled. And there was a special guide to do the cooking. Nevertheless, our life was pleasantly informal. We were relaxed with each other. We had a lovely time.

I have not mentioned reading books, stimulating conversations with the adults or an awakening of my intellectual life because there was nothing to report. I was too busy for such things. My father's intellectual interests hardly touched me in those early days. Yet I remember that it was considered a good thing to have interests and that reading was one of the most important of them. Although reading itself made little impres-sion on me, the idea of reading did. The practice eventually caught up with the idea well along in my teens. In my younger days, one of my father's favorite stories made me conscious that the world was divided between those who read books and those who didn't, and there was no question which side I was expected to join. The story had to do with Nanan and Grandpa's library at Elm Court, their Lenox estate.

Elm Court was larger and more lavish than High Lawn, although it did not have a farm attached to it. It did have, however, extensive greenhouses and a whole wing of the main house just for guests. The huge library was used as a secondary living room on less elegant occasions or when only the family was present. Its walls were lined with shelves which were loaded with splendidly bound volumes arranged in so orderly a fashion that they appeared to be unread. According to my father, they were unread. At some point in my early childhood, the room had been redecorated, and Grandpa had asked my father to fill it with books. The latter turned to his friend Charles Lauriat, a well-known Boston bookdealer, and conveyed to him the only instructions Grandpa had given him: there were X number of shelf feet to be filled and the dominant decor of the room was pale green, a color to be matched and complemented by the bindings. Not a word was said about authors or contents. The instructions were faithfully carried out; the outward appearance of the books was exactly what my grandparents and their advisers had wanted. My father, however, enjoyed telling us that he and Mr. Lauriat had had a grand time, even though nobody would ever appreciate it, putting together a fine collection of the world's best literature.

From *From Right To Left* by Frederick V. Field. Lawrence Hill & Co., 1983.

ROBERT UNDERWOOD JOHNSON

Robert Underwood Johnson (1853-1937) was a distinguished editor who followed Richard Watson Gilder of Tyringham as editor of The Century, *the foremost intellectual journal of the country in the latter half of the last and the early years of this century. He was influential in the conservation and national parks movement, and active in war relief and peace efforts, as well as being a prolific poet. "The Housatonic at Stockbridge" inspired Charles Ives's song and tone-poem of the same name.*

To the Housatonic at Stockbridge

Contented river! in thy dreamy realm —
    The cloudy willow and the plumy elm:
    They call thee English, thinking thus to mate
Their musing streams that, oft with pause sedate,
Linger through misty meadows for a glance
At haunted tower or turret of romance.
Beware their praise who rashly would deny
To our New World its true tranquillity.
Our "New World"? Nay, say rather to our Old
(Let truth and freedom make us doubly bold);
Tell them: A thousand silent years before
Their sea-born isle — at every virgin shore
Dripping like Aphrodite's tresses — rose,
Here, 'neath her purple veil, deep slept Repose,
To be awakened but by wail of war.
About thy cradle under yonder hill,
Before thou knewest bridge, or dam, or mill,
Soft winds of starlight whispered heavenly lore,
Which, like our childhood's, all the workday toil
Cannot efface, nor long its beauty soil.
Thou hast grown human laboring with men
At wheel and spindle; sorrow dost thou ken;
Yet dost thou still the unshaken stars behold,
Calm to their calm returning, as of old.
Thus, like a gentle nature that grows strong
In meditation for the strife with wrong,
Thou show'st the peace that only tumult can;
Surely, serener river never ran.

Thou beautiful! From every dreamy hill
What eye but wanders with thee at thy will,
Imagining thy silver course unseen
Convoyed by two attendant streams of green
In bending lines, — like half-expected swerves
Of swaying music, or those perfect curves
We call the robin; making harmony
With many a new-found treasure of the eye:
With meadows, marging smoothly rounded hills
Where Nature teemingly the myth fulfills
Of many-breasted Plenty; with the blue,
That to the zenith fades through triple hue,
Pledge of the constant day; with clouds of white,
That haunt the horizons with their blooms of light,
And when the east with rosy eve is glowing
Seem like full cheeks of zephyrs gently blowing.

Contented river! and yet over-shy
To mask thy beauty from the eager eye;
Hast thou a thought to hide from field and town?
In some deep current of the sunlit brown
Art thou disquieted — still uncontent
With praise from thy Homeric bard, who lent
The world the placidness thou gavest him?
Thee Bryant loved when life was at its brim;
And when the wine was falling, in thy wood
Of sturdy willows like a Druid stood.
Oh, for his touch on this o'er-throbbing time,
His hand upon the hectic brow of Rhyme,
Cooling its fevered passion to a pace
To lead, to stir, to reinspire the race!

Ah! there's a restive ripple, and the swift
Red leaves — September's firstlings — faster drift;
Betwixt twin aisles of prayer they seem to pass
(One green, one greenly mirrored in thy glass).
Wouldst thou away, dear stream? Come, whisper near!
I also of much resting have a fear:
Let me to-morrow thy companion be
By fall and shallow to the adventurous sea!

From *Poems of 50 Years* by Robert Underwood Johnson. Published by the author, 1931.

AUSTIN HAIGHT

From his boyhood in the last decades of the last century, Austin Haight loved the outdoors — hunting, fishing, watching the annual Trinity-Williams football game, operating the family farm in New Lebanon Center — and telling wonderful stories. He was the sort of person who paid attention to life in a way that brought a rich sense of adventure to him every day. Here, in recollecting an "old-timer," he recalls a vanished era in the Berkshires.

Bill Day, Veteran Sportsman

Old Bill Day has been a professional hunter since he was first able to carry a gun and used to get his ears cuffed for missing a flying partridge. He has been a trout fisherman for several years longer. He was "learned" how to shoot birds; I was taught. Between the two methods there is a vast difference.

One afternoon, after I had missed three birds straight, firing six shells, Bill gave me a demonstration of being "learned" — that is, all but the ear cuffing. For perfectly obvious reasons, much of this has to be blank.

It started with a yell. "Hey, there, you little ____! You're wastin' a h____ of a lot of powder." He rushed at me and pretended to bat me over the head. "Now get on, and if you miss the next one I'll kick you all the way home." As I turned to go he took a soft but healthy swing with his big foot at my rear.

"There!" he said. "That's the way the old man broke me in, and I wasn't half as big as you are, either. Wish you could have seen the gun I had, too. It was a muzzle-loader, o' course. Someone had got snow or mud in the barrels and bursted them; so I guess that they were not over twenty inches long after they was cut down. It scattered so that you had to shoot awful quick."

We sat down in the autumn sunshine, for I loved to make a break in the hunt and hear Bill talk of those days of boyhood.

"How did your father teach you to catch trout?" I asked.

"Oh, that was easy. Someone would want a mess of fish, and he would root me out of bed at daylight and say, 'Git out and go fishin', and don't come back until you have the basket full — about twelve pounds.' I jest had to get 'em, but I always done it fair. No, sir; in all these years I ain't snared a bird, trapped a fox or took a trout, except on a hook. It ain't 'cause I don't know how. I've seen hundreds of birds snared and trout netted. I jest didn't like that way. It ain't no fun; and if you have to make a livin' thataway, why not get all the fun there is in it?"

This is the reason I have always liked Bill. He has been a hunter and fisherman for the market all of his life, yet I have never known him to be other than a sportsman, one who observed the game laws as they narrowed his season of operation. If anyone can point a finger at him, it might be due to the fees he accepts from persons whom he has guided. These are sometimes influenced by the net results of the day and indirectly is selling. Three dollars a day for services and two extra is about one dollar per pound for five pounds of trout, but it must be remembered that he guided his man all day and probably fished only the hard places. If his man fired a box of shells at birds, without a hit, two extra dollars might be called a consideration for the two birds he killed and gave to the man.

Whatever you call it, the fish were taken in a manner appropriate to the season, and the birds were fairly shot on the wing. Bill is a Simon-pure sportsman and the most remarkable shot I have ever known.

The first time I saw him was on a brook some forty years ago. I was a youngster fishing with worms one bright day in the latter part of June. Suddenly an eight-inch trout was dangled in front of my face and someone asked, "Why didn't ye catch this one?"

Turning, my startled look disclosed a smiling man towering over me. He was six feet tall, straight and lean. His twinkling eyes were partially hidden by shaggy brows and a battered felt hat that was still gray in spots. On the raveled band were trout flies.

His blue work shirt was crossed by a leather strap which suspended the largest fish basket I have ever seen; as a guess, it would hold fifteen pounds of trout. His long legs were incased in common work pants which hung from a leather belt with a huge brass buckle. His trouser legs were tucked into high woolen socks. A pair of rubber brogans, such as men wore over felt boots in those days, completed his costume. He was wet nearly to the waist.

"Guess I scairt ye," he laughed as he lighted his pipe.

"Yes, sir; kind of," was my bashful reply.

"Got any fish? Course ye ain't, fishin' with bait a day like this," was his answer to his own question. "Ye ought to have a rig like this for low water and a bright day. Trout don't eat worms except on high water. Why, your bait there jest gags 'em."

I looked at his rig with interest. It was a three-piece rod made of lancewood and about nine feet long. As he waved it absent-mindedly I could see that it was limber in action, nickel-mounted and had a small nickel reel below the grip. The line was what we called in those days "oiled silk," with a leader on it about two feet long. This was made from the snells of broken hooks and flies. His single fly was a large Brown Hackle. Seeming to be at a loss for words but desiring to help me, he continued: "Put your pole in the bushes and watch me. I'll show ye how it's done."

I have never seen another man use a fly just as Bill did. He did not cast often; he simply held his rod high and let the current do the work. The fly was always high on the water and traveled across the ripples as he waved his rod back and forth. It may have been the inexperience of the trout or his art — I have never known, and I have never been successful in following his example — but he took fish after fish. I could see the need of his large basket.

I followed him for half a mile, picking up points that have remained with me to this day. One was the use of the anal fin for bait.

A fish rose short to his fly.

"Ah, ah," mumbled Bill. "He didn't want it. I'll fix him!"

Off came the fly and on went a hook. From his basket he took a trout. Cutting off the anal fin with a fair amount of meat, he placed this on the hook. He cast well below where the trout rose and retrieved the lure with a jerky motion, keeping it several inches under water. It was taken at once, and the fish was landed.

"Got to give 'em what they want, and some want different things. I like the fly best, though." He was replacing it as he talked.

I left him then and did not see him again for nearly two years.

Our second meeting was as unexpected as the first. I was at the grist-mill about the middle of September. A man drove a gray horse hitched to a buckboard into the mill-shed and asked permission to leave it there for the rest of the day. While he was unhitching I asked the miller his name.

"Why, don't you know him? That's Bill Day. He's the best shot and the best fisherman in the county. Makes a livin' at it, too. Always has and always will. The whole family just hunt and fish for the hotels, pay their bills and have a good time doin' it."

After the horse was cared for, I saw him take a hunting coat and a shotgun from under the seat, and I recognized my fly-fishing friend. He put on the coat and, picking up the gun, walked to the mill with a peculiar stride that I soon found could cover the ground. He seemed to bend his knees a little and simply glide.

Addressing the miller, he asked, "What's the damages?" pointing with his thumb in the general direction of the shed.

"Oh, that's all right, Bill. No damages," said the miller.

Pulling from the depths of his hip pocket a money bag, he handed over a quarter. "Give old Kit a mess of grain and a drink at noon, will ye? She ain't missed a meal since I owned her. I'll pay ye now 'cause I might get shot before I get back," he laughed.

"All right, Bill," chuckled the miller. "Goin' after some birds?"

"Yes, I guess I'll try to hit a few. Can't shoot as good as I used to — I seem so nervous." Turning to me, he asked, "Want to come along and play dog?"

Did I want to go? The honor of being asked was enough. You bet I did!

As we walked toward the nearest woods he asked me if I had seen any pa'tridges about, and we headed for a little run where I had seen some.

As we neared the place he halted. "Now we'll jest take it easy, and you do as I tell ye. We'll see if we can't get a few. Can't shoot as good as I used to, but you scare 'em up and I'll do my best. Now wait here until I whistle, and then come through. If a bird gets up, holler, jest so I can be expectin' it."

Presently I heard the signal and started my first drive. Instinctively I seemed to know I had to cover ground, and I traveled back and forth in the bushes like a spaniel. I had not gone far when a bird rose. Half frightened, I ducked my head and then remembered I was to give warning.

"Here comes one," I shouted.

There was a pause and then a shot. I waited for him to reload and continued. A second bird went up. Again I shouted, and again a shot. I repeated this six times.

When I came to the opening he was standing in, I was an excited boy, and Bill was smiling. "That's pretty good for a start. Ye did well," he said in his soft, easy way.

"How many did you get?" I panted.

"Don't know," he continued, "but you go over by that walnut tree and see how many you can find. All I ain't missed are layin' thar. I'll stay here so's to mark the spot."

I did as he told me and picked up five perfectly dead birds.

"Waal, that's all but one. I may have missed her — there's a lot of air around a flyin' bird. Jest go on a little further. I thought she acted awful dead as she came down."

Sure enough, there was the bird "with its feet up to heaven and dead as a mackerel," as I have heard Bill say so many times.

I repeated this operation in cover after cover during the rest of the day, and that man shot eleven birds without a miss. For a "nervous" person, that is pretty good work, especially in thick September foliage.

On the way home he thanked me for my help and wanted to pay me for my "trouble," but I had been too honored to accept a fee for my services.

As we walked on I was surprised to hear him say: "I wanted one more; I got an order for twelve. Well, if ye can't get 'em, ye can't. Guess someone will have to eat salt pork."

Just think of going after twelve birds, in September, with a ten-year-old boy for a dog!

That is how I became acquainted with Bill, and from that day grew a strong friendship, now ripened by years and the memory of our many hunts together. Often I go to his home, nine miles away, to hear him yarn about the days when he hunted for the market. Always there is the spirit of sport in his stories; all of his hunting and fishing has been for the pure love of it. The commercial side never enters into the talk. He had to have ammunition and tackle, but these were incidental to the sport itself.

In the days when selling birds and trout was lawful, Bill and his brother used to have a contract with some hotel in a neighboring city. This was always verbal, but just as binding as if written. It provided that the purchaser should handle all the birds Bill and his brother could get, take delivery at his house at intervals frequent enough to prevent spoiling, furnish ammunition, and pay a certain sum in cash each week. They received credit for this game at the rate of 50 cents for partridges and $1 per dozen for woodcock. Flickers were taken at the same rate per dozen and served by the hotel in place of woodcock. Trout were worth 50 cents per pound and were called for every day, but paid for once a week.

These prices were paid prior to 1890. A few years later these figures were doubled. Today bootleg game brings sums that are out of all proportion to its worth. I have heard of partridges selling from $5 a pair to $5 apiece, and trout as high as $2 per pound.

Bill never kept track of his totals. Only one year can he recall the number of birds he sold. At the time of the final settling the hotel proprietor had remarked, "Well, boys, if you had killed two more, you would have had an even thousand."

Think of 998 birds from the 15th of September to the 31st of January! Bill and his brother never hunted on Sunday, and it is a safe estimate that there were 20 stormy days during these 4 1/2 months. That leaves a total of 122 hunting days. Bill estimated that they had killed only about 150 woodcock, as the smaller birds were not worth bothering with. Therefore, the average kill of partridges was nearly 7 a day, and I believe it would have been nearer 10 a day for a shorter length of time.

This was not a bad income, for the average wage for labor was $1 and woodchopping brought only 50 cents a cord. I shudder to think of the birds they could have killed with better guns and ammunition.

During the latter part of the bird season and throughout the winter, Bill used to set deadfalls for mink, the only animal I have known him to trap. He tended these traps while he was hunting birds or foxes, and they were so carefully concealed that few men ever saw them. With mink and foxes worth from $5 to $10 each, his winter hunting was profitable. The fox pelts were good until the latter part of February, but by that time the guard hairs became broken and the fur dull. In the case of mink, the pelts were prime until warm weather. With the advent of April he began his trout fishing, which lasted until September 1st.

As he said one time, "If you call all this work, I only get two weeks' vacation, from September 1st to the 15th, jest long enough to let my toenails grow a little."

Once laws were passed prohibiting the sale of game and fish, it seemed that Bill would be out of a job and have to work as others did. It was not long before he was guiding. Three dollars a day was his fee when I first knew him, and he gave his man the birds he killed or enough to make a legal bag. If you killed your own limit, he kept his birds and held you in far higher respect.

My brother and I have hunted with him many times, both as a guide and a companion. Some of these days are the brightest in my memory, and others the weariest. We used to threaten to put a ball and chain on him to slow down his awful speed. He could cover more ground than any man I ever saw. I feel perfectly safe in saying that, alone or with his brother, he would average fifteen miles a day, and I have known him to go twenty-two on a single fox hunt.

One day, about 1900, we wanted to give a dinner, and we made Bill a special offer. It was that we would give him $10 if we got ten birds, but only the usual $3 if we failed. Bill was off like a shot, and most of the time that day we were either so winded we could not shoot or too tired. We killed one bird to his nine.

The next time we made a very different proposition. It was that he should have $10 if we killed ten birds, and we were to give him credit for a missed bird which in his estimation he thought we should have killed. This only applied to birds he drove to us, not to birds we walked up. How he fed them to us!

My brother was an exceptional shot, and still is, for that matter. I will admit to hitting 50 per cent of my shots. This brought results that were all that could be desired. Those were days any old partridge hunter would like to look back on, yet we never went with him more than once or twice a season. Our home grounds were also good then.

For some time I kept track of Bill's shots while he was with us. I recall eight hunts in six years. All of them were when he was guide and had to shoot our "leavin's," as he called them. These were at birds that did not fly to us or just clean cases of "wiping our eyes." During these hunts he killed thirteen birds with fourteen shells — not a single miss!

One day my brother raised a bird some distance in front of Bill, who was inside the woods on a road that ran to the outside. Neither of them had a shot as the bird started, but Bill put his gun to his shoulder and began to swing as it flew down the edge, out of sight. When his gun came to the opening, he fired, and the bird flew into the shot. That is one of the most spectacular shots he ever made, but he has done it several times. I have never shot a bird that way.

We were good friends. Once in a while a hunter would disappoint him, and then he would call me on the phone. "Hey, boy, do you and your little brother (he is thirteen years my senior) want to hunt for fun today? I can come down or you up. It won't cost you a cent."

We always "went up," for we did not want that man in our birds. This was a case of every man for himself, and such shooting! Once my brother "wiped his eye," and I thought Bill would cry. This was really due to a new gun.

Bill was the darnedest man to swap guns I have ever seen — once a week or once a month. He never had the same one long. Talk about a gun fitting a man! Here is a man who fits any gun. I have seen him beat a man at the traps, swap guns and do it again. When he was about seventy, he shot three strings of twenty-five targets for a seventy-two; the other three were dusted. I have seen him do as well with three different guns — "jest tryin' 'em out."

He is a scarred veteran now. One foot is minus some toes, a part of his right arm is gone, and his back is sprinkled with shot that have been there for years — all due to the carelessness that comes with long use of firearms.

When he was taken to the hospital at the time of his arm accident, he was told that he would have to submit to an amputation.

"That means that you want to cut it off?" he asked.

"Yes," he was told.

"Well, you can't do it. I'd rather die first. What's a one-armed hunter good for?"

He fought the entire staff and was so suspicious of their motives that he would not take an anaesthetic while his arm was being dressed. What he suffered no one knows, but he saved his arm.

It is all a joke now, just like all the rest of his mishaps. Even when he almost killed his brother, he had to joke. Let him tell it.

"The day I pricked Art a bird was flyin' low, and I had to swing awful quick to get a shot at it. He hadn't ought to have been where he was. I told him where to go and supposed he was thar. Anyway, I shot, and then I heard a devilish yell, and there was Arty, only about ten rods away a-wallerin' on the ground. I see I had hit him; so I picked up the bird and walked over to where he was layin', and I says, 'Did I hit ye?' He sort of wiggled and grunted. Then I says to him, 'Are ye sufferin'?' and he looked at me and says, 'You're d____ right!' and grunts again. I see he wasn't bleedin' none, and I says to him, 'Are ye sufferin' enough so's I better give ye the other barrel?' Gosh, ye should have seen him get up then! I thought he was goin' to shoot me. Guess he would have if I hadn't been so close.

"No, he wasn't hurt bad — kind of winded; only had about a dozen No. 6's in his back. Got 'em yet, but he's forgot about it by now. We picked some out with a pin, but most of them were too deep to get at; so we left 'em."

One time I asked Bill what had been his best bag for a single day. I knew he had done some awful execution. He laughed. "Oh, I never kept no track; guess that twenty-eight was about the best. It was funny that day. I had Chet drivin' for me, and down Bone Lane he got into a bunch. They come across nice, in ones and twos. I was 'most smothered with the feathers, but I got all eleven of them. They all fell in one place; I guess that a horse blanket would have covered the lot. I've done that once before, but I never got a dozen. I guess I could have if the birds hadn't give out. In them days we used to get bunches of them in the fall. It was jest a case of findin' 'em and hittin' 'em."

One evening we were returning from a day's hunt. The sun was almost down, and the moon was just showing over the hill to the east. We had nine birds between us, and the day seemed to be done.

Bill was quiet as we trudged along. Finally he halted. "Say, boys, down in them alders there's a bird. If I could make it fly into the moon, I think I could see it and get a shot. Wait here. I'm goin' to try."

We laughed at him as he scuttled off. Presently there was the roar of wings, a pause and then a shot. We listened. There was a faint thud of a falling body.

"That's ten!" shouted Bill.

I have never heard him brag about himself, his gun or his hound. He hated to hear others boast.

One day a friend sent a stranger out from the city to hunt with him, and the first thing the man did was to tell how good a shot he was. Bill told me afterward: "Thinks I, you ain't as good as ye tell, or ye wouldn't be tellin' — you'd be showin' — but if you be, why go shoot the birds. I'll feed 'em to ye."

All that day he drove bird after bird to that man, who could not hit a thing. Every shot Bill had he deliberately missed. "Gosh, I missed seven birds that day — more than all last year," he chuckled.

These are a few pages from this man's life of many years in the woods and along the brooks. A quiet, honest friend and one of the finest sportsmen with whom I have ever hunted or fished.

From *The Biography of a Sportsman* by Austin D. Haight. Thomas Y. Crowell, 1939.

MARY ALLEN HULBERT

In 1890, Mrs. Mary Allen Hulbert, a cosmopolitan socialite of Duluth, married Thomas B. Peck, a wealthy textile manufacturer of Pittsfield. She was a widow with one son and he a widower with three small children, and the merged families moved into the Peck mansion on East Street. In 1907 Mrs. Peck met Woodrow Wilson in Bermuda and their friendship resulted in a lengthy correspondence. (Wilson wrote her 224 letters in all.) When the first Mrs. Wilson died in 1914, it was widely anticipated that Mrs. Peck, who had divorced Mr. Peck in 1912, would become First Lady, but Wilson married Mrs. Galt instead. His correspondence with Mrs. Peck became known and subjected her to considerable gossip and unfair notoriety during the presidential election campaign of 1916. Her fortunes thereafter declined and she ended up in Hollywood. Her autobiography affords a glimpse of the '90s lifestyle of the second and third generations of Berkshire industrialists who had amassed fortunes in paper and textiles.

Mrs. Peck of East Street

Upon our arrival in Pittsfield I saw East Street for the first time. Later I learned to know and love it, but that bleak winter night it looked drear and my heart was heavy. I wanted my little son in my arms and the warm love I had left behind, and left for what? As the sleigh, drawn by a dashing pair of horses, circled the park, even the jingle of the bells seemed to mock me. The sky was black above the great leafless elms. We turned into the icy drive leading to the red-brick house that was to be my home.

As we waited at the door my heart sank lower, the bare branches creaked and tossed in the wind, but the door opened and Mr. Peck's father and sister came forward from the drawing room to greet us, and, within, flowers gave a festive air. Two of Mr. Peck's three children were there. The elder girl of eight had lived with her maternal grandfather since her mother's death while Mr. Peck's sister cared for his home and the other children, a daughter of six and a boy nearly four. The little girl was sweet and dear, the boy an unhealthy child who had been, as I found out not long after, drugged by his nurse. I found a bushel of empty paregoric bottles tucked away under the eaves of the attic.

Presently dinner was announced. I was asked to take my proper place at the table, but there was such a tragic look in the sister's lovely eyes that I begged her to keep it. She had been so utterly devoted to the children and to making her brother comfortable, and had enjoyed, for the first time in her life, the freedom of being a mistress of a home. I suffered with her in the thought that she must now give it all up to another woman.

Mr. Peck had told me, on the train, that his father and mother had lived together in the homestead, sat at the table and seen their children grow from youth to manhood and womanhood, and had not spoken to each other for twenty years — never once through all those long years. Mr. Peck, Senior, whom I found on hand to greet me, left us about ten-thirty, and, a few minutes later, a little black-garbed figure, my husband's mother, slipped in to greet the new daughter-in-law. Such a frail shrinking little thing she was — Elizabeth Dowse Peck — very fine brown hair waving above her broad white brow; brown eyes looking large in a white face, with skin the texture of a rose. They all seemed cruel to her, without reason I thought, but I could not judge yet — one must be with people to know them.

Just up the street lived the sister of Mrs. Peck — they did not speak either. "Not a talkative family, apparently, these Dowses," I said to myself. Later, sometimes, I was not addressed by Mr. Peck for long intervals. At first I was hurt, but I learned to laugh at it and treat it as the manifestation of this New England family's idiosyncrasy. Normally he was kind, especially in sickness.

In time I took part in various Pittsfield social activities, and I always recall, with pleasure, how, as a member of the musical club, I worked up Dvorák's "Sonatina" for Violin and Piano which is really a *duo* for the two instruments, not a feeble "also ran" for the piano.

The Pittsfield Golf and Country Club was organized in our little drawing room in the red-brick house. Mr. and Mrs. Walter Hawkins, Mr. and Mrs. Edward Pollock, Dr. Colt, Mr. George Tucker and myself met to put into action a plan to give Pittsfield this much needed social and sport activity. Mr. Peck refused to be with us or to have anything to do with the matter, as, indeed, did many others who are now, or were, officially active in that beautiful club. I fancy they were jealous of their exquisite Pittsfield of the past and must have resented anything that brought in the more crowded activities of the great outer world. I understood better when lumbering street cars came through our beautiful East Street, shattering its peaceful quiet.

Periodically I entertained the "Free Will Society," a church missionary activity. Mr. Peck's grandmother had been president of the society in her day. Its meetings were great occasions, sewing machines busy stitching for the poor in near and far missions, barrels of clothing galore — then a nourishing tea. So many of the dears were fragile old ladies. Then, too, I had been brought up on this sort of thing, my mother having been president of the "Benevolent Society," both in Grand Rapids and Duluth.

Mrs. Mary Allen Hulbert Peck in 1890.
The Berkshire Athenaeum, Local History Department

Many interesting, delightful persons, not only those living in Pittsfield but visitors too, made our life varied. We were hospitably inclined and gave many dinners, to say nothing of luncheons terminating in the ever-pleasant game of auction bridge; we went to good plays at the theater on South Street, and music was heard in Pittsfield even before Elizabeth Coolidge's great plan made the place a Mecca for musicians. Mr. Hamilton Mabie was with us occasionally, always happily our guest when in town. He came to make his delightful addresses before the Wednesday Morning Club (never held by any chance on Wednesday). The following morning after we had all talked well into the night (or rather he had talked and we had been his listeners), he would sit beside the fire, with the snow outside or the early spring or autumn coloring delighting his artistic sense, and read the *Springfield Republican*. He loved to read, so he said, the news from Athol, Peru Mountain, and Becket.

East Street was a Mary E. Wilkins or Margaret Deland story in itself. The Longfellow house (recently demolished, alas, to make way for a public school) was just across the street, at the corner of Appleton Avenue. Further along lived "Miss Maria," a generous and thoughtful lady in her own New England story-book way. She had a horse and two-seated surrey in which she took certain less fortunate friends to drive on certain days. One of the friends whose day was Thursday began to grow fat. Miss Maria looked at her critically one day, and, at the end of the drive, she said: "Mary, I'm sorry, you are now overweight; I cannot allow this horse to pull more than a certain number of pounds, so do not expect me next Thursday."

I can see too, another old lady, "Miss Emma," coming down East Street, dressed all in pale mauves and blues and pinks, with bits of rare old lace and ribbons a-fluttering and with soft white curls under her lace-ruched bonnet. Her mind grew confused in her later years; one day I heard her accuse her family physician of ruining her life; and he, a saint on earth if ever there was one, only said: "Now, Miss Emma, you know you don't mean that."

Gertrude Watson was a Pittsfield friend I had met in Rome, but I remembered her — tall, fair, with her hair loosely coiffed; her dress of blue with rare old lace; her lovely smile revealing an enchanting dimple; altogether a delightful personality. I had never forgotten her in all those years. Then, too, she was further impressed upon my mind because I later saw a painting of her that Elihu Vedder had just finished. No wonder I was delighted to find her again in Pittsfield.

Pittsfield always rather looked down on Lenox — "it was the habitation of the merely rich!" I've always chuckled a little to myself when I remember a letter from Europe that came directly to me addressed: "Mrs. Peck, Pittsfield near Lenox, U. S. America."

The Country Club flourished after the initial work was finished by the undaunted seven who started forth from our drawing room, each of us with a long list of people to see, hear and persuade to contribute. We rented a little farm not far from the center of Pittsfield and the entertainment committee, of which I was a member, prepared and carried to the farm every Saturday for two years a tea, until the struggling club should get on its feet. We took out food, maids, china — everything. Also the entertainment committee donated furnishings and made the little farmhouse attractive. We had good golf on a nine-hole course; I even won a cup from Mrs. Edward Manice, who was our star golfer — by a fluke, alas!

Several years later, the club bought the beautiful old estate on which was the house of Revolutionary times called "Broad Hall," the scene of Holmes' *Elsie Venner*. This purchase nearly broke my heart for I wanted that place, how I wanted it no one but myself ever knew, except possibly Mr. Thomas Peck, into whose ears I poured my supplications and arguments. He could sell the red-brick house, I argued, for fourteen thousand dollars; the price of the Broad Hall estate, at that time, was twenty-eight thousand — half payment down. I planned that the house, which was too near the road, could be moved to the top of the hill under some beautiful elms whence we could see the little lake lying below — what a wonderful place for the children! Over one hundred acres if I remember right. I further suggested that we could keep enough acreage to maintain our own privacy and still be able to sell enough to others desirous of living further out from Pittsfield to more than pay the required balance. I did not "sell" him the idea.

I had the promoter-pioneer blood of the West in my veins, but evidently not salesmanship. Money (or the lack of it) is an awful nuisance and such a mean limitation. When I measure my expenditure with my desires I'm the most economical person in the world. I really do not want money for self-gratification, but I used to want it most awfully for the creation of lovely things and had the impatience of youth against waiting. Possibly, too, a Micawber-like feeling that something would turn up, if I were permitted to carry out my plans.

After Mr. Peck's father's death we moved into the homestead just across East Street from our little red-brick house, and I had a grand time repainting it and making a few changes I thought necessary as well as resurrecting the old garden. I became much interested in my garden in Pittsfield. All the garden lore I must have absorbed as I trudged about with my Grandmother Allen in her own garden seemed to come back to me, and the place grew lovely. Even the children liked to saunter and sit in it and I was "nutty" about it, they said, and they used to pull me into the house when they thought me overtired. Nice children, they were.

Our gardener was a thin, tall New Englander, with a face like a russet apple with cheeks pink tinged; a real flower lover, so much so that he grew quite resentful when I insisted that he take out some flourishing, blooming plant that didn't fit my color scheme. We always had a little tussle of wills; when I insisted, he yielded, but remained melancholy all day. Sometimes he would plead, "Poor little feller, he's bloomin' so nice — it seems a pity to kill him." At last I couldn't bear his suffering, so I gave him a place in the kitchen garden for his loves and all was well, but he never failed to say, as he transplanted, "There, little feller, you'd never know'd you was moved." Dear old "Miller," he has gone and, where my garden bloomed, there is an oil station.

Mine was a dear old house with large square rooms and a long dining room running the whole width of the house, with a butler's pantry and kitchen large enough for several modern apartments. I was then an ardent germ chaser, and I breathed a sigh of thankfulness when the workmen removed eight layers of paper from behind the wainscoting of the bathrooms.

Mr. Peck associated its rooms with events of which I knew nothing, but I was keen on its possibilities and we had some quite heated arguments as to the use of the southeast room. Mr. Peck said No, that it could not possibly be made light and used for a book-living room as I wished. Too dark and gloomy! It was perfect for funerals and I could use it as a drawing room if I wished. My reply was to say, in a coldly superior manner, that I failed to see how a room with two large south and two east windows and a large fireplace could be dark. I won, but he never quite got over his astonishment at our living room's brightness and cheer. I think the eight funerals he remembered of his little brothers and sisters starting from this room had darkened it in his eyes. (Before they ceased speaking, Mrs. Jabez Peck had presented her husband with eleven children!) The room opposite I had made into a drawing room and used it as a background for my old French prints, Lowestoft bowls and for flowers in Bristol glass. With candlelight on the old gilt-framed mirrors, the mahogany and satinwood furniture of the eighteenth century, it was a charming room.

From *The Story of Mrs. Peck* by Mary Allen Hulbert. Minton, Balch & Co., 1933.

The Accessible Paradise
1914 to 1990

EDNA ST. VINCENT MILLAY

Edna St. Vincent Millay (1892-1950) won celebrity as the liberated-woman poet of the hedonistic 1920s ("I burn my candle at both ends ..."). In 1925 she and her husband Eugen Jan Boissevain, an importer of Dutch East Indies products, bought "Steepletop" near the Massachusetts line in Austerlitz, New York, and fixed it up as their permanent home.

Renovating Steepletop

July 22, 1925

Dearest Mummie:

Here we are, in one of the loveliest places in the world, I am sure, working like Trojans, dogs, slaves, etc., having chimneys put in, & plumbing put in, & a garage built, etc. — We are crazy about it — & I have so many things on my mind at this moment that must be done before I'm an hour older, — you know how it is — that I hardly know if I am writing with a pen or with a screw-driver. — You & Kay & Howard are all invited to come to see us when next you are in these parts again — one at a time or all at once, but the most restful time to come would be after a couple of months — just now there is a little too much mortaring & tearing down of old building going on, & a guest is likely to be pressed into service laying a floor or digging a hole for the septic tank. —

I have written the Corn Exchange Bank to transfer one hundred dollars from my account to yours. You will probably receive a notice of it in a few days. Make it go as far as you can, darling. Our expenses are staggering just now. The furnace & bathroom alone come to a thousand dollars. It's terrible, simply terrible. But it's going to be a sweet place when it's finished — and it's ours, all ours, about seven hundred acres of land & a lovely house, & no rent to pay, only a nice gentlemanly mortgage to keep shaving a slice off.

We're so excited about it we are nearly daft in the bean — kidney bean, lima bean, string-bean, butter-bean — you dow whad I bean — ha! ha! ha! — I'm off! — (Now you understand what I have been trying to tell you, that I am very interested in & pleased with the place that Eugen & I have bought.)

Please write me at the above address *soon*. Much love to you all three, from us, Ugin & Edner.

I shall come across your little kid's book presently & mail it to you. Just now Gawd knows where anything is.

Respectfully yours, Sefe, Litt. D.

From *Letters of Edna St. Vincent Millay*. Edited by Allan Ross Macdougall. Harper & Bros., 1952.

Poems

MIST IN THE VALLEY

These hills, to hurt me more,
   That am hurt already enough, —
   Having left the sea behind,
Having turned suddenly and left the shore
That I had loved beyond all words, even a song's words, to convey,

And built me a house on upland acres,
Sweet with the pinxter, bright and rough
With the rusty blackbird long before the winter's done,
But smelling never of bayberry hot in the sun,
Nor ever loud with the pounding of the long white breakers, —

These hills, beneath the October moon,
Sit in the valley white with mist
Like islands in a quiet bay,

Jut out from shore into the mist,
Wooded with poplar dark as pine,
Like points of land into a quiet bay.

OCTOBER — AN ETCHING

There where the woodcock his long bill among the alders
Forward in level flight propels,
Tussocks of faded grass are islands in the pasture swamp
Where the small foot, if it be light as well, can pass
Dry-shod to rising ground.

Not so the boot of the hunter.
Chilly and black and halfway to the knee
Is the thick water there, heavy wading,
Uneven to the step; there the more cautious ones,
Pausing for a moment, break their guns.
There the white setter ticked with black
Sets forth with silky feathers on the bird's track
And wet to his pink skin and half his size comes back.

Cows are pastured there; they have made a path among the alders.
By now the keeper's boy has found
The chalk of the woodcock on the trampled ground.

FROM A TRAIN WINDOW

Precious in the light of the early sun the Housatonic
Between its not unscalable mountains flows.
Precious in the January morning the shabby fur of the cat-tails
    by the stream.
The farmer driving his horse to the feed-store for a sack of cracked
    corn
Is not in haste; there is no whip in the socket.

Pleasant enough, gay even, by no means sad
Is the rickety graveyard on the hill. Those are not cypress trees
Perpendicular among the lurching slabs, but cedars from the
    neighbourhood,
Native to this rocky land, self-sown. Precious
In the early light, reassuring
Is the grave-scarred hillside.
As if after all, the earth might know what it is about.

THE SNOW STORM

No hawk hangs over in this air:
The urgent snow is everywhere.
The wing adroiter than a sail
Must lean away from such a gale,
Abandoning its straight intent,
Or else expose tough ligament
And tender flesh to what before
Meant dampened feathers, nothing more.

Forceless upon our backs there fall
Infrequent flakes hexagonal,
Devised in many a curious style
To charm our safety for a while,
Where close to earth like mice we go
Under the horizontal snow.

From *Collected Poems* by Edna St. Vincent Millay. Edited by Norma Millay. Harper & Row, 1956.

LAUGHRAN VABER

Laughran ("Larry") Vaber, a retired media spokesman for General Electric and before that a radio and TV newscaster, got his first radio job as the telephone switchboard operator for a Syracuse radio station based on his West Stockbridge telephone experience. By the time he graduated from Syracuse University and returned to the Berkshires four years later, he was well-known throughout central New York as an on-air radio personality.

West Stockbridge Central

When modern technology breaks down and doesn't live up to invincible expectations, it's tempting to recall the "good old days" when the pace was slower, life was simpler, when machines didn't carry the burden of solving our problems. A time when the human touch made life more pleasant.

The latest dramatic example of technology's limits occurred last January when the huge computer breakdown crippled AT&T's long-distance phone service and disrupted much of the nation's communications.

One of those old-timers I grew up with in West Stockbridge said such a massive breakdown of technology made people feel helpless and vulnerable. "Why, just a few years ago," he recalled, "the only thing that interrupted telephone service would be fallen wires in a storm. There never was a time when you couldn't turn the crank on the box next to the phone and reach Mildred or Beatrice or Hazel in the central phone office. And they'd connect you whether you asked for your party by name or number. They'd give you the time, the weather, tell you where the fire was when the town siren blew and even let you know if you'd had any calls while you were out."

Yes, the central telephone operator of several decades ago in towns like West Stockbridge was taker of messages, provider of all sorts of information and a virtual human 911 emergency center, tracking down the local doctor, rounding up volunteer firemen, determining whether the local sheriff or the state police were needed to deal with an emergency and asking a neighbor to look in on an elderly shut-in who was not answering the phone.

I also get nostalgic about those days when the telephone office with its operator on duty was the communication and nerve center of the community. But nostalgia doesn't necessarily equate with the desire to turn the clock back. For the human touch of the telephone operator could also mean a chance for human failure and potential tragedy. I know, because I was a telephone operator in West Stockbridge nearly half a century ago.

Memories of telephone events in the '30s, '40s and '50s are vivid for me, as are the two-digit numbers of most phone subscribers of that period. Even today, as I exercise by jogging in the West Stockbridge cemetery, I play a game of matching the names on gravestones with the phone numbers belonging to those names. Such matching comes in handy, too, in helping remember other numbers. For instance, here's how I memorized the padlock combination of my gymnasium locker: to the right ... Troy's Garage (number 12); to the left ... Lee Lime Co. (number 2); to the right once again ... Baldwin's Hardware Store (number 37).

Jean Caston Chapman of Richmond, also a West Stockbridge operator in the 1940s, has the old numbers etched in her memory. She said that she recently decided for the fun of it to try and recall every predial phone number in town; she scored well.

West Stockbridge at the beginning of this century hardly resembled the town we see today. Automobile traffic, which today uses the north end of Main Street for U-turns, didn't disturb the cows and horses that used a large watering tub in the center of the turn. Electricity was as scarce as telephone service. Two local merchants in those days had strung telephone wires as part of their businesses. One was operated out of Baldwin's Hardware Store with about 40 customers on the line, each paying $8 per year. The second line, out of Kniffen's General Store, had about 20 customers.

This was the town in 1901 when my mother, one year old, arrived with her parents from Dutchess County, N.Y. My grandfather, the Rev. William Laughran DuBois, had been called to West Stockbridge as pastor of the Methodist Church, housed in what today is the Grange Hall. He also travelled by horse Sundays to preach at churches in State Line, West Center, Queechy Lake and, on a part-time basis, the South Congregational Church in Pittsfield. To help support his growing family he worked as town postmaster, mortician's helper and carpenter. The latter skill enabled him to build his own three-story house which still stands at the southern end of Main Street.

That house had just been completed when, in 1916, the New England Telephone and Telegraph Co. began a search for an agent who would have a then state-of-the-art switchboard installed in a private home and operate an NET&T agency, offering the town vastly improved and expanded service.

So the New England Bell company named my grandfather agent and set up shop on a 24-hour basis in my grandparents' home. It would remain there until the advent of dial phones 39 years later, the longest duration for a phone office in a private home in the history of NET&T.

Mildred DuBois, my mother, at the age of 16 took the first call in the new system on Memorial Day of 1916, saying "number please," just as she would say for the final call on October 26, 1955, when dial phones at last came to town.

Operators at "Central," Stockbridge. Clemens Kalischer

The new "state-of-the-art" equipment didn't change much during those 39 years. There never were flashing lights, only mechanical dime-size pieces of metal called "drops," assigned to each subscriber, which would drop on a hinge as a signal the customer wanted to place a call. The operator had approximately a dozen sets of cords with plugs on each end, the number of people in town who could talk at one time, and corresponding sets of keys to operate the cords. When a subscriber called the operator, the operator selected a set of cords, plugged one end into a receptacle lined up with the drop, said "number please," plugged the other end of the cord into the number requested, and then pulled the ringing key to activate the bell in the home or business being called. During power failures the operator had to generate electricity for each call by turning a hand crank simultaneous to pulling the ringing key.

Many phone subscribers had private lines and one or two pulls of the operator's ringing key would summon the party being called. Some rural party lines had as many as 15 subscribers on one line, which meant that only one of those 15 could use the phone at one time. Unless, of course, others on the line simply wanted to pick up their phones and listen to their neighbors' conversations. And anyone who ever had a party line in those days will testify that was fairly common.

In addition to connecting two parties, an operator monitored conversations to see if the parties were through talking so that a disconnect could be made, thus freeing the set of cords for other calls. The switchboard had a "monitor" button which could be pressed while the operator was listening to a conversation so that the subscribers could not hear the operator. But this monitor was seldom used in the normal screening of calls, and most subscribers could tell by the click of the operator's key or background noise in the central office that the operator was on the line. It was not at all unusual, in fact, to hear a subscriber warning the other person on the line to "watch it, I think the operator's listening."

Modern telephone technology has at times raised the issue of invasion of privacy. Neighbors often can overhear conversations on cordless phones, and devices are available to monitor auto-phone conversations.

Nevertheless, I'd venture a guess that the "good old days" offered telephone users less privacy that they have today. Operators of decades ago were officially warned about eavesdropping on conversations and repeating anything overheard. But an operator had a pretty good idea what was going on in town.

There were many times that a call would arouse an operator's curiosity and cause that call to be monitored. An excited caller saying, "Operator, get me the police!" would assuredly find the operator staying on the line to find out if any further emergency help was needed.

The telephone office also served as a mini long-distance office. For towns in central and southern Berkshire, operators in those communities were asked to ring the party being called, then note exact connect and disconnect times, calculate charges and mail billing tickets for each call at the end of the day to the main NET&T office in Springfield. All long-distance calls not in this small geographical area were handed to a long-distance operator in Pittsfield.

Only five West Stockbridge subscribers could talk at one time to out-of-town parties. The number of out-of-town circuits included three to Stockbridge, two to Lee and one to Richmond. Calls to all other towns had to be routed through these three communities. There never was a direct circuit to Pittsfield, for instance.

Collecting coins from the town's two or three pay phones also was the responsibility of the central office operator, and a prominent sign on the phones admonished callers not to deposit coins until the operator asked for them, for, there was no way coins could be returned. Frequently callers would explain they hadn't seen the sign and dropped coins in prematurely. They were usually given the benefit of the doubt and connected without being asked for more money.

For the 39 years that the "central" remained in the family home, the only pay phone not in a place of business and accessible 24 hours a day was on my grandparents' front porch. It was illuminated by the porch's coach light and had a lighted sign.

The only times I recall money changing hands in the West Stockbridge central office was bill-paying time, subscribers having the option of mailing their payment to Springfield or bringing it to "central." Traffic into the house for payments was augmented by the presence of another pay telephone in the office. People seemed to like the sociability of paying their bills, making their calls from the comfort of a nearby couch if they didn't require the privacy of a closed booth, and finally enjoying tea or coffee frequently offered by my grandmother.

One lady who in the 1930s had no phone on her farm in nearby Austerlitz, N.Y., frequently used the pay phone in the telephone office. As a youngster I was told by my mother and grandmother that the nice lady who let me sit on her lap wrote beautiful poems. In later years I therefore took a special interest in the writing of this renowned lady, Edna St. Vincent Millay.

Although my grandfather was NET&T's official agent, most of the responsibility for running the office fell to my grandmother since he added politics to his busy life and spent weekdays during most of the 1920s in Boston, where he served Southern Berkshire in the Massachusetts House of Representatives. When he died in 1934 he was succeeded by my grandmother, and although a few outside operators were hired, it remained pretty much a family affair, with the three children, then their spouses and then the grandchildren all learning how to "tend to" the switchboard and helping out in a pinch.

Holiday dinners always were at Grandmother's because the switchboard had to be covered. During dinner, in the dining room adjacent to the telephone board, one member of the family had to eat with a headset on, the plug that connected the headset to the switchboard lying in the lap so that the designated operator could leave the table to answer calls.

The only diary that I ever kept as a youth was from 1940, my 11th year, where I find notations about relieving my grandmother at the switchboard. During my high school years, my grandmother, who for years had taken the all-night duty, became increasingly hard-of-hearing and felt she should no longer take responsibility for hearing the bell which through the night would awaken the sleeping operator should there be such a rare call. I eagerly took the job.

Five nights a week I would go on duty at 10 o'clock; take the dwindling late-evening calls, and then around midnight, before retiring to a nearby bedroom, activate a large and loud bell that would ring and wake me on the rare occasions anyone used their phones after midnight.

Most nights my sleep would be undisturbed until around 6 a.m. That was about the time of the first call every morning when the owner of Crane Lake Camp would call a Pittsfield bakery to order the day's supply of bread.

Earlier I mentioned that human failure held the potential for tragedy. Fortunately, no tragedy occurred, but one night during those high school years I failed in my duties, and because of the potential for serious consequences, I've never forgotten it.

One night after retiring I did have a call, waited until the conversation was finished, disconnected it and went back to bed, without reactivating the bell. Like turning off the alarm clock, going back to sleep and oversleeping. Later that same night, or early morning, there was another call, someone from Pittsfield trying to get a West Stockbridge number. The Pittsfield operator repeatedly asked operators in Stockbridge, Lee and Richmond, the only towns with direct circuits to my switchboard, to see if they could reach West Stockbridge.

The night telephone operator in Stockbridge was Richard Thorsell who slept and operated the switchboard at the central office on Elm Street. He arranged for someone to replace him, got dressed and drove to West Stockbridge where he pounded on the front door of my grandmother's house, finally waking the chagrined teen-age operator.

Although failure like mine that night had frightening potential consequences, there are some individuals today who say they still miss the personalized service of the old central telephone office.

"There were no answering machines in those days," Mrs. William Persing remarked recently. She's the widow of the only doctor West Stockbridge had for many years. "We really relied on the phone office," she said, recalling how she would call central to say that the doctor was on a house call and she was going shopping, could calls and messages be accumulated by the operator?

Today's volunteer firemen would be lost without their radio network, but there are still a few firemen around who recall it was the telephone operator who helped spread the word of a fire by calling selected volunteers and giving the location of a fire while other volunteers, having heard the town siren, called the operator.

The oldest living West Stockbridge telephone operator is Mrs. Malcolm Wheeler who, as a teenager in the 1920s, was probably the first non-family person hired. She recalls subscribers, ready to hang out a wash, calling central to see if any rain had been forecast. She also recalls her 1923 wedding in the front parlor of my grandparents' home performed by her boss, my grandfather. She recalls that someone participating in the ceremony was standing in the background, wearing a switchboard headset, ready to dash back at the sound of a buzzer.

In the last few of those 39 years that New England Telephone kept its agency in my grandparents' West Stockbridge home, business increased to the point that a second switchboard was placed alongside the original, and during peak hours the so-called traffic required two operators at a time. Because of the increased business, perhaps service became a bit less personalized. Newer operators wouldn't be expected to memorize an increasing amount of numbers and asked, rather than hinted, that subscribers try to use their directories. Message-taking became rarer, and night operators seldom slept the entire night without interruption.

Yet, in the autumn of 1955 when the equipment for the switchover to dial service was nearly in place, the community responded in an emotional farewell to the old service and to the people who had provided it.

Thirty-five years have passed since then. Now we have computers and fax machines connected by phone. We have cellular phones in our cars and are able to call anyone in the world within seconds, whether we're calling from six miles in the sky or a thousand miles at sea.

And yet, there was something about those days of the crank telephone, perhaps a piece of the human factor, that no amount of technology can ever replace. The best way to describe it is to recall a comment made by one very old lady a few years after the switch to dial telephones. She had no family, few friends and was confined to her home. "Oh, how I miss that old phone. I'd get so lonely, so I'd give that phone a crank. Then I'd pick up the receiver and hear, 'Number please.' I'd ask her if she had time to chat. She never said no, or if the switchboard was very busy she'd tell me she would call back. And she always did. Of course, I have television now, but it's just not the same."

From *The Berkshire Eagle*, May 1990 Berkshires Week.

WALTER PRITCHARD EATON

Walter Pritchard Eaton (1878-1957), drama critic for the New York Tribune *and the* New York Sun, *and from 1933-1947 professor of drama at Yale, was a tireless and much-loved Berkshire enthusiast. He lived in Stockbridge and later established himself at Twin Fires, his farm in Egremont, which he made well-known through his long-running country-life columns in the* Berkshire Eagle, *his many books of nature appreciation, and his popular lecturing on garden and drama topics. He also wrote a shelf-full of boys' books* (The Boy Scouts in the Berkshires, The Boy Scouts in the Green Mountains, The Boy Scouts in the White Mountains, ... on Katahdin, ... in the Dismal Swamp, ... in Death Valley, *etc.).*

First Visit to the Berkshires

The high plateau of the [Berkshire] Barrier is the region of almost forgotten villages, of abandoned farms, of second-growth forest repossessing land once cleared by the pioneers, of ancient roads now choked and often impassable, and of wide prospects from the hills over an undulating sea of treetops.

It was this region I first knew in 1899, before I had ever seen Stockbridge. The season was September, and I decided on a walking trip before going back to college. I took the Fitchburg train out of Boston on a hot, sticky day, and presently we were lurching up the gorge of the Deerfield River. I alighted at a station called Zoar, a few miles short of the tunnel, and drew a deep breath of fresh air. The stage driver was expecting me. His "stage" was a battered carry-all, and after a laconic greeting we began climbing the road northward beside the noisy waters of Pelham Brook.

"How far is it to Rowe?" I asked.

"Ten miles up, two miles down," said he which added to the right figure.

Up and up we plodded. The air grew cooler and cooler. I could smell the sweet water of the brook, or fancied I could. Finally we leveled off on the village street, where there were a sawmill, a few houses, a little stone church, and a general store. Thence the road ran uphill again to the old center, where I could glimpse the spire of the ancient church, now abandoned.

"This must be the highest town in the state," said I.

The driver pointed with his whip in a northeasterly direction. "They do say the cemetery in North Heath over there is the highest p'int o' cultivated ground in Massachusetts," he replied.

I boarded with Mrs. Browning, a lively widow generally called The Mayor, who, when not listening on the new party line, regaled me with local legends. Her summer boarders had departed, and only a highly personable young school teacher just out of Normal School shared with me the hospitality of the house. But she was busy by day, and for two weeks I tramped the country either alone or with the Unitarian minister — for oddly enough the Rowe church had been led out of Calvinism a century before by its pastor, the Rev. Preserved Smith. It was so remote from the beaten tracks that the ecclesiastical powers did not discover what he was up to until too late.

The minister took me one day through three miles of woods with no hint of our destination and then watched my face as we suddenly emerged from the trees on the very lip of a precipice that plunged down eight hundred feet to the Deerfield River, where it flows south out of Vermont. On the other side of the canyon — for it is truly that — rose a precipitous wall. Down at the bottom beside the river was the track of a railroad, generally known as the Hoot, Toot, and Whistle, running up toward Monroe Bridge — the Hoosac Tunnel and Wilmington. It has long since been abandoned for passenger service.

Coronado could hardly have been more surprised to emerge on the rim of the Grand Canyon than I was to come upon this splendid gorge in the state of Massachusetts. There was, of course, a jutting rock on the rim called Pulpit Rock, or the Devil's Pulpit by some, a name which annoyed my guide.

"Why blame the Devil for the work of erosion?" said he. "And why find anything evil in such a noble prospect? I should like to preach God's word from this pulpit, to all the peoples."

"They'd have to sit pretty far down," said I, and he reluctantly agreed.

Returning, we climbed a high pasture above the village to look down on the clustered roofs of the village, the ravine of Pelham Brook, and northward to the blue pyramid of Haystack in Vermont. From here, too, we could see a green patch on a domed hill which was, perhaps, the lofty cemetery of North Heath. It looked like cultivated ground, at any rate. There was no sound in the gathering twilight but a distant cow bell. The air was cool and fresh as only mountain air can be. The weariness of a hot summer's toil on a newspaper sloughed off my spirit, and suddenly I wanted to live always in this place and go up on this pasture at sunset.

"Time enough for that when you are fifty," said my guide. "But it's a beautiful land."

(Incidentally, I came back to the Berkshires to live when I was thirty-two. I got impatient.)

The next day I tramped over Hoosac Mountain through the tiny hamlet of Florida. There was no Mohawk Trail Highway in those days. The old dirt road climbed right up, crossed the plateau not far from the smoking ventilator shaft of the tunnel, and then plunged straight down to North Adams. I plunged with it into the ugly industrial town and took a trolley to the ivied precincts of Williamstown, to find myself in the midst of arriving Freshmen who were being "rushed" for fraternities. The hilltop silence, the panorama of woods and fields and far mountains, the smoke of the little village nestled by its brook, the smell of kerosene and calico from the general store, the racy speech of Mayor Browning, were suddenly far away. I took a night train through the tunnel and tramped up in the dark by Pelham Brook, which sang to me as it raced down from the hills. I felt oddly as if I were going home.

Such was my introduction to the Berkshires, and I am glad of it. It taught me something of the extent of the region, gave me a dramatic glimpse of its wilder aspects, but above all took me back into an earlier period when the hill towns were in the van of pioneer migration, were inhabited by sturdy and self-sufficient people whose farms were flung like mantles over the shoulders of the hills and whose sawmills whined by a hundred streams.

After the coming of the railroads and the subsequent decline of the hill towns, many of them became almost isolated until the building of state roads after World War I. Until then there were but two paved roads crossing the Barrier, from east to west, and none connecting the villages. The old roads went straight uphill and straight down again into deep hollows bogged with spring mud.

From *The Berkshires*. Edited by Roderick Peattie. Vanguard Press, 1948.

Cellar-Holes

Does anyone besides myself, I wonder, collect cellar-holes? You might suppose they would be a rather difficult thing to collect, but they are not, in my part of the world, at any rate. They might be somewhat cumbersome to assemble in one place, and somewhat crumbly also; but why should a collection be assembled in one place? Why not leave each choice piece in its original setting, and visit it from time to time as the mood invites? That is what I do with my cellar-holes. More than two hundred miles separate the northern and southern specimens, though the bulk of the collection is scattered in a portion of one county in my native state. I could visit nearly all of them in a day, if the roads were good. But the roads are not good; some, indeed, are as overgrown with verdure as the cellar-holes themselves, and can be negotiated only on foot. That assures me a privacy, however, which quite justifies my assumption of ownership.

I call them my cellar-holes because I alone visit them and treasure them and muse over their story when I know it, — which is not often, — or invent a story for them otherwise; an even more delightful occupation. Let other men rave of their first folios, their banister-back chairs, their Wedgwood urns, their Renaissance chests; give me my cellar-holes, bramble-edged and full of crumbling brick and rotten wood, melancholy reminders, at the front of some ancient clearing by the forgotten road, of a vanished race, an altered civilization, lovely with fireweed, home now of a woodchuck, silent and wistful in face of the reinvading forest.

Cold Spring River Road (now Route 7) in Williamstown. Stockbridge Historical Society

AN ABANDONED VILLAGE

Following the abandoned road we are already upon, we shall come in time into a road that is not abandoned — though, were you in a car, especially if it were your own car, you might think that it ought to be. This road takes us to the ancient village green of what was once our most prosperous town. It crests the world, at an altitude of 1700 feet, and the very dirt of the highway has followed the inhabitants down into the valley, leaving a long stretch of naked rock to mark the road. In this village were once, a century ago, four stores, three churches, and a town hall. At least, so I am told by the ancient gazetteers. I have discovered one of the stores, now occupied by hay, and the cellar-hole of the last church to remain standing. The rest are quite gone. Of the fine Colonial dwellings, two are evidently used at times as summer homes. One is the residence of a family of Polish Jews. The rest are abandoned and falling into desolate decay. Between two of them — one, no doubt, formerly the parsonage — a flight of marble steps leads up to a broad door-stone, and you step from that — into the cellar-hole of the church. This edifice burned not many years ago, and thoroughly, so there is no pile of rotting timbers in the hole; only pink fireweed and a few charred beams.

You look across the cavity and the clearings behind it, — now growing up to weeds and scrub birch, — over mile after mile of rolling hills and shadowed ravines, country almost as forlorn as this in the immediate neighborhood — all because Stevenson invented the locomotive, and this country is seventeen miles from the nearest railroad. A fine and sturdy civilization came up here and conquered these hilltops, bringing the graces of architecture, the strength and sanctions of religion. And now they have gone back again, like a wave that rises only to recede. Their cellar-holes are their monuments. I have often been moved to preach from those marble steps, with the fireweed for congregation; but the inhabitant of the village, coming into his front yard with the dog, invariably discouraged me with his suspicious glances.

THE GOODALES' SKY FARM

Again we leave a pleasant village on the plain and climb steadily for six miles, rising more than a thousand feet, through a water-worn gorge in the abrupt and heavily wooded mountainside, with the tumbling brook ever beside us, now far below the road and lifting up its voice from the shadows of the hemlocks, now almost laving the wheel-ruts. Halfway up, a spring gushes from a bank, amid a bed of maiden-hair, and a mossy hollowed log conducts its water into a yet mossier wooden trough. Just as the road at last breaks over the final "thank-you-marm," and enters on an upland plateau quite invisible from the valley, you will note again the telltale formal planting of aged maples by the wayside, and the no less telltale banks of day-lily spears. There is an old orchard here, too, across the road, in what was once a clearing, the poor, neglected trees still struggling bravely to renew their life in a wilderness of suckers from the base of the dead branches.

Just back of the largest maples, where the day lilies mass in profusion, is the cellar-hole. An entire colony of young trees has started up in the bottom. No trace of woodwork is left. The house has all gone back to compost, save the foundation stones. Yet here, and not so long ago, either, as time runs, books were once written — books of poetry by two little girls, which were published by a famous firm in New York and read by all our parents. The little girls knew little of life; they wrote about the flowers, the trees, the coming of spring, of summer, the first reds of autumn, the first winter storms. Standing here on their doorstep, beneath the maples, they looked back down the deep ravine, — more easily than we can do to-day, for the clearing was larger, — and saw life, not only as something adult and beyond their experience, but as something far away and far below, something lived under a faint haze down there on the valley floor. You will find a hint of this now and again in their poems, as always you will find the suggestion of their mother's presence behind them, their mother who loved flowers and whose hands, no doubt, set out the first clumps of these day lilies which have now preempted a whole section of the roadside. I dug a clump of them up one spring, and transplanted it into my garden, in remembrance of that strange flowering of the arts on the bleak hilltop a generation ago. I call them my literary lilies. The lilies and the cellar-hole are all that is left of Sky Farm.

From *On Yankee Hilltops* by Walter Pritchard Eaton. W.A. Wilde, 1933.

COLLINS MILES

Many Berkshire families preserve remarkable collections of family letters and papers, but few, if any, are more complete and extensive than that of the Miles family of Egremont and Mount Washington. The letters of Collins Loewe "Pete" Miles (1909-1989) to his brother Lemuel give a glimpse of the daily concerns of a young man establishing himself as a carpenter, painter, and cabinet maker during the Depression. Lemuel had gone to California to work for an uncle near Sacramento, but returned to do farm work in Great Barrington. During the '40s, Collins Miles introduced the chain-saw and the portable gasoline-powered sawmill to Mount Washington lumbering operations, and in 1950 founded the Copake Lumber and Supply Company in Copake, New York.

Mill housing in Adams, c. 1940. Courtesy of The Berkshire Eagle

Depression Letters

Mt. Washington, Mass.
Oct. 21, 1932

Dear Lem,

Here's hoping you had a pleasant journey by train to the west. Thanks a lot for the loan — I'll make it up sometime, just now it saved me from drawing what little I have from the Savings Bank.
Mother is home, and the ol' man has a Mrs. Linsley from Gt. Barrington at home doing the work. I took her to Pittsfield yesterday (Thurs 20th) to see some Doctors from the Riggs Foundation, in Pittsfield, they are Spe-

cialists in spinal and brain diseases, I got no satisfaction at all from them, but I think I will take her up once more as a last resort. I think she feels much better, anyway she <u>looks</u> much better.

I wish you to give my regards to Uncle Gary [Miles] and tell him that if everything continues as well as it has the past few years, I am coming to California, just for a visit.

Marion [his sister, Marion Hopkins] and the kids are down home occasionally, and I think I will go up and spend the night Sat. I'm working Sun just to finish up a job to get paid.

Just now, the weather is fairly pleasant, the end of five continuous days of rain.

Write and tell me what your job is, I'll be interested in that, don't take a job that isolates you from other people too much. Work <u>with</u> people even if you only pay expenses. The hunting season started here yesterday, very few hunters up here, because the land is all posted. I'm not going yet, too busy as usual. A little later in the season.

Just for fun tell me when you get this letter. It will leave Mt. Washington at noon Sat. Oct 22.

Then I'll try one by air-mail.

    Sincerely

    Pete

To Mr. L.D. Miles
Care of G. Miles
Galt, Cal.

        Mt. Washington, Mass.
        Nov. 7, 1932

Dear Lem,

I will mark the time this letter is posted in Gt. Barrington. Just for fun remember the time and day it reaches you.

I haven't heard from you, but I take it for granted that you are wrapped up in your new job.

Mother is a little better I think. Clarence Brainard's mother is there just now. Marion & the kids are O.K. too. Mother and I stopped in there one day when we were going to Pittsfield.

Seth [Hopkins] is going to make me a truck of some description, and I expect to start building my house soon — I've decided that if Hoover is elected I'll build it, and if he isn't I will take a chance anyway. I just heard him speak from Elko, Nev. and am firmly convinced that he should continue to direct the country. Write — when you get time of course, I will be glad to hear about California, and what your job is.

Business has been very good of late but just now, for the first time in two years I have practically nothing to do — I have but I would rather keep it until later in the season.

I send my best regards to Uncle Gary whom I hope to meet sometime, and remain

Sincerely,
Pete

To Mr. Lemuel D. Miles
Care of G.A. Miles
Galt, California

Mt. Washington
March 14, 1934

Dear Lem,

You see it takes some time for my mail to get in and out of here, it's quite all right with me, glad to have you come up for a visit. I'll keep you busy, don't worry about that any.

I'm not doing anything to amount to anything yet, I painted a couple of days up at Weaver's Mon & Tue. I've been trying to build a place to keep my car in for some time, I have yet to chink it, build 2 doors & fix a window. Then I must build a body for my truck. Then I'll start in earnest on Mack's cabin.

It should be quite warm by then. I had my winter vacation some time ago. Spent a week with Bill Miles, drove out to the New England Sportsman Show in Boston while I was there. Spent two weeks with Mark.

Perhaps you should leave some of your junk down there, just to save moving it. I leave that to you.

I've got one rear wheel off the car now but I can come after you most any time. I've been monkeying with the brakes, cleaning them out and such.

Mervin shot a 19 lb. wild-cat Monday — no Tuesday. I went with him today, but lost the track in a hell of a snow-storm, about 2 inches fell.

Sincerely
Collins

To Mr. Lemuel D. Miles
Great Barrington, Mass.
R.F.D.

["Mack" is Clifford Mark; "Mervin" is Mervin Whitbeck, both residents of Mt. Washington.]

April 4, 1934

Dear Lem,

I suppose by now you are thoroughly established in your new surroundings. I expect to go to work soon on Mack's place, as the frost is out of the ground enough to dig now. The roads are a hell of a mess up here now, I haven't had a chance to go down home lately. I've finally got a place to keep my car inside. I built the doors for my garage a couple of days ago.

I'll be glad to go to work, cause I'm so dam broke I couldn't buy a free lunch. Because you went to work so soon after quitting one job, bears out my theory that if one wants to find work, really wants to work I've never yet seen when he couldn't.

But sometime, when you are changing jobs, why don't you try something besides farming?

Of course it's become a habit now I suppose, and is therefore much easier for you, than one not used to farming.

I stayed at Mervin's last night (where I am now) and as Jim [Mervin Whitbeck's son] won't let me alone I'll have to go eat breakfast, he will be quiet there.

Sincerely
Peter

To Mr. Lemuel D. Miles
Gt. Barrington, Mass
c/o John Broderick, "Chadwick Farm"

Postmarked April 26, 1934
Mt. Washington, Mass.

Dear Lem,

I'm returning your loan, and many thanks. I missed the mailman today (Tuesday) so this is two days behind time.

Old John Diamond has forgotten more about pick sharpening than Broderick knows now, Broderick says you can't weld steel on picks — you can weld anything on to anything.

Zeke [Whitbeck] is working for me now on Cliff's [Mack] cellar hole. I've pushed a pick and shovel for eight hrs., drove to Copake & brought back a kid (he's 21) to stay here & fuss around the place for a week or so. I think I have a little garden for rabbit & deer fodder.

I paid .15¢ for 13 carrots & 24¢ for 2 heads lettuce tonight. I had 6 deer on my place one morning a while ago — all in one bunch.

I worked 11 hrs. over at the Berkshire Club Ground, for Mr. [Jack] Droege Sunday — I left here at 7:45 and got home at 7.30.

He's the fellow I built the fireplace for last fall.

It's a water system this time.

After May 1st the mail comes every day.

> Sincerely
> Collins

To Mr. Lemuel D. Miles
"Chadwick Farm"
Gt. Barrington, Mass

Mon. Eve.
Postmarked April 16, 1935

Dear Lem:

Thanks a lot for the loan, I'm sorry I had to take it. I usually have enough to do business with but was short for a while. I got a check for $100 a couple of days later & spent it all in 2 days.

I'm ready to start the fireplace in Mack's cabin room. We had 2 in. of snow tonite early in the evening.

Say, there were a lot of brads in that box of yours, they'll help a lot. I'd like to send you another dollar for them but the best I can do is offer you and anyone you care to bring a good dinner some Sunday.

> Sincerely,
> Pete

To Mr. Lemuel D. Miles
Gt. Barrington, Mass
R.F.D

From the letters of Collins Loewe "Pete" Miles (1909-1989) to his brother Lemuel, in the collection of the Miles family of Egremont and Mount Washington.

GERTRUDE ROBINSON SMITH

A descendant of Cotton Mather, Miss Gertrude Robinson Smith of Glendale was an executive of extraordinary effectiveness. She directed the United States side of Edith Wharton's war-relief fund-raising campaign during World War I, and later raised the millions to build the New York headquarters of the American Women's Association, which she headed for seventeen years.

When the idea of holding a festival of symphonic music was broached as one measure for countering the effects of the Depression in the Berkshires, she took over its promotion with characteristic energy and dispatch, as may be seen in this initial organizing letter sent to 150 "representative" women in the communities inside the 40-mile radius she circled around Stockbridge on a road map.

A Letter From Miss Smith

June 18, 1934

Dear Mrs. Taylor:

I am sure you will agree with me that there are few things artistically more enchanting than listening to a beautiful symphony orchestra on a summer evening outdoors under the stars.

Such an opportunity is being offered the Berkshires by Mr. Henry Hadley, our own American composer and conductor, provided we can interest the necessary audience. The plan is to have the concerts at the Hanna Farm on Route 41 between Stockbridge and Lenox on August 23, 25 and 26. The subscription prices covering the entire Festival of three concerts would be $5 and $3 depending on location. Mr. Hadley will bring an orchestra of 64 men from the New York Philharmonic Symphony Orchestra and hopes at two of the concerts to be able to have well known soloists.

As the concerts seem to be of great interest to our community, I am asking a representative woman from each locality to come to my house on Tuesday, June 26 at 4 o'clock to hear Mr. Hadley outline the plan. There will be no guarantee funds asked from anyone. If, after careful discussion we all agree that we want the concerts, then we will organize to dispose of the moderately priced subscriptions to insure success.

It is my privilege to have been asked by Mr. Hadley to present the idea to our community. I am more than happy to do so and I hope that you will be interested and able to come to the meeting on the 26th.

> Very cordially yours,
> Gertrude Robinson Smith

From *Music Under the Stars* by John G.W. Mahanna. Berkshire Symphonic Festival, 1953.

ANNIE ZUCCO HARRISON

Annie Zucco Harrison of Great Barrington worked at Rising Paper Company in Housatonic for 46 years, from 1926 until 1972. In 1974 she was interviewed by James S. Turner of Simon's Rock for an oral history project. Here are excerpts of her recollections of working in the paper mill.

Working at Rising Paper

BUGS IN THE PAPER

In the summertime, especially on the night shift, they would have lots and lots of bugs in their paper. Sometimes out of every ream, you'd get 40, 45 sheets of paper that you'd have to throw out on account of the bugs. And they tried yellow bulbs, and electric screens, they tried everything, to eliminate them. And it was a shame, because a whole big sheet of paper with one little bug would have to come out.

FAITHFUL EMPLOYEES

Well, the younger years, most everybody there either had a mother working up in the rag room, or a father working in the beater room, or washer, or somewhere, some part of the mill. Most every family had two, three, or four working there at one time or another. Six of us in my family, not all at once, but three at one time a lot of times, and it just seemed as though it was one big family — that everybody knew everybody, and that those that came usually stayed. The women stayed until they had children and had to leave, and then they'd come right back in there, and the men just stayed on for years and years. It's not like today, the young help comes and leaves. These men stayed forty, forty-five, some even to fifty years. And the women, up in the rag room, the very faithful, they stayed for years, too. And the fun we used to have, we worked hard. But we played too.

And the fellows, when no bosses were around, we used to all take a turn riding around the finishing room in the broke box.

When I first went there, in the winter [in 1926], there was nothing doing much, so all the girls used to bring either their sewing, tatting, embroidering in; the older ones would sit in a corner and chat, or read a book. But that went on every day: girls sewing, and talking, and then come spring we'd go out and walk over the trestle, down in the field and around, and when it was summer, they'd have a croquet set set outside, or we could play softball outside, or baseball. And then, the younger ones would sit on the banks of the river and just put our feet in the water and cool off a little bit, way down below the raceway there. There was lots and lots of things to do in the summer, outside: we'd go down and look for pussywillows, or flowers, anything. We only had an hour, but just to get out, where there was fresh air, we would go. And then the following winter, they had a victrola put up in a room, and the girls used to bring records in, and then we'd have our lunch out there, and then they'd shove the tables in a corner and everybody'd get up and dance, that wanted to. Then eventually, they did away with that. People started going home for lunch. At first, everybody stayed for lunch, because there was no time to go home. Nobody had cars in them days, and everybody stayed there for lunch.

A GOOD PLACE TO WORK

When I went there there was no vacation, not at first, but I think in '33 and '34, I think they started then. You got a week. And I think you had to be there five years.

I always felt good about working there.

B. D. Rising was just fine, and so was the Rising Paper Company president, Mr. Moses. Of course, we got more after he was there, they gave more benefits and things, when he owned it.

Every year we'd have a meeting, and they'd decide where they wanted to bowl. The first year ('33 or '34) we bowled up in Lee. And the second year in Canaan. We'd take a vote, wherever we'd want to bowl. Well, if anybody didn't have a way to go, which people didn't have cars in them days, they'd have a sheet of paper down on the bulletin board, and anyone that didn't have a way, that wanted to go, would put their name. And by the time it came the night to go bowling, everybody'd have a way. Even the President would take us sometimes, if we didn't have a way to go.

Mr. Moses used to have a banquet at the Red Lion Inn, every year, around Halloween, in October, and it was beautiful. Everybody went, and everybody had a corsage, and the men had cigarettes, that Mr. Moses put on every table, and it was just wonderful. They danced there, after they'd done eating. And if anybody didn't have a ride there, they'd get you a way up, and back.

From a 1974 interview with Annie Zucco Harrison, by James S. Turner.

JAMES GOULD COZZENS

James Gould Cozzens (1903-1978), one of the 20th century's finest novelists, went to Kent School and returned to the Berkshires to live in Williamstown after the great success of his 1957 novel, By Love Possessed. *The extract here is from his earlier novel,* The Last Adam *(1933), about a doctor in a crossroads town along the Housatonic in the Connecticut Berkshires.*

Ringing Doctor Bull

The snow storm, which began at dawn on Tuesday, February 17th, and did not stop when darkness came, extended over all New England. It covered the state of Connecticut with more than a foot of snow. As early as noon, Tuesday, United States Highway No. 6W, passing through New Winton, had become practically impassable. Wednesday morning the snowplows were out. Thursday was warmer. The thin coat of snow left by the big scrapers melted off. Thursday night the wind went around west while the surface dried. Friday, under clear, intensely cold skies, US6W's three lane concrete was clean again from Long Island Sound to the Massachusetts line.

With the storm had come a necessary halt in motor traffic. Both Wednesday and Thursday it was scanty and uncertain. Friday, fine and sunny, all the main roads were crowded by the delayed appearance of heavy vehicles; 150 h.p. tank trucks distributing gasoline crawled out from their depots; the five-ton truck-and-trailer combinations supplying chain grocery stores took the road. Although the day was one of the coldest of the winter, a remarkable number of private cars came out, too.

Through the wide bay window to her right, May Tupping could find a moment from time to time to watch, across the corner of the New Winton green, this never quite ceasing procession. She could amuse herself by noticing the number plates. Bound north went plate after yellow New York plate. Bound south passed the frequent green plates of Massachusetts, the dingy ultramarine of Vermont. From both directions appeared a scattering of white number plates; presumably from New Hampshire when they came down, and from Rhode Island when they came up. She saw one which she knew was Maine's black and white; and one which was probably New Jersey, but the colors happened that year to be practically the same as Connecticut's own.

Two of the gasoline trucks paused at Weems' garage, thrust their hoses into the buried storage tanks for a few minutes before moving on, but most of the traffic had no business in New Winton. Cars going through as fast as they could flickered behind the bare elms on the west side of the green all afternoon. At the south corner the rigid batteries of pointed arrows turned a few west to cross the river; but, as a rule, May could make a safe bet with herself. She knew what each southbound driver was going to do before he did. Abreast of the white board, suspended from a neat signpost arm and carrying the black inscription: *New Winton, 1701*, a discovery would be made. At that point, driving, one saw both that the bridge road was deserted, and that US6W, leaving New Winton, dipped gently, stretched a level, exhilaratingly straight two miles to the river bend. Each car suddenly went much faster. Given the book on her lap, the various colors of the number plates, and this little ingenuous trick practiced so faithfully by driver after driver, May Tupping managed to pass the time.

"I'm sorry, Mrs. Talbot," May Tupping said, "Doctor Bull does not answer."

Her right hand twitched the plug from 11. On the other line there was a halt, a sort of silent whine, while Mrs. Talbot's harassed mind wrestled the vain little it could with her worry. "Well," she said in necessary surrender, "well, all right, May —"

May released the key, dropped the plug back. Looking away from the electric glow shining off the complex surface of the switchboard, she saw three New York plates succeed each other, but abstractedly, concerned about Mamie Talbot. She wished that she could be surer that these calls of Mrs. Talbot's were just Mrs. Talbot's nervousness. Whether by nature, or because of the amazingly bad luck she had, Mrs. Talbot was always upset, apprehensive, hysterically expecting the worst. You couldn't tell what she really meant by Mamie having a bad turn. In Mrs. Talbot's words, Mamie didn't rouse. A person with pneumonia was naturally pretty sick, might not feel like rousing every time Mrs. Talbot had a mind to rouse her.

Still, with nothing else to do, May presently plugged in 11 again. Doctor Bull's house was at the other end of the green, and if she were looking she could see his car arrive. But she might not be looking; he could have come while she had her eyes on the number plates. Then, too, car or no car, Mrs. Cole might have got back from wherever she was. Or she might even have been in the house all the time. Mrs. Cole was very absent-minded, and if she happened to have a door closed, she might not realize that the telephone bell meant anything. It was even possible, May thought privately, that Mrs. Cole would simply decide to be deaf. Though she seemed quite able to keep house for the doctor, who was her nephew, and to go unescorted to the motion pictures in Sansbury, people said that she was ninety years old. Perhaps at that incredible age you ceased to see the use of answering telephones if you had anything better to do.

Whether the old lady was at Sansbury in a motion picture theatre, or merely letting the phone ring while she philosophically puttered about the kitchen, made very little difference. Soon, tired of the throb of the futile ringing, May disconnected, sat passive again, regarding the book in her lap. It was the sixteenth volume of a set of books in the library. The set was said to contain everything ever written with which an educated person should be familiar and volume by volume May was getting through it. She let her eyes focus, reading again, for she was not yet tired of it: "— *My marks and scars I carry with me to be a witness for me, that I have fought his battles who now will be my rewarder. When the day that he must go hence was come, many accompanied him to the river side, into which as he went he said, Death, where is thy sting? And as he went down deeper, he said, Grave, where is thy victory? So he passed over, and all the trumpets sounded for him on the other side.*"

How Mrs. Talbot got on at all, May didn't know. Mrs. Talbot took in a certain amount of laundry work, but most of what money they had Mamie made laboriously in the Bannings' kitchen, washing dishes and doing things that the cook and the maid did not care to do. May doubted if she were paid very much, especially when Mamie got her keep and clothes which Virginia Banning no longer wanted. Of course, it let Mamie get away from her mother, but May was astonished that Mamie could stand it, even so. Mrs. Banning made her go to the Episcopal church. Mrs. Banning also told her that she would lose her job if she went out evenings with a man.

The man, May learned from Doris Clark, who had Morning on the switchboard, had been Donald Maxwell. Donald worked for Miss Cardmaker on the hill. Very coarse in moments of intimacy, Doris said that she would eat her hat if Mamie (the phrase was Doris's) hadn't been laid. "Listen, I *know* Donald," she explained.

May didn't doubt that anything Mamie might have been, Doris had been first. Both the Clarks and the Maxwells lived in the handful of houses a mile or so west of the river known as Truro. It wasn't that Doris resented it; she seemed to take a personal pride in Donald's achievements. Like her sister, Clara, who had 2nd Night on the switchboard, Doris showed a quality which May Tupping could only describe as horrid. A good sample of it was the brazen use both of them made of a building company's calendar on the far wall, and minute pencil checks for a calculation which May felt violated decent reticences.

Disquieted, not liking her thoughts, either of the Clark girls, or of

Mamie's illness, or Mrs. Talbot's misery, May looked down now, read once more: "— *though with great difficulty I am got hither, yet now I do not repent me of all the trouble I have been at to arrive where I am* —" A kind of courage and sober cheerfulness seemed to come to her out of the fine plain words in simple succession. Looking through the window, she could see over the veranda rail, down the short slope of lawn under snow; then, the packed soiled snow of the uncleared side road; the snow, clean again, deep and undisturbed, blanketing the elongated trapezoid of the green. At the far corner, diagonally across from the carefully kept high hedges of the Bannings' place, was the old Congregational church, standing on the green itself. It was all white, with six tall multiple-paned windows on this side; four plain white columns on the front; and a steeple rising beautifully from two polygon lanterns. Down at this end was only a pedestal, lonely; and more lonely still, on top of it stood the stiff, a little less than life-size figure of a Civil War soldier.

While May looked now, into sight at the corner came a low gray car, traveling north very fast. Its top was down. It was occupied by a single fur-coated driver. Guy Banning, she recognized, up from college for the Washington's Birthday week end. He must have been going some, for two hours ago he was still in New Haven, telephoning his mother that he was coming. May watched the gray car pass all the way up the green, turn into the Bannings' hidden drive. Though Guy would probably have to think a minute to be sure of her name, it pleased May to consider how much she knew about him. She even knew all about the gray car. Although it had been built in Europe and had cost ten thousand dollars, Guy had managed to buy it from another Yale boy for only a few hundred. Getting gas at the garage, he told Harry Weems about it, and Harry told Joe, and Joe told her. Harry had gone over the engine and was ready to admit that it was a fine car; he'd never seen one to touch it. It was five or six years old, but it was so well made that it was just as good as new.

Her reflection was interrupted. Turning off US6W to pass right in front of her came a big scarlet truck. The closed doors of its cab bore the gold words *Interstate Light & Power Company*. May reached and plugged in 145. "Mr. Snyder," she said, over the bend of the Cobble to the power line construction camp, "that truck of yours is just going by now ... you're welcome."

She had hardly finished speaking when, distinct even indoors here, she heard the long arrogant whistle of a locomotive, warning motors which might be approaching the bad crossing US6W made a half mile north. That must be a freight train; and she concluded, glad to have something more to think about, that they would better side-track it. The evening train, upbound, ought to be already at Sansbury. She waited a minute, still looking out, and presently she saw the locomotive's voluminous plumes of steam jetting above the bare tree tops, an intenser white on the sharp snowy slope of the Cobble behind. The train itself she could not see because of the houses, the hedges and trees on the rise of ground to the east of the green. Very dimly, peals from a swinging bell reached her. Yes, she decided, relieved; they were going to side-track it. The puffing crash of steam expelled in new, laborious movement sounded. The round white plumes went back past the station roof.

Presently it would be dusk. At some point the western hill shadow, coming silently up the fields from the river, had reached the green. The slanting flood of sun diminished, finally was gone. It was perfectly light still, a sunless lucid light with no direct source. The sky was a hard northern blue; sun itself shone a bright sad orange on the crest of the Cobble. Increasing cold could be guessed from an elusive, fragile clarity of air in the valley shadows. By contrast, the heat about her permeated May; it seemed to sink to her bones, pleasurably, the way cold painfully does. She hoped it would stay there, that she could absorb it and carry it home and keep it in the cold of the kitchen. The kitchen floor was practically on the ground, and the inside of the walls had never been finished so you couldn't expect an oil cooking stove to help much. All the while she worked, May's hands were either aching with cold or seared with heat. She only hoped it would be warm in the living room where Joe had his bed.

On the switchboard the first position pilot light awoke. She cut off the buzzing, noted that it was 44. "Oh," said a surprised voice, "that you, May? Well, May, would you ring Doc Bull? Pa" — it was Sal Peters, down the river, and she seemed exasperated — "ain't a bit well —"

The plug went into 11 and, ringing, May listened, suddenly hopeful, meaning to mention Mrs. Talbot too, if he answered; or if Mrs. Cole had come back and knew where the doctor was. She rang it for a full minute. "I'm sorry, Mrs. Peters," she said. "Doctor Bull isn't there."

From *The Last Adam* by James Gould Cozzens. Harcourt Brace, 1922.

WPA GUIDE

In 1939 the Federal Writers' Project of the Works Progress Administration produced a still-useful guide to the Berkshires. The project's anonymous writers included innumerable lively stories as well as ably researched information.

Gold in the Berkshires

Gold in Berkshire! Gold in old Greylock, on its sides and back! Gold in its pockets and piled in masses on its shoulders! Gold in the town of *ADAMS!* GOLD! ... GOLD! ... GOLD! Words that have sent more than one man stumbling up the mountain trails, past the ruined hut of the old hermit who lived high up on the mountainside, back in the 1700's. Whenever he made one of his rare visits to the Adams general store, he paid for his purchases with nuggets and gold dust. When asked where he found the treasure, the old man would wink craftily. Or he would draw the questioner to one side. Then with his withered lips close to an eager ear, he would whisper, "I'll tell you next time. Ha! Ha! Ha!" The old hermit never told. There was a storm, a winter blizzard. After it was over, the old man was found frozen to death.

In the 1700's Greylock was not ready to yield the bright streak in its veins. Nor in the 1800's. The twentieth century finds it still reluctant. Experts have declared their belief in the existence of a mineral belt extending from the north down through New England into the Carolinas and Georgia, and Berkshire County lies directly in its path. But mining engineers unanimously agree that Greylock's gold is present in such small quantities that it would cost more than it is worth to get it out.

Through the years many Berkshire men have hacked into Greylock, and every one has come away disappointed. They left yawning holes in the mountain's sides — holes into which many of them poured their strength, their youth, and their money. There is a twenty-foot pit on the center slope of Greylock, still barely discernible, and higher up, the deep excavation made by the Quakers.

In 1901 the gold fever again rose high and the Greylock Mining and Milling Company was organized. Shares were sold to all comers — ten thousand of them at fifty cents a share. It was proposed that a shaft be sunk in the Notch on Greylock, and the gold in "them thar hills" was promised as a certainty to all investors. Although the futile venture cost shareholders five thousand dollars, undeterred residents dug a thirty-foot hole in 1916.

One seeker after riches found himself left with something far worse than poverty.

"Can you tell me what this is?" the fellow asked a distinguished Boston chemist. He held out a box of mineral specimens.

"Why, yes," replied the chemist lightly, "it's a box of iron pyrites."

"Pyrites? Well, what's it worth?"

"Oh, nothing, nothing at all," said the chemist, amused.

"Nothing!" There was agony in the cry. "Nothing! But, God bless my soul, sir, there's a woman back in my town who owns a whole hill of this stuff!"

"Well, you'd better warn her before she goes trying to mine it for gold. 'Fool's gold' is another name for iron pyrites, my friend," observed the expert. "Warn *her?*" the man groaned. "Why didn't someone warn *me*? I've gone and married her!"

From *The Berkshire Hills: A WPA Guide* by Members of the Federal Writers' Project of the Works Progress Administration. The Berkshire Hills Conference, 1939.

BARTLETT HENDRICKS

Bartlett Hendricks of Lanesborough was curator of natural history at the Berkshire Museum from 1932 until his retirement in 1989. One of the original organizers of skiing in the Berkshires in the '30s, pioneering skiing on Mt. Greylock's Thunderbolt Trail and at what is now Jiminy Peak, he loves exploring the Berkshires in all seasons.

Berkshire Dirt Roads

A Berkshire dirt road at its best offers a riding surface that in comfort and sheer pleasure no hard surface can equal. True, you should avoid most back roads in winter, and all of them during the spring thaw or at the time of one of our infrequent and never too serious summer droughts. But at all other times country roads can be explored not only because they are the means of reaching some of our brightest destinations but also for the stimulation that such driving can bring to a tired mind and a jaded imagination.

It isn't necessary to make your will before winding up the family buggy for an exploratory twirl of our secondary roads, but a few sensible precautions are advisable. Carry a pail or a large can. Wrap it in an old rug or burlap bag and place it in the storage trunk so it won't rattle. Even if your motor never gets thirsty on the hills, at least you can pick berries into the container. And while *you* will never be so unfortunate as to be stuck in the mud, the rug or burlap may prove handy should you have to change a tire. It is wise to have a short but stout plank to prevent your jack from sinking into soft ground, and twenty-five feet of strong rope is useful and may be the means by which you are able to tow another car to the nearest service station. Almost as important as your county map is a compass, preferably the type that fastens to the dashboard, if you expect to do most of your hiking within sight of your car. To supplement your map, get a set of the United States Geological Survey maps of Berkshire County. These are inexpensive and may be obtained from a few local stores or ordered from Washington. Put a flashlight in your glove compartment and carry binoculars and a camera, if you have them. Finally, as a last precaution, tape or wire an extra key on the outside of the car, hidden, but not where you can't remember where you put it.

Among some people who should know better, I have developed a modest reputation for my knowledge of our country roads. When they ride with me I simply barge along as though I knew all the time exactly where I was going. Although I can visualize the topography of the Berkshires well enough to have a general idea as to about where I am, I frequently haven't the foggiest notion of where I am headed or, indeed, from whence I have come. I have been known to arrive at the end of no fewer than six dead-end roads in a single day. This is hard to pass off, but I generally succeed by claiming that I knew it all the time but wanted to show the passengers the view.

All private and dead-end roads should be clearly marked, and all routes, even the most minor, should be identified, but until they are you can have the satisfaction of being an explorer. In your moments of indecision, remember Christopher Columbus; he didn't know where he was going, he had no idea where he was, and he hadn't the remotest knowledge of where he had been, but he had a whale of a time! And so can you. When I return from a new trip I mark the route in red on my map, and I derive much quiet pleasure from seeing the red lines grow and planning future trips to fresh territory.

From *The Berkshires*. Edited by Roderick Peattie. Vanguard Press, 1948.

Mount Greylock from Fred Mason Road, Cheshire. Courtesy of The Berkshire Eagle

ALBERT SPALDING

The first American violinist to gain a major international reputation, Albert Spalding (1888-1953), son of the co-founder of the sporting goods company, named his "small stone house" in Great Barrington "Aston Magna," from which the music festival takes its name.

"Hoboken of the Berkshires"

In 1925 Mary and I digressed from our usual habit of spending the summers in England. The magnet that deflected us was a small stone house hidden away under tall pine trees on the crest of one of the mountainous ridges of the Berkshire Hills in western Massachusetts. It had been built by Charles Freer of Detroit, the railroad magnate whose business successes had been only an apprenticeship to his real vocation — the study and collection of Oriental art, chiefly Chinese. The museum in Washington, D.C., which bears his name is the realization of that mission.

He was born in Kingston, New York, in circumstances bordering on actual poverty. His taste in art had its beginnings in a passionate love of the beauties of Nature. This particular hilltop — then a woody wilderness — had been the goal of many a trek to enjoy the lovely view that takes in the many miles of valley southward. This hill rises abruptly to the west of the town of Great Barrington, and, once you are deep in its forest fastness, it is difficult to believe that the varied activities of three or four thousand people are going on below.

Freer never lived to enjoy this home; he died when it was barely completed. It was left to his assistant and collaborator in his great collection, Katherine Rhoades, who is a warm friend of ours, and it was from her that we rented and eventually bought the house. After we saw it we never wanted to live anywhere else.

The house presents a modest appearance but has rooms of generous proportions. Though conveniently near the town, it feels remote from everything but Nature. Its greatest glory is its array of majestic pine trees, carefully stripped of their lower branches and approaching the sky before spreading their canopy of green shade. It is a place around which the circle of contentment has been drawn.

We found that most of our neighboring friends and acquaintances lived about eight miles to the north of us, in Stockbridge. They rather raised their eyebrows at the little industrial town of Great Barrington, and we were often chided on our imprudent choice. Midway between the two towns there is a miniature Alpine pass flanked by a rocky elevation called

Monument Mountain; Alexander Sedgwick called this "The Great Divide." Why had we put ourselves beyond the Divide? We patiently explained over and over again that it was the attraction of a particular site, a particular house, that had drawn us, rather than the choice of an elite community.

Albert Spalding at Aston Magna. Courtesy of The Berkshire Eagle

One day at luncheon I found myself next to a charming lady who militantly posed this question: "And just what prompted you, Mr. Spalding, to settle in Great Barrington?"

Having carelessly failed to catch the lady's name, I rashly replied: "I'm not sure. ... Perhaps merely to avoid Stockbridge!"

The temperature dropped suddenly, though I then had no idea why. But when I told Mary of this passage of arms — "And who," she demanded, torn between amusement and horror, "*who* did you think was talking to you?"

I didn't know. Who?

"Only a member of the Inner Circle of Stockbridge — Mrs. Sedgwick herself! Really, you *are* impossible!"

In time, owing to Mary's unfailing tact and Sedgwick magnanimity, we succeeded in living it down. We may have been granted, too, some of that special indulgence accorded to people who live in what I call the "Hoboken of the Berkshires."

Life in this pleasant, rolling countryside moves at a more leisurely pace than prevails in most of our other vacation areas. We used almost daily to round off the afternoon with some tennis. I was so bold, at about that time, as to enter my name in the annual club tournament. Now my tennis is respectable for a fiddler, though hardly of a quality to carry me far. But the participants that year were all only moderately good, and I had the luck to push through to the finals. At this point I met the previous year's holder, who played a soft but irritatingly steady game. He quickly had me facing defeat. The score was one set and five games to two in his favor. Perhaps a little too sure of his victory, my opponent unconsciously relaxed a little; at the same time I lashed out with the sort of shots that come off only occasionally. Luck was with me, however, and those shots found the lines and the corners, where formerly they had been going wild. Much to my surprise, I won the match.

This minor triumph had an amusing sequel. The win was, apparently, a popular one, particularly with Joyce, the club steward. And he saw to it the following season that I had one of the best lockers, and busied himself as an unexpected press-agent on my behalf. One day I heard him being interviewed over the telephone by the local correspondent of the *New York Times*. After covering the golfing news, he conveyed this amazing intelligence: "Mr. Spalding has just come in from the tennis courts; he is our best player!" (A gross exaggeration; this year there were any number of better players.) "Yes, the name is S-P-A-L-D-I-N-G .... Yes — Mr. *Albert* Spalding .... Yes — I believe he does play the violin, too ...."

When I told Bill Tilden this story he could not resist using it — probably elaborating it. As it got retold, my victory gained in size appallingly and I acquired an altogether unjustified reputation for tennis prowess. When ultimately it reached *Time Magazine*, I was astonished to learn that I was the New England champion! It is quite impossible to stem this kind of avalanche. Denials are of no use; they merely create firmer belief.

The summers came always too swiftly to a close. Once the days begin to shorten, time seems to telescope itself, and before you know it another concert season is at hand.

From *Rise to Follow* by Albert Spalding. Henry Holt & Co., 1946.

THEODORE GIDDINGS

Theodore Giddings, Berkshire newspaperman and sportsman whose columns on hunting and fishing have appeared for over four decades in the Berkshire Eagle, *lives in Lenox.*

Hop Brook

West of Otis is Tyringham, and north of it is Becket, where two of the best streams in the Central Berkshire District patrolled by Conservation Officer Almon H. Griffin are found. Mr. Griffin rates the Hop Brook in Tyringham and the west branch of the Westfield River in Becket among the five top trout waters in his territory. The others are Muddy Brook, Stockbridge; Greenwater Brook, Lee; and Cone Brook, Richmond. Mr. Griffin's bases in selecting these streams are: good water, high food content, natural reproduction evident, good carry-over of trout from year to year, and high creel census.

Stocked with brook trout, Hop Brook comes into Tyringham from Otis and picks up sixteen small feeder streams as it flows westerly into Lee, where it joins the Housatonic River. A landmark on the brook is the Steadman Rake Shop, operated until recently by the same family for five generations. Since Garfield, nearly every president of the United States has been presented a Steadman rake. Two rakes were given to President Coolidge while he was visiting his family's farm at Plymouth, Vermont.

"Handmade of native hickory," said Congressman Allen T. Treadway of Stockbridge as he passed the rakes over to Mr. Coolidge.

"This part's ash," replied the President dryly, as he ran his hand carefully over the handle.

A classic "local angle" headline appeared in the *Berkshire Eagle* one day. "May Have Fished Here," it read, telling of some notable person who had made news that day. The person was not President Cleveland, because he actually did "fish here" — in Hop Brook. President Cleveland's wife, Frances Folsom, was a friend of Richard Watson Gilder, editor of *Scribner's Magazine,* who built Four Brooks Farm in Tyringham in 1898. While the Clevelands were guests of the Gilders at the farm, the President went fishing and is reported to have had good luck.

Conservation Officer Griffin's district was patrolled for many years by the late William W. Sargood of Lee, affectionately known by Berkshire sportsmen as "Uncle Bill." He and Fred R. Ziegler of Pittsfield and Arthur M. Nichols of North Adams were among the pioneer "game wardens" in the county. One of Mr. Sargood's favorite stories concerned a Tyringham incident. "Uncle Bill" was looking over the streams one day shortly before the trout season opened when he came upon a boy fishing in a pool. The youngster had a pole in his hand and pulled the line out of the water to show the law enforcement officer that there was nothing on it.

"Catch anything?" inquired "Uncle Bill."

"Nope," replied the juvenile. "There's a big sucker in here but he won't bite."

"What's that other line over there?" asked the game warden, pointing to a taut line tied onto a twig and extending out into the pool.

"Oh, nothing much," the youth answered nervously. "Well, let's see, just for the fun of it," suggested "Uncle Bill."

He walked over and pulled in the line, which had a deeply-hooked brook trout on it.

"Don't you know that it is against the law to catch trout now?" said Mr. Sargood reproachfully.

"Yes, I do," replied the boy. "But you see, every time I tried to catch the big sucker, that trout kept stealing the worm off my hook. So I caught him and tied him up there, and I was goin' to let him go as soon as I caught the sucker."

From *The Berkshires*. Edited by Roderick Peattie. Vanguard Press, 1948.

Marshall W. Steadman at Steadman Rake Factory. Tyringham, c. 1930. Berkshire County Historical Society Collection

MORGAN BULKELEY

Naturalist, essayist, and poet, Morgan Bulkeley formerly farmed in the town of Mount Washington and for many years wrote a popular column on country life for the Berkshire Eagle. *He now lives in Pittsfield.*

Down, Once Up

Where woods have shaded out the apple trees,
You've seen a long-deserted cellar hole,
Half-choked with tumbled rock and raspberries,
Spilling mats of lilies on the knoll.

Like sunken grave, it makes a mournful scar
That many forces are at work to fill:
Leaves, rain, the prying root, the cold crowbar
Of frost, the woodchuck's paw, all work downhill.

Once things went up, like the small boy
Reluctantly exploring in the dark,
Guarding his candle like a precious toy;
He'd sooner lose his life than lose its spark.

But he'd not be a laughing-stock.
Beneath the spidery beams, he took the dares
And plunged his arm into the icy crock
To seize some pork for greens — and ran upstairs.

From *Mountain Farm* by Morgan Bulkeley. Hollow Spring Press, 1985.

KATHARINE ANNIN

Katharine Huntington Annin's weekly columns in the Berkshire Eagle *delighted readers for over thirty years. This is the last one she wrote.*

By Buckboard to England Brothers

Richmond, December 1, 1987

I suppose there are not too many people around Pittsfield now whose memories of North Street go back as far as mine do, but I have been thinking back to my early childhood when my family first began spending summers in Richmond.

Doing errands in Pittsfield involved an all-day expedition. We would drive to a shed in West Pittsfield where we could leave our horse and buckboard while we proceeded by the trolley into town. (The trolley line was supposedly going to be continued, a few miles each year, but the increasing number of automobiles put an end to that project.)

By the time we got to North Street it was lunch time, and fortunately England's had a very nice restaurant on its top floor. We would try to get a table by one of the rear windows where we could look down over the railroad tracks and Jubilee Hill. Then we would proceed with our shopping up and down North Street, accumulating our packages in a convenient walk-in area with a lot of shelves near England's front door. Nobody seemed to mind if bundles we temporarily left there came from Wallace's, Kennedy and McGinnis, or Holden and Stone across the street, or from Kelsey's grocery for that matter.

The drug store, which I think was always next to England's, supplied us with a refreshing ice-cream soda before we started home, and if that store didn't have whatever pharmaceutical item we were looking for we could probably find it by walking a block farther up the street to Bence's. We would be well loaded with bundles by the time we stood on the sidewalk waiting for the trolley car that would take us back to our horse and buckboard in West Pittsfield.

I sometimes wondered whether Star (named for the white spot on his forehead), ever wondered where we had been. One last errand would be to get some meat or fish from Mr. Chojnowski, whose store stood just at the end of the track where the trolley turned around. Otherwise, we would have to wait for the one day a week when his wagon came through Richmond and stopped at our door.

From *The Berkshire Eagle*, December 1, 1987.

BURTON BERNSTEIN

For half a century, Leonard Bernstein never failed to ignite excitement at Tanglewood. It was there in the shed, now named for his mentor of 50 years before, that he made his last public appearance on the podium, two months before his death on October 14, 1990. Here his brother Burton recalls "Lenny's" first summers at Koussevitzky's Berkshire Music Center.

Bernstein at Tanglewood

Of equal professional importance were the next two summers. Serge Koussevitzky and the Boston Symphony had been presenting concerts for several summers at Tanglewood, an estate in the Berkshires bequeathed to the orchestra, and in 1940 Koussevitzky inaugurated the Berkshire Music Center as an adjunct to Tanglewood. According to his plan, worthy young musicians of various disciplines would study with a distinguished faculty in pleasant natural surroundings; student conductors — an elite few, supervised by Koussevitzky himself — would actually practice their skills with a full-size student orchestra. Thanks to strong letters of recommendation, Lenny was chosen as one of three student conductors in the inaugural year. Falling under the spell of Koussevitzky (whose expressive nineteenth-century manner affected even the groundskeepers of Tanglewood), Lenny was soaring from the start, as a letter home, written soon after his arrival there, indicates:

Dearest Folks —

... I have never seen such a beautiful setup in my life. I've been conducting the orchestra every morning, & I'm playing my first concert tomorrow night. Kouss gave me the hardest & longest number of all — the Second Symphony of Randall Thompson. 30 minutes long — a modern American work — as my first performance. And Kouss is so pleased with my work. He likes me & works very hard with me in our private sessions. He is the most marvelous man — a beautiful spirit that never lags or fails — that inspires me terrifically. And he told me he is convinced that I have a wonderful gift, & he is already making me a great conductor. (I actually rode in his car with him today!) He has wonderful teaching ability, which I never expected — & is very hard to please — so that when he says he is pleased I know it means something. I am so thrilled — have never been more happy & satisfied. The orchestra likes me very much, best of all the conductors, & responds so beautifully in rehearsal. Of course, the concert tomorrow night (Shabbas, yet!) will tell whether I can keep my head in performance. We've been working very hard — you're always going like mad here — no time to think of how tired you are or how little you slept last night — the inspiration of this Center is terrific enough to keep you going with no sleep at all. I'm so excited about tomorrow night — I wish you could all be here — it's so important to me — & Kouss is banking on it to convince him that he's right — if it goes well there's no telling what may happen ...

Please come up — I think I'll be conducting every Friday night & rehearsing every morning — please come up —

All my love —

Lenny

Jennie was beside herself with pleasure, and even Sam couldn't help feeling stirrings of pride in his son, the apparent favorite of Koussevitzky. But who was this Koussevitzky, so rapidly becoming another father to Lenny, usurping Sam's rightful place? Sam knew that Koussevitzky, like him, had been born a Russian Jew, but, unlike Sam, had converted to Christianity in order to further his musical career in the motherland. What kind of man was this, who would do such a thing? And would he try to convert Lenny in order to further his career? (Sam didn't know it then, but Koussevitzky was already hinting to his Lenyushka that Leonard S. Burns would be a more presentable name for a conductor, the "S" being for Samuelovich. Lenny thought about it for a while and then put the idea out of his mind.) Sam needn't have worried about his son's Jewishness, which was so irrevocably a part of him that even Koussevitzky had no influence on it. Indeed, just the previous year Lenny had begun to compose a piece for soprano and orchestra based on the Book of Lamentations, and it was dedicated to "my father." There was nachas for you! But still Sam felt jealous, indignant, and, worst of all, impotent. Lenny was being lost to him, and there wasn't much he could do about it — except control the purse strings. When Sam finally drove Jennie, Shirley, and me to Tanglewood from Sharon, it was obvious that everything Lenny had said in his letter was true. The place seemed to have been invented for him alone.

There followed another rigorous year at Curtis and another glorious summer at Tanglewood, at which Lenny was clearly recognized as *the* protege of Koussevitzky — perhaps someday, it was rumored, the heir, if the board of trustees of the Boston Symphony could ever defy tradition and appoint a young American as conductor. It was only a fantasy rumor, not to be seriously discussed. And with the draft, Lenny's career would likely take a military turn. However, at his first Army physical he was classified 4-F because of chronic asthma. (The Army doctor who thus deferred him happened to be a celebrated asthma specialist.) It was humiliating and frustrating for Lenny not to be in uniform while just about everybody else was preparing for war, but there was nothing to be done.

In the fall of 1941, he was a twenty-three-year-old trained and promising musician with no place to go. He returned to Boston, where the gray presence of the Samuel Bernstein Hair Company hung heavily in the air. Koussevitzky tried his best to help. He arranged to have Lenny play as soloist in the Boston Symphony's premiere of a piano concerto by Carlos Chavez, but union problems cancelled the performance. In desperation, Lenny wangled enough money out of Sam to rent a drafty studio on Huntington Avenue, and he sent out announcements that he was available as a piano teacher. Sam assumed that this venture would fail — making Lenny a candidate once again for his business, just a couple of miles away — and Sam was right. Lenny's studio came into formal existence just two days before Pearl Harbor was attacked, and piano lessons were not top public priority that week. He was rejected by the military, by piano students, and, it seemed, by the entire world. He worked on his compositions (a clarinet sonata and the Lamentations piece), played a few minor-league concerts, and took some encouragement from his close relationship with Koussevitzky. One notable bright spot during the dreary winter was the appearance of Adolph Green and Betty Comden as performers in "My Dear Public," a calamitous musical by the composer-lyricist Irving Caesar, which was trying out in Boston. It was the first professional theater I had ever seen, and it baffled my ten-year-old mind no less than it did the adult audience's. I can safely say that from its opening number to its finale, nobody knew for sure what was happening on stage. (Irving Caesar was also the author of the enigmatic words for the song "Tea for Two.")

The summer of 1942 brought some cheer. Lenny returned to Tanglewood (its last full season for the duration) not as a student but as the assistant to Koussevitzky, with teaching responsibilities. But when the summer ended he was back in the bind. Reopening the Huntington Avenue studio would be flirting with fiscal and emotional disaster so he tried New York again, a last stab at the big time. New York was even grimmer than Boston. It marked a period that Lenny has referred to as "my Valley Forge." From a cheap furnished room, he went forth looking for work, any work. What he found was the occasional odd job: vocal coach, rehearsal pianist, dollar-an-hour piano teacher, and — to contribute to the war effort — performer for the soldiers at Fort Dix, New Jersey. Through the auspices of Irving Caesar, he landed a steady twenty-five-dollar-a-week position with a music publisher, transcribing jazz improvisations, arranging songs for piano, and writing original pop tunes, under the name "Lenny Amber." That job at least rescued him from the ultimate defeat of returning to Boston and Sam's business. He had some money to live on and some time to compose. His piece for soprano and orchestra, based on the Book of Lamentations, had developed into the "Jeremiah Symphony." He entered it in a competition for American music which was sponsored by the New England Conservatory, but it didn't win the prize, and, worse yet, Koussevitzky didn't think much of it. But it won some points with Sam, who relished its Jewish thematic material and its dedication to him.

Although there was no formal Tanglewood season the following summer, Koussevitzky was spending the warm months at his estate, Seranak, overlooking the Tanglewood grounds. He invited Lenny to visit and help him with a benefit there for the Red Cross. Lenny, his prospects apparently no brighter, arrived at Seranak on the day before his twenty-fifth birthday and was informed by Koussevitzky that Artur Rodzinski, the recently appointed music director of the New York Philharmonic, wished to see him. Rodzinski owned a farm in nearby Stockbridge, where Lenny met the conductor on his birthday morning. They chatted amiably in an asthma-inducing hayfield, while the wheezing Lenny wondered why he had been summoned. At last, it was made clear. Rodzinski abruptly declared that he had seen Lenny conduct the Tanglewood student orchestra the summer before, and he had since come to believe that Lenny would be right for the post of assistant conductor of the New York Philharmonic. Besides, said Rodzinski, who was a confirmed Buchmanite and claimed to communicate directly with the Lord, God had told him to "take Bernstein." One did not argue with divine intervention. Lenny became the assistant conductor of the Philharmonic, without so much as an audition before a professional orchestra. It was one hell of a birthday present.

From *Family Matters* by Burton Bernstein. Simon & Schuster, 1982.

THOMAS WHITBREAD

Thomas Whitbread grew up in Cummington. He teaches English at the University of Texas.

Country Blessing

I know how it must be, anywhere
In the United States, where through roads run
Through villages. I was a child in one,
Paper Mill Village, village without a square,
With one paved road, Route 9, going everywhere
In two directions, toward West Cummington
Or else East Windsor. I knew all the fun
It was possible to have bicycling there.

And I knew there, and know how it must be
Anywhere, in bed, tucked in, early at night,
To wait, awake, awaiting, before sleep,
The incontestable future, adult, free,
And far-seeing, in the lights, brilliantly bright,
Of the nine o'clock bus going by my soul to keep.

From *Four Infinitives* by Thomas Whitbread. Harper & Row, 1964.

WILLIAM CARLOS WILLIAMS

Katharine Frazier, a concert artist who taught at Smith and Mount Holyoke, in 1923 established the Cummington School (later Community) of the Arts near the Bryant Homestead in Cummington. Among those who worked there were Alan Hovhaness, Marianne Moore, Alan Tate, Malcolm Cowley, Robert Pack, Diane Arbus, William de Kooning, and Helen Frankenthaler.

In 1939 Frazier invited poet and graphic designer Harry Duncan to establish a press at the school. Duncan developed the Cummington Press into one of the finest hand-press imprints, publishing now-much-sought-after editions of such writers as Wallace Stevens, Robert Lowell, Rainer Maria Rilke, R.P. Blackmur, and William Carlos Williams. In this letter to Stevens, Williams relates his visit to Duncan. Later Duncan moved the press to the University of Iowa.

Harry Duncan and the Cummington Press

July 24, 1944

Dear Wally:

My vacation for this year is past and I passed through Hartford (standing) about a month ago on my way to Bennington College to talk to the girls there who laughed so hard I could hardly finish the poem. But they were nice. Maybe later in the season I'll be in Connecticut again. If ever I am there again I will look you up for I'd like very much to see you.

I have a small book of verse being brought out by the boys at Cummington. I had never met Duncan so stopped off there on my way to Bennington. He is very earnest and makes very attractive books. Have you ever been there? If not, go — when you want to get away from things — you'll enjoy the people and the place: the birthplace of William Cullen Bryant, completely off the earth. A hell of a place to get to. Train to Northampton then bus from there to Cummington, then walk up the mountain. I took a taxi rather than wait four hours for the bus — and drew a very nice girl driver in a black dress. Ask her if she remembers me.

    Sincerely,
    Bill

From *Selected Letters of William Carlos Williams*. Edited by John C. Thirlwall. Astor-Honor, 1957.

JAMES THURBER

New Yorker *humorist James Thurber (1894-1961) lived in Cornwall, Connecticut, on the Housatonic branch of the New York, New Haven, and Hartford Railroad, which he makes the setting of this parody of World War II spy movies.*

The Lady on 142

The train was twenty minutes late, we found out when we bought our tickets, so we sat down on a bench in the little waiting room of the Cornwall Bridge station. It was too hot outside in the sun. This midsummer Saturday had got off to a sulky start, and now, at three in the afternoon, it sat, sticky and restive, in our laps.

There were several others besides Sylvia and myself waiting for the train to get in from Pittsfield: a colored woman who fanned herself with a *Daily News*, a young lady in her twenties reading a book, a slender, tanned man sucking dreamily on the stem of an unlighted pipe. In the centre of the room, leaning against a high iron radiator, a small girl stared at each of us in turn, her mouth open, as if she had never seen people before. The place had the familiar, pleasant smell of railroad stations in the country, of something compounded of wood and leather and smoke. In the cramped space behind the ticket window, a telegraph instrument clicked intermittently, and once or twice a phone rang and the station-master answered it briefly. I couldn't hear what he said.

I was glad, on such a day, that we were going only as far as Gaylordsville, the third stop down the line, twenty-two minutes away. The stationmaster had told us that our tickets were the first tickets to Gaylordsville he had ever sold. I was idly pondering this small distinction when a train whistle blew in the distance. We all got to our feet, but the stationmaster came out of his cubbyhole and told us it was not our train but the 12:45 from New York, northbound. Presently the train thundered in like a hurricane and sighed ponderously to a stop. The stationmaster went out onto the platform and came back after a minute or two. The train got heavily under way again, for Canaan.

I was opening a pack of cigarettes when I heard the stationmaster talking on the phone again. This time his words came out clearly. He kept repeating one sentence. He was saying, "Conductor Reagan on 142 has the lady the office was asking about." The person on the other end of the line did not appear to get the meaning of the sentence. The stationmaster repeated it and hung up. For some reason, I figured that he did not understand it either.

Sylvia's eyes had the lost, reflective look they wear when she is trying to remember in what box she packed the Christmas-tree ornaments. The expressions on the faces of the colored woman, the young lady, and the man with the pipe had not changed. The little staring girl had gone away.

Our train was not due for another five minutes, and I sat back and began trying to reconstruct the lady on 142, the lady Conductor Reagan had, the lady the office was asking about. I moved nearer to Sylvia and whispered, "See if the trains are numbered in your timetable." She got the timetable out of her handbag and looked at it. "One forty-two," she said, "is the 12:45 from New York." This was the train that had gone by a few minutes before. "The woman was taken sick," said Sylvia. "They are probably arranging to have a doctor or her family meet her."

The colored woman looked around at her briefly. The young woman, who had been chewing gum, stopped chewing. The man with the pipe seemed oblivious. I lighted a cigarette and sat thinking. "The woman on 142," I said to Sylvia, finally, "might be almost anything, but she definitely is not sick." The only person who did not stare at me was the man with the pipe. Sylvia gave me her temperature-taking look, a cross between anxiety and vexation. Just then our train whistled and we all stood up. I picked up our two bags and Sylvia took the sack of string beans we had picked for the Connells.

When the train came clanking in, I said in Sylvia's ear, "He'll sit near us. You watch." "Who? Who will?" she said. "The stranger," I told her, "the man with the pipe."

Sylvia laughed. "He's not a stranger," she said. "He works for the Breeds." I was certain that he didn't. Women like to place people; every stranger reminds them of somebody.

The man with the pipe was sitting three seats in front of us, across the aisle, when we got settled. I indicated him with a nod of my head. Sylvia took a book out of the top of her overnight bag and opened it. "What's the matter with you?" she demanded. I looked around before replying. A sleepy man and woman sat across from us. Two middle-aged women in the seat in front of us were discussing the severe griping pain one of them had experienced as the result of an inflamed diverticulum. A slim, dark-eyed young woman sat in the seat behind us. She was alone.

"The trouble with women," I began, "is that they explain everything by illness. I have a theory that we would be celebrating the twelfth of May or even the sixteenth of April as Independence Day if Mrs. Jefferson hadn't got the idea her husband had a fever and put him to bed."

Sylvia found her place in the book. "We've been all through that before," she said. "Why couldn't the woman on 142 be sick?"

That was easy, I told her. "Conductor Reagan," I said, "got off the train at Cornwall Bridge and spoke to the stationmaster. 'I've got the woman the office was asking about,' he said."

Sylvia cut in. "He said 'lady.'"

I gave the little laugh that annoys her. "All conductors say 'lady,'" I explained. "Now, if a woman had got sick on the train, Reagan would have said, 'A woman got sick on my train. Tell the office.' What must have happened is that Reagan found, somewhere between Kent and Cornwall Bridge, a woman the office had been looking for."

Sylvia didn't close her book, but she looked up. "Maybe she got sick before she got on the train, and the office was worried," said Sylvia. She was not giving the problem close attention.

"If the office knew she got on the train," I said patiently, "they wouldn't have asked Reagan to let them know if he found her. They would have told him about her when she got on." Sylvia resumed her reading.

"Let's stay out of it," she said. "It isn't any of our business."

I hunted for my Chiclets but couldn't find them. "It might be everybody's business," I said, "every patriot's."

"I know, I know," said Sylvia. "You think she's a spy. Well, I still think she's sick."

I ignored that. "Every conductor on the line has been asked to look out for her," I said. "Reagan found her. She won't be met by her family. She'll be met by the FBI."

"Or the OPA," said Sylvia. "Alfred Hitchcock things don't happen on the New York, New Haven & Hartford."

I saw the conductor coming from the other end of the coach. "I'm going to tell the conductor," I said, "that Reagan on 142 has got the woman."

"No, you're not," said Sylvia. "You're not going to get us mixed up in this. He probably knows anyway."

The conductor, short, stocky, silvery-haired, and silent, took up our tickets. He looked like a kindly Ickes. Sylvia, who had stiffened, relaxed when I let him go by without a word about the woman on 142. "He looks exactly as if he knew where the Maltese Falcon is hidden, doesn't he?" said Sylvia, with the laugh that annoys me.

"Nevertheless," I pointed out, "you said a little while ago that he probably knows about the woman on 142. If she's just sick, why should they tell the conductor on *this* train? I'll rest more easily when I know that they've actually got her."

Sylvia kept on reading as if she hadn't heard me. I leaned my head against the back of the seat and closed my eyes.

A summer afternoon train from Stockbridge to New York. Clemens Kalischer

The train was slowing down noisily and a brakeman was yelling "Kent! Kent!" when I felt a small, cold pressure against my shoulder. "Oh," the voice of the woman in the seat behind me said, "I've dropped my copy of *Coronet* under your seat." She leaned closer and her voice became low and hard. "Get off here, Mister," she said.

"We're going to Gaylordsville," I said.

"You and your wife are getting off here, Mister," she said.

I reached for the suitcases on the rack. "What do you want, for heaven's sake?" asked Sylvia.

"We're getting off here," I told her.

"Are you *really* crazy?" she demanded. "This is only Kent."

"Come on, sister," said the woman's voice. "You take the overnight bag and the beans. You take the big bag, Mister."

Sylvia was furious. "I *knew* you'd get us into this," she said to me, "shouting about spies at the top of your voice."

That made me angry. "You're the one that mentioned spies," I told her. "I didn't."

"You kept talking about it and talking about it," said Sylvia.

"Come on, get off, the two of you," said the cold, hard voice.

We got off. As I helped Sylvia down the steps, I said, "We know too much."

"Oh, shut up," she said.

We didn't have far to go. A big black limousine waited a few steps away. Behind the wheel sat a heavy-set foreigner with cruel lips and small eyes. He scowled when he saw us. "The boss don't want nobody up deh," he said.

"It's all right, Karl," said the woman. "Get in," she told us.

We climbed into the back seat. She sat between us, with the gun in her hand. It was a handsome, jewelled derringer.

"Alice will be waiting for us at Gaylordsville," said Sylvia, "in all this heat."

The house was a long, low, rambling building, reached at the end of a poplar-lined drive. "Never mind the bags," said the woman. Sylvia took the string beans and her book and we got out. Two huge mastiffs came bounding off the terrace, snarling. "Down, Mata!" said the woman. "Down, Pedro!" They slunk away, still snarling.

Sylvia and I sat side by side on a sofa in a large, handsomely appointed living room. Across from us, in a chair, lounged a tall man with heavily lidded black eyes and long, sensitive fingers. Against the door through which we had entered the room leaned a thin, undersized young man, with his hands in the pockets of his coat and a cigarette hanging from his lower lip. He had a drawn, sallow face and his small, half-closed eyes stared at us incuriously. In a corner of the room, a squat, swarthy man twiddled with the dials of a radio. The woman paced up and down, smoking a cigarette in a long holder.

"Well, Gail," said the lounging man in a soft voice, "to what do we owe thees unexpected visit?"

Gail kept pacing. "They got Sandra," she said finally.

The lounging man did not change expression. "Who got Sandra, Gail?" he asked softly.

"Reagan, on 142," said Gail.

The squat, swarthy man jumped to his feet. "All da time Egypt say keel dees Reagan!" he shouted. "All da time Egypt say bomp off dees Reagan!"

The lounging man did not look at him. "Sit down, Egypt," he said quietly. The swarthy man sat down. Gail went on talking.

"The punk here shot off his mouth," she said. "He was wise." I looked at the man leaning against the door.

"She means you," said Sylvia, and laughed.

"The dame was dumb," Gail went on. "She thought the lady on the train was sick."

I laughed. "She means you," I said to Sylvia.

"The punk was blowing his top all over the train," said Gail. "I had to bring 'em along."

Sylvia, who had the beans on her lap, began breaking and stringing them. "Well, my dear lady," said the lounging man, "a mos' homely leetle tawtch."

"Wozza totch?" demanded Egypt.

"Touch," I told him.

Gail sat down in a chair. "Who's going to rub 'em out?" she asked.

"Freddy," said the lounging man. Egypt was on his feet again.

"Na! Na!" he shouted. "Na da ponk! Da ponk bomp off da las' seex, seven peop'!"

The lounging man looked at him. Egypt paled and sat down.

"I thought you were the punk," said Sylvia. I looked at her coldly.

"I know where I have seen you before," I said to the lounging man. "It was at Zagreb in 1927. Tilden took you in straight sets, six-love, six-love, six-love."

The man's eyes glittered. "I theenk I bomp off thees man myself," he said.

Freddy walked over and handed the lounging man an automatic. At this moment, the door Freddy had been leaning against burst open and in rushed the man with the pipe, shouting, "Gail! Gail! Gail!" ...

"Gaylordsville! Gaylordsville!" bawled the brakeman. Sylvia was shaking me by the arm. "Quit moaning," she said. "Everybody is looking at you." I rubbed my forehead with a handkerchief. "Hurry up!" said Sylvia. "They don't stop here long." I pulled the bags down and we got off.

"Have you got the beans?" I asked Sylvia.

Alice Connell was waiting for us. On the way to their home in the car, Sylvia began to tell Alice about the woman on 142. I didn't say anything.

"He thought she was a spy," said Sylvia.

They both laughed. "She probably got sick on the train," said Alice. "They were probably arranging for a doctor to meet her at the station."

"That's just what I told him," said Sylvia.

I lighted a cigarette. "The lady on 142," I said firmly, "was definitely not sick."

"Oh, Lord," said Sylvia, "here we go again."

From *The Thurber Carnival* by James Thurber. Harper & Row, 1975.

JAMES MACGREGOR BURNS

Pulitzer-Prize-winning historian James MacGregor Burns is Woodrow Wilson Professor of Government Emeritus at Williams College.

Shays's Rebellion

Western Massachusetts, late January 1787. Down the long sloping shoulders of the Berkshire Mountains they headed west through the bitter night, stumbling over frozen ruts, picking their way around deep drifts of snow. Some carried muskets, others hickory clubs, others nothing. Many wore old Revolutionary War uniforms, now decked out with the sprig of hemlock that marked them as rebels. Careless and cocksure they had been, but now gall and despair hung over them as heavy as the enveloping night. They and hundreds like them were fleeing for their lives, looking for places to hide.

These men were rebels against ex-rebels. Only a few years before, they had been fighting the redcoats at Bunker Hill, joining General Stark in the rout of the enemy at Bennington, helping young Colonel Henry Knox's troops pull fifty tons of cannon and mortars, captured from the British at Ticonderoga, across these same frozen wastes. They had fought in comradeship with men from Boston and other towns in the populous east. All had been revolutionaries together, in a glorious and victorious cause. Now they were fighting their old comrades, dying before their cannon, hunting for cover like animals.

The trouble had been brewing for years. Life had been hard enough during the Revolution, but independence had first brought a flush of prosperity, then worse times than ever. The people and their governments alike struggled under crushing debts. Much of the Revolutionary specie was hopelessly irredeemable. People were still paying for the war through steep taxes. The farmers in central and western Massachusetts felt they had suffered the most, for their farms, cattle, even their plows could be taken for unpaid debts. Some debtors had been thrown into jail and had languished there, while family and friends desperately scrounged for money that could not be found.

Out of the despair and suffering a deep hatred had welled in the broad farms along the Connecticut and the settlements in the Berkshires. Hatred for the sheriffs and other minions of the law who flung neighbors into jail. Hatred for the judges who could sign orders that might wipe out a man's entire property. Hatred for the scheming lawyers who connived in all this, and battened on it. Hatred above all for the rich people in

Boston, the merchants and bankers who seemed to control the governor
and the state legislature. No single leader mobilized this hatred. Farmers
and laborers rallied around local men with names like Job Shattuck, Eli
Parsons, Luke Day. Dan Shays emerged as the most visible leader, but the
uprising was as natural and indigenous as any peasants' revolt in Europe.
The malcontents could not know that history would call them members
of "Shays's Rebellion." They called themselves Regulators.

Their tactic was simple: close up the courts. Time and again, during
the late summer and early fall of 1786, roughhewn men by the hundreds
crowded into or around courthouses, while judges and sheriffs stood by
seething and helpless. The authorities feared to call out the local militia,
knowing the men would desert in droves. Most of the occupations were
peaceful, even jocular and festive, reaching a high point when debtors
were turned out of jail. Most of these debtors were proud men, property
owners, voters. They had served as soldiers and junior officers in the
Revolution. They were seeking to redress grievances, not to topple governments. Some men of substance — doctors, deacons, even judges —
backed the Regulators; many poor persons feared the uprisings. But in
general, a man's property and source of income placed him on one side or
the other. Hence the conflict divided town and country officials, neighbors, even families.

Then, as the weather turned bitter in the late fall, so did the mood of
the combatants. The attitude of the authorities shifted from the impla-
cable to the near-hysterical. Alarmists exaggerated the strength of the
Regulators. Rumors flew about that Boston or some other eastern town
would be attacked. A respectable Bostonian reported that "We are now in
a State of anarchy and confusion bordering on a Civil War." Boston
propagandists spread reports that British agents in Canada were secretly
backing the rebels. So the Regulators were now treasonable as well as
illegal. The state suspended habeas corpus and raised an army, but lack-
ing public funds had to turn to local "gentlemen" for loans to finance it.
An anonymous dissident responded in kind:

"This is to lett the gentellmen of Boston [know?] that wee Country
men will not pay taxes, as the think," he wrote Governor Bowdoin in a
crude, scrawling hand. "But Lett them send the Constabel to us and we'll
nock him down for ofering to come near us. If you Dont lower the taxes
we'll pull down the town house about you ears. It shall not stand long
then or else they shall be blood spilt. We country men will not be imposed
on. We fought of our Libery as well as you did...."

From *Vineyard of Liberty* by James MacGregor Burns. Alfred A. Knopf, 1982.

CHRISTOPHER RAND

Journalist Christopher Rand (1912-1968) was the son of the distinguished portrait painter Ellen Emmet Rand of Salisbury, Connecticut, and the cousin of playwright Robert Emmet Sherwood, whose mother lived in Stockbridge. He was a staff writer for the New Yorker, *where his study of the southern Berkshires,* The Changing Landscape, *first appeared.*

Berkshire Iron Industry

My cabin home of last summer — on the plateau where join the New York, Connecticut, and Massachusetts borders — was especially near two features of that height, called Bear Mountain and Sage's Ravine. The brook by my cabin fed into the latter. The brook itself was small; I could nearly step across it, and its trout seemed rarely to grow beyond five inches long. Yet Sage's Ravine, a half mile lower, to the east, was a big and awesome thing, with falls and rapids plunging into deep, dark pools — creating a moist, mysterious, cool atmosphere in the shade of ancient hemlocks. One imagined that the stream had been working there forever, wearing down the stone. In the Ravine's upper part the water was baffled again and again by rocks, but lower down it fell more sharply — so steeply that one could hardly follow it on foot. In that lower part it had cut a deep magnificent V-shaped gorge; it was, in fact, still cutting it, for the gorge's sides were lined with avalanches, with fallen — undermined — old trees, and with wild new growth arising in their places. The Ravine followed the Connecticut-Massachusetts line and made a thorough division between those states — more distinct, by far, than political boundaries elsewhere in that wilderness. And also, dropping swiftly a thousand feet, it linked the heights to the lowlands stretching off around them.

Bear Mountain, the other nearby feature, rose steeply to the Ravine's south — the brook-bank climbing past my cabin went on upward, at a good angle, to join the mountain's flank. The mountain's summit was a dome of rock, which throughout my childhood, and much earlier, had always been called the highest point in Connecticut. That honor had since been stripped away by some debunking surveyor, who had pronounced a nearby hillside, rising into Massachusetts, a few feet higher where it crossed the border. Yet still Bear Mountain looked higher than that other point, and it was far grander and had a better view. It also boasted a monument, a big tower of dark stones tapering inward, like Tibetan architecture, as it rose. The tower, which could be seen for miles in all directions, bore a plaque saying it stood on Connecticut's "highest ground" and had been built in 1885 by a certain Owen Travis. Early in the summer Owen Travis was just a name to me, but later I found that he had been a celebrated mason in the nineteenth-century community, long since vanished, on that plateau.

Lenox Iron Works in Lenoxdale, 1875. Courtesy of The Berkshire Eagle

I used to go up on Bear Mountain, sometimes to pick huckleberries, sometimes merely to get the sunlight denied me, round my cabin, by the canopy of trees. The mountaintop was sparse and open — big stone ledges with pockets, now and then, of dirt and organic matter. The wind could blow hard up there; the sun could beat down; and often the soil, resting so thinly on the bedrock, would be parched. Only the smallest of trees — scrub oak, pitch pine, and small gray birches — grew there. The pines, especially, were distorted by the wind — leaning, as in a Japanese garden, with their neat round needle-clusters — emerald green — disposed artistically on their limbs. The wind would sigh in the little pines as I walked near them, and all around I would have a feeling of space. On a good day I could see the Catskills, thirty miles away across the Hudson. I could see up into Vermont. I could all but see New York and Boston. Those places would be off on the horizon. Then short of them, down below me, would lie the open farmland of Dutchess, Litchfield, and Berkshire counties. And short of that, again, would be the plateau on which Bear Mountain stood — it was a rolling woodland, green and spongy-looking, with other knobs rising from it here and there — all smoothly rounded, like the curves of a Maillol nude.

A veritable sea it was of woodland — its green leaves the drops of water — yet it hadn't always been that way. In the nineteenth century the plateau had been deforested, again and again, for charcoal; and also in that century it had bustled with an iron industry. The iron turned out there had been rated among the world's best; it had been favored especially for gunmetal and shipfittings — the anchors of the *Constitution* and its sister ship, the *Constellation*, had been forged there on the heights. The furnace that had smelted the iron was still standing last summer — I passed it often, three miles to my cabin's south — but it had not smudged the plateau air (according to some reports) since 1847, when the molten iron had reputedly "frozen" in its hearth, forming a "salamander" that the owners had not thought worth while removing. I remembered the furnace, a handsome old ruin, from my childhood. It had then been crumbling away and had been deemed unsafe to climb on, but then just recently — in 1961 — it had been renovated by a local mason, Peter Brazzale, with the backing of a local philanthropist; and so now it was a monument.

It was a rugged, archaic-looking block of masonry, thirty feet high, according to the records, and thirty by twenty-four feet at its base. It was made of the dark local stone put together without mortar, and on two of its faces there were openings, one for letting the molten iron out. These were in the shape of "false" arches; each had been built, that is, by merely sloping its two sides together till a broad stone lintel could be placed on top to join them. The work looked primitive, partly because of these false arches, yet at the same time strong and massive, like much prehistoric architecture in the Old World. Originally the masonry had been held together, in a precautionary way, by wooden beams and iron tie-bars. In the restoration the beams had been replaced by old telephone poles, running across the different faces, and these, for all their size, looked properly to scale. The whole structure in its loneliness — it stood beside a mountain brook near a dirt mountain road — was an impressive, enigmatic reminder of the past.

While camping on the plateau I had already learned something of the old charcoal-burning there, and now I began to study the iron business, which had combined with it to make the heights, now such a wilderness, into a hive of industry. I could find no one alive, of course, who remembered 1847, but I did find some documents on the iron — pamphlets and articles written by metallurgists or local historians. Also I found one local historian in person: the late Julia Pettee, then aged 90, who was descended from a Mount Riga iron-master, who had long been a professional librarian, and who had done much research on the old Salisbury — she was still doing it, in fact, last summer. I began consulting Miss Pettee and the documents, and from them I pieced together this story.

Iron-making began early in America. The technique, used in Europe for centuries, was known to the colonists, and they vitally needed its fruits — needed nails, horseshoes, pots, pans, muskets, farm tools, and other ironware. Besides this they had an export market, in England, because iron-making in those days used charcoal — lots of it — and the British forests were hard pressed. So American leaders promoted the industry from early times. By 1647 or 1648 John Winthrop, Jr., son of the Massachusetts governor, had two blast-furnaces going near Boston. The same John Winthrop became governor of Connecticut in 1657, and a year later he built a furnace just east of New Haven. Throughout the next century other furnaces went up in Massachusetts, Connecticut, and elsewhere on the Atlantic seaboard. The ore they smelted was apt to be indifferent — often it was "bog ore" dredged up from nearby ponds — but something useful could always be made from it.

Not until 1732 was ore discovered in Salisbury. The Salisbury region, at the meeting of the three states, had been slow in getting settled because it was at the end of the line from wherever one approached it. If one approached from New York one would go up the Hudson to Livingston Manor, well above Poughkeepsie, and then travel eastward to the farthest edge of the Livingston domain — to a nomansland, indeed, where the Livingstons were virtually at war with the New Englanders. And if one approached from Boston or New Haven one would go southwest or northwest, as the case might be, to the limits of civilization as conceived of in those centers. The Salisbury corner was known in Connecticut as the Western Lands or the Greenwoods, and when its iron was discovered it was inhabited only by Indians, one English colonist, and a few Dutch families who had come in from the Hudson. The iron seems to have sped up Salisbury's development, indeed, rather as the Gold Rush sped up California's.

In my researches I have come on several encomiums of the Salisbury ore: it was "as good as any found in the United States"; it was "the richest this side of Sweden"; it was "perhaps unexcelled in the world, according to the Smithsonian Institute." I have also heard it praised by Salisbury neighbors who know something about it. There may be an element of local pride in these judgments, yet it does seem that Salisbury iron had outstanding qualities — especially it must have had durability under repeated shock, for it was highly prized for guns and, later on, for railroad car-wheels. The news of its discovery, in 1732, is said to have traveled fast and far — even to Europe — but the ore was not exploited in much quantity at first, perhaps because Salisbury lacked even wagon-tracks then to link it with the outside world. Pack-horses would presumably have taken any exported ore — or iron or ironware — to the Hudson, the closest navigable waterway, which was twenty-odd miles distant as the crow flies. So only small forges or "bloomeries" were used at first, these beating out objects in scant volume.

Then in 1762 a real blast-furnace, comparable to the later Mount Riga one, was built in a part of Salisbury township that is now called Lakeville, but was called Furnace Village through the early nineteenth century. The furnace — it has since disappeared — was built by three entrepreneurs, one being Ethan Allen, a Connecticut man who later moved to Vermont and led the Green Mountain Boys there. They placed it near the outlet of Lake Wononscopomuc or Lakeville Lake, where there was a good fall of water to power the blast. In the decade after its launching the enterprise had its ups and downs, and it changed hands more than once. Ethan Allen sold out in 1765, to a partner, and was fined shortly afterward for beating the latter up (Allen, a big, irrepressible man, soon to be a famous guerrilla, was in repeated trouble during his Salisbury phase). When the Revolution began the furnace was controlled by a Tory sympathizer, who sailed off to England, after which it was taken over by the Connecticut authorities on behalf of the war effort. They kept it busy overtime making iron for munitions, especially cannon. Salisbury was well placed as an arsenal of democracy, being fairly safe from attack, but also near important war theaters like the Upper Hudson Valley, where Burgoyne was campaigning in 1777. Many workmen came to Furnace Village from elsewhere, and many hogsheads of rum were brought in to keep them going. Cannon were made here by pouring molten iron into a cast — of clay, straw, rags, and other materials — that was set nose up in the ground with tamped sand around it. The moulding produced a solid chunk of cannon shape that, when cool enough, was taken to a nearby shed for boring. There it was hung under the roof, muzzle down, and lowered till it came into contact with an erect drill turned by a horse walking round and round it — the weight of the gun itself, gradually lowered, supplied the pressure for the boring. Later the finished gun would be fired at a nearby hill for testing, and many cannon-balls have since been found embedded in this hill, which is now covered by houses, a school, and an undertaking parlor.

Other munitions made at Lakeville during the Revolution included mortars, grenades, swivel-guns, and camp-kettles. An iron chain was stretched across the Hudson during the war, as a defense against British ships, and Salisbury ore was used in it; but, according to Miss Pettee, the smelting and fabricating were done elsewhere. (The British seized this chain, incidentally, and later took it to Gibraltar, where they used it for protecting the moles.)

Mount Riga, the plateau of my obsession, played only a minor part in these early events. A small forge was built there in the late eighteenth century, and Miss Pettee believed that charcoal was being burned on the heights as early as 1750. But the place was too remote, still, for big-time war industry; and then when peace came, as so often happens, doldrums came with it. The colonial furnace capacity had been expanded in the war, and now there was an industrial pause while the new states argued about their unity. It was not till 1810 that the furnace was built on Mount Riga, and even today one meets with doubts on the wisdom of its placement there. The question must have been nicely balanced. A furnace in those days needed to be in touch with five things: water-power, charcoal, iron ore, limestone, and, of course, a market for its output. In one recent pamphlet, by a metallurgist, I have read that water-power was the governing consideration, and Mount Riga scored high in that regard; it had two lakes, the upper feeding into the lower, and the lower into the dashing brook near which the furnace was built. The site was also good for charcoal — with many square miles of almost level woodland at its door — but for ore and limestone it was poorer. Five main ore-beds were discovered eventually in Salisbury, the greatest being at Ore Hill on the present Route 44, between Lakeville and Millerton, N.Y. All these mines were near Mount Riga, but near its base only, and the ore had to be carried upward a thousand feet in altitude and three or four miles in ground distance; in the beginning at least this too was done by pack-horses on mountain trails. It was the same for the limestone, except that this had to be carried still farther across the lowlands. And finally, of course, the finished products had to come down off the mountain to be sold, though some writers have called this an advantage. Once wagon-roads got developed, these writers say, the teams transporting ironware or pigs could get a flying start — a first few miles of easy, downhill hauling — toward such far objectives as the Hudson.

Anyway the furnace was built on the mountain, and it boomed there in the early nineteenth century, a period when Eastern industry was developing fast (if mainly by the old techniques) and the West was still wild and remote — the Erie Canal was not opened till 1825, when Mount Riga's furnace was in mid-career. The furnace was a bridge, in a way, between the colonial and modern technologies — or it was a vestige of the former on the brink of modern times — and to study it helps one understand that changeful moment in our history.

The furnace, then as now, was but a stone's throw from the dam of the lower Mount Riga lake, and in between stood a water-wheel that drove a huge pair of leather bellows (long since vanished) to supply the blast. Then downstream, a few score yards below the furnace, was another dam (its crude remains are still there) that supplied blast air, and perhaps motive power, for secondary installations, principally two forges.

I have read that these works, all together, "blazed for half a mile along the stream," which today is only a babbling sylvan affair. The old furnace — then as now — stood several yards from the stream itself, up a slope to its south; and behind it, still more southerly, rose — and rises — a considerable hill. On this hill lived most of the furnace workers, and on it were stored the operation's raw materials. The charcoal, brought in on wagons from the surrounding plateau, was kept in sheds for dryness, while the ore and limestone were stockpiled in the open. Then from that stockpile area a ramp led out northward to the furnace, and over it repeated batches of the ore, the lime, and the charcoal were carried — some writers say by horse-carts, some by man-pushed wheelbarrows — to be dumped into the smelting process.

Though block-shaped on the outside the furnace had a vertical cavity within that was cylindrical save for bulging a good deal in the middle. The cylinder's narrow top was relatively cool, and it was here that the materials were dumped. They then descended gradually, heating and mixing the while, through the broad midriff (it was sixteen feet in diameter) and into the narrow bottom, which was called the hearth. The blast of fresh air forced by the bellows, came in, from the side, near the hearth's top and promoted intense burning there. The charcoal fueled this and supplied carbon to the iron; the limestone supplied other ingredients and also drew off certain impurities from the ore. Then in time the good molten iron collected down in the hearth while the impurities, also in liquid form, floated on top of it. These would be drawn off at their level — to cool eventually and become slag — and the metal would be tapped at intervals, by the opening of a door in the hearth, to flow out into moulds on the slope below.

It was vital, I have read, that the mixture keep moving down through the bulging cylinder, and one danger was that the hunks of charcoal, ore, and limestone would jam there and form an arch. If this happened the arch had to be broken quickly, say by poking from above, before the molten stuff lower down, supporting it, was withdrawn. Otherwise the arch might crash destructively into the emptiness, or it might simply stay there, becoming more solid all the time, and make it necessary to rebuild the furnace. Another danger was that the ore — through, say, failure of the blast — might cool in the hearth: might "freeze" there and form a salamander, as such plugs of congealed iron were called. This too would make rebuilding necessary (or abandonment, as possibly in the case of Mount Riga). And then a third danger, less to the furnace than the workers, was from the noxious gases generated in the smelting. To cope with this the gases were drawn off, upward through a vent, where they continued burning, torchlike, in the air. By day this torch "was suspended over the furnace top like a mystical oriflamme," I have read in a description of one old furnace, "and at night it served as a beacon, lighting up the countryside." It must have been a gorgeous sight, and so must the tapping of the hearth itself, which was apparently done by dark sometimes — one can imagine the blazing metal come raging and roaring out then on the primitive mountaintop.

It raged out into main-stem channels called sows and thence into side ones called pigs, which nosed up to the former like piglets to their nursing mother (thus the phrase pig-iron was born). The moulds were of sand, with enough clay mixed in to keep them shapely, but not enough so they would bake into tile under the hot metal. There was water in the mixture too, but again not enough to cause a steam explosion — the whole pig-and-sow area, in fact, was roofed over to keep out rain water, which might have had the same effect. The hot iron ran through the sows into the pigs, guided by attendants called puddlers. Then it cooled into usable bars, but not without picking up sand in the process. Most materials handled at the furnace were weighed in gross tons of 2240 pounds but the pigs were weighed in ones of 2268, the extra twenty-eight pounds being a sand allowance.

Mount Riga was able to process about half of its pig-iron to a further stage in the two forges downstream from the furnace. One forge made big things like anchors, cauldrons, and plows. The other made "chains, garden and farm tools, hinges, latches, kitchen utensils and miscellaneous small wares." Pig-iron was also further refined into standard bars that were shipped off to fabricators elsewhere. Many bars went to the U.S. arsenals at Harper's Ferry and Springfield, Mass., to be used for musket barrels. The Springfield bars traveled all the way — sixty miles — by team and wagon. Those for Harper's Ferry were teamed over to the Hudson and went on down by tow-boat. Other bars were sent to the Collins axe company, at Collinsville near Hartford, and still others to a scythe-factory then in business on the Salisbury lowlands, near where Sage's Ravine comes down. There was a settlement there called Hammertown — in honor of the scythe industry's clangs and bangs — but those noises have long been stilled and the settlement itself has vanished.

Products of the Mount Riga forges, or of others contemporary with them, can still be seen in Salisbury. The late Mr. Joe Pickert, for instance, near the former Hammertown, had an old monkey-wrench that looked almost like modern sculpture; it had a curved, roughly beaten handle about three feet long and a simple, ingenious method of adjustment. Mrs. George Haas has a puddler's tool that looks like a massive, long-handled frying-pan. Some of the old cauldrons are still around too. One stands, as a watering-trough, on the mountain road near the old furnace. Another serves as a mammoth geranium pot outside the Haases' motel, the Ironmaster's Lodge, near Lakeville. The cauldron on the mountain is about three feet across and is round-bodied, thick, and heavy — rusty too now, of course. Those cauldrons were used, among other things, for army camp-kettles, for soap-making, and for the rendering of whale-blubber. Whaling boats worked out of the Hudson in the early nineteenth century — basing, say, at Poughkeepsie and they often carried Salisbury kettles, mounted atop brick stoves, out on their decks. They would cook their blubber while at sea.

The most notable Riga forgings were probably the anchors. Anchors of the superior Salisbury iron were used not only by the *Constitution* and *Constellation*, but by many other ships, including two frigates built in New York for the Greeks in their war of liberation (the Salisbury ironmakers sent the Greeks a big case of muskets too). The anchors were tested on the mountaintop by being hoisted on tripods and then dropped to the ground — if they survived this they were pronounced O.K. and would be dragged off to the Hudson (each by six oxen in the early days). If the anchors were for the U.S. Navy, officers would travel to Mount Riga to observe the testing; and some writers have concluded that gay, lavish balls must have been held there on these occasions. I have found no other evidence for such balls, though, and I suspect that what might be called the Ozymandias or Jamshyd convention of ruin treatment has been at work here.

> They say the lion and the lizard keep
> The courts where Jamshyd gloried and drank deep.

Mount Riga is well fixed for the lion and the lizard — in the form of bobcats and rattlesnakes — but the courts of Jamshyd take imagining. The best documented old splendor I have detected in the Riga community was embodied in its general store, which reputedly had four clerks and was better stocked, with items brought back by team from the Hudson, than were the lowland villages round about. If a Salisbury woman wanted a silk dress, I have read, she had to go up on the mountain to get it. That is hardly Jamshyd, yet it is a far cry from the lonely peace of the townsite today.

Some half dozen old houses do still remain on Mount Riga, chiefly on the hill above the furnace. Deserted in winter, they are used as summer camps by families drawn to the lake. Without maintenance by such families they would have surely gone the way, by now, of the other houses there, which have left nothing behind but old foundations and cellar-holes, perhaps with half-wild lilacs or apple-trees near by. If one prowls around the site, as I have done, one finds many of these traces — finds evidence of an extensive settlement, including a fair amount of open farmland, this now delineated by old stone walls in the forest. I have read that the villagers grew wheat, flax, rye, and potatoes in the days of the furnace. They must have also raised garden vegetables and kept pigs, chickens, and cows. But the mountain's soil is thin and its growing season short; they must have turned to the lowlands for many things.

I have been told, I think reliably, that there were some fifty houses in Riga Village or near it on the plateau. I have also read that a new school built there in 1820 took care of seventy-one pupils. And the late Phil Warner, a devotee of the mountain, said that he heard Mrs. Thurston, one of the old inhabitants, tell his mother in the early 1900s — at age about eighty — how she had often looked out of her window, long ago, and seen two hundred men on the way to work. These things suggest a population of several hundred souls, if not a thousand. It seems likely that men predominated in the community — such a boom town in so rough surroundings — and this is further indicated by the presence of two extra large foundations near the furnace, which probably, I am told, supported boarding-houses. Many of the Riga men — the Raggies — were good hunters and fishermen, and their own life was probably on the wild side too. I have read about one temperance meeting in Riga Village, after which all the liquor in the store was thrown into the stream. But no doubt it was soon replenished. There was a big payroll on the mountain in boom times, and Salisbury men have always thought liquor a good investment.

The derivation of Mount Riga's name, and that of Riga Village, is a puzzle. Catharine Maria Sedgwick, a mid-nineteenth-century novelist of nearby Stockbridge, Mass., wrote a moralistic tale about a young Raggy called *The Boy of Mount Righi*. She said the eminence had been named, by Swiss immigrants living there, after a Mount Righi in their own country. Miss Julia Pettee, on the other hand, has said it was named after the Baltic Riga by Latvian and Russian immigrants who had come to the mountain as charcoal-burners — she cited a tradition in her family to this effect. However, there are no Swiss, Latvian, or Russian names in the old Riga Village cemetery, nor do the Raggy descendants on the Salisbury low-lands have such names. Without exception their nomenclature seems to be English, Dutch, and French — the last reflecting, no doubt, a south-ward drift of Canadian woodsmen. The Raggies seem, in fact, to have had colonial blood of unexcelled purity, and the name Riga presumably has another explanation. It might, one supposes, be a back-formation from the word Raggy itself. If poor charcoal-burners were living on the moun-tain as early as 1750, which Miss Pettee believed, there must have been ample time, in the next century, for them to get the name Raggy and their domain that of Ragga. Riga can still be pronounced almost Ragga, in fact — the one thing it can't be called is Reega; it is Ryega or something toward Ragga from that. (This etymology is pure speculation, of course. Yet the name invites speculation. It seems, for instance, unlike any Indian names in the neighborhood. What can it be then?)

Government maps, incidentally, apply the name Mount Riga only to a small peak at the south edge of the Riga plateau. But this is not the current usage of the region. In Salisbury, "Mount Riga" means at least the Connecticut and New York State parts of the whole eminence, which covers about fifty square miles and is called, officially, the Taconic Range. Often the term takes in the Massachusetts part as well (and one hears the word Raggy applied to the woodsmen of Mount Washington, Mass., a still-alive community).

In my Salisbury boyhood I was enchanted by the idea of the Raggies. The Raggy spirit seemed to me then — as it still does — romantic, independent, and rich in flavor. But I could not have defined what a Raggy was, and I think this is true of many Salisbury people. There is a tendency nowadays to think that anyone who has lived in the township fairly long, and has a reasonably carefree attitude, should be called a Raggy; and from that point the concept moves, through various stages and various minds, to the other limit, the purist one, where Raggies are only those who live the old-time woodsman life on the mountain itself. In this latter sense there have really been no Raggies, in Connecticut at least, for the past half century.

While staying on the mountain last summer, and thinking about it, I concluded that the term made most sense if it were confined to people who had actually lived on Riga or to their descendants still living near by — to families with names like Surdam, Ostrander, Rosseter, and Ball, which are seen on gravestones in the Mount Riga cemetery, or like Bonhotel and Brazee, which, though not found there, are celebrated for a mountain background. There are many with such names still in Salisbury. Often they live on the lower slopes of Mount Riga itself — in the upper edges of the settlements around it — and it is they, by and large, who are still the good woodsmen of our town (or who were that — one of them, now in his late fifties, told me last summer that he had walked everywhere on the mountain as a youth, but had years ago been weaned of that habit, or ability, by the automobile).

It is the Raggies, too, who have supplied the town's most vivid folklore. Some of this has been written up, even scurrilously — I have read allegations in print of disreputable, hillbilly Raggy ways; of incest, for instance, and of diets monotonous with woodchuck. Other, less hostile items of folklore are passed on orally in Salisbury. There was, for instance, the man who told his wife one Sunday that he was going to a ball-game in Salisbury village, who did go to it, but who drifted off later to upstate New York, and stayed there for seven years without bothering to write; when he finally came home, after this long absence, his wife looked up from her work and merely asked him what the score of the game had been. There was also the old lady who became chair-bound late in life and who used to pass the months by hatching out eggs, two at a time, in her bosom. Tales like this filled my imagination when I was a boy, and so did the feats of strength and woodcraft attributed to Raggy men. Among the gayest moments of my boyhood were those of attendance at Raggy square-dances, with Raggy callers and fiddlers, and among the nicest people I have known were Raggy men who worked on my father's farm. In my vagueness I didn't identify them strictly then as Raggies, but last summer I pinned them down more closely: at least two former charcoal-burners had come into my life then, and at least two charcoal-burner's sons who had been born on the mountain. To me these men have always seemed admirable, kind, and gentle. Since the age of twelve fate has kept me from Salisbury most of the time — and often from America too — but the ideal of the Raggies has stayed with me; and my judgment of other peoples, whether Chinese, Tibetans, Greeks, or urban Americans, has always, I think, been colored by it.

From *The Changing Landscape* by Christopher Rand. Oxford University Press, 1968.

JUDITH McGAW

Judith McGaw became interested in the Berkshire paper industry while a history teacher in Pittsfield. She is now a professor at the University of Pennsylvania with a special interest in the history of technology.

The Mill Towns Transformed

January 23, 1857, began as a rather typical Berkshire winter night, bitterly cold and windy. Then, at 1:30 A.M., the Lee Congregational Church bell began ringing unexpectedly, awakening the sleeping citizens and startling those paper mill hands working night tour. In response, members of the recently organized volunteer fire company, including both paper mill workers and mill owners, rushed out into the bitter night. They dragged the new "Water Witch" fire engine to a spot opposite the blazing block of stores at the south end of Main Street and began pumping with all their might. But hostile nature frustrated their combined efforts. Howling winds fanned the blaze. Intense cold froze the water as it fell.

The fire still burned brightly when the new town clock, one hundred feet away in the old church steeple, struck three. Shortly thereafter, as the assembled citizens watched with horror, a gust of wind picked up a flaming shingle from the business block and deposited it on the cupola above the clock and bell. The fire fighters had no way to reach the tower, no way to douse the flames. Several minutes later the clock and the bell plummeted to the earth. By 5:00 A.M. nothing remained of the church except two or three cords of charred wood. The rest was ashes. The imposing fifty-six-year-old landmark, where many local citizens had worshipped and most had gathered annually for the town meeting, no longer stood at the center of town life.

The fiery destruction of the Lee Congregational Church can serve as a convenient symbol for the transformation of the paper mill towns after 1857. Like the citizens of Lee in January 1857, Berkshire paper makers suffered a rude awakening in the years after mechanization. Although their machines were running smoothly, alarming new problems drew them outside the mills and forced them to confront their limitations in the face of nature. Berkshire's resources, so long deemed inexhaustible, now appeared inadequate. Chronic shortages of fiber, fuel, process water, and waterpower recurrently plagued mill owners. Moreover, familiar but uncontrollable natural forces aggravated their situation. Local rivers periodically froze, flooded, or dried up, and between 1857 and 1885 twenty-

six devastating fires reduced local mills to ashes and their costly machines to scrap. Berkshire County's three oldest mills — Zenas Crane's
original mill, the Church brothers' first Lee mill, and David Carson's Old
Red Mill — all disappeared from the local landscape.

Just as the fire began in the business block but created a baffling
dilemma when it spread without warning to the church tower, so the new
production dilemmas mill owners faced after mechanization resulted
directly and unexpectedly from the mechanical productivity they had
wrought. And like the volunteer fire company, mill owners found their
impressive technological preparation insufficient when confronting un-
anticipated new problems. Initially, like the firemen vainly pumping
water into the howling wind, mill owners tried to mitigate the impending
crisis by repeating familiar behaviors: they sought out more rags, fuel,
sizing, and springs; built more dams; and expanded existing mill structures. Ultimately, however, they found that traditional solutions fell short
when addressing novel problems.

With substantial investments at stake, mill owners managed to solve
the problems of scarce resources, inadequate power, and devastating fire.
But unlike mechanization, the new technological solutions they adopted
brought to the mill towns physical changes as dramatic as the old church's
destruction. Berkshire paper makers pioneered the American manufacture of wood pulp newsprint, but at the coast of deforesting local hill-
sides. They introduced new chemicals to economize on traditional raw
materials, but understood their use so poorly that they frequently pol-
luted local rivers. After flooding hundreds of acres to increase water
power, they supplemented waterwheels with steam engines, burned up
more of the local forests, and exhausted steam and smoke into the village
air. Finally, they constructed enormous new fire-resistant buildings to
concentrate production and replace mills that had burned. These imposing structures dominated the local landscape, their steam whistles replaced the church bell as the loudest local voice, and their numerous
workers crowded the once quiet village streets. By 1885 the mill towns
had been transformed.

From *Most Wonderful Machine* by Judith McGaw. Princeton University Press, 1987.

WILLIAM JAY SMITH

Poet William Jay Smith of Cummington has won wide international acclaim for his work and has taught poetry at a large number of colleges and universities. He is not alone in being a fancier of Berkshire morels nor in avoiding indicating even vaguely where he finds these "feasts of air."

Morels

A wet gray day — rain falling slowly, mist over the
    valley, mountains dark circumflex smudges in the distance —

Apple blossoms just gone by, the branches feathery still
    as if fluttering with half-visible antennae —

A day in May like so many in these green mountains, and
    I went out just as I had last year

At the same time, and found them there under the big maples —
    by the bend in the road — right where they had stood

Last year and the year before that, risen from the dark duff
    of the woods, emerging at odd angles

From spores hidden by curled and matted leaves, a fringe of
    rain on the grass around them,

Beads of rain on the mounded leaves and mosses round them,

Not in a ring themselves but ringed by jack-in-the-pulpits
    with deep eggplant-colored stripes;

Not ringed but rare, not gilled but polyp-like, having
    sprung up overnight —

These mushrooms of the gods, resembling human organs
    uprooted, rooted only on the air,

Looking like lungs wrenched from the human body, lungs
    reversed, not breathing internally

But being the externalization of breath itself, these
   spicy, twisted cones,

These perforated brown-white asparagus tips — these morels,
   smelling of wet graham crackers mixed with maple leaves;

And, reaching down by the pale green fern shoots, I nipped
   their pulpy stems at the base

And dropped them into a paper bag — a damp brown bag (their
   color) — and carried

Them (weighing absolutely nothing) down the hill and into
   the house; you held them

Under cold bubbling water and sliced them with a surgeon's
   stroke clean through,

And sautéed them over a low flame, butter-brown; and we ate
   them then and there —

Tasting of the sweet damp woods and of the rain one inch
   above the meadow:

It was like feasting upon air.

From *The Traveler's Tree: New and Selected Poems* by William Jay Smith. Persea Books, 1980.

NORMAN ROCKWELL

Everybody loved Norman Rockwell and his wife Molly; it was impossible not to. His account of his dinner at the White House shows why — his self-deprecation, his genial humor, his feeling for the goodness of ordinary people. These are the qualities that, combined with his unsurpassed technical ability, made him America's favorite illustrator.

From Stockbridge to Washington

MOVING TO STOCKBRIDGE

In 1953 I left Arlington and moved to Stockbridge, Massachusetts. Restlessness again. And then I was having trouble with my work and thought that maybe a change of scene would help me. It didn't. I sank deeper into the muck. I was dissatisfied, doubted my ability; decisions made in the morning evaporated by three o'clock. I started to lean on advice, not sort it out, using the good, rejecting the bad. Among those I listened to were several psychiatrists from the Austin Riggs Center, a psychiatric institution in Stockbridge. And that, finally, was how I recovered from the crisis.

I don't think I'm what you'd call a temperamental artist. For over forty years I've done commercial work, which involves deadlines and various other restrictions. I've painted over three hundred *Post* covers; I've done the Boy Scout calendar for thirty-four years; I've handled many advertising accounts for long periods — for instance, Massachusetts Mutual Insurance Company for twelve years. No, you can't say I'm temperamental or flighty. But every so often I get into a hassle over my work. I get all tied up in a knot. Why, I don't know. Usually I work my way through the crisis by myself. And it's a slow business, rather like getting up in the middle of the night in a strange house and trying to find the light switch. You bump into tables, bruising your shins; bang your head on doors; stumble over rugs; groping, straining your eyes, and all the while feeling that maybe the next step will be into nothing and you'll tumble down a stairway you can't see and split your skull.

But in Stockbridge, for the first time, it wasn't, to my relief, like that. Because I got to talking with Erik H. Erikson, a psychoanalyst on the staff of Austin Riggs Center. Sort of casually to begin with, but pretty soon I found myself seeing him regularly. He helped me to understand the crisis. And I came through it rather more easily than I would have plodding along by myself.

I wasn't mentally ill or anything like that. I don't think I would have cracked up. But you don't have to be desperately sick, on the point of death, before you call the doctor. I sure owe a lot to Erik Erikson.

My first studio in Stockbridge was right in the center of town — two rooms over Sullivan's meat market. (I became poverty-proud: another illustrator would tell me about his new twenty-thousand-dollar studio. Then, "Where's your studio?" he'd ask. "Oh," I'd say, "it's over the local meat market. Just two small rooms.") After a while I knew everybody in town.

THE WHITE HOUSE CALLS

One afternoon, returning from a morning spent searching for a model in Pittsfield, I found three or four people talking excitedly at the foot of the stairs leading to my studio. "Hey, Norman," one of them said as I got out of my car, "we've been looking everywhere for you. The White House is on the phone." "What d'you suppose they want?" asked another. Four or five more people ran up. (News spreads fast in a small town.) I dashed upstairs. It was a secretary on the White House staff; she wanted to know if I could attend a stag dinner to be given by President Eisenhower at the White House. I said yes, I could, and she asked me to keep it confidential.

I rushed right out to tell Mary, mystifying the crowd at the foot of the stairs, for when they asked me what the White House had wanted I frowned and looked mysterious, saying, "Top secret."

A couple of days later I received a note from the President inviting me to dinner. I quickly posted my reply — "I'd be delighted" — and ran home to dig out my tuxedo. But as I pulled it from a steamer trunk in the attic a cloud of moths flew up. The sleeves were tattered, the seat ragged, and the lapels threadbare. I hurried to a local haberdasher to buy a new one.

When I tried on his best tuxedo I thought it looked kind of cheap. It was blue ("Midnight blue," said the clerk, "the latest thing"), not black, and the silk lapels dropped in fat, glittering curves to the waist, which was encircled by a cummerbund. "You're sure it's fashionable?" I asked. "Oh yes," said the clerk. "That's the shawl collar. A cummerbund is à la mode." So, in spite of my misgivings, I bought the tuxedo.

That wasn't the end of my preparations. I figured to be pretty nervous, maybe even scared, at the dinner. And, I thought, supposing my mouth dries up and my throat clogs and I'm unable to speak? What then? … What then? Why then you'll be ashamed of yourself.

Well, I thought after several minutes of agonized imaginings ("Hello," says the President — "Gargle," say I, tongue-tied), take precautions then.

I repaired to the office of Dr. Donald Campbell. Again medical science came to my rescue. This time with what is known as a "happy" pill.

Norman Rockwell and Tom Carey, Stockbridge's indispensable all-purpose delivery man.
Clemens Kalischer

"Take it twenty minutes before you go to the White House," said Dr. Campbell, "and you won't be afraid of a thing. It obliterates apprehension, tension, and dread."

Armed with my pill — pea green — and my tuxedo — midnight blue — I went off to Washington. You are, I said to myself on the plane, bulwarked against catastrophe. Even the state dining room (which Ben Hibbs had told me was awe-inspiringly magnificent) can't lump your throat or quake your knees. And I opened my stud box and gazed fondly at my pill, nestled securely in a wad of cotton.

On arriving at the Statler Hotel, I inquired how long it took to drive from the hotel to the White House. Upstairs in my room I worked out a schedule. Then I sat down on the bed to wait.

After a while I decided that the clock had stopped. I called the operator. No, the clock hadn't stopped. I cleaned my pipe. I counted the panes in the window. I recited all the poetry I could remember. I whistled, hummed, and swung my feet back and forth, back and forth. Pretty soon the bottom dropped out of my stomach. I began to feel lightheaded. The clock ticked. I waited. I thought I wouldn't make it; I'd collapse with nervous exhaustion.

But finally it was six-thirty, exactly one hour before the dinner. I gave my tuxedo to the valet to press. At seven o'clock he brought it back. As I fumbled for a tip I noticed him looking at the tuxedo queerly, as one might look at a mongoose if one turned the corner of Fifth Avenue and Fifty-third Street and stumbled on it during rush hour. "What's the matter?" I asked. "Nothing, sir, nothing," said the valet, instantly recovering the customary blank stare of a valet waiting for a tip. "There is," I said. "The tux isn't right, is it?" "Well, sir," said the valet, "I might say that I have never seen that *particular* shade of blue before." "Oh, Lord," I said, handing him his tip, "I knew it." And after he'd left I stared morosely at my reflection in the shiny lapels of the tuxedo, patting the pill in my coat pocket and thinking, At least you've got that; you may look like a fool but you'll feel like Grant at Appomattox.

I marched into the bathroom, drew a glass of water, and shook the pill out of its box into my hand, where it landed on its edge and promptly rolled into the sink and down the drain....

"In fifteen years," I said out loud, "I'll laugh at that." And, stunned, I went into the bedroom, pulled on my extraordinary tux, tied my tie, and went downstairs.

As I reached the taxi stand outside the hotel a battered old cab chugged up, clanking and rattling. At the wheel was a stout, robust, middle-aged woman with a chauffeur's cap cocked rakishly over one eye. The doorman waved her away. I signaled her to stop, feeling in my tender state that we two, the cab and I, victims of adversity, should stick together.

"Where to, mister?" asked the driver.

"The White House," I replied, still in a daze.

"My land!" she exploded heartily. "You going to the *White House?* Whatta you going to do *there?"*

"I'm going to dinner," I said, recovering somewhat under this onslaught of good nature.

"Wow!" she exclaimed. "I ain't *ever* before taken nobody to the White House before. I'll get ya there in five minutes flat." And the cab leaped forward with a roar like a wounded rhinoceros.

"Wait!" I yelled. "Hold on. I don't want to be early. What I want you to do is go up to the White House and then drive back and forth in front of it until the dot of seven-thirty."

"Okay, mister," she said.

While we were cruising up and down Pennsylvania Avenue she asked, "What's your name? You famous?"

"I do covers for the *Saturday Evening Post*," I said. "My name's Norman Rockwell."

"Ha!" she said. "I've seen your stuff. You scared?"

"Yes," I said, studying my watch. "Get ready now, it's almost time ... NOW!"

We turned into the White House gate and jolted to a stop. The guards checked my invitation. We continued up the circular drive, waited while a chauffeur helped a gentleman out of a large black limousine, and then jerked forward, the cab backfiring, and halted before the entrance. A crowd of secret service men and flunkies was standing on the steps and beside the white pillars. I paid the fare and started up the steps. "Hey, Mr. Rockwell," boomed a voice behind me. I turned around. The cab driver was leaning across her cab and waving at me. "Good luck, Mr. Rockwell," she shouted, "good luck." The secret service men and the flunkies laughed. I waved back. "Thanks," I called.

A secretary ushered me upstairs and into a sitting room. I almost panicked as I crossed the threshold, for all the tuxedos were black with thin, dull lapels, and there wasn't a cummerbund in sight. But a minute later President Eisenhower greeted me warmly and I felt right at home.

Then the President, raising his voice a trifle, welcomed us. He went on to explain the purpose of his stag dinners. As President he is forced to spend most of his time with politicians, generals, statesmen, and experts, discussing weighty problems. Once in a while he likes to forget the cares of state and relax for an evening with people he enjoys talking to. His stag dinners are informal get-togethers, he told us, adding that he hoped we would not talk to the press about the dinner. In the past a guest had done so and it had been very embarrassing. "I feel that this is a personal get-together with people I like," he said, "and I'd like it to stay that way."

So I'm afraid it's going to be an anticlimax, because I don't feel that I should discuss what went on that evening, though I can say that I had a fine, easy time and enjoyed myself very much.

When we were about to leave the table after dinner I wanted to take the place card, matches, and menu as souvenirs. But I hesitated, afraid of looking silly. Then, glancing around, I discovered that all the other guests had taken theirs. So I took mine.

And after leaving the President, as we were standing on the steps of the White House, we sounded like a bunch of kids discussing the high school football hero. A secretary had told us that our evening had lasted *one half hour longer* than any of the President's other informal evenings. We were delighted and flattered. Which shows how President Eisenhower affects people. You just can't help liking him.

I have one dark, deep confession to make. Before each place at the dinner table was a small jackknife, a present from the President to each guest. There was no inscription on the knife, however. So when I arrived at Penn Station the next day I walked up Eighth Avenue to a jeweler's. "Could you engrave 'From DDE to NR' on this knife?" I asked the jeweler. "Sure," he said, "have it for you tomorrow." "I'll give you twenty dollars if you can get it done for me today," I said. "Sold," he said. That night at home I showed my knife to Mary and the boys. "See," I said proudly," 'From DDE to NR.' How about that?" They were very impressed. And during the next few months, whenever I took out my knife, always being careful to show the inscription, people would ask, "DDE? Is that President Eisenhower? Where'd you get that knife?" So I'd get a chance to describe my evening at the White House. Ah, vanity, vanity, thy name is Norman.

———————

From *My Life as an Illustrator* by Norman Rockwell. Doubleday, 1960.

HAL BORLAND

From his Housatonic farm in Salisbury, Connecticut, Hal Borland dispatched a weekly nature editorial to the New York Sunday Times *for 36 years, from 1942 until his death in 1978. He also wrote a weekly "Our Berkshires" column for 21 years for the* Berkshire Eagle, *where the following first appeared.*

Hill Country Observations

THE BOG

We stopped at a small bogland the other evening and parked the car and went on foot to look and listen. It was just at sunset, and on the hillside beyond the swamp a barred owl was hooting softly. It was quite a way off and at first I thought I was hearing a mourning dove. But it was an owl, all right. Sometimes, at a distance, an owl will sound like a dove, and the doves have been calling so much and the owls so little that I was confused.

In the meadow that sloped down to the bog were a few patches of bluets, *Houstonia caerulea*, which some call Quaker Ladies and some call Innocence. They were like little patches of fog in the grass, for they grew close and bloomed generously. The tiny four-petaled flowers were so white, so sparsely touched with any shade of blue, that I wondered again why anyone ever called them bluets. And down at the wet margin the swamp violets were full of deep purple blossom, one of the richest colors that early May has to offer.

But it was the bog itself we had come to see.

Red-wings challenged us, a small flock of them. They circled and scolded and flashed their crimson epaulettes, and they perched on the stalks of last year's cattails, swaying precariously. The old cattails were fluffed into smoky-looking tufts, ragged out by wind and winter and perhaps by the early nest builders too. But at the base of each stalk rose the bright green of new growth, the blades that will make the bog a green jungle by July. Among them was the darker green of blue flag, the wild iris, which will color the swampland in another month with its big blossoms. At this stage the blades of iris and cattail look much alike, except that the cattails are somewhat narrower and a lighter, yellowish green. And among them were still narrower blades of one of the bur reeds, I couldn't be sure which but guessed at the variety known as *symplex*, the smaller one. The blades looked like rank grass.

On and around the little tussocks that were above the water were marsh marigolds, nearly all of them in bloom. Some were up to their ears in water, the leaves seeming to float and the blossoms only a little higher. They are web-footed cousins of the common buttercups and the Latin name, *Caltha palustris*, means marsh-cup. Botanically, they are also cousins of the columbine; but that is one of those things I have to take on faith. I don't really believe it, though I know it is true. I do believe that the marsh marigold flower is one of the loveliest golden yellows I ever saw anywhere.

And on the tussocks themselves were great masses of skunk cabbage leaves, big as elephant ears, gaudy, extravagant and primitive. And among them I could see others of the *Arum* family, with their dark-striped spathes, a number of light green, plantain-like leaves of sweet flag, and an occasional dart-shaped leaf of the arrow arum.

On the far margin of the little bog were two tall elms, trembling on the verge of leaf, still lacy in tufts of young seed, and beneath them were clumps of willow brush where the inch-long leaves had already begun to hide the finished catkins. And alder brush was tufting out in leaf, still hung with the little cone-like seed cases from last year. From somewhere nearby a hyla shrilled and I thought he was the last member of the peeper chorus that was so loud two weeks ago. But from down at the other end of the bog came an answer in a voice so high it sounded like falsetto. No chorus, though.

The water caught the glow of sunset and turned from pewter gray to opalescent. The opalescence was fire-dappled with specks of lettuce-green that caught some lively light and almost glistened. Duck-weed, finer than the finest confetti, drifted in the luminous water.

There was a dark movement back among the cattails. As we watched, a big brown muskrat swam into the open, the V of ripples from his nose like long, silvery whiskers. He swam toward the bank where we stood, quietly as a shadow; and suddenly he saw us and dived with a plop and left only a swirling of the opalescent water.

We turned and went back to the car. I always feel close to beginnings in a bogland; especially at dusk, I feel as though I stood on the brink of ancient days when warm seas washed the first land and aquatic life was making its first venture away from the mother element, Water. Even here in the Berkshire Hills, bog life has a primitive aspect, a sense of elemental change. The very smell of a bog is fecund and fertile of mysterious and fundamental change.

I get the feeling, particularly at dusk, that anything can happen on the margin of a swampland. Outlandish things. There have been dusks when I was sure that if I waited on such a margin only another hour I would see a 30-foot Stegosaurus, complete with armor-plate scales, come wading out from among the reeds and cattails, trailing a million centuries behind him. I never have, but I still wouldn't bet that I never shall.

HOLLYHOCKS

Hollyhocks are in bloom and they, of all flowers, are typical of New England to me. That is in part because almost thirty years ago, on my first trip to New England, I seemed to see hollyhocks in every farmhouse dooryard and growing wild along many roadsides.

That first trip was made in July, on a vacation from a daily job in Philadelphia. I had two weeks in which to wander, and I drove up the west bank of the Hudson to Poughkeepsie, then turned northeast into Connecticut, not knowing that I was seeing the country I would some day call home. It was a strange land, placid in the July-hot valleys, green and cool on the hills. I came up through Salisbury and Canaan, on north through Great Barrington and Pittsfield, marveling at the maples, the stone walls, the plain farmhouses — and the hollyhocks. I went east along the Mohawk Trail, turned south on back roads, by-passed Springfield, Hartford, New Haven, and returned to Pennsylvania. I had seen a land new to me, old to American history. I knew I would come back eventually.

Remembering now, I think it was the tumbled hills of the Berkshires that most fascinated me. The hills, the stone walls, the small farms, the quiet villages, and the ubiquitous hollyhocks couldn't be forgotten. Now I know that these are only a few of the thousand things that are, to me, special to New England, and particularly to the Berkshire country, though not exclusively here.

The white church spires, the elms, the gracefully proportioned old houses, are traditional New England. Yet I have seen villages in Ohio, in Illinois, even in Oregon, that could be set down in Connecticut or Massachusetts and look completely at home. That is no accident. The early settlers in all those places were from New England and they took with them their village patterns and traditions. Early Oregonians even shipped pre-cut houses, complete with doors and windows, around Cape Horn so they might have the familiar homes of their tradition in that alien land. And I have seen towns in Kansas — they are called towns, not villages, out there — complete with central greens, white clapboard churches, classic houses, and hollyhocks in the dooryards. Free-staters, abolitionists, who went to eastern Kansas in the "Bloody '50s" of a century ago, established those towns in the pattern of their home villages here in Connecticut and Massachusetts.

But nowhere else is the combination quite the same. The snug farmhouses in the narrow valleys are different here — even though now so many of them have been taken over by summer folk or retired year-rounders from the cities. The stone walls are unique to New England, manmade monuments, actually, to the debris scattered over this land by the glaciers of twenty-five thousand years ago. The brooks, some of them unpolluted and relatively natural, hurry down the valleys and dawdle across the meadows in a particular rhythm and pattern. The maples and oaks thrive on the shallow topsoil and color in October as nowhere else in the world. Dandelions in spring, daisies and hawkweed in summer, goldenrod and asters in autumn, try the patience of New England farmers who cherish a clean meadow and a profitable crop of corn and oats. And hollyhocks bring a special glory to our door-yards in July.

Barbara, who is a Connecticut Yankee from away back, tells me that hollyhocks are not really special. Others try to tell me that hollyhocks are common because they are easily grown and persistent, and because they will tolerate neglect. The early farm wives, they say, had little time to pamper dooryard flowers. But I insist that hollyhocks were brought to New England for the same reason they were taken to Old England, for the sake of beauty, for the satisfaction of seeing those crinkled silken petals spread their color in midsummer. Hollyhocks, originally native to the Near East, were probably taken back to England by the Crusaders, who had an eye for beauty, floral as well as feminine. And they were brought here to New England by the very early colonists, not to eat or to provide an infusion to cure a fever or a bellyache, but just for beauty. Those settlers were tough and practical, but like all successful pioneers everywhere they had a streak of sentiment in them, thank goodness.

So here are the hollyhocks, New England as a stone wall or a Seth Thomas clock. They still come in the fine old whites and pinks and honest reds, as well as the newer shades. They are gnawed by Japanese beetles, infested with rust, get crown rot and root diseases, but they persist. If the year should ever come when they fail to bloom, something will have gone from New England, something lovely, something beautiful. But I doubt that such a time will come, for hollyhocks, like old New Englanders, are of a tough, enduring strain.

From *Hill Country Harvest* by Hal Borland. J.B. Lippincott, 1967.

GERARD CHAPMAN

Dean of local columnists in the Berkshire Eagle, *Gerard Chapman over the years has indefatigably tracked down the details on scores of interesting Berkshire personalities of the past, both famous and obscure. Here he writes about the Goodale sisters, once famous, now obscure.*

The "Apple Blossom Poets"

Just a century ago this fall, two young girls living in a remote corner of Berkshire County became nationally famous by virtue of their best-selling book of poetry. They were dubbed the "Apple Blossom Poets" because their first book, published in November 1878, was titled "Apple Blossoms: Verses of Two Children." The first edition sold out in three days.

They were Elaine and Dora Read Goodale, elder daughters of Henry Sterling and Dora Hill Read Goodale, who lived on the 700-acre Sky Farm in the upland town of Mount Washington. There Elaine was born October 9, 1863, and Dora October 29, 1866. There were also a younger brother and sister.

From their intellectual and refined parents, the girls drew a love of learning; they became adept in the nuances and rhythms of English and even knew some Greek and Latin. They loved to roam the woods and fields; were sensible of the wind, weather, sun and the changing seasons; and were inspired to limn their impressions in verse.

When Elaine and Dora were about ten and seven years old, they produced a monthly literary magazine for the family, called "Sky Farm Life," copied by Elaine on note paper sewed into pamphlet form. Some of their verses appeared in *St. Nicholas* magazine in 1877, and it was a selection of these and others that were issued as the book "Apple Blossoms" by G.P. Putnam's Sons, a major publisher, the next year.

The verses attracted attention throughout the United States; the book was extensively reviewed, and as *The Nation* said, "They are certainly remarkable productions in view of the circumstances." The *New York Post* ascribed to Dora's work "a freer spirit than that which breathes through Elaine's. She is more truly a child of nature than Elaine ... who is already passing from objective to subjective themes — that is, from the contemplation of what is going on before our eyes to the recording of that which takes place within us." And the *Berkshire Evening Eagle* said,"... tender grace and delicious delicacy of poetic expression ... make some of these passages like frost work on a windowpane...."

The success of that first book resulted in the appearance in 1879 of "In Berkshire With the Wild Flowers"; enlarged the following year, it was reissued as "Verses From Sky Farm." Next came "All Around the Year." Dora herself achieved distinction when her poem "The Hills of Berkshire," set to the tune of "Annie Laurie," was sung by those assembled for the tenth annual dinner of the Berkshire Society of New York in 1897. In that year also, she published the book "Heralds of Easter."

Elaine meanwhile had attended Harvard Annex (Radcliffe College), and when Gen. Samuel C. Armstrong visited Sky Farm, she became interested in the plight of the displaced Indians of the Western plains. Gen. Armstrong had been instrumental in the founding of what became Hampton Institute in Virginia, and Elaine taught there; in 1883, she edited its magazine *Southern Workman.*

In 1885, after a six-week tour of the Sioux reservation in the West, she published in the New York and Boston papers her observations on reservation life. The next year, she was appointed a teacher in the day school at White River Camp, Lower Brule Agency, in the Dakota Territory. In 1890-91, as supervisor of Indian schools, she visited more than 50 schools throughout Indian territory.

These trips took Elaine to the Pine Ridge Agency, where she met Dr. Charles Alexander Eastman. Born a Santee Sioux in Minnesota Territory in 1858, named first Hakadah and then Ohiyesa, he assumed his mother's maiden name, attended successively Beloit, Knox and Dartmouth colleges, and took a medical degree at Boston University in 1890.

Elaine and Charles were married June 18, 1891, at the Church of the Ascension in New York, and honeymooned at Sky Farm. He practiced among the Indians of the West and privately in St. Paul, and for the government, assigned simple, Anglicized names to Sioux Indians to simplify claims procedures.

In 1915, he and Elaine established a girls' camp in New Hampshire; but as he was frequently absent, the operation of the camp and the upbringing of their six children fell to Elaine, who became disenchanted. In 1921, they separated, he going to live with his son Ohiyesa in Michigan. He died in Detroit January 8, 1939.

Charles and Elaine had been prolific authors over the years, with many books published, singly or jointly; but her essential part as talented writer was revealed by Charles' failure to publish anything after the separation.

Giving up the camp in 1925, Elaine became prominent as a spokeswoman for liberal causes and as a dissident member of the DAR, forcefully opposed its blacklisting of persons deemed "unpatriotic." In 1935, she addressed the problems of women over forty in her book "Hundred

Maples." She died in a nursing home in Hadley, Mass., December 22 1953, and is buried in Spring Grove Cemetery in Florence. Two daughters live in Northampton.

Dora Read Goodale never married. She was a prolific writer, publishing many articles, poems and stories. She was a pioneer in community health in the Cumberland Mountains (in what today we call "Appalachia"), and from 1920 to 1946 taught in the Uplands Sanatorium at Pleasant Hill, Tenn., of which institution she became a director. In 1941, many of the verses she published while there were gathered into a pamphlet, "Mountain Dooryards," which she expanded into a book in 1946.

In 1927, Dora traveled in France and Germany for six months, for the most part alone, sending back observations and commentary which appeared in newspapers in a continuing series. Later, she was at the Sanford School in Redding Ridge, Conn., where she lived with her mother. After some 15 years in a nursing home, she died in Dunn Loring, Fairfax County, Va., December 12, 1953 — ten days before Elaine's death hundreds of miles north. Dora is buried beside her mother in the Center Cemetery in Redding.

What must surely be the greater part of the writings of the two sisters — poems, articles, fiction and books — exists in clippings, typescripts and holographs in seven boxes of material in the Sophia Smith Collection in the Women's History Archive at Smith College in Northampton. Dr. Eastman's biography was done as a master's dissertation in 1975 at the University of North Dakota, and a paper exploring the reliability of his historical books appeared last year in *American Indian Quarterly*.

From *The Berkshire Eagle*, September 21, 1978.

BERNADETTE MAYER

Avant-garde poet Bernadette Mayer and her family lived in Lenox during the 70s. One day in their carless life in the center of town forms the subject of her extraordinary long poem, "Midwinter Day," from which the following is taken.

Lenox on December 22, 1978

But why do we live here?
                              Incorporated in 1767,
This town's not very old like hotdogs and Pampers
Everybody who visits us finds it kind of unwitting
To walk around a town like any other, just a place
Except it's New England which is defended, tight and cold
I'd rather live someplace higher, warmer and a little freer
Where money was like matches and words were wine
But as it is Lenox is okay for us as a family,
Two writers and two babies each of whom have each other
Still somehow beyond the community of local people
Some of whom are limited, bigoted, stodgy or mean
Others among them love nature and certain kinds of art
And a man we know who lives alone here says he's lonely
He just reads, drinks, keeps a journal and sniffs cocaine
The town adolescents shout and skid around in their cars
And leave half-empty bottles of Jack Daniels in the park
The high school imported a black man from Harlem to play on
Their championship basketball team, the Lenox Millionaires
And the rumor is the schools are so bad the students
Don't always learn to really read and write in sentences
Hockey's a big thing I don't know anything about it
Alot of cars have "Lenox Scholardollar Day" stickers
Which means they want to give money to the un-athletic kids
Zoning, sewers and taxes concern all the owners of private property
And the town is run tightly with an eye to tourists' money

But there's no other industry except for G. E.
                              Lewis' mother
Says we're snobs and we only think about poetry
                              It's true
There's something about America that's unthinkable

Like the style my mother thought she ought to be accustomed to
Because her mother had convinced her she was better than all this
Whatever this is, but not good enough to slough off the religion
Of the simple joys of poverty, humility and fear
                                        And so
She gave my economic father the business religiously
And they both died young having said, if we didn't spend this money
To go on a vacation, we might have to spend it if we got sick
Without understanding that once bereft we've more to lose
And energy in the world mainly comes
From the hearts of the homeostatic people in it
Who hopscotch around, either picking up the stone or kicking it
And should be left alone without invasions or savings
Though there are masses and classes of people,
                                        I don't deny it
What but the impulse to move and speak
                                Can change the world
Where should we move
                        Who is this person speaking
Who am I speaking to
                        To you whom I love,
                                        Can I say that?
I can't stand to watch the people leaving
Shear Design, that's the hairdressers' place, looking like
The Man from Atlantis or Farrah Fawcett Majors or like
Men who invidiously wish to be like
                                The unspeakable Shah of Iran
In their dealings with the world
                                Now withdrawing, now attainable,
Rich with a drastic face for the hopelessly bitter people
Or the old story of the ludicrous young man in business
Flattering the aging woman with the greed of his attention
To further and simultaneously subvert the relentless image
Of the attitude of his mother to his father
                                Maybe here
My own moralism smacks of my neighbors' inherited tight-lipped looks,
These judgmental rugged individuals tense in the rigid morning
Like a memory of a funeral
                        Good day
                                I'll defend your dismay
Parents, come to the hurricane
To protest the children learning in the usual way

To eat and adore
        No that's not what I saw!
                    Just beyond
The civilized town are places everyone goes by car,
Sears, Zayre's and King's, Stop 'n' Shop and the Price Chopper
Which is cheaper because they don't use union labor
Big mothers steer carts with kids past the things
And something called malls are the big thing now
With indoor gardens and no windows where whole families can go
Even on the weekends for pleasure and to buy things
But the malls seem to ruin the lives of the local people
And are all caught up in hideous deals with fraudulent corporations
From the outside these agglomerations look like artless spaceships
Buried into the ground surrounded by cars and some trees in space
And one of the problems with them is that such blatant flatness
Creates winds so fierce in winter one cannot walk
Inside are millions of the objects of novelty and fast-food to eat
In imitation of being rich like kings and being brought things,
Of being surfeited and entertained like queens vomiting
To be able to assimilate more which there isn't room for
In the spaceless closeted private-property house rendered valuable
Lately by the inability to see another house from it
Though in a state like this it's nice to be alone
                              I'll trade you

We go on anyway
                The hotel's deserted today
                          Red berries,
This is the windiest corner of our walk, the most bitter,
The southern boundary of the circumscribed town, branches fallen
On each heart of every man and woman if they are they (invasion
Of the body snatchers) they seem to walk more tentatively
                                As we do
Like a step on the ice of the wisdom of the temperamental sky
Like cars go fast because they mean everything headfirst
Like need and desire, money fame and all kinds of love
Now to creep without aggression or the protected passion
Of a real man or woman through this pile of beautiful ice
As if to slip away means nothing,
                    Has no word or expression
Like the baby's desire to swallow all the eggshells
Like nesting birds
                The strollers make a roar

Except for cars
We practically see only white or black or gray today
We look and we see
Peripatetic
Like the police the police,
If it were noon the noon siren would just have frightened us,
Voting, the energetic town government, so clean and full of men
Who make sure the eyes of the people if nothing worse avoid
Flashing and neon signs and flagrant cheap posters and designs,
Street vendors and the uncut grass
Last summer
They even cut down the only blackberry bush in town
And the library had to lose its two dramatic elms
It's 12:15 p.m.
Everything circumscribed but what of nature's still around,
No place any different but for the limits of fear and love,
We love to walk for the rhythm of the heights to write
Going forward on foot by sights leaves the self alone at home
Something might happen or nothing, old lines, I might even die,
Ice and storms could crack the maples in their immobile ages,
Sentimental telephone cables are buried in the center of town
Not with a view to Mount Greylock
You've done all this before
Nothing happens
Let's go over it again
You've walked around
We're turning nearer home we meet the librarian who's got
An interesting hat, if it's not too cold or hot
We see the whole town every day, two square blocks
With alleys, shortcuts, the town clock and two weathercocks,
The Lemon Tree, Cimini's, the Crazy Horse, Lilac Park,
The first dentist, the dramatic post office, the Academy landmark,
Amoco Station, Dr. Tosk's, Loeb's Foodmart, Hagyard's Drugs,
Mole and Mole, the Lenox Library, Whitestone Photo, two icy fireplugs,
Two banks, Curtis Hotel, Town Hall, firehouse, police station,
Dee's Department Store, Four Seasons Travel-bus stop combination,
Different Drummer, Coffee Break, Candlelight Inn, Gateways Inn,
Community Center, Kelly's Irish Inn, Paddlewicker, Village Inn,
Nora's, Little Anthony's, David Herrick's, the pizza place,
The Arcadian Shop, Lucy Lou's, the second dentist, an empty space,
Spiritus Mundi, Clearwater, the greasy spoon, Michele the baker,
Buxton's Hardware, Elm Court Florists, the Bookstore, the shoemaker,

Heritage House, Just a Second, I've skipped the churches & Church
    Street
Between Housatonic and Franklin where the two package stores meet
The Golden Needle, Mainstream Woodworks, the former Yoghurt
    Rhapsody,
Glad Rags, The Restaurant, the laundromat and an art gallery,
I skipped Hawthorne Press which is off the main route
And the nursery school though we often go by foot

From *Midwinter Day* by Bernadette Mayer. Turtle Island Foundation, 1982.

MILTON BASS

Milton Bass, a native of Pittsfield, for many years arts and entertainment editor of the Berkshire Eagle, *is a novelist who lives in Richmond. This excerpt from* Not Quite a Hero *exemplifies the good humor of his rapid narrative style and his insight into the way politics happen in the Berkshires.*

Mayor of the City

The inaugural speech went well. Costain had "adapted" most of it from a "state of the state" address given by the governor of California to his legislature, and he could see heads nodding in approval among the audience of two hundred as he spoke about "budget austerity" and "holding the line on expenditures while going forward on services" and "closing the drawers of bureaucracy" (he knew it was an infantile joke but was a victim of its cleverness) and "resisting inflation" and "increasing employment" and "seeing to the needs of the aged, the retired and the sick."

The years of speaking at sports banquets had given him an easy manner before an audience, and he enjoyed being the focus of four hundred eyes. The applause verged on the enthusiastic, and he drew a big laugh when he invited everyone to have a cup of coffee and a piece of cake in the lobby "because it's the last free thing you're going to get in my administration."

The receiving line had been scheduled to run until 2 P.M., but by 1:15 it was obvious that the well-wishers had run dry and the snow-covered individuals coming through the portals had other business than to congratulate the new mayor.

Costain broke off his conversation with the president of the Junior Chamber of Commerce and strolled over to his wife, who was chatting with two female municipal employees.

"Well," he said, "would any of you ladies like another piece of cake?"

"Oh, no, thank, you, Your Honor," said the older of the pair. "We still have the water bills to get out." And they scurried off.

"No sense your hanging around any longer," said Costain to his wife. "It looks like the party's over."

"Who's going to clean up?" she asked, looking over at the littered table with the crumpled paper cups and crumb-strewn plates.

"Not you," he said. "The mayor's wife gets Mondays off and doesn't have to do windows. You take the car and go on home and be grateful we don't have to go to a coffee tonight."

"How will you get home?"

"I'll grab a cab or hitch a ride."

"Call and I'll come pick you up."

"No. They're talking about a foot of snow before it stops, and we can't afford to have the mayor's wife in an accident on his first day in office. I'll get home."

"Is it all right to kiss you good-bye?"

He almost said, "Better not." Almost. But then he leaned down and planted a solid one right on her soft red lips. Someone gave a bark of a laugh behind them, but he didn't turn. Bill Costain and his wife always kissed when they left each other's presence and when they reentered each other's presence, sometimes if it was only to go in another room. The mayor and his wife were going to continue the practice.

"This is about as far as we ought to go in the hall," he said to her. "I'll let you know later how private my office is."

Her face pinked a bit as she smiled at him, covering her embarrassment by making an elaborate business of drawing on her gloves.

"You'd better watch it," she said. "Your constituents might not appreciate your sense of humor."

He walked down the hall to the corner suite, where Mrs. Cain sat glowering behind the desk on which rested a simple sign telling the world that this was the "Mayor's Secretary." Mrs. Cain had worked for former Mayor Albert T. Blandford during all four of his administrations and was even more bitter than he about his loss to the young upstart. Since his pay had ceased at 10 A.M. that day, former Mayor Blandford had not felt it incumbent upon him to even attend the ceremony of his successor. Good sportsmanship had never been one of Albert T. Blandford's qualities, which in some part accounted for the host of enemies he had built up in four terms of office and his subsequent loss of that office to a young man who had excelled in sportsmanship.

But Mrs. Cain's salary did depend on her showing up at City Hall at a nominally respectable hour each weekday morning (Blandford had taken breakfast coffee at three different politically oriented restaurants and never reached his office before 9:30 A.M.), and she had remained at her desk all during the inauguration and subsequent receiving line festivities, slipping out only once to snatch a cup of coffee to go with the contents of her brown lunch bag.

"And you're Mrs. Cain," said Costain, holding out his hand to her.

She looked at his hand for a moment, then tremulously placed her own forward, never permitting him a firm hold, but grabbing it almost immediately back. At the side of her desk was a large cardboard box filled with pictures, small china and plastic figurines, pen sets, blotters, all the trifles acquired by Albert T. Blandford in eight years' tenure.

"Any instructions for me?" asked Costain.

"What?"

"This is all new to me," he said, waving his arm around the area. "You're the only one here with experience. Is there anything I ought to know about at this particular moment?"

"No, nothing."

"Then I'll just go in my office and start being mayor," he said, almost backing out of her presence into the adjoining room. The thought of spending the next two years with that at his portal gave Costain an uneasy feeling in his stomach, but he pushed her out of his mind as he gazed around the huge rectangle that was to be his domain. The buff-covered walls made no secret of where Blandford had hung his pictures, and the dust on the shelves and bookcases showed how the former mayor never had need to consult any of the volumes placed there for reference.

The desk was of good quality and size with a high-backed leather chair commensurate to the office. Costain folded himself into it carefully as he had become accustomed to with all chairs. Not bad, not bad at all. Better than the chair and the cubbyhole at Globemaster Electronics at any rate.

"I am the mayor of all the people," he said to the room. The room kept its counsel. Through the windows he could see the snow falling heavily, stifling all sound.

Is this it? he wondered. Why wasn't the phone ringing? Why weren't all kinds of people bustling in with reports, questions, whatever? Could he just sit here for the next two years and draw his twenty-four thousand dollars per and let the rest of the world go by? That is supposedly what Albert T. Blandford had done for the past eight years. That was the campaign attack by the forces of William S. Costain. Do something. Get Stockton moving again. Well, the time had come. What do you do? What do you move?

Now to business. What business? He sat at the desk again and pondered the future. If they weren't going to come to the mountain, the mountain had better fall on them. A meeting. Should he call a meeting of all department heads and outline his plans? What plans? All the plans of the campaign — more jobs, cut costs, help the aged, the infirm. How? How do you follow through on the promises? Where were the jobs? Suppose somebody asked him where the jobs were? Out there. The jobs are out there.

No. No meeting today. He picked up the phone and dialed the 0. He started counting by the fourth ring and was up to sixteen before the female voice said, "Yes?"

It wasn't even a pleasant yes. If anything, it was a rather disagreeable yes.

"Does it always take this long for you to answer a ring?" he asked.

"Who is this?" the disagreeable yesser asked in even more disagreeable tones.

"It's Bill Costain."

"Who?"

"Bill Costain."

"The mayor?"

"Yes."

"Uh ... I'm sorry, Mr. Mayor; but all the lines were tied up, and I was on a long-distance call. What is it you want?"

"Who is in charge of maintenance here? Like for painting a room."

"That would be Ron Blakely."

"Would you ring him, please?"

The voice that answered the sixth ring said that Ron Blakely was in the building somewhere and that he would be told the mayor was looking for him. The looking didn't take long because just as Costain was about to lift the receiver of the telephone to call his wife, there was a knock on the door, and in came a man who was obviously in charge of maintenance.

"I'm Ron Blakely, Mr. Mayor," he said, waving a folded carpenter's rule in a form of acknowledgment. A husky man somewhere in his early forties, the face creased from squinting at sun and the glare of snow. A hunter. A fisherman. Owner of a four-wheel-drive vehicle. "You said you wanted to see me?"

Costain unfolded from his chair. *First name or mister? Probably a snowmobiler. Looked like he just might be a snowmobiler. First name.*

"Yes, Ron," he said. "I was just wondering how much trouble it would be to give this room a coat of paint. Looks like it hasn't had one in quite a while."

"Hasn't," snorted Blakely. "Old Blandford liked to put on he was saving the taxpayers money. Kept telling everybody how a coat of paint saved was a coat of paint earned or some such thing like that. Made my building look like it wasn't rightly cared for. You can't blame me for the looks of this room, Mr. Mayor."

"How about blue?" asked Costain. "Have you got a nice blue?"

"I got any kind of blue you want, Mr. Mayor."

Costain liked the third blue chip he was shown, and arrangements were made so that the scrubbing of the barnacles and the subsequent painting would not interfere with the smooth sailing of the ship of state.

Costain sank back in his chair again, his first official act a complete success, and was reaching for the phone when it rang. He looked at it quizzically, wondering who might be calling him, and then smiled as he realized he could find out by picking it up.

"Mr. Mayor?"

"Yes."

"This is Chief Ahearn."

The chief had been noticeably present at the swearing-in ceremonies, resplendent in full blue uniform and white gloves, his pink face and azure eyes shining like a spotlight from the sea of faces.

"Yes, Chief?"

"I noticed that Mrs. Costain drove off a while back and was wondering how you were going to get home this evening."

Did the man have a Gestapo system working out of City Hall? Were the mayor and his wife to be under constant surveillance? Costain wasn't sure whether or not he should feel annoyed.

"I hadn't thought much about it, Chief. Either my wife will come back and get me or I'll take a cab."

"That snow is pretty thick out there, Mr. Mayor, and they're talking about ten to fourteen inches. Why don't I have one of the cars zip you home whenever you're ready?"

"Well, I don't know. Is that kind of thing, uh, done?"

"Oh, yes, sir, all the time. You're the commander in chief of the place now, and it's part of our job to see that you're mobile at all times and able to get back and forth to your headquarters."

So this is war.

"Well, Chief," said Costain, "I thought I would go home about a quarter past five."

"There will be a car outside waiting for you," said the chief.

And so there was. When Costain walked out into the blinding snowstorm, a black and white was parked at the curb, white smoke curling out of the exhaust pipe and a burly blue figure at the wheel.

They went up to the bedroom and listened to the eleven o'clock news on the radio while they were undressing, but there was no mention of the inauguration. There had been several accidents on the icy roads, from which one young man had died, and the weather for the next day was to be cold and windy.

Costain could barely keep his eyes open as he lay on the bed and watched his wife do her usual last-minute tuckings and retrievings. His sleep the night before had been fitful as he went over his speech while lying awake in the darkness and in his dreams when he dozed off. As usual, the anticipation had been much worse than the actuality. A piece of cake.

"Good night, Mr. Mayor," said Wanda, putting out the light and kissing him in practically the same motion.

"Good night, Mrs. Mayor," he mumbled, sliding off instantly into a deep sleep, so deep that Wanda had to nudge him awake to the point where he, too, could hear the ringing of the phone. It was pitch black, and the room was cold. The luminous face of the clock radio showed that it was twenty minutes past one. The phone continued ringing.

"Answer the phone, Billy," said Wanda. "There must be something terribly wrong."

He picked up the receiver but could not get out the word. Why would anyone be calling at this hour?

"Hello," he finally managed.

"I can't get up my street," said a harsh voice in his ear.

"Hello," said Costain.

"The whole goddamned street is blocked with snow," the voice screamed.

"Who is this?" asked Costain.

"A taxpayer," yelled the voice. "That's who it is. A taxpayer. And the whole goddamned street is blocked with snow, and the goddamned truck hasn't been through here once with the plow."

"What do you want?"

"I want my street plowed, that's what I want. So I can get home after work. You work eight goddamn hours breaking your ass, and then you can't even get home. What the hell kind of a city is this? What do we pay taxes for?"

"Why are you calling me?" yelled Costain, his own voice rising in anger as he realized that the man had lifted a few at a bar before starting for home.

"You're the fucking mayor, ain't ya?"

"What?"

"You're the fucking mayor of this fucking city. It's your job to see that the fucking streets are plowed."

The crash of the receiver jolted Costain's ear as he sat there.

From *Not Quite A Hero* by Milton Bass. G.P. Putnam's Sons, 1977.

AMANDA CROSS

A surprising number of talented mystery writers either live in the Berkshires, have used the region as the setting of their stories, or both — for example, Hugh Wheeler of Monterey (alias Patrick Quentin, Q. Patrick, and Jonathan Stagge), Richard Stevenson of Lanesborough, and Amanda Cross — in real life, Carolyn Heilbrun, a distinguished professor of English at Columbia who weekends and summers at her home in Alford. In this excerpt from The James Joyce Murder, *she introduces a confirmed New Yorker to a Berkshire native.*

Meeting Mrs. Bradford

When he had shut the gate behind him, he saw Kate, reading in a lounge chair under a tree. "Does the schedule permit of conversation now?" he asked.

"It had better. Mary Bradford is on her way to bring back the vinegar and partake of a cup of coffee."

"I, too," said Reed, collapsing into a chair, "have had an encounter. With Mary Bradford's husband."

"I know that already, you urban innocent. Mary Bradford saw you leap on the machinery, apparently waited to see if your intentions were homicidal, and determining that they weren't, decided to find out what you had said to her husband before he got the chance to tell her himself."

"You make her sound a most attractive lady. Has she no redeeming features — salt of the earth, perhaps, a natural bonhomie, a certain physical vigor?"

"Most of her physical vigor, as you shall soon hear, is in her voice. To hear her tell it, nobody works as hard as she, nobody contributes so much to society and receives so little from it, nobody has so much rectitude, propriety and good old-fashioned morality. Since her golden rule is 'Do unto Mary Bradford as Mary Bradford would like you to do unto her,' it is difficult to see whence her high moral tone. But don't let me prejudice you. What did you talk about with Brad?"

"As it happens, I was so busy having my teeth shaken out of my head, and observing the wonders of mechanized farming, that we didn't say very much. My shoes are covered with cow dung, and my spirit is oppressed."

"Reed. Have we got you down with our noisy ways? As I hope you could see this morning, our household is not really as mad as it seemed yesterday. This *is* peaceful, isn't it?"

"All events have conspired to rob me of my self-respect. I left New York yesterday feeling rested, vigorous and able, in my own way, to cope. Ever since I chugged up your beastly driveway I have been reminded of my ignorance, dipped in cow dung, made to appear effete next to some sunburned monster of masculinity on a tractor, and finally doomed, it seems, to listen to the chatter of the sunburned monster's wife."

"You don't fool me for a minute," Kate said. "Your masculinity and self-respect are no more in danger from today's events than they have ever been. You may be suffering from a surplus of fresh air — I know the feeling. Reed, I think what I cherish most about you is that calm assurance that does not need to prove itself. As to the cow dung, although it may be ruining a good pair of shoes, its price is above rubies and the envy of all gardeners. Pasquale will scrape it off your shoes and put it around a flower."

"Kate, the truth of the matter is, I had rather hoped ..." But the sudden entrance of a car into the driveway dashed the hope, or left it unexpressed. "Do you mean she drove up from just down the road?" Reed asked in amazement.

"No one ever walks in the country, except city folk. Hard-working farmers have no time for such foolishness. Hello, Mary," Kate called, getting to her feet. "May I introduce Mr. Amhearst. Mrs. Bradford."

"I guessed it was you in the guest room this morning when I came to get the cows. You can always tell when there's someone in the guest room because the windows are open then, and the blinds down, which of course they aren't when the room's empty. Ah, I thought, Kate Fansler has another guest. I bet it's a young man, she prefers men guests. I prefer women, who make their beds and don't expect to be waited on hand and foot, but then Kate has all those servants, so that probably isn't a consideration with her — I do envy people with help, but of course they all want to be paid a fortune and not do a thing — that dreadful Mrs. Pasquale down the road came in to help me once, talking, talking all day long, and I ended up doing all the work myself. No point to that."

Reed, who had risen, scarcely knew which part of this diatribe to respond to, if, indeed, any response was necessary.

"I hear you're a district attorney," Mary Bradford said.

Reed now stared at her in total amazement. He caught Kate's eye and saw her shrug, a shrug which said, "I didn't tell her."

"Shall we go in the house and have a cup of coffee?" said Kate, moving firmly toward the door.

"I really shouldn't," Mary Bradford said, following her. "I've baskets of raspberries to make into jam, and these days, of course, I'm my own hired man; then, if I don't get to clean the upstairs soon, we'll simply have to move out of it, and Brad, of course, is worse than the children, throwing his clothes around — I always get a sock right up in the vacuum cleaner, 'Look,' I say, 'I'm not the only person around here capable of picking things up ...'" Reed paused on the back porch to remove his shoes and socks and entered the house with bare feet. His normal impulse would have been to go to his room for another pair of shoes and socks, but the thought of allowing his naked feet to become grist to Mary Bradford's mill was too strong. He began to understand the effect Mary Bradford had on people. The woman positively tempted one to behave in an improper manner in order to provide her with material. This was an effect of undue propriety, shading off into prurience, which Reed had not personally observed before, and it fascinated him.

They settled themselves around the dining room table: everyone soon had a cup of coffee. Reed had the strange sensation of taking part in some aboriginal ritual. He wiggled his toes quite happily, and wondered what on earth Mary Bradford would find to say next.

"I call it shocking and improper behavior," she said, accepting one of Kate's cigarettes. "I've given up smoking," she added, lighting it. "Naturally, it's nobody's business what a man does in his own house, I suppose, but he rides up the road with them in a convertible, bold as you please, and what goes on in a big house like that on a weekend, all those girls. An orgy. I wouldn't be surprised," she added with a significant look, "if there were drugs. Drink of course goes without saying. One morning all those people are going to get up to do something, and find they can't stagger further than the nearest bottle."

"Are we discussing someone I know?" Reed asked in a voice straining so hard for innocence it sounded simpering to his own ears.

"The district attorney's office of Berkshire County ought to know about him," Mary Bradford said with emphasis. "But of course they haven't even got time to pick up these people who speed down the road, going fifty miles an hour right past a sign saying 'Children. Go Slow.' I have to lock my children in the house when the summer people come, I don't mind telling you."

"The boy I saw rocketing by this morning didn't look like 'summer people' to me," Reed said.

"That white trash," Mary Bradford snorted, identifying the car in question with no difficulty. "A new baby every year, and not enough sense or money to care for the ones they have. Who wouldn't have eighteen children if it weren't a question of buying them shoes?"

"How many do you have?" Reed asked. He was curious to discover if Mary Bradford ever stopped talking long enough to answer a question.

Kate merely sat back, smiling. Clearly she had been through all this several times before.

"Two," Mary Bradford said. "And they're properly dressed and not allowed to run around picking up whatever they take a fancy to. Of course, once that camp opens and all those lazy parents who send their children to the day camp come rushing up the road, it's impossible to cross over to our barn safely. But then, we're just farmers, and no one worries about farmers. You have to learn how to go on welfare, or get some union to support you, to succeed these days. Well, I must get back and make Brad's lunch. He'll just have to have peanut butter sandwiches. With all those raspberries to do there isn't time to prepare anything." She talked her way out of the house and into her car, pausing to make statements and then to digress from them at extraordinary length until, when she had finally backed the car out, Reed felt that he had survived an air raid, and that someone ought to sound the all clear.

"What sort of meal," Reed asked, "is lunch around here? If you think you catch a note of trepidation in my voice, it is definitely there. Kate, my sweet, I long for you to return to civilization, and I shall hope to commandeer hours of your time when you do, but I am afraid that I'm too frail a being altogether to withstand the rigors of the rural life. I don't know which is more horrifying, really, being bounced about on a tractor, wallowing in manure, or listening to the conversation of that angel of light from down the road. Not only is she malicious and suffering from logorrhea, she doesn't even conclude a thought. Who is that sybaritic chap down the road with the girls and the orgies?"

Kate laughed, "A very amusing character, as it happens, who's coming to dinner tonight. He's stopped in several times with invitations, and I finally proffered one. Just as you insist on trotting around in your bare feet, giving Mary Bradford loads to say when next she shares a cup of coffee with a neighbor, so Mr. Mulligan goes out of his way to act like an inebriated playboy. As a matter of fact, I've talked with him long enough to gather that he's a full professor of English and has published a good many books of literary criticism. Please don't go, Reed. Stay at least until tomorrow, meet Mr. Mulligan, and let us try to restore your faith in the countryside. It has its charms, you know. Open fires, silence, long lonely walks, beauty that sometimes takes one's breath away."

"I noticed the beauty on my tractor ride. Would you care to take one of those lonely walks? As a matter of fact, I set one foot on the road this morning and was nearly run down by the industrial revolution."

"Let's take some sandwiches, which I promise will not be peanut butter, and have lunch at the top of that hill. The brown dog will probably accompany us, but otherwise it should be quite peaceful. Of course, Mary

Bradford will undoubtedly see us go, and conclude The Worst."

"I shall look on it as a moral obligation to render one of Mary Bradford's suspicions correct. I feel quite inspired. All right, all right, I'm going to get on some shoes."

"And I shall get the sandwiches."

From *The James Joyce Murder* by Amanda Cross. E.P. Dutton, 1982.

RICHARD WILBUR

Richard Wilbur of Cummington was invested as Poet Laureate of the United States in September 1987. He has received many other honors and awards, including the Pulitzer Prize, National Book Award, Bollinger Award, Edna St. Vincent Millay Award, and Ford Foundation Award. Distinguished as a translator and teacher, he is a past president of the American Institute of Arts and Letters and a member of the American Academy of Arts and Sciences. Here are some of his poems on Berkshire observations.

Poems

ORCHARD TREES, JANUARY

It's not the case, though some might wish it so
Who from a window watch the blizzard blow

White riot through their branches vague and stark,
That they keep snug beneath their pelted bark.

They take affliction in until it jells
To crystal ice between their frozen cells,

And each of them is inwardly a vault
Of jewels rigorous and free of fault,

Unglimpsed by us until in May it bears
A sudden crop of green-pronged solitaires.

SHAD-TIME

Though between sullen hills,
Flat intervales, harsh-bristled bank and bank,
The widening river-surface fills
With sky-depth cold and blank,

The shadblow's white racemes
Burst here or there at random, scaled with red,
As when the spitting fuse of dreams
Lights in a vacant head,

Or as the Thracian strings,
Descending past the bedrock's muted staves,

Picked out the signatures of things
            Even in death's own caves.

            Shadblow; in farthest air
Toss three unsettled birds; where naked ledge
        Buckles the surge is a green glare
            Of moss at the water's edge;

            And in this eddy here
A russet disc of maple-pollen spins.
        With such brave poverties the year
            Unstoppably begins.

            It is a day to guess
What wide-deploying motives of delight
        Concert great fields of emptiness
            Beneath the mesh of sight,

            So that this boulder, this
Scored obstacle atilt in whittling spray,
        This swarm of shadows, this abyss
            In which pure numbers play,

            Though cloudily astrew
As rivers soon shall be with scattered roe,
        Instant by instant chooses to
            Affirm itself and flow.

HAMLEN BROOK

            At the alder-darkened brink
Where the stream slows to a lucid jet
I lean to the water, dinting its top with sweat,
            And see, before I can drink,

            A startled inchling trout
Of spotted near-transparency,
Trawling a shadow solider than he.
            He swerves now, darting out

            To where, in a flicked slew
Of sparks and glittering silt, he weaves

Through stream-bed rocks, disturbing foundered leaves,
            And butts then out of view

            Beneath a sliding glass
        Crazed by the skimming of a brace
Of burnished dragon-flies across its face,
            In which deep cloudlets pass

            And a white precipice
        Of mirrored birch-trees plunges down
Toward where the azures of the zenith drown.
            How shall I drink all this?

            Joy's trick is to supply
        Dry lips with what can cool and slake,
Leaving them dumbstruck also with an ache
            Nothing can satisfy.

                    DODWELLS ROAD
            (CUMMINGTON, MASSACHUSETTS)

I jog up out of the woods
To the crown of the road, and slow to a swagger there,
The wind harsh and cool to my throat,
A good ache in my rib-cage.

Loud burden of streams at run-off,
And the sun's rocket frazzled in blown tree-heads:
Still I am part of that great going,
Though I stroll now, and am watchful.

Where the road turns and debouches,
The land sinks westward into exhausted pasture.
From fields which yield to aspen now
And pine at last will shadow,

Boy-shouts reach me, and barking.
What is the thing which men will not surrender?
It is what they have never had, I think,
Or missed in its true season,

So that their thoughts turn in
At the same roadhouse nightly, the same cloister,
The wild mouth of the same brave river
Never now to be charted.

You, whoever you are,
If you want to walk with me you must step lively.
I run, too, when the mood offers,
Though the god of that has left me.

But why in the hell spoil it?
I make a clean gift of my young running
To the two boys who break into view,
Hurdling the rocks and racing,

Their dog dodging before them
This way and that, his yaps flushing a pheasant
Who lifts now from the blustery grass
Flying full tilt already.

SONNET

The winter deepening, the hay all in,
The barn fat with cattle, the apple-crop
Conveyed to market or the fragrant bin,
He thinks the time has come to make a stop,

And sinks half-grudging in his firelit seat,
Though with his heavy body's full consent,
In what would be the posture of defeat,
But for that look of rigorous content.

Outside, the night dives down like one great crow
Against his cast-off clothing where it stands
Up to the knees in miles of hustled snow,

Flapping and jumping like a kind of fire,
And floating skyward its abandoned hands
In gestures of invincible desire.

From *New and Collected Poems* by Richard Wilbur. Harcourt Brace Jovanovich, 1988.

PAUL METCALF

Paul Metcalf is a poet, novelist, essayist, literary critic, and lecturer. He lives in Becket.

Stampers and Hawkers

On August 1st this past summer — Herman Melville's birthday — the U.S. Postal Service held ceremonies in New Bedford in connection with the first-day issue of a new Melville stamp, part of the literary arts series. As one of Melville's surviving descendants — I am a great-grandson — I was invited to attend, representing the family.

My wife and I drove down the day before. It was a typical sweltering summer day. We checked into the Whaler Inn, kindness of the New Bedford Post Office, and made tracks as fast as we could for Horseneck Beach and a swim in one of the two great oceans on which Melville had voyaged.

The next day blossomed even hotter: a soggy, blistering day, and even at the harbor there was not a breath of wind. We made our way to the Whaling Museum, where, an hour before the stamps were to go on sale, the collectors were already lining up. We were escorted to the director's office where we drank coffee and hobnobbed with some of the visiting dignitaries. These included the assistant postmaster general from Washington; the postmaster of New Bedford; the mayor of New Bedford; a rear admiral from the Coast Guard; the president of the Melville Society; a chaplain; the port director of customs; assorted other local postmasters; etc. Among such I was a sort of minister without portfolio, with nothing but my bloodline to offer — and feeling a little bit silly about it.

At the appointed hour, we were lined up military fashion and marched through what had now become a seething mob of stamp collectors, to the auditorium, where we took our chairs on the platform. Gracing the ceremonies were the First Marine Band and Ceremonial Guard, in full button-down regalia — on this steamy, steamy hot day! Following opening remarks, we had the presentation of colors, the National Anthem and the invocation. We were patriotic and blessed, and ready to sail into a sea of speeches — which indeed followed. (During one of these, Dr. Milton Stern, president of the Melville Society, scribbled a note on an envelope and slipped it to me: "What do you think Melville would have made of all this?" I wrote back, putting it in quotes: "I don't believe it!")

To vary the program, we had a group of musical selections: a rousing performance of "Stars and Stripes Forever," and some semi-classical pieces, with that peculiar tone that occurs when a good military band tries to be "aesthetic."

With the conclusion of the final speech, and the presentation of albums, we filed out of the auditorium, and I thought, that's that.

But that was not that. That was just the beginning. There occurred now a phenomenon that left me shaken, and that still somewhat mystifies me. There were more than four hundred in the auditorium, most of them stamp collectors, and, picking me out from among the other dignitaries, a swarm of them descended on me, seemingly all at once, all shoving programs and ballpoints under my nose, demanding my autograph. I'm as vain as the next man, and anyone who asks for my autograph generally has my attention. But this turned into a mob scene, I scribbled and scribbled and scribbled, the sweat of my brow fogging my glasses, and I began to think to myself: Who are these people? What do they think they're getting? I'm three generations removed from The Great Man, and yet they seem to think they're getting a piece of Him, as though I were Herman himself signing their programs. One insistent woman demanded that I sign six — "for the grandchildren." After nearly an hour of this, when my fingers were cramping and my legs felt rubbery, the last of these strange souls finally departed.

We were collected once more and made our way over sunbaked sidewalks to the harborside. Here we boarded the U.S. Coast Guard cutter *Unimak* and sat down at tables on the afterdeck. Without benefit of canopy or awning, we lunched on elegant broiled haddock under the broiling, broiling sun — and listened to more speeches. My wife thought she was going to faint.

When it was finally over, the crew stood at attention and piped us ashore.

We drove back to the Whaler Inn, slithered out of our sopping clothes and into bathing suits, and headed once more for Horseneck and a cleansing, cooling plunge into the waves. Swimming under water and on the surface, bobbing with the waves, bodysurfing, I thought again of that swarm of locusts that had descended on me. I thought of Dr. Stern's question: "What do you think Melville would have made of all this?" I recalled that *Moby-Dick* had been published in 1851, when Melville was thirty-two; that it was panned by the critics and sold poorly; that Melville lived and wrote for another forty years after this, and died in almost complete obscurity; and that still another thirty years passed before interest in *Moby-Dick* began to develop. I thought: suppose it had been Melville himself, and not I, who had signed all those programs? What, indeed, would he have made of it?

Finishing our swim, we went back to the Whaler Inn for a dinner of

motel fish and an evening watching the Red Sox lose another one on
television.

. There are some things in this world that are just too mad to contemplate.

The Melville clan gathers on Melville's piazza at Arrowhead, 1987.
Courtesy of The Berkshire Eagle

I have no idea whose birthday falls on September 16th. But that day,
here in the Berkshires, blossomed sparkling clear. Following a day and
night of humidity and rain, a weather front passed through, and the
morning air was fresh and crisp, with a northwest breeze. I had become
interested in the migration pattern of hawks and discovered to my surprise that we were only a forty-five-minute drive from two of the better
spots in the northeast from which to observe these flights.

We had gone first to Mt. Tom — or, more properly, Goat Peak,
adjacent to Tom. Here there is a steel tower rising above the treetops, and
the platform at the top offers a panoramic view: the Connecticut River
valley, with the oxbow; Mt. Monadnock; the tall buildings of the University of Massachusetts; Westover, Northampton, Easthampton, Holyoke,
Springfield and Hartford. It had been a beautiful sunny day, but the
hawk flights were disappointing: only a few birds, and these at a distance. The greatest excitement came from an eagle — whether immature
bald or golden could not be determined. (My fellow observers, all strangers to me, were obviously experts, with years of study and watching
behind them.)

This day — September 16 — we decided to go to another spot, also
nearby. It is simply a hilltop, located in — ah, no, dear readers: I think I
shall keep this to myself. It is one of the most spectacularly beautiful and

apparently little-known spots here in the Berkshires, and if I locate it and publicize it, you and your family and friends will discover it and flock to it, and it will cease to be what it is now: the top of the world, in a near-perfect state of nature.

It is just a bare hilltop, and not particularly high, an easy climb from the road. It is spectacular, though, because the land around it is all slightly lower, and one looks for miles and miles and miles in any direction before discovering a higher configuration, so that the sky is an enormous blue bowl, and one stands on the hilltop at the center of what seems a near-perfect circle. Well-known mountains were visible, some at a great distance, but I shall not name them, dear readers, for there lurks among you someone with a cartographic mind who would use this information to help pinpoint our hilltop.

There were two hawk-watchers present when we arrived, and perhaps eight or ten others showed up as the morning wore on. They were all carrying picnic lunches, folding chairs, and the inevitable binoculars; they were there for the day, to make an official count for their local chapter of the Audubon Society.

On the platform at Mt. Tom, and here on this hilltop, I became aware at once of a rare kind of camaraderie. It was rare in that it mixed openness and friendliness with respect for one's privacy. In both places, we were outsiders: amateurs among experts. I quickly discovered that if I wanted to be alone with my thoughts, or with the birds, or with nature, they would leave me alone; but if I wanted to ask questions or share perceptions, they were more than helpful, going out of their way to indoctrinate us into the wonderful world of hawks, without being patronizing or condescending.

At Mt. Tom I had been wearing my Red Sox cap, and this brought me into conversation with some of the men, mostly older, all of whom were dedicated baseball fans, as well as bird-watchers. I thought of John Kieran, the late sportswriter for the *New York Times*, who was also a serious bird-watcher and naturalist. I have meditated some on this affinity, between bird-watching and baseball.

Here on the hilltop, we had come only for the morning, had not brought lunch. Our new friends opened their picnic boxes, offered to share with us. We politely declined.

At both places, I observed and tried to speculate on the backgrounds of these people. They seemed to come from different walks of life, some giving evidence of the "advantages," others clearly from the working class. They were brought together by their single compelling interest.

I felt, too, that their response to the world of birds was an aesthetic experience; but, in most cases, it was the single aesthetic in their lives.

These were not gallerygoers, poetry readers, music lovers, but their artistic passion was every bit as powerful. One of my favorites among them was a young man in ragged jeans, a work shirt, a baseball cap on backwards, and his hair in a pony tail. He described what is called a "kettle" of hawks rising in a thermal wind, reaching the top, and then, one by one, peeling off: "That's neat," he said. "Neat." That single monosyllable said it all.

When we first arrived, the sky was clear, with only a few clouds on the horizon. Although the sun was warm, it was breezy and cool enough for a down jacket. Initially, the hawks were few and distant. We stood or sat among the low-bush blueberries, conversed casually, and scanned the horizon. The first excitement was a flight of twelve broadwings, directly overhead. By now some wispy cumulous clouds had spread over us, and we lay on our backs looking directly up at the seemingly chaotic, swiftly moving patterns of flight, in and out among the blue of the sky, and the white and soft gray of the clouds. The birds were near enough to be seen with the naked eye, but to be seen much better of course through the glasses. The whole flight lasted only a few moments, and they were gone.

Later there was a much larger kettle, again directly overhead. As before, we lay on our backs, the glasses lifted and lowered, lifted and lowered. This flight lasted for several minutes, and the official count came to 214. If you think that's a lot, dear readers, consider on 13 September 1983, at Mt. Wachusett, during the space of one hour — 12 noon to 1 P.M. — the official count of broadwinged hawks came to 16,216! No such prodigious numbers at our hilltop. Still, the few minutes that it took those 214 to pass were strangely exciting.

At Mt. Tom we had been disappointed because the birds were few, and distant. Here, the birds were more plentiful, but similarly distant; and it occurred to me that that's part of the aesthetic, the excitement: those magnificent creatures, swirling, soaring, rising, diving — keeping their distance. Closer, they would lose their wildness, which was their signal virtue.

A little after midday we took our leave. On the way home my wife pointed out to me how strange was the contrast between these two events of our summer: New Bedford and the hawk-watch.

Strange, indeed.

First, the weather, that framework in which all events occur, and which is seldom far from the attention of a New Englander: there was the cloying, steamy humidity of New Bedford ... and the brisk, dry, early-fall warmth-and-chill on the hilltop.

I thought of Herman Melville, the man whom we were presumably celebrating in New Bedford, the man whose restless, roaming spirit carried him to the South Seas ... as the instinct of the broadwings overhead led them in their southward migration.

I thought of the people: the stampers and the hawkers. The stampers, cornering me, crowding me, clutching their programs and ballpoints in their sweaty palms, seemed a people possessed, as though fighting an unseen enemy, seeking security in their collections and autographs. The hawkers, on the other hand, were without an ax to grind.

There was the almost military formality of the ceremonies in New Bedford, vis-a-vis the relaxed informality, both at Mt. Tom and the hilltop.

For the stampers, there seemed some demonic significance in possessing a family member's autograph. I wondered: suppose I were to tell the hawkers who my great-grandfather was? I imagine they would be polite about it, but I doubt that they would really care. I would neither rise nor fall in their estimation. And the hawks themselves wouldn't give a tinker's damn!

These thoughts give me great pleasure.

From *Where Do You Put The Horse* by Paul Metcalf. Dalkey Archive Press, 1986.

STEPHEN SANDY

Stephen Sandy lives in North Bennington, Vermont, and teaches at Bennington College. Among many other honors, he was named the university poet at the ceremonies marking Harvard's 350th anniversary.

Riding to Greylock

Two schoolboys behind still talk
about their winter vacation
while I ransack my bags.
Here is my Edwardian
boy's nature book, "The Romance
of Animal Crafts," but the Mohawk

Trail has seen better days,
our Bonanza bus zigzags
an icy curve; no one
could read now. And I admit
it: I have lost my keys.
They're gone. So here I sit

desiring them, wondering
in which snowdrift they are.
Across the hills Mt. Greylock hulks
like a beached whale,
flooded by air. The bare
branches mullion the fields.

Coupin writes how curious
the nests of field mice were,
houses woven at home,
ingenious; neat. Are mice
unreconciled as us
to losing things in the snow?

There's no romance in ant
hotels you can be sure,
nor in these great showplaces
of the pleasing coral polyps.
But if their buildings can't
leave me a vision of

myself, forget them. The dams
of the sedulous, crafty beaver
delight me. Soon I note
a "beaver vernacular";
then in her tale for children
some spinster gives them trappings

— hearth rugs and pillow shams,
the sort of thing we heard
and half believed in childhood.
Then, we compared our lot
with the beaver or the witch,
thought hard which one we'd choose

to be (and which was which!).
It's dangerous to think
of animals as stuffed
toys, stunted people; just as
children, carefully coiffed
and propped in old photos

— baby fogeys — are hideous,
vain midgets like Tom Thumb.
All this is fallacy
of course; pathetic and
old hat. How did I come
to this? Because I feel

defenseless today? A fish
out of water, a snail
without a shell? A boy
without his key!
                    They've turned
the heat off now; it's cold.
That wakes you up! I wish

I had not watched the old
lady in black on the ice
outside the bus collapse
in stroke or heart attack!
When I stopped there, too near,
I saw each ebbing synapse

snap; her face pass fear,
stiffen and loosen at once,
blue with the deep eye-shadow
of death. That lying there
like a rag doll grown huge,
adulterated, slack

at the seams (as where the rouge
spots on her cheeks seemed cotton
patches coming loose),
that had to happen. But
to think of someone dying
becoming some recluse

of his old self, and gladly!
What if she had been able
and willing? A priest had called
for her name (he must perform
last rites) and no one helped.
The crowd was behaving badly.

Maybe the lady chose
it this way, ready to shed
her frilly skin; to lie back,
savaged. The willingness
of an animal to be dead
when it must; a flower's; the dog's

eye in a fading rose!
          These fields half overgrown
lie caulked with snow now, choke
on their abandoned bones
of stalk and stubble. The bus
rocks me; or when I doze

knocks me awake. In Greylock's
shadow now, we're nearly there,
where I will hunt for my keys.
The boys are silent. Then, "O!
there was a fox, a red fox
on the soccer field! On the snow!"

From *Riding to Greylock* by Stephen Sandy. Alfred A. Knopf, 1983.

WALTER HOWARD

After an international career in journalism, Walter Howard returned to the Berkshires to operate the family dairy farm in Tyringham. At the time of his death in 1987 he was the editor of the op-ed page of the Berkshire Eagle.

Riding the Milk Truck

You have them, you love them, you feed them, you milk them every morning. Then the milk gets picked up, and in the afternoon you start all over again. Curiosity ate at my soul: Where did the milk go? So the other day I rode along with Richard Barrett's tanker to find out.

Barrett's Route No. 1 starts at his depot on South Onota Street in Pittsfield, every other day at 9 a.m. I rolled out really early, got the girls milked and skidded into the yard with seconds to spare.

Route 1, the flagship route in Barrett's countywide network, is run with a new and powerful Transtar II cab pulling what's got to be the most highly polished milk tanker in New England. I could (and, alas, should) shave in its reflection. With Bob Osterhout behind the wheel, today we are going to pick up about 18 tons of milk from nine farms scattered around the county, and deliver the load to Yankee Milk Cooperative's processing plant in West Springfield.

Barrett's five trucks collect from 44 farms in the Berkshires. Most are picked up every other day; a few, whose cups runneth over otherwise, have to be collected daily.

Each farm, by law, must store its milk in a bulk tank refrigerated to about 37 degrees F. With each pickup, a sample of milk from the farm is bottled, identified and sent to the cooperative's laboratory for analysis. Violation of various minimum standards can bring to the farm a swarm of inspectors from any state in the Northeast where the milk might ultimately be sold. This, and I speak from the heart, is to be avoided.

First stop, at 9:30 a.m., is Silvio Rotti's farm on Fort Hill Avenue, an island of greenery on the outskirts of Pittsfield. Silvio is a courteous host and gives me a quick tour of his barns while Bob pumps the Rotti herd's production out of the tank and into the trailer. The cows are cleaning up better hay than I feed mine.

We are waved out of the yard and head toward Richmond and the Walter Iwanowicz farm on Summit Road. I adjust slowly to the novelty of riding 10 feet above the asphalt. From here, people's lives are laid bare.

Hedgerows cannot conceal the yards that haven't been cleaned up yet, the unmade beds or the dishes still in the sink. I can't resist looking in as we roll by.

Very good farm, says the inspector's report at this second stop. I can see why. The place is immaculate. Mr. and Mrs. Iwanowicz are just finishing cleanup of their milking equipment when we arrive. While their tank empties into our tanker, Iwanowicz and I commiserate about inflation, mortgages and the bad goings-on in Washington.

From there, it's a short run to the Deinlein farm, something of a rarity nowadays. Mr. Deinlein has a small herd of milking Shorthorns. Backing into his yard isn't easy. Bob misses on the first try — "lost it," he growls — but makes it on the second. A skillful performance.

One could argue that economics in 1979 don't justify stopping at a small farm like this. Picking up a few hundred pounds of milk takes just as long as pumping a few tons someplace else. Maybe so, but these few cows are there, and the land they graze on is being used. Strike them off the list, and another farm bites the dust.

Bob recalls to me, as we head toward West Stockbridge, that as recently as 20 years ago many of the stops on his route were still milk-can stops, three or four cans per stop, and that there weren't miles to travel between stops. Times have changed. Houses have sprouted where the pastures were; and on the front steps of the houses, painted black and filled with geraniums, are those milk cans that Bob used to pick up.

The next stop darned near finishes me. Bob suddenly turns off Monument Valley Road, east of Great Barrington, roars over a precipice, and comes to a stop in midair. We are at the Hoskeer farm, if I dare get out and look around without roping myself to the trailer. I do, and am glad, for the view is spectacular, and Mr. Hoskeer's tank is brimming — a beautiful sight. One more cow in milk and he'll be running over. I envy him.

We are now approaching familiar territory. The Tryon farm in Monterey is the next stop before we hit home base in Tyringham. A winding climb uphill leads Bob and me to speculate how it will be in that blizzard next January. He hasn't run this route in winter yet.

As we climb yet another hill toward my farm, I pray silently that the Howard herd hasn't pulled its ritual weekly jailbreak and scattered all over the road. They haven't, thank God, and our pickup for a change is routine, although my small Jerseys shrivel into uddered gnomes seen from the cab of Transtar II.

We are now in the homestretch. Next stop: Hale Brothers' Sunset Farm. The Hales are renowned for their maple syrup, but they also have a good herd. Their reverse-S driveway, a real pistol, presented a psychological barrier to a trailer rig for years. Barrett's crew shattered that barrier a few weeks ago by getting a trailer in without scratching a building. This meant that a smaller "straight job" no longer had to make a special run from Pittsfield to pick up the milk. Today is Bob's first attempt to negotiate the curves with Transtar II and its trailer, the longest in the fleet. He does it with ease.

After this, the Mitchell farm just down the road seems like duck soup, and from there we head for Frank Carrington's on the outskirts of Lee. Frank is fixing his fences (which is what I should be doing) when we pull in. His tankful completes our load, and we head for the Pike with about 18 tons of milk behind us. Capacity is 25 tons, and Bob will probably be hauling close to that in a few weeks when our cows hit that nice green grass and really start putting out. It's called the spring flush, and for haulers and distributors alike, it can cause problems.

King of the Pike, I enjoy watching all those little cars scramble out of Transtar's way as we head east to the Yankee plant in West Springfield. We are due there at 3 p.m. and pull in seven minutes late — mostly because Bob has treated me to a sandwich en route.

Harris trailers, unburdened, are heading out. A Zabco straight job from over in the valley is unloading when we arrive. Many of these are old veterans, scarred from battles with potholes, fallen trees and winter barnyard ice. Barrett's No. 1 stands out in this crowd like a gleaming moonraker. We are the last truck of the day. It will take about two hours to pump us out, wash and sanitize us for tomorrow's run.

En route, I have noticed that Bob values cleanliness. Now, armed with brushes, mops and high-pressure hoses, he attacks an empty Transtar II like a scouring archangel. If we arrived a little dusty after our swing through Western Massachusetts, going home clean, by God.

Precisely at 6 p.m. we roll into Exit 2 at Lee. The only smokey on the return trip leapt the divider at marker No. 13 and for greener pastures eastbound, so we are home free. I find it a long day. And we had perfect weather. What would it be like in the worst of winter? Yet it must be done; rarely does a Berkshire farmer have to dump his milk.

As I roll slowly out of bed next morning to face the herd I feel kind of late, though for me I'm not. Bob has been on the road an hour already, heading for Burlington. It's all in a day's work.

Tyringham's Steeplechase

Among the many mansions in my father's house, the Union Church of Tyringham suits me better than most. It presides over the town without commanding it: a visible presence whose proportions match the community it serves.

Many New England towns cannot make this claim. They are saddled either with high-steepled monuments to sectarian arrogance, or damp mushrooms of humility where the meek whisper their hosannas and think guilty thoughts. Somewhere between is the right answer to what a house of worship should be. I think those who built our church had the answer.

Trial and error had something to do with this. The present church, built in 1844, was the fourth of five houses of worship built in Tyringham, and is the only remaining one. The township was settled in 1739 and then included what has since become the town of Monterey, six miles to the south of Tyringham center.

At the outset, church services were held in Monterey — somewhat sporadically. Ministers came and went. Supporting a church was a town budget item in the days before church and state went their separate ways, and it carried a very low priority. The Rev. Adonijah Bidwell, who graced the pulpit for longer than most, was moved to complain that his flock had dwindled to four or five, because the town fathers refused to replace missing window lights in the church, which made it rather breezy in winter.

Insult was added to injury when Bidwell learned that his pastoral salary, which he hadn't received for four years, went instead to support the activities of the Minutemen, off in eastern Massachusetts firing shots heard round the world: "... but to come to another reason; I have preached in this town four years for which I have had no reward but understand me I don't mean that four whole years is due but three years and about three-quarters of year's salary is due...." Did he get paid? We don't know.

His successors, variously Methodists, Baptists and Congregationalists, didn't fare much better. There were more than 50 who preached for a pittance in Tyringham during the 19th century. One, the Rev. Delos Lull (would he have changed his name for a television contract?), almost tasted glory in 1859 when a parishioner gave him a pickled ham, ready to be smoked, or to be stolen. "The ham could not have removed itself," he commented as he stared into an empty smoke barrel some time afterward.

When the present church was raised in 1844, at a cost of $6,000, it served a Methodist congregation. The Baptists worshipped down the road. Their church burnt in 1873 — some said, "due not to divine but to human agency" — and was rebuilt immediately. Early in this century, Tyringham's population having shrunk to a fraction of its industrial-age apogee, the two small congregations joined forces under the benevolent carapace of the Union Church. And so it has remained to this day.

Two years ago, an important part of that carapace — the steeple — showed visible signs of interior ailments that had, apparently, been weakening the structure for years. The Church Committee studied the problem and, faced with the necessity of raising $12,000 for repairs, decided to accept the challenge. It isn't easy for a town with a population of fewer than 300 to raise that kind of money, particularly during a recession. But a preliminary letter of appeal brought in $5,500 in contributions, which encouraged the church's Steeple Committee to press on. Included was a large donation from Edward N. Perkins Sr., who spent many summers in Tyringham and who died this past winter just short of his 100th birthday. Mr. Perkins was a devout Episcopalian and by his own admission didn't care very much what went on inside a Union Church, but he cared very much how it looked on the outside.

Eighty foundations, supposedly interested in the preservation of New England church architecture, were solicited. One responded, in a small way. The committee then turned to better friends, the neighbors and former residents of Tyringham.

In the spring of 1982, a letter soliciting funds in addition to the $8,300 already raised was sent out, over the signature of John McLennan, the chairman of the Steeple Fund. For by then the cost estimate for repairs had passed the $15,000 mark and was still climbing. As so often happens during surgery on an old building, removal of exterior trim revealed unexpected corruption on the inside.

There were moments of discouragement, but there was also Millicent McIntosh, of Tyringham. The former president of Barnard College admits that she had never raised a nickel before she took on that top educational assignment. Since then, she has raised many nickels, and that talent went to work for the steeple.

Two evenings of play readings were held in the church. The George Gilders opened their newly built octagon to the curious (we keep to ourselves, but open houses are irresistible). Carolyn Canon stitched a patchwork quilt and personally sold the raffle tickets for it. Marcia Eisenberg, a trained genealogist, gave a course in tracing family histories. The Church Committee served several church suppers. The Hop Brook Community Club, the Valley Club, the Volunteer Fire Company and its Ladies Auxiliary all pitched in. Suzette Alsop donated 10 percent of the sale price of paintings by her, sold at a show in the fall of 1982. Robert Brown, an engineer, climbed up the staging every night to check on progress. And so it went.

By the end of last year, the total cost of restoration had risen to $28,000, but the end was in sight. So was the Steeple Committee's goal: A final letter, in February of this year, announced a homestretch effort to collect the last $2,661. The goal was met, indeed exceeded by more than $1,000, which is set aside for various church maintenance problems.

On Sunday evening, July 10, the newly restored steeple will be dedicated. The Rev. Richard O'Hara, pastor of the church during the great campaign, will return for the ceremony from his new post in Lynn. There will be many good things to eat, and many people to eat them — and a general sense of pride that nearly $30,000 had, in fact, been raised to save the steeple.

How this averages out among the population of a small town is a calculation that shouldn't be made. It does, however, suggest a sense of generosity which would have paid poor Rev. Bidwell's salary many times over. And it says something about support for an institution to which you may not necessarily belong but which is, nevertheless, there when you need it. Luckily for us, the darker side of Puritanism had pretty well leached out of our forefathers' souls by the time they traveled westward to settle the Berkshire townships in the mid-18th century. The steak roast which raises funds today for a worthy cause is much more wholesome, though perhaps more expensive, than its antecedent entertainment, the burning of a witch.

Which isn't to say that the sheep now graze safely and quietly on their side of the fence. There are those (I among them) who miss the traditional words of the King James Bible at church services. Others who take issue with views on world affairs, uttered from the pulpit. At least disagreement no longer consigns one to hellfire and damnation.

One approaches the center of Tyringham from Lee to the north, past Break Neck Road and down Paper Mill Hill. In winter, the church is visible from the northern edge of town. Or, from Otis to the southeast, one descends Braden Hill, past Sodom Road, the Monterey Road, and sees the church with rather less warning. There are four large wooden columns but no windows at the front. The steeple, now secure for a while, is actually a double-tiered cupola, with 12 smaller columns supporting each tier. There are four tall windows on each side of the church. Across a narrow road is the Tyringham Cemetery, at whose center stood the first church in town.

I particularly like to see it at night, coming home from Lee. The front is well lit and makes the church appear larger than it is. That's all right, too, because darkness puts extra demands on a symbol of sanctuary, and a little help that enlarges the image somewhat, not too much, is a good thing.

From *Sisyphus in the Hayfield* by Walter Howard. Cobble Press, 1988.

STEPHEN PHILBRICK

Poet Stephen Philbrick operates a sizable sheep farm in Cummington.

Poems

FATTENING DORSET SHEEP

Famous death is so blank
   And the cracked corn spills so sweet,
   Catching in the noils of the wooly noggins.
The leader of the wethers walks the plank
Of the long trough, trying to eat everything, even his feet.

Who are these pale faces kept behind
In the dark barn these days of fire?
They are lambs in fall who fell
Too late to fatten in time,
The survivors of spring who grew too slow to die.

Their world is once, they have no mind to wander.
One spring to milk, one mumbled summer of pasture noise,
One fall to fatten.
Then in the acetylene air of winter
He'll shear them, the never ewes and the wethers, those ammonia boys

Who never know how soft it falls,
The wool rich as meat.
Who never know how swift it stuns,
The gun that makes their small, straw world
Go black, big and instant.

Before dinner he stops to wash his lanolin hands.
There is a hunger that bleats, there is a whiff of rain. Something walks
with him, something he almost thought —
About how much a sheep, and how much a man understands
And how different it hits them in the brain.

CLEARING BRIARS

Wherever briars fall is fertile ground.
They have a way of moving that legs have never found.
They run rings around a garden and insinuate that trees
Grow tall because they're dull, and dense because they're sound.
My shears whispered said and done, but the briars insinuate with ease

That I am the angel of solid interests: the oak and ax
And afterblow of work: it's true, I count the cracks
I made in the heap and sea of briars that crown the solid ground.
But even their dead eel around my straight attacks.
They have a way of living that blades have never found.

Laboring through their evil green to show the land its shape,
I saw a mercy in the briars that turned my work to rape.
The creeping things that live on edges, and under and behind
Take shelter in the briars; birds and toads tick slower, hairs sleep
    on the nape.
Whatever briars hide is not lost but found. My sight was much
    sharper than my mind.
They have a way of keeping that the heart will have to find.

———————

From *No Goodbye* by Stephen Philbrick. Horizon Press, 1982.

ROY BLOUNT, JR.

Humorist Roy Blount, Jr., lives in Mill River. Author of About Three Bricks Shy of a Load, What Men Don't Tell Women, *and* One Fell Soup, or, I'm Just a Bug on the Windshield of Life, *his most recent book is* Camels are Easy, Comedy's Hard.

A Berkshire Ditty

W hen communication's irksome
I adjourn to pastures Berksome
Where, in fact, I live.
Rolling hills and folk laconic
Round about the Housatonic
Make me positive
Life is more than hype and neon.
Here I plop what's left of me on
Slopes, and feel them give.

Written by Roy Blount, Jr., for *The Berkshire Book*. Berkshire House Publishers, 1986.

Why I Live Where I Live, If I Do

M ill River's population has been in decline since the eighteenth century. I guess the per capita income has risen some since then but not dramatically. There haven't been any mills in Mill River to speak of since the railroad bypassed us shortly after the invention of the railroad, but there is a river, the Konkapot, which makes a sound — konkapotkonkapotkonkapot, only more liquid — that we can hear from our house at night. Nothing else public in town is running after six.

Our place is not precisely bucolic (a three-minute walk to town hall) or urban (next to town hall lives a cow) or suburban (a local man sold his entire lawn for topsoil a few years ago). In just over two hours by car I can be in Gotham, but on the other hand our dogs fight porcupines.

We have plenty of dogs: two. Because we live next to an expanse of woods, our dogs come home looking like porcupines and smelling like skunks. We might as well let the porcupines and the skunks themselves come on inside. One morning recently we opened the door to let the dogs in, and here came one of them barreling home from way back up the dirt road, running and beaming, running and beaming *wham* she was ambushed and knocked flying by Colonel, the neighboring husky, but scrabble roll scramble she was back up running and beaming, beaming and running, closer and closer, running beaming indoors *plangk plonk plang* she was up on top of the piano. She never did that before. And that was our more nearly ordinary dog. We are always trying to figure out what our other dog looks like. I say she looks like President Benjamin Harrison in the face and, overall, like something drawn by Hugh Lofting, author and illustrator of the Dr. Dolittle books. My wife says she looks like the Flying Nun. That's one thing to do in Mill River, sit around discussing what your dog looks like.

We live on the outskirts of Mill River, but it's a short-skirted town. I walk to the store in three and a half minutes. Get the *Times*, the *Daily News*, the *Globe*. And the mail. And liquor. And manila envelopes. And produce. And lock washers. And great meat. Jim, an excellent butcher, taught Gary.

Except for having your car fixed or inspected by Jack or Eldred Stanton, that's about all there is to do right in town (I mentioned going to the library). But on our property I can always cut firewood or screw around with the compost. We have more than an acre of trees, quite a few of which are dead. Chop one of those dried-out boys down with an ax, drag it up to the house past the bemused horse, saw it up with a Swedish handsaw, split the logs with a good old American splitting maul. A person likes to *whang*! Right? Not too many opportunities to *whang*, more than enough to be *whanged*, in the city.

The satisfactions of compost are more rarefied. Compost, to me, is a lot like writing. Sometimes our heap doesn't seem to want to break down. "I like compost," I will yell at it. "But not very mulch!" Or, "Dust thou art, to dust returneth, was not spoken of my soil!" Our compost never — at least not while I'm watching it — steams. You hear about piles that emit visible rays of heat, but that is a pleasure I've been denied. Still and all, I take pride in our down-to-earth clump of decadence. There are various ways — apparatus, structure — you can rig up your compost so it works faster. I don't get into any of that. My whole interest is mix.

Flat beer, bones, ashes from the wood stove, tobacco spit, coffee grounds, shredded *Timeses* and *Newses* and *Globes*, stale birthday cake, grass clippings, bad fruit, burned popcorn, struck matches, butts of cigars from Art Rooney, our horse's manure, spoiled hay, etiolated broccoli, black zucchini, lobster shells, fish eyes, the pet sand crabs that froze, mice the cats couldn't finish, olive pits, finger blood, hair from each of our combs and brushes, dish-rinse water, peels, hulls, parings, stems, twigs, leaves, bark, sawdust, eggshells, fingernail clippings, pencil sharpenings, moldy applesauce, weeds, sand, month-old bread, live worms (many of them descended from five dozen I got at Hugh Carter's worm farm in Plains), corncobs, apple cores, dust, pine straw, wine dregs, tea bags, string, crusts, crumbs, sardine oil, melon rinds, artichoke chokes, shrimp legs. A *great heterogeneity of tissues,* coming together to create a richness, like unsavory influences forming a style.

I am open to the accusation that I see compost as an end in itself. But we do grow some real red damn tomatoes such as you can't get in the stores. And potatoes, beans, lettuce, collards, onions, squash, cauliflower, eggplant, carrots, peppers. *Dirt* in your own backyard, producing things you eat. Makes you wonder.

Don't have to be on no committees in Mill River. Don't have to do no socializing without enthusiasm. Do have all these hills, vales, falls, deer, grosbeaks, and woodchucks. Low property taxes. Never have to wait for a tennis court. Right-off-the-stalk sweet corn. Kind of people around who, if you or your car turns into ice, which you or it is likely to do during at least six of the year's months, will help you get thawed. And we don't worry about burglary — we real, local residents don't. It's true, some of these city people have had their weekend places broken into. I didn't do it.

From *What Men Don't Tell Women* by Roy Blount, Jr. Little Brown & Co., in association with The Atlantic Monthly Press.

BARRY STERNLIEB

Poet Barry Sternlieb lives in Richmond and teaches in Pittsfield. He is the publisher of Mad River Press.

Poems

NO SUCH THING

Morning peaks
    clear and dry
      on the loud wavelength
   of Canada geese
near the pond, hitting
full height across Malnotti's field
where it's easy to pass
one life through the eye
of another,
     moving,
as if any direction could match
this hot clover smell,
     toward ten Holstein heifers
who spook
and head uphill.
Taken together
their clean black and white hides,
    none exactly alike,
make the same
rhythm inside us, the same blindness
we look for in thinking nothing
the same.
Almost at our fingertips:
    how the buzzard floats!
Wind wrings a hush
out of shallow grass
the cows go back to,
the same grass that draws us down
    where sun
and water couple
swearing no such thing
as too long
in coming.

TAKING STOCK

At minus twenty, silence
wears the rough grain
of hills into sun,

everything around here
taut as the angle
between northeast and north.

These days we keep
close to home, our hearts
holed up like animals underground.

Where is the pleasure
of bearing winter
if not in the raw clarity,

sheer glare, or even stillness
that can't be thought?
As far as this place goes

the book of cold,
worth its weight in ignorance,
does for always
what always does for us.

IN DEER SEASON

In deer season he becomes a doe
moving through the orchard,
belly full of apples,
smelling woodsmoke and frost,
hearing old leaves curl,
taking what light has to give
across the last rise,
everything kindled by the unseen
egg in a run of sperm.

From *Thinning The Rows* by Barry Sternlieb. Brooding Heron Press, 1990.

DON GIFFORD

Don Gifford is Professor of English and Class of 1956 Professor of American Studies Emeritus at Williams College. In The Farther Shore: A Natural History of Perception, *from which the following observation of his corner of the Berkshires is taken, he weaves the rich and unusual insights of a lifetime's concern with literature together with clear-sighted analysis of contemporary life.*

At Home in the "Placeless Cosmopolis"

THE VIEW FROM THE WORKTABLE

Seated at this worktable I can, of course, try to describe "the landscape that radiates from me accordingly." My study faces east from the second floor of a house set down in a hollow 640 feet above sea level. From the windows and the skylight of this house and study in summer, the horizon lines are pushed up by deciduous trees. In winter, the horizon lines (except those established by the white pines to the north) decline a few degrees, and we can catch glimpses of the hills beyond. The house is surrounded by the asymmetry of its L-shaped lawn and its amoeboid flower gardens; there is no longer sufficient sun-space for vegetables. The lawn flows into other lawns without much fence or screen on what amounts to an eighteen-family island, bounded south, east, and north by two streams, Buxton Brook and Hemlock Brook, and shut in by the town's Westlawn Cemetery up the hill to the west. It's even more of an island now that the bridge over Hemlock Brook that was our access has given in to the age on its plaque, 1910. The "temporary" detour circles up through the cemetery to exit between the white gateposts that glimmer at night like the ivory gate "Without a flaw," as Virgil said, "and yet false dreams are sent / Through this one by ghosts to the upper world."

AN ISLAND TOWNSHIP

This creek-bottom cul-de-sac sits on the periphery of Williams College in the village of Williamstown. College and village have their political identity only by inclusion in the Town of Williamstown. The township in turn is geographically enisled in a bowl formed by the Taconic Mountains to the west and southwest, the Berkshire Hills to the south, the Greylock massif east and southeast, and the southern foothills of the Green Mountains to the north.

This island township has its own wayward microclimate, oblivious to the weather forecasts computerized in Albany, New York, thirty miles to the west, or in Springfield, Massachusetts, in the Connecticut Valley fifty-five miles to the southeast. According to conventional wisdom, weather systems on this continent generally move on axis from west to east. The mountains that define this valley (2.4 miles to the east, 1.8 miles to the west) are on axis north to south with east-west ridges like thresholds 1.6 miles to the north and 4.6 miles to the south. "A meteorological toilet bowl" is the received witticism about this extinct lake bottom (Lake Bascom disappeared when the last glacier withdrew). Like many of the microclimates in this country, ours was once monitored by a one-man weather station, until the Nixon administration, in a fit of cost cutting, decided that only macroclimates and the sites of major airports were of interest to its Commerce Department. Shutting down the one-man stations banned the clutter of wayward microclimates from the computer loops. Something in this should, as Thoreau once said, "serve a parable-maker one day."

THE NEIGHBORHOOD

My neighbors are a mix of types and classes: a retired steeplejack and his wife; an art-museum custodian and his wife, a registered nurse, and their two daughters; a grandfather who doubles as bartender and motel nightclerk, his wife, and a daughter who cleans for several families we know in town (and brings back the news) and mothers her only child, a daughter; a young woman who owns and manages several boutiques; a somewhat older woman pursuing a career as a professional writer; a professor of mathematics and his wife; and twelve other families scattered across that range. Gentrification has set its seal on eight of the eighteen houses down here, and many of our neighbors probably couldn't afford to buy their houses from themselves in today's real-estate market, as we probably couldn't. All the signs promise further gentrification in this out-of-the-way cluster of what were once low-cost, affordable houses. These houses themselves displaced a scattering of small houses, the cabins of what was once a black ghetto. One of those cabins, once enlarged and twice refurbished, remains.

In its way, this island constitutes a neighborhood, neighborly in its manners and behavior, informed both by the impulse to affirm others and lend a hand and by the necessary contraries of irritations, jealousies, and gossip. Not an ersatz neighborhood like a condominium or some other variation of contemporary barracks life, this is an organism that cuts its own lawns, shovels its snow, and changes over time.

TOWN AND GOWN

Up in the village, there is a similar mix of types and classes but with a greater display of affluence and, in the case of one neighborhood, more poverty and dereliction. The college dominates village life and is the principal employer. There are the inevitable town-gown fault lines, enlivened by seasonal outbreaks of conspiracy theory. From September to May, there is the noisy presence of two thousand handsome and intelligent young men and women, most of them affluent, and this creates certain distortions. For some of us, the two thousand represent eternal youth and complicate the processes of our aging. The merchants, and many townspeople, find them an arrogant and irritating bunch, but the students are amusing too and a fairly consistent, usually gratifying, surprise in person and in the classroom.

I am, of course, gown, but I move about on a first-name basis in town with merchants and shopkeepers and bankers and public servants and with those who help us out with our carpentry and painting and plumbing and electrical and landscape problems. In a closet way I am town as well — my mother (1895-1982) was born in a boarding house for the families of textile workers in North Adams, five miles to the east; her father (1872-1922) was born in an ironmaster's house in Lanesboro, fourteen miles to the south; her mother (1873-1954) was born twenty-eight miles down-country in West Stockbridge. But I stay in the closet because I've been in residence here only since 1951, and my childhood roots (the Gifford ones that count locally) are in and around Schenectady, thirty-seven miles to the west.

There are fracture zones other than town and gown. The French-Canadian church remained French-speaking until twenty years ago and still regards itself as the church of the poor and downtrodden. The Irish-Catholic Saint Patrick's houses the rich. The town is bedroom for owners, managers, and other high-level employees of industries and businesses in northern Berkshire County. Increasingly, there are the affluent more-than-visitors among us, retirees, second-home and weekend-home people who see Williamstown as a haven "away from it all" but with the many amenities created by the college, by two impressive art museums, by a lively tradition of summer theater, and by music here in the winter and nearby in the summer. A strange expression, "to get away from it all." Some of us live here year-round under the impression that this is where it all is.

TOURISTS

Many of us feel, probably mistakenly, that these affluent immigrants will eventually take over and hold us hostage, as the hordes of tourists do when they dispossess us on weekends and turn our village into a quaint boutique during the peak seasons: summer, fall (foliage), winter (skiing). Tourists anywhere tend to be a bother to the locals because they don't speak the language, because they mess up traffic patterns and crowd the shops and sidewalks, and because they're always so rich (having prepared to indulge themselves by saving up at home). In sum, all these outlanders and intruders make us feel more native than we actually are.

The general store becomes a museum. Clemens Kalischer

"OUTSIDERS"

Our village, town, and county are "outside," as Daniel Shays, preaching rebellion two hundred years ago, said they would be as long as the state capital is in what he called "merchant- and lawyer-infested Boston." There the capital remains, and there, when they think of western Massachusetts, they think of the place where the voters are, in the growing megalopolis of the Connecticut Valley, a little more than an hour to the east of us. As well conditioned outsiders, we don't expect our bridge to be fixed any time soon; if the time ever comes, we expect to battle once again a Boston-based department of public works that wants to treat this little cul-de-sac to a bridge appropriate to an interstate highway. But that outsider status and experience has its rewards — in the intuitive sympathy that informs the traveler from Williamstown when he visits the outsider places of other geographies: Cornwall, Wales, Ireland, Brittany, Provence, Catalonia, the Basque country, and many of the corners of the Third World.

"THE MEGALOPOLITAN DIASPORA"

If I look up from my worktable and try to define the edges and circumferences of my worlds, the walls of this study dissolve. The circumferences project beyond the farthest imaginable horizons before I can chart location or direction or diameter or the speed of their regression. Even in this haven, this outside, we are not stationary people or sojourners in Arcadia, despite what the affluent immigrants and other visitors might think. Instead, we are urban nomads, people of what David Jones has called "the shapeless cosmopolis and of the megalopolitan diaspora." When immigration and tourism threaten to overwhelm, our impulse is to declare once again that we are country people with our own special brand of calm and considerate understanding, quite the opposite of the harried intelligence of the city dwellers. But our urbanity, or rather the suburbanity we share in the coast-to-coast suburb of this country, betrays us into this world without edges, this city intelligence, which we share with the interlopers. (Only the ghettos remain urban in the old-fashioned sense, and rural simplicity is at least a generation ago.)

In 1951, the telephone at my elbow had a three-digit number with a telephone operator to handle every call, whether local or national, at the manual switchboard in a storefront near the post office downtown. To-day, the reach of this instrument is extraordinary: eleven digits will fetch any corner of this country; thirteen digits and the fetch is global. But the intermediary presence of a telephone operator has faded into a shadow world outside of town.

The computer keyboard under my fingers was made in Japan. It uses mini floppy disks "made in Japan and assembled in the U.S.A." Power comes out of the wall to run this machine and the letter-quality printer that tractor-feeds paper made in Canada. That power also runs a host of other things all over the house: lights and television and hi-fi and radios and clocks and ovens and cooking pans and the thirty-odd electric motors that power the labor-saving network of this house.* That power comes unseen from an electrical utility that generates and sells power to us and buys and sells power from and to other utilities in an arrangement called the New England Power Pool. The pool is in turn an interlocking and overlapping system of grids and confusions that derive from the differing regulatory policies of the six New England states and from the contrast-

---

* Four for the furnace; two for the workshop; six in the kitchen for the odd jobs of squeezing, blending, and chopping; one each for the refrigerator and the freezer; one in the dishwasher; one in the washing machine; one each in the two vacuum cleaners; one in the sewing machine; one each for the record turntable, tape deck, and VCR; two for the solar-exchanger pumps; one for the weed cutter; one for the hair dryer; one for the convection oven; one in a large fan; one in a small electric heater; and that doesn't count the compact-disc player or the battery chargers for the lawn mower, edger, and car.

ing long- and short-term profit motives of the several utility companies involved.

The hydroelectric station at Shelburne Falls on the Deerfield River, less than twenty-five miles to the east of us, could supply (and on emergency occasions has supplied) the electricity needs of this geographically isolated pocket. But there is a nuclear-energy plant at Rowe, ten miles this side of Shelburne Falls. Why there, where it's not needed locally? Because that nuclear plant was one of the first and, in case of accident, Rowe was appropriately remote from population centers of any political significance. The not-in-my-backyard chorus wouldn't have been very large and could safely have been overruled. The electric grid is organized in the same way. When grid-wide power shortages occur, the chances are that backwater towns like ours will get blacked-out or browned-out first.

Most of the technology and energy that sustains my home is located offstage in a circumferenceless space of power and manufacturing and service stations, in distribution and disposal systems that have their edges not only outside the house and village but also outside the state, the region and, more and more frequently, the nation. The repair services that keep the power coming out of the wall and the electronic signals coming over the wires are headquartered and dispatched from centers a two-hour drive away from here, their voices full of astonishment and disbelief when we've been cut off by a storm they haven't seen or felt. An exception is the wood, our primary source of winter heat, that now awaits stacking in its three-cord mound beneath my study window. It comes from a woodlot two miles away. I can visit that woodlot in a walking afternoon as I cannot even identify, let alone visit, the sources of the electricity that comes out of the wall or of the natural gas that powers the kitchen stove.

ANOTHER EDGE DISSOLVES

Last spring, another edge, another contact was suddenly removed: the twice weekly home delivery of milk and eggs stopped. A link with the past was cut, and therefore the past was evoked. In the 1920s, the milkman made daily rounds from his farm on the plateau above the lake where we spent the summers. He dipped the milk from the forty-quart can with a pint measure. I don't remember the year when he shrugged in complaint, but state law would henceforth require him to bottle and cap his milk with the label Raw prominent. (There was much fear of contracting tuberculosis from raw milk in the 1920s.) In town, the horse-drawn vans of the dairyman and the baker and the iceman made their daily rounds; the fruit and vegetable cart called in season; the butcher's wagon came three times a week, but his meat was not dependable; the fishmonger was a Friday regular. In addition to all those shops that paused at our door, there was the corner grocery a three-minute walk away. What remains as the edges dissolve in this village sixty years later? Two small supermarkets, each two automobile miles away, and one gourmet food and produce store one mile away. All three offer year-round meats, fish, fruits, and vegetables without regard to what's in season, and therefore all three blur the edges of space and time that might otherwise limit and define our world.

THE PASSIVITY OF DEPENDENCE

The stock image of New England village life is of a tight-knit, gossipy combination of neighborly comfort and tyranny. On occasion that image fits. But the anonymity and edgelessness of modern urban life is everywhere in the fabric of this subrural, suburban life. The village contacts dissolve, and the remoteness of the they on whom the dailyness of our home lives depends means that we have little or no influence on the choices being made in our name, the anonymous policies designed to serve us. If this were a tight-knit village in a regional world, the tyranny of that anonymity and remoteness might well constitute the conditions for rebellion. Daniel Shays and his Berkshire County contemporaries thought so in 1787, when the remoteness of the state authorities in Boston and the confiscatory taxes they demanded sparked rebellion. But the passivity induced by the comfort and leisure of our urban dependencies renders such an observation ludicrous.

And so, without edge or circumference, is there no margin to our lives, no room for marginalia? Again, are we on the fringe or at the center? This house in this village, my center, is on the fringe of the nation, if it exists for the nation at all. The economy of this household is on the fringe of political economy, hardly a factor in the wealth of nations.

But I am centered, for all of that want of circumference. As a human being, I am more or less midway in the mammalian scale between the smallest of the shrews and the great blue whale, and perceptually I move about in a timespace midway between that of the atoms and that of the stars, realms so remote that I can't perceive them without the speculative mediation of instruments. Centered. And orbiting on the fringe of this "placeless cosmopolis."

From *The Farther Shore: A Natural History of Perception* by Don Gifford. The Atlantic Monthly Press, 1990.

TAD AMES

Tad Ames, a journalist and environmentalist, is assistant director of the Berkshire Natural Resources Council.

Beauty Past Compare

Pittsfield, November 4, 1990

A few Thursdays ago, after the big lightning storm, I went out for a walk around the rain-slicked city. Midnight had come and gone, and the wet streets were quiet, but not dead. Behind glass, in caged light, the kid in the Mobil station watched TV with one eye and looked over his girlfriend with the other. A soft rain dropped past the street lamps.

Through the city I walked. An occasional car hissed by, floating through the procession of soaked brick buildings huddled up along the sidewalks. The stream never stops on Pittsfield's North Street, but it slows. It was past midnight. News from that time of the night can't make the next day's paper.

Amid the blue air of the Salt and Pepper, I ordered the breakfast special. The waitress made a fresh pot of coffee. A young man came in, sat down and asked the next guy down to pass him the paper. It was the Thursday paper. Friday's wasn't out yet. "I've already read this," said the young man. He started to read it again.

On the way home, I stopped on the First Street railroad bridge to watch the trains go by. It was after 1 a.m. A long, long train headed west. Standing up on the bridge in the misting rain, I kept thinking the last car had come, but then another would slide out from the shadow under the bridge until suddenly the track was empty and the lights pulled away down the line. When that train was gone, another steamed up and moved east, the interval between the clacks growing shorter as it picked up speed.

I ran home across the Common, flicking mud from my heels. A soft rain came down. Street lights cast their bloodless glow over the houses and storefronts. Everything was quiet and brilliant in the wet. I passed under a cigarette billboard. This is what it said: "Alive with pleasure."

Halloween morning came up clear and cold. Before work, I had to walk over to East Street on auto business. It was crisp out, but anyone could tell it would warm up. The sun wasn't over the trees for a minute before the frost began to give way.

I walked out Elm Street, looking for the little footbridge that crosses the river and goes over to one of the parking lots on East Street. I'd found it once before, but I wasn't having any luck this time. I followed a couple of dead ends, saw some kids going off to school, a young woman coming out of her upstairs apartment with a cup of coffee and puffy eyes. I saw a vase full of silk flowers trapped in the space between dropped venetian blinds and a condensation-draped window. That was it.

Finally, I found Hathaway Street, with its bridge, and crossed the river. Opposite Hermann Alexander's, I stopped and looked east through a chain link fence. An asphalt GE parking lot stretched out before me, maybe one-sixth full, light posts strung out like optimistic sentinels. Beyond that, reposing in the low sun, stacks and brick and belching steam, sprawled GE itself. It was not yet 9 a.m., and my heart was at once breathing and breaking with the ache of sad industrial beauty. What expectations lay beneath the spread of asphalt. What hope climbed in the rising courses of brick! What hope!

I picked up my car, which the mechanic had rescued from near terminal immobility. He thought I could get it through the winter, at least. "Car like that," he said, "drive it till it pukes."

Out on the road, revitalized with a new clutch, the car bucked under me. The sky was blue, and there was no wind. I rolled the window down. The air was right there, right up clean against your skin as you passed the transmission shops and the churches and the sloping old houses. Some people pass through here and see a dead old city. They don't see the hills in the morning. They don't see the dreams. I was on my way to work, and I passed under the cigarette sign. Here's what it said: "Alive with pleasure."

———————

From *The Berkshire Eagle*, November 4, 1990.

Credits and Sources

William Hubbard: Major Talcott's Raid, 1676
From *The History of the Indian Wars in New England from the First Settlement to the Termination of the War with King Philip, in 1677*. By The Reverend William Hubbard, Minister of Ipswich. Boston, 1677.
    Konkapot et al.: The Housatonack Deed
From *Indian Deeds of Hampden County*. Edited by Harry Andrew Wright. Springfield, Massachusetts, 1905.
    Benjamin Wadsworth: Journey to Albany
From *Wadsworth's Journal* in Massachusetts Historical Society Collections, Volume 1, 4th Series, 1851.
    Jonathan Edwards: Sermon to Stockbridge Indians
From *Selections from the Unpublished Writings of Jonathan Edwards, of America*. Transcribed by Alexander B. Grosart. Edinburgh, 1865.
    Esther Edwards Burr: Excerpts from Rankin's Bogus Journal
From *Esther Burr's Journal*. Edited by Jeremiah Eames Rankin. Washington, 1903.
    Excerpts from the Authentic Journal, 1956
From *Esther Edward Burr: Journal, 1754-1757*. Edited by Carol Karlsen and Laurie Krompacker. Yale University Press, 1984.
    Henriette-Lucy Dillon, Marquise De La Tour Du Pin: The Last Night in the Wilderness
From *Memoirs of Madame de la Tour du Pin*. Translated by Felice Harcourt. Harville Press, 1969.
    Timothy Dwight: Travels in New England
From *Travels in New-England and New-York* by Timothy Dwight. Edited by Barbara Miller Solomon. Harvard University Press, 1969.
    Zenas Crane: Advertisement
From *The Pittsfield Sun*, 1801.
    William Cullen Bryant: Poems
From *Poetical Works* by William Cullen Bryant. Thomas Y. Crowell, 1893.
    Letters
From *The Letters of William Cullen Bryant*, Volume I. Edited by W.C. Bryant III and T.G. Voss. Fordham University Press, 1975.
    John H.B. Latrobe: March Through the Berkshires
From *Journal of A March, Performed By the Corps of Cadets of the United States Military Academy, In the Year Eighteen Hundred and Twenty-One*. Ward M. Gazlay, Newburgh, New York, 1822.
    Special thanks to the Special Collections Division, U.S. Military Academy Library, West Point, New York.
    Elkanah Watson: The Berkshire Agricultural Society
From *History of The Berkshire Agricultural Society* by Elkanah Watson. E&E Hosford, Albany, 1819.
    David Dudley Field: Berkshire Insects
From *A History of the County of Berkshire, Massachusetts* by David Dudley Field. Pittsfield, 1829.
    Thomas Melvill: The Condition of Pittsfield's Schools
From *Report of the Committee on Schools*, April 17, 1837.
    Catharine Maria Sedgwick: A Hill Town Encounter
From *A New-England Tale* by Catharine Maria Sedgwick. E. Bliss and E. White, New York, 1822.
    The Sacrifice
From *Hope Leslie* by Catharine Maria Sedgwick. White, Gallaher, and White, New York, 1827.
    Autobiographical Selections

From *Life and Letters of Catharine Maria Sedgwick*. Edited by Mary E. Dewey. Harper & Bros., New York, 1872.

Harriet Martineau: Notable Berkshirites
From *Autobiography* by Harriet Martineau. J.R. Osgood, 1877.
From *Retrospect of Western Travel* by Harriet Martineau. Saunders and Otley, London, 1838.

Fanny Appleton: Berkshire Letters
From *Mrs. Longfellow: Selected Letters and Journals of Fanny Appleton Longfellow*. Edited by Edward Wagenknecht. Longman Green & Co., 1956.

Henry Wadsworth Longfellow: The Old Clock on the Stairs
From *The Belfry of Bruges and Other Poems* by Henry Wadsworth Longfellow. J. Owen, 1846.
The Influence of Scenery on the Mind
From *Kavanaugh* by Henry Wadsworth Longfellow. Ticknor, Reed & Fields, Boston, 1849.

Harriet Beecher Stowe: How We Kept Thanksgiving at Oldtown
From *Oldtown Folks* by Harriet Beecher Stowe. Fields, Osgood, Boston, 1869.

Francis Parkman: Through the Berkshires by Train in 1842
Berkshire Journal of 1844
From *Journals of Francis Parkman*. Massachusetts Historical Society.
Attack on Fort Massachusetts
From *A Half Century of Conflict* by Francis Parkman. Little, Brown, 1897.

Henry David Thoreau: With Luke Rice of Florida
Alone on Greylock's Summit
From *A Week on the Concord and Merrimack Rivers* by Henry David Thoreau. James Monroe, Boston and Cambridge, 1849.

Susan B. Warner: Queechy Scenes
From *Queechy* by Susan B. Warner. J.P. Lippincott, 1895.

Mark Hopkins: Sermon
From *The Berkshire Jubilee* celebrated at Pittsfield, August 1844.

Frances Anne Kemble: Letters
From *Records of Later Life* by Frances Anne Kemble. Henry Holt & Co., 1882.
Jubilee Ode
From *The Berkshire Jubilee* by Frances Anne Kemble (Mrs. F.K. Butler). 1844.
More Letters
From *Further Records 1848-1883: A Series of Letters* by Frances Anne Kemble. Henry Holt & Co., 1891.

Thomas Robbins: Diary Excerpts
From *Diaries of Thomas Robbins*. Edited by Increase Tarbox, 1888.

Charles Dickens: A Visit to Mount Lebanon
From *American Notes* by Charles Dickens. Estes & Lauriat, 1892.

Ralph Waldo Emerson: Journal Excerpts
From *Journals and Miscellaneous Notebooks of Ralph Waldo Emerson*. Belknap Press of Harvard University Press, 1971.

Oliver Wendell Holmes: Scenes from Berkshire Localities
From *Elsie Venner* by Oliver Wendell Holmes. Houghton, Mifflin, 1883.
Memories of Pittsfield
From *Life & Letters of Oliver Wendell Holmes*, Volume I, by J.T. Morse. Houghton Mifflin, 1896.

Nathaniel Hawthorne: Journal Extracts, 1838 and 1850-1851
The Julian Diaries
From *The American Notebooks* of Nathaniel Hawthorne. Edited by Randall Stewart. Yale University Press, 1932.
Ethan Brand: A Chapter from an Abortive Romance
Written in 1847. First published in the "Boston Weekly Museum," January 1850.

Herman Melville: Selected Letters
From *Letters of Herman Melville*. Edited by Merrill Davis and William Gilman. Yale University Press, 1960.

North From Otis
From *Israel Potter* by Herman Melville. G.P. Putnam & Co., 1855.
Cock-A-Doodle-Doo!
First published in *Harper's Magazine*, 1853.
Poems
From *The Works of Herman Melville*. Constable, London, 1922.
Dedication
From "Weeds and Wildings," probably written in 1891. Published posthumously in 1924.
Evert A. Duyckinck: Picnic Letters
From *Glimpses of Herman Melville's Life in Pittsfield 1850-51; Some Unpublished Letters of Evert A. Duyckinck* by Luther Stearns Mansfield (Williams College); reprinted from American Literature, Vol. 9 No. 1, March 1937.
James T. Fields: The Picnic
From *Yesterdays With Authors* by James T. Fields. Osgood & Co., 1873.
J.E.A. Smith: Pages from Pittsfield's History
From *History of Pittsfield* by J.E.A. Smith. Lee and Shepard, 1869.
The Richmond Boulder Trains
From *Taghconic* by "Godfrey Greylock" (J.E.A. Smith). Eagle Printing & Binding, 1908.
Henry Ward Beecher: Mid-October Days
From *Star Papers, or, Experiencing Art and Nature* by Henry Ward Beecher. J.C. Derby, New York, 1855.
Washington Gladden: Williams in 1856
From *Recollections* by Washington Gladden. Houghton Mifflin, 1909.
Henry Wheeler Shaw (Josh Billings): The Bliss ov Living up in New Ashford
From *Josh Billings: His Works, Complete*. G.W. Carlton & Co., 1876.
Dora Goodale: Our Chickens
From *Apple Blossoms: Verses of Two Children* by Elaine Goodale and Dora Read Goodale. G.P. Putnam's, New York, 1879.
W.E.B. Du Bois: By A Golden River
From *Darkwater* by W.E.B. Du Bois. Harcourt Brace, 1921.
Growing Up in Great Barrington
From *Autobiography* by W.E.B. Du Bois. International Publishers, 1968.
From Great Barrington to the Wider World
From *Dusk of Dawn* by W.E.B. Du Bois. Harcourt Brace, 1940.
Letter Home
From *The Correspondence of W.E.B. Du Bois*, Volume I. Edited by Herbert Aptheker. University of Massachusetts Press, 1973.
Edith Wharton: Life at The Mount
From *A Backward Glance* by Edith Wharton. William R. Tyler, 1962,
Excerpts from *Summer*
From *Summer* by Edith Wharton. Harper & Row Perennial Library. Reprinted by arrangement with D. Appleton & Co.
Moonrise Over Tyringham
From Artemis to Arcturus by Edith Wharton. Charles Scribner, 1909.
Xingu
From *Xingu and Other Stories* by Edith Wharton. Scribner's, 1916.
Henry James: The Berkshire Scene
From *The American Scene* by Henry James. Chapman and Hall, 1907.
Ellery Sedgwick: Happy Valley
From *The Happy Profession* by Ellery Sedgwick. Little Brown, 1946.
Adele Sloane: A Perfect Week
From *Maverick in Mauve* by Florence Adele Sloane, with commentary by Louis Auchincloss. Doubleday, 1983.
Frederick Vanderbilt Field: The Elegance of High Lawn
From *From Right To Left* by Frederick V. Field. Lawrence Hill & Co., 1983.

Robert Underwood Johnson: To the Housatonic at Stockbridge
From *Poems of 50 Years* by Robert Underwood Johnson. Published by the author, 1931.
Austin Haight: Bill Day, Veteran Sportsman
From *The Biography of a Sportsman* by Austin D. Haight. Thomas Y. Crowell, 1939.
Mary Allen Hulbert: Mrs. Peck of East Street
From *The Story of Mrs. Peck* by Mary Allen Hulbert. Minton, Balch & Co., 1933.
Edna St. Vincent Millay: Letters
From *Letters of Edna St. Vincent Millay*. Edited by Allan Ross Macdougall. Harper & Bros., 1952.
Poems
From *Collected Poems* by Edna St. Vincent Millay. Edited by Norma Millay. Harper & Row, 1956.
Laughran Vaber: West Stockbridge Central
From *The Berkshire Eagle*, May 1990 Berkshires Week.
Walter Pritchard Eaton: First Visit to the Berkshires
From *The Berkshires*. Edited by Roderick Peattie. Vanguard Press, 1948.
Cellar-Holes
From *On Yankee Hilltops* by Walter Pritchard Eaton. W.A. Wilde, 1933.
Collins Miles: Depression Letters
From the letters of Collins Loewe "Pete" Miles (1909-1989) to his brother Lemuel, in the collection of the Miles family of Egremont and Mount Washington.
Gertrude Robinson Smith: A Letter From Miss Smith
From *Music Under the Stars* by John G.W. Mahanna. Berkshire Symphonic Festival, 1953.
Annie Zucco Harrison: Working at Rising Paper
From a 1974 interview with Annie Zucco Harrison, by James S. Turner.
James Gould Cozzens: Ringing Doctor Bull
From *The Last Adam* by James Gould Cozzens. Harcourt Brace, 1922.
WPA Guide: Gold in the Berkshires
From *The Berkshire Hills: A WPA Guide* by Members of the Federal Writers' Project of the Works Progress Administration. The Berkshire Hills Conference, 1939.
Bartlett Hendricks: Berkshire Dirt Roads
From *The Berkshires*. Edited by Roderick Peattie. Vanguard Press, 1948.
Albert Spalding: "Hoboken of the Berkshires"
From *Rise to Follow* by Albert Spalding. Henry Holt & Co., 1946.
Theodore Giddings: Hop Brook
From *The Berkshires*. Edited by Roderick Peattie. Vanguard Press, 1948.
Morgan Bulkeley: Down, Once Up
From *Mountain Farm* by Morgan Bulkeley. Hollow Spring Press, 1985.
Katharine Annin: By Buckboard to England Brothers
From *The Berkshire Eagle*, December 1, 1987.
Burton Bernstein: Bernstein at Tanglewood
From *Family Matters* by Burton Bernstein. Simon & Schuster, 1982.
Thomas Whitbread: Country Blessing
From *Four Infinitives* by Thomas Whitbread. Harper & Row, 1964.
William Carlos Williams: Harry Duncan and the Cummington Press
From *Selected Letters of William Carlos Williams*. Edited by John C. Thirlwall. Astor-Honor, 1957.
James Thurber: The Lady on 142
From *The Thurber Carnival* by James Thurber. Harper & Row, 1975.
James MacGregor Burns: Shays's Rebellion
From *Vineyard of Liberty* by James MacGregor Burns. Alfred A. Knopf, 1982.
Christopher Rand: Berkshire Iron Industry
From *The Changing Landscape* by Christopher Rand. Oxford University Press, 1968.
Judith McGaw: The Mill Towns Transformed
From *Most Wonderful Machine* by Judith McGaw. Princeton University Press, 1987.

William Jay Smith: Morels
From *The Traveler's Tree: New and Selected Poems* by William Jay Smith. Persea Books, 1980.
Norman Rockwell: From Stockbridge to Washington
From *My Life as an Illustrator* by Norman Rockwell. Doubleday, 1960.
Hal Borland: Hill Country Observations
From *Hill Country Harvest* by Hal Borland. J.B. Lippincott, 1967.
Gerard Chapman: The "Apple Blossom Poets"
From *The Berkshire Eagle*, September 21, 1978.
Bernadette Mayer: Lenox on December 22, 1978
From *Midwinter Day* by Bernadette Meyer. Turtle Island Foundation, 1982.
Milton Bass: Mayor of the City
From *Not Quite A Hero* by Milton Bass. G.P. Putnam's Sons, 1977.
Amanda Cross: Meeting Mrs. Bradford
From *The James Joyce Murder* by Amanda Cross. E.P. Dutton, 1982.
Richard Wilbur: Poems
From *New and Collected Poems* by Richard Wilbur. Harcourt Brace Jovanovich, 1988.
Paul Metcalf: Stampers and Hawkers
From *Where Do You Put The Horse* by Paul Metcalf. Dalkey Archive Press, 1986.
Stephen Sandy: Riding to Greylock
From *Riding to Greylock* by Stephen Sandy. Alfred A. Knopf, 1983.
Walter Howard: Riding the Milk Truck
Tyringham's Steeplechase
From *Sisyphus in the Hayfield* by Walter Howard. Cobble Press, 1988.
Stephen Philbrick: Poems
From *No Goodbye* by Stephen Philbrick. Horizon Press, 1982.
Roy Blount, Jr.: A Berkshire Ditty
Written by Roy Blount, Jr., for *The Berkshire Book*. Berkshire House Publishers, 1986.
Why I Live Where I Live, If I Do
From *What Men Don't Tell Women* by Roy Blount, Jr. Little Brown & Co., in association with The Atlantic Monthly Press.
Barry Steinlieb: Poems
From *Thinning The Rows* by Barry Sternlieb. Brooding Heron Press, 1990.
Don Gifford: At Home in the "Placeless Cosmopolis"
From *The Farther Shore: A Natural History of Perception* by Don Gifford. The Atlantic Monthly Press, 1990.
Tad Ames: Beauty Past Compare
From *The Berkshire Eagle*, November 4, 1990.

Richard Nunley is a graduate of Dartmouth and Cambridge, and has lived in the Berkshires since 1957. He teaches English at Berkshire Community College and is a weekly columnist for the *Berkshire Eagle*. He has lectured frequently on writers in the Berkshires.

Michael McCurdy is an artist, illustrator, and author. His wood engravings have appeared in trade books and limited editions for both adults and children. His most recent titles include *The Old Man and the Fiddle* and *American Tall Tales*. He lives in Great Barrington, Massachusetts.

Clemens Kalischer, free-lance photographer, contributed many of the contemporary photographs in *The Berkshire Reader*. His work has been in a variety of international publications, and he has exhibited at the Metropolitan Museum and the Museum of Modern Art. He maintains the Image Gallery in Stockbridge, Massachusetts, which presents contemporary visual artists.

Production services by Quality Printing, Pittsfield, Massachusetts, and by Ripinsky & Co., Newtown, Connecticut.